The Dragon Nimbus Novels Volume III

THE
DRAGON NIMBUS
NOVELS
VOLUME III

THE RENEGADE DRAGON
THE WIZARD'S TREASURE

Irene Radford

DAW BOOKS, INC.
DONALD A. WOLLHEIM, FOUNDER
375 Hudson Street, New York, NY 10014

ELIZABETH R. WOLLHEIM
SHEILA E. GILBERT
PUBLISHERS
http://www.dawbooks.com

First Paperback Printing, January 2008
1 2 3 4 5 6 7 8 9

Introduction

Welcome to a world where dragons are real and magic works. If you are new to the Dragon Nimbus, pull up a chair and join us as we revel in tales that have touched my heart more than anything else I've written under any pen name. If you are returning after an absence, I am very happy to have you back.

This is a world that began with a Christmas gift of a blown glass dragon. The dragon sat proudly on the knick-knack shelf for several months, loved and admired, reluctantly dusted, and totally inert. Then one night at dinner my son remarked, "You know, Mom, I think dragons are born all dark, like that little pewter dragon, then they get more silvery as they grow up until they are as clear as glass." The dragon came to life for me.

Out of that chance remark came first one book, then three, five, seven, and finally ten. I built a career on these books and loved every minute of the process. These characters still live in my mind many years after they jumped into their stories and dragged me along with them.

Many thanks to DAW Books and my editor Sheila Gilbert for reviving *The Dragon Nimbus* a lucky thirteen years after they first debuted.

With these omnibus volumes, you can read about the dragons with crystal fur that directs your eye elsewhere yet defies you to look anywhere else. Wonderful dragons full of wit and wisdom. Magic abounds. Magicians and mundanes alike learn about their world and special life lessons as they explore dragon lore past and present. The books will be presented in the order in which they were written, and the order that makes the most sense of the entwined tales.

So, sit back and enjoy with me.

And may reading take you soaring with Dragons.

Irene Radford
Welches, OR

THE
RENEGADE
DRAGON

This book is dedicated to the memory of Cindy Carver, Susan Holzworth, Jo Clayton, and Barbara Martin, dear friends who departed this plane of existence too early but left me with a wonderful legacy. Thanks to them I have learned to have faith in myself. Now I just hope I can live up to their expectations.

Prologue

Midmorning of Saawheen, the Holy Day of Remembrance, in late autumn of the second year of the Reign of Quinnault Darville de Draconis, Dragon Blessed King of Coronnan; a meadow west of Coronnan City

Shayla stretched her wings wide, catching a shift in air currents as she cruised the length of the waterway humans call the River Coronnan. Her twelve dragonets had just eaten a bemouth, one of the ferocious fish that inhabited the depths of the Great Bay. Even though her babies drowsed with full tummies, she knew they'd awaken again soon, clamoring for more fresh meat to feed their growing bodies. In the meantime, she took this rare free time to enjoy a few moments of peace and freedom, allowing the air currents to guide her constant search for food.

She scanned the ground for likely game. All of the cows and sheep the humans had set out as a tithe for the dragons looked too scrawny to feed her hungry babies.

The nimbus of dragons had agreed among themselves to allow the herds to increase before culling. Generations of war and privation had taken a toll on both dragons and humans. They would all thrive better if the dragons hunted wild game for a few more years.

Shayla, oh, Shayla, I need your help. A human mind called to the dragon. *Shayla, hurry. I need you.*

Shayla listened closely to the summons. The plea of a woman with a deep problem. A problem dragons couldn't ignore.

She knew the mind calling her away from her leisurely glide around the Great Bay. The female named Maarie Kaathliin, called Katie by those close to her, had mated with dragon-blessed King Quinnault at the same time Shayla had flown a nuptial ritual with five male dragons. Queen Katie had proved to be a formidable woman nearly worthy of leading a dragon nimbus.

(How may I assist?) Shayla banked her wings and circled until she located Katie. The queen stood at the edge of a large field, cradling her baby in her arms. Shayla recognized the other humans who rested nearby after a meal. She grabbed the meaning of their word "picnic" from the mind of King Quinnault. She still didn't understand the difference between eating in the lair or eating in the field. Dragons did both and had no word to separate the two.

She narrowed her telepathic communication so that only the queen could hear her. King Quinnault and his sister Myrilandel were openly receptive to dragon thoughts. Powwell, the fledgling magician who played with Myrilandel's daughter, could hear less. Yaala, a descendant of the renegade dragon—who shall forever more remain nameless—could hear all too much if she opened her mind to her heritage.

Shayla grieved a moment that Nimbulan, Myrilandel's husband, had lost his magic and thus his ability to communicate with dragons. The loss of that magic had aged and saddened him greatly this past year. She had enjoyed his logic and humor—which often mimicked wisdom.

Shayla, I have explained and pleaded with these people for many moons. They refuse to recognize a danger that threatens us all. Can you give them a dragon dream of great import? Katie asked.

(Dragon dreams are dangerous, to yourself and those you hold dear.) Shayla backwinged, puzzled by the request.

I know that, Shayla. I do not ask for a dream that will lead them astray, only teach them a valuable lesson.

(Such as?)

Take a memory from me and make it real to those around me.

Shayla saw the terrible images within Katie's mind and

nearly fled to the void between the planes of existence. *(Why do you wish to share this memory? You should flee it as you fled your homeworld.)*

The same danger I fled is on its way to this planet unless we stop it now. We must not destroy this world called Kardia Hodos as my people destroyed Terra.

(Agreed.) Shayla fought her own reluctance to relive the memory in vision form. This was a lesson the foolish humans must learn—now, before they made grave mistakes.

(The dragon spirit within Myrilandel makes her immune to dragon dreams,) Shayla stalled. *(She is influential among many of those you must reach with this lesson. The woman-child, Yaala, needs to live this vision more than most, but her dragon ancestry will make her immune as well. She lives apart from their society and does not know how to value the nimbus of humans.)*

Myri can pluck the memory of this dragon dream from Nimbulan's mind, Katie replied. Her thoughts bordered on frantic. *Powwell, the journeyman magician, will share his knowledge with Yaala, as he shares everything with her. They are friends despite her separateness from others. If Nimbulan, Quinnault, and the journeyman magician experience what terrorizes my people, they will act upon it.*

(For a dragon dream this troubling, I must land.) Shayla worried gravely for the future of her humans should this dragon dream come to pass on Kardia Hodos. She positioned herself so that sunlight arced rainbows through her all color/no color wings as she circled and landed.

The dragonets would nap a while longer. And if they woke, hungry and screaming for more food, they would have to wait. This dragon dream needed to be imparted soon, or it would be too late.

The other humans jumped up, pointing toward her. Joy filled them as they rushed to greet the dragon. Amaranth, Myrilandel's daughter, clapped her hands and crawled toward the pretty display of colored light refracting through the dragon's wings.

"Shayla, I would like to introduce you to Marilell, my daughter." King Quinnault bowed deeply, gesturing to the infant in Katie's arms. "Katie and I ask your dragon blessing on our firstborn." He draped an arm around his mate and female child, pulling them close to his side. With his free hand he caressed Shayla's muzzle.

The dragon allowed her eyelids to droop as she leaned into the king's caress. She savored his affection, knowing how the dragon dream she was about to give him might frighten him into ending all further communication with dragons.

Myrilandel lifted Amaranth onto Shayla's outstretched forearm. The physical resemblance between Myrilandel and Quinnault had grown stronger since Shayla's daughter had borne a child and forgotten her need to fly with dragons; her silvery-blond hair had become more golden and her long, sharp facial features had softened with maturity and pregnancy. But Shayla knew that the spirit of a purple-tipped dragon still resided in the body of the king's sister. A spirit that would always demand release. She had survived one such near transformation due only to the love of her mate.

Yaala, too, could experience the need to become a purple-tipped dragon, though a dozen and more generations separated her from her heritage. Was that why the young woman stood back, refusing to approach another dragon?

Shayla peered at the infant Queen Katie held. The new mother bit her lip a little.

"You'll get used to dragons, dear. Their size is intimidating, but their hearts are pure," Quinnault chuckled.

(My daughter calls you friend. The king my nimbus has adopted as one of our own calls you lover. You may trust me with your daughter,) Shayla reassured the queen.

The fledgling magician edged closer. Shayla sensed the man-boy drinking in the magical energy she emitted. She needed him closer yet.

Yaala lingered by the distant tree. So be it. She would not live the vision of a dragon dream whether she stood close or far.

(The child Marilell is worthy of her parents. She will make a strong leader of your nimbus,) Shayla announced to all who could hear her. She kept an eye on Powwell, willing him to draw closer while she chatted with Quinnault and Katie.

Quinnault raised an eyebrow at that suggestion. So did

Nimbulan after the dragon message was passed on to him verbally. Shayla allowed herself a moment of humor. One day, humans would learn that females could govern unruly males quite well.

Al last Powwell stepped within a dozen talon lengths of the others. Close enough.

Once more Shayla dipped into Katie's mind and wrested the awful memory from her.

Immediately the humans plunged into another world. A stifling world of stale air tainted by artificial materials and chemicals. A filthy haze kept them from seeing the sky. Some kind of unnatural barrier stood between them and the haze. But the barrier trapped clean air, made it stale despite mechanical beasts that scrubbed it and stirred it in imitation of the wind.

More mechanical beasts grunted and whined in a wild cacophony of sound. Humans walked around cautiously, eyes searching every corner for danger. They wore strange clothing, like artificial skin in muddy colors that flattered nothing and highlighted many unattractive features. Across their muzzles they had draped coverings in the same vague colors as their clothing. Each step was listless, hesitant. They kept their arms close to their bodies rather than swinging them freely in confident strides. As they approached buildings or other people, they shied away from the briefest physical contact.

The observers from Coronnan shifted their startled gazes from the drab people to the dazzling buildings made of metal and glass. So much precious glass! Each window represented a Coronnite lord's entire fortune. While the wonder slowly abated, the watchers all wrinkled their noses at the strange-smelling air. They stared at the frightened inhabitants in bewilderment.

An old woman walked a slow, unsteady path between the wondrous buildings. Her wrinkled skin looked waxy and pale with more ailments than just advanced age. She stopped often, swaying with weakness and indecision. Her swollen hands and feet made her progress awkward. A large man with some vivacity still in his step veered sharply to avoid contact with her. He quickened his steps and increased his vigilant watch.

Another man carried his small son as he hastened through the crowd. Despite the urgency in his manner, his feet shuffled as if he had not the strength to lift them clear of the walkway. "Help me find a doctor," he called to one and all. "My son is sick. Someone, anyone, help me find a doctor." The little boy breathed raggedly. The bloating of his extremities had faded, leaving him gaunt and wasted. His skin stretched too tightly over his facial bones, taking on a waxy, bluish tinge. The father dashed futilely from one person to the next.

An older man whose broad shoulders suggested an earlier athletic build gone to waste screamed, tearing his mask away. He gasped for air. More air. Never enough air. His eyes bulged. Blood seeped from his mouth, nose, and ears. His limbs convulsed. He thrashed at all who came within reach. The pulse in his throat raced until it could beat no more.

Everyone, including the wobbling woman and the man with the sick child, ran away from the hideous sight of the dying man.

Katie wept, burying her face against her husband's shoulder.

Nimbulan reached for the ailing man, needing to help him, offer him whatever healing and comfort he could. He would never reach the phantom man who no longer existed except in Katie's memory. Nimbulan looked for Myrilandel to lend her magic to the healing effort. She couldn't follow him into the dragon vision and didn't see death all around her.

Shayla noted with gratitude that Myrilandel's daughter Amaranth also seemed immune to the dragon dream.

Nimbulan beat his fists against the ground in frustration. He didn't realize he touched the clean grass and dirt of Kardia Hodos rather than the smooth, poured-stone surface on the strange and dangerous world of the dragon dream.

Quinnault held Katie back from the vision, needing to shelter her from these unknown dangers. Their daughter slept, dreaming her own dreams, too young to recognize the images.

The fledgling magician backed away from the illusory dying man in horror but couldn't escape the dragon dream. He ran away from the images. His instincts took him toward

Yaala, though he could not see her through the dream. Shayla pressed the dream deeper into his mind so that he would never forget and would instantly be aware of the cause of this man's death. He needed every detail imprinted on his mind so that he could relate it accurately to Yaala who stood numbly by his side, clutching his hand.

At last, when the dead man ceased twitching, a machine looking like a giant square spider emerged from a glass doorway, gliding several talon lengths above the ground. It hummed to itself as it flashed several different colored lights over the victim. Beeping noises followed the lights. One slender arm, clawed like the giant pincer of a bay crawler, poked the man.

The dead man could no longer respond to the probe. Then two metal arms slid out from the machine's belly, scooped him up, and the machine glided off to an unknown destination. A second machine emerged, very similar to the first, but smaller. It sprayed the ground where the dead man had been with a foul-smelling liquid.

Some of the deadly humors that had killed the man died in the obnoxious substance. Most. Not all. Shayla and Katie both knew now that nothing, not even all elixir distilled from the Tambootie tree could kill *all* of that plague.

"Someone has brought the seeds of this plague to Coronnan," Katie announced.

And Shayla knew that she and the other dragons would have to break a centuries-old taboo to prevent the spread of the plague. A member of the dragon nimbus would have to go to Hanassa, the home of the renegade dragon, where the seeds of the plague lay dormant, waiting for a catalyst to bring them to life.

Chapter 1

Early afternoon of Saawheen, outside the meeting chamber of the Council of Provinces, Palace Reveta Tristile, Coronnan City

Journeyman Magician Bessel skidded to a halt outside the door to the chamber where the Council of Provinces met in urgent session. He took a moment to steady his ragged breath and straighten his hastily donned formal blue robes. A gravy stain in the middle of his chest refused to stay hidden among the folds. He hadn't worn the robe in moons. Master Scarface, head of the Commune of Magicians, usually excluded his Senior Journeyman from every meeting.

"*S'murghit!* I have the right to stand behind Master Magician Scarface's left shoulder, observing, advising," he muttered angrily. Master Nimbulan had never treated his assistants and students as if they did not exist.

Then Bessel straightened his shoulders. "I have to make a good impression on the master today. I can't give him reason to exclude me anymore," he stated firmly as he adjusted the folds one more time, trying to cover the stain. It defied concealment.

He grounded his staff and channeled a touch of magic through it to the stain. His eyes blurred as he found the greasy molecules and loosened their hold on the fabric. In a moment brown flecks dropped to the stone floor.

"While I'm at it, might as well get rid of the wrinkles." A little more magic added crispness to the folds and straightened the line of the robe. But he didn't have time to add fibers to the shoulder seams and neckline to cover the weight he'd gained since he'd worn the robe last. He looked as respectable as possible on such short notice.

Taking one last deep breath that sounded more like a sigh, Bessel calmly opened the door of the large chamber to find all twelve lords, their magician advisers, King Quinnault and Queen Maarie Kaathliin with Scarface as their adviser, seated at the round table in the center of the chamber.

Bessel looked at the forest of magician's staffs standing at regular intervals throughout the room. *My staff will never have those distinguishing twists and whorls within the wood grain,* he moaned to himself. No matter how much magic he channeled through his tool, it remained straight and smooth. *How can I ever fit in, truly belong, if I can't make my own staff behave? Maybe if I search the library again, I can find a trick to get the twisting started.* He sighed long-ingly as he looked at Scarface's elaborately knotted staff.

Nimbulan and his wife Myrilandel stood against the wall adjacent to the door with Powwell, their adopted son. Those three looked grim, almost frightened. So did the king and queen. Myrilandel, ambassador from the dragon nimbus, should be seated next to her brother, King Quinnault, not standing in near exile against the wall.

But she was the only ambassador present. Whatever had triggered this urgent meeting involved internal matters.

All of the most powerful people in the kingdom had gathered in one room at the same time. That didn't happen often. Bessell couldn't remember it happening since King Quinnault's coronation nearly two years ago, not even his wedding a little over a year ago had brought every lord and magician to the capital city. For both events every ambassador had been present. Now only Myrilandel. Why?

The late afternoon sunlight streamed through the rare glass windows in the chamber. In a few hours, when the last of the light left this bright autumn day of Saawheen, the Holy Day of Remembrance would begin. All of these people should be at home with their families or preparing for solemn religious rituals. Instead, they crowded into this room, whispering quietly among themselves.

Bessel strained his listening senses to pick up the conversations, but he could not catch more than an occasional word unless he dipped into the speakers' minds. He'd wait for official announcements rather than violate another's privacy.

He took one step to the right, toward Master Scarface. Powwell snagged his sleeve and shook his head slightly. So slightly, Bessel doubted anyone else in the room noticed.

Then Bessel took one look at the Senior Magician's scowl and decided to stand next to Powwell, well away from Scarface. The Senior Magician looked furious even before he noticed Bessel's late entrance. The scar that gave him his nickname stretched whitely from temple to temple across the bridge of his nose; a sure sign of deep concentration or distress. He kept his eyes half closed as if in great pain.

If I had a place to hide where HE couldn't find me, I think I would, Bessel sent to Powwell on a tight telepathic signal so that none of the magicians in the room could overhear—especially Scarface.

So would we. I wonder who is going to end up with kitchen duty for two moons when this is done? Powwell returned on an equally tight line. His eyes looked more haunted than usual and his hollow cheeks seemed almost gaunt with strain. He carried his hedgehog familiar in his hand rather than hidden in his pocket, a sure sign of disquiet. Since having to leave his sister Kalen behind in Hanassa last year, the familiar seemed the only being capable of giving Powwell comfort. Even his friendship with Yaala sometimes failed to help him.

Bessel understood Powwell's sense of emptiness at the loss of his only family.

Kitchen duty is preferable to being thrown out of here with no place to go and no other magician allowed to take us in, Bessel returned, praying that he would not become the victim of Scarface's wrath. Two senior apprentices had lost their place in the University of Magicians last moon for seemingly minor infractions. They'd been with the University almost as long as Bessel, having started under Nimbulan's tutelage.

Where is Yaala? he asked, noting the absence of Powwell's dear friend, the exiled Princess of Hanassa. She should be sitting next to Queen Maarie Kaathliin. The royal couple had practically adopted Yaala as a foster sister and kept her close to them on all official occasions.

Powwell shrugged as if he did not know, but he clenched his fist around his hedgehog familiar, allowing the sharp quills to prick his skin until a drop of bright blood seeped through his fingers.

Who are they waiting on? Bessel tried a different line of questioning. He counted heads.

"Excuse my tardiness. I was detained with important communications," King Kinnsell, the queen's father, said. He stood squarely in the doorway, waiting for acknowledgment from every person in the room.

That didn't take long. The leader from the mysterious land of Terrania dominated any room he graced with his presence. His aura shimmered in tightly controlled layers of color that mimicked a rainbow. No one had that bright array in precisely measured sections. Not normally. Kinnsell used his aura to project authority when realistically he had none. Even the bright sunlight seemed to concentrate on him, making his expensive golden brocade tunic glow.

What is he doing here? Bessel asked Powwell.

The younger magician shrugged again.

Kinnsell moved around the huge table to stand between King Quinnault and Scarface. His posture radiated confidence and authority. He held his right hand beside him as if he curved his fingers over the knob of a short walking stick. As he gazed about the room and nodded to several individuals, he brought his hand back slightly, adjusting the angle of the imaginary stick.

Bessel shook his head at the curious gesture. He was used to watching magicians for a signature gesture to indicate deep thought or information gathering. This hand position was new to him.

Scarface stooped to whisper something to King Quinnault. He had to lean awkwardly around King Kinnsell to do so. The Senior Magician's scowl deepened.

"Now that everyone is gathered, I have unsettling news to relate," King Quinnault announced from his demi-throne.

Queen Maarie Kaathliin touched her husband's hand in silent reminder of something. They both searched the room with their eyes, finally resting their gazes on Nimbulan and Myrilandel.

"Where is Yaala?" Quinnault asked. "She is part of this."

"I dismissed the woman," Scarface said succinctly. "Her information is secondhand and therefore invalid. And so is Ambassador Myrilandel's."

"My sister is ambassador for the dragons. Her presence is required!" Quinnault replied angrily.

Both Myrilandel and Nimbulan remained quiet, eyes averted from the lords and magicians who stared at her. Perhaps they did not see Quinnault's gesture to make a place for them at his side.

The queen opened her mouth to speak. Before she could utter a sound, King Kinnsell spoke again. "We have enough witnesses to proceed." He smiled and wiggled his fingers as if tapping the imaginary stick.

Who was running this meeting? Bessel tried hard to keep his face bland and unsurprised. He checked with his True-Sight to make sure Kinnsell did not hold an invisible magical tool. He didn't.

"Witnesses, Your Grace?" Lord Hanic asked of Kinnsell and not his king. An edge of defiance tinged his aura.

Bessel didn't expect anything else from the border lord who questioned everything and withheld his vote in Council until he knew which side would win. He sided with Lord Balthazaan against the king more often than not. Hanic's magician, Red Beetle—because his red eyebrows formed an unbroken V on his brow like the beetle with similar markings—whispered encouragement to his lord.

"The dragons have given us a dragon dream of great importance," Quinnault replied, reasserting his authority in the room.

A dragon dream! Bessel stood a little straighter, letting magic enhance all of his senses.

Whispers broke out around the room. Very few humans experienced a dragon dream. Fewer still understood the visions that seemed so real the receiver believed he lived the images generated by a dragon's mind.

"We have decisions to make based on this dragon dream."

Quinnault raised his voice above the babble. The attention of those present returned to him. Silence prevailed once more.

Then, slowly and in simple words, the king related how he and the queen had taken a picnic outside the city with their friends. Quinnault related the details of the dream in compelling and minute detail. The sounds of the machines chugging out the filth that provided a breeding ground for the plague dominated his tale. Looks of horror crossed the faces of lords and magicians alike. Bessel felt a tightness in his chest and a heaviness in his gut.

What if that terrible plague came to Coronnan?

"He forgot the smell," Powwell whispered. The hedgehog wiggled its nose in its funny circular motion, emphasizing the unpleasantness of the scent. For the first time, Bessel noticed a rusty coloration on the tip of his spines. Almost like dried blood. He wondered if it were natural or a result of Powwell habitually squeezing his familiar so tightly that he bled onto the spines.

"What smell?" he asked, breathing heavily to shake off the fear of the plague and the smell of Powwell's blood on the hedgehog's spines. He should know if the plague had come to Coronnan. He was Senior Journeyman. He had access to information most mundanes couldn't dream of, but this was the first he'd heard of disease run rampant.

"The smell of the plague," Powwell replied, still whispering. "Metallic, acidic, and yet syrupy sweet. Like nothing born on this world that I know of." The hedgehog hunched and bristled its spines.

"You mentioned glass, fortunes in glass windows," Lord Balthazaan half stood, leaning closer to the king. "If Terrania is so rich and powerful to use glass so carelessly, why haven't we used the queen's connections to exploit their wealth?" He banged his heavy ring bearing the family crest upon the table for emphasis.

Balthazaan's magician adviser, Humpback, waggled his staff as if he used that medium to communicate with his lord. Then he leaned closer to Red Beetle while they consulted secretively.

Bessel wished he could eavesdrop.

Behind the king, Kinnsell smiled in satisfaction. He thrust

his broad chest out a little, like a lumbird in a mating display. Bessel nearly forgot how short the man was compared to most of the lords and magicians. Every man in the room—lord and magician alike—kept looking toward King Kinnsell as if needing him to confirm every statement. He had become the natural focus in the room by standing above the royal couple, separating them from their chief adviser. Bessel almost believed the projected image of Kinnsell's political power and importance to the entire kingdom.

Then he remembered Queen Katie's generous dowry. King Kinnsell had worked a miracle last year, creating a port city overnight out of four islands in the Great Bay; he had left Coronnan with a machine to help navigate the mudflats between Coronnan City and the port. Maritime trade in Coronnan had quadrupled since that time. How Terrania benefited from the gift had remained a closely guarded secret.

Would that secret and the true bride price be jeopardized by the removal of that one precious machine from Coronnan?

Get the conversation back to the plague. It's more important than Terrania or glass, Bessel sent to Scarface.

The Senior Magician reared his head back in surprise, glaring at Bessel angrily. *Where did you come from?* his startled thoughts leaked directly into Bessel's mind. Then the Senior Magician calmly folded his hands in front of him, on the big table. *You do not need to remind me of our priorities, young man. I am Senior Magician, you but my assistant.*

Scarface cleared his throat loudly, scanned the room to make certaiun he had everyone's attention, and finally spoke. "Glass and wealth mean nothing if we all die of this mysterious disease."

Kinnsell pushed his hand forward, giving his imaginary stick a new angle as he frowned at Scarface for interrupting.

"True," Quinnault said on a sigh of relief. "We must send dispatches to all parts of Coronnan seeking information. Any unusual illnesses must be reported."

"And the presence of any foreign machines must also be reported," Queen Maarie Kaathliin interjected. "Machines seem to make life easier. But one machine leads to another and another until we are slaves to them and their pollution taints all of our lives. The pollution is the food for the plague, and when it runs out of tainted air, it turns on people. We have loyal magicians who can help us better than any machine. We do not need technology to build a good life, a stable economy, and a healthy populace."

And as long as the magicians served a purpose in Coronnan, Bessel would have the Commune and access to their library. He didn't want to think about a world where impersonal machines replaced a human magician.

"Aren't you overreacting, daughter?" Kinnsell rested a parental hand on her shoulder. His other hand pushed farther forward. The reprimand in his voice was unmistakable.

Bessel needed to know the origin of Kinnsell's gesture. How could he understand the man and his motives if he didn't know why he held his hand that particular way?

"No," Queen Katie replied. "Our people have lived with the plague so long we no longer know the warning signs. Terrania has become so dependent upon technology her people don't know how to, and don't want to, live without it, even though the pollution generated by those machines causes many, many deaths," she replied, shaking off his touch.

The two glared at each other a long moment.

Bessel wanted to crawl under the table to avoid this embarrassing family squabble. He'd had enough of those at home—a place he sincerely wanted to forget. The Commune was home now.

"I wish all of you could have personally experienced the dragon dream," King Quinnault said. "But since Shayla only granted this vision of potential disaster to a few of us, then you must accept my word that we face dangerous times, my lords. Very dangerous. Now, please, disperse to your religious and family duties properly warned and forearmed with knowledge."

Attend me, I have tasks for you, Scarface ordered Bessel telepathically.

Bessel nodded his acceptance of the order. So did Powwell.

Behind Quinnault King Kinnsell scowled. He jerked his

head several times in brief nods of signal to several people in the room. The gesture happened so fast Bessel missed who replied and who didn't.

He sensed a tension and defiance in the air, almost tasted it like Powwell had tasted the scent of the plague in the dragon dream.

Chapter 2

*Two hours before sunset on the Holy Day of
Remembrance, outside the meeting chamber of
the Council of Provinces, Palace Reveta Tristile,
Coronnan City*

Powwell followed Scarface out of the Council chamber.
Curiosity burned within him. For the past year, since
he had escaped the outlaw city of Hanassa with Scarface
and the others, the Senior Magician had gone out of his
way to avoid noticing Powwell, or any other student who
had come to the University under Nimbulan's tutelage. He
wouldn't even allow mention of Rollett, the journeyman
magician who had failed to escape the city of outlaws, let
alone discuss a rescue attempt.

Powwell was afraid his search for his lost sister Kalen
would take him back to Hanassa. The city had almost killed
him. If he ever saw the inside of the collapsed volcano
again, he was almost glad Rollett would be there to help.
If Rollett still lived.

"Powwell, you spend far too much time in the library pur-
suing your own research. I need you and Bessel to go on a
quest together," Scarface said. He refused to meet Powwell's stare of astonishment. "You'll have to lose your dependence upon a familiar to complete the quest, though.
Get rid of that nasty little creature."

Powwell tucked Thorny into his tunic pocket as he
clenched his jaw against an angry retort. Scarface had no
patience or understanding of the unique relationship be-

tween a magician and a familiar. If given a choice between working with his familiar or his staff, Powwell had to choose Thorny.

When he could control his words, he replied, "I've only been a journeyman for a few weeks, sir. The Commune can't send me on a master's quest yet." He had too many things to learn in the library before he embarked on his own quest—one that had nothing to do with Scarface or the welfare of the Commune.

"What kind of quest, sir?" Bessel asked.

Scarface shifted his attention to the older journeyman. "Gilby has been missing six moons in his search for Jaanus, another journeyman magician who has been missing for well over a year. I need you to find them both and bring them back. Coronnan cannot afford to lose any more magicians, especially if a plague threatens us."

"Sound reasoning, Aaddler," Nimbulan said from behind them. "But I think retrieving Rollett from Hanassa would be a more successful quest." His tone left Powwell with the impression he had more to say on the subject. Nimbulan's left hand came up, palm out, fingers slightly curled—his old magical gesture used as an extra sense to gather information or concentrate his thoughts.

Tension flowed out of Powwell at the sound of his adopted father's voice. Nimbulan would look out for his best interests, even if Scarface had forgotten how.

If only the old man could take him into the void to search out Kalen . . .

"We all know your obsession for keeping your students close to you, even though you have nothing left to teach them," Scarface snarled in contempt. "What else do you hesitate to say?"

"Bessel is your Senior Journeyman. He has responsibilities here," Nimbulan replied.

"I have apprentices who can take over his duties."

"Apprentices, sir, not journeymen," Bessel said, his voice and posture quite apologetic. "Apprentices don't have the training yet to help you with the younger students, to prepare your potions for special spells, to monitor your glass for important summons, or to research new spells for you.

They aren't mature enough to sit quietly in Council meetings, observing the reactions and whisperings of the lords and ambassadors."

Powwell almost applauded Bessel for speaking up for himself, something the Senior Journeyman rarely did—if you could find him outside the library. Bessel spent more time in the treasure trove of knowledge than Powwell did.

Nimbulan nodded encouragement to Bessel to continue.

"I would be happy to hasten the studies and exercises of some of the older apprentices, sir, so that they are ready for advancement when I am ready for my master's quest."

Powwell almost snorted in disgust at Bessel's humble tone and posture. As usual, Bessel seemed more interested in compromise just to keep his place in the University rather than fight for what he knew to be right.

"It is not your place to question my orders. Either of you." Scarface's clenched lips turned as white as his scar. The anger that always simmered within him seemed ready to explode.

"But it is their place, as the only two journeymen available, to offer observations to help you in your decisions," Nimbulan said. "I trained them to think and not just to obey orders blindly." His face worked as if he held back a big smile.

Powwell wanted to grin, too. Scarface had shown exemplary administrative skills in guiding the Commune this last year. He had stepped into the vacuum left when Nimbulan lost his magic and nearly his life. But Scarface's temper had won him few friends.

"I won't accept your quest, sir," Powwell replied. He stared directly into Scarface's hooded eyes so the man would know his determination. Thorny squirmed within his pocket, suddenly uncomfortable with Powwell's boldness. "I have made no secret that as soon as I figure out where she is, I will leave here to rescue my sister. If no other method exists to find her, I must prepare myself to enter the void to seek out her life force."

Powwell would know her distinctive orange-and-brown signature colors in any guise. Now that he was close to learning a way to find his sister, he wouldn't let Scarface interrupt his quest.

"Powwell, the void is far too dangerous!" Bessel protested. He looked almost as white with fear as Scarface did with anger.

"To enter the void, you must tap illegal magic," Nimbulan reminded him. "Your oath to the Commune prevents you from using those powers."

"You took oaths of obedience to me, young man. You owe me and the Commune." Scarface returned Powwell's stare.

"No, sir. I took an oath of loyalty to the Commune, Coronnan, and my king. I can best fulfill that oath by returning Kalen to the people who love and care for her. She has a valuable talent. If necessary, I'll go to Hanassa to find her. While I'm there, I can investigate what happened to Rollett—a stronger and more experienced magician than either Gilby or Jaanus."

"I do not believe you can assist anyone but yourself on such a wild lumbird chase. If your sister lives, her talent is based upon rogue magic. She must remain in exile from Coronnan. But your sister is dead. We both watched her fall into the pit of boiling lava along with Yaassima, the Kaalipha of Hanassa."

"But Yaassima went into the void between the planes of existence, not the pit. The dragons spat her out again in our presence. Yaassima was thrown into the pit before Kalen. Therefore, I must presume my sister lives."

"You tread on dangerous ground, Powwell. If you flirt with rogue magic to enter the void, then you betray the Commune and me, your master."

"Nimbulan is my master, no other."

Scarface raised his fist as if to strike Powwell.

Powwell reached out with his magic, stopping Scarface's fist in midair.

Thorny bristled, stabbing Powwell through layers of clothing. Powwell absorbed the pain, letting it fuel his magic.

"Consider yourself confined to your rooms except for kitchen duty until further notice. I must think on a proper punishment for this defiance," Scarface ground out, still unable to move his hand against Powwell. The Senior Magician wouldn't think about lowering his hand, only smashing Powwell's restraints.

Powwell turned his back on the Senior Magician and walked away without releasing Scarface's fist. If Scarface had realized that Powwell had tapped illegal powers—through Thorny—retribution would be swift and terrible.

I guess I've severed all my ties to the Commune and Coronnan with that little act of defiance. Severed his access to the library and the information there that might lead him to Kalen as well.

*   *   *

Inside the meeting chamber of the Council of Provinces

Walk with me, Katie, Quinnault said telepathically, as he rose from the council table. *I need to stretch my legs before my mind will settle and sort through this mess.*

Katie looked quickly around the room to see if any of the magicians present had eavesdropped. She knew that even if they had, they were honor-bound to respect the privacy of the royal couple and wouldn't show awareness of the communication.

Yes, Scarecrow, Katie replied. She slipped her hand into his, surprised by the chill in his fingers. *We both need fresh air and quiet.*

Quiet is something we'll never have while we live in Palace Reveta Tristile. Quinnault chuckled beneath his words. Around them they could hear hammering, stones scraping on each other, as the almost continuous building on the palace and the city within the new capital expanded almost daily.

"Where shall we walk?" Quinnault asked in tones just barely above a whisper.

"Somewhere without a dozen attending guards, courtiers, magicians, and ambassadors," she replied equally quietly.

"Not in this lifetime. We rule, and therefore our lives belong to the masses not ourselves." The king sighed.

"I know. 'Tis the same in my home. I just wish we could have a few moments away from politics."

Katie felt the tension in her husband at her words.

"I wasn't born a politician, Katie. I cannot lie and am

always surprised and hurt when others lie to me. No book exists that will teach me how to bend the truth like a politician." A look of bewilderment crossed his face.

"I understand you must select suitable mares to mate with Buan," she announced to the room at large.

Quinnault's eyes lit. *Good idea. Others will follow us, but you have removed the outing from the realm of politics.*

Not entirely. The ambassador from SeLenicca has a mare he wants to breed with your stallion, and so does Jorghe-Rosse from Rossemeyer.

"Buan has enough stamina to satisfy both and more." Quinnault chuckled again. He lengthened his stride as if he couldn't get out of the stuffy chamber fast enough. Katie nearly ran to keep up with him, never letting go of his hand, especially now that it warmed under her touch.

New buildings, many still shrouded in scaffolding, seemed to sprout like stalks of new wheat on every island comprising Coronnan City.

Two years ago, before Katie came to Coronnan as his bride, he had been lord of these islands. His stark defensive tower was now an extensive palace and administrative center. Simple farmhouses and vegetable crops had given way to dwellings and workshops for craftsmen thrown up almost overnight, elegant townhouses for politicians, and temples—dozens and dozens of little temples to serve the growing populace of the new capital of Coronnan.

This city represented her husband's dream of peace for Coronnan and an important place for this country within the world marketplace.

But he'd never planned to be king. She had been raised for her role as a member of a royal family that had ruled a galactic empire for many generations.

Quinnault nodded casually to the city dwellers as he passed them on his way to the nearest bridge. "Time was, I could name them all and their children. Now I know only one out of ten," he muttered.

Katie squeezed his hand in reassurance. "You know more of them than my grandfather ever tried to learn of his immediate household. It's important for us to maintain contact with the people we govern."

Quinnault smiled at her with that special half quirk of his mouth. Her pulse quickened in wonder and awe at her love for him.

They crossed the bridge in the market square. Vendors closing up their booths before the commencement of the holy day and late customers alike stopped to bow or curtsey to the royal couple. Children ran about caring little for the dignity of those who followed the king and queen at a discreet distance.

A flicker of movement in Katie's peripheral vision caught her attention. Just another bystander, propping himself up against the corner of a building. But not just any bystander. She nodded slightly to him and suppressed another smile. Liam Francis, her youngest brother, come to check on her—though they both knew he should not be on planet.

Her father should not be here either, but he was always a law unto himself.

A tiny bit of Katie's homesickness dissolved. She did miss her family. She almost gestured for Liam Francis to join her. At the last instant she dropped her hand. He blew her a kiss and melted into the crowd, one more slim young man among many—though he stood almost a head shorter than most.

One of the ladies rushed to the queen's side and shooed the children away.

"Let them play," Katie said, catching an unsteady toddler trying to follow his older siblings. She cuddled the child close for a moment. "We should have brought Marilell. She needs to get out of the palace more and breathe fresh air."

"We took her on the picnic. She's had enough fresh air for one day and needs a nap." Quinnault brushed a stray curl off Katie's face with his long fingers. "You need a break from constant mothering. We need time together before our next child comes. Any sign of making me a father again?"

Katie shook her head regretfully.

The courtiers stepped back one pace, giving them a small illusion of privacy. The guards who hovered around the edges paused as well, surveying the marketplace with restless, wary eyes.

Liam Francis popped up on the other side of the thoroughfare, then vanished again. Her homesickness came back to Katie with a sickening jolt.

Quinnault squeezed her hand this time, as if he sensed her loneliness among this bustling crowd.

She sighed. As long as she had her husband and daughter she had a family. But the only time she and Quinnault were ever truly alone together was in bed. And she wasn't certain the servants didn't listen then, too.

Oh, how she longed to snag Liam Francis and sit quietly by the fire with a mug of mulled wine while catching up on the latest gossip from home.

The parade of people followed Quinnault and Katie as they crossed a dozen islands between the palace and the mainland. As they stepped up on the last bridge, Katie paused a moment to look back. Their entourage had grown to include a number of curiosity seekers. Some nibbled food and sipped ale from the numerous markets along the route. Musicians played lively tunes in rhythm with their steps—or had they started marching in time with the music? A few people began an impromptu dance, others lifted their voices in songs.

"I've never known a people so ready to turn any event into a party." Katie gazed at them in amazement. Her foot tapped the dancing rhythm. Was that her brother kicking up his heels with a local woman on the fringes of the crowd?

"After three generations of civil war, the common people have learned to grab enjoyment whenever they can, despite the feuds and jockeying for power at court," Quinnault replied. "I want to give my people reasons to rejoice every day. They deserve it."

"Do you suppose it would be beneath our royal dignity to join the dancing?" She would love to maneuver close to Liam Francis and exchange a few words, maybe dance a few steps with him, just like at parties back home.

"Considering that I would tread on your feet and likely slip and fall on my bum, yes, this free-spirited dancing is definitely beneath my dignity." Quinnault chuckled openly.

Much of the daily strain of ruling slid from his face, replacing worry lines with youthful humor.

Katie hid a laugh behind her hand. The image of her tall

husband sprawling in the mud, long legs tangled in the hem of her skirts presented a decided contrast to his normal public demeanor.

Quinnault's mind tickled hers with silent laughter. He, too, enjoyed the image of himself as the gangling scarecrow of his youth. He still thought of himself as that awkward young man yanked from his quiet life of study in a monastery to govern his family's lands, out of place and bewildered by the enormity of his duty.

"You've never quite grown into your feet, have you?" she asked quietly.

"I'm not familiar with that expression." He continued smiling and nodding his head in time with the music.

"Children and dogs tend to have feet out of proportion to their bodies. They are awkward until their bodies grow to match the feet. Once their proportions match, they become as graceful in mind as in body."

"Ah, yes, they do. Frankly, Katie, I've grown into my feet." He looked down at the monstrous boots that covered them. "But I haven't grown into my role as king."

"Yes, you have, my dear. The people adore you."

"My very minimal magical talent as an empath qualified me for my chosen life path as a priest. I understand what the people endure, and sometimes I can help them heal. But the politicians who make the government work talk circles around me. They lie and hide the truth behind rivers of words. I get lost in the words that mean too many things at the same time."

"Most people are mystified by those wordstorms." Katie gazed lovingly into his eyes, wondering how her alien education might help him deal with the professional wordsmiths.

Shouting in the middle of the crowd disrupted her thoughts. An argument grew around a knot of younger men. She checked to make sure her brother was not one of them. Back home he would be the first to wade into a brawl, fists and feet flying, loving the game of breaking heads to break up the fight. Liam Francis had vanished again. No sign of Sean Michael or Jamie Patrick either.

One of the disputants, clothed in a gaudy orange shirt with purple piping, threw an overripe pear at his neighbor.

The fruit splattered the more sober unbleached linen shirt of a dark-haired man who stood a little taller than most of the crowd. He responded by throwing the remains of his ale into Orange-shirt's face.

Both followed through with fists. Their neighbors joined the spreading brawl.

"Guards, go and break this up. Disperse the people before this spreads even further," Quinnault ordered.

Half of the armed escort dispersed through the crowd.

Katie clutched her husband's arm, frightened, as the anger spread and engulfed the people standing closest to the bridge. Angry thoughts blasted through her mental armor. The emotions behind the fight made her toes curl and brought lumbird bumps to her spine.

She'd experienced this sensation only once before, when an assassin had crept into her room the night before her wedding. He'd used magic to instill fear in her, a terror so great she lay immobile, defenseless against his attack.

"Come, Your Grace," the sergeant-at-arms suggested. ":I'll escort you to the royal stables. You'll be safe there."

"Take Her Grace back to the palace by whatever back routes you can find," Quinnault replied. He patted Katie's hand. "I'll follow by a different route with the others. We'll be safer attracting less attention with smaller parties."

"No, Quinnault," Katie said quietly but with determination. "We both need to stay. Someone is amplifying the crowd's emotions with magic to further their own political agenda. Listen to the argument. Listen hard. We need to stop this here and now!"

"Filthy foreigner!" Orange-shirt yelled. "How dare you think of marrying off your daughter to my son. I'll not taint our bloodline with Rovers."

Strange, Orange-shirt dressed more like a Rover than the man he accused.

"Rovers steal our children as well as our hard-earned dragini." That voice came from a different quarter altogether. The angry emotions swelled, as if being manipulated by a master hand.

The assassin who had used her own emotions against Katie had been a Rover.

Confusion muddled her thoughts. Who was behind this?

"Rovers will rape and control your mind with their magic worse than any Commune Magician." That voice came from an ordinary woman with muddy blond hair, no Rover coloring in her face or clothing.

"Bad enough we have to put up with a foreign queen and her prancing lumbird father. We don't need Rovers and them desert mercenaries freeloading off our bounty. We don't need a foreign queen controlling our king," Orange-shirt called to the crowd in general.

Katie bristled. Beside her, Quinnault clenched his jaw. A muscle jumped in his cheek, and the pulse in his neck beat too rapidly.

The few remaining courtiers in their party gasped at the audacity of the crowd voicing these sentiments in front of the royal couple. Most of the dignitaries had dispersed at the first sign of trouble.

"We need a new king," Orange-shirt yelled above the noise of the crowd. "We need a king who doesn't bow to foreign interests."

"Kill all foreigners!"

Chapter 3

*Late afternoon, Saawheen, on the Long Bridge to
the mainland, Coronnan City*

"**S**peak to them, Quinnault. End this before the violence
spreads!" Katie tugged at her husband's arm. The moisture on her brow and back turned icy with fear.

The guards surrounded them, swords drawn. Tension made
their arms twitch.

If any one of them drew so much as a drop of blood, all
hope of exerting calm would disappear.

Quinnault stared at her, gathering his thoughts. Then he
nodded his head and took a deep breath.

"My people." Quinnault raised his arms above his head
as he spoke the words in a voice that carried to the far
reaches of the crowd.

A few people paid heed and ceased their babble.

"Stand higher on the bridge so that more people can see
you," Katie urged him. Hope sprouted in her chest at the
crowd's initial response to him.

He took two steps back to the center of the arched span.
His height and the elevation made him stand well above
everyone. "My people, listen to me!" he commanded again
in ringing tones worthy of a battlefield—or a pulpit.

Katie immediately felt calmer, more confident. Apparently so did the mob. Quiet spread in gentle ripples.

So this was Quinnault's magic talent. Nothing overt
enough for him to be called a magician, but enough—and
perhaps the best talent for a man with aspirations to the

priesthood or to leading a diverse populace through tribulation.

"Listen to me, please. You must cease this violence!"

Katie saw three men pause with hands upraised, ready to strike. But they didn't complete their blows.

"I understand your fears," Quinnault said. "I lived through the wars, I fought alongside you when rival lords threatened these islands. And when peace came within our grasp, you declared me king. You, the people, decided I should lead you because you knew I would bring the warring factions together in compromise." Quinnault paused a moment to let his words sink in.

"Now we must all work together to maintain that peace. We must fight those who would disrupt that peace from *within* as well as without."

Men and women stared in disbelief at missiles of food and stones and tools and clubs they clutched in their hands. A woman in the front ranks deliberately put down the palm-sized rock she had been ready to lob at the man standing next to her. Her neighbor pocketed the hammer he held poised to defend himself.

Quinnault breathed deeply.

So you noticed that someone manipulated their emotions with magic, Katie commented on a tight mental line. Best if the magician in the crowd did not eavesdrop.

Magic? Quinnault cocked an eyebrow at her. His slightly bemused expression could not hide his unease from her.

Katie searched the crowd for signs of the man with the gaudy orange shirt with purple piping. She should have been able to pick him out in a moment among the more soberly dressed folk.

I sense magic and conspiracy in this brawl. Someone deliberately fed fear into these people.

"Disperse to your homes now to celebrate Sawheen, our Holy Day of Remembrance," Quinnault commanded. "You are good people. You don't need to listen to those who would use you to fight their fears. You need only live your lives in peace. A peace we have fought for. But now the fighting must cease."

"What about the foreigners? What about . . . ?"

Katie searched the crowd for the speaker. It sounded a lot like Orange-shirt, but she couldn't be sure. The voice seemed to come from all directions, followed by ripples of unease. She spotted Liam Francis working his way through the crowd with deliberation. Sean Michael and Jamie Patrick approached from other directions, their bright red hair obvious beacons in the mob. She hoped they honed in on the disruptive magician.

"If you notice people from other lands crowding our city, be assured they bring trade, they bring friendship. I work with their leaders to avoid another war. We all work for peace and prosperity," Quinnault responded.

A mood of calm followed his words, more overwhelming than the anonymous voice.

Katie bit her lip in confusion. Was it right for her husband to use magic to influence the crowd in the same manner another had used magic to bring the crowd to riot?

(Sometimes, Katie, one must fight fire with fire or magic with magic,) a dragon voice reminded her.

"What do we do now, Quinnault?" she asked. Her brothers disappeared again, swallowed up in the mass of people. She had no idea if they found their quarry or not.

"We need to know who started this and why," Quinnault replied. "My investigators must ask questions and keep their eyes and ears open for more signs of trouble. I'm certain there will be more."

*   *   *

Sunset, neighborhood temple three islands west of Palace Reveta Tristile, Coronnan City

Katie sank to her knees on the cold stone floor of the little neighborhood temple. The last rays of sunlight streamed through the high narrow windows, adding luster to the icon tapestry of the three Stargods descending upon a cloud of silver flame on the back wall of the sanctuary. Beside her, Quinnault bowed his head and murmured the prayers for the dead. Nimbulan, Myri, and Yaala occupied the space just behind the royal couple. Around them—with a buffer zone of empty space out of respect for Quinnault and Katie—the entire congregation recited the same petitions.

A red-robed priest joined Katie in her prayers. She glanced briefly at him. He kept the cowl of his garment over his head, concealing his face. Unusual that anyone not of the royal entourage would come so close.

The priest jostled her elbow slightly as he made a very Terran sign of the cross, touching head, heart, and both shoulders. She'd grown used to the locals using almost the same gesture but with a different invocation from the one she'd learned as an infant back home.

"Almost like being at home," the priest whispered in a Terran accent.

"I should have known you'd show up eventually, Sean Michael," she whispered back to her older brother—the middle one in age of her three siblings. "You aren't supposed to be here. We agreed, no more family contact. We take no more chances contaminating this culture."

"Have to check up on my baby sister." He bowed his head again to avoid Quinnault's inquisitive look.

"Liam Francis already did."

"Ah, but our youngest brother has not reported back to us. I suspect he has found a tavern and a lady to entertain him for the evening. Like the dark-eyed beauty over there." He gestured with his chin toward a woman with Rover coloring and Rover-gaudy clothing strung with chains of coins who knelt directly behind Nimbulan.

"Or Liam Francis may have gone looking for a disruptive magician. I thought I saw you and Jamie Patrick following the same psychic scent."

Sean Michael raised a rusty red eyebrow at her. "We found nothing."

"Could you look again?"

He nodded. "And when may I see my favorite niece, the Princess Marilell?"

"In the morning." Katie nudged him sharply with her elbow, a familiar gesture to quiet him during church services.

"Kinnsell is not reporting in to the mother ship either. I really came to haul him back home, but I couldn't resist the opportunity to see you, little sister." He brushed her fingertips gently with his own.

The brief caress filled her with warmth and a longing to hug him close.

A moment later he slipped away, barely noticed by anyone but herself. A void of loneliness opened in her belly.

Someone I should know? Quinnault asked her. He dropped his hand to clasp hers. His love channeled through the physical contatct.

One of my brothers, she replied. She used to think mind-to-mind communications with her brothers came easily. But compared to the intimate contact with her husband, family telepathy seemed a great effort. No wonder her brother had whispered.

Your family isn't supposed to be here, Quinnault said.

Neither is my father. Sean Michael came to take Kinnsell home.

Odd place to look for your father. I've never known him to show the least interest in our customs.

Kinnsell is only interested in himself.

And causing trouble.

Hush, beloved. Our part is coming up. Katie clasped a spray of bright flowers she had laid on the floor beside her earlier. When the priest signaled her forward, she rose and placed the small bouquet of autumnal blossoms on the plain stone altar. "In memory of my mother who passed beyond this plane of existence five years ago. May she find peace beyond the void," she recited the ritual.

Quinnault followed her with petitions for a long string of deceased relatives.

Together they bowed to the altar and returned to their places.

Then Nimbulan, Myri, and the rest of the congregation followed suit.

"Who is that woman?" Katie asked, nodding toward the flamboyant woman with a cloud of dark hair and clear ivory skin that her brother had noticed. The two men who placed flowers on the altar immediately after her could only be Liam Francis and Sean Michael. Where was Jamie Patrick hiding? And Kinnsell? She was surprised her father hadn't found the exotically beautiful woman yet.

"Her name is Maia. She came out of Hanassa last year with Nimbulan," Quinnault replied quietly. "She has some claim on him. We shelter her here in this sanctuary with magical armor all around so that others of her kind cannot spy on us through her without her knowledge or consent."

"She does not seem happy. What if she decides to leave?"

"I do not know. I only hope that if she chooses to leave, she will return to her clan and not remain to be manipulated by the Rovers who wish us ill."

A wave of distorted images washed over Katie. Her sense of now and then, up and down, real and unreal, swirled around her in a tornado of bright colors and broken images. Her father, Maia, a shuttlecraft from the mother ship. Dragons, dragons everywhere. And a purple cloud so dark it seemed almost black engulfing them all.

She swayed dizzily.

"Katie!" Quinnault wrapped both arms around her, holding her upright.

"Scarecrow. I see trouble. I've never had a premonition before, but I see trouble surrounding that woman. Disaster cloaks her aura and it centers around my family somehow."

*   *   *

Saawheen Evening, in the home of Myrilandel,
Ambassador for the Dragon Nimbus to
Coronnan, Coronnan City

Powwell searched Yaala's eyes for support, compassion, anything but the fear that lingered there.

"This is very dangerous, Powwell," Bessel said quietly from the desk in Nimbulan's study. "Neither of us has much experience with the void. The spell is illegal. I'm not prepared to sacrifice everything to help you find your sister."

"You don't have to work the spell, only monitor me and bring me back if I get into trouble. You're the only magician I trust, Bessel."

"I'll monitor you, Powwell," Yaala said quietly from her window seat. The autumnal sunset backlit her fair hair and skin giving her the illusion of ethereal fragility. Her heavy brocade gown nearly overwhelmed her slight figure. It reflected the current fashion of muted Kardia tones. Bronze and green flecked the gold fabric. Those colors looked wonderful on Queen Katie with her red hair and green eyes, so everyone at court wore them.

Yaala needed light blues and pinks to flatter her. She also needed a warmer climate. Desert born and bred, she shivered in the drafty window seat. And yet she clung to the light filtering through the oiled parchment pane.

Powwell vowed to take her home again. As soon as he found Kalen. Yaala deserved the best. More than he could give her.

"You don't have the magic to drag me out of the void, Yaala," Powwell replied. He clasped her hand in reassurance. "I'll be all right. I've researched this extensively."

"Shouldn't we wait for Master Nimbulan to return from temple?" Bessel fiddled with one of the master's pens. "He'd be able to monitor you. He knows what you are up against."

"But he has no magic either."

"What if Scarface finds out what we're doing? This spell requires rogue magic. The whole thing is illegal." Bessel began tapping the pen against Nimbulan's desk.

"That's why we're doing it in Myrilandel's house. She's the ambassador for the dragons. This house, the embassy, is foreign territory. We aren't in Coronnan, so the spell isn't illegal here."

Neither Bessel nor Yaala looked reassured by the argument.

"I need you, Bessel. And I'm running out of time. I've wasted moons and moons trying to figure out where to look for Kalen without going into the void. I've tried to abide by the rules of the Commune. Now Scarface has dismissed me from the Commune. He's cut off my access to the library, to the entire University. I'm a magician outside the Commune; therefore I have to either apologize to him or leave Coronnan by midnight. I have to search the void here and now. Either you help me, Bessel, or I do it alone with only Thorny to guide me." He petted the little hedgehog within his tunic pocket.

"Start your trance, Powwell. Best we get this over with before I lose my courage."

Powwell sat cross-legged on the floor, placing Thorny on his right thigh, within easy reach. In an emergency, his familiar could bristle his spines, jabbing Powwell back into his body and this reality. He took a deep breath on three counts, clearing his mind of the room, his companions, every stray thought except his purpose. He let go of the dragon magic he kept stored in his body and found a silvery blue ley line deep within the planet to feed him magical energy. Calm spread through him like warm honey. He took a second breath on the same three counts, holding it three counts, and then releasing it on three counts. The absolute blackness of the void flickered around his peripheral vision. He resisted the urge to plunge into the emptiness between the planes of existence. A third breath took him deeper into his trance. Yaala and Bessel became illusory ghosts to his perceptions. Nothing existed in this reality except Thorny who remained a solid and familiar presence.

The void beckoned him with the soft music of the stars. He almost recognized the melody, needed to hear more to fit the alluring pieces together.

I'll tether you to this existence with the umbilical of your life force while you search, Bessel said directly into his thoughts.

Powwell merged with the blank nothingness of the void. All sense of his body, of direction, of his planetary orientation evaporated. Nothing existed but his mind.

He fought a momentary panic that he might become lost, never find his way back or forward into his next existence. Then Thorny's emotional touch reassured him.

On the heels of the panic came awareness of dozens of bright umbilical cords representing the life forces of all the lives he had encountered. He picked out Nimbulan's blue easily. Though the life force had faded since the last time Powwell had viewed it with his master, the blue still dominated Powwell's life. Myrilandel's crystal and silver wrapped around Nimbulan's blue, essentially binding them together into one being.

Bessel's braid of bright blue and red trailed away from

his perceptions, a ladder to climb back into his body if he needed help.

He searched for Kalen, expecting her life force to entwine with his own. An undefined silver cord tinged with lavender wrapped around Powwell with no trace of his sister's orange and brown. Yaala? He looked more closely at the dull silver of his own life, seeking a hint of color. Magicians rarely saw their personal signature colors.

A brighter crystal life danced around Powwell's own life force, just out of reach. Only Shayla, the nearly invisible female dragon could be such a pure crystal. She influenced all the lives in Coronnan without becoming a part of any.

Powwell relaxed, accepting Shayla as his guide and mentor during this journey.

(What do you seek?)

I search for my sister who is lost to me, Powwell replied to the directionless voice that filled the void as well as his mind—perhaps his mind and the void were the same thing. His thoughts threatened to drift into idle speculation. The void invited him to explore each new tangent. Thorny prodded him with a mental jab—like a spine pricking his skin. Powwell yanked himself back to his quest.

(Is she truly lost, or do you not know where to look?) A typically cryptic dragon observation.

Kalen was thrown into the lava core of Hanassa as the dragongate opened, but before it was fully formed. Her companion went into the void. The dragons spat that one out again. I must presume my sister drifts alone in the void as well.

Powwell sensed alarm and wariness in the crystal life force the moment he mentioned Hanassa, the city of outlaws, and the dragongate, the magical portal that could take a traveler away from Hanassa to any number of locations.

(If the one you seek entered the void from Hanassa, then if she finds her way out again without assistance, she must return to Hanassa. Give up your search. She will not welcome being found.)

I have to find her. I am not complete without her. She is my only kin.

(She may be your kin no longer. Seek others to fulfill you. Seek in your heart for the source of the emptiness you feel.)

I can't. I have to find Kalen. I promised her.

(Look within yourself before you venture into the realm of the renegade dragon.)

Powwell fell back into his body with a stomach-wrenching jolt.

A red haze with black sparkles lingered in his vision as Bessel and Yaala solidified before him.

Powwell shook his head to clear his eyes. Deep within the heart of the haze, a shrouded drop of orange and brown lingered and then turned deep purple that darkened into black. A heartbeat later it shrank to nothing. The haze retracted from the others, forming a mist around himself and Thorny, like an aura.

Thorny hummed a welcome and relaxed his hunched spines.

"Wake up, Powwell. Come back, Powwell!" Bessel slapped his face to rouse him. "Leave the void behind you, Powwell."

"Is my magical signature red with black sparkles?" Powwell asked. The words came out slurred. He felt almost drunk with fatigue and light-headedness. He reached out his hand toward Yaala, needing her touch to anchor him.

"You saw your own colors?" Bessel replied. His mouth gaped open in awe.

"Yes, at the last moment as I came back to my body. Yours are a red-and-blue braid."

"I've been told as much," Bessel agreed. "I wish I could see them."

"I saw all of our colors, but I couldn't find Kalen in the void. As I returned, I saw her orange-and-brown life force greatly diminished and shrouded in purple. A purple so dark it was almost black."

"Hanassa," Yaala breathed the word in a frightened hiss.

"Shayla told me I had to beware the renegade dragon. I have to go to Hanassa to find my sister. Did she mean I have to go to the city or to the only dragon exiled from the nimbus?"

"Both," Yaala said. "But first you have to find a way into the city. Land access was destroyed in the kardiaquake as we left the city. The dragongate has either shifted its portals or is broken."

"Scarface has had round-the-clock watches at all the

known portals in Coronnan," Bessel reminded him. "None of them have opened in over a year. If the dragongate still exists, you'll have to find a new opening to get into the city."

"I'll find one. Somehow. I hope Rollett is still there to help."

"You'd better hope Rollett is still alive. Hanassa kills outsiders," Yaala reminded him.

"The renegade dragon or the city?"

"Both."

Chapter 4

*Dawn, after Saawheen, University of Magicians
residential wing, Coronnan City*

Powwell crept out of his cell in the journeyman's section
of the University. Fortunately, only one other cell was
occupied at this end. Five cells remained empty until more
apprentices earned journeyman status. Bessel snored softly
in the last room on the corridor, next to the staircase leading up to the masters' suites and down to the kitchen and
refectory. Behind Powwell, the fifteen apprentice cells were
much more crowded, sometimes four or five young men
bunking in a single cell smaller than Powwell's room. He
didn't like leaving Bessel alone, the only journeyman in the
complex, the only buffer between Scarface's temper and
the vulnerable apprentices.

His mission would not wait, and he would not apologize
to Scarface for his disobedience.

The morning air smelled clean and damp, as if it were
just awakening to new adventures. Powwell yawned briefly
and stretched. Longingly he looked back at his rumpled
bed. No. He'd come too far. His decisions had been made
moons ago when he left his sister in Hanassa.

Resolutely, he shouldered his pack and pulled Thorny
out of his tunic pocket. The little hedgehog tried to curl
into a tight ball. Normally nocturnal, dawn signaled his preferred sleep time. Powwell roused him with a thought. Reluctantly, Thorny uncurled and wiggled his nose. The scent
of fresh bread baking, heightened by Thorny's keen nose,
made Powwell's stomach growl.

Guillia, the cook, housekeeper, and surrogate mother for the University—and also Kalen's mother, but not Powwell's—had probably been awake for hours preparing the hearty breakfast required by magicians who burned tremendous amounts of energy working their talents for the good of the kingdom.

Silently, Powwell crept down the stairs. At the bottom of the stairwell, he turned left into the now enclosed corridor, then immediately left again, and stepped down three uneven stairs to the kitchen. When Nimbulan first established the University in the abandoned monastery, this room had been the kitchen where Powwell and two other apprentices gathered with Journeymen Bessel, Rollett, and Master Nimbulan. Jaanus and Gilby, the missing journeymen had been there also, along with Old Lyman the librarian. The cooking fire kept them warm in the drafty abandoned monastery during that first long winter.

Powwell smiled in memory of the bonds of friendship and loyalty they had all formed. His mouth watered for the taste of the Tambootie flavoring his tea. The University would never lace any food or drink with the Tambootie again.

He hated leaving Bessel and Lyman alone with Scarface. Only those two remained from the days when Nimbulan ran the University with a strict but loving paternal air. He'd made the University into a family. Scarface turned it into a stern and unforgiving institution.

"One day you'll learn, Scarface, that the strongest family is one that is bound together by silken cords of love. Some members may leave, but they will return when needed. You prefer to force your fellows to follow you with iron chains of control. Once we escape, we'll never return to you," he muttered as he skirted the long dining tables on his way to the new kitchen, separated from the refectory by a short passage.

Out of long habit, he paused and probed the kitchen with his magic before entering. The years of constant warfare during his youth had made him cautious. The time he had spent as a slave in Hanassa had taught him suspicion. A curious vacancy beyond the door made the hair on his nape stand up. Thorny hunched, all of his spines bristled.

Someone had built a bubble of armor around themselves to keep a conversation very private.

That had never stopped Powwell before. He'd survived war, slavery, Hanassa, and Scarface by learning to eavesdrop. Of course, the armor erected by two magicians using dragon magic might be harder to penetrate than one maintained by a solitary magician. He'd just have to probe deeper.

Powwell opened the door to the kitchen, making sure his magic silenced the hinges and prevented a cool draft from announcing an intruder. He breathed in the welcoming scent of fresh bread, bacon, and dried fruit stewing in wine and spices. Quickly he silenced his growling stomach.

He searched the room, brightened by cooking fires, for any distortions of light. There, to the left of the hearth in the chimney nook, shadows gathered more deeply than they should. Only a light shell of armor surrounded the magicians since the only other person in the room was Guillia who was presumed to have no magic other than her instinct for providing wonderful meals for empty stomachs precisely when needed.

A quick probe of red-and-black light, showing Powwell's unique signature very nicely now that he knew how to see his own colors, and he ducked back into the passageway, leaving the door ajar a tiny crack.

"Bessel was right to refuse the quest! Scarface needs him to help with all the new apprentices he brings in by the sledgeload," Red Beetle hissed.

Powwell heard the click as the middle-aged man snapped his fingers while he talked. He made a sound very like the red beetle he was named for.

Briefly, Powwell wondered if he kept one of the stinky insects in his pocket as a familiar. Wouldn't that set Scarface on his ear if he did! He'd have to outlaw one of his staunchest supporters.

"Bessel is so insecure about being outcast he'll fall under Scarface's total control in no time," Red Beetle finished.

"And I say we cannot take a chance on having any outsiders in the University and Commune. We must purge our membership." A small thud followed Humpback's words. Powwell could almost see the stoop-shouldered magician who advised lord Balthazaan ramming his staff up and down with each word. His awkward posture made him rely on his basic tool of magic as a walking stick as well as a channel for his spells.

"We don't have to worry about Powwell any longer. His magic is stronger than Bessel's and he's more independent." Red Beetle said.

"Too creative with his spells by half. Powwell always has to be different." Humpback pounded his staff against the flagstones.

"Well, Scarface formally dismissed him. He has to be out of Coronnan in three days or face trial and imprisonment, possibly execution. 'Tis a good law, no magic or magicians without Commune sanction," Red Beetle replied.

So, the removal from the University of everyone who had studied or worked with Nimbulan was an actual conspiracy rather than merely Scarface lashing out at what he could never totally control. Powwell had suspected as much moons ago.

"Once we have total control over all the members of the Commune, the rest of Coronnan will fall into our hands. The ineffective king and Council of Provinces will be obsolete. We will have order governed by dragon magic at last," Humpback said decisively.

Total control of the kingdom? The Commune wasn't supposed to work that way. They provided *neutral* advisers to the king and lords.

What could Powwell do to stop them?

Nothing.

Good thing he was headed to Hanassa as soon as he found an entrance into the closed city deep in an ancient volcanic caldera. If Rollett still lived, Powwell could send him home to help Nimbulan, Lyman, and Bessel fight this conspiracy, too.

Should he warn Bessel?

If Bessel didn't know about the conspiracy now, he would not listen to Powwell's warning.

"Sorry, Bessel, I can't stick around to help you. But you'll land on your feet. You always do, though you might not think so. I'll send Rollett back to help," he whispered to his absent friend, "because I've got to find Kalen and this is the only way to do it."

He listened a few more moments as the magicians planned how they would advise their lords to coincide with Scarface's policies. That wasn't supposed to be the way the system worked. The magician advisers should be neutral observers. Politics should not taint the Commune and the University. But they did.

Then the two master magicians left the kitchen, without glancing at Powwell. They each munched on thick slabs of bread slathered with brambleberry jam.

When he could no longer hear their steps on the flagstone passageway, Powwell slipped into the kitchen.

"I've packed a journey bag for you," Guillia said without preamble. "You'll find my girl."

"I'm going to try," Powwell replied, raising his eyebrows at the woman's perception. He hefted the pack on the worktable, almost as big and heavy as the one he already carried with his books and clothes and tools. How had she known he'd need rations for a long trek on his own.

"She's alive. I can sense that." Guillia removed a large pan full of crisp bacon from the hearthstone.

"Do you have magic after all, Guillia?" Powwell asked, snitching a rasher of bacon. It burned his fingers, and he juggled the hot meat back and forth between his palms until it had cooled enough to eat.

"Just a mother's instinct." She scooped the remaining bacon onto a serving platter with a long-handled fork.

Powwell stole another handful.

"If Yaala asks, tell her I'll meet her in the clearing by spring. Tell her . . ."

"I know what to tell her, lad. Now, best you be off before *they*," she jerked her head in the direction Red Beetle and Humpback had walked, "come back and find you still here."

"Did you hear them talking, Guillia?" Powwell asked as he kissed her cheek in thanks.

" 'Course I did. Their paltry armor wouldn't keep out a mouse let alone a woman who needs to know what transpires in this University. They don't like women, so they pretend I'm not here. Though they'll scream loud enough if I'm two heartbeats late with their meals. Now scoot. Just find my girl and make sure she's safe."

"I'll do that, Guillia. For you. For both of us, I'll find Kalen and I'll find Rollett. Then we'll come back and take care of Scarface."

"Just find Kalen. I don't want my little girl left alone without family or friends."

"No one deserves to be without family. I just hope Bessel is as lucky as I am to find both when he's forced to leave here."

"I'll watch over him while he's here, lad. Though I suspect he'll leave, too, 'afore long. All the boys here are like sons to me. As long as Scarface lets me stay, I'll watch over all of them."

*   *   *

Early spring, a mining village in Balthasaan, South of Coronnan City

Bessel trudged up the hill toward the mining village and his parents' home. He didn't want to be here. But Scarface had insisted he come. The message from home requesting his presence had been urgent.

Bessel stared hard at his father standing in the open doorway of the family home. Old memories of pain and loneliness clouded his awareness of here and now.

Spring sunshine warmed his back but he might as well be facing the winter blizzard that had shrouded the village the last time he saw it. The snow had masked the black dust that permeated everything for miles around. But it hadn't hidden the blackness in his father's heart.

Bessel would never think of him as his father again.

"So you've come back," Maydon said tersely. The squarely built man Bessel had once called "Da" blocked the doorway. His stance did not invite Bessel within, despite the urgency of his message.

Maydon balanced his weight on one leg and crutches. He'd lost the left leg from the knee down years ago. Now he looked as if he'd rather use the crutches for weapons than walking aids.

"I was told to come back." Bessel looked toward the path he had just followed to the house, wishing he could reverse directions. New growth of flowers and grasses poked through the pervasive dust. Soon they, too, would be coated in the awful stuff.

Bessel wanted to cough just thinking about the dust.

"And you always obey orders, I suppose," Maydon sneered.

"You ordered me away from your home eight years ago. I obeyed you then. Now I obey the Senior Magician of the Commune of Magicians. He ordered me to visit my mother on her deathbed." Bessel's oath of loyalty and obedience meant a great deal to him.

He'd skirted disobedience in helping Powwell access the void last winter. No one had heard from Powwell since then, five full moons. Now Bessel followed orders without question rather than risk exile from the fellowship of the magicians.

He couldn't walk away from the home and family the Commune represented as Powwell had.

"Why did you request that the Commune release me from my important studies for this visit?" Bessel asked Maydon after a long moment of hostile silence.

"Book learning never served anyone but greedy magicians. Besides, she asked for you."

"Then I'd best go inside and see her."

Neither man moved.

"Aren't you going to use your *s'murghin'* magic to force me to back up?" the one-legged man challenged his son, never letting his contempt lessen in his voice or posture.

"No."

"Why not?" Surprise loosened Maydon's fierce grip on his crutches a little.

"I won't contaminate my mind or my honor by touching your ugly thoughts," Bessel replied. He wanted to believe that his family had become hostile toward Bessel's magic talent because they didn't understand it. They'd never encountered a magician before, other than the Battlemages attached to the armies that periodically pillaged the mines and the village.

"Watch your mouth, boy. I'm your da, your family."

"You ceased being my father the night you threw me into the teeth of a winter storm to fend for myself." For the first time, Bessel noticed that his father's stocky frame, formerly rotund, had wasted to tough sinew and bone. His eyes looked too bright, and an unnatural flush rode high on his cheeks and brow. His hands were swollen where he clutched the crutches.

The once substantial stone home looked as frail and neglected as its owner. But then, Maydon had always considered his job as accountant for the mines a poor second to working the mines themselves, even though the job brought in a great deal more money—enough to build this house for the family.

"Did you know I was captured by outlaws?" Bessel continued. Bitterness nearly choked him. "They had a magician of sorts with them who wrapped a spell around me so that I couldn't use my magic to escape. Did you know that those outlaws used me as their toy for two weeks until I was sold at auction?" He clung to the warm memory of Nimbulan marching into the outlaw camp and outbidding all the others for the right to exploit Bessel's talent, to enslave him, and abuse him.

But Nimbulan hadn't exploited anything. Instead he'd given Bessel the love and understanding to use his talent wisely. Nimbulan had become more of a father to him than Maydon had ever been.

"Only what you deserve, Magician," Maydon spat the title, staring at Bessel, lips pursed so tightly they lost all color.

"Maydon, come quickly," a woman called from inside the house. "Maydon, she needs you."

Bessel recognized his aunt's voice. Baarben had lived with her brother's family for as long as Bessel could remember. He bit back a cry of welcome for the woman who had been as much a mother to him as his own mother.

Maydon stepped back into the house. His expression of fierce rejection of his son faded into anxiety.

Bessel followed him, being careful not to touch his father. They hadn't touched since the day Bessel had used his magic to free his father from a mine accident. The heavy rocks and timbers that pinned Maydon had cost him his leg. But Bessel had saved his life.

Maydon had declared that without the leg he wasn't certain he had a life. He'd blamed Bessel and the boy's cursed magic talent for saving him.

Every time Bessel remembered what outlaws had done to him, he wished he hadn't levitated beams and rocks from his father's leg, hadn't made it possible for the other miners to rescue him.

The moment Bessel passed the doorframe, a strange smell stopped him short. He should recognize it. What? The memory escaped him, slipping in and out of his mind like a dragon. One moment it was there, almost tangible, and then the light shifted and it was gone.

He hesitated to enter the house until he understood the smell. Something told him it was dangerous.

The sound of his aunt's loud weeping finally drew him inward.

The smell intensified as he neared the common room. His mother lay on a low bed beside the hearth. She shivered with intense chill in the overly warm room. Fever flushed her skin.

Baarben threw a handful of herbs onto the open fire. Aromatic smoke rose, filling the room. Bessel identified five different herbs that should reduce fever and ease painful joints. Baarben hadn't included the Tambootie in the mixture. It had unique curative powers to anyone with a hint of magical talent but was toxic to mundanes. Should he suggest that she add some? The family must have some magic talent for him to have inherited it.

Maydon seemed more comfortable breathing the astringent essence of the plants. They had no effect on the dying woman by the hearth.

"Did he come, Maydon? Did my baby come home?" Bessel's mother whispered. She gripped her husband's tunic with a wasted, clawlike hand.

"I've come home, M'ma." Bessel knelt beside her. He realized he didn't even know her given name. She'd always been "M'ma" or "Mer Maydon" in his mind.

"Bessel, my baby." Her voice trailed off and a tiny smile touched her lips. Then a fit of coughing grabbed her until unconsciousness claimed her.

"She'll die happy now. You can go," Maydon said. He stared into the flames rather than look at his son.

"She should have a true healer! Why didn't you send to Lord Balthazaan?" Every lord had a magician adviser, a magician healer, and a magician priest assigned to his province. Even if Balthazaan and Humpback were out of the province, the healer and priest should be available.

"There are too many people dying of this strange disease." Aunt Baarben touched Bessel's sleeve in sympathy. "Even the lord's family and household suffer. It takes the old, the young, and pregnant women first. But no one is immune."

"I haven't the healing talent, but I'll see what I can do." Bessel touched his mother's face with exploratory fingers. He wasn't a strong magician. Without illegally tapping a ley line, what could he do other than give his mother a little strength? Even when he'd gathered a full portion of dragon magic, he had trouble joining with the other magicians to increase the power of the joint spell by orders of magnitude. Lately he'd had trouble gathering any dragon magic at all, almost as if there wasn't enough left to go around.

He'd give M'ma all of his strength if he could. That had to be enough until he could summon a healer. She couldn't die. Not yet. Not until he'd made peace with her, made certain she knew that he blamed only his father for his estrangement.

"You'll keep your filthy magic away from her!" Maydon roared, slapping Bessel's hand away. "Let her die in peace and pass to her next existence without interference."

Bessel stared at his left hand a moment, the one his father had slapped away. A dominant left hand had marked him as a potential magician from earliest childhood. Deliberately he closed the offending hand into a fist and drove it into Maydon's jaw.

Maydon reared back. His crutches fell to the slate floor. He flailed clumsily as his body joined the crutches.

"Fewer than half of all left-handers are magicians and less than half of all magicians are left-handed. You condemned me as a magician before you had any true evidence," Bessel said quietly. "And I will help my mother if I can."

"Bessel, your father is a cripple. He can't defend himself.

He can't work the mines anymore. You should have compassion." Baarben rushed to help her brother stand.

"He's so crippled he made a small fortune keeping the
accounts for the mines after the accident. He's so crippled
he fathered five more children on my mother, each one
diminishing her strength a little more, making her vulnerable to this hideous disease. Look at her! She's pregnant
again. That's why she hasn't the strength to fight it." Bessel
returned his attention to what little he knew about healing.

If only he had some Tambootie leaves in his pouch . . .
He'd heard rumors that Queen Maarie Kaathliin's father
needed the Tambootie to cure a plague in his homeland.

Was this the same plague? The disease caused by machines? He hoped not, but he recalled a grove of Tambootie that grew nearby. He'd stolen some of the leaves as a
child and experimented with them until his father had exiled him from the family. Once he eased the fever and
strengthened his mother a little, he'd fetch the leaves of
the tree of magic.

If he tapped a ley line, he could effect some repairs to
her body to buy him more time.

No. The Commune had valid reasons for outlawing rogue
magic.

He inhaled deeply on three counts, held it three counts,
and exhaled on the same rhythm. His body relaxed. He
repeated the exercise, and his mind drifted away from the
confines of bone and flesh. A third deep breath brought
him within reach of the void between the planes of existence.

*(There are lessons to be learned in the void. Do not enter
unless you are prepared to expose the truth,)* a voice whispered into the back of his mind.

As he hesitated to join with the allure of the void, a ley
line filled with magical energy pulsed beneath the ground
near the center of the village.

He reached out to tap the line, let it flood him with
strength.

Revulsion replaced the magical energy. NO! He couldn't
use ley lines and he couldn't access the void. Powwell had
had to leave the protection of the Commune in order to

use rogue magic in his search for Kalen. Bessel couldn't risk his membership in the Commune.

Dragon magic had limitations, especially when a magician worked alone. But when the Commune worked in concert, their magnified spells could overpower any solitary magician. They could impose rules and regulations, ethics and honor, on all magicians. Rogue magicians had perpetuated civil war in Coronnan for three generations, all in their quest for power, until Nimbulan had discovered dragon magic and created a lasting peace with King Quinnault's help.

Bessel risked the wrath of the Commune and the dragons if he violated their most sacred law. He had to help his mother using only legal magic, no matter how limited.

Breathe in, one, two, three. Hold, one, two, three. Breathe out, one, two, three. This time he concentrated on remaining in contact with the flow of dragon energies within his body. Power tingled in his fingertips. He ran his hand down the length of his mother's wasted body, keeping a thin cushion of energy between his hand and her skin. The heat of her fever, the disintegration and bleeding within her lungs, the irregular rhythm of her heart pulsed at his sensitized hand.

He felt the rupturing of blood vessels deep within her body. His mind saw her internal organs collapsing.

No part of her body was free of the disease.

"Oh, M'ma," he wailed. "I can't help you." If he'd come earlier. If he could tap a ley line to give him the magical energy to repair some of her vital organs . . . But he could not do it. He would not bring rogue magic back into Coronnan—even to help his mother.

Chapter 5

*Early spring, the road below Myrilandel's clearing
that runs across the pass from Coronnan into
Rossemeyer, southeastern corner of Coronnan*

Yaala clutched Powwell's hand in eager anticipation. His
palm was as hot and moist as her own.

The long winter of waiting for the pass to clear had
ended. Spring had burst forth in this remote mountain pass
a few days ago. The time had come to take the next long
step in reclaiming her heritage.

At last she was going home to Hanassa, the only place
she belonged. She daydreamed of clearing the city of mercenaries, outlaws, thieves, and murderers, making it a haven
for the innocent refugees of war and poverty rather than a
lawless haven for those who caused war and poverty. With
the help of the machines hidden deep within the lava tube
tunnels of the old volcano crater, she could turn Hanassa
into a prosperous industrial city with honest work for all.
She'd make the people of Hanassa her family.

Quinnault and Katie had taught her that such ideals
could exist. It was more than her mother, the late and unlamented Kaalipha of Hanassa, had taught her in her entire
life.

"Wait for it," Powwell hissed. "Feel the hot wind? It's
opening. I found a new portal for the dragongate!"

"Amazing," Yaala replied. She stared unblinking, mouth
slightly agape, at the shimmer of distortion within an arch-
shaped shadow.

"We can get into Hanassa now. All these moons of

searching are over." Powwell breathed on a deep sigh. "Kalen won't have to wait for rescue any longer."

He hugged Yaala hard. His eagerness to risk his life to rescue his half sister irritated Yaala. She'd never loved or been loved by anyone with such intensity.

"I can restart my machines and take control of Hanassa," she said, thinking of the only things that mattered to her—other than her friendship with Powwell. "We've had to wait so long, I didn't think this moment would ever come." She refused to believe Powwell's tale of the terrible dragon dream Shayla had given him last autumn. Yaala's machines used volcanic heat to create steam rather than burning fossil fuels. Her machines did not provide the pollution the disease spores fed upon. She was the engineer. She should know.

Why should she trust a dragon anyway? Shayla and Hanassa the Renegade had been born into the same nimbus, might very well have been part of the same litter. The nimbus had exiled Hanassa—the only dragon in their long history to require such punishment. The once purple dragon had taken human form and founded a city for other renegades. Depredations perpetrated by Hanassa and his followers had plagued the rest of Kardia Hodos for centuries.

She would end their tyranny of terror once and for all.

Yaala pulled her spine away from the outcropping of rock. The jagged stones fit her bizarre spinal structure as if carved for her. In all of her twenty-one years she'd never been able to rest her back against any surface. Her spinal bumps, residual traits of her dragon heritage, had defined her erect posture and set her apart from other humans. Her mother, Yaassima, had treated the minor deformity as a badge of honor. But then, the late Kaalipha of Hanassa had wanted to be more dragon than human.

In the end, both dragons and humans had rejected her.

Yaala didn't want to die like her mother, lost and alone, reviled by one and all. She clung to Powwell's arm as they watched the magical portal take form.

"After the kardiaquakes and partial openings I found these past five moons, I was afraid we'd never be able to use the dragongate to get back into Hanassa." Powwell turned his rare grin on her. His entire face lit with joy. All those hours spent with maps and pins and calculations finally come to fruit."

Yaala returned the smile. "I'm going home. I'll be able to fire up Old Bertha and get the 'tricity flowing again. I know I can."

"You don't want to do that, Yaala. Remember the dragon dream," Powwell warned.

Yaala ignored him. They'd argued about her machines endlessly since he'd come to her in Myrilandel's clearing where she had waited for him. She *would* restart whatever machines she could repair.

The air shimmered within the arch-shaped shadow created by a rocky overhang and a spreading oak tree heavy with mistletoe. Hot air, born of a volcano, blasted forth from the center of the shadow, replacing the last remnants of winter chill on this bright day. Colors swirled within the darkness of the shadow. Red, green, blue, black, yellow. More red and even more black.

Between one eye blink and the next, the colors within the shadow solidified into the image of red sandstone cliffs surrounding a murky lake, waters black with a strange substance floating on its surface. In the distance, a volcano belched hot ash in a tall column that reached for the sky.

"It's not Hanassa!" Yaala yelled, hauling Powwell back from stepping through the imagery into the unknown landscape. "We can't go there, Powwell."

"Of course it's Hanassa. The gate always returns to Hanassa and nowhere else. See the path leading up the cliff to the plateau. It's Hanassa. I have to rescue Kalen. We're going now!" The fifteen-year-old journeyman magician grabbed her arm and yanked her forward until she stumbled through the blast of swirling colors toward the alien scene.

"But the path is outside of Hanassa. The dragongate is supposed to take us into the heart of the mountain!" Her words evaporated in the rush of hot wind.

A vortex of spiraling energy caught Yaala. Up and down, right and left, now and then, distorted, blended, became one and shifted. Disorientation lurched in her stomach, then numbed the back of her neck. She needed to curl into a fetal ball but couldn't find her feet.

More hot air hit her in the face. She blinked away the fine grit of volcanic ash that blurred her eyes. She sat on the hot red sand beside the strange black lake.

"This isn't Hanassa. We have to go back." Yaala scrambled for the rapidly fading gateway. Her knees sank into loose sand. She couldn't rise or crawl fast enough. The cool green and brown of a forested road in Coronnan on the other side of the dragongate swirled into a kaleidoscope of colors. The air stilled and around her the temperature rose.

The smell of sulfur intensified; the smell of Hanassa. But this wasn't the city of outlaws her mother had ruled with a bloody fist.

Sweat broke out on Yaala's brow and back, almost as if she was still in the pit beneath the hidden city of outlaws.

Her generators and transformers were in the pit. She had to return to them, get them working again in order to claim her heritage.

"Where are we, Powwell?" she breathed the words, careful not to inhale any of the dust that permeated the air. Her fair scalp beneath her pale hair puckered and she knew she risked sunburn and dehydration even with the heavy ash haze.

"I—I'm not sure where we are." The young magician turned a full circle. He chewed his lower lip and ran a hand through his thick mass of curly dark hair in indecision. His gray eyes took on a cloudy look, mimicking the sky. A flutter of movement within his tunic pocket indicated his hedgehog familiar didn't like this place any better than Yaala did.

She hoped Thorny pricked Powwell deeply with his sharp spines.

"Why did we use that portal? I told you something was wrong." Yaala was also scanning the red-and-black horizon for anything resembling a familiar landscape. A dark speck soared in the distance, near the belching volcano. A dragon? Her dominant spinal bumps prickled, like a dog's ruff standing on end when faced with unknown dangers.

She could see nothing but miles and miles of wind-sculpted sand dunes and baby mountains reaching all the way to the distant horizon where the very active volcano belched again in a shower of spark and more black ash. The dragon disappeared within the dark cloud. Yaala ducked instinctively, even though the hot wind blew the dangerous fumes away from them.

"The dragongate is only supposed to work one way on this end," Powwell mused. "From Hanassa, you can go 'most anywhere if you wait for the right opening. But all of the destinations lead back to Hanassa and nowhere else. We should be in the tunnel overlooking the lava core."

"Well, we found an active volcano. But that's the only resemblance to Hanassa—which blew its top and collapsed into a caldera aeons ago."

"Oh, Kalen, I've failed to find you once again." Powwell beat his fist and his forehead into the hot sand. "How much longer can she hold out in the pit, or the void, or wherever she's hiding?"

"How long can we last here, with only a few journey rations?" Yaala shifted uncomfortably. Ash hazed the sun like a thick fog, but didn't deflect much heat. Nor did it provide any moisture. Her exposed hands and face dried and withered under the burning sun. She wondered if the sand was hot enough to burn through her trews and boots.

"At least we know the gate didn't disappear altogether after the kardiaquake." Yaala touched Powwell's smooth back with tentative fingers.

They had survived a lot together in the last year and a half. He'd been as much a victim of her mother's cruelty as Yaala had in the slave pit below Hanassa.

Thorny poked his nose out of Powwell's tunic pocket. Powwell caressed the hedgehog's relaxed spines and murmured comforting words to the creature.

Yaala knew a moment of painful loneliness. She would never have a familiar. No magic coursed within her veins, no matter how many generations of dragons limbed her family tree. She had no family left. The machines in the volcanic pit beneath the city of Hanassa had been more friendly, predictable, and faithful than her mother. She'd rather study the fascinating intricacies of her machines and the 'tricity they generated than trust a pet for companionship.

Powwell loved the funny little hedgehog so much he kept Thorny's discarded spines. Even on this long journey, Powwell kept the dried spines wrapped in a silk wallet inside his belt pouch.

She shook her head to clear it of the puzzle of magicians and their familiars. She had to think clearly and hopefully.

"Don't give up yet, Powwell. The dragongate may open again in a few moments. We don't know what kind of damage occurred in that kardiaquake just before we left Hanassa."

"What if the dragongate takes weeks to open again at this location? I was sure my calculations were correct. I found the portal. It should open to the pit in Hanassa and nowhere else. So where are we?"

Yaala scanned the land once more. Something about the way the sandy plateau dropped off into a steep cliff, and the narrow valley behind her seemed familiar, but distorted. They sat atop a small mountain. The black lake rippled and shivered. A moment later the land beneath them shifted and quaked. The lake waters rose a few inches and spread. Steam spouted up from the depths. Something . . .

"Maybe we are in Hanassa. But Hanassa of long, long ago, when the volcano was first forming. That lake might lie atop the core of lava at the heart of the mountain."

"But Shayla said that the dragongate only distorts distance, not time. She should know. She's a dragon." Thorny poked his nose out of Powwell's pocket and wiggled it in agreement.

"Dragons don't know everything." Yaala glared at Powwell. "And they don't always tell the truth." Her mother hadn't known how to separate truth from her own desires. Her ancestor, Hanassa, had begun the bloody tradition of reign by terror in the city.

"Dragons know a lot more than they tell."

"Dragons and magicians aren't equal to my machines." Machines couldn't be as evil as Shayla and Queen Maarie Kaathliin pretended in the infamous dragon dream. Resentment of Powwell for ramming two magicians' staffs into the guts of her beloved generator as a diversion for their escape from Hanassa rose sharply within her. She thought she'd forgiven him, understood the necessity of his actions. But now . . . now she wanted to strangle him. Then love him back to life.

What did she truly feel? It didn't matter. She couldn't trust emotions. Especially her own. Machines didn't have emotions.

"Well, I broke the machines with mundane tricks. I didn't even need magic," Powwell replied, sifting the hot sand through his fingers. "And I'm glad I broke them. Machines create pollution that feeds the plague spores. And when they run out of pollution, they turn on people and start eating them from the inside out."

"That's a myth created by the queen to keep technology out of Coronnan. Technology that would replace magicians and give power to every mundane. Besides, Coronnan doesn't have any machines to create pollution, so the plague can't thrive."

Powwell glared at her, then returned his attention to running his fingers through the sand. "Maybe these sands will tell me something. They've been here a long time. A memory of time distortion might be embedded in them." He took three deep, slow breaths, triggering a magical trance. The sand continued to drift through his fingers.

His eyes rolled up and his face took on the blank look of a deep trance. "Fire. Fire burning deep within the Kardia. Fire spreading upward. Fire melting rock. Icy air shattering. Fire. Ice. Time. Time . . ." he chanted in a voice much deeper than his own.

His words sent chills down her spine, despite the heat. "We have to find Rollett and send him back to help Scarface. Don't lose track of Kalen. You came to rescue your sister and Rollett," she interrupted his meditation. Concern for his childhood idol and his half sister should snap him out of the trance.

Powwell didn't reply. He shuddered as he pushed himself back into awareness. He jerked his hand away from the sand as if it burned his skin.

"Rollett can take care of himself. Kalen is much more vulnerable, so young, so untrained. . . ."

His priorities had always centered on Kalen. And yet . . .

Didn't he feel 'tricity shooting through his veins like she did when they touched, even casually?

"Well, we aren't going anywhere until the dragongate opens again." Yaala grimaced as the Kardia shifted beneath her feet again. If they didn't get out of here soon, the vol-cano might erupt, with them in the middle of the explosion.

"The gate can't open again until the ash clears and the sun creates an arch-shaped shadow for the gate to form in," Powell reminded her. "The arch is crucial."

"That could take a lifetime or three," she replied.

Chapter 6

Ancient plateau of Hanassa, time unknown

Powwell paused before hefting another rock to scan the arid landscape around the plateau. Off in the distance a winged ceature drifted on a rising air current. A dragon?

Help me! he called, trying desperately to contact the being with his mind.

His head remained empty of outside thoughts. Either it wasn't a dragon, or the dragons in this place didn't recognize the need to maintain contact with humans.

The sands, when he sifted them through his fingers, had told him only of fierce eruptions and cyclonic winds over a long period of time. Yaala had interrupted him before he'd had time to sort through the images to see if this had once been Hanassa, or would be at some time in the future. His gut told him the dragongate had returned him to Hanassa, but the portal had destroyed his planetary orientation—or maybe the time shift had. He had no idea where the magnetic poles lay, which was closest, what phase of the moon they entered or which season.

He returned to his self-appointed task and dropped a heavy piece of black rock onto the red sandstone where he thought the dragongate had been. He added a second and third rock to the growing pile that came close to matching the pile two long strides to his left. Maybe, if he could get the piles high enough, he could get something akin to an arch shape for the dragongate to form in.

He couldn't tell for sure, but he thought the portal had to open and close on the exact same coordinates each time.

But then again, maybe it only needed to be in the same vicinity.

If the natural shadows wouldn't form an arch, he'd make one. No matter how long it took. The passage of the sun told him that he and Yaala had only been in this landscape less than one day. His magic senses insisted they had spent a week or more here. Magnetic poles tugged at him from all directions.

To verify his time sense, he'd set up a kind of sundial around the piles of rocks. The sun moved far too slowly.

He and Yaala were trapped here in this alien landscape without food or water beyond their meager journey rations or protection from the merciless sun.

If only he'd had more time to study the dragongate back in his days of slavery in Hanassa. If only he'd kept a tighter hold on Kalen to keep her from running after Wiggles, her ferret familiar, as he and Yaala and the others had escaped Hanassa through the dragonate over a year ago. If only . . .

Guilt and "if onlys" didn't change the fact that he'd made a serious error in judgment when he stepped through the dragongate this time. But the gate had always worked the same way.

(No it hasn't always worked the same. The destinations changed. The frequency of opening changed,) a voice in the back of his head reminded him—a dragon or his conscience? He looked around for the source. Maybe the dragon in the distance had heard his cry for help after all.

The only living being he saw was Yaala. She sat huddled in the tiny shadow of a boulder watching him work. The few large rocks on this plateau offered her scant protection from the diffuse rays pouring through the ash haze.

Powwell's darker skin fared a little better than Yaala's. The backs of his hands had begun to darken and redden, though. They'd both have painful blisters before long.

She had draped a kerchief over her head, knotting it above her left ear, Rover style. She'd worn the same head-gear in the pit, protecting herself from the intense heat of the lava core. Now she needed it as a barrier between her fair skin and the pounding rays of light. But the kerchief didn't shade her eyes or protect her face.

He hated the thought of her reverting to the grimy desert

rat who had first befriended him in the pit. She'd remained aloof from everyone but him in Coronnan City. Her mother had outlawed her and condemned her to the pit. Yaala had nothing and no one outside of Hanassa. Now he had delayed her return to Hanassa and her beloved machines. Would she ever truly belong anywhere?

Wasn't that a definition of a renegade?

The kardia shifted beneath Powwell's feet. Not much. A precursor to the main shock. He braced himself for the rolling disturbance, like being aboard a ship in a storm. Just a little quake this time. No new fissures opened in the dry ground. But the movement disrupted his balance. He sat down heavily. Instinctively, he reached with his magic to find the nearest pole for a sense of where and when to reestablish his equilibrium. Nothing. The moon and seasons eluded him as well.

All he knew was the relentless sun. They had to get out of here soon.

Thirst tasted sour in his throat. He sipped a little of his dwindling water supply. They each had a leather container of water and a pack of journey food, enough to take them from one village to the next in Coronnan.

His waterskin seemed far too light. Not enough to last in this searing heat. He thought he'd rationed his water wisely, only taking a few sips each hour as marked on his sundial.

"Powwell, I see shadows!" Yaala called. She rose from her crouched position beside a boulder.

"Shadows? Where?" He peered at the few boulders, willing their shade to expand.

Hot wind sand-blasted his face. The sun seemed brighter. Less ash obscured the horizon. The wind increased, grew hotter yet. It came from his left away from the direction he'd placed his cairns of rocks.

He turned in place, awakening all of his senses for hints of change. A shimmering distortion, like a mirage in a distant heat haze, grew between himself and Yaala within the minuscule puddle of shade cast by the nearest boulder.

"The gate is opening!" Yaala dashed toward him, through the forming gate, and disappeared within the shifting swirls of light! Just like Kalen had when she'd been thrown into the lava core before the dragongate fully formed.

"Yaala!" he screamed and dove after her. He couldn't let her die in the volatile gate. Stargods only knew where she'd end up. They had to complete this quest together.

Loneliness and despair swamped him. He'd not lose another dear one.

* * *

Mining village in Balthazaan Province, south of Coronnan City

Bessel sensed the grief of his gathered siblings. Nine all told counting himself. They stood in a circle around their mother's bed in descending order by age maintaining the ritual death watch.

He watched the grief play over the faces of his oldest brother and two older sisters, the ones he knew from his childhood. They choked back sobs and closed their eyes against tears. He did, too, as much for the lost companionship of his family as for the death of their mother. The fourth young adult in the circle, another sister one year younger than himself, had been only a small child when he left the mining village. He barely remembered her.

The five siblings born after his father's accident in the mine wept openly, darting glances of fear toward their father. Maydon had always ruled the family with a heavy fist and violent temper.

Anger replaced Bessel's grief. Anger that these youngsters had to stand and watch M'ma die. They had said their good-byes to her during her last moments of consciousness. Why did they have to bow to tradition and watch blood trickle from M'ma's mouth and ears while knowing they could do nothing to help? Why couldn't Maydon release them to grieve in quiet privacy until it was all over?

M'ma started coughing again, weakly. Baarben rushed to help her sister-in-law sit up. The children made space for her in the circle. None of them knew how to ease the insistent blockage in their mother's lungs. No one in this mining village learned anything more than their assigned place in life allowed. Maiden aunts were expected to nurse the family's ills. Aunt Baarben was the one who must help M'ma sit up, not the children who stood closer.

But it was late for anyone to help M'ma. She opened her mouth for one last inhalation. Blood streamed from her mouth. She opened her eyes wide, seeing nothing. Then she collapsed. Her life's spirit exited her body.

"Bring her back. You've got to make her live again!" Maydon pounded on Bessel's shoulder. "You're a magician, bring her back to life."

All of Bessel's siblings looked at him, hope brimming in their eyes along with their tears.

"I can't." Bessel bowed his head. "Even if I could, the Stargods forbid reanimating a dead body for any reason."

"I'll get Lord Balthazaan's magicians to compel you to do it. Make your mother live again!" Maydon grabbed Bessel's shoulders and shook him hard, letting his crutches fall to the floor. For a moment, he was entirely dependent upon his estranged son.

Bessel didn't let his small smile of triumph touch his face. Because of the trauma of his experiences in the outlaw camp, no magician had since been able to compel him to do anything he didn't want to do.

"No such spell of reanimation exits. Your ignorance assigns me more power and fewer ethics than any true magician could hope for." Gently, Bessel removed his father's hands from his shoulders, then restored the man's crutches. "If I could have helped her, I would have done it hours ago while she still lived." But he might have helped her, if he'd had the courage to tap a ley line and access the void.

The healer would have come from Lord Balthazaan's castle if Bessel had asked. He'd have come to help another magician. But Bessel wasn't a true magician yet. He hadn't achieved master status.

He was still an outsider looking in. Never more than in this large family that shared his blood but not his talent or his experiences.

"Can't or won't?" Maydon sneered at Bessel. "You can hurt me any way you like, I'm the one who threw you and your cursed talent to the wolves. Kill me if you must, but don't hurt your mother. Bring her back!"

"I can't. No matter what you think, I am not all-powerful. Nor will I break sacred laws."

Bessel walked out of his father's house, not once looking back. Bitterness and regret were his only companions.

S'murghit! The Stargods had taught the first magicians how to cure a plague. Where was that knowledge when he needed it?

Certainly no one in the village knew the first thing about true healing. Midwives and maiden aunts knew how to use a few herbs and poultices. They could bandage wounds and set broken limbs. None of them knew how to read to learn more. Maydon had taught his children a little ciphering, enough to keep household accounts. Nothing more. Tradition said they needed no more. None of them had ever expressed a dream of achieving anything more than their father had or than Lord Balthazaan expected of them.

And now a plague beset them, and their ignorance was killing them.

The strange scent he had detected in his father's house assailed him again. Stronger, deeper. The village was filled with it along with the black coal dust from the deep mine. Was the dust a kind of pollution for the plague to feed upon?

He stopped in the center of the pathway between houses and turned a full circle. His magic talent bristled a warning deep inside him.

Death stalked this community, just as it had stalked the strangers in the dragon dream Shayla had given Powwell, Master Nimbulan, and the king and queen. Everyone in the Commune had heard of the dream in the minutest detail. Powwell had been most specific about the scent of the plague, relaying it to his classmates in direct telepathic communication. *That* was the familiar smell.

Queen Maarie Kaathliin's plague had come to Coronnan, and no one knew how to cure it.

Chapter 7

Midnight, forested knoll outside Coronnan City

Kinnsell O'Hara scanned the forest landscape uncertainly. Why did these primitive bushies always insist upon clandestine meetings in the midst of all of these trees? And they always chose midnight, when civilized men should conduct delicate negotiations over a fine port wine in cozy dens furnished with large, well-padded chairs. Not standing out in the cold wind freezing their arses off.

He felt naked without the protective walls of a building, or his shuttle, or the atmosphere domes of cities back home. But this wasn't home. This was a primitive world where the locals believed that magic worked and dragons were real.

Even the king here was addressed as "Your Grace" because he ruled by the grace of the dragons. Kings should have majesty, as well as grace.

He shuddered in the chill night air. He couldn't leave the country of Coronnan and the planet Kardia Hodos fast enough. Just as soon as he accomplished what he'd come here to do, he'd hightail it away from all this open space and unconfined air and back to civilization.

But his mission would guarantee that he would be the next emperor of the Terran Galactic Empire. None of the other candidates—any of his three siblings and all of their combined children could find themselves elected emperor—knew how to keep the sprawling territories bound together into a cohesive unit. None of them valued the fresh food produced on planets such as this one. They all believed tanked food sufficient to sustain life. None of them understood that truly enjoying life meant unique tastes, unique experiences, and the hope that every citizen might eventually be able to enjoy them. If that hope died—no matter how remote—the citizens had the power to depose the central government. Then the TGE would fracture into dozens of scattered autonomous and warring worlds.

Control would vanish. Briefly, he thrust his right hand forward as if guiding the joystick of a shuttle in atmosphere flight. By dropping the nose a little, he could regain control of airspeed. Then he eased his hand back, control reasserted.

Kinnsell intended to maintain control, starting with the bushie lords and his far too independent daughter.

A rustle of underbrush off to his left told him that someone—or something—large and clumsy approached. His heart climbed into his throat. Suddenly all of the local tales of predatory gray bears, spotted saber cats, and . . . and dragons didn't seem so preposterous.

Something eerie about the place sent his imagination into overdrive, dredging up childhood horror stories of monsters under the bed.

The night breeze chilled his skin despite the heavy layers of protective clothing. He swallowed his fears and checked his scanner. The readings indicated one human, leading some kind of riding beast. Steeds they called them. The locals couldn't even remember the proper name for a horse. Not that Terra had been home to any horses outside natural history museums for many generations.

Kinnsell relaxed. His overactive imagination had tricked him once more. His daughter Katie had the same tendency. Now that she was queen of this backwater, she could give vent to her storytelling without the hindrance of civilized conventions.

She hadn't been on the planet a full day when she started filling his head with tales of dragons.

Imagine, the girl actually claimed she had seen and touched a dragon! A huge beast with crystal fur and telepathic capabilities had "blessed" her marriage to Quinnault. Didn't she know that every myth and legend made dragons—sacred or evil—reptiles with jewel-colored scales?

Even his pragmatic and obedient sons had spouted tales of magical creatures and enchantresses after visiting their sister. Kinnsell had ordered all three of them to remain aboard the mother ship. He hoped Katie's egalitarian attitudes hadn't contaminated them. Otherwise they might all challenge him for the crown of the emperor when Kinnsell's father finally died. The old man was taking his own sweet time about it. The Terran Galactic Empire grew shakier every year. It needed Kinnsell's firm hand on the joystick to guide it back to prosperity.

"Master Varn?" the approaching human spoke confidently, as if he could see in the dark. Maybe he could. The locals constantly surprised Kinnsell with their uncanny abilities.

Kinnsell quickly donned the heavily veiled headdress that kept his identity as a human from a different planet concealed. He hated the costume of layer upon layer of wispy chiffon. But the family insisted. This world must not be tainted by knowledge of its Terran past or by technology and pollution. Soon he'd end the charade. The TGE needed the fresh food produced by this world. But not tonight. He'd not reveal himself or his mission to this bushie noble with delusions of grandeur. Not until Kinnsell had control of the situation.

" 'Tis, I, Chieftain of the Varns," Kinnsell replied in solemn tones suitable to an awesome being of unknown origin and proportions.

"Do you have enough wealth to bribe me to release my entire plantation of the Tambootie?" The man's voice didn't show any sign of deference or awe in the face of one of the legendary Varn traders.

A niggle of disappointment knotted at the base of Kinnsell's spine. His ancestors had started the cult of the Stargods here. His people should appear as gods to these primitives! Instead he was forced by an outdated covenant to effect this ghostly appearance.

But he needed the Tambootie. Lots of it. A lot more than King Quinnault and his own daughter had been willing to give him.

The plague raged throughout the TGE; Tambootie was the only known cure. If he had enough of the weed, he could eliminate the disease forever—as it should have been when genetic scientists first realized their experimental microbe not only ate toxic waste and air pollution, it ate the toxins within human bodies that had built up over generations of uncontrolled industrial waste. And then ate the human hosts.

"I have seeds that will triple your yield of grains," Kinnsell intoned. "Provided the Tambootie is from the spring harvest, and not fallen leaves from last autumn."

"Seeds won't do me much good. Most of my land is crags and ravines." The bushie noble spat into the dirt on the forest floor.

"I have sheep embryos that when grown will yield wool so long it will spin almost as fine as silk."

"Embryos? What are they?"

"Fertilized eggs you implant into the uterus of a female sheep."

"Demon spawn!" The man shuddered and made a curious flapping gesture with crossed wrists. His heavy signet ring glinted in the moonlight.

Kinnsell realized the man did not wear a traditional seal set into the ring. Instead, the fine silverwork represented an elaborate and twisted knot reminiscent of his Celtic ancestors on Terra. He suddenly knew lust for that ring. He'd have it on his own hand before he left this backwater for home. His hand thrust forward, reasserting control.

"I'll not impregnate my good sheep with demon spirits." The lord continued. "I'll continue feeding the *s'murghin'* dragons my Tambootie rather than deal with demons."

"Can you mine your land?" Kinnsell was running out of options. His hand remained forward, still trying to regain control. He hadn't much left on his mother ship that would help these people—or bribe them.

"My mines were played out generations ago. Not enough iron and copper left to make it worth hauling the slag to the surface." The man's eyes shifted to the side, sure indication he lied.

He had coal. Coal that could fuel industrial plants—here or elsewhere. Kinnsell had smelled the dust the last time he visited Balthazaan.

He smiled and swallowed any lingering loyalty to the

anachronistic family covenant. His hand came back in a position of smooth flight. "I can give you tools that will cut through solid rock to the hidden veins of ore."

The lord's eyes opened wide in greed, then narrowed in speculation. "What good are those tools if my miners don't know where the veins are?" He twisted his ring. A sign of agitation or greed?

"I have a second tool that senses the presence of precious metals, iron and coal as well." Kinnsell's mind brightened at the thought of gleaming steel, a commodity of increasing scarcity now that the largest iron-producing colonies had domed their cities and abandoned their mines in favor of full citizenship in the TGE. Now that he'd transgressed a little against the family covenant, he might as well go all the way. "But for the tools, I'll need more than the plantation of the Tambootie trees in trade."

"I haven't got much else. The wars stripped me of everything but a few worthless acres and a bunch of daughters."

"Then with your first profits from the veins of ore *my* tools find for you, you must buy every ton of surplus grain you can find." The Empire needed food more than additional supplies of steel.

"Surpluses are supposed to go to the king. Security against drought, he says." A note of disgust tinged the man's reply. He abandoned twisting his ring to clench his fist and shake it in anger.

Kinnsell got a better look at the ring and coveted it more. He also knew he could exploit the lord's emotion. King Quinnault's foresight in preparing for a drought still five years off—if the normal weather cycle prevailed—had been denounced as ludicrous by his shortsighted nobles. They wanted profit. Now.

"My people suffer from drought now," Kinnsell said. A drought of resources of their own making, not weather induced. He couldn't change a situation created almost a thousand years ago, but he could profit from his society's policy of stripping planets and moving on. "We need the grain now. Your king doesn't need surplus food until a new drought hits you. Droughts are the whims of the Stargods. The next one may never come, or it may be delayed."

"Or it might come tomorrow. I'm not certain incurring

the king's wrath by giving up so much Tambootie and selling surplus food is worth a few sledgeloads of ore."

"No mere mortal can tell for sure when a drought will come." Kinnsell fought to keep the desperation out of his voice. These bushies weren't easy to corrupt. Or rather, they were so corrupt already he couldn't turn their vices to his own benefit. The benefit of the TGE, he corrected himself. "You haven't hoarded surpluses before and your people always survived. A year's delay in adhering to the king's new laws won't hurt."

"Give me some reasons not to obey these new laws now. I did just fine in the old days making my own laws and ruling my lands by myself without inference from any king."

Kinnsell swallowed a sharp retort that the lord hadn't done "just fine" during the generations of war. Instead he said, "King Quinnault is like a fanatical priest. He wants everyone to believe as he does without variation and without logical explanations. He doesn't want the good of the country, he wants control of your lives, your resources, your minds." Kinnsell paused a moment to let that thought sink in. "The sooner Quinnault is brought down, the sooner you can go back to making a profit any way you see fit."

"The other lords and I signed agreements to support him. The people love him. Chancy thing to depose him." The bushie lord was back to twisting the ring.

"The people love him now because they don't truly know him. He won't let them see the truth of his need to control every aspect of life in Kardia Hodos—including their thoughts. How do you think he quelled that riot last autumn if not by mind control? You must show them the truth. Then you will be free to sell your resources for a profit rather than pay the king's useless taxes."

"You'll trade me rock cutting tools and ore finders?" The bushie noble tapped his lip with his forefinger as if mulling over the possibilities.

Kinnsell sincerely wished his telepathy could penetrate the man's mind. The locals like this lord with dark hair and olive skin, similar to the natives of the Mediterranean on Terra, seemed totally impervious to the family talent. The ones with fairer coloring opened easily to telepathic probes—unless they had psi powers that allowed them to pretend to be magicians. He hadn't met anyone with Asian or African features to know how widespread the natural shields were. Each race resided on a different continent here; except for the ones like this lord. They wandered the whole planet like Gypsies.

"You Varns always trade in diamonds. If I had some diamonds, I could buy my neighbor's surplus tomorrow," the bushie lord suggested. "You wouldn't have to wait until I reopened the mines and found a viable vein of ore, then found a market for it and sold it."

"A sudden influx of gems will shout to all of Kardia Hodos that you have traded with Varns. King Quinnault will look closely at your plantations of the Tambootie to see if you have violated your covenant with the dragons."

The noble crossed himself and murmured a prayer. Then he crossed his wrists and flapped his hands.

Kinnsell wished he knew the origin of that bizarre gesture.

"Dragons and magicians have never done me any favors. Don't see why I should give up a tithe of land to the trees of magic, and another tithe of my few sheep to the dragons."

"You shouldn't have to give up anything to charlatan magicians and nonexistent dragons." Kinnsell pressed the man toward a decision. "My mining tools will work better than magic."

The noble's eyes gleamed with greed.

"You get the Tambootie and the grain when I sell the first load of ore."

"I need the Tambootie now."

"I need working capital now."

"Gold. I'll give you gold."

"How much?"

"One hundred coins the size of your thumbnail."

"Coins from where? Merchants don't take every mintage."

"The coins of Varnicia, the spice merchants, are good everywhere." Kinnsell knew how to counterfeit those.

"And hint of Varn origin, just like diamonds."

"Then the coins of Jihab, the jewel merchants."

"Tainted by Maffisto assassins. You guarantee your tools will serve me better than magicians?"

"My tools will eliminate the need for magicians. You and

your kind will be free of them once and for all." *And with improved technology, I'll have a planet producing enough food to feed three civilized worlds. We'll export the coal and iron to industrial worlds and leave more men to work the land.*

"Gold bullion will do. I can sell it anywhere."

"Done. I'll take your signet ring as surety . . ."

"I have neighbors willing to trade grain and Tambootie for freedom from magicians." The lord totally ignored Kinnsell's last request. "They trust me to bargain for them. I have a list of what they need." The bushie pulled a long roll of parchment from his tunic. A very long roll, indeed. "I found a man to write it who failed as a magician apprentice. He stayed at the cursed University long enough to learn to read but not much else."

Kinnsell licked his lips eagerly. He'd have this planet mechanized and shipping massive surpluses within a decade. But he didn't think he'd ever inform the locals of their right to dome their cities and join the Empire as full citizens. Terra needed food, not more citizens. He needed the crown that this world's food could give him. His hand came back, soaring higher in his personal agenda.

Briefly he wondered if he should lift the ban on reading and writing on this world. Not yet. The lcoals might learn too much too fast.

*   *   *

University of Magicians Library, Coronnan City

Bessel stared at the strange paragraph in the old text. He'd been shelving books for Master Lyman when his talent insisted he open this book and read. The pages had fallen open right where he read and reread the same paragraph.

A person with the healing talent can diminish the effects of disease by symbolically exchanging blood with the patient.

What? How? He had to read further. The three other books he cradled in his arms dropped to the floor with a resounding thud. He ignored the echoes in the normally hushed library. Several apprentices looked up from their studies. Bessel didn't care how much attention he attracted, or about the sniggers of the other students.

He knew his pudgy hands were clumsy. That didn't matter. This book offered a clue to the end of the plague. If he found out how to do this, maybe he could get permission to return to Lord Balthazaan's disease-ridden province. He couldn't save his mother, but he might save some of the others before the plague spread any farther. And he wouldn't have to tap a ley line or access the void to do it.

He grabbed the book with both hands and stumbled over the fallen books to the nearest study desk. He was already reading when he plunked down on the stool.

> The healer must first trigger a middling trance being careful not to fall too deep in thrall with the void. While still in contact with his body and his mind, the healer takes his ritual dagger in his left hand and carefully cuts across the right palm of the patient. Then he must repeat the cut on his own left palm. The ritual dagger may then be placed upon a silk scarf to await later cleansing. The healer must place his left palm across the patient's right hand, making sure to align the cuts. With his free hand the healer must bind the hands together with a pristine white bandage, also made of silk.
>
> If the healer has been properly trained and successfully passed the trial by Tambootie smoke, no contagion will spread to his own body, though all mundanes within the room become infected.

Bessel turned the page for the ritual words that would complete the healing spell. The next three pages had been torn from the binding.

He flipped back and forth in the book seeking the missing pages. Ragged edges at irregular intervals testified to several more clumps of pages that had been removed. Whoever had mutilated the book had done it hastily, not taking time to cut the pages cleanly.

Who? Who would damage a precious book?

"Master Lyman?" he asked in a hushed voice. The Master Librarian should be nearby. He rarely left his beloved books. Bessel often wondered if the old man ate and slept in the library as well.

Journeymen whispered legends into the ears of awed apprentices that Old Lyman ate only knowledge and never slept.

"Yes?" Master Lyman peered at Bessel through an opening in the bookshelves. He seemed to have simply moved books aside rather than walk a few feet around the shelving unit.

"Master Lyman, have you read this book?"

"Title and author?" Lyman scrunched up his wizened face in thought.

"*Ceremonies of Symbolic Magic* written by one Kimmer, a scribe from the south. I think this was copied from the original text." Bessel stared at the fine tooling on the leather cover. Traces of gold leaf still clung to the ancient embossed lettering.

"Kimmer? Ah, yes. Kimmer of the south. A fine scholar and one of our most prolific authors. Sadly, I have not had time to read this text." Lyman started to shove books back into place, withdrawing from Bessel's presence.

"Uh, Master Lyman?"

"You have another question?" Lyman poked his head back into the shelf opening. "Two questions in one sitting from the same student? Could it be that one of you is beginning to think enough to ask questions?"

"Master Lyman, someone has torn some pages from this book. Who would do such a thing?" Distress made Bessel's voice rise in pitch and volume. He immediately lowered it to a more appropriate whisper. "I think I've found a reference to early blood magic. It was used for healing rather than power! This is important."

"Hush, boy. You must never say that out loud! I told Powwell the same thing when he read from this text. I also told him to hide this book." Lyman scuttled around the bookshelves and grabbed the book away from Bessel. His funny, old-fashioned tunic that hung to his knees and he'd belted on the outside to hold up his trews made him appear more a harmless gnome than a powerful and wise magician.

Had Powwell removed the crucial pages from the book? Why? Surely he wouldn't need blood magic to rescue his sister. But then, in Hanassa, maybe he would.

The main door to the library banged open. Master Scarface stood framed by the massive double doorway. The scar that gave him his cognomen made a vivid red pathway from temple to temple across the bridge of his nose.

"Out!" he commanded. The scar bleached white, clear evidence of the tension he kept carefully contained. "All of you students out of here now. The masters have important work to do. We cannot be disturbed."

A dozen apprentices gathered up their books, scrolls, and writing implements in preparation for leaving.

"Don't take anything with you. Leave the books behind. Just get out of here. Now."

While I still have the courage to do this. Scarface's stray thought penetrated Bessel's mind. What was the Senior Magician going to do?

"Quickly, boy, hide the book and get yourself away by the postern door." Lyman thrust the book back into Bessel's hands and shoved him toward the back corner of the three-story-high room that filled the entire central wing of the U-shaped University building. "Hide yourself well without magic. He'll smell your magic if you use it."

"Lyman, show yourself," Scarface ordered as he stalked into the library. Three master magicians, all of them new since Scarface had taken over leadership of the Commune a year ago, followed closely upon his heels. All of the master magicians seemed more willing to follow Scarface than make a decision on their own. That was how Scarface had become Senior. No one else wanted to do it.

"Yes, Master Aaddler?" Lyman stepped in front of Bessel, giving the journeyman cover for his quick retreat.

Bessel kept his ears open and his magical senses alert as he sought a dark corner for himself and his book. He knew he needed to hear the truth beneath the spoken words.

The Senior Magician winced at the use of his true name. Since he had taken over, all of the masters had adopted working names and reserved true names for only the most solemn occasions.

"The books must be separated by categories," Scarface

said, looking directly into Lyman's eyes rather than at the books. The intensity of his gaze suggested he attempted to influence Lyman with magic.

"They already are cataloged and categorized." Lyman didn't falter or succumb to the mental manipulation.

"For the safety of the Commune and those who seek knowledge here, a further separation is required. The queen's dragon dream foretells danger in the knowledge contained within these books."

The three satellite magicians moved to flank Scarface, becoming a solid wall of determination.

"I have studied the matter. We can no longer delay in removing dangerous information from the reach of vulnerable apprentices."

"Dangerous as in . . . ?" Lyman remained firmly in place, blocking the other magicians.

"All references to rogue magic must be placed where only master magicians can access them. All references to machines that mimic magic must be set aside for later culling," Scarface announced. "None of my students have need of this forbidden knowledge."

"You are going to ban books?" Lyman asked. For the first time, Bessel watched the old man fumble for a retort that would misdirect or perplex. Lyman stood blinking, mouth agape. He radiated emotional pain.

"We must remove dangerous books from the hands of vulnerable children and those who would misuse the forbidden knowledge secreted therein."

Chapter 8

The void between the planes of existence

Pulsing energy jolted through Yaala, the only sensation available to her as numbing darkness enfolded her. She had no body, no perceptions, only thoughts and the rippling currents tingling her mind. Something akin to the 'tricity generated by her beloved machines beneath Hanassa. But different. Unnatural.

(Your 'tricity is unnatural. We belong here,) a voice said inside Yaala's head.

Where am I? she asked. She wanted to speak but had no mouth to form the words. Only her mind existed. Her mind and the voice.

She retained a brief memory of seeing the dragongate start to form and dashing forward to stand beside Powell. Then, before she could reach him, she fell into . . . nothing; nothing but the repeated jolts.

Her thoughts spun, seeking order out of nothing.

. *(You have found a place where you do not belong and cannot stay.)*

I have never belonged anywhere but with my machines. How do I return to them?

(Is that what you truly wish?)

I have no alternative.

(There are always alternatives.)

Then I make the choice to return to Hanassa. With Powell. The image of underground caverns filled with giant generators and transformers formed slowly in her memory.

Gradually, she completed the picture with all of the colors and sulfur smells she had lived with so long. Then she added the memory of Powwell following her about with tools and oil rags.

(That is the one place I cannot send you. Dragons do not venture near the realm of the renegade.)

Abruptly the voice disappeared. And Yaala was left alone in the nothingness, with only her mind and her memories. And the jolting energy.

All energy followed definite currents. She remembered that much from her study of the machines. Even when 'tricity appeared to flare in random directions, it followed some kind of pattern, using the air as a conduit when no wires existed.

Therefore this strange energy had a beginning and an end. She had but to follow it.

She took a moment (if time still existed, which she doubted) to study the patterns of the energy. At first, they seemed random and directionless. Gradually, she tuned her mind to the frequency of the flow. At last, she found a rhythm. It pulsed in her mind almost like music. Haunting and compelling.

(Follow me!) it seemed to say. *(Follow me home.)*

Her mind blended with the pseudo 'tricity and joined the pulsing dance it created out of nothing. A kind of joy filled her. If she'd had a body, she would have laughed.

Laughter. One of many things missing in her life. Yaassima had laughed, but only when cruelty lit her mind. Yaala had never found anything to laugh about in Hanassa, even as a small child. Fear had dominated every aspect of surviving the Kaalipha's strange whims and bloodlust.

Now Yaala laughed and understood that her life could never be complete until she put aside her fears. Yaassima was dead. Yaala's mother could no longer terrorize her. *I am free of her!* She laughed out loud, needing to include others in her mirth. But who?

Powwell, her only friend, was on that lonely desert plateau, lost in time. Nimbulan and Myrilandel were back in the capital. And she was lost in the void.

I don't want to be alone.

The energy swirled in a stronger vortex. Colors erupted

around her. Her limbs tingled as they had when she tumbled through the dragongate.

Abruptly she found herself sitting beside a large tree with a rocky overhang sheltering her from a spring rainstorm.

Evey joint in her intact body ached and rippled with the residual energy. Especially the base of her spine where she seemed to have landed on her butt on the hard forest floor.

"Was I in the magicians' void?" she asked whoever might be listening.

The tree branches whispered among themselves as the wind rose and the rain intensified. Their conversation meant nothing to her mundane senses.

She crawled to her knees, searching her surroundings for clues to her whereabouts. She needed a drink. The hours she had spent on the desert plateau had evaporated every spare drop of moisture from her.

She knew how to survive. And survive she must. Yaassima had taught her that. The only valuable lesson her mother could impart.

She knew how to survive alone.

The rocky overhang looked promising. Rain ran down the rocks in heavy rivulets. She lapped at them, refreshing her parched throat.

A small measure of strength returned to her with the influx of water. She drank more deeply and filled her waterskin.

Yaala crept deeper beneath the overhang until a large outcropping sheltered her back from the pelting rain and fierce wind. Her prominent spinal bumps fit nicely into the crevices as if made to fit her unique body form.

"Right back where I started from. Only this time I don't have Powwell." A deep ache opened within her, unrelated to the physical distress of her adventures.

"Powwell!" she howled, more alone than she'd ever been before. More alone than when Yaassima, her own mother, had executed Yaala's father and dipped her hands in the still warm blood.

"Oh, Powwell, find me, please. I don't want to be alone."

*   *   *

*The city of Hanassa, home of renegades, dragons,
magicians, and mundanes*

The kardia rumbled and rolled beneath Rollett's feet in
the hellish volcanic crater called Hanassa, home to mercenaries, political outlaws, thieves, murderers, and exiled
rogue magicians.

Stargods? Not again!

"Everyone out! Get out of the tunnel now!" he yelled
as he dashed forward. Two dozen men streamed past him,
each seeking the exit. Some of them showed signs of panic
as they ran. Rollett touched each man on the shoulder,
offering reassurance. They calmed down and cleared the
tunnel in an orderly fashion.

The confines of the excavation amplified the sensation of
motion from the quake. Dirt trickled through cracks in the
ceiling of the lava tube passage. Instantly Rollett scanned
the partially blocked tunnel with every sense available to
him.

He and his crews had almost reached the section where
three men had died the last time the only known exit from
Hanassa had collapsed on them.

"I won't sacrifice any more men to Piedro's bloodthirsty
god Simurgh," he proclaimed to any who might hear. "I
won't let this cursed city trap me any longer."

With his last words he slapped his hand onto the most
vulnerable crack. Before he'd had the chance to breathe
deeply twice, magic coursed through his fingers into the
unstable tunnel. On the third breath the calm of a light
trance descended in waves upon his muscles. His mind
floated free of the restrictions of his body. He followed his
magic into the walls of the ancient volcano.

He found the imbalance of broken layers of solidified
lava and aeons of dirt. A push here, leverage there, and
the tunnel stabilized at the same moment the kardia ceased
quaking.

Rollett returned reluctantly to his sweating and exhausted body.

"Is it safe, Rollett?" one of the masons whispered from
the tunnel entrance. Rollett had elevated the man from

captive slave to honored workman soon after they began the first digging-out of Hanassa.

"I think so. Give it a moment." He breathed deeply of the hot dry air, willing the air to feed his undernourished body and give him reserves of strength. He'd found no ley lines in this hellhole to replenish his magic. The dragons had deserted this part of the world centuries ago, taking their special magical energy with them. He had only himself to fuel his talent.

He drank deeply from the skin tied to his belt. The sulfur-laden water almost tasted good. He drank again until the rancid flavor made him gag. Then he knew he'd had enough. He'd learned his first week in Hanassa to avoid dehydration at all cost. Water was more precious than food these days.

Both were in short supply.

Without food and fresh water, he didn't have enough of himself left to give at the rate Hanassa used him up. Excavating the tunnel was their only hope to open the city to outside supplies.

"Why don't you just climb up the crater walls and slip through the holes in the fence?" the mason asked. His eyes kept returning to the tumble of dirt and boulders behind Rollett. The mason crossed himself and stepped back into the daylight.

Six moons ago, three men had died in the last cave-in. Rollett hadn't been close enough to stop it with magic then. He and his crew had lost nearly a year's work in a few moments of quaking kardia.

"You needn't fear the ghosts of those men. They died honestly." Rollett stood up and squared his shoulders. *But they are the last ones to die in this tunnel.*

"You've got the strength and courage to climb the crater," the mason encouraged him, returning to the issue Rollett couldn't explain to himself let alone to one of his crew.

"You have the strength to escape, too, friend. But I made some promises that keep me here. I intend to keep them."

"No one else in this cursed city believes in promises."

"And they have lost their belief in themselves. They have

lost control of their lives. Until I finish what .I set out to do, we must make do with the few supplies some of our comrades send through those gaps in the barbed fencing. Not enough to make life easy again, but enough to give Hanassa hope that we will burrow out of here."

He remembered the first time he had encountered the fence a year and a half ago. The climb up the outside slopes of the mountain in the desert heat without enough water and food had nearly killed both him and Nimbulan. Then the disappointment of encountering the unbroken line of barbed fencing had nearly ended their mission before it truly began. He and his master had been trying to break into Hanassa to rescue Nimbulan's wife. Now men braved the crater and the fence to break out of Hanassa.

"I hope you succeeded, Old Man," he whispered to his memory of Nimbulan. "I hope you found a way back to Coronnan where you can lead the Commune in the fight for justice and peace. I don't like to think you died in that last battle we fought together in the Justice Hall. Your body should have been among those we carted out and buried, but it wasn't. Though if you escaped, I don't know how."

Scarface, the Battlemage who had become a mercenary, had also disappeared that night. Rollett had never trusted the man, although Nimbulan had. Something about the way the man manipulated the camaraderie of his companions . . .

If you were responsible for making certain I got left behind, Scarface, I'll see that you pay in all of your next existences.

Rollett deliberately separated himself from past grief and suspicions. He needed all of his concentration here and now.

He probed the tunnel one more time with his magical senses. "It's safe to come back in, but you'll need to shore up the walls here and here." He pointed out the weakest spot to the hovering mason.

"I have decided that masonry and mortar require too much precious water," a newcomer said from the tunnel entrance.

"Would you rather watch your city starve, Kaaliph Piedro?'' Rollett asked the Rover who had grabbed power the moment the old Kaalipha had died, taking the previous Rover Chieftain and her pet Bloodmage with her.

Piedro's dark eyes narrowed, hardly veiling the animosity behind them. His lithe body betrayed him, he looked more than ready to spring upon Rollett like a legendary spotted saber cat. Then he twisted his head as if listening to a light tune borne on the wind. He shook himself a little and replaced the mask of reasonableness on his face and posture.

"I feed the city. My people work hard at cutting a stairway up the crater walls to the fence. We will have access to the outside world again, when I deem it safe,'' Piedro replied. "My Rover magic tells me that the outside world is not safe at the moment.''

Rollett couldn't penetrate the man's emotions with or without magic. Rovers had strange powers that few outsiders understood or could participate in. One had to have Rover blood to use Rover spells.

"Safe for you or safe for honest workers who were brought here as slaves against their will?'' Rollett asked, forcing an air of innocence into his tone. "You don't feed the city, Piedro. You keep us on starvation rations so you can pretend to control the rabble. But you are still sleek and strong. Where do you get your supplies if all the exits are blocked?''

He held back the anger that sent heat through his veins. He hadn't the strength to challenge Piedro openly. And now he'd exhausted himself holding the tunnel together during the kardiaquake.

What do you have hidden in the labyrinth beneath the palace, Piedro? He and the Rover Kaaliph stared at each other for a long moment, assessing, weighing, mutely challenging.

"Mix the mortar,'' Rollett ordered the mason. The broad man scuttled out of the tunnel. Rollett could taste the man's fear as it permeated the air.

Piedro licked his lips, savoring it.

"Invoking terror only gives an illusion of control,'' Rollett said, as much to himself as to the upstart Kaaliph. "You don't have Yaassima's cunning or her magic.'' The late Kaalipha had governed with a bloody fist. Infractions of her few rules met with swift and fatal retribution. But she had rules. Those who broke the rules knew the consequences.

Piedro made and broke his own laws on a whim. No one knew for sure what was legal and what wasn't. Like this tunnel. Yesterday Piedro had welcomed the efforts to dig out. He'd openly told Rollett that the excavation toward the outside world kept troublemakers too busy and tired to wreak havoc within the city—or foment open rebellion.

Rollet wondered why Piedro hadn't assassinated him yet. He'd had many opportunities in the last year and a half. Perhaps the Kaaliph feared that Rollett's men, who worked and lived as a cohesive unit, protecting each other, might rebel at the loss of their leader. Perhaps Piedro had secret plans to use this crew for something else. Perhaps . . .

The hair on the back of Rollett's neck rose in atavistic fear. He searched first for signs of a ghost. The blocked end of the tunnel remained quiet.

Slowly he turned back to the tunnel entrance, knowing who awaited his notice. A short figure stood beside Peidro. Her head barely reached the Rover's shoulder. A black lace veil covered her from head to toe. The intricate pattern of open and dense thread shifted with each movement, revealing haunting hints of a feminine figure robed in a finely cut black gown. A paler blob indicated the location of her face, but no hint of hair or eye color, distinguishing features, or age filtered through the veil.

She maintained a tighter control of her emotions and her aura than the cadre of Rovers who accompanied Piedro everywhere. Even if Rollett had the energy to spare to probe her, he knew from experience he'd find nothing. The probe would pass right through her.

Rover magic was mysterious. Her magic was unfathomable.

The woman rose up on tiptoe and whispered into Piedro's ear. In the year and a half since the Rover had seized power, no one but Piedro had heard her voice. All that anyone knew of her was that Piedro never went anywhere without her—except the brothels.

"I shall attend you in a moment, my dear." Piedro patted her hand solicitously. She backed away, as if floating in a mist of her veil.

"Leave this excavation, Rollett," Piedro ordered. "The great winged god Simurgh is hungry. His temple—the only temple remaining in all of Kardia Hodos dedicated to him—lies empty within my palace. Don't give me an excuse to feed him your blood. Much as I have enjoyed them, I grow weary of your challenges."

"Who ordered the end of this project, you or your consort?"

"I rule Hanassa. No one else!" Piedro screamed in a voice on the edge of hysteria.

Rollett merely raised one eyebrow in question.

"Guards, post five men here at all times. The work will cease immediately." Piedro turned on his heel and stalked out. His temper made little ripples in his aura, like watching air distortion around a hot flame.

"Move the next load of dirt to the latrine pit," Rollett ordered his work crew.

The guards looked at their hands. Two masons shouldered them aside, carrying buckets of fresh mortar. Other men followed with shovels and picks ready to attack the blockage.

The Rover guards moved outside and took up assigned posts but did not interfere with the work.

"Rumor has it that Piedro has a new supply of grain and dried fruit. Maybe a load of hams as well," a worker whispered to Rollett as he passed.

Rollett nodded slightly in acknowledgment. Every dark of the moon he heard the same rumor. Always the darkest night of the cycle.

"Tonight," he whispered to the next man who passed him.

"Three hours after midnight," the man mouthed, careful not to let any of Piedro's spies hear.

A presence behind Rollett prickled his senses. He reached over his shoulder and grabbed the first informant by the ear and wrestled him into an armlock.

"Stargods, how do you do that?" the prisoner gasped as he relaxed within the punishing grip.

"Never sneak up on a magician," Rollett warned. "Next time I might kill you with a thought before I check to see if you are friend or foe." Rollett grinned and relaxed his pressure on the man's windpipe enough to let him breath. But not enough to let him go.

"Yeah. Well you'd better be double careful tonight," the informant said, rubbing his throat. "I also heard Piedro started the rumor of new supplies in order to trap you. He's afraid to arrest and execute you, but if you died in honest battle stealing from him . . ."

"I'll remember that." Rollett released the man. Then he shuddered inwardly, keeping all traces of revulsion from his face. He'd spent too many years at Nimbulan's side learning that peace, honor, and justice must bind a society together. Violence came too easy for him these days.

"You'll make a good Kaaliph, Rollett," the mason said under his breath. "But you aren't ruthless enough to keep the job. You'll need the consort to help."

"Want to make a bet on that?" Rollett slammed the man up against the stone buttress, holding him a foot off the ground by the throat with one hand.

The mason's face began to pulse purple.

Rollett eased his grip enough for the man's feet to touch ground.

"No bets, Rollett," the mason gasped.

"Remember what happens to people who defy me. Now get to work."

He stalked out of the tunnel, disgusted with himself and with life in Hanassa.

Chapter 9

"**B**e safe, my love," Queen Maarie Kaathliin whispered as she leaned out the nursery window. She pressed her fingertips to her lips and blew a gentle kiss.

In the courtyard below, Quinnault looked up and smiled. He grabbed at the empty air as if catching the kiss. Then he opened his fist against his cheek, planting the caress where it belonged. With a jaunty wave he mounted Buan, his favorite stallion, and rode out the main gate of the palace courtyard.

The waiting company of royal soldiers leaped to their mounts and followed at a canter. They planned to escort a sledge caravan of foodstuffs and firewood to the beleaguered province of Lord Balthazaan. Thrice before, the much-needed supplies had been ambushed by well-organized outlaws and never seen again. The last had happened but days ago. The outlaws should not be quite so greedy for these supplies.

But Katie knew her husband chafed for the chance to confront and punish those thieves.

Quinnault might become lost in the wordstorms of politicians, but when action was called for, he responded readily with a worthy plan.

If only they could find the source of the disquiet in the capital city, she knew he'd form a good plan and act upon it. But vandals tore apart the scaffolding on new buildings, painted anti-foreign slogans on walls, and set fire to pungent offal in the doorways of foreign merchants and ran, leaving no clue to their identity.

Quinnault's dream of justice and peace in Coronnan faded with every act of sabotage.

Rumors gave the troublemakers a dozen different identities and motives. No one presented solid evidence.

The most frequent rumors claimed that the vandals as well as the outlaws attacking caravans were Rovers seeking revenge against Quinnault and the Commune for their exile from Coronnan along with all of the magicians who could not or would not gather dragon magic.

Other rumors spoke of foreign armies. Still others whispered that the dragons stole the food. The latter stories were always accompanied by the strange flapping gesture to ward against evil and a few crosses of the Stargods.

"None of those rumors can be true," Katie said to the air, pounding her fist against the window casement. "A magical border protects all of Coronnan from foreign troops and Rovers. And the dragons have no need for grain and fruit and pickled meat. Do you, Shayla?" She sent the last question telepathically as well as verbally.

But the dragons remained silent. For many weeks they'd been too busy to respond to Katie or Quinnault. She'd heard magicians complain about a lack of dragon magic to gather. Without dragon magic to impose ethics and honor upon magicians, Coronnan might very well dissolve into disastrous civil war once more. What transpired?

Katie moved to stand over her daughter's crib. "I miss the informal clutter of my family." She sighed heavily. Three times this past winter each of her brothers had visited her clandestinely. Each time she had hugged her sibling close, unwilling to let him go, though she knew she must. They had responsibilities back home.

She had not seen them for two moons. Perhaps they had gone home—taking their father with them. But it was unlike Liam Francis not to risk one final good-bye.

She had chosen her life with Quinnault—her beloved Scarecrow—on this rural planet with clean air and fresh food in exchange for the precious Tambootie to cure a plague. But she still missed her boisterous brothers and their adventures together. She'd never needed friends and lovers until she came here. Her family had filled every emotional need she had.

She must never see them again and must never communicate with them either. The family covenant forbade it. Kardia Hodos must remain free of the taint of technology and the plague.

Still, her brothers bent the covenant to check on her. The bonds of family went deeper than duty.

She gazed lovingly at her daughter, a true miracle of life. This eight-month-old bundle of hungry demands represented the future of this country and her family.

For a few moments, at least, Princess Marilell slept quietly, sucking her fist. Hungry even in sleep.

"Maybe you'll have a baby brother soon," Katie whispered to her daughter. She placed her hand protectively across her belly, hoping. . . .

She shot another question to the dragons. Still no answer. On the night Marilell had been conceived, the dragons had flown a nuptial flight as well. Shayla had told Katie the next morning that both matings had been successful.

Shayla wasn't due to mate again for at least another year. Katie hoped she didn't have to wait until then to become pregnant again.

"Maybe not having enough milk to nurse you, Marilell, is a blessing. Maybe I'll conceive again quickly. Perhaps I already have. No one back home will consider taking the time to nurse their own babies, so they have to resort to drugs and devices to keep from having too many children too soon. But here, children are a blessing rather than an inconvenience necessary for the continuation of the human race."

Or a frightening experience depending on the mother's exposure to the plague. The old, the very young, and pregnant women always contracted the plague first.

No one knew for certain what breakdown in their immune systems triggered a plague spore back into life. The genetically engineered microbes were supposed to eat only toxic waste until they ran out of food, then they should turn cannibalistic until only one remained and it starved to death. But the microbes mutated, turning into dormant spores until more pollution fed them, or they found bacteria and buildups of toxins within the human body a culinary delight.

The reports of illness devastating Lord Balthazaan's province, beginning at the coal mines with their heavy concentrations of mineral dust, had spread to include other regions—city and rural alike. If the problems resulted from privation, the caravan of supplies Quinnault led would help. They needed firsthand reports from the trusted officers with the caravan rather than reliance upon rumor.

Katie read every written report and listened closely to every rumor for similarities between the current illness and the Terran plague. She hoped the symptoms differed enough to rule out the plague. The people of Coronnan succumbed to a choking cough. Terra's plague caused all of the internal organs to hemorrhage. Eventually the patient either bled to death or drowned from blood filling the lungs.

The soldiers had orders to gather fallen branches and limbs along the route to supplement the loads of firewood. Nimbulan had added the request to include the Tambootie for bonfires in the central marketplace of afflicted villages and manors. Scarface had countermanded Nimbulan's request. Smoke from the Tambootie was toxic to mundanes. In this case, the cure could be worse than the disease.

Nimbulan had countered that only eating the raw leaves of the Tambootie had proved lethal to mundanes. Breathing the smoke was such a private ritual of magicians that no record of a mundane reacting to the smoke existed. If a distillation of the Tambootie proved safe to mundanes, then the smoke should be as well.

Who was right? Katie wanted to believe Nimbulan because he was a friend and had proved wise so many times in the past year. But Scarface sounded so logical. . . .

If only they knew for certain that the smoke would *safely* prevent the disease.

The queen traced the baby's cheek with her fingertip. Such soft skin, warm and pink. She vowed that her new home would never know the plague, never live in fear of bearing children lest the plague strike mother and child when most vulnerable.

Silently Katie moved away from the crib to a secret recess in the wall near the outside corner of the room. She pressed and twisted an imperfection in the stonework. The false face of the stone popped open on well-oiled hinges to reveal an opening about twenty centimeters square. Previous queens of Coronnan had secreted jewels and valuable documents here. Katie used the cache for more important equipment.

She withdrew a small computerized box, a vial of test strips, and a lancet. "Do I really need to do this every day?" she asked herself. She dreaded the painful pricks from the lancet more and more. Maybe today she would just put the equipment back in its hiding place. The anxious mother part of her insisted she proceed.

Once brought out of dormancy, the virus spread rapidly by the briefest human contact, devastating entire populations in a matter of weeks. Each carrier caused a mutation of the virus that was resistant to the previous generation of antibiotics. In seven centuries of fighting the plague, Terran scientists had found that only a distillation from the Tambootie tree cured the plague.

In all those generations, Katie's family had never lost a member to the plague. The O'Haras and a few other families had proved strangely immune to the disease. But the microbe mutated so quickly Katie dared not take a chance that the next bug would kill her and devastate her new home.

She had lived on bush worlds for three years before being dispatched to the distant planet known as Kardia Hodos. Aboard the space transport here, she had lived in a special isolation chamber with a different air supply from the rest of the ship. Was that long enough to know she was free of the plague?

No. She had to perform this small chore once every day for ten years to be sure. At least another four years of painful pricks from the tiny needle.

Katie washed her hands with the hard lye soap used by the common populace. She preferred the cleansing properties of this soap to the softer perfumed stuff favored by the local nobility. She winced as the lancet pricked her finger. A bright hanging drop of blood welled up from the minute wound. She touched the surface of the test strip with the blood and slipped the chemically treated slide into the meter.

The tiny computer whirred and hummed to itself as it checked her blood against a thousand tests, including iron levels, thyroid, cholesterol, blood sugar, and hormone levels for pregnancy. In less than a standard minute the machine beeped, satisfied that Katie's blood was clean of the plague, her red and white counts remained normal, and her hormones maintained a satisfactory level. She wasn't pregnant.

This tiny machine should be the only machine that would ever taint Kardia Hodos. And she would destroy it when she no longer needed it.

Except her father had given a sonar unit to the Guild of Bay Pilots. She wished she could sabotage that device. One bit of technology always led to another and another until the entire society was riddled with machines, synthetics, and pollution.

A knock on the door roused her from her silent contemplation.

"Come," she called. Getting servants to respect her privacy had been a long uphill battle, but at least now they knocked and announced themselves when entering. Getting them to leave her alone again was still a problem.

"Your Grace." Kaariin, the queen's personal maid, bobbed a quick curtsy. "King Kinnsell, your father, requests an audience." Her eyes shone wide with awe and a bit of terror.

Kinnsell had that effect on people. Most people. Katie hadn't allowed him to intimidate her since she was twelve and discovered that she had as much right to be elected emperor upon her grandfather's death as her father did.

"What are you doing here, Kinnsell?" she asked the shadowy figure in the hallway. "You left for Terra last autumn, right after the dragon dream." That had been his announced intention, but she'd seen Sean Michael and Jamie Patrick twice since then and Liam Francis three times. Jamie Patrick, the eldest, had told her Gramps had suffered a third heart attack near the Solstice and they might have to leave for home without notice to attend him.

Kinnsell nodded toward the servant in a gesture requesting privacy.

Katie almost asked Kaariin to stay, just to annoy her father. "I will interview King Kinnsell in the solar," Katie

said instead. She caressed her baby one more time and
moved toward the inner door that would take her to her
private suite.

"You will receive me here, Katie," Kinnsell boomed as
he pushed his way past the maid into the nursery, slamming
the door in Kaariin's face. He wore a local style of richly
brocaded tunic with plain dark trews and boots instead of
Varn veils and headdress. He intended to be seen as the
King of Terrania.

Marilell whimpered at the disturbance.

"Hush!" Katie commanded her father. "You've awakened the baby."

"Good. About time I had a chance to hold my granddaughter." He reached into the crib and lifted the baby to
his shoulder before Katie could intervene. "You know, if
you'd let me bring in a monitor, you wouldn't have to
spend so much time babysitting. You could get out of this
frigid palace, take part in the government, have a life."

"My child is my life!"

"Ah, Katie, all your fine education wasted on this primitive world. They don't even have the wheel, for God's
sake."

"Don't forget that at regular intervals this planet provides
enough surplus food to feed a civilized world for five years.
And never forget that this primitive world is protected by
family covenant. I can have you arrested and imprisoned by
Gramps and Uncle Ryan if you violate the pact."

"A nice solar heater would make this drafty old barn
more comfortable. I don't like the idea of my granddaughter being exposed to constant chill."

Katie sighed. Her father would only hear what he wanted
to hear.

"Natives thrive in their natural climate. The strongest
survive and build antibodies against *natural* ailments. Besides, the family covenant specifically forbids machines on
this planet. We've had this argument before, Kinnsell. Why
are you here?"

"I came to see my granddaughter."

"Why aren't you on Terra attending Gramps after his
heart attack? You should be delivering a load of much
needed Tambootie, that will make enough medicine to cure

a million or more people of the plague." She took a deep breath to control her temper. Then she resorted to sarcasm to keep from slapping some sense into him. "You'll never be elected emperor if you don't show your face on the homeworld more than once a decade. No one will remember you as savior of humanity unless you take credit for the cure."

"Pop recovered from his heart surgery quite nicely without me. He'll live another decade or more. Liam Francis and Sean Michael are delivering the Tambootie in my name. About time they made themselves useful."

"I'm happy to hear that Gramps is doing well." And she was. Of all of her vast family, Gramps was her favorite, the one whose ideas about protecting Kardia Hodos agreed most closely with her own. As for her brothers, any one of the three of them might ingratiate himself with the legislature by taking credit for finding a cure for the plague—Jamie Patrick most likely, but he hadn't been sent home. Every one of the family held more moderate views toward expansion and exploitation than Kinnsell. But not as conservative as Katie and Gramps.

"The joint legislature is certain to elect me emperor when I bring Kardia Hodos back into the fold of the Empire. Finders of lost Terran colonies are always highly regarded." Kinnsell preened while holding the baby away from him.

"No!" A wave of vertigo washed over Katie. "This world is protected by the family covenant. We've kept it secret for seven hundred years to protect it from outside influences."

"And I intend to follow another family tradition of bringing lost bush worlds back into the Empire. We need all the agriculture we can get to feed the civilized worlds, the important worlds. Besides, the rest of the Empire needs the Tambootie that only grows here in order to cure the plague once and for all. I think she's wet." He set Marilell back into the crib.

"You'll strip this planet as you've stripped others. You won't be satisfied until every known planet is a desert." The baby could wait a moment, she wasn't fussing.

"Not deserts. Domed and protected from the ravages of climates and natural disasters."

"And unable to produce food, only to consume it. Every domed atmosphere is a potential breeding ground for the plague."

"Not if I harvest the Tambootie." His right hand rode at a comfortable and easy position beside him.

Katie knew she'd not convince him of anything while he felt himself in control of the situation. Still, she had to try.

"Synthetic air and food mutate new viruses. You know that. There isn't enough Tambootie to cure every new mutation. And you'll take it all. I know you, Kinnsell. You'll take all of the Tambootie, right down to the roots. The dragons will die without the Tambootie supplementing their diet. Without dragons, there won't be any magic. Coronnan will perish without magic."

"There isn't any magic. Only psi powers." His hand nudged forward a fraction. Had she broken through his blockheaded opinions, even just a little?

"Little do you know, Kinnsell. Little do you know the miracles this planet offers. I forbid you to take anything from here. Not so much as a grain of dirt. The Commune will back my order and force you to obey. Now get out. Go home. Never darken my door again."

"In my own good time, daughter. When I've finished what I came here for."

"Over my dead body, Kinnsell!"

"If necessary."

* * *

Library of the University of Magicians, Coronnan City

"Start clearing a space in the gallery for the questionable books, Lyman," Scarface ordered.

Bessel considered slipping out the postern door. The noise of old wood and rusty hinges protesting being opened would alert Scarface to Bessel's presence in the library. The Senior Magician would know he'd been here and hunt down the book. Stargods only knew what he would do to Bessel once caught with a now forbidden book.

"We can block off access with locked gates, and I shall set the magical seal so that only I can open it." Scarface turned his back on the old librarian and pointed out the most inaccessible corners of the library.

"No," Lyman replied quietly. "I will not be a part of this. I am not strong enough to oppose you on my own, but I will not be a part of it."

Bessel sought a hiding place, any hiding place.

What was Scarface thinking, banning books? Nimbulan had made the library the focus of the entire University. Knowledge was valuable, any knowledge, in any form. Magicians keeping secrets had led to intense rivalries and many battles during three generations of civil war.

Now magicians had the responsibility to guide the rest of Coronnan through cooperation and sharing of knowledge. They couldn't do that unless they were the best educated men in the world; educated in all facets of life. How could they combat the dangerous machines if they didn't know their function and design? How could they negate a rogue magician if they did not know the nature of his spells?

Besides, Bessel was certain that information about the plague that had killed his mother could be found in one of these old books.

He couldn't help his mother. A tear threatened to choke him. She had loved him in her own distracted way. His father's prejudice had separated Bessel from the family. Not his mother. His father's prejudice and *ignorance*.

Bessel remembered something Myrilandel had told him about the time she had fled ignorant people who blamed her for all of their ills. People rarely looked up for a fugitive. They always looked down or at eye level.

He climbed. The bookshelves were massive constructions, ten feet high, each shelf a convenient step to the next.

As quietly as possible, he settled himself flat along the very top of the unit. He had only inches to spare between his back and the floor of the first gallery circling the perimeter of the library.

"If you won't help, then move aside, old man." Scarface waved Lyman out of his way. "I didn't expect one of Nimbulan's acolytes to agree with me. Fortunately there are few of you remaining to pester me with outlandish ideas. Coronnan will remain under my control with the blessing of dragon magic."

What? Coronnan would remain under Scarface's control. He hadn't said "the Commune." He'd said "Coronnan." The fine hairs along Bessel's spine tingled in warning.

Lyman hesitated long enough for Scarface's temper to whiten the scar on his face. At last Lyman bowed his head in submission and stepped aside.

"We must begin putting the forbidden books under the gallery, deeply shadowed," Scarface mused, staring at the upper shelves. "We'll move up into the galleries if we have to."

He waved to his three satellite magicians to begin work at the front of the three-story-high room. They separated and immediately began pulling books off the shelves. They carried each book to the center worktables, making neat stacks of them. They worked rapidly, removing more books than they left shelved. Probably Scarface had decided which books to cull before they began.

Bessel pressed himself deeper into the shadows between the wall and the gallery floor. His squarely-built body barely fit atop the shelving unit.

Scarface brought a ball of witchlight to hand and raised his arm to see deeper into the shadows.

"You there!" Scarface shouted, pointing directly at Bessel. "Why are you hiding up there?"

"Um . . . um . . . I was dusting and I got stuck." Bessel flushed with the awkward lie.

Scarface raised his eyebrows, making the scar white again, a sure sign that he concentrated hard on containing his temper.

"I think not, boy. More likely you sought a hiding place to take a clandestine nap. I knew you were lazy. This proves it. Come down from there. Now."

Bessel looked to Lyman for some kind of direction.

"Don't seek out the old man. He can't tell you what to do. I am Senior Magician. You are oath-bound to obey me without question."

Bessel made the awkward climb down. But as he shifted his legs to dangle over the edge of the shelves, he pushed the precious book deep into the waistband of his trews, covering it with his tunic. He willed it into invisibility. It seemed to shrink and flatten as he continued the climb down the shelves. Scarface wouldn't be able to find it even with his Sight-Beyond-Sight.

Chapter 10

A rise overlooking Coronnan City from the south

Kinnsell stood on a slight rise on the south shore mainland overlooking the islands of Coronnan City. The River Coronnan made a natural moat. But enemies had boats, and the inhabitants needed the bridges connecting the various islands to each other and the mainland. The city was vulnerable.

And he planned to take it if Katie and her husband defied him further. "Cursed family covenant is outdated, worthless. The Empire needs this planet. The Empire needs me at its head and this planet will give me the crown. I won't let my renegade daughter keep me from getting it." He spat into the ground. A new sense of freedom lifted a weight from his shoulders. His hand rode easily at his side.

The distances involved in transporting food to the civilized worlds had grown beyond practicality centuries ago. Tanked food kept the Empire fed, but its citizens craved real food and were willing to pay enormous sums for small tastes.

Kardia Hodos was the private storehouse of the emperor.

"What do you see down there that our best generals and Battlemages can't?" his companion asked. The bushie lord continued to twist his heavy ring nervously and had refused several times to part with it, no matter the bribe.

"I see a way for the Guild of Bay Pilots to transport troops into the heart of the city."

"We've tried that. The pilots aren't bribable."

"But they owe me greatly for the depth finding machine." Kinnsell had discarded the Varn costume. His followers needed to know his identity now that he openly worked to establish a power base. Starting with Lord Balthazaan who deeply resented Quinnault and his fakir friend Nimbulan.

"And I owe you for ore finders and rock cutters. What do the others owe you?"

"Five lords in your league of rebellion will discover every one of their ewes will bear twins or triplets that are bigger, healthier, and have longer wool than any beast they've seen before."

"The ones you could persuade to accept your demon magic. If word gets out how those lords became so rich in sheep, no one will buy anything from them. And it will be another full year before the promised wool is available."

"The hybrid wheat will pay off by the middle of summer." Kinnsell suppressed a cough. Talking dried his throat out. He wasn't used to all this cold raw air. He edged his hand forward.

"If the weather holds, the wheat harvest might be better than average. If the soil hasn't been depleted by overplanting. If the dragons don't burn our fields to dust because we gave you more of the Tambootie than King Quinnault authorized."

"Don't tell me you are so stupid you believe in the dragon myths!" Kinnsell shouted, pushing his hand farther forward. "What is it about this place that makes you all believe that simple psi powers are major magic and that dragons are real? Every contact we have put in Coronnan has forsaken our civilization and gone bush. Even my daughter. And she's supposed to be educated."

"You have obviously never come face-to-face with a dragon or one of the magicians who control them." The bushie lord made the curious flapping gesture with crossed wrists as he looked up. Was he truly scanning the heavens for sight of a dragon?

"None of your magicians will break down my shields and force a dragon illusion on me. I'll prove that the magicians are frauds. Then you won't have to put up with them. You can rely on your own intelligence and my machines." Kinnsell's hand came back to rest easily at his side.

"The lords will follow you if you manage to end the tyranny of the magicians and the dragons. We don't like them any better than you do. But the lords I speak for need proof of your powers before they commit to your cause."

A hot, angry flush burned Kinnsell's cheeks and brow. He was getting very tired of these bushie lords making demands on *him*.

"I set up one of your agents to start the riot that nearly ended all of the foreign treaties. I have given you times and locations and ambush plans for the loads of supplies going to the provinces. You have in turn sold the food on the black market at a tremendous profit. I presume last week's shipment is already on its way to the location of your choice. We can't allow Quinnault to deliver the current load either. Common people all over this hellhole begin to question Quinnault's ability to govern. His only support lies among the city's populace."

"He leads the new shipment with more guards than my soldiers can handle. He'll be seen as the great deliverer."

"Not if I give you a reason to call him and half his troops back before he travels half a day from the capital. The king shall fail in this mission as he has in every other."

"What reason? It will have to be compelling to bring the king back."

"I'll think of something." Like kidnapping Princess Marilell. As the baby's grandfather, he had the right to keep her every other weekend by Terran law. But he wouldn't bother to inform Katie of his plans.

"The lords want action now. They'll need proof of your powers and your sincerity to wait any longer to overthrow Quinnault."

"Like what?" Kinnsell braced himself for the next demand for tools and technology. If he kept this up, he wouldn't have enough left of his ship to fly back to civilization—which couldn't come too soon. He'd hoped to withhold a butane torch hot enough to burn the impurities out of the local sands so they could make decent glass until he'd run out of all other options. Was this the time to offer it?

The sky started to leak an annoying drizzle.

He'd be warm again as soon as he reached civilization. Warm and dry. Maybe then he'd stop coughing.

"The magicians keep a Rover woman prisoner in their University." The bushie lord eyed Kinnsell from beneath heavy black brows. Plots cooked deep within those eyes. Kinnsell wished he could read them.

"Free the Rover woman, and we will believe your technology is more powerful than magic." *Technology we can use to control you as well as the magicians and the king.*

Kinnsell couldn't help but overhear the man's thoughts. He smiled to himself. Not often did these locals let their natural shields slip. But when they did, he learned a lot.

Best he not let them know his own psi powers were strong and growing stronger.

Something about this planet . . .

"Very well. I will remove the woman from the University tomorrow after I have reconnoitered. Then I will show your craftsmen how to make a spinning wheel to handle all of the wool your new sheep will produce next spring."

"A Wheel!" the lord touched his head, heart, and each shoulder in the approved cross of the Stargods.

At least Kinnsell's ancestors had gotten something right in teaching these yokels the gesture of protection and prayer.

Then the lord crossed his wrists, left over right and flapped his hands in another ward against evil.

"The Stargods have forbidden the Wheel as well as reading and higher mathematics for all but magicians. Those two things are the keys to all evil." The lord backed away from Kinnsell, repeating the flapping gesture. When ten meters separated them, he turned and ran into the thick trees as fast as his fat legs and long robe allowed.

"Damn!" Kinnsell slammed his fist into the trunk of a tree. "Now I have to start all over again. Unless. . . ."

* * *

Ancient plateau of Hanassa, time unknown

Powwell ran into the dragongate. He banged his forehead against a wall of resistance. Hard. Stars burst behind his eyes. The alluring song of the gate rang in his ears with discordant notes, repulsing him rather than drawing him in.

Yaala had entered the vortex of time and distance while facing him. Her passage must have triggered something, blocking this angle.

He darted around the shadows and approached the swirling distortion from the other side. His eyes tried to follow the shifting landscape within the gate. He lost his focus, and his head swam. The kardia shifted beneath his feet once more, and he fell headlong into the pulsing spiral of blood red, fire green, and midnight black.

Thorny hunched within Powwell's pocket. The hedgehog's spines jabbed through Powwell's shirt. Thorny's blast of emotional upset followed the sharp pricks. First a plunge from the familiar landscape into the horrible desert. No water. Too much light. Uncertainty. Fear. Now this horrible pulsing energy again.

Thorny was not happy.

Powwell wasn't happy either. He had to find Yaala. Everything else in his life lost importance. He had to stay with Yaala.

Only this opening of the dragongate could lead him to Yaala or Kalen. He didn't know how to find Kalen without Yaala. He couldn't think beyond staying beside Yaala.

He prayed to the Stargods and whatever other forces might hear him that she hadn't triggered the gate too soon and ended up in the void without an anchor.

The colors grew more intense, stabbing into his eyes. Powwell clenched them shut. The pain lessened a little. He concentrated on refinding his planetary orientation, hoping to understand how the dragongate worked. Or where it was taking him.

Energy pulsed around him. He tumbled with it, losing all sense of up and down, right and left. Time and distance became meaningless. He had no idea where or when he traveled, only that he traversed a great distance.

Numbness filled his mind.

The dragongate held him seemingly forever.

Was that a moment of sleep?

He became aware of his body. No longer tumbling. Energy flowing around and with him, heat and light soothed the aches in his joints. And then . . .

And then there was green. Lots and lots of green. He

lay in it. Breathed its moisture. Luxuriated in the comfort of being home.

Home! Yes he was home, in Coronnan. The South Pole tugged at his feet, watery sunshine broke through the cloud cover. Sunset was still hours away.

But where was Yaala?

He looked around carefully, moving as little as possible. The rocky overhang looked the same as when they'd left it. Hours ago? Days ago?

No, the season hadn't changed by more than a few hours. Early spring. The dark of the moon tonight. Not quite noon now. The rain shower dissipated quite rapidly as sunshine broke through the clouds. The rain had just begun when they entered the dragongate for the first time at dawn.

So where was Yaala?

Strident voices pierced his ears. Angry men off to his left.

They probably walked the road that ran from Myrilandel's village over the pass into the Southern Mountains. It passed near Hanassa on its way to the desert kingdom of Rossemeyer.

Powwell listened closely.

Men shouted in a language he hadn't heard since before leaving Hanassa. Rovers! Stargods, he had to get out of here.

He heard a heavy sledge scraping the packed dirt of the road.

Powwell opened his senses with magic, striving to understand what was going on. He hoped Yaala wasn't the center of that argument. It sounded as if the men might come to blows in a moment.

"*S'murghin'* four-legged dimwit. Get over here!" a man shouted.

A steed screamed and stamped the ground.

Powwell heard the clang of iron shoes striking rock on the rough road. Not a Rover steed. Rovers didn't shoe their beasts.

A whip cracked. The steed roared in pain. Powwell felt the terror of the high-strung animal. Leather snapped and hooves pounded the road, disappearing in the opposite direction.

"Piedro's going to kill us now. He really wanted that steed, a second man said.

"The Kaaliph refuses to believe steeds are too smart to use the dragongate," the first man muttered.

The import of the words broke through Powwell's mind. Piedro must have taken the title of Kaaliph after all the other contenders had died.

The brief triumph Powwell had felt when he watched Yaassima and her pet Bloodmage murder each other faded to disgust. Hanassa had merely traded one ruthless leader for another.

Piedro now ruled the city; Piedro, the cruel one who had delighted in slamming his fists into Powwell's gut when he kidnapped him along with Kalen and Myrilandel a year and a half ago.

"We have to get these supplies through today. The gate won't open a true path again for another moon," the first man said with a grunt. "Let's move these sledges now. Lord Balthazaan is going to be right on our heels when he discovers how much we've stolen from him. When he hired us, he told us to leave most of this for him to sell on the black market."

"We left the lord extra jewels from Piedro's hoard. The lord can get more supplies from the king. We can't get anything but what we can carry through the dragongate until Rollett digs open the tunnel," the second man grunted as if hauling something very heavy.

"Well, you better hope Magician Rollett never gets the tunnel gate open, or we're out of a job."

"If Piedro wants the tunnel kept closed so he can play benevolent ruler by doling out food at starvation rations, why don't he just execute Rollett as a troublemaker?"

"Because the consort doesn't want Rollett dead yet. And what the consort wants, Piedro orders. Now move it. The dragongate opens in about two hundred heartbeats."

Powwell had to hide. He couldn't let these Rovers catch him at the entrance to the dragongate. But if he went too far, he'd lose the chance to get to Hanassa for another moon.

But where was Yaala? He couldn't go to Hanassa without her.

A light touch on his shoulder jerked him out of his confusing mind loop. Yaala stood over him, a finger to her lips for silence. She motioned for him to follow her.

Powwell scrambled to his feet. He resisted the urge to hug her. They hadn't time to indulge in emotional displays. He followed Yaala behind the outcrop of rock she favored just as the Rovers entered the opening in the trees.

We have to follow them, Powwell sent to his companion.

Yaala shook her head. She had no magic, so she couldn't talk to him mind to mind.

Yes. The gate won't open for another moon.

"Too dangerous," she mouthed. "Rovers."

I know. But if we are very quiet and step through the gate behind them, they won't look back. They never do. We can hide in the tunnels once we get through.

Yaala shook her head again. Tears of disappointment touched the corners of her eyes. She wiped them clear, then straightened her shoulders in determination. One quick jerk of her chin showed her willingness to risk following Powwell.

We're in this together.

"You're in this with me!" the first Rover said, grabbing Powwell by the back of his collar. "Did you forget, boy, that all Rovers have magic? I heard every word you thought. Piedro's gonna like the present we bring him. New victims to execute for his consort. That lady never gets enough blood. She's worse than Yaassima."

Chapter 11

"**I** won't be a Rover slave again!" Powwell screamed.

This time he would return to Hanassa of his own free will and in command of his actions, not the victim of kidnap. He'd rescue Kalen this time or die trying. But he'd never be a slave again.

He slammed his staff into the gut of the man who seemed to be in command of the raiding party.

The Rover countered by grabbing the twisted staff with both hands.

Powwell wrenched it away. His balance shifted back. He stumbled over Yaala. She thrust her hands against his back, pushing him onto the balls of his feet. He swung the staff end over end, clipping the second Rover in the jaw.

Thorny gibbered inside Powwell's pocket, afraid of Powwell's violent reaction. Powwell absorbed the pain from the tips of the hedgehog's sharp spines pricking his skin through his shirt and continued circling with his staff. Thorny wanted to be away from here. Powwell did, too. For different reasons.

Powwell maneuvered his opponent around until the Rover's back was to the overhang and he himself was in the open. The dragongate, when it opened, should be no more than two paces away.

Thorny didn't like that idea at all and hunched. His spines withdrew, then bristled with deeper penetration. Powwell renewed his attack on the Rover with sharpened senses and strength.

A third man and a fourth appeared in the forest opening from the direction of the road.

Yaala flung dirt in their eyes. She swung her pack in a broad circle, catching the first one alongside his temple. He teetered into the men behind, toppling them all.

The Rover leader still menaced Powwell with a knife. Powwell circled the staff one more time and brought it down atop the man's wrist. Wood cracked. Bone snapped. The man howled in pain and dropped his weapon.

"Hurry, Powwell, the dragongate opens," Yaala ducked the man with a bright red weal on his temple. She slid from behind the overhang into the arched shadow.

"Which scene?" Powwell didn't take his eyes off the Rovers. Two of the newcomers staggered upright with clubs and knives at the ready.

"The right scene. The right time," Yaala called back.

Powwell dove after her into the vortex of power that warped distance in an eye blink. He had to trust that Yaala was right this time. All of his instincts screamed to wait and view the other end of the portal himself.

He had to trust Yaala when he hated to trust anyone but himself and Thorny.

*   *   *

The pit beneath the city of Hanassa

Yaala hit the once-familiar ground running. Her balance reeled in the sudden blackness of the lava tube tunnel. A wall of air heated by the lava core greeted her, nearly searing her lungs. She could barely breathe. Walls pressed against her from all sides, much smaller than she remembered. She needed to clutch the jagged walls for support. She didn't dare. Powwell needed room to pass through the portal directly behind her. Could he use his magic to stop the Rovers from following?

What could she do to help her friend? Not much without tools.

Running footsteps behind her. Powwell. *Stargods, please let it be Powwell.*

The tunnel had changed shape after the kardiaquake.

Last time she had been through here, a person could turn around in the narrow confines. Now the walls seemed to grab and block her with every pace. Powwell would have trouble breathing in here. More trouble than usual when underground.

"Duck," she called back over her shoulder, hoping her friend wouldn't knock himself senseless on one of the protruding rocks. At least the tunnel was only ten paces long. It used to be thirty. Or was it a different tunnel? If the dragongate had switched openings, that would explain the changes in its patterns.

A lighter blackness signaled the opening of the tunnel into a huge cavern.

Flickering remnants of yellow light told her that at least one of the generators continued to power the lighting system.

The hulk of Old Bertha, the largest of the machines that generated 'tricity, sat huge and silent within the vast cavern. She looked bigger in the shadowy light, without definite edges and ends. The generator filled nearly the entire cavern with blackened metal and broken conduits. The pipe connecting the machine to an underground lake lay in three broken pieces. Steam erupted from the first open end where the pipe passed above the lava core of the volcano. Upon meeting the comparatively cooler air of the labyrinth, the steam spread out and condensed into water. A new lake formed beneath the pipe, rusting the other sections. Water dripped from every surface, compounding the accumulated rust on Old Bertha.

After only a year and a half, the damage looked beyond repair.

She didn't have time to grieve over the loss of the machine. She needed a tool, a weapon. Powwell had rammed two magician's staffs into the guts of Old Bertha to create a diversion when they escaped from here. The machine was now dead. The staffs served no other purpose now. She grabbed the exposed end of the one that had belonged to Nimbulan, instinctively trusting the tool used and shaped by the honorable old man over the one carried by Scarface.

The seven-foot shaft resisted her tugs. Clumps of rust broke free from the machine around the opening. She pulled again with a downward twist. The wood snapped.

She fell backward into a small pool of warm water as four feet of the staff broke free of the machine's grip.

A momentary pang of regret at the destruction of Nimbulan's staff touched her throat. Then she remembered he wouldn't be needing it again. He'd lost his magic in defense of Coronnan. But she needed a weapon. She scrambled to her feet, holding the staff horizontally in front of her.

Powwell erupted from the tunnel mouth and whirled to face whoever might follow.

One Rover pelted through the tight tunnel, screaming his rage. He held his club tight against his chest. The narrow walls and low ceilings hampered his movements.

Powwell drove his own staff straight into the man's eyes. The Rover ducked below the staff, coming up with club extended. Powwell jumped aside. The Rover kept running forward.

Yaala tripped him with the broken staff. He landed facedown in the spreading lake of hot water beneath the broken pipe. Much hotter than the isolated pool she had fallen into. He yelped and rolled to the side, keeping his face free of the steaming liquid.

Mist formed around the splashes. A cold mist. Everything else within the pit was hot. Stifling.

The mist grew, nearly solidified into a human form, but a veiled form without distinct features.

"The wraith!" Yaala said out loud. Chills ran up and down her spine. The fine hairs on her arms and the back of her neck stood on end in atavistic fear.

"With my head and heart and the strength of my shoulders, I renounce this evil." The Rover crossed himself repeatedly, scooting away from the apparition.

A ghostly white arm reached toward Powwell. Entreating. Lonely. Desperate for . . . something.

The Rover reacted first, running back into the tunnel.

He leaped through the dragongate as the inviting green of Coronnan swirled into the wild spiral of closure.

Powwell and Yaala followed their enemy, skidding to a halt on the crumbling ledge overlooking the flaring molten rock of the pit. They looked back over their shoulders.

The wraith approached slowly, still holding out a skeletal arm. The ghostly mist filled the narrow tunnel. Their only escape lay a thousand feet below in the boiling lava.

Chapter 12

The pit beneath the city of Hanassa

Shooting flames of boiling rock lulled Powwell into a kind of trance. He needed to step off the ledge, just one step and he would. . . . He deliberately pushed away the allure.

(Follow me. Find your destiny in me.) It sang to him like the haunting temptation of the void.

He closed his mind to the temptation and turned away.

The misty wraith stopped its pursuit the moment he turned to face it. But it still held out a ghostly arm entreatingly.

The mist flowed in the small currents and eddies of air around the humanlike figure at the center. The tendrils shaped into the suggestion of a long tail wrapped around the "feet" of the wraith. Other bits and pieces of opaque vapor suggested wings and spines, minus the distinctive single horn sprouting from the forehead like Shayla and her nimbus of dragons.

Powwell dismissed the dragon features and concentrated on the human body within. Yaassima had coveted draconic features. Yaala had inherited a few, like the prominent spinal bumps of vestigial spines, and an extra eyelid. Myrilandel, Shayla's daughter in human form, had the near colorless skin, hair, and eyes of a dragon. None of these women came close to a real dragon in awesome size and power. Nor did the wraith.

Yaala edged closer to him, away from the spectral being. He wrapped his arm around her waist, holding her close to his side. Whatever the wraith did to them, they'd face it together.

He took one step forward. The only way out. The wraith retreated one step as well.

Powwell tucked Yaala behind him, keeping her hand in his. The tunnel didn't offer enough room for them to walk side by side. She squeezed his hand in silent reassurance. He took another step forward and another.

The wraith flowed backward at an equal pace. The edges of the mist took on a darker hue. Hints of rosy purple? Powwell sensed alarm growing within the bizarre figure.

When they reached the big cavern, where the derelict machine sat like a monstrous spider presiding over the web of tunnels, he breathed a little easier. The wraith hadn't harmed him yet. It seemed almost afraid of him. Or for him?

In the distance he felt more than heard one small machine chugging away. That would explain the dim light. Little Liise, a docile generator who rarely broke down, worked at that particular rhythm. She supplied power to the lights down in the pit and nowhere else. The rest of Hanassa would be in darkness except for natural torches, candles, and oil lamps. Piedro, Kaaliph of Hanassa, wouldn't have enough 'tricity to mimic magic as Yaassima had.

"What do you want of us?" he asked the wraith quietly. His words echoed in the nearly silent cavern. They seemed strangely empty without the machines' constant *yeek kush kush* sounds.

The wraith twisted in upon itself. It raised both thin arms. The vague form suggested that it held its palms up, begging. The tail and wing illusions shrank. Was it writhing in pain? More like indecision or frustration.

"Do you need our help?" Yaala asked, slipping up beside Powwell. She kept her hand in his. The moisture on her palm told him how nervous she was. She should be comfortable here in this labyrinth of tunnels, the only home she had ever really known.

The wraith covered its face with ghostly hands and drifted apart, as mist before sunlight.

"What do you suppose she wanted?" Powwell breathed a sigh of relief.

"She?"

"I guess. I had the suggestion of a female beneath all that haze. I don't know why." He shrugged, not knowing how to examine the feminine feel of the wraith's pleading. He didn't mention the dragon illusion. Most likely it was just that, an illusion meant to trigger a response of respect and awe.

"Let's get out of here." Yaala tugged at his hand.

Powwell followed her slowly, oddly reluctant to leave the wraith that had once haunted him. He never thought he'd be hesitant to depart the inner chambers of the pit and the slavery he'd known here. Suddenly, he became aware of the miles of kardia pressing down upon him.

His breathing became shallow and labored. He needed air. He needed sunshine. He needed OUT! *Stargods, I hope the gate to the palace is open and unguarded.*

Satiric laughter echoed in his mind. A flicker of white tantalized his peripheral vision. Did the wraith taunt him with foreknowledge of the lack of exits?

* * *

Midafternoon, queen's solar, Palace Reveta Tristile, Coronnan City

"Random matings, solely for the sake of conceiving children are no longer appropriate for Spring Festival," Katie stated firmly to the five ladies gathered in her private solar.

"But, your Grace, Spring Festival has always been a time of betrothal. How are our young people to find the right mate if not in the rituals designed by the Stargods?" Lady Balthazaan turned pale with shock.

Katie doubted her Terran ancestors had contrived the ritual dance around a maypole—Festival Pylons they called them here—where the men danced in one direction and the women opposite, changing partners on the whim of the patterns called by village elders. Whichever partner one ended the dance with was their mate for the evening. If that one night together resulted in a child, then the union was blessed by the Stargods and the couple married on or before the Solstice. If no child was conceived, then the couple parted and tried again the next year.

Some of her ancestors probably sanctioned, maybe even participated in the dance. Few of them would have had the imagination to create it.

"The selection of a life mate is too important to leave to young people," Lady Hanic added. Like her husband, she always waited to see what others thought, then formed her opinion to match that of the strongest faction. "Such decisions are best determined by the Stargods."

The remaining three women nodded their heads in vigorous agreement.

"Did you participate in a Festival dance?" Katie asked all of the women.

"Of course not!" Lady Balthazaan gasped. She held her hand to her throat in dismay. "My marriage was a political union. The negotiations between our fathers went on for years."

"I would think a union that important should be left to the Stargods as well," Katie replied quietly, head down.

She played with her needlework a moment to keep her hands busy. All she ever did with her sewing was play and pretend she accomplished something. She'd never learned the fine art before coming to Coronnan. However, her afternoon gatherings with the ladies of the court seemed to demand she join them in the skill.

No one in the room spoke. Katie peeked to see the five women exchanging horrified glances, shaking their heads and biting their lips.

"Spring Festival is a good time to announce betrothals." Katie decided to partially agree with the women. "The dance is even a good way to introduce couples and to celebrate the joy of Spring. But children deserve a stable, loving family with parents who choose to be together rather than those who come together randomly. I do not want Festival in the capital city to degrade into an orgy."

"Our retainers will be most disappointed, Your Grace," Lady Nunio interjected.

"I'm certain young men and women who want to experiment with sex will find a way to do so. But let it be discreet and private."

"What of the young men going off to war? Many do not return. Festival is their only chance to sire a child," Lady Hanic asserted.

Strange that she, of all those present, would present an argument. Like her husband, she usually waited to support whatever side of an argument seemed likely to win.

"We are at peace, Lady Hanic. With luck and diplomacy, the men will not be marching off to war any time soon." Or did she know something Katie didn't?

"One of the reasons we have clung to Festival for so long is to replenish the unstable population due to generations of civil war," Lady Nunio said mildly. "We may have peace now, but we also have a disease running rampant that is killing as many as any major battle. But we lose women and children as well as men in their prime. We need a good Festival to bring hope back to the people."

Katie stilled in shock. She'd read reports of a few isolated cases of a disease felling many in a single village. A plague running rampant had never been mentioned. Who hid the information and why? Was it *the* plague?

"Your Grace!" Kaariin ran into the solar from the nursery. She wrung her hands in anxiety. Her face looked too pale. "Come quickly, Your Grace, the baby is sick."

Katie dropped her hopeless embroidery as she stood. "How?" she demanded, running toward the inner room.

"She coughs until her skin turns waxy and blue. I'm sorry, Your Grace. I've taken good care of her. I'm not responsible . . ." the girl babbled.

"Send a message for King Quinnault to return immediately." Katie dashed past her maid to her daughter's crib.

Sure enough, little Marilell coughed deeply again and again interspersed with whimpers of pain and bewilderment. Katie picked her up, patting her back in soothing circles. Too tired and weak to hold her head up, Marilell rested her head on her mother's shoulder and continued to cough.

Chapter 13

Midafternoon, royal nursery, Palace Reveta Tristile, Coronnan City

Katie looked carefully at her baby, searching for the cause of her illness. "Send for the king immediately, Kaariin," Katie commanded. The maid curtsied and ran down the corridor.

Marilell continued coughing, weaker now, gasping for breath between each spasm.

"Allow me, little sister," Jamie Patrick said emerging from the shadows behind the doorway. "I think I know what ails the child. My own Kevin did the same thing." He held out his arms for the baby.

Katie relinquished her daughter reluctantly. Only the deep love and trust between herself and her brother allowed her to part with her ailing child. He had a little more experience than she with two young children back home with his seldom seen and rarely acknowledged—by her father—wife.

"Thank the Stargods you're here. Is it . . . is it the plague?" she asked, almost afraid that if she voiced her deepest fears they would come true.

"Nothing quite so bizarre," her oldest brother replied. He sat on a nearby stool and draped the little princess over his knee.

Marilell screamed her distress.

"She gets enough air to protest whatever ails her," Nimbulan remarked from the doorway. He held his daughter, Amaranth, easily in the crook of his right arm while raising his left hand, palm outward, fingers slightly curved as if he still gathered magical information with the gesture.

Myrilandel stood beside him. "We were in the palace and interrupted Kaariin on her errand." She marched to stand over Jamie Patrick and the baby.

Jamie Patrick rapped the baby on the back with the flat of his hand. Marilell gasped and choked, spitting up a thin line of fluid. Another rap brought a whoosh of air from the baby's mouth along with a small metal object that rolled across the floor to land at Katie's feet.

"Lucky for all of us Kaariin noticed her distress so quickly. Much longer and the ring could have pushed farther down her throat and torn delicate tissues or choked her completely," Myrilandel commented as she nodded approval of the way Jamie Patrick rubbed the baby's back.

Katie stooped to pick up a man's ring lying at her feet. Intricately twisted silver strands distinguished it from an ordinary signet ring favored by the men of the court.

"I remember Amaranth trying to swallow a very large chunk of raw yampion when she was that age," Myrilandel said as she relieved Jamie Patrick of his sobbing burden. She cuddled the baby against her shoulder, cooing soothingly to the little princess before handing her over to her mother.

"Thank the Stargods you knew what to do, Jamie Patrick." Katie accepted the precious bundle of sobbing child. She held her daughter tightly against her shoulder as she introduced her friends to her brother.

"Sorry, I can't stay, sis. Kinnsell doesn't know I'm here and doesn't want me to contact you, but I had to say 'Hi,' one more time before we leave." Jamie Patrick bent slightly to kiss her cheek. Like most Terran men, he stood only half a head taller than Katie, and much shorter than most of the natives of this planet.

"Be careful, Jamie Patrick. Kinnsell is up to something." Katie caressed his lightly bearded cheek. He had sported a dapper little beard since he could grow one, convinced it added maturity and intrigue to his narrow face. His hair was more blond than red, and he'd said he felt washed out in comparison to the rest of the family.

"We'll be in touch, Katie. I wish we could drag Kinnsell out of here now, but our mission isn't complete."

"What mission?"

But he was gone, as quickly as he had come.

"What do we have here?" Nimbulan removed the slobber-covered ring from Katie's grasp. "Unusual design. I have seen something like it before." His graying eyebrows dipped into a sharp V as he frowned in concentration.

Myrilandel studied the entwined strands carefully.

"It looks Rover," she mused. "What do you think, Lan? You lived with Televarn's tribe an entire season."

"Possibly of Rover design. They do very distinctive work. But the memory that tugs at me is older. Much older." He shook his head sharply. "I'll remember at the least likely moment. Forcing the image into my mind won't help."

"Rover?" Katie gulped. "I've heard that the Rovers sometimes steal children. A . . . a kidnapper could have dropped the ring if disturbed in the act." The same legend of stolen children followed Gypsies and Tinkers back home— usually more myth born out of fear of strangers than from any basis in truth. Were the local version of those wanderers guilty of a heinous crime or victims of malicious gossip? She didn't know.

At the beginning of the riot last autumn, the man in the orange shirt had accused his neighbor of having Rover blood. But Orange-shirt's gaudy clothing more closely resembled Rover preferences than his victim's sober tans and browns.

What was going on here? Was there a connection between the riot and a stranger leaving a potentially lethal object in Marilell's crib, a simple piece of jewelry a teething baby would likely swallow and choke to death on?

"There's been no filthy Rovers in my nursery!" Kaariin protested from the doorway, wringing her hands. "I'd never leave my princess long enough for one of them to sneak in here." She stood straight, fists clenched proudly at her sides.

"No one is accusing you of negligence, child," Nimbulan said soothingly. "A true Rover needs only a heartbeat of time to work mischief."

"Who would do this, Nimbulan? Who would sneak past numerous guards and servants to try to steal my baby?" Katie hugged her daughter closer. Marilell squeaked in protest.

"Someone who wants to hurt you and Quinnault very much. Someone who seeks to control Coronnan by controlling you."

"Kinnsell collects odd bits of unusual jewelry. This is just the sort of thing that would appeal to him. He is also the one man no servant or guard would detain near the royal apartments," Katie whispered.

She had to warn Jamie Patrick. He had to take their father away now, not later, not when their mysterious mission had been completed. Now.

* * *

Late afternoon, on a royal passenger barge in the center of the Great Bay

A fragrant spring breeze drifted from the mainland toward the passenger barge traversing the Great Bay. Journeyman Magician Bessel inhaled deeply of the clean air colored with salt and new lilies. He stood on the top deck with five ambassadors and their ladies. Below and ahead of them a dozen oarsmen pulled the vessel toward shore by brute strength, helped only a little by a tide nearing its lowest ebb.

Master Scarface had assured Bessel that the deaths in his parents' village were isolated. Lord Balthazaan's greed and mismanagement had left his miners ill nourished. The storms and privations of winter had weakened the common people, leaving them vulnerable to all manner of diseases. No true plague ravaged Coronnan. Nor would it now that the books with references to technology had been isolated.

The Commune, meaning Scarface, was in control.

The disease that killed his mother couldn't have been the plague. He prayed it wasn't.

The flower-laden air replaced the stink of the plague in Bessel's memory.

Yet the scent, a mere hint of Powwell's telepathic rendition of the dragon dream, but very prevalent at Ma'ma's deathbed, continued to haunt him.

Every time Bessel voiced a doubt, Scarface reminded him that he need not concern himself with plagues and such. His duty to the Commune required he complete his diplomatic training, hence his presence on this barge.

But he still hadn't revealed the hiding place of the little book he'd been reading just before Scarface rearranged the library. A new iron gate with only one key and a personalized magical seal blocked off the now forbidden books. But the book with intriguing references to blood magic was safe in Bessel's room, hidden beneath a loose floor tile.

Scarface had been most generous in reassuring Bessel after the incident in the library. Bessel had expected punishment. Instead, Scarface had assigned him to this luxury barge. As ordered, Bessel listened to and observed five diplomats and their ladies while they toured the new port city at the edge of the deep water in the bay. For an entire day, Bessel had maintained a light trance so that his mind could understand the conversations conducted in five different languages, even if he couldn't understand the words themselves.

Fatigue dragged his shoulders nearly to his elbows and his eyelids drooped heavily. His stomach growled often. Soon he'd be back at the University where he could sleep and eat and then report to Scarface all that had transpired today.

The depth-finding machine at the center of the barge beeped quietly. One little beep every ten heartbeats. Bessel paused in his savoring of the warm breeze to examine the machine with all his senses. The steady beep told him that no hidden submerged obstacles or suddenly changing channels within the mudflats threatened the barge. But what other threats did the machine disguise? How could the Commune be sure the machine did not emit unseen plagues, much as dragons emitted unseen magic?

He wished the Guild of Bay Pilots was not dependent upon the machine to negotiate the mudflats between the port islands and Coronnan City.

But when King Kinnsell of Terrania had magically constructed the port city out of four natural islands as part of the queen's dowry, he had built jetties that changed the pattern of shifting channels within the mudflats of the inner Great Bay. The port city kept cargo vessels, passenger ships, and invading fleets safely in the depths of the outer bay. The Guild of Bay Pilots had the responsibility of ferrying legal cargo and passengers into Coronnan City. They had no way of learning the changes in the channels fast enough to fulfill that responsibility other than with the depth finder.

Queen Maarie Kaathliin would see to it that no other machines were introduced to this planet by her father. But what about this one?

Maybe Scarface had been right to ban certain books. If anyone understood precisely how the depth finder worked, they could duplicate it, adapt it to other uses. . . .

Bessel took a few moments to draw the warm sunshine on his back deep into his bones. In a few moments, when he could master his bouncing stomach, he'd look at the sparkling light on the shifting waters rather than the mysterious machine. The muck of the mudflats might be only a few fathoms below the water here, but the constantly changing waves disguised the depths. He had no focus to anchor his stomach or his magic. The staff in his hand was useless without that focus.

He put up with his queasy stomach and listened to the prattling of the ambassadors and ladies who shared the barge with him. Understanding would be so much easier if he just eavesdropped on their thoughts. But Nimbulan had drilled into him respect for the privacy of others.

Bessel hadn't even invaded his mother's mind to catch her dying wishes. He wished he had. He hadn't felt her love for many years, and he missed her more than he thought possible.

His stomach lurched with a new shift of the currents and tide. Power simmered within the kardia beneath the waves, begging him to tap it and calm his innards. The power could show him how the depth finder worked. He refused the invitation to rogue magic.

If he had refrained from tapping rogue magic to help his mother, he certainly wouldn't do it to make himself more comfortable.

From the look on the face of the new ambassador from Jihab, he didn't like the rising and lowering of the deck with each new wave any better than Bessel did. The portly man, who had made several fortunes as a jewel trader before turning to politics, blanched and clamped his teeth together. His normally ruddy skin took on the ghastly pallor of green akin to light-shy fungi in the back of a sea cave.

Bessel liked the jovial jeweler. The other four ambassadors, their ladies, and aides on the barge were all too aware of their own self-importance to pay him any attention. But Heinriiche Smeetsch had greeted Bessel politely and seemed genuinely interested in his studies to become a master magician. Bessel had even confided his secret wish to succeed Master Lyman as librarian.

He could think of no better way to protect the banned books and the knowledge they contained. *S'murghit,* how could Scarface be so sure the disease that felled Lord Balthazaan's province wasn't a plague that needed more than fresh supplies to cure it?

The beeping black box beside the pilot's chair at the exact center of the barge increased the frequency and intensity of its signal. Bessel sensed no change in the mudflats. But dragon magic was Air-based and didn't lend itself to Water-oriented spells. The Kardia-based rogue magic would be able to delve into the mysteries of the Bay.

Kardia and Water were teamed as were Air and Fire.

Raanald, the representative from the Guild of Bay Pilots, kicked his arcane machine. "*S'murghit,* I know these waters. There was nothing in this region yesterday to hinder our passage. We should be well beyond the bar. Two degrees starboard," he called to his helmsman. "*S'murghin'* machine. Why is it telling me to avoid a clear passage?"

Raanald brushed the folds of his gaudy maroon-and-gold uniform sleeve into a straight line, very aware of his elite calling. He knew the waters better than the machine did.

Or so his attitude indicated. If he knew the waters better than the machine, why risk having the machine at all?

"What does that beeping mean?" Bessel asked.

"The machine does not concern you, Magician." Raanald spat the last word as if it fouled his mouth.

Distrust of the man and the machine rose in Bessel.

Maybe that was just his stomach protesting the constant and uneven movement of the barge.

A wave lifted the shallow-bottomed vessel several feet, then dropped it into the trough. Ambassador Smeetsch spun in place, heaving his luncheon over the side.

Ambassador Jorghe-Rosse from Rossemeyer slapped his Jihabian counterpart heartily on the back, making a joke of his squeamishness.

Bessel might have laughed if his own meal rested more easily. Or if the depth-finding machine would stop beeping. It seemed to be getting louder and faster, warning of unseen submerged obstacles. The sandbar that ran parallel to the coastline changed dimensions every spring as the River Coronnan dumped tons of silt into the Bay. It changed again after every storm. Why was Raanald so certain they had navigated beyond it?

He edged closer to the black box, needing to read the arcane symbols and know what dangers it saw beneath the barge.

He ached to tap a ley line and let it fuel his magic senses. Then he'd know for certain what transpired.

No! Bessel reminded himself sternly. That would make him a rogue, an outcast, alone. He'd lose more than just his mother if he succumbed to the allure of rogue magic.

"Three degrees starboard," Raanald called again to the helmsman. Puzzlement creased his brow and clouded his eyes.

Another big wave caught the passenger vessel. The barge had been designed for negotiating very shallow water in calm weather and didn't have enough keel to stabilize it in rough seas.

"*S'murghin'* magicians, can't leave the weather alone!" Raanald glared hard at Bessel as he kicked the machine's black box housing.

The journeyman magician wanted to defend the Commune of Magicians, loudly and vehemently. The Commune didn't mess with the weather. They knew better than to upset the natural balances. The pilot was as ignorant and prejudiced as Bessel's father.

"Is there a problem, Master Pilot?" Ambassador Jorghe-

Rosse asked. He stood nearest to Raanald among the passengers milling about the luxury barge.

"Storm coming in. One we didn't know about." The surly pilot looked at Bessel again, affronted. "It's upsetting the tide and wind predictions." One of the duties of the Commune was to keep the local boatmen accurately informed of weather forecasts and changes.

"Pop up storms are not uncommon in spring and autumn," Bessel said. "No one can predict them. They do not last long and tend to hit small areas, leaving the coast a few miles away dry and clear." Could the coming storm have changed something in the water to upset the machine?

"Will we reach the docks before this storm hits?" asked the representative from Jihab. He looked over the side of the barge as if the little left in his stomach might want to join his luncheon.

"I've weathered a lot of these mage—spring storms," Raanald lectured, covering his word slip with grand gestures. "Especially during the wars." He glared at Bessel as if he were personally responsible for the generations of civil war as well as every storm. "They're tricky. Might pass us altogether and only ruffle the water a little. Like now." He kicked the waist-high black cylinder of the depth finder again.

The machine settled back into its normal calm beep. One every ten heartbeats.

Bessel raised his eyes to the sky in search of some trace of a coming storm. The sky had darkened perceptibly with a complete cloud cover that thickened by the moment.

Dragon magic told him the weather patterns easily, when he had reason to pay attention. Pressure dropped in the air to the immediate east. A rapid change of temperature. Wind rising, driving the storm cell toward land. Right over the top of the barge.

"You gentlemen had best take a seat inside the pavilion." Raanald sniffed the air. His eyes opened wide in alarm. The machine started beeping again, erratically.

Bessel peered over the man's shoulder, eager to know for himself what dangers awaited them.

"Get out of my way, you *s'murghin'* meddler. Wouldn't

have anything to worry about if you had kept your weather spells to yourself."

"I did nothing," Bessel finally said in his own defense. He'd had enough of keeping his mouth shut, though he knew his role as diplomatic observer required nothing more of him.

"Maybe not you, but your kind is always messing with the weather. Especially that scar-faced bastard." The pilot spat on the deck at Bessel's feet. "The Guild of Bay Pilots don't need you clogging up our channels and changing our tides. We got machines to take care of us. Royal machines. Five degrees to port," he corrected his previous course changes back to their original path.

If the machine is so important, why don't you trust it? Bessel kept his thoughts to himself.

The ambassadors and their ladies took seats on the benches fixed to the deck beneath an awning. The rising wind sent the cloth shelter flapping. Bessel remained at Raanald's shoulder, observing the flashing red lights across the bubble face of the black box. At first he couldn't make sense of the constantly changing display. Then he picked out stylized numbers in red beside the carefully printed words in white against a black background. The words meant nothing to him. Yet.

The numbers decreased on the left and piled up on the right at an alarming rate.

"I said, sit down, Magician," Raanald shouted with curled lip. But the anxiety in his eyes as he looked back to the beeping black box kept Bessel rooted in place. "Hard a port!" Raanald shouted.

The rudder and pole men in the rear quarter of the barge struggled with their tools.

A wave caught them crosswise. The deck tilted sharply to the left. Bessel grabbed the machine housing to brace himself. His staff tangled with his feet. He crossed his ankles to keep his most essential tool within reach.

The dignitaries slid down their benches into the flimsy railing of the luxury barge. Hard wood cracked and splintered. Fine silk gowns and robes flew in the rising wind. Limbs tangled. Ladies screamed and men gasped.

"I said *hard* a port," Raanald screamed.

The rudder man shoved his tiller, hard. Wood snapped as the rudder grounded in the bar. The tiller moved freely, disconnected from the rudder.

The barge swung sideways and leveled. The awning whipped away from its supports, flying toward shore in the rising wind. Another wave slapped across the deck, drenching the tangled passengers. They screamed again. Ambassador Jorghe-Rosse muttered a curse in his desert warrior language.

Bessel didn't need to know the words to understand the meaning. He closed his eyes and concentrated, breathing deeply. At the first deepening of his trance, he sent his magic into the damaged rudder. The wooden mechanism resisted his control. He concentrated harder. His stomach growled with hunger. His legs and back ached from the strain. Sweat broke out on his brow, washed away by the spray of the next huge wave that roared toward shore from the open sea.

If only he could tap a ley line to fuel his magic, he could handle the storm, the rudder, and the passengers. He couldn't. He wouldn't. He had to rely on his weak dragon magic.

Help! he called telepathically to any magician who might hear him. *I need help saving these people.*

A long pause of nothing. Sweat streamed from his brow and down his back as he wrestled with several options. None of them acceptable. He ached for permission to tap the forces he knew could help him. He knew it would never come.

Whatever happens, don't let anything happen to Jorghe-Rosse, Master Scarface returned to him when Bessel thought the emptiness in his head would last forever. *Peace depends upon Rossemeyer's goodwill. They are looking for excuses to invade us again. You must save their ambassador at all costs!*

His master's authoritative tone calmed Bessel a little. Concentration came a little easier. He had to get the barge back under control and into the deeper channel.

The strident beeping of the black box interrupted his thoughts.

"Stay off the bar. *Hard* a port, you *s'murghin'* swabbies.

I said *HARD!*" Raanald dashed from his station by the precious machine to the rudder. "I knew there was a bar here, but the machine said it was ten yards to port!"

An onerous shudder passed through the barge followed by a jerking halt. The deck canted wildly to the left, upsetting the already disoriented and disgruntled dignitaries again. They landed in a heap against the damaged railing. More of the slender wooden staves that formed the decorative fence broke. Several pieces of wood fell into the churning bay, swirled in the obstacle's eddies, and sank.

Ambassador Jorghe-Rosse bent over his lady, protecting her with his body. The next wave sent him crashing through the decorative wood into the thrashing waves.

Chapter 14

Bessel cast aside his formal magician's robe and heavy boots as he dove after the ambassador. He kept his staff pointed ahead of him, channeling his senses along it for greater awareness.

All of his instincts told him to stay aboard and solve the problem with dragon magic. Nimbulan had taught him problem solving. But he knew he'd not be able to tap enough communal magic to dissipate the obstacle that held the barge, calm the waves, and rescue the ambassador.

A mundane rescue first. Then he'd worry about the other dangers. Thank the Stargods he could swim.

Cold water enfolded him, numbing his thoughts and turning his limbs to jelly. He scanned the turbulent water for any trace of the ambassador's black robe.

Nothing.

With all of those layers of clothing and hidden weapons common to the desert dwelling mercenaries of Rossemeyer, Jorghe-Rosse could easily get dragged to the bottom and stuck in the mudflats.

Bessel dove deep. He forced his eyes open despite the salt sting. Murky water obscured his vision. Crosscurrents assaulted his already heavy limbs. He pushed his concentration into strong strokes that took him toward the obstacle. His planetary orientation kicked in and he "knew" where the buildup of mud, sand, and drifted debris trapped the barge and snared the ambassador.

A year and a half ago, Nimbulan and King Quinnault had fended off an invasion fleet from Rossemeyer by filling the inner bay with felled trees and other obstacles. Now, the rotting remains of one of those defensive trees trapped the ambassador. The barge had grounded on the bar to the side of the snag.

Bessel's lungs burned for air. He'd been down too long.

He poked at the assorted tree limbs and mud with the staff. A long white arm appeared before his red-hazed vision. The currents flattened Jorghe-Rosse against the snag, pining him more effectively than a boulder. Bessel reached out with his hands and his magic. He grabbed hold of cold fingers and wrist with one hand, being careful to stay above the ambassador and the crushing current as he struck out for the surface. He had to abandon the staff, but he knew it would follow him eventually.

Pressure built in his chest. His legs didn't want to kick. The limp hand slipped from his grasp.

He didn't have the strength or air to go back. At last his head broke the surface of the water. Icy needles of rain pelted his face. He closed his eyes against the pain and gulped air. A second deep inhalation and a third.

Without thinking, he triggered a trance and he saw the ley lines glimmering against his inner vision. No dragon magic came to him to replace the enticing power.

Protect the ambassador at all costs. Master Scarface's words pounded into his mind again.

Damn the rules. Peace in Coronnan depends upon this man's safety. I've got to save him any way I can.

Bessel grabbed the power and let it enhance his lungs and heartbeat. Then he dove again. Muddy water, churned by the storm and his own movements, cleared before him. He saw the pattern of the current that pinned the ambassador's body. His staff had grounded in the bar nearby.

Bessel grabbed the staff and wedged it between Jorghe-Rosse and the tree trunk. At the precise moment the current eased the tiniest bit, he thrust all of his weight onto the staff, prying a gap between the snag and the ambassador.

With new strength and agility, and a touch of levitation, Bessel yanked Jorghe-Rosse free.

Suddenly, the magician sensed semi-awareness rippling

through the drowning man. Like any drowning victim, Jorghe-Rosse fought the water, his rescuer, and his dimmed consciousness. He whipped his arms into a deadly rotation, seeking to strike whatever pinned him. His left fist connected with Bessel's jaw.

Starbursts exploded behind the magician's eyes. His grasp on the ambassador's wrist slipped. His contact with the ley line and his magic faded. He was lost in the murky, cold water without a sense of up and down.

Jorghe-Rosse gasped for air. But there was none.

Blackness crowded Bessel's vision. The cold numbed his body. He made one last desperate grab for the man he needed to save. His fingers tangled in cloth.

Enough. Aching in every joint, weakened by the blow to his jaw and loss of magic strength he struggled upward.

Finally, after what seemed like forever, he broke the surface. He wasted several moments just breathing. His lungs continued burning, protesting any movement.

Then Bessel struggled for the still trapped barge dragging Jorghe-Rosse behind him.

Anonymous hands reached to relieve him of the ambassador and then pulled Bessel aboard.

"Too late, *Magician*," Raanald sneered. "You drowned the ambassador. Now there'll be war with Rossemeyer. And you caused it."

*   *   *

The city of Hanassa, before midnight on the dark of the moon

Rollett paused in the shadows around one of the rock outcroppings that littered the caldera floor of the ancient volcano. Shacks and taverns surrounded each jumble of volcanic stone. From here he spied the palace entrance. Fifteen long paces separated him from the arched entrance within the cliff walls that rose from the city proper. The first Kaaliph had built his palace out of an existing cave system. The cool interior of the north wall made it the most desirable location within the natural walls of the city. Other important personages occupied other cave dwellings, like the Rover enclave. Most of the others had to settle for these makeshift dwellings against the massive boulders.

Darkness, darker than the dark night, filled the palace entrance. Yaassima had never allowed shadows anywhere near a vulnerable portal. She had ordered torches shifted every few minutes to illuminate different sectors and her guards firmly fixed in the doorway at all times. In the old days, an assassin or thief had no place to hide and no gaps to penetrate.

Piedro kept his torches stationary and his guards moving. He had Yaassima's ruthlessness but not her cunning. Rollett had discovered in the last year and a half that most Rovers rarely thought beyond "today." They loved the open road and met each day with joy at being alive, and each crisis as it came. Plans for "tomorrow" were useless because "tomorrow" might never come.

The Rovers trapped in Hanassa frequently indulged in violent brawls and self-inflicted wounds. The lack of open roads and a wandering way of life tore at their sanity.

Piedro exhibited the typical shortsightedness of his race. His capricious cruelty could be a sign of his growing loss of reason.

Rollett watched the seemingly random movements of the guards until he saw a pattern. Humans found comfort in routines. Hardened assassins, thieves, and terrorists imposed chaos but worked best within the limits of their own ordered regularity. Within a few moments Rollett knew when and how to walk through the front gate of the palace without challenge.

"One at a time, slide through the doorway on my command. Go all the way to the Justice Hall as quickly and quietly as you can. Don't wait for the rest of us until you get to the Justice Hall," he ordered the line of men hugging the wall behind him. "Now!" he pushed the first man forward.

One by one Rollett's raiders infiltrated the palace. Rollett feared that the prospect of fresh food might make them reckless. Fortunately, the caution bred into them by years of outlawry prevailed. In short order, Rollett was the only man left to enter.

He waited a few more heartbeats to make sure the

guards' pattern of movements held true. The man on the left, the one who carried a spear, faltered.

Rollett stopped in mid-step. His balance teetered. As quietly as he could, he planted both feet on the ground and recovered just before he fell flat on his face.

The guard scratched his crotch, belched, and moved on.

But now the guard on the right had turned in his patrol and faced the doorway.

Rollett held his breath, willing the guards to resume their normal pattern. Two more passes and a gap in their vigilance appeared again. Rollett wrapped a shadow around himself and slipped through. He'd only had to use a minor magic trick to divert the guards.

Too easy. He'd made eleven raids on the palace stores. In every one, he'd had to fight for each morsel of food he gained.

The hair on the back of his neck stood up. All the senses available to him jumped to alert. He paused at the first alcove inside the gateway to listen.

Nothing. So far, no one followed. He proceeded toward the rendezvous, watching every flicker of torchlight for signs of a trap.

By the time he had wound his way to the Justice Hall, all his senses tingled with uneasy rawness. Something was wrong. This was too easy.

He paused outside the broad archway leading into the largest chamber in the palace complex, the temple to the winged demon Simurgh—the only one left in all of Kardia Hodos. Locals called it the Justice Hall now. Rollett hadn't observed much justice dispensed from here—only cruel punishments by Yaassima and then her successors.

He listened with his ears and his mind, pinpointing each of his men as they sneezed, shuffled their feet, or murmured a question. So far, none of Piedro's guards shared the huge hall. Where were they? Usually he had to dodge a dozen or more just to get this far.

Slowly he eased around the archway, keeping his shadow cloak close and solid. He'd pay for the magic trick later in hunger and exhaustion. Better to be tired and hungry than dead.

Stargods! He wanted to get home. Ending the Great

Wars of Disruption and establishing the Commune of Magicians had been easier than trying to survive in Hanassa. Longing for Nimbulan and his friends in the Commune welled up in his throat, threatening to choke him.

He swallowed the emotion. Any emotion was dangerous right now. He needed to maintain tight control of himself if he hoped to survive tonight.

Once inside the hall, he remained close to the wall. Only his eyes moved. He peered into every crevice, nook, and shadow.

The hideous stone altar, with its hand and foot manacles at each corner, rested flush with the floor now. Piedro didn't know how to make it rise from its sunken position. The secret had died with Yaassima. The new Kaaliph still executed people, but the bloodletting lacked the aura of a religious ritual without the altar.

. If Piedro met an ignominious end in the near future, the worship of Simurgh might very well die with him.

The tapestry behind the dais to Rollett's left hung limp and tattered. Not enough of the peaceful alpine meadow with a waterfall scene remained to conceal an armed guard.

The room seemed empty except for Rollett's raiders.

He signaled quiet to the seven men as he stepped from the shadows. Keeping his back to the walls, he circled the room to the far side where a smaller door lay hidden behind another tapestry—this one portrayed an orgy in vivid and obscene detail.

All of his men waited for him to lead the way. Rollett paused and listened again. The interior corridor remained quiet and empty. He probed it with every mundane and magic sense available to him. But he didn't trust those senses tonight. They should have roused at least ten guards by this time. None of them patrolled their usual routes or slept in their usual hiding places.

Piedro had set a trap. Where?

If his men didn't need fresh food so desperately, he'd abandon the raid right here and now. By tomorrow night the new shipment would be moved somewhere more secure deep in the labyrinth of these caves. Rollett had yet to find that location. They had to steal the food tonight or not at all.

Rollett pointed to his eyes and ears, warning his men to be extra alert. Then he gestured for them to follow him silently.

The corridor sloped gently downward before curving to the right. Three smaller passageways opened on the left before they reached a major junction. The right-hand passageway sloped downward. The left continued straight ahead, level and wide open. From experience, they knew the easy path terminated in a dead end. He'd never explored to the right. The memory of the scent of fresh food drove him up the slope to the center.

Rollett's mouth began to salivate. He needed to run ahead and grab a handful of fruit and nuts. He could devour an entire ham by himself. Caution made him proceed slowly.

As he approached the last twist in the corridor, he held up his hand to halt the men. Once more he listened with every sense available to him. Quiet. Too quiet.

He waited through one hundred heartbeats. Still nothing. He listened for another one hundred heartbeats.

This time he heard what had been missing in the rest of the palace complex, the sound of soft uneven breathing. Several men waited just inside the open door of the storeroom.

Rollett held his breath. Did he dare go through with the raid? His stomach growled. They needed the food stored here.

But something more was wrong than just the presence of the guards lying in wait. The storeroom smelled wrong. It smelled empty of food.

The man just behind him shifted his posture forward. Rollett put out his hand to restrain him. Too late.

"Food!" The three men behind him broke into a howling run, clubs raised.

"Wait," Rollett ordered. They ignored him, too desperate to listen to anything.

He had no choice. He had to follow them into the trap, defend them any way he could. Staff raised, senses alert, he charged after his men. The remaining men in his gang unleashed daggers and boot knives as they, too, joined the fray.

Lights flashed inside the storeroom, blinding the raiders. Rollett resisted the urge to cover his eyes with his hands. He had other senses to compensate for the dazzle blindness. His men didn't have that advantage.

Even before his vision recovered, Rollett knew the battle was hopeless. He heard the screams of dying men as he blocked a sword slash with his staff. The metal bounced off the hardened and twisted wood.

Shadows took on substance before Rollett's eyes. He flipped his staff end over end, catching the attacking guard under the chin. The big man staggered back, flailing his arms.

Rollett's men didn't fare so well. He counted two down, bleeding heavily. The others were sorely pressed and outnumbered two to one.

"Retreat!" he called even as he swung his staff into the belly of a palace guard. "Retreat!"

Rollett followed his own order, backing out of the storeroom. Two guards pursued him closely.

Rollett spun and ran back down the curving corridor. He hated to leave his men. They'd have to fend for themselves. Those were the rules in Hanassa.

Loose sand on the floor turned slippery beneath his hurried footsteps. Rollett skidded into the junction. A wall of new guards blocked the main corridor back to the Justice Hall. He'd never break through them. Even with magic he'd be hard-pressed to battle them all.

And he had no more magic. His limited reserves had gone into shadows and concealment getting into the palace.

He increased his speed and his skid, turning the sharp corner into the unexplored downward slope.

Stargods! I hope this isn't another dead end. '

Sweat rolled down Rollett's back. His limbs grew heavy. His lungs labored to draw in the hot air and his heart pounded loudly in his ears. Almost as loud as the heavy footsteps pounding the dirt floor behind him.

The slope increased. The walls became rougher, more like a natural cave, without evidence of being smoothed or enlarged by man-made tools.

His footing grew precarious on the light covering of fine sand. But so did the guards' behind him. A sharp turn appeared before him. He tried to slow his steps and slammed into the wall. The loose sand upset his balance and kept him stumbling forward. He lunged in the new direction, trying to control his momentum. His feet flew out in different directions. He landed heavily on his side.

As he measured his length along the corridor, he rammed his head against the crossed iron bars of a locked gate.

Chapter 15

The pit beneath the city of Hanassa, time unknown

"All the caverns lead back to Old Bertha," Powwell said as he kicked one of the rusted pipes strewn about the huge cave. They'd been wandering for hours. Days? He didn't know anymore. Their trips through the dragongate had disrupted his time perception. He needed to eat and sleep before he could restore all of his senses.

"The caverns have always led back here," Yaala replied. Her eyes took on a glazed look of enthrallment. She grabbed the broken pipe and lovingly began to scrape rust off of it with her belt knife. The blade quickly dulled, but she ignored it, completely absorbed in her task and the plight of her machines.

"No, Yaala. The tunnels and caverns all led to the rim of the pit. This cavern only has one or two accesses overlooking the lava core. There are dozens of others. How do we get to them?" Powwell checked the exit tunnel that also gave access to the dragongate. So far, it hadn't opened again while he watched. Something was terribly wrong. The opening and closing had always been random, but rarely more than one hundred to one thousand heartbeats apart.

"Well, we found the living cavern. It's empty of people, but full of food. We'll be all right for now." Yaala continued to clean the broken pipe, frequently comparing the open end with the other pieces.

"Wake up, Yaala. Think. We have to get out of here." He grabbed her shoulders and shook her. She dropped the sections of pipe. Hot water splashed them both.

"We can't do anything without the machines. Old Bertha needs me," she protested when he stopped shaking her.

"Hanassa needs you, Yaala. The city needs a strong leader. The machines are nothing. They aren't power, they are tools."

She stared at him as if he were the most stupid being on Kardia Hodos.

"I need you, Yaala. I need you to help me find my little sister. I need your strength to keep me from lashing out and murdering everyone in your city until I find Kalen. *We* need to find Rollett and send him home to help Nimbulan. Now stop fussing with Old Bertha and help me find a way out of here."

She turned her head away not answering.

Powwell watched the access tunnel again for signs of the dragongate opening. But he maintained his grasp on her shoulders, needing the physical affirmation that they both still lived, still had quests to keep them going.

"There. That's two pieces together. I bet I can reconstruct the entire pipe. Then I'll clear the tube tunnels of debris and restring the wires to Liise. She doesn't give off much 'tricity, but I should be able to coax enough out of her to control some of the 'motes," Yaala said. "Perhaps we can use Liise to jump-start Old Bertha."

"What good are 'tricity and 'motes that mimic magic if we can't get out of the pit to use them? What use are they in helping me find Kalen? Especially if they carry the seed of the plague. You won't have a city to reclaim if your blasted machines breed a plague that kills everyone. Including us."

"*My* machines would never hurt anyone." Yaala wrestled away from his grasp and resumed her work with the rusted pipe. "I need to know more about 'tricity and Yaassima's gadgets before I reclaim my heritage."

Kalen, with her sullen silences and selfish need to control the people around her seemed more attractive to him now than Yaala obsessed with the generators and transformers.

He longed to tell his sister everything that had happened to him since their separation. She fed his ideas with twists and "what ifs" that gave him new insight into problems, and into life.

Had she grown in the last year? Did she still have Wiggles, her ferret familiar?

"Of course you have to find Kalen," Yaala said after several moments of silence. "You won't be happy until you do. Then you can come back here and help me with the machines."

"No, Yaala. I won't come back here, ever, once Kalen is free."

She didn't seem to hear him. The machines held her attention completely. Almost as if they threw a spell over her.

Becoming Kaalipha and ruling Hanassa was just an excuse to be close to her machines. He should have known this would happen. The machines were her family; she had returned to them. Would Powwell ever return to the Commune? Not without his sister.

"So why have the caverns changed? It takes more than one kardiaquake to move a labyrinth this large." Powwell decided to change the subject.

"Some of the tunnels have collapsed. Yes. Maybe we mistook the way out because of debris blocking the main exit from the living cavern." Yaala's eyes brightened a little as her thought processes moved away from her broken machines.

"Or maybe the wraith has disguised the exit so we can't leave," Powwell mused as he caught another glimpse of drifting white off to the side. He turned to look straight at the place where the wraith had been, but it—she?—had disappeared again.

"You go look, Powwell. I just want to check one thing. . . ."

"We're in this together, Yaala. Come. Now. You can play with your toys after we find a way out." He grabbed her hand and dragged her back toward the cavern that held the food stores. At one time it had been home to several hundred slaves including Yaala and himself. They'd all looked to Yaala for leadership. Had she been this obsessed then?

Powwell stopped at the first tunnel junction. He looked left. If his memory held true, he thought the tunnel narrowed and dead-ended. Then he looked right. The hairs on the back of his neck stood up. Thorny bristled and jabbed

Powwell with his spines, urging him left—away from the atavistic sense of dread in the right-hand tunnel. Something nasty awaited them. They needed to turn back, try a different direction. The hedgehog gibbered in panic. Powwell pushed forward through that tunnel anyway. The last three times he'd explored this area, he'd avoided the tunnels that made him too aware of the weight of tons of kardia pressing down on the flimsy cave system; too aware of the limited supply of air; too aware of his own mortality.

Powwell pressed on, pushing away his fears. He kept telling himself that the wraith wanted him to stay. She was making him and Thorny sense terrors that didn't truly exist.

They passed through the living cavern without pausing to drink from the foul-tasting stream. He'd drunk too much of the sulfurous water a year ago because there was nothing else to keep his body from withering into a pile of dust in the tremendous heat of the caverns. Even Thorny didn't beg for a drink.

At last the tunnels began to slope upward. The air freshened, and the temperature decreased. "I think we've found it, Yaala." He tugged on her hand to hurry. He couldn't get out of the caves too soon.

They slowed on the last slope upward to the gate. Instinctively, they hugged the shadows near the wall. Liise's yellow ceiling lights didn't reach this far, so they had to pick their way carefully over the uneven pathway. The glow behind them blinded them to the darkness in front.

Powwell closed his eyes and stretched his magic senses. He didn't have much dragon magic left. Thorny's sense of smell was probably more accurate than Powwell's True-Sight at this point.

"Thorny smells a human up ahead," he whispered, pausing to share the sense with his familiar. "Blood and sweat and fear."

"Who?" Yaala asked, peering into the darkness.

"Only one way to find out. Keep quiet." Slowly they crept forward, hands linked tightly together. Powwell stretched his other hand in front of him.

At last he grasped one of the metal crossbars of the gate. A glow of light from higher in the tunnel helped him distinguish the interlocking pattern. He found the square plate that housed the lock. Beneath the lock lay an inert figure, more rags than anything else.

Gently he prodded the head region of the lump.

"Huh?" a man shook his head and peered up with bleary eyes.

"Rollett?" Powwell asked. "I'd know those blond streaks in your black beard any day. Rollett, what are you doing here?"

"I should have died with the others," Rollett mumbled.

* * *

Near midnight at the gate between the pit and the Kaaliph of Hanassa's palace

Yaala stooped to look closer at the bundle of rags that spoke. The little bit of glow from the lower caverns showed lighter streaks in the man's dark beard and hair. By the same light she saw the glimmer of moisture in his eyes.

"I've got to go back. My men are dying up there." Rollett stirred as if he meant to stand, then collapsed against the iron bars of the gate again.

"Where are you hurt?" she asked him.

"I . . . maybe. I hurt all over. But wounds?" He patted his mid-region. His hands came up dry. "No blood." He shrugged. Then he winced as if his head hurt at the movement.

"Powwell, give me some light," she ordered.

"You've got to get out of here," Rollett whispered anxiously. "The guards are right behind me. They're out for blood. My blood. They already killed three of my men."

"The corridor is empty," Powwell said. He opened his clenched fist to reveal a ball of witchlight.

"What?" Rollett reared up on one elbow. He looked up the sloping path toward the palace, his aches and pains forgotten.

"Thorny doesn't smell anyone but us, and my magic isn't quivering—except for the wraith," Powwell said. The tiny hedgehog poked his funny head out of Powwell's pocket, wiggling his nose. He stayed out rather than darting back into cover, a sure sign that no one approached them.

"You sure? They were right on my heels, screaming to

kill me. Piedro laid a trap for me and my men. My men . . ." He groaned and lay back down again. "I've failed them. And myself."

"Is this the same Piedro who tried to assassinate the queen on the eve of her wedding?" Yaala asked. A gnawing suspicion grew deep within her. Piedro knew how the dragongate worked. He also had a confederate in King Quinnault's palace who helped him escape a magically sealed dungeon.

"What queen?" Rollett turned his piercing gaze on her.

"You haven't heard that King Quinnault married the Princess of Terrania," Powwell replied. "We didn't hear until we got back to Coronnan."

"You've been back? How? When?" Rollett pulled himself to his knees, using the crossbars of the gate for support.

In the last glow of witchlight, Yaala saw a deep bruise forming on the left side of Rollett's face, beginning at the temple. He had to hurt. Any movement would aggravate the pain.

She also couldn't help but notice the clean lines of high cheekbones and straight nose above his trimmed beard. An aristocratic face despite traces of a peasant background in his accent. He might have nothing to wear except rags, but he'd kept himself clean and well groomed. Admirable traits in the foul city above them.

"How did you get out?" Rollett demanded. "You've got to get me out of here. I can't stay here any longer. I've got to get out! I have to find a way to free my men." He shook the gate with all of his strength. The metal remained solidly closed. "I promised. . . ." His quiet words ended in a choke, almost a sob.

Powwell stared at his fellow magician without answering. Rollett had said nothing about Kalen, only about his men. Long moments of silence stretched between them.

"There is an exit near the lava core," Yaala finally said. "It's magic. Every once in a while the mouth of one of the little tunnels becomes a gateway to another part of the world. Within a few heartbeats you can be thousands of miles away. This end opens to myriad destinations, but all of the destinations lead only back to Hanassa. If the dragongate isn't open, you step into the boiling lava."

Rollett nodded in understanding, his eyes wide as he mulled over the possibilities. "That's how Nimbulan and Myri escaped last year. Yaassima must have used it to send her assassins and robbers anywhere in the world. Piedro can bring food and supplies in without going through the city. The dragongate must be why he has repeatedly blocked our attempts to construct exits from above. *He* doesn't need them, so he won't let us have them. But he won't give us access to the dragongate either."

"After the big kardiaquake last year, the dragongate changed," Powwell added. "It won't open again until the next dark of the moon."

"Nooooooo!" Rollett howled. "Don't tell me you came through the gate without the food. We won't be able to continue without the food."

"There is food down here. But we didn't bring anything other than the journey rations in our packs." Yaala thought back to the heavy sledges the Rovers had tried to bring through. Food for a starving city. Her city, if she could reclaim it. Would Rollett help or hinder her quest?

The city was probably more his than hers now. He'd lived and worked among the citizens for a year and a half. He'd helped them rebel against the new Kaaliph. They looked to him for leadership.

All she could claim were a few malfunctioning machines. *Did I risk my life and Powwell's to reclaim Hanassa, or merely to be near my machines?* she asked herself for the first time. She had to think about that for a while.

Who was more important—more like family—Powwell or Old Bertha? The big generator was dead, unrevivable.

Was there anything left of her city to reclaim?

All she knew at the moment was that Rollett triggered emotions in her that made her question everything.

Rollett's eyes brightened a bit, and his face calmed. "What kind of food?"

"The living cavern is full of flour and cereal grains, barrels of salted and pickled meat, dried fruit, root vegetables, and a little wine," she replied.

Powwell searched the ceiling with haunted eyes as the ground rumbled beneath them. He clutched the nearest wall, eyes closed and breathing deeply.

Stargods! What condition was the city in if kardiaquakes rocked it so frequently and Piedro withheld basic food supplies?

The kardia stopped shifting.

"So that's where Piedro has been hiding his regular stores. All of it is stale and a lot of it is infested with maggots." Rollett closed his eyes. His shoulders drooped. "It's better than nothing, but never enough. Piedro doles it out at starvation rations." He seemed to barely notice the kardiaquake.

"There's water down here, too," Yaala reminded him. She knew how limited the city wells could be if the surrounding mountains had been dry during the winter. The sweet water of Coronnan seemed too bland after drinking nothing but the heavy mineral and sulfur-laden water of Hanassa all of her life.

"Open this gate. I need to see what's here, what we need most up above." Rollett licked his lips and stared longingly over Yaala's shoulder toward the inner caverns.

"I don't know how to open that gate," Powwell replied. "Yaassima controlled it with 'tricity. No ordinary key can open it."

"Nimbulan broke and reset it when he escaped with Myri and the others," Yaala reminded him. "Piedro has been using it for more than a year."

"I could break it if I had enough strength to use my magic." Rollett shook the gate again.

The murmur of the stream grew louder. Not the stream after all. Voices coming from the upper corridor.

"The guards are coming!" Rollett swung around, his back pressed hard against the gate. "I'm trapped. Piedro will execute me for sure this time. His consort hasn't tasted blood in almost a week."

Chapter 16

Bessel trudged into the Great Hall of King Quinnault's palace. Chill bay water dripped from his trews, and his boots squished with every step. He'd thrown his formal robe back over his everyday trews and tunic, but it was almost as sodden as the rest of him. No amount of emptying his boots and wringing his socks would dry them.

Hours had passed, awaiting rescue and answering questions since he'd dragged Ambassador Jorghe-Rosse from Rossemeyer from the depths of the Bay.

Misery dogged his steps as much as the scraggly white mutt with long, curly fur that had followed him from the docks and kept pressing up against him. Bessel wanted to kick it out of the way, but it looked as depressed and lonely as he felt. He let it stay with him as he followed the other refugees from the barge.

Armed guards from both King Quinnault's personal guard and from Rossemeyer had met them as they docked.

Four stern-faced warriors from Rossemeyer led them from the docks into the palace. They carried their dead ambassador on a litter. Another four warriors flanked them protectively. Behind them came the other dignitaries and their ladies, still wet and chilled. The palace guard had given them warm blankets and cloaks. But no one had offered Bessel anything.

Except the dog. When it rubbed against Bessel, he felt a little warmer.

Jorghe-Rosse's lady stood a little apart, dry-eyed and chin jutting with determination. If she grieved, she didn't show it in her posture.

Bessel, the pilot, and the boatmen brought up the rear, along with the bedraggled dog. Bessel didn't need to read the sailors' minds to smell their fear. No one knew for certain how the new widow would avenge her husband's death. Only that she would.

Fires roared in the hearths at either end of the huge hall. The dignitaries gravitated to the bright warmth even at this late hour. Tapestries and flower bouquets gave the room an air of cozy invitation. King Quinnault and Queen Maarie Kaathliin had transformed their major reception area into a home that welcomed petitioners to the court rather than made them afraid of true justice in a cold and forbidding hall.

Bessel didn't think there could be justice as long as Rossemeyer was involved. The entire country of mercenaries made their own rules that had nothing to do with the rest of civilization.

The king and queen entered the hall through a small back door. The king still wore riding leathers flecked with steed foam, as if he'd driven his mount to extremes in his hurry to get here. Queen Maarie Kaathliin clutched her baby tightly as they made their way to the twin thrones on the low dais. She kept looking around anxiously. Usually she left the child with servants while she accompanied her husband on official business. Today she refused the nanny who kept reaching for the child.

Master Scarface and a few of the other master magicians marched into the room, pushing aside the crowd of courtiers. Scarface took up his position between the twin thrones. The other master magicians flanked the royal dais. Bessel tried to catch Scarface's gaze. The Senior Magician scanned every corner of the room except where Bessel stood.

Bessel sent a gentle mental query to his master. Scarface remained impassive and unresponsive.

Wind-drift, the master magician standing just to the right of the queen's throne, a man Bessel barely knew but who had become very close to Scarface in recent weeks, sent an inquisitive mental probe of his own toward Bessel's mind. Bessel saw it as a glowing yellow dart. It sped toward Bessel's right eye. A hair's breadth from contact the energy bolt stopped, turned, and backlashed to the sender at double speed. The magician reared back, clutching his eyes in pain.

Scarface opened his eyes wide in alarm. His scowl deepened.

Bessel shrugged. The magician hadn't asked permission. No magician had been able to read his mind without Bessel's prior consent since his experience with the outlaws as a child.

They'd exile him for sure now and he'd be alone, without the family of the Commune.

The dog plunked down on his foot. Maybe he wouldn't be totally alone. But a dog didn't make up for a family.

May I ask your version of the story? Please? Wind-drift asked politely. His wild red-gray mane, which usually stretched back from his face as if he stood in a strong wind, crackled with the energy of Bessel's backlashed probe.

Since you asked politely. Bessel opened his mind and let his memories of the afternoon pour forth.

Scarface still looked angry and puzzled. Was Wind-drift passing the images along to his senior or not? Wind-drift hadn't been with Scarface in the library separating the books. Maybe, just maybe, he could be trusted.

"My condolences, Madame," King Quinnault said as he rushed from his throne to take the hands of Lady Jorghe-Rosse. He radiated sympathy. "I, too, have lost many of those I loved. What can we do to show you and your husband the honor and respect due him?" His empathy reached out to include Bessel and the others.

"My husband earned honor as a general on the field of battle as must every man of Rossemeyer," Lady Jorghe-Rosse replied. "He did not die in battle as was his right." Something fanatical burned in the lady's eyes as she stared directly at Bessel.

A chill deeper than the numbing waters of the Bay formed a knot in his belly. Senior Magician Scarface's eyes echoed the lady's malevolent gaze.

"A death for a death," Lady Jorghe-Rosse demanded.

The queen gasped and wrapped her arms more completely around her baby. Everyone else in the Great Hall stared in stunned silence. Except the magicians. They nodded in agreement.

"I can't do that, Madame," Quinnault said, meeting the lady's gaze steadfastly.

"Then I must take what is due me." The dark-eyed woman whipped a dagger from the multiple folds of her black cloak. The rippled blade was as long as her forearm. Death at her hands would not be clean or swift. She raised it menacingly at the king.

The warriors dropped the corpse on the ground and drew their own vorpal blades.

Cold sweat broke out on Bessel's face and back.

He didn't want to die.

The dog took a protective stance in front of him, baring his teeth. A growl rumbled from his throat—much deeper and louder than a mutt that size should be able to issue. Bessel bent to touch the matted tangles that hid the animal's eyes. The growl turned to a low moan of pleasure.

If you stay with me, the first chore is a bath, he told the dog with his mind.

It dropped to the ground and buried its head beneath muddy paws. Bessel would have expected a similar reaction if he'd spoken out loud and the creature understood the word "bath."

"There must be no more death!" Queen Maarie Kaathliin gasped. No taller than an adolescent child, she moved beside her tall husband, keeping her gaze firmly on Lady Jorghe-Rosse. She still didn't relinquish the burden of her child to the maid who dogged her steps.

The ambassador's wife didn't put her blade away. She looked down at the red-haired queen, a tall dark lily disdaining a small wild rose.

"I will hear all of the evidence, Lady." Quinnault clamped long fingers over Lady Jorghe-Rosse's wrist. He squeezed until she dropped the blade. It landed among the rushes, clattering loudly in the stunned silence. "I will determine the cause of death. If 'twas murder, then justice will be served. If 'twas an accident, as I was told, then we will take no further action."

"I do not call that justice. I call that cowardice," Lady Jorghe-Rosse screamed, struggling to free her hand from the king's grasp.

"For that I am sorry, Lady. But that is the law."

"A law made by cowards for cowards. My king will go to war to honor my husband! I will have the death of the one who murdered my husband!"

We will have our justice as well, Scarface reminded Bessel. *You tapped illegal powers. The law will be served.* The magicians of the Commune echoed his thoughts.

*   *   *

The pit beneath Hanassa, time unknown

Powwell turned his head sharply, trying once again to see the wraith as it flitted about the tunnel, just out of sight, out of reach.

But not out of hearing distance.

She will desert you, the wraith whispered into Powwell's mind. *Look at how she is with this other man. Her eyes linger too long on his face, on his figure. Her hands touch him fondly through the bars. She never touched you like that.*

"Enough!" Powwell shouted, shaking off the insidious voice that had been plaguing him since they approached the gate. His words echoed in the caverns. Rollett and Yaala stared at him. The voices and footsteps farther up the corridor hesitated before thundering forward again.

Scrunching up his eyes and gathering all of his energies, Powwell threw a probe into the lock and shifted the tiny pieces of metal. It opened with an audible click.

Rollett nearly fell through the sudden opening. A misty form oozed through the small opening between the bars.

Thank you, the wraith chuckled and drifted away. *The iron has imprisoned me for too long. Now I can find my body.*

Rollett recovered and scrambled to reclose the gate before the Kaaliph's guards descended upon them. He stared after the misty white form, mouth slightly agape.

The nagging sense of dread in the back of Powwell's

neck and the need to hide deep within the caverns evaporated with the wraith. So did his mistrust of Yaala. She'd only shown the other magician concern for his well-being as she had helped Powwell his first few awful hours in the pit.

But Powwell's instinctive fear of being underground returned in full force. He needed all of his concentration to keep from running after the wraith without regard to the guards or the safety of his companions.

Thorny hunched his spines and wiggled uncomfortably in Powwell's pocket.

He swallowed his fears and thanked his familiar for the reminder. He'd lived down here before. He would survive if he kept his gibbering panic under control.

"We'll be safe down here for a while. We can hide," Powwell whispered, gesturing for Yaala and Rollett to follow him.

"We've got to lock the gate," Rollett protested. He moved his fingers trying to make the interior pieces respond to his depleted magic.

"The guards won't cross that barrier as long as it's closed," Yaala replied. "They're more afraid of this place than they are of the Kaaliph. Come on, I know a place to hide."

"I want to hear everything that has happened at home while I've been gone."

"You need to go home as soon as possible, Rollett. Nimbulan needs you to keep Scarface from ruining the Commune," Powwell added. "I can't go until I've found Kalen."

Together they ran back into the living cavern. Yaala searched briefly right and left, orienting herself in the dim light. Powwell kept part of his senses tuned to the curses and stumbles among the guards behind them.

True to Yaala's prediction six men slid to a halt before they collided with the gate. They opened their eyes wide in fear, chewed their lips and looked everywhere but at each other.

"The wraith has Rollett now. We won't get him back," one guard muttered.

"What are we going to tell Piedro?"

Tell him the truth, Powwell whispered into their minds, trying to mimic the wraith's voice. *Tell him his prey is lost in the pit. The dragongate swallowed him as well as the fresh food.*

The guards backed up slowly, keeping their eyes on the gate.

Thorny squirmed within Powwell's pocket. Together, they might have enough energy for one last trick. Slowly the gate opened, creaking ominously.

The guards turned and ran back the way they had come.

"They won't be back any time soon. We have time to rest and eat and plan," Powwell said.

"Plan what? The city is close to starvation. My men need another three moons to dig through the collapsed tunnel— if they'll follow me at all after I failed in this raid. Piedro plays at cutting a staircase up the walls of the crater but mostly blocks all attempts to climb out, and this mysterious dragongate of yours is closed for another moon." Rollett plunked himself down amidst the barrels of salted meat.

"I won't let Piedro have my city," Yaala said, standing with legs slightly apart and hands on hips. "I will do anything to regain control of my city." She thrust out her chin in a gesture highly reminiscent of her mother, the last Kaalipha of Hanassa. Not once did her eyes wander toward the inner caverns and her machines.

"Will you do *anything* to regain your city, Yaala?" Powwell asked, suddenly afraid for her. "Will you murder and exploit just to feel as if you have power over someone else? Will you become as bloodthirsty as your mother?"

Chills ran up and down his spine. The wraith hadn't scared him as much as the thought of Yaala wielding an executioner's sword.

Chapter 17

Bessel held his breath a moment, blocking out the malevolence behind Scarface's telepathic announcement. The long scar running from temple to temple whitened against his ruddy skin. Bessel needed no other communication to know how deeply committed the Senior Magician was to eliminating all use of rogue magic, by whatever means at hand.

Scarface had already started on the library. Possibly he'd used the queen's dragon dream about machines as an excuse to destroy books he'd already chosen as dangerous.

Bessel's execution or exile for using rogue magic was the only option by the law of the land and the law of the Commune. Scarface would make sure the king and Commune would offer no mercy.

He'd have total control of the Commune without interference from anyone who had begun under Nimbulan's benign management. Would control of all Coronnan be his next quest?

A great gulf of emptiness opened in the journeyman magician. Never again would he know the deep satisfaction of sharing magic with the Commune. Never again would the men open their lives and their souls to include him in the circle of magic. He'd almost rather die than live without that intense bond.

The dog sat up and licked Bessel's dangling fingers. Automatically, he scratched its ears. He felt more confident of his future when he touched the animal. *Are you going to be my familiar?* he asked it.

The dog replied with an enthusiastic lick of Bessel's hand. Together, magician and familiar backed up a step, away from Scarface. The symbolic distance they put between them and the Senior Magician widened immensely.

He couldn't allow Scarface to succeed in his plot to oust anyone in all of Coronnan—magician and mundane—who might oppose him.

Wind-drift smiled slightly. What did the man know? Bessel didn't dare try to read his mind.

A ripple of anticipation and dread passed through the crowd as King Quinnault and Lady Jorghe-Rosse faced each other in determined silence. The desert warriors who accompanied the lady waited patiently, swords drawn, for a signal from her to fight or withdraw.

"Excuse me," said a tall man verging on elderly from the back of the crowd.

Nimbulan! If anyone could sort out this mess, it was the retired Senior Magician.

He'd aged greatly in the year and a half since he'd lost his magic. His skin looked pale, and the wrinkles around his eyes had deepened. But he still stood straight and his step sounded firmly on the flooring stones beneath the rushes. His dark auburn hair had gone almost completely gray. Contentment shone from his eyes. He greatly enjoyed his new role of husband and father. Bessel half expected to see Nimbulan's daughter Amaranth toddling along behind him, or tucked under his arm. Certainly, his wife should be close by. The three were inseparable.

But he couldn't see Myrilandel or their child in the crowd. Where was she?

Scarface bowed slightly, barely deferring to Nimbulan. Wind-drift exchanged a curt nod with the retired magician. Quinnault released the widow's hands and also turned his attention to the newcomer. King and magician had become great friends during the long process of bringing peace and stability to Coronnan.

Were these two strong men strong enough and wise enough to keep Scarface under control?

The warriors from Rossemeyer wavered a fraction in

their defensive stance as Nimbulan passed them. They reasserted their hostile posture once more when the lady remained firm. They had faced Nimbulan the Battlemage and lost the last time Rossemeyer tried to capture Coronnan's rich resources.

"My condolences, Lady Rosselaara." Nimbulan bowed respectfully to the new widow; the first to grant her an identity other than as the ambassador's wife.

With a Rosse in front of her name, she had to be a royale, a king's sister or daughter, used to having her every whim granted. She'd also have influence with her government. Her family would rally around her.

Would the Commune support Bessel as firmly?

Not while Scarface led them.

Lady Rosselaara bent her head a little in acknowledgment of Nimbulan's greeting. The first indication that her neck didn't have a pole rammed down it.

Nimbulan stepped forward, never taking his eyes off of the widow. "As I understand it, Lady, your husband died fighting the Bay and a storm. Worthy adversaries for any warrior. Adversaries that have defeated more good men than I care to remember. He did not die without honor."

"I will have a death for a death. How does one kill a storm?" Lady Rosselaara cocked one eyebrow at Nimbulan.

The aging magician returned the gesture. "Magic will shift a storm elsewhere. Nothing can stop it altogether. But the magicians of Coronnan do not tamper with balances of nature. We strive only to predict storms and prepare for them."

"This magician conjured the storm!" The pilot pointed a finger at Bessel. "I know he did. I saw him ram his staff into the deck and roll up his eyes in a trance. I felt the Kardia shift beneath the Bay and move great obstacles that weren't there the day before. Then he spoke demon words. He called up the storm and drove *my* barge onto a bar of his own making."

"Is this true, boy?" Scarface wove his fingers in an intricate pattern—his habitual gesture for seeking information and truth.

"No, it is not true. I maintained a light trance so that I

could understand the conversations in five different languages. I would never call up a storm or create a bar of debris. Raanald tried to navigate around the bar, but it caught the rudder and snapped it. Then the waves caught us crosswise and threw the ambassador overboard. I found him plastered against one of the old tree snags from the last sea battle by the currents."

"Then why didn't my depth finder warn of the bar's proximity?" The pilot trembled all over in his anger.

"It did. You kept changing course erratically because you didn't trust it."

Stunned silence filled the room.

Bessel looked from Scarface to Nimbulan and back to the pilot, seeking a response, any kind of response.

"If you do not trust the machine, why should we use it at all?" King Quinnault asked. "Is the machine faulty?" He looked to his queen.

She shrugged her shoulders. The machine had come from her people, from distant and mythical Terrania.

The pilot glared at Bessel, his mouth clamped firmly shut.

"Then perhaps the pilot is the one who must answer for my husband's death," Lady Rosselaara said. "He will speak readily as my blade lops off pieces of his anatomy."

The pilot straightened his shoulders and stared back at her with all of the arrogance of his guild backing him up. He knew himself too valuable to Coronnan for King Quinnault to give him over to foreign justice.

"Answers will be found, Lady," Nimbulan intervened. "But by our methods. If anyone is found negligent in this matter, justice will be served."

"I don't care for justice, Magician. I care only for vengeance."

"Will the death of an innocent bring your husband back to life?"

"The death of a guilty man will give me back my husband's honor."

"Then if any are found guilty, you will be informed of his fate." Nimbulan returned her determined glare. "Go home now, Lady Rosselaara. Go home and grieve. Prepare your husband for his funeral rites."

"You have one day to deliver the guilty man to my door so that he may be buried beneath my husband. If he is not dead at this hour tomorrow, I will kill him." Lady Rosselaara turned on her heel and marched out of the room. The litter bearers exited with her, carrying their fallen ambassador. Her honor guard sheathed their swords, wheeled as one, and followed her.

No one needed to utter the "Or else," that followed her final words.

"Now what?" Quinnault asked of no one in particular. "We have conflicting testimony. We have the problem of an untrustworthy depth finder. I am open to suggestions, gentlemen."

"I never liked having to rely on any machine," Queen Maarie Kaathliin said. She shifted the baby to her shoulder, easier now that the foreigners had left. "We should learn to read the mudflats another way."

"Such as?" Scarface intoned, stepping forward to stand beside the king, his rightful place as Senior Magician. The place that Nimbulan resumed all too easily. Wind-drift held back.

"Where is your famous magic, Master Scarface?" The queen turned her gaze to the ugly man who had forsaken life as a Battlemage and mercenary to join the Commune. "Why can't your magicians plumb the depths of the Bay and chart the course for the barges?"

"We have tried, Madame." Scarface looked more fierce than regretful. He kept his accusatory gaze upon Bessel.

The young magician wished he could disappear. He tried fading into the background—a trick Nimbulan used often. But he couldn't tell if it worked.

"Again and again, we have tried," Scarface continued, finally looking away from Bessel toward the queen. "But dragon magic, legal magic, is more in tune with the elements of Air and Fire than with Water and Kardia. To delve into Water and Kardia deep enough to chart the channels we need rogue magic. Upon pain of death or exile, we cannot violate our covenant with Coronnan. Only dragon magic can be combined and amplified by many magicians working together. Only dragon magic can be controlled with ethics and honor." The Senior Magician repeated the first rule of the Commune, staring back at Bessel, daring him to admit his lapse in legal magic.

Bessel remembered the day he had taken his oath to king and Commune. At the time he had truly committed himself to obeying the laws of the Commune and Coronnan. Yet today he had violated one of the most basic of those laws. He had tapped a ley line, violated his oath.

Would he violate it further in order to stop Scarface's mad crusade to control all of Coronnan? He'd not be much help to anyone unless he stayed in the Commune.

If he hadn't tapped a ley line to help his mother, surely he would never do it again. Never! Couldn't the Commune give him some kind of probation rather than death or exile?

"Master Scarface, please have one of your magicians take statements from the boatmen and Journeyman Bessel," King Quinnault ordered. "I would know who speaks truth in the matter of the storms and the machine. Then I will need you in my office in one hour to plumb the depths of the diplomatic mess caused by Ambassador Jorghe-Rosse's death."

"Very good, Your Grace." Scarface bowed respectfully along with everyone else in the room as the king exited with his wife. The mundane courtiers and servants filed out of the Great Hall as well.

"I will discuss this matter with Myrilandel, the dragons' ambassador," Nimbulan said. A half smile lit his face. Of course he'd discuss it with Myrilandel, his wife. "There must be a way to read the Bay with magic, the same way we . . ." a look of sadness—nearly pain—crossed his face. "The same way the Commune uses magic senses to find veins of ore and tests the fertility of soil." He resumed his normal, dignified demeanor.

"There is another matter that must be discussed in private, among the magicians," Scarface intoned. "Bessel, you will come with me." Scarface beckoned his journeyman to follow him back to University Isle where the Commune would hold court.

Bessel couldn't move. All heat left his body.

"The pilot felt you use rogue magic, Bessel," Scarface

reminded all who listened. "You know the punishment for that infraction."

"You will take the word of a mundane and prejudiced witness as truth without so much as letting the boy defend himself?" Nimbulan asked. He shifted to stand beside Bessel.

The dog took up his protective stance in front of Bessel.

The journeyman appreciated the gesture of support, but knew his case was hopeless. Only the dog truly believed him.

"I, too, felt the kardia shift as Bessel tapped the power of a ley line," Scarface said. "He has no defense."

Chapter 18

*Past midnight, the route between Palace Reveta
Tristile and the University of Magicians,
Coronnan City*

Bessel sloshed behind Nimbulan all the way across the
bridge to University Isle. The bedraggled mutt kept
close to his heels every step of the way. It cringed away
from the other magicians as if expecting to be kicked and
beaten. Bessel kept close to Nimbulan, his old master,
gleaning some measure of temporary safety from his vi-
brant personality. But nothing could ease the dread eating
a hole in his gut. Very soon he would lose the Commune
forever. All because he had tapped illegal magic in a failed
attempt to save a life.

If he had succeeded, would Master Scarface consider
leniency?

Bessel doubted it. The Senior Magician of the Commune
was as inflexible in his expectations as Lady Rosselaara
of Rossemeyer.

Did he truly want to remain in the Commune with
Scarface at its head?

He had nowhere else to go. He needed the Commune
more than it needed him.

But someone had to stop Scarface.

More magicians joined the procession from the palace as
they neared the University. They closed in around Bessel,
excluding the shaggy mutt from their perimeter, as if they
knew it would help Bessel escape justice. The dog whined
and danced to penetrate the circle.

Bessel missed the creature already.

"Scarface will have trouble gathering enough magic to implement any punishment," Wind-drift muttered from behind Bessel.

"No one's seen a dragon in days. Not since Scarface removed most of the books from the library," Master Whitehands, head of the healers, replied. "I've got an apprentice watching the skies from atop the tower. He's really talented with FarSight. His reports of dragon activity are dismal. They haven't been seen hunting bemouths in the Bay. That's their favorite food and keeps the number of monsters down to tolerable levels. Our fisherfolk will be in trouble if the dragons don't return to hunting."

"We'll be in deeper trouble without any dragon magic to gather," Wind-drift reminded him.

Bessel turned around to ask a question, but the two masters had withdrawn from his proximity. Two potential allies against Scarface. Were there more?

"Did you hear that?" he whispered to Nimbulan as they proceeded through the University. The sound of many boots slapping the flagstone passageway nearly drowned out his words. But it didn't mask the angry barks of the mutt.

Nimbulan merely nodded, holding one finger to his lips to signal silence on the subject.

They proceeded in single file up winding stairs to the tower room above the classrooms. Bessel feared separation from Nimbulan. Behind him, he could hear the dog yipping as he followed the troop. The risers narrowed and steepened each step of the way. Up three flights they climbed. Bessel's heart beat faster, and his legs grew heavier. His drying clothes grew stiff and weighed heavily against his chilled skin. There didn't seem to be enough air in this tight stairwell.

At last Master Scarface passed his left hand over the lock of the tower room. The portal sprang open. Only the Senior Magician could work that spell alone. The other masters needed three different magical signatures to move the lock.

One by one they filed into the working room that was almost filled by a round black glass table. Bessel had been in this private enclave of masters only once before, the day the roof had been finished. Dragons had had to lift the unique and incredibly valuable black glass table onto the roof of the next lower level and then the room was built around it. The tower would have to be destroyed to move the table.

No one else in all of Kardia Hodos possessed any artifact made from so much glass. Only dragon fire burned hot enough to eliminate the impurities in sand, turning it into true glass that wasn't so brittle and flawed it shattered at the lightest touch. Dragons had made the table for the Commune. They had given it to Nimbulan in time for the former magician to work his last and greatest spell— protecting Coronnan with a magical border.

But Nimbulan had been forced to leave his magic embedded in the black glass. He'd made his choice, to save the life of his wife, Myrilandel, rather than save his talent.

His magic glowed within the table surface, casting blue highlights within the black glass.

Nimbulan touched the surface with reverent fingers. A look of aching loneliness crossed his face. Then he tucked his hands within the sleeves of his tunic and raised his head. No emotion crossed his face or radiated from his aura.

Bessel grew colder yet, trying to imagine his life without magic. He was about to learn what it felt like. Without the Commune and dragon magic he had nothing, was no one.

The dog whined and scratched at the closed door, reminding him that he had one friend. Bessel closed his ears to the dog's entreaty. He didn't dare trust its offer of faithful companionship. It, too, would desert him if Scarface stripped him of his magic.

Only Master Lyman was missing from the ranks of twenty master magicians come to pass judgment on Bessel. He wondered briefly if the master magicians—all new since Nimbulan's retirement—had shunned the old librarian because he hadn't cooperated with the banning of certain books. Bessel hoped not. The Commune needed Lyman's knowledge, wisdom, and gentle approach to diplomacy.

A measure of resolve replaced Bessel's momentary depression. He had to find a way to stay in the Commune. Coronnan needed him in a position to counter Scarface. He couldn't do that exiled or dead.

Each of the master magicians took a reserved chair placed around the massive table. The chair backs boasted vivid embroidery worked in each magician's signature colors. Every piece of needlework was as unique as the magician who sat in the chair. But together, with hands linked around the glass table, their magic and their souls blended, became one, amplified, and worked miracles.

I'll be a part of that miracle again. Somehow, some way, I've got to stay in the Commune.

"Arbitrary punishment is not our way, Bessel," Scarface said, almost kindly. "Do you have an explanation for your heinous actions?"

A glimmer of hope blossomed in Bessel's heart. "You told me to save the ambassador's life at all costs. The only way I could hope to do that was to see the current that trapped him and drag him free at a moment of slackening. I didn't have the time or strength to do it with mundane skills. Dragon magic did not respond to me beneath the waters of the Bay. I used the tools available."

"And still you failed."

"If I had tapped the ley line when I first sensed trouble, I might have been in time. I failed because I hesitated to use solitary magic."

"As well you should. Any use of rogue magic opens the doors to chaos. Only dragon magic allows many magicians to combine their powers and impose ethics, honor, and justice upon *all* magicians."

"I know, Master. And I am sorry for my transgression. It will not happen again." Bessel bowed his head, hoping Scarface would take the gesture of humility into account.

"Once you have tapped rogue powers, there is no going back. You will be tempted again and again. Others will find excuses to do so as well. We must make an example of you." Scarface's voice rose as his scar whitened.

Wind-drift placed a placating hand upon the Senior Magician's arm.

Scarface's jaw tightened and worked side to side as if he ground his teeth in a massive attempt to control his temper.

"Excuse me, Master Aaddler," Nimbulan interrupted. His use of the Senior Magician's true name signified the importance of his words. "There are more important issues before us than Bessel tapping a ley line in a desperate attempt to save a life."

"What more important issue can there be than violation of our most sacred law?" Scarface glared angrily at his former comrade. They'd been friends when they first escaped Hanassa. Now Scarface treated Nimbulan as a distrusted foe.

"There is, first, the issue of the pilot's mistrust of the depth finder. It seems to me he is the party at fault here. If he had listened to the machine's warning and taken precautions immediately, Ambassador Jorghe-Rosse might still be alive and Coronnan would not be facing probable war with Rossemeyer."

"A matter for politicians to decide."

"But we of the Commune are chief advisers to the politicians. *Neutral* advisers. We . . . You need to make decisions, investigate the machine and the Guild, and give all of the information to the king and the Council of Provinces."

"After we have dealt with the transgressions of one of our own. We must police our members so that hysterical and uninformed mundanes do not need to."

"Then you must begin by exiling yourself, Master Aaddler."

"What!" Several of the masters stood, pounding fists against the table. Outrage burst forth from their tightly controlled auras.

But Wind-drift remained calm. Who was this man? More importantly, where did his loyalties truly lie?

The dog yipped outside the door. His bark sounded strangely triumphant.

Hope and bewilderment glowed within Bessel at the same time. He stood a little straighter, grateful that Nimbulan befriended him.

The retired magician waved his hand for them to quiet. The masters obeyed, revealing a measure of respect for Nimbulan that Scarface had yet to earn.

"Continue with your explanation, please, Nimbulan," Scarface ordered, pointedly denying his accuser the right of a title or working name.

"For you to have felt the shift in the kardia caused by Bessel's tapping of a ley line, you, too, must have been using solitary magic. By your own laws, you also must face death or exile along with the boy you so boldly accuse."

* * *

Past midnight, outside the University of Magicians, Coronnan City

From the supporting buttress of an outside wall, Kinnsell watched the magicians—master frauds more like—wind up the staircase to their private enclave. Now was as good a time as any to rescue the Rover woman. Darkness shrouded the entire complex. He'd never have a better opportunity to avoid detection by the magicians.

He needed to get close enough to the members of the Commune to test the viability of their psi powers. Until then, he had to presume they used sleight of hand and other tricks to convince a gullible populace. But they still held a great deal of political and economic clout on this planet.

Silently, he crept through the long corridors of the ancient buildings. The oldest portion seemed to have been a single story built in a simple U shape around a central courtyard. The corridor that ran along the inside of the U and accessed the individual rooms showed signs of recent enclosure. He had expected to find twisting passageways and hidden staircases here. But each square room abutted the next neatly without unwarranted thickness of walls to accommodate secrets. Four staircases ascended to the recently added second and third stories; one at the end of each of the side wings and one on either end of the central and longest arm of the U. All seemed to have been built on straight lines with quarried stones, neatly squared to fit together. He'd investigate the outbuildings later—all very neat and square as well. Presumably, they housed storage and cooking facilities and nothing more.

Thick stone walls made him feel protected, almost as if he was back in civilization. Almost. These bushies, noble and peasant alike, had not yet discovered climate control, even inside their buildings. A few rooms made use of inefficient fireplaces or even, *shudder,* central hearths that lost more heat than they added. No wonder they wore so many clothes! Nearly a meter of stone between himself and the outside world offered some insulation. But he doubted he'd ever be warm on Kardia Hodos, not even in high summer.

He wouldn't think about the primitive—meaning nonexistent—plumbing. So far he had managed to trek back to his shuttle at regular intervals to take care of his own personal hygiene, though he'd rather have parked the vessel farther away from the city where it was less likely to be found.

Every room he encountered in the residential and classroom wings of the University seemed to have an overt purpose and no hidden ones. Only the library—which occupied the entire central section of the building—offered the suggestion of places to secrete a prisoner.

Where would they hide the woman the bushie lord insisted must be rescued to prove Kinnsell's technology stronger than the magicians' magic?

He'd watched the comings and goings of this place all day. Other than the cook, there didn't seem to be any women in the University complex. No serving women. No mistresses or wives. And certainly no prostitutes. Where?

In desperation he slid into the library, empty of students at this late hour, although a few lights still glowed. All of the masters had retreated to the tower room—the third story of the classroom wing. Presumably, the apprentices slept. Therefore, there should be no one to hinder his search.

A maze of old-fashioned books tantalized him. The musty smell of learning invaded his nose and spread into his veins like warm insulation gel. Books had been obsolete for storing and dispensing knowledge for almost one thousand Terran years. Yet, still, books persisted as a favored hobby and status symbol among a large majority of the population. Something sensuous about holding a book in your hands, caressing the cover, gazing at the *permanence* of the printed words upon paper (synthetic since the loss of pulp trees after the first doming of Terra).

These books looked to be the genuine thing. Some printed on real paper. Others on parchment. They were bound in embossed leather, carved wood, or etched bronze—the latter richly jeweled and engraved.

Kinnsell couldn't help himself. He had to touch the incredible artifacts of a bygone era. He had to open one, read from it, cherish it. Maybe he could steal one and take it home. He could sell it for the price of a bush world. But he'd keep it. He'd honor it. Read from it every day. And when he became emperor, he would return to this library and confiscate as many books as he wanted.

His hand rested comfortably by his side, easy with his control of the situation and his life.

"May I help you, King Kinnsell?" the face of a wizened old man appeared in the gap made by Kinnsell's removal of the tome he held protectively against his chest.

"Who are you?" Kinnsell asked, startled to find anyone hiding in this treasure trove. His right hand edged forward a bit, seeking control. "And how do you know my name?"

Quickly he checked his mental barriers to make sure no one could delve into his mind without his knowing. They seemed intact. But who knew what could happen on this bizarre planet that treasured books but disdained climate control and plumbing?

"Everyone knows the queen's father," the old man replied.

"But not everyone knows you. Who are you?" Kinnsell hated having to repeat himself. He should be able to pluck the man's entire life history from his mind with no effort.

Instead, he found only images of viewing Kardia Hodos from a great height, soaring on strong wings. He reveled in the sensation a moment, recalling glorious moments piloting his shuttle through atmosphere of the many planets he had visited. Cyber controls responded to the briefest thought, but he preferred the sense of control a joystick gave him. Either way, his shuttle gave him the illusion of true flight like a bird—or a dragon.

Then the feeling of hunger for meat dominated the old man's memories.

Yuck. No civilized person survived on a blood diet anymore.

Kinnsell shook himself free of the lingering taint of the old man's perversions.

"Now that you have dipped into my memories, are you any more enlightened than before?" the old man asked.

He rearranged some books on his side of the shelf to reveal more of his face and form. Slight, stoop-shouldered with age. Nearsighted, too, from the way he peered at Kinnsell.

"May I please know your name?" Kinnsell asked through gritted teeth. He didn't have time or patience for word games.

"Ah, the magic word. Please. Yes you may know my name. I am called Lyman, Master Librarian in this existence."

"This existence?" Another curious superstition among these people. There had been Terran cultures that believed in multiple incarnations. Bush planets abounded with odd cults. Kinnsell preferred the family tradition of one god, one life, and an afterlife in heaven. That was the accepted philosophy in a large proportion of the civilized worlds. The accepted religion lent itself to a hierarchy of priests who, in turn, could be controlled.

"You didn't come here to debate religion and the purpose of life." Lyman dismissed the subject with the wave of a gnarled hand. "What do you seek? I know all of the books treasured here. I can help you find almost any single volume."

"I'm just browsing."

"Or looking for something not normally found in a library."

"None of your business, Lyman. Just leave me in peace."

"Will you ever know peace?"

"Not until you leave me to my business."

"Your business is my business as long as you seek answers in this library."

Kinnsell wanted to scream in frustration. Instead, he turned abruptly and stalked off through the maze of bookshelves. He thrust his right hand forward and to the right. He'd hardly walked the length of two aisles when the little man appeared before him, blocking the path.

Kinnsell evaluated the now visible little man. He appreciated the fine cloth of the old-fashioned blue tunic that hung nearly to his knees, belted with a silk sash. Most men in Coronnan wore shorter tunics with a leather belt beneath to hold up their trousers—or trews as they called them.

"You won't find what you seek without me," Lyman said.

"I'll find her if I have to tear this building apart, stone by stone." But he'd not harm a single page of the precious books.

"Her? Ah, the only woman you could seek is Maia, the Rover woman."

Kinnsell held his breath a moment. Had he really let slip that vital piece of information? He must be more careful.

"I'm afraid we can't let you take her," Lyman continued. "Out of the question, entirely."

"I didn't expect you people to throw your prisoner at me."

"She's not a prisoner. She remains under our protection of her own free will."

"I've heard that one before."

"You don't understand. She truly wishes to stay under our protection. Strange people, these Rovers. All members of a clan are linked mind to mind. None of them can think or act without all of the others knowing about it. The leader of the clan—usually a powerful magician—directs all of their thoughts and actions, just like a political dictator but more effective because of the magic. They have no freedom as we understand it. We have managed to shield Maia from the manipulations of her wandering relatives. As long as she stays here, she is free of them."

"This entire planet has truly bizarre beliefs. That is the most outrageous yet."

"Is it? Why else would one of her relatives have coerced you into an impossible rescue attempt? They don't need her. They fear her position here because they cannot monitor or manipulate her actions. She does not spy upon us for her clan. Therefore, they believe she must be returned to them or be killed. You, King Kinnsell, are their tool for that purpose."

"I serve no man but myself."

"That's what you think. If you will excuse me, I must consult with the Commune about your uninvited wanderings." The old man grinned, ambled off among his beloved books, and was soon lost from Kinnsell's sight.

Chapter 19

*Past midnight in the tower room reserved for
Master Magicians in the University of Magicians,
Coronnan City*

"**I**mpossible!" Scarface screamed. He half stood from his thronelike chair. "I could never violate my oath to the Commune and revert to rogue magic. I am Senior Magician. I am in control of myself and this Commune at all times." He sat back again, composing his face.

But Bessel saw the tension in his shoulders and the whitening of the ugly scar.

"There is no other way you could have sensed a shift in the energies of the kardia when Bessel tapped a ley line. You must have been working rogue magic at the same time," Nimbulan replied blandly. A twinkle grew in the old man's eyes. He sucked in his cheeks as if suppressing a laugh. He was enjoying himself.

Bessel, however, didn't dare relax. His life and his career were still in jeopardy.

"Explain your outrageous accusation, Nimbulan." Scarface stared at the former Senior Magician.

All of the other master magicians remained absolutely silent. Only their eyes moved, shifting from Scarface to Nimbulan and over to Bessel, then back again.

"You put forth the theory yourself last year in a very learned document," Nimbulan continued. "Communal magic is tuned to Air and Fire much like a harp and flute can be tuned to blend their music together. Kardia and Water are similarly tuned—but to a different harmony that does not blend well with Air and Fire. For you to sense the changes in the Kardia energies, you must have been in tune with them. What were you doing in the first moments of the storm? The moment when, under orders, Bessel grabbed the only magical energy available to him in a mad attempt to rescue Ambassador Jorghe-Rosse."

Bessel watched Nimbulan cock one eyebrow in question. Then the former magician raised his left hand, palm outward, fingers slightly curved.

"I was . . . I was . . ." Scarface stammered. He glanced at each magician around the table, as if seeking inspiration. At last he looked Nimbulan directly in the eye and spoke. "I am not on trial here, Nimbulan. Journeyman Bessel is. If I was tuned to the kardia, I was not aware of it. Bessel knew precisely what he did and why."

The man lied. Bessel knew it in his gut as surely as he knew the dog waited for him outside the door.

"The why is important, too," Nimbulan reminded them all. "You told him to do whatever was necessary to save the ambassador."

"And he failed," Scarface concluded.

"At least I tried. And I almost drowned trying. None of you offered me any assistance or advice," Bessel accused. "Did you want the ambassador to die so that you could prove your superiority in another war?"

The chill of his wet clothes had penetrated to his bones hours ago. None of these judgmental masters had even offered him a towel, or a chair, or a hot drink. Yet here they sat, fat and warm and comfortable and dry.

"Would you have jumped into the storm-tossed Bay to rescue a foreign ambassador?" Nimbulan asked everyone in the room.

"I can't swim," Scarface whispered.

"Then how would you have carried out your own orders to save the ambassador at all costs?"

Silence rang around the room.

"Masters, come. We have a situation," Lyman called from the doorway. He breathed heavily as if he had run up all three flights of stairs to the workroom. A sparkle in his eyes indicated he had left much unsaid and that amused him.

The dog dashed between Lyman's legs to jump against
Bessel. He whined and yipped for attention until Bessel
picked up the smelly bundle of tangled curls. Warmth
began to penetrate his body immediately.

"What, Lyman?" Scarface demanded. Every muscle in
his body radiated his angry frustration.

"I have interrupted an attempt to free Maia from our
custody. The Rovers have hired a professional to do their
dirty work."

"Rovers in the capital? We cannot allow Rovers anywhere near Maia," Scarface said.

As one, the masters rose and rushed toward the door.
They appeared all too anxious to separate themselves from
the uncomfortable questions and accusations that had been
flung about.

Scarface grabbed Nimbulan and Bessel by their arms to
stay their retreat.

"This business is not finished. For now, Bessel is in your
custody, Nimbulan. See that he breaks no more laws. And
keep him away from me!"

"And what of yourself, Aaddler?" Nimbulan asked. His
left eyebrow rose again in query. "What laws will you break
before this business is finished?"

Bessel wished he had the confidence to confront the Senior Magician with his true name. But then, Nimbulan had
little to lose. He'd already lost his magic.

Bessel could lose everything. The dog licked his face.

Well maybe he wouldn't lose everything.

*   *   *

*The pit beneath the city of Hanassa, time
undetermined*

Noise pressed on Rollett's ears as he followed Yaala and
Powwell deep into the labyrinth of caverns. Yaala intrigued
him and irritated him. Something about her made the hairs
on his arms and his nape stand on end. He'd seen a lot of
horror this last year that did not make him as suspicious
as this.

He took a moment to study her in detail as she led the

way. She had the long face, straight nose, and wide-set eyes of Yaassima and Myrilandel. But her small stature and golden-blond hair did not suggest a relationship to the deceased Kaalipha of Hanassa. He'd heard enough horrific tales about Yaassima's need for blood to hope the young woman hadn't inherited that single trait from her mother. She had survived when everyone thought her executed.

How had she managed that?

By taking refuge in this hidden sanctuary with the machines. She moved through the labyrinth of caverns easily, familiarly. Every step took them deeper into the inner caverns and the source of the annoying *yeek kush kush* noise. Yaala's posture and stride loosened the closer they came.

He was reminded of how he had sought a kind of refuge with Nimbulan the Battlemage during the wars. Once he'd found relative safety, companionship, and comfort with the magicians, he hadn't wanted to venture out into the real world at all. For many years he'd found it difficult to even go into the markets for supplies on his own.

Then one day, a year and a half ago, Nimbulan had set out on the long journey to Hanassa in search of his kidnapped wife, Myrilandel, and their two adopted children, Powwell and Kalen. Rollett couldn't let him go alone. He could not let his fears confine him within the safe walls of the University of Magicians when Nimbulan needed him. Then Scarface had entered the picture and forced or coerced Nimbulan into leaving Rollett behind in Hanassa.

Powwell and Myrilandel had escaped with Nimbulan and Scarface, but not Rollett. And presumably not Kalen.

Powwell had confirmed Rollett's suspicions in his tale of Nimbulan's retirement and Scarface's elevation to senior. Scarface, ex-Battlemage and ex-mercenary, wouldn't be happy until he controlled every aspect of every life around him.

Rollett needed to go home. Now. But he also had a duty to his men here in Hanassa. They relied upon him, trusted him with their lives.

"Show me the machines," Rollett said grimly.

"Why?" Yaala asked. Suspicion darkened her pale blue eyes. They weren't as colorless as Yaassima's and were much more expressive. Dared he read her mind?

He couldn't afford to waste his magic. He'd wait until she did something threatening. Then he'd invade her mind and strip it of every bit of knowledge he needed to escape Hanassa once and for all. With his men.

"Show me the machines and how they work. I need to understand everything about them if I'm to overpower Piedro and get us out of here. The city won't last another moon until your dragongate opens and food can come through," Rollett finally said.

"I'm not leaving until I find Kalen." Powwell placed his hands on his hips and jutted his chin in the most decisive posture Rollett had seen in the boy.

"She's not in the city, Powwell. I'd know if she got left behind."

"You didn't know about the pit and the dragongate. You don't know the palace," Powwell replied. "She's here somewhere. I sense her presence." He lifted his nose almost as if sniffing for her distinctive scent. The hedgehog poked his head out of Powwell's pocket and mimicked his action.

Strange, Rollett always thought of familiars as belonging to women's magic. He'd found so much satisfaction working with the men in the Commune he'd needed no companion but his staff. He couldn't remember if Powwell was particularly gifted with dragon magic or not. The boy—almost a man now—had spent so little time at the University with the other apprentices and journeymen, that Rollett hadn't had enough time to truly know anything about him except his unusual attachment to the girl Kalen, his half sister.

"I'll show you what I can," Yaala finally said after spending a long moment looking longingly toward the machines and back toward the passageway into the city.

Which did she prefer, the machines or the power of the Kaalipha? He wished he could trust her. Or at least understand her motives. Later. He'd know everything about her before he put his next plan into action.

Rollett listened carefully to her detailed explanation of generators, transformers, resistors, and currents. Her rather plain face glowed with a special beauty when she spoke—almost like a proud mama showing off her numerous children.

A piece of him wanted to reach out and teach her how to trust again. But he didn't dare trust her, so why should she trust him?

He shook off the emotion and concentrated on her lecture—sermon?

Generators made the mysterious 'tricity from steam. Transformers changed the raw energy into a usable form, as a magician transformed dragon magic. Currents flowed through the wires. Magic flowed through a man's blood.

"I've used ley line magic to power my talent, and I've used dragon magic. 'Tricity isn't so different," he said.

"I thought the same thing," Powwell agreed. "But I've touched this power, and I don't think it's safe for men to use."

"Yaassima's tricks with lights, making the altar stone disappear, and her sudden appearances on the dais were all illusions powered by this 'tricity." Rollett confirmed Yaala's lesson.

"Yes." Yaala nodded slowly. She kept her eyes on Rollett, searching his face for something.

"Then we don't need magic, we need 'tricity to overpower Piedro and reclaim the city." Rollett mulled over a number of possibilities in his mind. Magic and 'tricity. 'Tricity and magic. Where did one end and the other begin?

Ideas begin to awaken in his brain. With ideas came plans and hope. But first he needed more information.

"I wonder if we can use 'motes to stabilize the dragongate?" he muttered.

Powwell's eyes went wide with speculation. "The gate worked often and well while the generators ran continuously. Now the dragongate has shifted, stalled. Maybe it doesn't have enough power to open more frequently, and it doesn't have the power to keep it locked in one time span."

Yaala shook her head in dismissal of the argument. "Yaassima had 'motes—triggers—hidden all over the palace, some in her jewelry," Yaala continued. "The 'tricity never touched her body, only the 'motes. She used them to channel the 'tricity into specific chores. The hollow rods used on the gate lock and to stun people at the entrance to the palace were also a kind of 'mote."

Rollett had experienced those hollow rods. The guards

struck a special rock with the wand to make them emit an ear-piercing sound that froze mundanes for long moments—but only made magicians uncomfortable. The guards used that time to search suspects and those who wished to enter Hanassa. They also used the wands as a kind of detector for metal weapons. An effective security device.

Yaassima's guards must have had some kind of protection from the sounds. Rollett wondered how to mimic that for his men.

"None of these tricks will help us get out of Hanassa," he sighed in resignation. There had to be another way; 'tricity was the key. "We can't slap a wand to stun the guards. Half of them are Rovers and immune to the sound." With their mind-to-mind connections, all Rovers had the possibility of magic even without the specific talent. "We need a dragon to dig us free or fly us over the rim of the crater."

"None of the dragons will come near Hanassa," Powwell reminded him.

"Yeah, I know. They say that Hanassa, the renegade dragon, still rules here," Rollett replied.

"How can that be?" Yaala looked at them both, eyes wide with wonder. But her pointed chin trembled with a touch of fear. "My ancestor took human form and founded this city over seven hundred years ago. Once in human form, he had to live and die a normal life span."

"Dragons are very long-lived. Lyman told me that a dragon can live a thousand years or more." Rollett began to pace. He circled the generator, the one Yaala called Liise, touching it occasionally, trying to understand the how and why of Hanassa the renegade dragon. Hanassa had stolen the machines from the Stargods and used them to mimic the magic of the three divine brothers.

"Dragons live a long time in dragon form," Powwell corrected him. "When they take human bodies, like Myrilandel did, then they are limited to the life span of the body."

"But Myrilandel borrowed an existing human body. She didn't shapechange," Rollett argued. "When her body dies, her spirit could move to a new body if she chooses."

Stunned silence greeted that statement.

"Couldn't she?" Rollett repeated.

"Yes, she could," Yaala whispered. "I don't think she would want to, though, because she has embraced the limitations of humanity."

"What if Hanassa never accepted his human body as anything but a temporary host?" Bizarre thoughts plunged into Rollett's mind faster than he could assimilate them all. "What if Hanassa's spirit hides in these caverns waiting for a likely body to inhabit, then steals the body until he no longer needs it or it dies?"

"The wraith," Powwell and Yaala said together.

Chapter 20

Before dawn, Library in the University of Magicians, Coronnan City

Kinnsell walked to the back of the library. He stretched his stride, covering the twenty-five meters in short order. He ignored the tantalizing shelves of books along the way. He didn't have time to dawdle and read titles, caress bindings, or smell the unique combination of old paper, ink, and leather.

Iron bars blocked his exit. Behind the locked cage stood another library, as large or larger than the front portion. The stairway to the gallery and more books also lay behind the gate. Deep shadows hid these books from casual view. Kinnsell needed a lot more light to read the spines of even the closest volumes.

"More secrets?" he asked the books. They didn't reply. Not that he expected them to. He shook his head. Of course the magicians had to lock away most of their knowledge. The only way they could maintain control of the populace was to keep them ignorant.

"Education will be the first thing I introduce to these people once I am in control. Then the wheel. After that, progress will be unlimited. They'll thank me in the end."

He pulled a small, zippered wallet from inside his tunic. He brushed a dozen tiny tools made of the finest alloys with his fingertips. A hooked probe about the size of a toothpick seemed the proper piece to pick the lock. He could have used his telekinetic powers to manipulate the lock, but those skills didn't come as easily to him as telepathy. He might need his strength later, to free the woman.

The hair on the back of his wrist stood up in alarm as he inserted the probe. What? Cautiously, he channeled a little of his psi powers along the probe and met a wall of resistance.

"Aha!" He smiled. The master magicians had set the lock with telekinetic powers. Only stronger powers would release it. Presuming, of course, the opener used his mind instead of a key.

Kinnsell swallowed the atavistic fear that shot along the probe and up his arm. Merely the power of suggestion. His technology had to be stronger than the magicians' psi powers. This was just the first test of his skills.

With a little fiddling, the lock tumblers shifted under the probe. The gate swung open on well-oiled hinges. Kinnsell slipped through the opening and relocked the gate with the probe. He shook off the lingering tingle of distaste that infected his fingertips. The next person through here would find the lock much easier to manipulate.

Thousands of books lay between himself and whatever exit he might find back here. He wanted to linger and learn from them. Not enough time today.

"I'll be back," he promised himself. "I'll own all of you before I'm done with this planet. And I'll know why the magicians hide you. When I am emperor, I shall make books a priority. E-readers are efficient, but books are life." He caressed a book spine and moved on.

Half the wealthy merchants, nobility, and financiers in the Empire collected books. They would lobby for his election on that proclamation alone.

Sure enough, a small postern door lay secluded in a dark corner, almost hidden among the shadows between the stacks of shelves. He thought he'd spotted it during his search of the exterior grounds of the University. He bent low to lift the antiquated latch. The little door refused to budge.

"Mere locks won't stop me." But the mechanism resisted his tools. He turned his concentration on the lock. This was a trick his family didn't know about. No one in the O'Hara family had been able to use telekinesis since the first Mary Kathleen seven hundred years ago. But Kinnsell could. He'd kept his talent hidden all his life, using it to keep a competitive edge over the other contenders to the imperial throne.

The lock yielded to his mental touch after only a few moments of concentration. He should be panting and sweating with fatigue. Instead he felt as if he'd opened the lock using only mundane means.

Curious. What was it with this planet? He could eavesdrop on mundanes with little or no effort—except the bushie lord. And now locks moved at the merest thought. But magicians, men who merely had strong psi talents, could block out his strongest efforts to read their minds.

He had a glimmer of an idea of why his family went bush so readily on Kardia Hodos. Would the augmented powers stay with him after he returned to Terra? No one could oppose his election to the imperial crown if it did. And if he met opposition, he'd just change their minds for them.

He slipped through the doorway—so small and narrow even he had to duck, and he was several inches shorter than the bushie natives. As he straightened his back and drew a deep breath, he caught sight of the cook running from the kitchen building behind the residential wing to his right. The only woman allowed on University Island, and now she was running away in the middle of the night. She should be busy fixing the next meal for the hundred or more magicians and apprentices. Curious.

Well, he searched for a woman who should be secreted in the University but wasn't. Why not follow the only woman who did live here?

Guillia. He plucked her name from her mind quite easily. She was mundane, then. Her thoughts were more chaotic than most women suffering PMS. Something about a conspiracy . . .

More curious. A conspiracy within the Commune might serve him well. "A house divided . . ."

The woman led him along a convoluted path across several bridges and down streets that were barely wide enough to call alleys. During the day, these streets were crowded enough to be called major thoroughfares.

Even at this early hour numerous people moved about, finishing up late business in the taverns, the end of gatherings, and parties in the homes of the wealthy, getting ready for morning trade. Kinnsell felt comfortable for the first time since coming to this disgusting planet. His rapid pace stirred his blood until he was quite warm. Crowds pressed in on him. Wonderful crowds of people. That's what he missed about the bush. Civilized planets were crowded. No one was ever truly alone in a domed city. He heard a thousand different hearts beating the staccato rhythm of life and sighed with relief.

Guillia almost slipped away from him in shadows cast by torches and candle lanterns. But he'd touched her mind. She couldn't elude him long. There, two blocks ahead, she turned into a tidy little stone building with a tall steeple reaching toward the heavens.

A church? Ah, yes. His esteemed ancestors had started the cult of the Stargods here. They'd modeled it after their own beloved faith, merely substituting the three O'Hara brothers for the Holy Trinity of the Father, Son, and Holy Spirit. Of course the churches would have steeples and the natives would make the sign of the cross as a ward against evil.

Kinnsell stepped into the nave of the church. He paused a moment, waiting for his eyes to adjust to the dim interior and to catch his breath. One of the many things he intended to change on this planet was the minuscule windows in the churches. They deserved tall stained glass panels. He would definitely leave the augmented butane torch with his bushie lord. He'd make a fortune melting local sands into fine glass. The limited capacity of the fuel tank would make him greedy and eager to serve Kinnsell again in return for a refill.

Kinnsell moved from the dim porch into the nave where a hundred candles lit the worship space. Out of long habit, Kinnsell touched his head, heart, and both shoulders then bent one knee in obeisance to the altar. So what if he worshiped a different god than the ones revered here? The intent was the same.

He searched the open space for signs of Guillia. If the natives used pews, they had cleared them away after their last worship service. He saw no hiding places in the square room. Not even pillars to support the roof.

His skin prickled as if someone looked over his shoulder. He looked in all directions. Something more than pews was missing from this church: crosses. No crucifix hung above the altar, no wings extended from the nave to make the building into a cross. The icons on the walls, too, were devoid of crosses. How could these people believe in an afterlife—which he knew they did—without the dominant symbol of faith?

But then they didn't believe their god had died for them and then resurrected to a new life. They knew only that their Stargods had cured a plague and given a select few psi powers—what they called magic.

He shuddered and crossed himself again and again to make up for the lack of religious symbols and for the blasphemy of his ancestors.

The sense of being watched increased. He needed to get out of here.

"Are you looking for someone?" a woman asked quietly from behind him.

Kinnsell whirled to confront her. A short woman looked up at him through liquid black eyes. Her thick black hair was bound into a neat bun at the back of her head. A delicate mole lay just to the right of her mouth, enticing him to kiss her.

She looked so small and lonely he needed to enfold her in his arms, protect her, love her. . . .

Kinnsell checked his lustful response to her. He'd met women like her before. They used their minor psi talent to entice men, mold them to their will. Once alerted to their mental entrapment, he knew how to build barriers against it.

Then he noticed the olive tones of her skin and the bright red, purple, and black of her clothing. She wore large hoops in her ears and a dozen bangles on each arm. Just like the gypsies back home on Terra.

"Are you Maia?" He spoke as quietly as she had. His heart beat double time in excitement. This task was proving easier than he expected. He hadn't even had to rouse the woman from sleep. The bushie lord would have his captive and Kinnsell would have the entire planet at his disposal.

He needed to cough and control his breathing.

"Who are you?" She backed up, looking about for an avenue of escape, or to make certain he had brought no accomplices with him. She looked like a frightened deer he'd seen in pictures of old Terra. Another ruse.

"I won't hurt you, Maia. I've come to help. I'll take you home if you want." He held out a hand to her, inviting her to trust him. He used his own talent to persuade her.

"Who are you?" she asked again. Her shoulders relaxed a little, but she did not take his hand.

Kinnsell tried a light mind probe. She was as well armored as the bushie lord. No wonder she didn't fall for her own tricks used against her.

"I am an emissary from the Stargods come to rescue you." He swallowed the lie as easily as every other lie he told in and out of church.

* * *

Before dawn, tower room reserved for Master Magicians, University of Magicians, Coronnan City

Bessel clutched the wet dog against his chest, almost as a talisman. Nimbulan led the way down the three flights of stairs to the University courtyard.

"What's going to happen to me now, Master Nimbulan?" he asked as the other master magicians angled off toward the library.

"Nothing, I hope," Nimbulan replied, proceeding into the open air. He headed across the circle of the courtyard. His long stride seemed shorter than usual and his feet dragged a little. Was that a trace of puffiness in his fingers?

Bessel had known the former magician for most of his life. They had survived together through years of hard living during the Great Wars of Disruption. Huge armies had protected them then, but only because Nimbulan had been the strongest, most cunning Battlemage of his generation.

The tremendous effort of working great battle magic had depleted his energies and life force time and again.

He deserved his retirement. But could Coronnan afford to let him retire as long as Scarface ran the Commune?

A few clouds scudded away in the brisk wind. No other traces of the storm lingered.

The dog licked his face and squirmed to be let down. Bessel placed him on the damp stones reluctantly. Already he missed the reassuring warmth of the dog.

"Master Scarface entrusted me to you until the matter is settled," Bessel reminded the older man. He petted the dog, trying to postpone separation as well as decision.

"Then you will continue your studies from my home rather than here at the University. We have plenty of room in that great barn of a house Myri inherited from the dragons, especially now that Powwell is gone." Nimbulan paused to stare at the mongrel. He wrinkled his nose at the smell of wet dog. "I hope you aren't planning to bring *that* with you." He pointed accusingly at the dog.

"I don't know. It followed me when we left the docks." Bessel stooped to continue caressing the dog. In a way it seemed they belonged together. The bedraggled mutt looked up at him adoringly and licked his hand.

"Myri won't let it in her house until it has had a bath. I'm not sure I want the thing around. I've never had a use for familiars. My staff was always enough. . . ." He looked up at the sky and gulped back his emotions.

"My familiar." Suddenly Bessel knew that by announcing the bond between himself and the dog he had completed the process of adoption. They belonged together like the family he'd never truly had. Even the Commune had not offered him the trust and companionship this scruffy mutt did.

Bessel looked at the dog in a new light. "I wonder why it waited until now to adopt me? Not many magicians have familiars anymore." Perhaps the dog had sensed his magic only when he tapped the ley line. Perhaps the relationship of magician and familiar depended upon rogue magic.

"That's a question we can puzzle out later, along with other matters. Gather your things and meet me at the house in the morning, after you've cleaned up yourself and the dog. I wonder if the dragons have replaced familiars . . . ?" Nimbulan turned and wandered off into the city. He kept his left hand up, palm out while he pondered whatever great thoughts filled his head.

No matter how depleted Nimbulan's body, his mind obviously continued as bright and active as ever.

"Come on, dog. Do you have a name? I can't keep calling you dog." Bessel beckoned the animal to follow him.

Mopplewogger. The word came clearly into Bessel's head.

"That is a bizarre name. Mopplewogger. I wonder what it means."

Pictures of a long-legged and sleek water dog standing in the prow of a fishing boat filled his vision.

"Sorry, dog. You don't quite fit the picture."

The dog sat abruptly with a depressed look, if a face truly existed beneath the tangled ropes of muddy curls.

The mind picture the dog sent Bessel abruptly switched to show an even larger dog jumping from the boat to assist a fisherman battling a bemouth, one of the voracious giants that inhabited the outer depths of the Bay.

"If you say so, Mopplewogger," he chuckled. "That's how you see yourself. Maybe you are as brave and loyal as those dogs even though you're less than half the size and all that wet fur would weigh you down in the water. C'mon, we both need a bath, some sleep, and something to eat before we present ourselves to Master Nimbulan and Ambassador Myrilandel. She talks to dragons. Maybe she can answer some questions for me."

Chapter 21

Before dawn, neighborhood temple near the
University of Magicians, Coronnan City

"**H**ome? You'll take me back to Televarn?" Maia bounced into Kinnsell's arms.

"Whatever you wish, my dear." *Whoever Televarn is, he's a lucky man.* He held the young woman close against his chest a moment, breathing in her delicious feminine scent. He hadn't been with a woman for quite a while. Surely his current wife would forgive him one lapse considering the wealth and prestige he would take home to Terra. It was not as if he were replacing his wife with a younger woman with a bigger dowry and better political connections.

He'd done that three times before and was tired of the game. His current wife suited him fine. She'd make an elegant empress.

Then the significance of the name Maia had given her man at home hit him between the eyes. Televarn: one who speaks to Varns. He'd run into a swarthy man of that name once on a mission to Kardia Hodos about a decade ago. The man was incapable of telling the truth, would betray anyone for the right coins, and drove a hard bargain, harder than any other trader Kinnsell had come across anywhere in the galaxy. He was also one of the most beautiful men Kinnsell had ever seen. No wonder Maia wanted to return to him.

Kinnsell certainly wouldn't take this delicious woman anywhere near Televarn until he'd finished with her.

"Do you have possessions you must gather? We must

leave immediately." He'd take her to his ship, just outside the city. They'd have privacy for a while and then he'd move the little shuttle to make her think they traveled where she wished. But he'd take her only as far as the home of the bushie lord who bargained almost as fiercely as Televarn had.

"Possessions?" Maia laughed. She shook her head, setting the hoop earrings to bouncing. Her breasts strained against her black bodice.

Kinnsell wanted to rip the restrictive cloth away and free those full, ripe breasts. They'd fill his hands nicely.

He clenched his hands into fists and kept them firmly at his sides. She must have strong psi powers to go along with her allure. He swore to himself not to fall victim to her. He'd use her the way she wanted to use him.

"I am a Rover," Maia announced proudly. "Rovers wear their wealth. There is nothing more valuable than my freedom. Ah, to wander the roads of the world again. Televarn will wish to rove again after so many years in Hanassa. He was never truly meant to remain in the city of outlaws as their Kaaliph. I will remind him of the wonders of the road." She closed her eyes and smiled dreamily.

"Then we will leave now." Kinnsell grabbed Maia's hand, caressing her palm with his thumb. He drew her fingers to his lips, drinking in the lush smell and taste of her, telling himself that this was what she expected, so why not enjoy flirting with her. His breathing went ragged again, and he coughed to steady it.

Finally, he set his left hand to the back of her waist while keeping her hand bound in his right and headed out of the church.

"We can't go that way." Maia held back. She tugged his hand rather than releasing it. "*They* watch me. We must use a different door. And then find a place to hide until sunset tomorrow. The dawn comes, and with the light their power increases." Her eyes went wide with fear.

"Who prevents you from leaving a church?"

"The magicians. They watch every move I make while they claim to protect me from my own people. They invade my privacy worse than Televarn ever did with his mind in my mind all of the time. The magicians hate women and will kill me if they catch me outside the sanctuary of this building." She hissed as if her words, like the magicians, were tainted with venom.

"Is there another way out of here?" Kinnsell didn't trust his psychic shields to hide them from a truly powerful magician. He should have noticed a spy with psi powers lingering around the outside of the church. He'd have to learn the trick of extending mental invisibility to another person, something the magicians used all the time in protecting their king—the compromising weakling Katie had married.

"Of course there is another way out. The priests and magicians think it secret, but I found it." She seemed to include priests within the same category as magicians, both menacing and dirty.

"Then why haven't you left before this? You have friends and allies waiting for you."

"Getting out of this sanctuary is one thing. Staying hidden while I escape the city is another. But you will protect me." She caressed his cheek and pursed her lips as if expecting to be kissed.

Kinnsell leaned closer, more than willing to oblige. She smiled so very sweet, promised so much. . . .

He shook himself free of her spell.

"We must be quiet." Maia pressed a finger to her full lips. Her eyes sparkled with mischief. "The priest consoles the cook from the University. She comes here often, supposedly to check on me, but mostly to confess to the very handsome priest. I would confess to him, too, but he prefers his women fair and docile. We can learn something the magicians do not wish the world to know." She tiptoed toward the altar and a small postern door.

"Eavesdrop on a confession?" Kinnsell gulped back his sudden apprehension. He had to keep reminding himself these people didn't believe in the faith that had sustained his family for more generations than anyone could count.

"Knowledge is power, and power is more valuable than any wealth," Maia reminded him.

"That is a concept I can appreciate." A concept his sons could never comprehend. He'd hoped that Katie had learned it. But she, too, had opted to hide on this bush world rather than seek political power. True power.

Thankfully, his current wife understood. She'd forgive his lapse in fidelity for the sake of knowledge and power.

Together, he and Maia moved toward the altar. A large tapestry showing the three Stargod brothers descending to Kardia Hodos upon a silver flame covered the area immediately behind the slab of blue marble. The cold flames in the woven picture looked amazingly like an antique space shuttle. The murmur of quiet voices filtered through the beautiful needlework. Kinnsell looked closer and realized the tapestry separated the main worship area from another room.

The feminine voice became tearful. The masculine voice whispered soothing comfort.

Kinnsell and Maia listened closer.

"Scarface threw me out! I'm not to return to his island again. Not even to visit my husband," the woman wailed.

"He must have had a reason. Have you been remiss in your duties as cook?" The priest kept his voice neutral.

"I provide amply for my boys at the University. I feed the Masters even better, but does he appreciate my efforts, my talents? No. He says that women distract his magicians from their true calling. He says that women represent the old magic and that all traces of it must be eradicated. He told me to be gone before dawn."

"That is a serious change from what I was taught in my early training as a magician, before I opted for the priesthood."

Kinnsell remembered that all the priests and healers in this world must first be magicians. Their first loyalty would always be to the Commune. The woman Guillia might have made a mistake taking her problem to a priest.

"I am not to return to the island again, not even to retrieve my belongings or kiss my husband good-bye. I have lived there three years. It is my home! And my mundane children must leave, too. Nimbulan promised them an education. They can't learn to read and cipher anywhere but at the University. What is to become of us? We have no place to go!"

"Guillia, only magicians may learn to read. That is the law of the Stargods. Scarface is correct in removing your sons from the school. But surely your husband will support you? He can buy you and the children a house on another island. He can live there and work at the University."

"You don't know Stuuvart very well." The woman snorted in disgust. "He's more interested in counting his crates and barrels in the storeroom than in the welfare of his family."

Kinnsell had heard enough. The Senior Magician sought to consolidate his power by evicting all the women from the University, in the name of removing all traces of the old magic—whatever that was. He'd condemned a journeyman magician for using that old magic in an effort to save a drowning man. What would be his next step in controlling everything in this miserable country?

The library. The storehouse of all knowledge accumulated since the Stargods had left the family book collection here seven hundred years ago. Over half of it was locked away already. How long before its existence—even protected by iron bars and telekinetic locks—proved too dangerous and Scarface destroyed the wonderful treasure trove of books?

Kinnsell had to go back and save all of those wonderful books. *His books!* But he had to get Maia away from here in order to win the support of the lords. How much time did he have?

*   *   *

Near dawn the morning after the dark of the moon, the pit beneath the city of Hanassa

"The spirit of Hanassa used my mother's body!" Yaala exclaimed. That explained why Yaassima had executed her consort for no reason and exiled her own daughter—her only child and heir. Hanassa controlled the city and thirsted only for blood and more blood. Hanassa didn't need an heir, he would simply invade the next convenient body.

Did the spirit displaced by Hanassa become the next wraith that haunted the pit?

Relief made Yaala's knees tremble and her head light. She need not fear falling into the pattern of her mother's ruthlessness because the Yaassima she knew hadn't been her mother.

"But the wraith was here in the pit before Yaassima died, Yaala," Powwell argued.

"The wraith we knew was my mother's spirit. And now it is someone else's." Yaala glared at Powwell as if begging him not to shatter her brief moment of looking toward her future with something akin to confidence and hope.

"Who is the wraith now? We have to know who, so we can deal with Hanassa in that person's body," Rollett reminded them. "Neither the wraith nor Piedro is going to allow us to just walk out of Hanassa."

Powwell's face looked bland and empty. Thorny retreated deep into his pocket. Both sure signs that he knew more than he told. Yaala knew from experience he wouldn't tell until he was ready.

"This is all very interesting. But I need food and sleep before I can think any further." Rollett yawned.

Yaala heard his jaw crack as he repeated the yawn and scrunched up his eyes. He opened them again reluctantly.

Suddenly he looked vulnerable and young. The last year in Hanassa had aged him beyond his twenty or so years. At first glance, she had thought him closer to thirty. But he couldn't be that old and still a journeyman. Young men either progressed to master or left the University while still quite young.

"Take what you need from the living cavern. There are pallets there, too. Don't forget to drink," Yaala reminded Rollett. She fell back into the attitude of authority. For years, the denizens of the pit had obeyed her without question. Her mother's guards had respected her and feared the accidents she arranged for those who defied her. Yaala pushed aside the notion that she could be as ruthless as the late Kaalipha of Hanassa.

"I need you healthy and strong when we go above," she added to her orders to Rollett. Once we have deposed Piedro, I'll do all I can to help you return to Coronnan. Hanassa needs Coronnan's strength and resources to become truly independent again."

"Do what you can to fix those blasted machines, Yaala,"

Rollett said over his shoulder as he stumbled toward the large living cavern. "I think I know how to make use of them. I'll need your machines to end the tyranny of Piedro and the consort. They probably sabotaged the tunnel every time we came close to the exit."

"Yes." Warmth began to glow in the pit of Yaala's stomach. With the machines operating again, she could do anything. She could resume control of her life as long as she had the machines.

She turned to speak to Powwell. Her words died in her open mouth as the wraith flew into the cavern, circling them again and again.

I want my body back. I want it back now! He can't have it. It's mine! The wraith's hysterical gibbering invaded Yaala's mind, driving out all coherent thought.

Chapter 22

Neighborhood temple near Palace Reveta Tristile,
Coronnan City

True to her word, Maia led Kinnsell to a small ventilation grate in an outside wall of the church. She tugged on the metal bars. They came loose with little effort.

Kinnsell saw places where the hinges had been scraped clean of rust. She must have been planning her escape for some time.

The young woman wriggled through the small opening with little effort. The sight of her enticing bottom squirming about made his blood pressure rise. He swallowed his desire and concentrated on following her.

He had trouble getting his wide shoulders clear of the metal framework. The small opening pressed against his back and chest. He had to cough several times to relieve the pressure in his lungs. At last he squirmed free. A coughing fit made him stagger until he'd relieved the ache.

His elegant brocade tunic suffered almost as much as his breathing. Well, he wouldn't need it once he got back to his ship and resumed his heavy Varn costume. At least then he'd be warm. The layers and layers of thin veils insulated better than the fur lining of his bushie clothes.

"Where is Televarn now?" Maia asked in a hushed whisper.

"I'm not certain. He moves around a lot," Kinnsell twisted the truth as he knew it only a little. Why did he feel uncomfortable lying to this woman? Making the truth fit his own needs had never bothered him before. "We'll have to go to my ship and contact him from there." The shadows grew long. He didn't have a portable torch to light the way to his hiding place. They'd have to hole up somewhere tonight. Unless Maia could see in the dark like the bushie lord and half the population of this cursed planet.

Wherever they spent the remainder of the night, Kinnsell intended to spend it in Maia's arms. Her posture, her attitude, her very being promised him many exotic delights; things his wife had forgotten as soon as she said "I do."

"You will work a summons spell at your ship?" Maia's eyes grew wide. "Then you are a Master Magician, too!"

"Y . . . yes. What do you mean 'too'? Who else do you know that is also a magician?"

"Why, Televarn, of course." She sucked on her cheeks and avoided his gaze.

She was lying. Someone else very close to her was a magician.

Kinnsell crept behind her on tiptoe until they had put several streets and alleys between them and the church. The sensation of being watched grew stronger with each step he took. He searched the area with his eyes and ears as well as his psychic senses. Nothing. He couldn't find anyone watching them, not even the few remaining people on the streets at this chill quiet hour before dawn.

He had to concentrate hard to see where he placed his feet. Maia kept darting in and out of his view as she slipped from shadow to shadow—just like a magician—an illusionist. He had to keep reminding himself that the magicians here, just like the entertainment magicians back home, were merely actors who specialized in tricking their audiences.

When he could no longer see the church or its tall spire among the jumble of rooftops, he breathed a little easier. But the chill of unease wouldn't leave him. He still felt as if someone spied upon his every move. A less determined person would have gone back to the church to end the disquieting sensations.

He prided himself on his determination and kept walking.

Kinnsell stumbled over an uneven paving stone. Maia stepped confidently ahead, surefooted and swift.

The darkness intensified. The hair on Kinnsell's nape stood up in atavistic fear. If he didn't find shelter soon, he'd start prattling about dragons just like Katie.

By the time they reached the last bridge out of the city onto the southern mainland, Kinnsell breathed heavily. Sweat rolled down his back and under his arms, but he didn't feel warm. The tightness in his chest increased with each step. He'd have to let a cough loose soon. But the noise would echo loudly through these empty streets, betraying their position to any watcher. If he could only hang on until they crossed this last bridge.

The night breeze increased. Kinnsell began to shiver. He prayed that shelter awaited him close by.

New storm clouds built up in the outer bay. The air temperature seemed to drop dramatically. He didn't make it beyond the center span of the bridge before an explosive bark erupted from deep within his lungs. Again and again his lungs tried to expel building fluid and failed. He couldn't drag in enough air. He clung weakly to the bridge railing. His knees wobbled and dizziness assailed him.

Thankfully, this wasn't the plague. His family had always been immune through countless mutations, as were several other clans. Scientists hadn't yet found the genetic code that allowed them to combat the dreaded disease.

This must be some obnoxious ailment caused by exposure to the elements. He hoped the antibiotics he had aboard the shuttle would counter it.

"You are ill, Master Kinnsell?" Maia stood beside him, one hand on his shoulder.

Warmth invaded his system from that hand. The cough eased enough for him to breathe.

"I'm all right now. I'm just not used to the air here."

"Yes, the city is filthy. Better we take to the road where we can breathe free." She tugged on his sleeve. "But the road will wait for tomorrow or the next day. The road will always be there, we have but to set foot on it. For tonight, I know an inn."

Slowly, Kinnsell followed her across the last few steps to the shore. Up ahead, rushlights sparkled in the growing darkness. The cold, damp river mist hadn't reached the lights yet.

He paused to look up at the stars, as bright as the torches. Humans on Terra hadn't been able to see stars from their homeworld for many centuries. Long before the first domes went up, pollution had obscured the night sky. He wished he could see Terra's sun from here; know that he was still a part of the Empire and civilization.

"What will the inn cost us for a room and a hot meal?" he asked, as the thatch of a roof showed black against the dark night sky. He fingered the stash of local coins he carried. He had no idea what each one represented in the true value of goods and labor.

"He will charge you nothing." Maia skipped lightly, twitching her bottom. The movement sent her petticoats swaying.

Kinnsell watched her with growing interest. She hadn't objected to the idea of one room for the two of them. Perhaps she flirted as seriously as he.

One hundred long and wearying paces later, Maia pushed open the drooping gate into the inn courtyard. Kinnsell followed her into the open space, too weary to handle the heavy wooden gate. A painted sign showing a green-haired and seaweed-clothed water witch swung in the breeze, creaking on rusted hinges.

"The Bay Hag Inn," Maia said, sweeping a hand in the direction of the sign.

Kinnsell peered closer for any indication of written words on the creaking slab of wood that swayed in the predawn breeze. Only the picture stared back at him. Maia had read the picture. Only magicians on this world had the knowledge to read words.

A few listless stable hands groomed shabby, knock-kneed steeds. The cook yelled from the kitchen, something about evicting witch cats. Kinnsell couldn't make out all of her words through her thick peasant accent. Guests sang a drunken ditty quite loudly in the common room, with total disregard for key and tone—or the hour.

The stench of unwashed bodies, crowded horses, and stale chamber pots sent Kinnsell into a new coughing fit. He bent over, clutching his knees in an effort to remain on his feet.

"You have to stop this, Master." Maia rubbed his back

solicitously. "The innkeeper won't let you stay here if he thinks you carry the plague that ravages the interior provinces."

"I don't have the bloody plague, Maia. Believe me, I'd know if I did." A niggle of doubt tried to insert itself in his mind. He pushed it away. In these filthy conditions, disease must run rampant. But whatever felled the populace, they couldn't have the same plague that decimated the civilized worlds. Local conditions wouldn't support that plague. Anything else, he could cure with a few antibiotics once he reached his ship. Tomorrow. They'd walk there first thing in the morning.

"Tomorrow we hire steeds to take us to your ship," Maia continued. "They will travel much faster than walking."

"I'll be damned if I bruise my backside on one of those beasts!" Kinnsell straightened from his coughing crouch. "If the inn can't provide anything better than those nags, I'll walk." The energy of anger and insulted pride gave him the strength to walk into the inn.

"I'll do the asking, Master Kinnsell. The innkeeper will not refuse me." Maia stepped in front of him as a paunchy, middle-aged man wearing a stained apron approached. He reeked of meat and stale ale.

Kinnsell almost gagged. He had to remind himself that on bush worlds people had to eat meat to survive. The prejudice of civilized cultures against blood diets was only valid on civilized planets.

Maia sidled up to the innkeeper. She draped herself around him, clutching his shoulder as she caressed his cheek with delicate fingertips.

"A private room and a meal for the gentleman?" The innkeeper eyed Kinnsell briefly, then turned his attention back to Maia's lips that hovered much too close to his own. "And for you, my lady, clean sheets and mulled wine in my cot." He grabbed the Rover woman around the waist, pulled her close, and kissed her soundly.

"But, but . . ." Kinnsell gasped. How could she pay for their bed and board by . . . by . . . She owed him—Kinnsell. He'd rescued her. She had no right to peddle her body to this filthy commoner.

Kinnsell narrowed his eyes seeking a suitable revenge.

He pushed his right hand forward striving to gain control of the situation and his emotions.

"Do not worry, Master Kinnsell. I will join you later. When you are rested." Maia smiled at him.

Kinnsell relaxed his posture. Let them think him placated.

She and the innkeeper ambled away, arms draped around each other familiarly, hands exploring bottoms and breasts already.

"But . . . but . . ." Kinnsell continued protesting for their benefit. Frankly he was relieved he would not have to perform just yet. This nagging cough left him tired and weak-kneed.

A very young blonde maid took his hand and led him up rickety stairs to the private room tucked under the steeply sloping eaves.

"I'll stay with you, Master," she offered, staring at him with huge blue eyes.

She couldn't be more than fourteen, a child. Barbarians!

He rammed his hand all the way forward. For once the gesture did nothing to help him.

Kinnsell slammed the door in the girl's face. The walls shook and the tiny shuttered window rattled from the force of his blow on the door panels. A mouse and loose straw dropped on his head from the thatch. He coughed again from the dust that filled his nose and mouth.

* * *

Noon, the University of Magicians, Coronnan City

Bessel and Mopplewogger slept until noon. They grabbed a handful of bacon and bread as they ducked out the back door. After an easy trip through the bustling city, they passed Jorghe-Rosse's embassy on the way to their new abode. Already blood-red mourning wreaths adorned all the doors. Cloth banners of the same blood red were draped from every window. Warriors from Rossemeyer expected to die in battle, therefore the color of freshly spilled blood represented death.

The dog scuttled past the house. Bessel followed as rapidly. Mopplewogger radiated fear that invaded Bessel. Just as they passed the dwelling, a man clad in the voluminous black robes and tall turban of Rossemeyer stepped onto the front stoop. The long strand of black cloth that normally draped from the turban across the man's face hung limply to his shoulder. A fierce frown drew the man's mouth into an expression of malevolence. He watched Bessel and his familiar through eyes narrowed in calculation. Then he unsheathed his serrated short﹒sword from the depths of his robe.

Bessel willed himself invisible.

You are dead, the warrior mouthed the words and stepped down to the street level. He maintained eye contact with each step.

Mopplewogger yipped and scooted forward, his bobbed tail tucked down.

Bessel ran after him.

The warrior didn't follow. Lady Rosselaara had given King Quinnault one day to produce a suitable victim for her harsh justice. Bessel had until midnight—if the desert mercenaries counted time the same way the rest of the world did. Somehow, Bessel knew they counted time to fit their own desires. They would wait for King Quinnault's justice only if it suited them.

Still looking over his shoulder, Bessel scuttled around an imposing townhouse half an island away. He knocked on Myrilandel's and Nimbulan's kitchen door with more urgency than was probably necessary. He wanted to be indoors and out of sight of any potential assassins. Since he could not fade from view with magic, he'd hide behind mundane walls.

Most of the houses on this island belonged to various ambassadorial parties. A few foreign merchants with enough wealth to buy one of these tall narrow dwellings had settled near their ambassadors. Dragon gold had purchased one of the slate-fronted houses for Myrilandel, their ambassador to the humans.

Nimbulan, Myrilandel, and their daughter Amaranth lived somewhat more modestly than their neighbors, with few if any servants, rarely giving lavish parties or hosting large retinues of their followers. Dragons didn't need to court favor with politically powerful people. People needed to keep the dragons happy.

But if no dragons had been seen in several days, did that mean the dragons were not happy with humans right now?

At last Myrilandel opened her kitchen door to Bessel's rapid knock. He continued looking over his shoulder for signs of pursuit.

The dragon's ambassador carried a broom and wore a simple peasant gown with a kerchief hiding her white-blond hair. Nimbulan was nowhere in sight. Bessel ducked into the warm room with the dog tangling his feet.

"I will not have dogs fouling my clean kitchen," Myrilandel announced, herding Mopplewogger back toward the door with the broom. He scooted around the broom and hid under the long worktable.

"He's not just a dog!" Bessel defended his new friend. "He's my familiar."

"Well, a familiar is different," Myrilandel peered at the dog through slitted eyes, as if assessing him with her magic. "I lost my Amaranth over a year ago, and I still miss him. Even naming my baby girl after my familiar didn't fill all of the gap his death left. What's this one's name?"

"He calls himself Mopplewogger."

"What in this existence is a Mopplewogger?" Nimbulan asked, coming into the kitchen with his daughter tucked under his arm. The little girl giggled around a damp thumb stuck into her mouth.

"Some kind of water dog," Bessel replied.

"Looks more like a dust mop with a nose and tail." Myrilandel shook her head. "Mopsie, I think."

The dog looked up at the shortening of his name, wiggling from nose to tail and back again.

"Pick a bedroom for yourself and Mopsie." Nimbulan gestured toward the stairs. "Then join me in the study, I'd like to assess your progress before we commence on new courses."

"Pick a room close to an exit for the dog," Myrilandel added. "You'll have to open doors for him, and you'll get tired of walking up and down those stairs in the middle of the night. Believe me, I know what it's like to be owned by a familiar."

"Uh, sir, I think I might need to learn something about self-defense and disguises." Bessel paused in his retreat toward the back stairs—the servants' stairs in any other household. If Myrilandel made use of any servant except an occasional nanny, Bessel had never seen them.

"Why?" Nimbulan dropped the arm he'd been gesturing with. "Has someone from the University threatened you?"

"No, sir. I had to pass the Rossemeyerian Embassy on the way here. One of their warriors came outside and watched me very closely. He unsheathed his sword and said something, but I couldn't hear the words."

Why didn't he admit that he knew what the man had said? Maybe the man hadn't said the words, only thought them.

"Did you read his intentions in his mind?"

"No, sir. I won't eavesdrop unless invited." An embarrassing flush heated Bessel's face.

"Even to save your life?" Nimbulan raised one eyebrow in question.

"I . . . I don't know. I've never been that desperate."

"Think about it while you settle in. And think about invisibility spells. I used to be quite good at hiding myself while in full view of those I wished to escape. Sometimes I didn't even need magic." The elderly man chuckled as he set his daughter onto her feet. He knelt before her and tousled her hair. "But I'll never escape you, Ammie."

The little girl laughed wildly.

Bessel wondered how much Nimbulan could teach him now that he'd replaced his magic with a loving family. Then his old teacher stood, slowly unbending his limbs. A grimace of pain crossed his face and he coughed.

Chapter 23

Afternoon, the pit beneath the city of Hanassa

"**A**re you sure this thing will work?" Powwell asked as he eyed the little black 'mote suspiciously. He held the box so the wraith could view it, too. The misty apparition hadn't left him for more than a few seconds since she'd returned, not even while they slept and ate. The iron gate had remained opened after the guards left. She could come and go as she pleased. So why didn't she go?

At least she'd ceased her wailing.

"I'm not sure of anything," Yaala replied. She repeatedly touched various parts of Little Liise, the generator that chugged happily along converting steam to 'tricity. Mostly Yaala fiddled with a control panel she had exposed on one end of the machine. "Touch the left button and see what happens."

Powwell held his finger over the button she indicated. Sometime in the past it had been painted red. Generations of use had worn the paint off and there were only a few wisps of color left to suggest its purpose. He closed his eyes and pushed hard on the button.

"Nothing's happening." Rollett scanned the caverns, holding out his staff as a sensor. He seemed unaware of the wraith hovering right in front of him.

"Wait a moment," Yaala advised as she fussed with buttons and switches on the nearby transformer. "Push it again."

Powwell pushed the button.

Still nothing.

"Point the 'mote toward the light control panel embedded in the wall." Yaala heaved a sigh of resignation. "I thought you knew a 'mote had to have a purpose and line-of-sight contact with its objective."

"Now we know," Rollett replied with a grin. "Just like FarSight. The magic lets you see farther than your eyes alone, but you have to be in line of sight."

Powwell and Rollett looked at each other. They both shrugged. More and more, 'tricity sounded like magic. But Powwell knew it wasn't magic. It was dangerous to touch, dangerous to any but the most expert engineer—Yaala.

And the machines would let the plague into Coronnan. He knew that the moment he smelled the metallic/chemical taint in the air beneath the pervasive sulfur when they arrived by the dragongate. He'd never forget the smell of the plague in the dragon dream.

The wraith wrinkled the part of its face that might be a nose, mimicking his own action.

Powwell pushed the button again, trying to ignore the wraith. The lights dimmed to a faint glow. Heavy darkness crept closer to him. His senses started adding up the grains of dirt and piles of rock in the mountain above him.

The wraith cooed gentle comfort into his mind, just like Kalen had.

"Now push the green button, the one on the right," Yaala instructed, before he succumbed to panic.

She looked happy, so Powwell guessed the 'mote and the machines behaved as she expected. He obeyed her instructions, remembering to keep the 'mote pointed at the control panel. The lights gradually brightened. He continued to hold the button. More lights flickered on.

For the first time, Powwell felt a lightening of the weight on his chest that came from being underground in the dim caverns. The wraith hadn't helped him as Kalen had.

"Will this 'mote do anything else?" Rollett asked, inspecting the device.

"What do you want it to do?" Yaala turned to look at him, hands on hips.

Powwell wondered why she looked so exasperated, so

confrontational with Rollett. She loved talking about 'tricity and her machines. But she seemed almost afraid to give Rollett any more information than she had to.

Afraid of Rollett? They were on the same side, weren't they?

"Will it make the altar stone rise up from the floor of the Justice Hall?"

"Probably."

"Will it allow me to appear on the dais without prior warning?"

"No. But I think it is tuned to a bank of lights in the ceiling to create a blinding flash in front of the dais so you can get through the tapestry of the waterfall before dazzle-blindness wears off anyone in the Justice Hall." Yaala took the 'mote back from Powwell and fiddled with it. "Yaassima liked all her 'motes tuned to the same frequency so she could use them interchangeably. This one should work on everything."

"Then let's go above," Powwell said. He started walking toward the exit before he finished speaking. He couldn't get out of the pit soon enough. The wraith floated close by.

You'll help me get my body back now. He can't have it. I'll do my best.

Yaala's 'motes wouldn't help him evict Hanassa from Kalen's body. He needed magic, strong magic. Only magic would save Kalen and get them all out again. He'd make Yaala come back to Coronnan with him and Rollett. She didn't really belong in Hanassa. No honest person did.

The next few hours could get very messy. Probably bloody, too.

*   *   *

Afternoon, the pit beneath the city of Hanassa

"This is just a reconnaissance mission," Rollett stated firmly. "We don't take any chances and we stay hidden as much as possible." He fixed a stern gaze on Powwell and Yaala in turn. The men of Hanassa usually flinched in fear when he stared at them like that.

Powwell and Yaala returned his gaze steadily. Each nodded briefly, decisively. They'd obey him this time because his plans coincided with their own.

"At the first hint of trouble, or if anyone recognizes you, head back here immediately. Don't wait. Don't try anything. Just come back here where it's safe."

"We know, Rollett. You've repeated it a dozen times," Powwell said impatiently. "Repeating it isn't going to help me find Kalen."

Rollett almost grabbed Powwell by the throat to intimidate some respect into him.

And hated himself for his instinctive reliance upon violence. What good could he do back home if he had truly succumbed to the violence inherent in Hanassa?

"Let's go. No sense wasting any more time with old instructions and older arguments." Yaala moved between the two. She placed a restraining hand on the chest of each man.

Rollett mastered his violent reaction. New respect for the woman cooled his temper further. She'd make an admirable leader in a civilized land. But here, among the lawless, she'd need help. His help. Should he stay?

He indulged in a closer examination of Yaala's face. She had washed off some of the journey grime and combed her blond hair, leaving it flowing free and soft rather than hiding behind the ugly kerchief knotted Rover style over one ear. Striking rather than beautiful with her long features and pale skin. He looked forward to seeing her dressed as a woman rather than a sexless ruffian. And hoped his desire would fade with the realization she had little or no figure to entice a man.

He didn't have the time or energy to waste on a woman.

He didn't know how much longer he could tolerate the city or the way the city had shaped him this past year.

"Our first task is to try the 'mote on the gate." Rollett marched forward, holding the 'mote in the palm of his hand. "Is there a way we can keep Piedro from opening the gate with magic or a key, Yaala? If he can't get to the food, he'll be in big trouble in the city. That will shift the balance of power. Food and escape are the only currencies in Hanassa." He aimed the little black box at various control panels as they passed. Lights came on and diminished as he pressed the buttons.

"I'll be interested to see who the veiled consort sides with if we manage that shift of power," Powwell mused. He kept looking over his shoulder as if he saw something or someone the other two couldn't perceive.

"So will I," Yaala joined in. "From what you've said, Rollett, she's the one who directs Piedro's every move. He strikes me as a man with ambition but not a lot of forethought. If we take out the consort, he'll be indecisive."

"The consort is the one I plan to watch most closely on this mission. Remember we just watch and learn this time." Rollett approached the gate slowly. He listened with all of his senses for evidence of Piedro's Rover guards.

He heard a mouse scuttle through the dust. A snake slithered behind it. The corridor remained quiet except for those tiny sounds. He checked the light quality for evidence of body heat or auras—though Rovers managed to suppress the visible radiation of heat and energy from their bodies. Last of all, he opened his mind to stray thoughts. Rovers had great armor around their minds when they traveled to places where they were a persecuted minority. But here in Hanassa, where one of their own ruled, the tribe had become lazy.

Silence except for the small rustlings of creatures who belonged down here and the subtle shift of rock and dirt.

The hair on the back of his neck stood up, and his stomach lurched in apprehension. "Kardiaquake coming," he warned the others, grabbing a wall well clear of the gate.

Powwell and Yaala pressed themselves against the wall of solid rock beside him. Interestingly, Yaala faced the rock while he and Powwell instinctively faced outward so they could watch for falling hazards and dodge them if necessary. He edged closer to Yaala so that he could shove her away from danger if necessary.

The ground beneath his feet seemed to roll. The corridor wall across from him rippled. Then quiet descended. He waited for the crash of a passageway collapsing. A few rocks rolled together, nothing bigger.

"How'd you know about that?" Powwell asked, pushing

himself away from the wall. He touched Yaala's shoulder gently as a signal for safety.

"I was listening for evidence of the guards. I heard the shift in the kardia," Rollett replied, still listening to the kardia for an aftershock.

"If we could maintain a light listening trance, we could predict all of the kardiaquakes. We could awe the populace into obeying us rather than Piedro." Powwell bit his lower lip and ran his hand through his hair in thought.

"Takes too much energy without a dragon or ley lines. I've tried it," Rollett dismissed the notion. "Come on. We've wasted enough time. Let's see what Piedro is up to."

When they had passed through the gate and closed it behind them, Yaala pulled a new 'mote from her inside tunic pocket. How many did she have? "When you use magic to open a lock, you just move the inside pieces around until they fit a pattern that releases it. Right?"

Puzzled, Rollett looked to Powwell. How did she know so much about the process of magic? He thought those secrets were kept from mundanes. Powwell shrugged and grimaced.

"Correct," Rollett replied, looking over Yaala's shoulder as she flipped open the black casing with a tool she kept hidden in a pouch tied to her waist.

"That's what a key does. And that's what a 'mote does." Yaala fussed with the insides a little. "So what we have to do is make the closure a puzzle."

"Rovers are canny with puzzles. They don't think in straight lines," Rollett said, watching her closely.

"If I reverse the polarity, and retune the resonance . . ."

Rollett felt more than heard a high-pitched hum in the back of his head. He tried duplicating it in the back of his throat. Too deep. He moved the vibration higher into his sinuses. Closer.

"There. Now we can open the gate with this 'mote and only this one, but Piedro will probably exhaust himself trying to manipulate the lock with magic and there is no mechanical keyhole.

"Will the wands the guards used to carry work on it?" Powwell ran his fingertips over the metal plate that housed the lock. A faint red aura followed his hand.

"Not anymore. They are tuned differently." Yaala pock-eted the 'mote and marched up the corridor with quick, decisive steps.

Rollett had to stretch his stride to catch up to her. He hadn't had time to fix the exact pitch of the hum in his mind.

At the junction, Rollett paused. He wanted to dash into the Justice Hall and confront Piedro but knew that course would only lead to more trouble than he could handle.

"Storeroom first," he mouthed. His two comrades fol-lowed him up the slope to the site of last night's ambush.

The room echoed emptily. If any foodstuffs had been stored here, they were gone now. Someone had even wiped the room clean of remnant aura traces. No telling who had been here and who hadn't.

He closed down his magic senses quickly, ruthlessly con-serving his energy.

Silently he motioned the others to follow him. At the junction again, Yaala stepped into the dead-end tunnel. "Dead end," Rollett whispered. He waved her back along the main corridor.

"Hidden staircase behind a door. I can open the door with your 'mote," she returned.

"Next trip. I need to see what is happening among the guards first." Rollett clamped down on his curiosity. Every-thing of import happened in the Justice Hall. Everyone in the city passed through there at some point of almost every day.

"I think you need to see what is up there," Yaala replied, stepping resolutely into the corridor.

"Wait, Yaala," Powwell said as he chased after her. His aura seemed to detach from him and follow like a ghost. The wraith?

Stargods! Was the wraith trying to steal Powwell's body?

Then Rollett paused and smiled. The wraith was Kalen, Powwell's sister, almost his alter ego. That meant that Ha-nassa was in Kalen's body, the consort. He knew he'd never trusted the veiled woman for more reasons than the obvi-ous. Kalen was immature, self-centered, manipulative, and sneaky. A prime candidate for the renegade dragon to use.

"We're supposed to stay together!" Rollett rushed to keep up.

"Then follow me. I know what I'm doing." Yaala threw the last words over her shoulder as a challenge.

Gritting his teeth, Rollett marched behind her that last two dozen paces to the dead end. He searched the apparently blank wall with all of his senses and found nothing. Powwell shrugged at him in confusion. He probably couldn't find anything there either.

Yaala grinned at him in sarcastic triumph as she held up a 'mote and pointed it at the top right corner of the end wall.

Slowly the rocks behind him groaned and protested. The noise became louder as rust and inertia fought with the overwhelming command of the 'mote.

Rollett resisted the urge to cross himself. Yaassima could have hidden any number of dead bodies behind that stone door.

Instead, the weak light from the corridor behind them revealed a narrow staircase that wound upward. "How far up does it go?" he asked when he'd found the nerve to speak again. A tiny bit of respect replaced some of his distrust of her.

"Nearly to the top of the crater wall," Yaala replied, setting her foot on the first step.

"I've seen small openings up there. I thought they were windows to parts of the palace." Rollett followed her as closely as he could without stepping on her.

"Windows, yes. But this is the only entrance to that part of the palace. I don't know that Yaassima knew of the treasure hidden up there."

"Treasure? Don't let Piedro or his people hear about this or we'll be dead in a moment for the knowledge." This time Rollett did cross himself. Piedro's greed for power would kill the entire city. In the Rover culture, money and jewels represented power to be hoarded.

"Not this treasure."

Yaala paused for breath on the first landing, fifteen steps above the corridor. At the next landing, twenty steps above the first, the passage narrowed. Rollett had to slide up the steps sideways. At the fourth landing they all bent double, gasping for breath in the rarified air.

And then finally, after the sixth landing, sunlight filtered down from the top.

Rollett squeezed past Yaala to greet the refreshing light of dawn. Dazzle-blinded at first by the natural light after the dim stairwell, he couldn't see anything beyond the five narrow windows cut into the stone walls. His magic sensed openness around him. He closed his eyes and let the light bathe him a few moments. Then, slowly, he opened them again to better awareness of his surroundings.

"Books!" Powwell gasped from behind him.

"Almost as many books as the library back at the University," Yaala said. "This is the true legacy of Hanassa."

Chapter 24

*Early morning the next day, queen's solar, Palace
Reveta Tristile, Coronnan City*

"**N**imbulan, Scarface, I need Bessel to escort me into
the country on a quest," Queen Maarie Kaathliin
said to her dear friend and the Senior Magician. She had
summoned them to her private solar at first light. Now the
sun hovered barely an hour above the horizon. She couldn't
wait any longer to counter her father's manipulations. Dis-
covery of the ring that had nearly choked Marilell had been
followed closely by the diplomatic crises over the death of
Ambassador Jorghe-Rosse. Katie had spent the entire next
day with Quinnault and his Council investigating the incident. They had concluded the accident and death were caused
by the storm.

Now she had to take action to end Kinnsell's manipulations for his own gain. She had no doubt the kidnapping
attempt was tied to her father's quest to become the next
emperor of the Terran Galactic Empire.

The Rover ring that had nearly killed Marilell could have
slipped off his hand or he could have put it there deliberately. He loved exotic jewelry and picked up new trinkets
wherever he traveled. Kinnsell was perfectly capable of kidnapping his own granddaughter and using her as hostage
to his ambitions.

"Bessel may not leave the confines of Myrilandel's
home," Scarface replied. He looked steadily at the wall
behind Katie's right shoulder rather than at her.

"Look at me and tell me that," Katie demanded. She

didn't like acting the authoritative queen among her friends, but Scarface had ceased acting like a friend several moons ago.

The Senior Magician glanced briefly at her face then turned his gaze back to the wall. "Bessel is under suspicion for several crimes. He may not leave Myrilandel's home until my investigation is complete, Your Grace."

"Then release him to my custody." Only Bessel would do. He was the only young magician left who had begun his training with Nimbulan; the only magician she trusted to be uninfluenced by Scarface's surly attitude. Scarface was so like her father when he needed to control everything and everyone around him.

She needed Nimbulan to pressure Scarface into giving his permission for Bessel to join her. Nimbulan seemed the only man left who could influence Scarface. If a way existed for the king and Council of Provinces to oust the Senior Magician, Katie could not find it in the written laws of the land. The Commune was independent from the government. They had to work with Scarface no matter how stubborn and prejudiced he became.

"Impossible. I will not release Bessel from confinement until this matter is settled," Scarface replied, just as authoritative as she. And just as inflexible.

"Nothing is impossible. I need that journeyman and only him." She'd be damned if she'd explain herself to the Senior Magician. Of late, his good-natured ability to organize and lead had turned sour and demanding. What was wrong with him? One would almost think that the Commune and University resisted his control. . . .

Hmm. Maybe. Something to think about. Later.

"The only reason Bessel remains alive and in Coronnan is because *I* have granted him probation until my investigation is complete," Scarface continued. "He worked rogue magic. By law he may not leave his sanctuary until judgment is handed down."

Katie looked to Nimbulan for confirmation. He nodded the truth of his replacement's statement. Scarface only looked more sour and determined to defy her. Very well, she'd maneuver around the Senior Magician and his blasted Commune.

"Bessel has knowledge that I require. I will interview him." And then convince Quinnault to grant him a pardon if necessary to keep him close to her on her quest. Powwell would have been a better choice, he had actually lived the dragon dream with them. But he had disappeared the day after the dragon dream. Yaala had never returned to court from Myrilandel's clearing last winter. Presumably, she followed Powwell (or led him) into Hanassa.

Frustration gnawed at Katie. If she knew her father, she hadn't much time to thwart his plans. She couldn't do anything while cooped up here at court. And she dared not venture out without the protection of at least one magician. Was frail Old Lyman hearty enough to ride with her?

"Then, I fear, Your Grace, you must wait until I have completed my investigation to interview him," Scarface replied. He looked as if he intended to stalk out of the solar without waiting for permission to withdraw from the royal presence.

"You'd best hurry your investigation, then. I intend to ride on my mission within the hour with Bessel at my side."

"At your own risk, madam." Scarface deigned to glance briefly at her, then back at the wall behind her left shoulder.

Katie tilted her head in question but didn't dignify the remark with words.

Scarface sighed and then explained. "Bessel is out of control."

"I thought he exercised admirable control," Katie remarked. "His testimony in Council yesterday was most concise and logical." She needed to draw Scarface out, get him to say something, anything, that would give her a clue as to why he had become so implacable of late. Then she'd know how to appeal to his better judgment and have him release the journeyman magician.

"You cannot know, Your Grace, the evil in the power that tempts him."

"Explain it to me, then."

Scarface shuddered deeply. Then he looked to the door and to Nimbulan for some kind of reprieve. Resignedly, he turned back to Katie.

"Imagine, if you can, being forced to watch renegade

soldiers torturing your closest family for information they did not have. Imagine yourself bound and gagged by magic so powerful you cannot even close your eyes to the carnage wrought in the name of justice. Then picture the glee on the faces of those same magicians as they revel in the pain of their victims, draw power from their screams of agony. And nothing could stop them except another magician more powerful than they. These magicians forced me to become a Battlemage. As soon as I had enough power to escape them, I ran to Hanassa to become a mercenary rather than continue to wreck havoc in their employ. Nothing could control the terror these men brought to Kardia Hodos until the dragons blessed us with their magic. Dragon magic allows—no, demands—that many magicians with honor in their souls combine their powers and amplify them beyond the dreams of the most powerful solitary magicians and control them. I must control Bessel. I must control all solitary magicians who attempt to bring down the Commune."

"Don't you mean that the Commune must control those who attempt to bring down the Commune?" Katie raised her eyebrows and stared at Scarface, daring him to countermand her.

Scarface did not look away as he spoke again. "I lead the Commune. The responsibility for its failures and its successes are mine."

"Bessel is one young man who respects both you and the Commune," Nimbulan protested. "He would never . . . ."

"He used rogue magic once. He will use it again. The lure of the ley lines is addicting. He will learn to fear the Commune because we must prevent him from tapping illegal sources of power. With fear comes hatred and the need to destroy. I have seen the pattern before." Scarface sighed deeply as if Bessel's one action was a deep personal insult.

"The Commune can control Bessel. He is more valuable as an ally than an enemy," Nimbulan argued.

"I have no choice. The young man must remain in his sanctuary or be declared a fugitive from justice, subject to immediate execution by any who can capture him."

"I have requested an interview with Bessel as part of the investigation, Master Aaddler. I am your queen. You may interpret that request as an order." By invoking his true name, Katie hoped to force him to answer. She'd use every trick at her disposal to have Bessel as her escort, but she wouldn't stoop to reading Scarface's mind, even if she were able to penetrate his personal armor—which she doubted she could.

Scarface merely stared at the wall, not intimidated in the least by her.

Nimbulan stared at Scarface, jaw slightly agape. Then he closed it with an audible click of his teeth. The silent tension among them grew almost like a living thing that squeezed the air out of the room.

"I will bring Bessel to you, Your Grace," Nimbulan said defiantly.

"I could force you into exile for violating the law of the Commune," Scarface snarled at Nimbulan.

"No, you can't. I'm not a magician anymore."

For the first time since he'd lost his magic, Nimbulan didn't shrink from admitting it. Katie wanted to applaud him.

"You have taken binding oaths. Be warned, Nimbulan, you are in contempt of the Commune. Both you and Bessel had best watch yourselves." Scarface stalked out without even bowing to his queen. "I refuse Bessel permission to leave his sanctuary. If he flees my authority, he announces to one and all his guilt in the matter of Ambassador Jorghe-Rosse's death. If he steps outside of Myrilandel's home, he is fugitive," he added as he disappeared through the doorway.

"Is there any way I can have that man demoted to the scullery?" Katie asked.

"Not without a major mutiny within the Commune," Nimbulan replied with a smile that more closely resembled a grimace. His skin looked too pale, almost clammy. She knew from experience he'd never admit to pain.

"I don't know what has gotten into Scarface. He used to be so pleasant to work with," she said rather than acknowledge infirmity in stalwart Nimbulan.

"Responsibility weighs heavily on Scarface's shoulders. Guilt, too, I guess. His past is full of contradictions."

"Enough of that man, Nimbulan. I need your journeyman on this mission."

"Does this have something to do with the dragon dream you had Shayla impose upon us last autumn?"

"Yes, it does." How much more did she dare reveal to him? Telling him her father's plans for bringing Kardia Hodos into the Terran Empire felt very much like betrayal of her family. But her family as a whole would not accept Kinnsell's actions. Surely her brothers could see through their father's plans and intervene?

And after that? Though her heart ached to hold Liam Francis, Sean Michael, and Jamie Patrick close against her heart one more time, she knew she had to give them up.

She had come to Kardia Hodos hoping for safety from the plague. She had found love and friendship beyond her hopes.

She couldn't help but smile at her love for Quinnault which grew daily beyond her wildest expectation.

"Scarface has sent all of the magicians who came to the Commune as my friends into retirement. My journeymen and apprentices have been dispatched on meaningless quests and never returned. Now he condemns Bessel without trial for an offense that Scarface himself is guilty of." Nimbulan bowed his head sadly.

"What?"

"Yes." Nimbulan nodded. "I don't know how or why, but Scarface was in deep communion with rogue magic at the time of the storm. He couldn't have sensed Bessel's tapping a ley line otherwise. And there was something strange about that storm. . . ."

"Could Scarface have manipulated the storm for reasons we cannot guess?"

"Possibly. He wants to exile or execute Bessel without a trial, but that seems very out of character considering the story he just told us. Something strange is going on here. We must watch him very carefully." Nimbulan paused while he looked out the window. "I presume you need a magician as bodyguard on this quest of yours?"

"Yes."

"Bessel is threatened by both the Commune and Rossemeyer. I will defy Scarface and send the boy with you. But he is not a strong magician. You need someone else as well."

"Someone I trust, and I no longer trust anyone under Scarface's influence."

"Myrilandel does not use her magic often, but she is strong when she needs to be. With the diplomatic immunity you granted her, she may use her solitary magic to protect you."

"I couldn't take her away from you, Nimbulan."

"Then I must go with you as well. Amaranth is old enough to be left with some trusted friends. The cheese maker in our market square has many children of her own and always welcomes Amaranth into her household. How long will we be gone?"

"I don't know. A few hours, perhaps a day or two." Her father wouldn't have parked his shuttle very far from the capital. He didn't enjoy walking and hated riding steeds.

"Is your husband in agreement with your plan? And what of your young daughter, Queen Maarie Kaathliin?"

"My husband will agree when he learns you will join us. I just wish he could come, too. I need his strength and clear sight where my emotions might get the better of me." One of them had to stay with Marilell, to protect her from Kinnsell or whoever threatened her.

"Now is not a good time for Quinnault to be absent from the capital. Leave the expedition with me. I will make the arrangements and see to it that Scarface gives Bessel permission to leave the city. Do you know which direction we will travel?"

"We head south, I think."

"Just what are we searching for?"

"Once before, many generations ago, three O'Hara brothers came to Kardia Hodos and cured a virulent disease. I just hope my brothers can arrive in time to prevent the next plague."

* * *

Early morning, the hidden library in Hanassa's palace

"Books, the knowledge of the ages," Rollett whispered, too awestruck to raise his voice. He reached a tentative hand to brush his fingertips across the spine of the nearest volume.

The faintest whisper of power tingled against his skin.

"Books," Powwell repeated. He rushed into the room and started reading titles. He pulled volume after volume from the shelves. Dust rose in massive swirls like columns of smoke.

Rollett choked back a cough. Powwell barked from deep in his lungs, stirring the dust into a wilder storm.

"Have you read these books?" Rollett asked Yaala.

"I . . . ah . . . I don't know how to read. Yaassima didn't think it a skill I would find valuable. But the last engineer taught me to read diagrams. Each engineer has passed on the knowledge of this library to his successor." She pulled a tall volume from a shelf just to the right of the entrance—easily grabbed by a person who had only a stolen moment to get in and get out. She opened the well-worn book to a page in the middle. Lines snaked around the pages in geometric patterns. At certain intervals blobs and crosses indicated something important. Yaala traced the pattern with her finger.

"This is a circuit board inside one of the 'motes."

Rollett looked at her blankly.

"The lines are wires. This is a resistor, and this a switch," she explained, pointing out the various symbols. "This diagram is greatly magnified so I can learn the exact pattern and find broken places in the 'mote."

"Look, Rollett, this is an herbal remedy book compiled by Kimmer—he's the scribe who wrote so many of the books in the University library." Powwell thumbed through the small volume quickly. "And this is a . . . *Stargods!* This is a journal of one of the Stargods. In the original hand! Do you know how valuable this information is? We have to get these books back to the University."

"No!" Yaala protested, much too loudly. "These books are *mine*. Hanassa stole them from the Stargods along with the machines and willed them to his descendants. They are mine!"

"To what purpose?" Powwell returned angrily. "The books serve no one but you, and you can't even read. The world needs this information."

"The books remain here, protected and secure. The only people who can come here revere the books. They don't burn or ban them." Yaala faced him, hands on hips, lips pursed in determination.

Rollett stared at her a moment, struck by the intensity of her commitment.

"Who is burning and banning books?" Rollett asked.

"No one," Powwell answered.

"Scarface has talked in the Council of Provinces about putting certain books behind locked doors to keep the knowledge contained within them from falling into the wrong hands," Yaala answered. "He'll destroy them, mark my words, I know that man. He'll destroy anything he can't control. I will never allow him to control these books."

"These books must remain hidden a while longer," Rollett agreed. He'd discuss ownership of the books with her later. She must see that knowledge and, therefore, the books belonged to all. "We can't move this many books until we know how we are going to escape Hanassa." *If we escape Hanassa.* "We have to scout the city better, we have to know what we are up against. That is knowledge more immediately valuable than this entire library of collected learning."

I have to save these books as well as my people in the city, Rollett thought to himself.

For this treasure I might agree to stay in Hanassa. With Yaala at his side if she wouldn't yield to him?

That thought brought him up short. He wanted nothing more than to be gone from this city with or without the daughter of the late, unlamented Yaassima. But if he opened the city to the outside world, then the library would be available to all magicians, priests, and healers. He could rule the library—but he'd have to rule Hanassa as well.

The image of Yaala standing by his side, helping him govern, kept replacing the image of him presiding over the library. He pushed it aside, concentrating on the here and now. He had to depose the current ruler of Hanassa and make an escape route—or open an entrance.

"Let's go find out what Piedro is up to." He turned his back on the wonderful treasure and marched back down the turret stair. When he reached the first landing, he heard

Yaala's and Powwell's footsteps following him sluggishly—reluctantly?

Back in the main corridor, Rollett waited for his companions to catch up. He noted a rectangular book-sized bulge in Powwell's tunic, right below the pocket occupied by Thorny. Rollett decided to ignore the theft temporarily.

A little farther along, they found the wall of tapestries that hid the side entrance to the Justice Hall. The last time Rollett had been through this doorway, he'd led a dozen men on a raid. How many of them had survived the trap laid by Piedro?

He held back an obscene tapestry while Powwell poked his head and his magic sense through the doorway. The younger man stopped short, gagging.

"What?" Yaala pushed her way past him. She turned back to Rollett, eyes wide, throat working convulsively, skin pale and sweating.

Rollett swallowed his sudden fear and looked as well. He immediately wished he hadn't.

The severed heads of two of his informers lay atop the raised altar stone, still dripping blood.

Chapter 25

Early morning, the second day after the dark of the moon, in the home of Myrilandel, Ambassador from the Nimbus of Dragons

Bessel slipped out of Myrilandel's house early. He needed to retrieve a few more personal belongings, and he wanted another look in the library. No one had told him he had to stay in the house, just out of Scarface's way, and the day looked too warm and fair to spend it indoors.

After the full day of testifying before the Council of Provinces or being locked in Nimbulan's study reviewing his magical education, both he and Mopsie were ready for some fresh air and exercise.

He'd broken his fast alone on some mixed grains that had stewed into a wonderful cereal overnight. A little dried fruit and thick cream in the bowl had filled his belly nicely. Even Guillia at the University—wonderful cook though she was—didn't have quite the right touch with cereal that Myrilandel did.

Mopsie hadn't liked the cereal, but he'd loved the juicy bone Myri had given him last night, and he'd lapped up a bowl of cream this morning as if he hadn't eaten in a moon or more.

Myri and Nimbulan had stayed up late last night talking over Bessel's report of Scarface's removal of books from library circulation, the investigation of Jorghe-Rosse's death, Scarface's increasingly fanatical policies, and the seeming absence of the dragons. Myrilandel had commented that the dragons still spoke to her but from a great distance.

They gave no explanation for wandering farther afield than usual in their hunting. Bessel hadn't been able to stay awake until they came to some conclusion. He presumed they still slept this morning. He and Mopsie had had the kitchen to themselves.

The dog ran a little ahead of Bessel and back again along the road. "Are you scouting ahead for me, Mopsie?" The dog wiggled his hind end and extended his pink tongue in a happy grin. Bessel drew a scent picture from the dog's mind of all the other dogs who had passed this way, piddling on appropriate marking spots. He was amazed at the varied information carried with each scent. "You are a terrible gossip, Mopsie."

The dog agreed and ran off again.

They headed away from Ambassador Jorghe-Rosse's home. The trip to the University would take at least half an hour longer this way, but Bessel wasn't about to risk attracting the attention of the vindictive warriors again. He hoped Lady Rosselaara had accepted the Council's verdict of death by accident.

The city came to life as they walked. Merchants emerged from their homes setting up booths along the major thoroughfares. Smells of cooking meats, baking bread, and stewing fruits tantalized Bessel. Mopsie enhanced each scent and noise for him. Bessel's other senses of sight and touch amplified as well. He turned circles as he walked, appreciating life as he hadn't in many years.

Mopsie licked his chops and stopped to sniff at the butcher's tent.

"Sorry, pup, I can't afford to buy you a bone today. You've eaten well enough for now." He scratched the dog's ears in compensation for the lack of another treat. As a journeyman magician, he was entitled to a small allowance, payable at the full moon, his portion of the fees paid for services the Commune as a whole gave the public. He'd spent most of his savings on a special crystal for his favorite small wand. Magical tools and healing herbs were the only expenses he should have. The University supplied everything else.

Would he still be a magician come the next full moon and payday?

Mopsie growled a warning. Bessel stopped in his tracks, seeking the source of danger.

Smoke. He smelled fresh hot smoke, uncontrolled and spreading. Where?

Just ahead, thick black smoke roiled out of the carpenter's shop. People gathered to gawk and scream and stand in the way of those who sought to escape the fire.

"Water!" Bessel cried. He grabbed a burly man by the shoulders and shook him out of his staring panic. "Bring water. Form a line with buckets. You know how to do this."

The man blinked his eyes clear of panic and confusion, then nodded his understanding. He grabbed a bucket from the nearby blacksmith and headed for the river. Other men followed. The women brought blankets and soothing salves for the carpenter and his family. Everyone moved quickly, organized—once the trance of panic was broken.

King Quinnault, before these people had made him king, had drilled them in simple ways to defend their homes from attack. Fire had been a favorite weapon during the Great Wars of Disruption.

Bessel took a place in the line of bucket bearers. A team at the river filled any available vessel with water and passed them up the line to the fire.

Three men, garbed in black with trim of bright purple and teal blue, stood to the side watching through hooded eyes. Their dark hair and tanned skin hinted of exotic breeding. Rovers? They leaned casually against the wall of the weaver's shop. But their stance told of wariness.

As one, they heaved themselves away from the wall and approached the carpenter.

Leery of the men's intent, Bessel opened his senses to them. Mopsie crept closer to the men, adding his keener hearing to Bessel's.

"Remember what happens to people who don't pay up," one of the black-clad men whispered to the carpenter.

"The king's guards will protect us," the carpenter protested.

"Who do you think we bribe with your money?" the men replied, laughing. "Spread the word to your neighbors. Ten dragini each moon and we won't burn you out. Another five at quarter day festivals and we keep the tax collector from darkening your door."

"But the tax is only two drageen each quarter day!" the carpenter wailed.

The men just laughed and strolled away.

A chill ran down Bessel's back. He needed to tell someone about this dangerous racket. But who? As a magician, he should report directly to Scarface. The Senior Magician wouldn't listen to him. Nor could Bessel get close to the king. And the king's guards seemed to be in the pay of the extortionists.

Who? Maybe Nimbulan had enough influence to get to the root of the problem. Later. The old man needed and deserved his sleep.

What could he do? Throw a truth spell on the culprits for the name of their leader. But then what? He didn't have the resources to tackle the gang on his own. He also needed time and privacy to work the truth spell. The gaudily clad men wandered through the marketplace, keeping well within the crowds.

Puzzled and wary, Bessel moved along in his quest to get to the library. The locals had the fire well in hand, they didn't need him now.

No one seemed to heed his leaving the line of bucket bearers. As if he'd never been there.

"You'll have to be quiet in the library, Mopsie. We're going to retrieve a couple of forbidden books. I hope they will answer my questions. I need to know more about invisibility spells and about navigating the Great Bay, as well as more about the plague." He added Rovers to his list of subjects to investigate. If the despised wanderers did lead the extortion racket, how did they get into Coronnan through the magical border and why hadn't they been arrested before this?

Didn't Nimbulan, and therefore, his cousin Lord Balthazaan, have Rover blood in their ancestry? That was how Nimbulan had been able to work Rover magic the season he lived with Televarn's clan. Rumor placed a number of Rover-bred retainers in Balthazaan's entourage. Their magic depended upon a common link in their blood. If a person with Rover blood in his heritage stood on one side of the border, could he link with Rovers on the other side of the magic wall to negate the protective barrier? Bessel filed that idea away for later examination along with the possibility of Rover criminals terrorizing Coronnan City.

Back to his primary concerns. Raanald, the barge pilot, hadn't trusted the depth finder. Either his distrust or a malfunction in the machine had led to disaster. There had to be a better way to navigate the mudflats of the inner bay, even in storms and shifting channels.

Mopsie yipped an agreement with him. He sent Bessel a mind picture of a sleek water dog standing in the prow of a fishing boat again.

"I'm sure you'd have been a big help, Mopsie." Bessel swallowed his chuckle. His image of the long ropes of Mopsie's curls soaked and matted by salt water on the short-legged body didn't quite match the dog's view of himself.

"Dust mop, indeed," Bessel muttered as he noted Mopsie's fur brushing the packed dirt of the road. "You'll need another bath tonight, and every night."

Mopsie tucked his tail between his legs and drooped his floppy ears. Yesterday, Bessel had to carry the dog into the sunken stone bathtub with him. The dog wouldn't go near the water otherwise. "If you hate baths so much, how come you think you belong in a boat on the Bay?"

Mopsie just wiggled his entire behind along with his stubby tail.

They crossed the first bridge. Mopsie stopped in the center of the span and looked longingly at the churning River Coronnan below. "Not this time, pup. We haven't time to take a swim today. It isn't warm enough either." Spring might have come, but the river was fed by snow melt deep in the mountains to the west. Bessel only enjoyed swimming in high summer when the chilly water was a refreshing change from the sultry weather.

As he hopped down the step at the end of the bridge, Bessel fingered the linchpin hidden beneath the railing. In case of invasion, all of the bridges connecting the myriad islands of Coronnan City could be collapsed as the inhabitants retreated inward to the palace and University. Invaders would have to resort to boats to follow them.

This linchpin had been oiled recently. Maintaining the

release mechanism was one of the duties of the Guild of Bay Pilots. The Commune made a practice of checking their diligence frequently.

The next bridge showed signs of rust on the linchpins on both ends. Bessel paused to look closer to see how neglected the mechanism was. He didn't pay any attention to the foot traffic going in both directions across the span.

Then Mopsie barked a serious warning. The dog tugged at the hem of his trews then nipped him lightly on the calf. "What is it, Mopsie?" Bessel glanced up from his inspection, looking for another fire.

The dog kept tugging him away from the bridge.

"I am duty bound to inform you that you die here and now so that you may know I am the instrument of justice!" A black-robed warrior ran toward him, vorpal sword raised.

Chapter 26

Early morning, the streets of Coronnan City

Bessel ran. He ducked and dodged through the crowded marketplace. The assassin from Rossemeyer followed close on his heels.

Why was it that when he wanted to be noticed, especially by the Commune, no one seemed to know he was in the room, but now, when he desperately needed to hide, an assassin spotted him easily in this large milling crowd?

People screamed and ran in illogical directions as the assassin cursed and brandished his weapon. Bessel used the confusion to put a human barrier between himself and the black-clad warrior. Desperately, he overturned crates of tubers. The hard vegetable balls scattered and rolled, tripping several of the running cityfolk.

And still the assassin followed, sword raised and ready. "Single-minded wild tusker," Bessel mumbled as he ran around a cart piled high with cone roots. He snatched two as he ran and tucked them away for a snack later. He'd need the sugars to replace energy depleted by running and any magic he had to throw to save himself.

At the candle maker's booth, a little girl stood in the middle of the path, frozen in place. She screamed her fear. Bessel stumbled to avoid bowling her over.

The assassin gained three paces before Bessel recovered his balance. The point of the man's sword slashed the back of Bessel's tunic.

Fear gave him new energy and a burst of speed. He reached the next bridge. Without thinking of the consequences, he pulled the linchpin the moment he and Mopsie cleared the last span. The bridge collapsed into the river.

The warrior had magnificent reflexes. He clung to the handrail, pulling himself along it until he reached the ropes that remained connected to the support posts on Bessel's end of the bridge. Then he proceeded to shinny up the rope, the sword now clutched in his teeth.

"Stargods, even the river doesn't slow him down." Bessel took off again. He had to cross only two more bridges to reach University Isle. He'd find refuge there. No one, not even an assassin from Rossemeyer, would follow a magician into the enclave of the Commune.

All Bessel needed was one other magician within reach. Once they made physical contact, the magic within both of them would amplify and grow. They could erect defensive spells to repel the warrior and his lethal sword.

If he reached the University in time.

Alone, he didn't have a chance of gathering enough magic to throw an effective spell.

Before Bessel had run one hundred paces, the warrior regained solid ground. Water dripped from his heavy robes. He grabbed them with his free hand, keeping the wet cloth from tangling his legs.

Mopsie yipped from the doorway of a ramshackle tavern. Safety? Bessel followed his familiar, trusting him with his life.

The dimly lit common room was nearly empty at this time of day. A dozen plank tables stretched the length and breadth of the open space, with little room to walk between.

Mopsie scooted beneath them, toward the back corner. Bessel dropped to all fours and followed. Deep in the shadowy corner a small metal grate was set into the wall next to the floor. Most of the older buildings on the islands had these primitive drainage gates. In winter and in times of high water, they were shuttered both inside and out. In summer, open grates offered some air circulation. After a flood, the grate would allow water to drain from the building. Some industrious city dwellers used the grates as a drain after washing slate or tile floors.

The tavern owner had unlatched the grate and swept

refuse through it into the common midden in the back alley. He hadn't refastened the bolts. A buildup of rust on the latches would make locking them difficult.

Mopsie paused only long enough for Bessel to push the grate up. The dog darted through just as the assassin entered the tavern. Bessel didn't linger.

Rusty latches scraped his arms as he wiggled and twisted through the small opening. His slashed tunic caught on imperfections in the metal frame. He heard it rip more as he squeezed his shoulders into the open.

His butt stuck. Curse those extra portions of sweet yampion pie and candied cone roots Guillia heaped on hungry magicians.

Someone clamped a heavy hand on Bessel's boot. He didn't wait to see who. Ignoring scrapes and bruises, he pushed through the opening, leaving his boot behind.

Limping, Bessel sprinted to the next bridge, collapsed it before crossing, and ran for a different one half an island away. He didn't wait to see if the assassin fell for his decoy.

His detour took him onto Palace Isle. He aimed for the palace gate, hoping the guards would protect him. Today was open petitions in court. Anyone could walk into or out of the Great Hall without notice. All of the guards were inside. He didn't have time to dive into the crowds and demand protection from King Quinnault.

And the king might have decided to bow to diplomatic pressure from Rossemeyer and declare him guilty.

Bessel cursed his ill luck and continued to the old causeway. Centuries of high tides and winter storms had almost completed the work of separating Palace Isle from University Isle. Mopsie leaped across the first break in the stepping stones with no hesitation. Bessel followed his familiar, again trusting the dog's instincts for good footing. Jagged rocks cut his bare foot, but he continued on, knowing his only refuge from the assassin was with the Commune.

Shouts and hurried footsteps told him the warrior with the drawn sword hadn't been fooled by the decoy for long.

"Help me!" Bessel cried, panting for breath as he jumped the last few feet onto University Isle. "Masters of the Commune, help me. Help a fellow magician!" He added a little magic to speed his cry to the proper ears. His talent barely responded. All of his energy went into running for the safety of the buildings.

Scarface stepped into the main entryway, arms crossed, face grim, eyes nearly closed with some carefully contained emotion. "What are you doing here?" he asked.

"An assassin from Rossemeyer is after me. I need your protection," Bessel panted as he skidded to a halt in front of the Senior Magician. He bent double trying to catch his breath.

"You were told to stay with Nimbulan." Scarface made a solid barrier in front of the door and sanctuary.

"I forgot some of my things." Bessel looked anxiously over his shoulder. The assassin stalked across the new bridge that connected University Isle to the Palace. He carried his sword lightly. A triumphant smile split his dark face.

"I'm a member of the Commune. You must protect me, Senior Magician Aaddler!"

"You are but a journeyman, not a full member of the Commune. I have decreed you exiled from the Commune until the issue of your use of rogue magic is resolved. Protect yourself." Scarface whirled and slammed the door in Bessel's face.

* * *

Palace Reveta Tristile courtyard, early morning

"May I help you mount your steed, Your Grace?" King Quinnault asked his queen, tugging his forelock and bowing deeply, like any of the stable hands who might have offered the same service.

"What do you think you are doing, Scarecrow?" Katie whispered to him. She tugged on his cupped hands, trying to get him to stand upright.

"I'm helping my wife mount her steed. And a noble steed it is, even if it is barely big enough to mount a child," he replied with a grin. The king's matching white steed stood nearby, head and shoulders taller than the queen's mount.

"But you're dressed for riding. And Buan is saddled and anxious for a hard run." She eyed the beast's restless feet, as big as dinner platters and unmindful of any human appendage that might get beneath him.

"I'm going with you, love."

"Please don't do this to me, Scarecrow. You've got to stay and find a solution to Lady Rosselaara's demands. And . . . and we can't leave Marilell alone. I don't trust anyone."

"I'm only going as far as Myrilandel's house with you. Then I'll come back and search the laws and old treaties for a precedent that will placate the widow. And I'm bringing the baby with me." He gestured at the maid who stood near the doorway with the squirming princess firmly clasped in her arms. A full escort of guards waited beside her, also ready to ride.

"I can't take all those guards with me. I need secrecy. You know what my father is like, what technology he controls. We can't let these men see it."

Quinnault's face took on the closed, emotionless look she knew too well. His stubborn face. No sense in arguing with him. Short of a full-scale invasion within the next ten minutes, he'd not change his mind. She couldn't change it for him, even if she used her telepathy.

"Maarie Kaathliin, the absence of an armed escort while you ride about the country is a clear signal that something special occurs. I won't let you go alone."

"I'm going for a ride with friends. I don't need an armed escort when I have a magician with me. They will interfere with my mission."

"The armed escort has orders to stay well behind you. They are sworn to secrecy. They have proved their loyalty time and again. I trust them with my life, so should you."

Katie bit her lip. She couldn't think of a single argument to sway him.

"I thought I was meeting Nimbulan, Myri, and Bessel here." Only the two steeds stood in the forecourt. She had expected to have to walk to the mainland stable rather than have the mounts ready for her less than an hour after her interview with Nimbulan and Scarface.

"We'll meet them at their home on the way out of the city. South, you said?" Quinnault bent once more, holding out cupped hands to assist Katie into the saddle.

She placed her left foot into his palms as she grabbed the saddlehorn. She barely had time to swing her right leg over the steed's back to keep from plummeting over it and onto the cobblestones on the other side.

"Easy, Scarecrow!" she gasped as she fought for balance.

"Sorry, love. Your steed is a lot shorter than I'm used to." His grin didn't reach his eyes.

"And I'm shorter than an adolescent child!" Back home, small stature and efficient metabolism were assets in a resource-deprived culture. Here, those qualities made her the butt of many jokes.

But the easy banter didn't break the tension she sensed in him.

"Quinnault, I need to do this privately. My father is dangerous. If your escort even glimpses the nature of his vessel, everything will change . . . for the worse."

He turned to mount Buan in one swift movement, ignoring her comments. Then he reached down to take Marilell from the maid. When the baby sat before him in the saddle, happily cooing, he spoke. "I changed my mind. I'm going with you. We'll leave the baby with Amaranth and her nanny for the day. Safer, I think, than the palace today. You think your father left his conveyance to the south of here?"

"Scarecrow, stay here, please!"

His stubborn face became more intense.

Katie heaved a sigh of resignation. "The land is more wooded and hilly. He'll want to keep his ship hidden. The land north and east of the city is open fields. To the west is open river plains." Shuttle design hadn't changed enough in the last seven hundred years to make the vessel substantially different from the paintings and tapestries depicting the Stargods descending from the heavens in a cloud of silver flame.

If anyone ever associated Kinnsell and his miracle machines with the beloved Stargods, no one would reject Kinnsell's bid for political and economic power through mechanization. And with mechanization would come colonists from the Terran Empire.

The plague would follow in short order. If it hadn't come

already. Most of the plague reports originated in mining villages. Were coal dust and iron filings enough pollution to give the microbe a breeding ground?

She wished she could do this alone. But the medieval culture that didn't depend upon technology and therefore didn't develop a plague breeding ground, demanded that neither she nor Quinnault step beyond the privacy of their bedchamber without an escort.

"Ship? Wouldn't he be on the Bay?" Quinnault asked.

"A different kind of ship than you've ever seen before, Quinnault. It sails through air, not water. And it contains many wonders that mimic magic and go beyond. I'll use those wonders to send a summons spell of sorts to my brothers. They are the only ones who might persuade Kinnsell to leave here before he changes our lives and our culture irrevocably." Hopefully, Jamie Patrick was either aboard or carried communications to the crew of the mother ship. With any luck at all, her two younger brothers might have returned from Terra as well.

Katie dug her heels decisively into the steed's flanks. It fairly leaped forward, speeding through the palace gates.

Quinnault followed close on her heels.

No route through Coronnan City was direct. For reasons of defense, the bridges rarely lined up and never connected three islands directly. Crowded streets on market day presented numerous delays to foot and mounted traffic alike.

"What is that?" Kate pointed to the smoke-blackened remains of a shop that had once held a dwelling above it. Both halves had been gutted. People stood before it, looking lost and bewildered, including a family of five draped in blankets. The father had lost his eyebrows in the fire. The three children sniveled quietly, noses running, eyes blinking rapidly, too cowed by disaster to cry out loud. The mother huddled beneath her blanket, staring blankly, heedless of her husband and children.

"Fire. Happens too often in the city. Wooden buildings, dry thatch, all crowded too close. We're lucky it didn't spread and take out the entire island," Quinnault replied.

Katie bit her lip, needing to stop and comfort the victims. But she didn't have time. Neighbors seemed to have the matter in hand.

"Remind me to send a basket of food and clothing when we return." She looked anxiously at Quinnault.

He nodded abruptly, eyes fixed on something in the burned-out ruins.

"What is it, Quinnault?" Then she saw it. A sigil of warning painted in blood red on the side wall of the building. Soot couldn't obliterate it.

With a gesture, Quinnault sent one of the guards to investigate. "I want a full report when we return. I expect answers and the name of a suspect. This has happened too often," he commanded. "And send the family food, blankets, clothing, whatever they need to get them through until they rebuild." Then he turned his attention back to Katie and his daughter. "Not much farther, love. Nimbulan and Myri live only two isles away."

"Who is sabotaging our city, Quinnault?" But Katie did not need an answer. Only Kinnsell could be so devious. He wanted control of Coronnan even if it meant deposing his own daughter and son-in-law. She couldn't waste any more time finding his shuttle and stopping his campaign. Kinnsell had had most of yesterday and all morning to work his mischief and move his ship.

By the time Katie and Quinnault negotiated the narrow streets, nearly an hour had passed since they'd left the palace. They reined in their steeds before the narrow row house occupied by Ambassador Myrilandel of the Dragon Nimbus and Nimbulan, her consort.

"Where is Bessel?" Katie asked as they reined in before the ambassador's house.

"I haven't seen him all morning," Nimbulan replied. "At first, I thought he'd only taken the dog for a walk but he hasn't returned."

"He and his familiar ate and left early," Myri said, eyeing the large hired steed her husband held for her. "I heard him say something about the library."

"We don't have time to go all the way back to University Isle," Katie fretted. But she needed the magician. Kinnsell would know how to break through any mundane force field she set up around the shuttle to keep him out. She needed Bessel to set a psychic barrier until the O'Hara brothers arrived and removed their father from Kardia Hodos.

"We'll manage without the boy," Nimbulan said, urging Myri toward her mount. "He'll be safe in the library. Even Scarface wouldn't forbid him access to the library."

"I'd rather walk," Myri said with a disdainful look at the hired steed her husband held for her. He hugged her close, and whispered something in her ear.

"You'll be safe. This steed will not throw you."

Myrilandel's hands moved to her belly in an age-old protective gesture.

Could she be . . . ?

No. Nimbulan would have said something in their earlier interview.

"We have to move fast. You won't be able to keep up," Katie said, still eyeing her friend for subtle signs of change in her face and physique.

"Not be able to keep up?" Myri cocked one eyebrow. A grin of mischief twinkled in her eyes. "I have friends in high places, remember?" She cast her gaze upward.

Nimbulan and Quinnault also looked up, scanning for the presence of a dragon.

"Will your dragons help us search?" Katie asked. Her mind kept jerking away from her immediate surroundings, back to her father.

What was Kinnsell up to? Who were his allies? She really needed Bessel's magic to keep Kinnsell from fleeing on the shuttle to someplace neither she nor the dragons could find.

She prayed her brothers would come quickly. Any brother would do who would haul Kinnsell back to the mother ship and home. Preferably Sean Michael. The middle brother showed more responsibility and logic than the other two siblings combined.

"Picture carefully, in full detail, what you search for," Myri instructed. "Rouussin is cruising the Bay and is willing to indulge us." Humor made her mouth twitch. Dragon moods were always unpredictable. Rouussin, the aging red-tipped dragon, tended to view humans as children he could spoil with treasures and treats even though he rarely understood the purposes behind their requests.

Katie sensed the dragon's feather-light mind touch. (*I am with you, Little One.*)

Carefully, Katie built a picture in her memory of a sleek

shuttlecraft like the one that had brought her to Coronnan last year. As long as two dragons, but no higher than one. Stubby wings, pointed nose with a band of windows, like six eyes, above. Tail fins surrounded the engine ports. Last, she remembered to add a silvery metal sheath covered in translucent porcelain scales.

(*That is a strange dragon, indeed, Little One,*) Rouussin chuckled.

A dragon that threatens to go rogue. If we do not find it soon, dragons will no longer have a home on Kardia Hodos. My father will see to that.

Chapter 27

*Near noon two days after the dark of the moon,
Bay Hag Inn, on the south shore of Coronnan
City*

Kinnsell stuffed wads of coarse linen sheet over his ears
to block out the noise. An obnoxious bird announced
the morning repeatedly. Each crow call grew louder than
the last. The bird kept blaring his greeting to the sun with
no signs of tiring of his duty.

He'd wakened and dozed a number of times only to be
roused again, most rudely, by the bird.

A civilized world would have alarm clocks that beeped
gently or played soothing music to bring the sleeper gradually to wakefulness. Or a man as politically powerful and
wealthy as Kinnsell O'Hara would hire a valet to wake him
at a civilized hour.

Dawn was not a civilized hour.

The light filtering through the shuttered window seemed
too bright for dawn. What time was it anyway?

Kinnsell rolled over on the lumpy bed, refusing to open
his eyes. The other side of the narrow straw-stuffed mattress was empty. Barely wider than a ship's berth, the cot
still had plenty of room to share with an intimate friend
when neither one required privacy and touching delighted
rather than offended.

Where was Maia? She had promised to join him when
she finished with the innkeeper.

He glared at the smooth layer of blankets beside him!
Then he threw the covers off the bed and stood up. None

of last night's fatigue and heaviness in his chest lingered. He needed a good breakfast and a hot shower with real water, not the sonic sprays required during space travel.

Then he'd deal with Maia and her disloyalty. If he didn't need the woman as hostage for the bush lord's loyalty, he'd dump her here within easy distance of the capital for the magicians to find her again.

But the bushie was tricky enough to hold Marilell, Kinnsell's granddaughter, hostage as well as his loyalty in return for Maia.

"I should have kidnapped the child myself, rather than trusting any local." But Katie's servants had been on the alert for him. He'd not sneak into or out of the palace easily, where Lord Balthazaan and his wife had free passage through the place.

"Ah, you have arisen at last, Master Kinnsell," Maia said, entering the room with a cloth-covered tray in her hands. She fairly bounced as she walked, and her black eyes sparkled.

"I thought I locked that door," Kinnsell snapped at her.

"You did. But you opened it again for me when I returned to you at midnight. As I promised." Her eyes narrowed seductively. "Then we broke our fast together and you slept again while I moved about the inn, asking questions. I have learned a great deal."

"I bet you have." Kinnsell glanced at the bed. She hadn't slept there. Her scent didn't linger on the sheets, nor were there any stains left by sex. She lied. He gnashed his teeth, wishing he could leave her here. Not yet. But soon, she'd know his revenge.

"I have ordered a hot bath for you, Master Kinnsell. You slept through the one I offered yesterday. It will be ready for you by the time you break your fast." She whipped the cloth off the tray to reveal fresh bread, hot from the oven, salted fish, creamy cheese, and a bowl full of berries that had been dried and reconstituted in a rich sauce that smelled of wine and cloves. His mouth watered.

"Peasant food," he sneered.

Yesterday? Had he slept through an entire day and two nights? Not likely.

His stomach growled its emptiness and then twisted into

an acidic rejection of any food. How long since he'd eaten? A day and two nights?

He couldn't think of food. He had to know how he had lost so much time to sleep. But it smelled delicious, and his stomach grumbled again with hunger.

" 'Tis the same meal ordered every morning by Master Magician Nimbulan and he comes from the most aristocratic of families. He's first cousin to Lord Balthazaan," Maia protested. She stared at the food and then looked up to Kinnsell with troubled eyes. All trace of pleasure left her expression.

"Does everyone on this planet—er, in this country—eat such coarse bread? Can't you mill finer flour than that." Kinnsell wanted to make her squirm under his displeasure even though he longed to grab huge bites of the stuff.

" 'Tis the spent wheat from brewing ale. The king considers this bread a delicacy!" A fat tear rolled down her cheek. She pouted, pursing her lips forward in invitation for him to kiss away her sadness.

Recognizing the ploy of women everywhere—with or without the spell of allure from psi powers—Kinnsell obeyed. Just this once he'd allow her to believe herself in control of their relationship. He brushed away the tear with his fingers and kissed the corner of her mouth. He dropped a second kiss on the enticing mole just to the right of her mouth, then another and another. . . .

Stop this! he ordered himself. "If the king eats this bread, then I will, too," he said breathlessly, wanting to taste more of her. But he must regain control of himself and of her. "See if you can hurry the bath. We must leave as soon as possible," he added less gently.

Maia rewarded him with a brilliant smile. "Soon I will be home, among my own people, and you will be hailed a hero for rescuing me." She kissed him soundly. "I will wash your back," she said with a new huskiness in her voice. "And your front."

Kinnsell swallowed his desire. He hadn't time to linger this morning. He'd lost too much time already. Katie must be frantic over the loss of her daughter.

He wouldn't take Maia to the bushie lord until he'd satiated the burning ache of desire in his gut. His granddaughter was safe. Even the conniving members of the king's Council wouldn't hurt the child, a mere baby and a girl. Now, if Katie had had the good sense to give birth to a son first, the child would be heir and therefore a threat to the rebellious lords.

The bread tasted nutty with a delightful complexity. It satisfied his hunger and settled the too-hungry-sick feeling quite readily. Kinnsell pushed aside the fish. The cheese would have to suffice for protein. Normally he wouldn't eat milk products, but the meal contained no legumes to complete the amino acid chain. The flavor burst on his tongue, promising new delights. The berries in their wine sauce were worthy of a royal banquet back home.

Maybe he'd linger on this planet a little longer, sample the delights of its cuisine—so much better than ship rations and tanked food. Fresh food was, after all, the primary reason for nurturing this planet. He'd also indulge himself with Maia for as long as he wanted. No need to hurry back to Terra and his cold and unloving but politically powerful wife until he'd secured a power base on Kardia Hodos. But he had to check in with the mother ship soon, or they'd send a search party. He didn't need any of his crew— especially his sons—questioning or sabotaging his work to bring this planet back under Terra's influence. Sean Michael and Liam Francis were due back any time now. The boys might even rescue Marilell from Balthazaan before Kinnsell reclaimed her.

He hurried through the bath despite Maia's attempts to climb into the little tub with him. The water didn't stay hot long and the heaviness threatened to return to his chest.

By the time Kinnsell and Maia walked out of the Bay Hag Inn, the sun rode high and raised steam on the damp cobblestones. A spring returned to his step that he hadn't felt in many years. Maia kept up with him, prattling stories about great adventures of the road. Most of her stories centered around the mysterious Televarn, chief of her clan. He tuned her out and concentrated on what to tell the bushie lord and when.

After about two kilometers, they reached the cutoff from the Great South Road. Kinnsell eagerly turned west. "Not far now, my dear," he said with a smile. Within half an hour he'd be back in his shuttle, an island of civilization on this planet of chaos.

Maia stopped abruptly, pressing her temples with anxious fingertips.

"We must go this way." She took two hesitant steps on the Great South Road. "We must hurry. They need us." She dropped her hands and stared blankly toward the south. Her eyes glazed over as if blinded by a trance.

Kinnsell had seen similar reactions to hypnosis. What kind of latent suggestion had the magicians put upon her?

"The clan of Televarn needs us," she chanted. "Televarn is dead. Long live the clan." Two more steps and she fell to her knees.

"Noooooo!" she wailed, pressing her hands to her temples once more. "He can't be dead. If Televarn is dead, then who has been inside my head this year and more? Who directs me?" She cried and tore her hair, still kneeling in the road. "I didn't believe them when the magicians told me Televarn died. I didn't dare believe them because his voice was still inside my head. He murdered the Kaalipha. I saw him do it. I saw him twist the poisoned knife in Yaassima's gut. He has to be alive!"

Kinnsell stared at her gape-mouthed as she pounded the ground with her fists. She stumbled to her feet and started running.

"That is not what happened," Kinnsell grabbed her shoulders, ready to shake some sense into her. He tried to remember the details of the tales told about the events in Hanassa when he'd first brought Katie here a year and a half ago. "Yaassima turned the knife in time and killed Televarn. Yaasaima died later. Now come along, this way," He tried to lift her to her feet. A deep cough made him release her.

"Follow me. We have to go west. We have to get to my ship." The cough passed. Kinnsell grabbed her around the waist and lifted her to her feet. She kicked his shins and bit at his restraining hands, never ceasing her wails and moans of distress.

"Televarn can't be dead! I know they lie to me!"

"Where do we have to go in such a hurry, Maia? Tell me where, and I will take you there in an instant," Kinnsell soothed. He couldn't let her escape now. Not when he was so close to commanding the full loyalty of the bush lords.

"You know the secret of the transport spell?" Maia ceased her struggles so suddenly Kinnsell almost fell forward on top of her.

He shifted his balance and loosened his hold a little. The spurt of activity renewed the tightness in his chest. He held his breath a moment to control the cough. He'd be comfortable and warm as soon as he reached the shuttle. Then the cough would go away. He only felt overheated and chilled at the same time because this damned planet was so bloody cold, without the slightest knowledge of climate control.

"Not a transport spell," he replied when he controlled his breathing once more. He sought a metaphor the woman would understand. "I control a dragon. A very special dragon that lets me hide inside her. She will take us wherever you want to go. But first we have to get to her."

"A dragon!" Maia crossed her wrists, right over left, and flapped her hands in the bizarre ward against evil. Her eyes grew wide with respect and . . . and terror. "You control the renegade dragon, Hanassa?"

"Whatever. Now come along this side path. We have to get to my dragon before she flies away on her own." He doubted Jamie Patrick would order the shuttle returned to the mother ship by remote, but he never knew what his sons might do. One day soon he'd have to beat some discipline into them—as he should have when they were little, but he was too busy courting political favor to bother with children then.

He kept his arm around Maia's waist as they returned the few steps to the barely maintained side path. Deep shadows from overhanging trees cloaked them. Kinnsell shuddered in atavistic fear of the unknown darkness. He kept up a prattle of words to mask his uneasiness. "My dragon will shelter us and give us hot food and drink and comfortable beds until dark. Then she will fly away with us. Anywhere you want to go." *As long as it's to the castle of my bushie lord. Once I show you to him, I'll control the majority of King Quinnault's Council and the king's daughter. I'll direct when and where technology is introduced. And I'll collect tithes from these bushies as well as the rewards*

*of bringing this world back into the fold of Terra's Empire.
None of my relatives stand a chance of winning the election
as emperor once I bring this planet back into the fold.*

"I have never touched a dragon before. But I have seen
one," Maia said, caressing his face with gentle fingers. "I
did not trust the dragon. I could not penetrate her thoughts.
But she touched mine. She blocked out Televarn's voice,
and I did not know what to do without him." Her wonderful hands slid down his back. "You can replace Televarn
in my mind. Your talent is strong, Master Kinnsell. You
can replace Televarn in the minds of all the Rovers. Your
control of the Rovers can extend to all those who have
even a trace of Rover blood in their veins, like Nimbulan
and Lord Balthazaan."

Heat flooded Kinnsell's veins wherever she touched him.
He recognized the subtle psi power and allowed himself to
enjoy her for a moment. Her words brought a smile to
his face as well. His family enjoyed a similar mind-to-mind
contact. But the O'Hara clan had better control, no one
person could remain in the mind of another without permission. These Rovers needed a leader to direct them. Kinnsell
was willing to employ them if they bent to his control as
easily as the rest of this planet. He lengthened his stride.

"You will not be able to penetrate my dragon's thoughts.
Only I can do that," he said, warming to his story. Cyber
controls could be defined as a form of mind-to-mind contact.

The nagging cough returned.

Maia touched his temple with the fingertips of her right
hand and his chest with the flat of her left hand. Heat
radiated from the points of contact. An electric buzz shot
through his veins. The cough eased. She lingered, not releasing her healing touch. His vision narrowed, blotting out
all but Maia. His thoughts focused on her bright beauty.

He raised his hand from her waist to the swell of her
breast. She didn't pull away. He risked opening his palm
to cup her fullness. Her nipple budded tight beneath his
fingertips. His heart beat loudly within his ears, pounding
out a staccato rhythm.

He turned her within his arms and kissed her deeply. She
opened to him, moaning her pleasure. This trip did have
some benefits, after all.

He stepped off the path into the dense underbrush. They could linger a while. No one would find his ship. They had plenty of time before they had to meet the lords at sunset.

"This way!" a feminine voice shouted over the sound of many steeds' hooves pounding the packed dirt of the road. His passion had deafened him to their approach.

Not just any feminine voice commanded this small cavalcade. His daughter, Mary Kathleen O'Hara, led the charge. Led them straight past him along the path that ran only to his shuttle.

*   *   *

Late morning, University Isle, Coronnan City

Bessel wasted one heartbeat of time staring at the door Scarface had just slammed in his face.

The assassin roared in triumph as he dashed across the bridge, sword raised.

"C'mon Mopsie. Let's see if you are truly a water dog." Bessel ran for the nearest river access and dove in.

Mopsie ran for the assassin, growling.

Bessel caught a brief glimpse of the little dog leaping for the man's sword hand. His teeth latched onto the wrist, forcing the assassin to drop his weapon.

Then cold, muddy waters closed over Bessel's head. The swift current pulled him down, down, down.

Bessel let the river current carry him as he swam upward. He shook water from his eyes while he kept his hands and feet moving. He heard another splash and looked back toward the bridge. Mopsie landed in the water in a great spray that dampened the assassin on the bridge.

"Good boy, Mopsie," Bessel called to his familiar. "You gave me time to escape."

The bedraggled dog paddled strongly toward Bessel. He yipped a greeting and aimed to intercept his master.

"You are the most pathetic looking mutt." Bessel couldn't help grinning broadly at the sight of all that soaking fur streaked with mud. No wonder the dog had looked so forlorn and lost when they first found each other on the docks.

Mopsie had been swimming in the Bay while Bessel had tried to rescue the ambassador.

"Maybe you are a water dog after all, pup." With determined strokes, Bessel set out for the mainland to the south of the city.

Mopsie growled a warning. Bessel looked about him for signs of the assassin. He saw the black-clad warrior on the bridge of University Isle shaking his fist at Bessel. Then the warrior scrambled toward the nearby dock where the University kept several boats tied.

Bessel swam with long strokes away from the continuing menace. The river offered hundreds of hiding places but few landings big enough for a boat. He knew he could escape the assassin as long as he stayed in the river.

Already the cold water sapped his strength and set his teeth chattering. He had to find shelter quickly. He headed for a series of aits hidden behind University Isle. Some of the tiny, temporary islands had withstood the river and the weather long enough to grow tall grasses and scrubby trees. He might not be able to build a fire to warm and dry himself and the dog for several hours yet. But he'd be able to get out of the water and probably out of the wind.

Mopsie barked again.

"What?" he asked the dog, treading water. He had to work at staying in one place in the strong current, but he didn't dare proceed until he knew the next danger.

Two quick barks. Bessel automatically looked left. He dove down and away from a heavy tree branch before it connected with his head.

"Thanks, Mopsie," he said when he resurfaced beside his new friend. He took a moment to scratch the dog's ears. "Now how did I know that two yips means left? And I suppose one means right?"

Mopsie barked once in agreement.

"Do you know any fishermen we can hide out with until it's safe to go back to Master Nimbulan?"

The dog barked one more time.

Chapter 28

Late morning, side trail off the Great South Road

Katie dug her heels into her steed's flanks. "We can't be late," she mumbled to herself. "We can't be late." Her words took on the rhythm of hooves striking the roadway.

She yanked the reins for the animal to turn left along the side path. Roussin told her the path had been widened from a deer trail by Rovers who used to camp in the clearing where Kinnsell had landed his shuttle.

Foam flecked her steed's mouth around the bit. Sweat gleamed along its neck. But its breathing and cadence remained steady. She'd driven the steed hard since Roussin had shown Myri the location of the bizarre dragon in a small clearing south and west of the city.

Quinnault led the way through this wilderness. Nimbulan and Myri kept up with them, through Myri looked decidedly green at the corners of her mouth and the edges of her pinched nose. Their mounts showed similar signs of fatigue. The guards lagged behind, but they kept her within sight until just before she turned off the main road.

Deep shadows darkened her vision the moment they left the road for the woods. She clung to the reins, praying the steed sensed the trail better than she.

She should have come yesterday, or the day before when Kinnsell first made his threats to bring technology to Kardia Hodos, when she'd first thought Kinnsell might own the ring that choked Marilell. But then Ambassador Jorghe-Rosse had died and caused a diplomatic crisis. By the time she and Quinnault had dismissed the emergency Council meeting, dawn of the next day hovered on the horizon.

Then they had spent an entire day hearing conflicting testimony and weighing evidence.

Anxiety gnawed at her. Rouussin said the shuttle was still in the clearing. Where was Kinnsell, and what was he up to?

Katie couldn't tell what or who lurked beneath the thick tree canopy. Just enough light filtered through the interwoven branches overhead to allow undergrowth to flourish.

No time to give in to her fears now. Nimbulan and Myrilandel and Quinnault were behind her. Quinnault rode ahead, slashing at encroaching branches and vines. They would protect her from the childhood monsters that leaped from her imagination into the trees. That wasn't really a Sasquatch and its mate beneath that oak. The last of the legendary pairs of Bigfoot had been captured and held in a protective zoo just after the first atmosphere domes had been constructed. The pair had failed to breed in captivity so none could have been transplanted to Kardia Hodos with the first terraforming project.

The shadows were just shadows.

They pelted up the narrow track for another kilometer—she had to think in miles she reminded herself. They traveled less than a mile. The dense forest opened. More light came through the canopy. The trees were younger, farther apart. Saber ferns and brambleberry bushes filled in the blanks between trunks. The rich scent of thick humus and fresh leaves about to burst forth from winter's sleep filled Katie's senses. She slowed the steed.

Her companions slowed, too. Not far now. Katie searched for signs of the shuttle's passage through the trees.

A path of singed branches led the way better than the track they followed. Only a shuttle's engine could have burned its way through the trees at that level, along that trajectory. Kinnsell hadn't been careful about damaging the forest when he landed.

Marsh plants dominated the foliage. Underground springs softened the soil. The steed slowed more on its own, picking its way carefully around treacherous mud.

A glint of silver caught Katie's eye. She kneed the horse forward, too anxious to worry about the footing.

Two tall Tambootie trees, stripped of their leaf buds, formed an archway to a wide clearing. A small pool reflected green light onto the side of the sleek shuttle. The landing pods had sunk deep into the soft ground. Sunk so deep Kinnsell would burn twice the normal amount of fuel breaking free.

The soft red glow of the alarm light blinked steadily beneath the hatch keypad. No one was within the shuttle. Kinnsell's footprints had been obscured by rain and the passage of wild animals at least two full days ago.

"Leave it to Kinnsell to choose his landing for convenience rather than safety." She almost laughed in relief.

"Watch the mud, Katie," Quinnault warned, dismounting before she could.

"This is indeed a strange dragon," Myri gasped. She crossed herself, paused, then made the more ancient ward of flapping hands over crossed wrists.

"But this dragon does not breathe and has no mind of its own," Katie replied. "It presents no danger until a human enters it and starts the engines. It is but a machine."

The wind and rain and natural cleansing agents in the environment could cope with the pollution left behind by one shuttle. But when the populace learned of the miracles of technology represented by those who flew shuttles, they always wanted more. The people wanted to control the forces of nature with technology. They didn't want to leave such powers only to magicians. Technology made mundanes the equals of magicians. Technology led to pollution. Bodies adapted to pollution, built up toxins in their body. The plague virus ate pollution in the air, the water, and inside human bodies. When it ran out of toxins, it ate living tissues and spread to the next host with minimal contact.

Kinnsell had to be stopped before he contaminated the entire world.

"I hope he hasn't changed the security codes," she said, marching toward the craft. Quinnault surveyed around the shuttle. Myri and Nimbulan came right behind her, holding hands like young lovers. Myri blushed and cupped her belly protectively again.

Before Katie reached the hatch, her boots sank into the soft mud. She lifted one foot carefully, wondering where to step next. The hatch and its keypad lock had sunk to a level she could easily reach, if she could get to it.

"We need solid ground," Katie looked around for inspiration.

"Branches," Nimbulan said. "We'll cut some of those everblue boughs and lay them across the path. That should secure Katie's footing. She weighs the least of any of us. I've only my short sword with me. It will have to do." He unsheathed his basic weapon/tool. Quinnault did the same.

"My dagger is sharp. I'll help." Myri pulled her own blade out of her hip sheath.

In short order they laid a dozen branches across the mud. Nimbulan breathed heavily, strain showed around his eyes, and his skin looked waxy pale from the small exertion.

Katie looked to Myrilandel to see if she noticed the undue fatigue in the older man. Her friend already placed her hand upon her husband's chest. A faint eldritch glow of blue healing connected them.

Nimbulan pushed her hand away after only a moment. The blue light lingered, stretched thin, still connecting them. They both stared at her hand in silence for a long moment. "You can't, love. Not now. 'Tis too dangerous for you to use your magic."

She glared at him with a determined set to her chin. Then Nimbulan nodded his head in acceptance. She raised her hand again but held it several finger-lengths away from his chest. The light blazed again, then died gradually. Nimbulan's face remained quite pale, but his breathing came easier.

Katie turned her attention back to the shuttle. If anyone could keep Nimbulan healthy, it was Myrilandel. She'd brought him back to life before.

There was only one reason why Nimbulan would not wish her to use her healing talent. She must be newly pregnant and feared to hurt the baby's development.

The fanning twigs of the cut branches with their blue needles spread out in front of Katie's feet and wove together in a blanket only a little paler than a clear summer sky. Katie stepped gingerly on the thickest portion of the branches. They sank a little into the mud, but held before her boots suffered any more damage.

She reached up and touched the flat keypad. Seven, one, eight, two, seven, two, eight, one. A soft whirring sound signaled the hatch opening to her command.

A blast of stale air greeted her. She wrinkled her nose at the slightly metallic, almost chemical scent of recycled air. The smell of home.

"Isn't that the same smell Shayla gave us in her dragon dream?" Nimbulan asked, holding a hand over his mouth and nose.

"Yes," Katie agreed, startled by the revelation. Quickly, she placed a fold of her heavy riding skirt across her face, then jabbed the close command on the hatch. The smell had become so ingrained in her memories of home, she had hardly noticed it in the dream. Now that she had inhaled nothing but the fresh air of Kardia Hodos she recognized the truth. This recycled air contained the scent of the plague.

"We have to leave right now. I can't risk contaminating myself or you with any more exposure." Katie gulped back her tears of fear and disappointment.

*   *   *

Near noon, side trail off the Great South Road

Kinnsell watched Katie and her entourage ride back down the path toward the road. Katie sobbed quietly.

What had happened to upset Katie so? She never gave way to her true emotions in public. Always, *always,* she found a way to convert a bad situation into laughter. In all her twenty-five years, Kinnsell had only caught his daughter crying once. The day he divorced her mother and married his pregnant mistress.

"We'll bring incendiary materials back to cleanse us of that . . . that . . ." the older man in the party said. His shoulders slumped in defeat. Nimbulan, the trusted magician who deceived the lot of them by claiming he'd lost his magic. Psi powers didn't get lost. But sometimes they hid for a while.

Nimbulan's skin looked waxy with a blue tinge around his lips. His fingers had swollen where he gripped the reins tightly. Probably just a heart condition. It had to be just a heart condition and not the first symptoms of the plague. Ill health would mask psi powers. The magician had lost his psi powers over a year ago. The length of the illness suggested a heart condition. The plague didn't linger that long once it chose a victim. Usually.

But the unpredictability of the plague and its mutations often devastated entire city domes before the first diagnosis.

"I will prepare a cleansing ritual for all of us before we destroy that renegade dragon you call a shuttle, Katie," said the tall blonde woman who always clung to Nimbulan's side. Myrilandel, rumored to be half dragon. "Meet me by the mainland stand of Tambootie trees. South of the first bridge." She kneed her steed and galloped ahead of the rest. No expression animated her face. Only the defiant stiffness of her very erect spine suggested any emotion at all.

A few more paces took the mounted party out of sight and out of earshot. Kinnsell stood up, brushing dead leaves and dirt off his brocade tunic and plush trews.

"Come, Maia. We have to hurry." So much for his plans to lie with the sultry woman before taking off. He had no intention of being anywhere in the vicinity when his treacherous daughter returned with the materials to torch the shuttle.

Katie's party and their steeds had churned the muddy path into a sopping mire. Kinnsell picked his way carefully along the sides until he reached the clearing. If these stupid bush dwellers had the sense to install climate control, he wouldn't have to ruin a decent set of boots!

He held his breath against a new round of coughing as the mud seeped through to his socks and chilled his feet and legs.

"Stargods protect me!" Maia exclaimed. She stared straight ahead, eyes wide. Over and over she crossed herself, followed by the bizarre gesture of crossed wrists and flapping hands.

Kinnsell followed her stunned gaze. He saw the shuttle

where he'd parked it, settled only slightly deeper in the mud than he remembered. Weak sunlight sparkled on the silvery tiles of the hull. The glare made him squint and lower his gaze.

"What is your problem, woman?" He faced Maia, hands on hips, aggravation and unease making him snap his words.

Maia pointed at the shuttle. Her mouth formed the word "dragon" but no sound emerged.

"That is my ship. I told you it is a kind of a dragon."

"A . . . a . . . atop the silver thing," she choked.

Kinnsell glanced again in the direction she pointed. Then he looked away again quickly. The glare hurt. "The sunlight reflects the silver skin, makes it brighter, just like sunlight on water."

"Not that. A real dragon. A real dragon is perched atop the silver one!"

Maia backed up as if she wanted to flee but didn't dare take her eyes off the thing that frightened her.

"Nonsense. There are no real dragons. Only my mechanical one." Kinnsell tried again to look at the shuttle.

This time a slight shift of the sparkling light made it a little easier to observe more closely. Something big did indeed perch atop the shuttle. Something almost transparent but with just a hint of silver revealing the massive bulk. Bright red outlined the extended wings and claws.

Then the standing dragon opened its mouth and roared. Flames burst forth from behind teeth as long as daggers.

Kinnsell almost wet his pants as he ran back down the path toward the road.

Chapter 29

Late Morning, Kaalipha's Palace, city of Hanassa

Powwell ignored the sounds of Yaala vomiting out in the corridor. He thought she'd would have grown used to this sort of thing by now.

But did anyone ever get used to violent and bloody death?

Rollett didn't look any better than Yaala, but at least he kept his breakfast down. "They were my men. They depended on me, and I failed them." Rollett swallowed nervously.

"They chose to live in Hanassa, a city of murderers, thieves, extortionists, rapists, and every other kind of criminal you can name. They came here because they couldn't, or wouldn't, obey the laws of the outside world. As long as they lived here, they couldn't hope for a clean death in old age," Powwell reminded him.

"Not all of them. Some of them came here as slaves—like you. They didn't have a choice. They relied on *me!*"

"I haven't time to hold your hand, Rollett, and make you feel better about yourself." Powwell resolutely swallowed his revulsion and stepped into the Justice Hall, senses alert to any danger or presence.

His resources had worn thin again. He pushed the limits of his magic for his own safety.

When he was certain no one hid in or around the huge room, Powwell crept forward. He clung to the shadows as long as possible. Thorny gibbered in his pocket. The hedgehog didn't like the smell of blood. They needed to scuttle away in the dark tunnels and hide.

Powwell hushed his familiar. He didn't like the smell of blood and fear either. But he had to find Kalen—or rather Kalen's body. The wraith was the only thing left of his sister. He had to use his magic to help Kalen regain her body. She couldn't do it alone. The blood on the altar could give him valuable information.

At last he took the remaining four long strides between the back wall and the raised altar below the dais.

"How'd they raise this stone without 'motes?" he asked. "There's a lot of blood on the manacles, so they managed to open and close them, too."

Rollett shrugged. Yaala wept silently in the corridor.

Powwell screwed up his courage and touched the coagulating blood with sensitive fingertips.

Power jolted up his hand and into his arm as if he had touched a ley line. He sucked up the energy greedily. And with the power came knowledge. The last moments of the dead man's life flashed across his mind.

Pain, humiliation, fear. Accelerated heartbeat. Quivering panic. Then a sharp agony in the back of his neck. Sharp awareness that this was the end. Almost a sense of relief. A flash of bright light and sudden awareness . . . Blackness.

Powwell lived through the shaking limbs and cold sweat only slightly distanced from the events. When his heartbeat returned to normal, he replayed the events through his memory, watching for glimpses of the people around the execution. He recognized Piedro standing on the dais as he passed judgment for treachery. The Kaaliph hadn't changed much since he'd helped Televarn kidnap Powwell, Myri, and Kalen a year and a half ago.

Powwell watched through the dead man's memories an entire clan of Rovers dancing around the altar stone in a stylized ritual. The magical power they generated from the dance raised the altar stone. Rough hands from behind forced his hands into the manacles at one end. His partner faced him at the other end, equally afraid, mumbling prayers to a dozen different gods. Then he shared the sensation of the cold stone on his throat as the outlaw was forced to bend over the substitute executioner's block.

But when he tried to focus on the figure beside the new Kaaliph of Hanassa, his eyes slid up, down, and sideways. He couldn't examine any feature of the vaguely feminine creature. As if Kalen had merged with a dragon!

A sharp pricking pain in his chest brought him back to the reality of the deserted Justice Hall. Thorny wiggled uncomfortably in his pocket. Fully extended spines threatened to rip holes in the sturdy cloth of Powwell's tunic. Something akin to a sob of grief shook both of them.

Powwell jerked his hand away from the altar. Blood still dripped from his fingertips. Power continued to tingle through him. He hated the thought that he gained from the terror of a man's death. He'd only known one Bloodmage. The thrill of harvesting power from pain and terror had driven that man to insane abuses of his magic.

"Thanks for reminding me, Thorny. Keep reminding me of the cost of this power." He caressed his familiar through his pocket until the hedgehog relaxed his spines and Powwell could safely pet him directly.

"What did you learn?" Rollett asked from the shadowed doorway.

Yaala remained in the corridor. Her squeamishness at the grisly deaths encouraged Powwell that she would not revert to her mother's cruel methods. Or Hanassa's— whoever had governed the Kaalipha's body.

"I'm not sure," he replied to his fellow magician. "The images are complex and distorted. I need time to sort through them. Let's scout the royal suite through Yaala's back door. I think we need to concentrate on Piedro and his consort. They have to have a weakness." He stalled.

He couldn't reveal all that he'd learned—the wraith would take the knowledge and try to regain her body alone. She wouldn't succeed and might kill herself with the effort. Nor could he let the others know that he was now in full possession of his magic. He wasn't even sure he could force himself to use this magic since it was powered by blood.

He wanted to run away from the power and curl up into a tight ball, just like Thorny. He didn't dare.

"I don't think you are going to spy on anyone, young magician," a man snarled from the back of the dais. Piedro stepped through the waterfall tapestry. "You escaped my slave pens once before. You'll not live long enough to do so again."

Two dozen Rover guards crowded into the room from the main doorway, swords, arrows, and 'mote wands aimed at his heart.

Then Powwell saw the consort standing next to Piedro. Black SeLenese lace of finest silk covered her from head to toe. A shift in the open pattern of the lace revealed her gray eyes and the ferret familiar draped across her left shoulder.

The wraith howled and dove for the consort. Hanassa, within Kalen's body raised her right hand within the lace veil and wiggled her fingers in a mocking shooing gesture.

The wraith screamed in agony and scuttled through the exit, back toward the pit and safety.

Powwell wanted to run after her, but found his feet unable to move, pinned by magic.

The consort laughed hysterically at his predicament.

Now, big brother, we are together again, Kalen's voice, but darker, throatier, penetrated his mind like iced water.

You aren't my sister!

* * *

Justice Hall, city of Hanassa.

"Run!" Yaala screamed. "Move, Powwell, move *s'murghit!*" She hit every 'mote secreted upon her person in hopes one would respond.

The altar rumbled as it slowly lowered, stone scraping stone. Lights exploded on and off around the room. The dais retreated and advanced in random jerks. The waterfall tapestry fluttered.

She backed into the corridor, still slamming her fingers against the various 'motes. She couldn't see a thing. The bright lights continued flashing before her eyes, even when they plunged the Justice Hall into darkness. But she had to make room for Powwell and Rollett to get through the narrow back door.

Two bodies brushed past her. She prayed they were her two friends.

A large hand grabbed her left arm and propelled her

backward. Every dragon instinct bred into her demanded she fight the man who held her. A deeper emotion knew that Rollett protected her, keeping his body between her and the advancing Rovers.

He'd do the same for any of his men.

She had to trust his magic senses to get them back to the pit and safety. Her eyes hadn't adjusted yet.

"Powwell?" she asked breathlessly when they had turned two corners and the corridor was beginning to come into focus.

"Here," the young man replied from right beside her. "Your screams helped me break the enthrallment." She heard a high-pitched chatter above the sound of their footfalls and her heart pounding in her ears. Thorny told her that he, too, accompanied them.

"We're all together," Rollett reassured her. He shifted position, dragging her in his wake rather than pushing her. "Get ready to open the gate in a hurry. We won't have much time to get through to safety."

Yaala pulled two 'motes from her left pocket. Which one operated the gate? She couldn't remember. Maybe it was one of the three black boxes in her right pocket. Or the two tucked into her breast band. They all looked alike.

"Catch!" She tossed 'motes to each of her friends. "Push every button you can until the gate opens."

Rollett let go her arm to grab two small black boxes out of the air. Yaala felt an immediate chill from the loss of his touch. That frightened her almost as much as the sight of Rover guards brandishing wands that she thought only she could control.

Yaala pushed buttons frantically as the gate came into view. Her feet slid on the loose sand of the corridor. She struggled to maintain her balance while continuing to push buttons.

At last the gate creaked open.

Powwell drew alongside her, 'mote pointed directly at the gate. He must have the proper one.

No time to think, only to escape to the other side of the gate.

"I will protect you, men, from the wraith. Don't let the gate stop you," Piedro called from behind the refugees.

Rollett reached the crossed iron bars first. He grabbed the gate, ready to slam it closed as soon as Yaala and Powwell passed through.

Powwell skidded on the sand, sliding out of control. He slammed into the bars, in the far corner away from the opening. He dropped the 'mote.

The guards pelted forward, barely ten paces away.

Yaala grabbed Powwell's tunic and dragged him through the gateway. Without thinking, she scooped up the black box and aimed it at the lock.

"Stargods, I hope it's not broken," she prayed.

Rollett slammed the gate closed, pressing all of his weight against it.

Archers followed the initial wave of guards. The nearest Rover raised his belt knife ready to throw it the last three paces into Rollett's back.

She turned off the lights.

Three very long heartbeats later, Yaala heard the lock snick tight.

Then they were off again, deep into the labyrinth of caverns. As they passed through the living cavern, the sounds of pursuit died down. At least the gate had slowed the Rovers.

"We've got to keep moving. I don't trust that lock," Rollett panted. He bent over, hands clasping his knees as he tried to ease his breathing. "Piedro is a very powerful magician. I felt his spells all around me. My armor almost collapsed under his assault."

"The lock will hold," Yaala reassured him. Still she headed toward the caverns where her machines resided.

"We're too late. We can't hide anywhere, and your cursed machines won't help." Powwell stared blankly toward the gate and the clang of wands against the metal bars. "The consort is too strong. She overpowered my blood magic to hold me in thrall. She's even corrupted Kalen's ferret familiar. That takes more magic than any one of us could dream of. Nothing will stop the renegade dragon from killing all of us. Not 'tricity, not magic, nothing."

Chapter 30

*Early afternoon, the northern edge of the River
Coronnan near the Great Bay, outside
Coronnan City*

Bessel hauled himself out of the river near the confluence
with the Great Bay. He'd run out of islands. The assassin had kept the stolen boat within sight for most of the
length of the river. When Bessel managed to get out of
sight of the warrior and crawl out of the water, the islands
around him were flat, low, and lacking enough vegetation
to hide him.

The coast north of the city offered him better refuge than
any of the temporary aits. Here, at least, he could find
shelter from the rising wind under a tree or behind a
sand dune.

Mopsie trudged out of the water beside him. He hung
his head tiredly for a few moments before shaking. Bessel
was too tired and cold to duck the spray. What was a little
more water when half the river weighed down his clothes?

The other half of the river matted Mopsie's long ropes
of fur.

Bessel followed the dog's example and wrung some of
the dripping water from his tunic. He shed his socks and
twisted them somewhat drier. He looked at his cold-reddened toes mournfully. "I'd better let the socks dry a
bit before putting them back on. Stargods only know where
my other boot ended up."

A muddy and rocky beach stretched before them, separating the bay from the land. A few gentle grass-covered hills marked the end of farmland and the beginning of the mudflats.

"Where to now, Mopsie?" Bessel asked, looking over his shoulder for traces of the assassin or of habitation.

Mopsie yipped once and trotted forward, angling to the right. After half a dozen paces, he stopped again to shake. The other half of the river burst free of his fur.

"You still look a mess, pup." Bessel ducked the spray this time. When the dog had finished and trotted forward again, Bessel shared a sense of lightness and freedom with the dog. "Is that what a familiar does, Mopsie, shares everything, the good and the bad?"

Mopsie grinned his agreement, his little pink tongue making a bright splash in the middle of the muddy white fur. The dog continued along the beach, looking back expectantly. Bessel followed, trusting his familiar as he had trusted few human beings except Master Nimbulan.

Shortly the dog's ears perked up a bit, and he raised his nose to sniff the wind. Bessel did, too. Woodsmoke drifted gently toward his nose. Woodsmoke permeated with salt and . . . and fish! Mopsie yipped happily and bounded forward.

Bessel's stomach growled, so he followed.

Along the beach a short distance and deep in one of the numerous coves on the uneven coastline, a group of three fishermen huddled around a small driftwood fire. The men had hauled their small boat above the ebbing tide line and turned it over to keep the interior dry. Bessel sensed rain on the wind and shivered anew.

Three sleek, long-legged dogs raised their heads from their paws, eyes and ears alert, but not menacing.

"Have you enough fish to share with a stranger?" Bessel asked politely. He stopped well away from the fire. Mopsie hung behind him rather than challenge the larger dogs.

"Looks like you're as much flotsam as man," one of the men laughed. Deep lines creased his face around the eyes from a lifetime of peering closely at the water in all weathers. A broken tooth showed when he grinned. Otherwise he looked healthy, reasonably well fed, and no more ragged than any other man of his profession.

"I feel like a piece of waterlogged driftwood," Bessel replied.

"Then come, sit by the fire, and warm yourself a bit. There's fish aplenty if you don't mind picking out the bones," the fisherman said. He gestured Bessel closer. The dogs lowered their heads but kept their eyes and ears on Bessel and Mopsie.

"Well, hello, pup!" a second fisherman greeted Mopsie. He held out a hand for the dog to sniff. "Where you been hiding these last few days?"

"Mopsie adopted me two days ago," Bessel said. He plunked down next to the second man. "Do you know where my fam . . . dog came from?"

"Them Guild of Bay Pilots turned out all their dogs when they got that fancy machine. Said they didn't need dogs to sense the currents anymore." The first fisherman spat into the mud in disgust. "Name's Leauman, and this here's Aguiir and Waaterrsoon." He gestured right and left to indicate his companions.

"I'm Bessel, and I'm very interested in learning more about your dogs." As if on cue, the three large dogs rocked and stretched onto their feet, then ambled over to sniff Mopsie.

Nose to nose, nose to tail, they introduced themselves. When Mopsie had been approved, they all wrestled a few moments, tugging on ears and nipping tails. But then they settled around the fire, each dog at the feet of his master.

"I don't understand. Can dogs smell underwater?" Bessel mused. He rested his elbow on one knee and propped up his suddenly heavy head with his hand.

Mopsie stretched and shifted, edging marginally closer to the fire and the fish cooking on a spit above it. Leauman smiled at the dog and then at Bessel. One of the dogs growled low in his throat at Mopsie. The little dog gazed back with wide innocent eyes and dropped his head onto his paws. A moment later he repeated the maneuver. This time the warning growls were louder. Mopsie had the grace to look guilty, but he didn't back away from his intended prize.

"What's to understand about Mopplewoggers? The dogs

stand in the bow of the boat and yip once for starboard,
twice for port. We follow the dogs and never run aground.
Ignore the dogs and you run afoul of a sandbar or flotsam,
just like that stupid pilot, Raanald, two days ago. If he'd
kept his dog and not bothered with the machine, he wouldn't
have lost his passenger and brought this country to the
brink of war." Aguiir hawked and spat again.

Bessel cringed a little, not knowing if he should mention
that he had ridden on the barge with Raanald two days ago.

"Mopsie doesn't look like a Mopplewogger," Bessel said,
caressing his familiar's silky ears in an attempt to keep him
from creeping closer to the fire and their dinner.

"Yeah, he was a surprise all right," Leauman laughed.
"One of the pilot's dogs was in heat when she got turned
loose. She must have mated with half a dozen strays around
the port. Every pup came out different."

"Is one of your dogs Mopsie's dam?" Bessel inspected
each of the lounging animals for any trace of resemblance
to his dog.

"Naw," Waaterrsoon spoke for the first time. "My
Swabby brought the bitch home with him. She's heavy with
pups again. This time I made sure she only mated with
Swabby." He petted his dog vigorously, possessively.

"What about Mopsie?" Bessel asked. "Why was he running loose on the docks eager to follow anyone home?"

Not just anyone! They all looked at him strangely, their
thoughts as clear in Bessel's mind as if they had shouted
them aloud.

"If you don't know why you've been claimed by a Mopplewogger, then you aren't ready to partner one," Leauman
stated. He abruptly ended the conversation by reaching for
one of the fish spitted above the flames. The sweet meat
nearly fell from the bones. He cupped a hand beneath it,
to keep the flesh from dropping into the flames. Gently he
blew on it to cool it, then fed a morsel to his dog before
eating himself.

The other two fishermen did the same. Only then did
Bessel take his own fish. Mopsie sat up, brushing his tail
rapidly in the mud. By this time his fur was more black
than white. Like the others, Bessel fed the dog first, recognizing the importance of a familiar in his life.

Mopsie had found him when he most needed a friend and defender. Could the dog sense the future? Maybe he just sensed emotions and recognized in Bessel similar needs to his own.

These men and their dogs had welcomed him, fed him, and offered the warmth of their fire; more consideration than Scarface and the Commune of Magicians had offered one of their own.

"If Raanald had kept his dog on board the barge, then he wouldn't have relied on the confused readings of the depth finder. If he had listened to a dog, he probably would have avoided grounding on the sandbar, Jorghe-Rosse wouldn't have fallen into the bay, I wouldn't have had to resort to rogue magic to rescue him, and I'd still be a part of the Commune," Bessel sorted the chain of events out loud, no longer caring who heard and who didn't.

"But if it had happened that way, you wouldn't have needed Mopsie and he wouldn't have found you," Leauman added.

"I think all of Coronnan needs to know more about the bay fishermen and their dogs," Bessel said. Surely one of the many books in the library discussed the unique relationship.

Probably one of the books Scarface had locked away.

"No one but us needed to know before this," Aguiir said.

"But we never had to choose between faithful dogs and machines before," Bessel added. "We never had the Commune declare certain knowledge forbidden to everyone, including magicians, before." Without that knowledge, the plague could come to Coronnan and they'd have no defense against it.

"I've got to go back and save those books. We can't afford to let Scarface lock them away forever."

"Someone chased you and Mopsie into the river, boy. Whatever you're running from is still waiting for you in the city," Leauman warned.

"I know. I have to accept that risk. The books are more important. Protecting Coronnan from men like Scarface and Raanald is more important. If I'd had time to investigate invisibility spells, this would be a lot easier."

*   *   *

Noon, shuttle clearing off the Great South Road

"Stop, Master Kinnsell, the dragon can't hurt you," Maia called.

Kinnsell slowed his steps as he moved away from the shuttle. He looked all around him very carefully before coming to a complete stop.

His lungs burned from his sudden burst of speed. He dragged in air, trying desperately not to cough. Cold sweat beaded on his skin and his knees shook so badly that he almost couldn't stand.

"It's only a little dragon. It won't hurt you," Maia reassured him again.

Rational thought began to filter back into his brain. "It looked mighty big and dangerous to me." Kinnsell felt his forehead. Perhaps his coughing bouts had induced a temporary fever. He had to have imagined the beast sitting atop his shuttle. Dragons did not exist.

"Certainly, dragons look dangerous," Maia laughed. "But they are oath-bound to protect humans. That is part of their covenant with the magicians."

Then Maia had seen the beast, too. Had one of Katie's companions left a post-hypnotic suggestion on them so they'd stay away from the shuttle?

Kinnsell relaxed a little, content with his logical explanation for the sight of the silver-and-red monster with fiery breath. He turned back toward the clearing.

"You're right, Maia. The dragon can't hurt us." It didn't exist. "But it might tell my daughter that you and I escaped, so perhaps we'd best begin our journey." He held out his arms to escort her back to the shuttle.

Fortunately the draconic illusion had disappeared by the time they entered the clearing again. Kinnsell marched up to the shuttle hatch, resolved to be on his way within moments.

He ran his fingers over the lock keypad. It did not respond to his usual codes. Eight, one, seven, two, seven, two, eight, one. He'd used the same code for years. Why didn't the bloody hatch open? He drummed his fingers on the metal/ceramic alloy of the hull. What random numbers would Katie use to reset the lock? He tried her birthday, his code backward, the coordinates for Earth, the coordinates for Kardia Hodos—he had to try those twice before he got the numbers right—and a straightforward one, two, three, four, five, six. Nothing worked.

"Dammit!" He kicked the hatch.

"Perhaps I can decipher her spell," Maia suggested, quietly. "A woman knows another woman's mind."

"Go ahead and try. But Katie is devious in her logic. There are thousands of combinations she could have chosen." He stepped aside while the dark-eyed woman stared at the numbered keys.

She stared a long time. Finally, she looked away rubbing her eyes and shifting her feet up and down in the mud. "Piedro says he cannot channel magic through me unless there is a second Rover with me. Piedro has replaced Televarn as head of the clan. I do not like him as well as Televarn, but he is satisfactory as a lover and his voice is strong in my head." She closed her eyes and looked off into the distance.

Lover? Had Maia slept with every man on the planet? He frowned, wanting to push her aside and handle the lock himself. He also wanted to drag her down in the mud and prove that he was a better lover than the Rover trash who invaded her mind.

"Tonight we will be together, King Kinnsell." Maia caressed his face. Then she abruptly returned her attention to the lock.

She lied. He knew she had no intention of willingly sharing a bed with him, no matter what she promised. Kinnsell realized Maia would never tell the truth if a lie sounded better, and she would not tell the whole truth if she must tell any of it.

She stared hard at the keypad for a long moment. "I cannot see the heat of Her Grace's hand on the puzzle. Your heat has masked it."

Kinnsell slammed his fist into the hatch. The first assault

of pain turned into a numbing ache. The clamminess returned to his skin. He jerked his hand away and sucked on his abused knuckles. They looked alarmingly swollen.

"There are other ways of unraveling a puzzle, though." Maia flashed a radiant smile at him.

Kinnsell forgot the pain in his fist, the growing anxiety inside his gut, and the pressure in his chest. He forgot her lies and deceit. "Tonight, my dear. Get that hatch open, and tonight we will celebrate in safe comfort."

"Yes. Tonight Piedro will reward you for returning me to the clan. Tonight we will celebrate in Hanassa."

"Just open the hatch, and I will command this dragon to fly us to safety." He couldn't remember if the bushie lord had named his castle Hanassa or something else. Many small details eluded him. Had he remembered the right codes for the lock? No matter. He would pilot the shuttle and take her where he wanted to go and nowhere else. Maia had no say in their destination.

Maia concentrated on the keypad one more time. This time she held her palm in front of it, a hair's breadth away. Her eyes rolled up and her expression went blank.

Then she reached her other hand inside her bodice, deep into her cleavage and out again so quickly Kinnsell almost didn't see her gesture.

But he followed her swift movements closely.

Still gazing at the lock in a trancelike state, Maia pulled a small twist of wire free of her garments. She inserted the tool into the very narrow crack that defined the doorway. A few seconds later the hatch clicked and slid open.

If he hadn't known better, Kinnsell would not have seen her pick the lock. But . . . "Electronic locks can't be picked," he gasped.

"A lock is a lock, and all locks can be picked." Maia giggled in triumph. "Now show me this wondrous dragon, Lord Kinnsell. I would make friends with the strange beast."

"Why not?" Kinnsell gestured Maia into the shuttle while suppressing a new bout of coughing. His lungs had been quiet for hours. Why now? Probably the molds and other nasty fungi growing in the mud had triggered an allergic reaction.

The warm, slightly metallic tasting air rushed to envelop him in familiarity. It smelled of home and comfort and safety. He drank deeply of it as he stepped through the portal into the passenger cabin.

Maia stopped short just inside the door. She stared at the comfortable blue upholstered benches that converted to beds, the softly blinking lights of the electronic readers and game boards, the food synthesizer that converted any vegetable matter into tasty dishes.

"What sort of magic do you wield, Master Kinnsell?" she whispered, too awestruck to move.

"The magic of technology," he replied seductively into her ear. "Settle in one of the benches and fasten the restraints. We'll take off in a minute."

"Don't leave me alone inside this strange monster, Master Kinnsell." Maia's eyes remained wide open. Her pupils contracted in terror, leaving the liquid brown iris to plead with him.

"Very well, my dear." Kinnsell patted her hand and drew her forward into the bridge area. "Sit there." He motioned her to the copilot's seat. She couldn't inadvertently change any of the controls unless he turned them over to her by voice command to the computer. A copilot could take control if the biosensors determined the pilot was dead or unconscious, but that wouldn't happen on the quick hop to the bush lord's castle.

Kinnsell drew the safety strap over his head and shoulders, fastening it on the clip between his legs. Maia mimicked his actions, hiking up her skirts and petticoats to reveal most of her trim thighs. Kinnsell had to gulp back his desire once again. His eyes did not want to return to the control board.

Finally he remembered what he needed to do. He cleared the viewscreen so that they could look out and see the real-time scene around them. Then he ran his fingers over the touchpads and began the firing sequence. Automatically he set his destination coordinates into the auto pilot. No need for the cyber-control headset. They were only going a short distance and not nearing a suborbital altitude. Almost instantly, the atmosphere jets roared to life.

Maia reared back in surprise. But when Kinnsell proceeded

calmly with the launch sequence, she relaxed, studying everything. He knew she'd never figure out the complexities of flying the shuttle. She couldn't even read, let alone understand the mathematics of navigation.

He fondled the joystick lovingly. Certainly he could use the touchpads to fly the shuttle. Most pilots did or they used the supersensitive cyber controls. But his family had always had an affinity for the joystick, preferring to sense the craft's movements and vibrations through the palm of their hand and the seat of their pants rather than the technological array before their eyes.

Kinnsell monitored the gauges. When the engines had enough power and fuel, he eased the joystick back. The engines roared again, straining to respond. He looked at the surrounding trees through the viewscreen. The craft did not move.

"What?" he asked the computer.

The displays told him that the weight of the mud on the stabilizing feet of the shuttle trapped them.

He eased the stick back again while rocking it side to side. The trees seemed to shift and waver in front of him. Like riding on a teeter-totter. The shuttle jerked back and forth but still did not lift. The engines continued straining. He burned fuel at an enormous rate.

Pressure built in Kinnsell's chest. His head seemed detached from his body. He had trouble focusing his eyes.

Still, he continued rocking the craft to loosen the cursed mud. Another reason to erect climate control on this planet—or at least construct decent landing pads.

"Perhaps the dragon is back. If it is sitting atop your dragon, the extra weight would make flight difficult," Maia suggested.

"There are no such things as dragons," Kinnsell asserted through gritted teeth. He continued rocking the craft. Seesaw. The trees swayed before his eyes.

Was that a tiny bit of lift?

Yes, he was breaking free. He wasted more fuel compensating for the planet's gravity. He eased the shuttle up to treetop level. The shuttle remained unsteady, shaking as badly as his hands. He ignored the weakness and the need to cough and the sweat pouring into his eyes.

When he had finally cleared the trees, he looked for his compass and couldn't find it. The array of lights and numbers on the control panel blurred and doubled and redoubled. He closed his eyes hard, and blinked several times.

"Wake up, Master Kinnsell. Wake up. You are losing control of the dragon!" Maia screamed in his ear.

Kinnsell roused slightly, shaking his head to clear it. Chills racked his body suddenly. His eyes blurred again.

"Autopilot. Set autopilot," he said. To his own ears each forced word took on new shades of meaning. Had he really told Maia to set the autopilot or had he named the colors of dragon wingtips? No, he had named each of his four children by wife number one and their three half siblings by numbers two and three. Number four, Marjorie, didn't like children.

Seesaw Marjorie Daw.

"Master Kinnsell!" Maia screeched again. "You must control the dragon, we are going to crash!"

Chapter 31

Noon, the pit beneath the city of Hanassa

Rollett watched Powwell walk resolutely toward the cavern he said housed the dragongate. Depression weighed heavily on the boy's shoulders. His skin looked waxy and pale in the unnatural light.

That strange misty aura still clung to Powwell's silhouette. Suddenly Rollett knew that Kalen had become the wraith while Hanassa inhabited her body. Now she kept close to her brother, demanding his help.

"Can we force Hanassa to relinquish Kalen's body?" Rollett asked, determined to push the boy into action. He couldn't allow one setback to force him to give up. If he'd done that, he'd have committed suicide a year and a half ago. But now he was out of resources. The city was out of time. They had to act.

Powwell shrugged, studying the bloody stains on his fingers. The dried blood looked black against his increasingly pale skin. He kept his back to Yaala and Rollett. But he tilted his head much as Myrilandel did when she listened to dragons. Did the wraith whisper to Powwell?

"We haven't time for arguing over spells and joined spirits," Yaala reminded them as she peered back along their escape routes. "The food in the living cavern will slow the guards down a little, but if Hanassa rules the consort's—Kalen's—body, then she'll drive the Rovers deeper and deeper until they find us. Hanassa knows these passageways better than I do."

"Does Hanassa know the dragongate?" Powwell whirled to confront them. Hope animated his eyes and his posture.

"He/she must if she's been down here for centuries," Rollett said.

"But does Hanassa *understand* the dragongate?" A wide grin split Powwell's face—a grin that spoke more of malice than of mirth.

"Can anyone understand it?" Yaala returned. "It changed and doesn't work like it used to. Who knows when it will open again, or change again?" She fell into step beside Powwell as they headed into the large cavern with the broken generator named Old Bertha.

Rollett followed the others, needing to stay with them lest he become lost and fall victim to the Rovers who searched for them. Escape was within his grasp only if he stayed with Yaala and Powwell.

Hope. He felt it in his bones.

Freedom. He tasted it in the air.

A haunting song almost within hearing drew him into the cavern more than the presence of his comrades.

Powwell stood in the opening of a small tunnel off the huge cavern. He braced his arms against the sides of the archway, staring into the blackness beyond. A bright flare of red from deep within the tunnel as well as the increased heat told Rollett that they neared the lava core—and the elusive dragongate. The song intensified. If only he could remember it, all of his questions would be answered.

"That's not the way to the dragongate," Yaala called to Powwell. She remained next to the vast hulk of the dead generator, touching it, as a mother caressed a wayward toddler.

Rollett gulped back a sudden surge of desire. The image of Yaala touching a child—his child—filled his imagination with longing.

No. She wanted to stay in Hanassa and rule it. He needed to go home. But he'd come back for his men, make sure they had the option of escape.

Yaala rested her head on the dead hulk of the machine. He wanted to reach out to her, let her grieve for the loss of the machine. Jerking himself back three steps from her, he forced his hands to his sides. He didn't know Yaala, didn't dare trust her with his fragile emotions. He hadn't known a woman's companionship during this entire long year and a half in Hanassa. The only women available were either hardened outlaws or disease-ridden prostitutes. He wouldn't touch either, no matter how much he longed to. Now Yaala enticed him, probably because she was clean, vulnerable, and lovely.

"This isn't the way we came through the dragongate this last time." Powwell's statement dragged Rollett's attention away from his momentary desire and back to the problem at hand.

"We came through that tunnel." Yaala pointed to a smaller opening adjacent to the one Powwell stared into. "I remember landing in that puddle near the broken pipe."

"But this is the way we left Hanassa last year." Powwell gestured toward the tunnel he leaned into. "I didn't recognize it before because of the partial collapse of the opening."

Yaala looked back and forth between the tunnel openings, confusion written all over her face.

Rollett examined both openings minutely and saw little difference other than the position in relation to Old Bertha.

"Look, the gate is opening!" Powwell called as he dived into the tunnel.

"Opening?" Rollett gasped. "We can escape right now?" His heart pounded in his ears. He plunged into the passage right behind Powwell, ahead of Yaala. "Home. I need to go home." If the opening led to home, then he could come back for his men. He could attack Piedro later, with refreshed magic and reinforcements from the Commune.

He smelled cool dampness. The hot red flares from the lava core swirled into a myriad of colors muted by a soft, soothing blue-white and deep gray. The song that called him grew louder.

"Not yet!" Powwell blocked his path with his staff.

Desperate to be gone from Hanassa and the men who pursued him, Rollett whipped his own staff around to confront Powwell in a fighting stance. "Out of my way, boy!" A red haze of anger blinded him to all but the need to escape.

"We don't leave without my sister!" Powwell snarled.

"Stop it, both of you!" Yaala warned in a hissing whisper. "Hanassa will hear you. Besides, that scene is resolving into . . . into, Stargods, it's underwater! Look at that bemouth. It will eat us alive." She backed out of the tunnel, hands crossed in front of her face, protecting herself from sprays of salt water.

Powwell shifted his stance just enough to see the watery blue landscape behind him while also keeping Rollett from charging past. "Deep water," he said succinctly. "We have to wait for the right scene. We have to wait for Kalen."

"Does this mean the dragongate isn't broken?" Yaala edged up behind Rollett, but she didn't try to come between the two men who remained ready to swing their staffs at each other.

Her warmth filled Rollett's back with comfort. He relaxed his stance a fraction. Some of the desperate need to escape dribbled out of him. He could go on a little longer. He needed to help Yaala depose Piedro so that he could rescue his men.

"It means the gate has changed. It opens to different locations than before," Powwell replied. "Maybe none of them are safe."

"This way!" A Rover-accented voice yelled from across the large cavern. "They're hiding in that tunnel."

"Keep them away from the dragongate," Piedro called back.

Rollett turned quickly, keeping his staff at the ready. Trapped! They were trapped in the tiny tunnel, barely wide enough to wield his staff. And Powwell just stood there with a feral snarl of satisfaction on his face.

Anger and frustration boiled up within Rollett. The only escape seemed to be the mysterious dragongate behind them. But one wrong step would put them into the lava core.

Powwell moved up beside him, shoving Yaala against the wall and out of their way. He held up his bloody right hand in a spell gesture. The hedgehog familiar keened an earpiercing wail and dived deep into Powwell's pocket, his spines fully erect.

The entire tunnel smelled of old blood and fear. Powwell's skin grew paler yet. A blue tinge developed around his lips and the edges of his nose. He started to sweat heavily.

Powwell drew his strength from blood magic!

Rollett swallowed heavily, convulsively to keep his bile in his stomach where it belonged. He'd had more than enough experience with the Bloodmage Moncriith. The thought of drawing power from the blood, pain, and fear of another living being revolted him physically and emotionally.

But he recognized that they had few other choices. If blood magic would keep Piedro and the consort at bay until they could step through the dragongate to safety, then so be it.

Powwell began chanting under his breath.

Always sensitive to music, Rollett listened hard to the spell.

"What are you doing, Powwell? You're enticing them this way!"

Chapter 32

Afternoon, the pit beneath the city of Hanassa

"**S**end the consort to me," Powwell called to the Rovers gathering in the large cavern. "My death will not appease Simurgh unless it is the consort herself who kills me. She must taste my blood!"

Inside his pocket, Thorny hunched and bristled his spines as far out as he could. The sharp tips penetrated Powwell's tunic, pricking his skin. Powwell inhaled sharply at the ache in his heart and the sensitivity of his skin. But no blood flowed from the tiny wounds.

That's right, Thorny, he whispered with his mind to his familiar. *Just the way we rehearsed it.*

"What are you doing?" Rollett and Yaala each grabbed one of Powwell's arms, dragging him back. Back toward the dragongate.

Powwell smiled inwardly as he caught a glimpse of the reds and black of the desert scene forming within the portal—so very similar to the scene the other gate had taken him and Yaala to, but different. This one opened into the same time as where he stood. The other one had drifted in time, taking Powwell and Yaala to Hanassa of many aeons ago.

Both deserts would not support human life for long. And if the dragongate held true to its previous patterns, it would cycle through many inhospitable locations before opening into someplace green—maybe Coronnan, maybe someplace else.

At the mouth of the tunnel, a black-veiled figure emerged into the uncertain light.

"Is that what you really want, Powwell?" the consort asked. Her voice grated harshly in the confines of the tunnel. Kalen's voice, but not her voice, deeper, harsher. "Do you want your sister to be the one to consign you to your next existence in the most unpleasant way I can think of?"

Slowly, the girl/woman removed the black lace veil. She dropped the priceless silk on the rough floor. It rippled as it fell, like cool water over a waterfall. Gravel and sand snagged the fine threads.

Powwell looked into his sister's gray eyes, so like his own and yet . . .

Wiggles, Kalen's ferret familiar remained draped across her left shoulder, unmoving. Powwell lifted one eyebrow at it.

"You killed the ferret and stuffed it because it would not stay with Hanassa, the renegade dragon. You are not as powerful as you want others to believe. Does the wraith haunt you? Does she keep you awake at night whispering of aching emptiness at the death of Wiggles?" He took another step back, pushing Yaala and Rollett against the wall. Only he stood between the consort and the dragongate.

Hot wind shot through the gate, caressing Powwell's skin with the enticement of escape.

He shut his mind to the need to turn and run through the opening, no matter where it took him. But he noticed Yaala and Rollett edging closer and closer to the inhospitable scene.

"Kalen died, leaving her body behind for me. I am Hanassa. I have always been Hanassa!" the consort proclaimed. She lifted her arms, palm outward as if embracing the entire volcano.

"Then, Hanassa, you will have to come get me. You won't be satisfied until you have my blood on your hands and in your mouth!"

She took four long paces closer to Powwell, not enough.

Thorny squirmed and pressed himself closer to Powwell's chest. A tiny drop of blood trickled down Powwell's chest, over his heart. The sharp lance of pain, brief though it was, sent power singing through his veins, enhancing the fading energy he'd gathered from the severed heads.

"Come and get me, Kalen. Join me in the pit of hell!"

Powwell teetered on the edge of the pit. Boiling rock flared upward. The heat nearly seared his back. Sweat poured down his face and made his palms slick.

"Powwell, stop this. I beg you," Yaala tried to pull him away from the edge. "You're my only friend, I can't let you do this."

Powwell closed his eyes rather than look at her. He knew if he saw tears in her eyes—tears in the eyes of a woman who never cried, who had survived horrors he could only imagine—he'd throw away his carefully laid plans.

"It's the only way to save Kalen, Yaala. If this doesn't work, stay with Rollett. You can trust him."

"Thanks, but no thanks," Rollett said, stepping beside him. "I'll help you, but I'm taking the next portal through the dragongate."

Powwell smiled his acknowledgment as he opened his mind a fraction to allow Rollett a brief glimpse of his plan.

"Do you have a death wish, boy?" Rollett raised his dark eyebrows.

"He must. He asked me to kill him," the consort said, only three paces away. "Give me your sword, Piedro. I shall execute this intruder myself."

"Aren't you going to rip out my throat with your bare hands? That's the way a dragon kills," Powwell taunted. "And you are a dragon in spirit, Hanassa. The purple-tipped dragon instincts still drive you. You hunger for fresh meat, cooked by your own flames."

Hanassa licked her lips. A drop of drool trickled from the corner of her mouth. She swallowed heavily as if tasting sweet, fresh meat. Kalen's features twisted into something alien and ugly. Any trace of the little girl had vanished beneath Hanassa's lusts.

"But you'll never have your own dragon flames again," Powwell continued. He and Rollett eased aside just a little, offering Hanassa a tantalizing glimpse of the scene beyond the dragongate. "The real dragon nimbus won't let you have a dragon body again. They won't let you fly out of this hellhole that is your prison. Your only escape is to steal a human body and walk out of here. But the humans won't let you live among them as long as you drink their blood."

Hanassa edged closer. Her nose worked as if scenting freedom in the desert on the other side of the dragongate.

The hot wind died. The gate began to close.

"You're more a prisoner here than we are, Hanassa," Rollett added his taunts to Powwell's. "We can step through the dragongate anytime we wish. Can you?"

"It's closing!" Hanassa wailed. She dashed toward them just as the red and black of the desert swirled into a myraid other colors.

"Not again!" Kalen screamed as her body hurtled over the edge of the pit.

A white mist enveloped her mundane body.

"Now!" Powwell commanded as he wrapped a magic net around his sister. "Grab her."

He sensed Rollett's diminished magic reaching to ensnare the young girl before she fell into the boiling lava a thousand feet below. Tendrils of power snaked and looped together, the dark red and deep sea-blue knots of Rollett's magic cradled one side of Kalen. Powwell's red and sparkling black held the other in a net of energy.

Powwell had to open his mind further so that he and Rollett could work together. Every instinct inside him shouted to keep his secrets, keep this other man from learning how much he had enjoyed gathering blood magic.

"Help me, Powwell!" Kalen, the true Kalen, screamed. "Don't let me die in the pit again."

Powwell closed his eyes and gritted his teeth. He sought closer contact with Rollett's mind. Their thoughts mingled, settled on a common need. Together they strained to haul Kalen back to the safety of the ledge.

At last Powwell held Kalen in his arms and opened his eyes. His sister. The only family he had left. The child/ woman who completed his every thought and made sense of his ragged emotions.

She turned to him, opening wide gray eyes to him in gratitude.

Don't let it get control of me, she pleaded. Her mental voice blended sweetly with his thoughts, filling a void that had existed since he'd been forced to leave her behind in this very tunnel over a year ago.

"Thank you," she said in Hanassa's harsh voice several

tones deeper than Kalen's. The white mist separated from her body once more. The wraith sobbed her disappointment.

Powwell's heart nearly broke in grief.

A self-satisfied smirk replaced the gratitude in Hanassa's expression. "I read your mind, Powwell." She caressed his face with long, talonlike nails that raked his skin but did not draw blood. "I knew what you planned the moment you shared your thoughts with Rollett. I let Kalen have her body for a few moments, so you would rescue her. Then I took it back. Now you are truly my prisoner, and I shall execute you properly."

Chapter 33

Katie breathed deeply of the redolent smoke from the Tambootie wood fire. The queen, Nimbulan, and Myri stood in a circle around a small campfire deep in the woods south and west of the city. Their escort stood well back from this stand of Tambootie trees, backs turned to avoid breathing any of the smoke.

Across the fire from her, Nimbulan swayed under the hallucinogens in the wood sap. Flame released those chemicals in uneven doses. They had no way of controlling how much each of them breathed in. But they needed Tambootie in their systems to combat the plague virus they might have inhaled. Katie didn't have time to distill proper and controlled doses and then return to the shuttle before Kinnsell departed with it.

Nimbulan's face grew paler as Myri's flushed with heat and distorted perceptions. Quinnault seemingly remained impervious to the hallucinogens in the smoke. He'd endured this before, when progressing from apprentice to journeyman in his priestly studies. Or maybe he simply knew how to flow with changes. Katie stopped fighting the splotches of improbable colors that filled her vision. She allowed the smoke to infiltrate her every pore and corpuscle.

The world spun around her. She lost contact with her

feet. Her arms rose level with her shoulders. She turned her palms up to embrace the sky. She could almost reach out and touch the clouds. Dense air seemed to enclose her in a vortex of color, lifting her higher above the others.

Visions of soaring above the clouds of Coronnan layered over her real-time sight of this mundane clearing and the ritual campfire. Cool air wafted beneath her arms/wings. Warm thermal currents guided her feet/tail. Sparkling crystal outlined all within sight.

Upward she soared, higher and higher toward the bright sun and the blackness of space beyond. The miracle of flight enticed her farther and farther away from her companions, and yet she did not fear the loneliness of where she traveled.

Suddenly absolute darkness enfolded her. All sensation of flight vanished. Sensory input ceased. Her body disappeared. All she had left was her mind and . . . and the dragons.

A dozen dragon thoughts invaded her mind, whispering secrets of past, present, and future. The meaning of her existence—of all of humanity—seemed just beyond the next confidence.

She listened carefully, certain she would understand soon. Thoughts of her aborted attempt to contact her brothers, her loyalty to her husband and friends, her duty to keep Coronnan and all of Kardia Hodos free of the taint of technology vanished. She had only her mind and the dragons.

(What questions do you bring to the void between the planes of existence?) a voice asked her. It seemed to reverberate and compound into a dozen voices, yet it spoke with the authority of one.

I need—I need to banish all traces of the plague from this world.

(Then you demand the death of one you hold dear.)

Memories of Katie's father arguing before the imperial legislature; Kinnsell ordering the servants; Daddy reprimanding her for some childhood infraction, filled her with a sad bitterness.

I have not loved my father in a long time.

(He is your father.)

His sperm sired me. But he never stayed home long enough to be a father. My mother raised us alone until Kinnsell put her aside for his pregnant mistress. Then my brothers became more father to me than Kinnsell ever was.

(He is your father.)

I wanted to love him. He wouldn't let me. His ambitions and greed got in the way.

(He is your father.)

Every contact with him created greater bitterness between us.

(You cannot love where you do not recognize the truth. He is your father.)

I cannot love him. He won't let me.

(Then you are not ready to recognize the truth.)

With a stomach-wrenching jolt, Katie returned to her body. She swayed on her feet. Gravity weighed too heavily on her limbs after the freedom of flight to the void.

"I have got to sit," she mumbled as her bottom found the ground. Almost sick to her stomach, she dropped her head between her knees, breathing shallowly to keep any more Tambootie smoke from penetrating her lungs.

"Katie!" Quinnault knelt beside her, seemingly unaffected by the smoke. He hugged her close, offering her an anchor to reality.

"What did you see in the smoke?" he asked after a moment of silence.

"Dragons."

"Dragons!" Myrilandel and Nimbulan exclaimed together.

"What have we done to her?" Myrilandel turned stricken eyes on her husband.

"Perhaps we have made a magician of her," Nimbulan said softly, almost below hearing. He didn't move any closer.

"This is what Scarface fears in lighting bonfires of the Tambootie in plague-affected villages," Quinnault added. "The smoke will enhance minor talents, make untrained magicians of minor talents who cannot be controlled."

"We must never mention this again," Katie said fiercely. "Women can only weave rogue magic. I will be condemned by the Council and Commune. I will be forced into exile with my daughter. The people will demand Quinnault marry another." Tears threatened to choke her.

Quinnault gathered her closer in a fierce embrace. "I will never give you up, Katie."

"If we have awakened magical powers within you, Katie, I will give you enough training to hide those powers," Nimbulan said.

Katie looked up at the sadness in his voice. The world spun a moment, then settled. Crystal continued to outline everything she saw. Her eyes focused in sharper detail than she ever thought possible.

Nimbulan moved slowly, almost painfully. The crystal light around the edges of his life flared sharply in orange and black. Blue tinged his lips and spread to his pinched nostrils. He clutched his swollen left hand in the center of his chest. His right arm hung limply by his side.

"Lan!" Myri jumped from her crouched position beside Katie to catch Nimbulan as he crumpled to the ground.

Overhead, Kinnsell's shuttle roared in a low and erratic trajectory.

Katie spared a half glance at the wavering path of the shuttle. The metal/ceramic craft listed to the left and dragged its tail.

"Don't crash, Daddy. I'm not finished with you!" she screamed at him.

Then quite suddenly the jet engines gave way to rockets and the shuttle rose in a new trajectory straight south toward a polar orbit. With the shuttle went her last hope of communicating with her brothers, her last hope of intervening before her father set loose the seeds of the plague on this planet.

She turned her attention back to the people she could help. Nimbulan lay unmoving on the ground. Myri wept silently by his side, holding his limp hand with the blue-tinged fingernails. "I am so sorry, Lan. I dare not help you. The life within me has just begun. We agreed not to taint your son with magic."

Katie realized in that moment that her father also took with him access to all of the advanced medical equipment aboard the mother ship—equipment that might save Nimbulan's life.

*   *   *

Late afternoon, Coronnan City

Bessel crept through the city, Mopsie at his heels. He crossed bridge after bridge, winding among the islands in a convoluted path that confused him as much as anyone who might follow him.

The fishermen had given him dry, mostly clean clothing, but no boots. They usually went barefoot. The yellow tunic and white trews seemed overly bright to Bessel. But the fishermen assured him the clothes represented safety to them. The bright colors were easier to see underwater, should one of them fall overboard. And the colors held no resemblance to the sober blue of the Commune. He'd look like any other fisherman gone to market.

He bypassed the University and its library twice. As long as Scarface ruled that enclave, he'd never be able to delve into the treasure trove of knowledge without help.

As long as Scarface ruled the Commune of Magicians, Bessel would not return, even if invited. He knew the truth now. He was a rogue magician with a familiar. Nimbulan might overlook his crime, but Scarface never would.

Finally, when both he and Mopsie knew that none of the assassins from Rossemeyer had spotted them, he turned toward Ambassador Row. Footsore and exhausted, he limped down several side streets to avoid passing in front of the Rossemeyerian Embassy.

Myrilandel's tall, narrow stone house looked blank and uninviting. The barest flicker of smoke emerged from the tall chimneys at either end of the building, as if all the fires had been banked. Bessel knew that Myrilandel and Nimbulan rarely used the formal rooms at the front of the dwelling. Life centered in the kitchen for them.

Myrilandel should have stoked the kitchen fire by now to prepare the simple evening meal. Unless the family dined at the palace with her brother the king.

Bessel and his familiar scooted down an alley to approach the house from the rear. Closed shutters and a firmly locked door greeted him. Fortunately, he remembered the sequence for opening the lock with magic. Nimbulan had given him that key last night. This was supposed to be his home until the issue of rogue magic and the death of Jorghe-Rosse had been settled.

The settlement meant nothing now.

A chill of unease and stale smoke rippled across Bessel's senses as he stepped down into the kitchen. A mixing bowl and several baking ingredients lay neatly on the worktable, as if set out ahead of time; so, too, were a pile of tubers and cone roots ready for chopping.

But no one greeted him. No one sang while working.

"Anyone here?" he asked the empty room. The fire remained a bank of smoldering coals. The house smelled empty.

Wherever Myrilandel and Nimbulan had gone, they had taken Amaranth with them. Not unusual.

"Well, if we are hungry, Mopsie, I'd best set about fixing something.

"Woof," Mopsie agreed. He waddled over to the pantry door and sniffed eagerly.

"Why did I know you'd be hungry, pup?" Bessel opened the door and followed the dog to the trapdoor leading to the cool cellar. The leftovers of last night's stew should be in the shallow underground room. Mopsie jumped down the four steps and found the covered pot before Bessel could bring a ball of witchlight to his hand for better visibility. Myri had left a bone beside the pot on the shelf, just above Mopsie's reach.

"If I give you the bone, do you promise to be neat with it? I can't have you messing up Myri's kitchen."

Mopsie sat politely and wagged his tail across the stone floor.

"Take it up to the mudroom, then." Bessel handed the bone—longer than the dog's head was wide—to Mopsie. The dog grabbed it with eager teeth and trotted up the stairs.

There he stopped and growled, dropping the bone to bare his teeth in warning.

Bessel set the stew pot back on the shelf very slowly, very quietly. Then he consciously set his magical armor in place. Spells would dissipate before reaching him. Mundane weapons should bounce off him—if he could hold the protection in place long enough. He wasn't used to relying upon ley lines to fuel his spells.

Cautiously, he mounted the first step. The armor sharpened his sight enough to spot the weaknesses in the wooden board that might creak and betray his presence.

His head and shoulders cleared the trapdoor entrance. He searched the pantry with every sense available to him. Once certain that no one had entered the little room and nothing stood between him and an exit, he doused his witchlight and climbed up the remaining three steps.

He paused at the closed door to the kitchen and listened. Someone moved about, restlessly, picking things up and putting them down again.

Who examined the kitchen so precisely?

Then the intruder bumped into the table. He mumbled a curse, barely audible to mundane ears. The wood groaned and a knife clattered against the floor. Four thuds suggested some of the vegetables had followed the knife.

Whoever prowled the room didn't know it well.

Mopsie crawled to the door, belly down, neck fur raised, and teeth bared.

Bessel put aside all of his reticence from invasion of privacy and opened his mind.

"Where have you been, boy?" Lyman angrily threw open the pantry door. "And where are Nimbulan and Myrilandel? The house is as empty and silent as a grave. Do you mind telling me why you and that scruffy mutt are hiding in the pantry like thieves?"

Bessel sagged with relief, leaning against the doorjamb.

"I don't know where anyone is, and I was looking for supper when my familiar warned me of an intruder. Why are you here? I didn't think you ever left the library." Certainly he hadn't left it long enough to keep up with current fashion. His knee-length tunics and silk sash were the objects of many apprentice jokes.

"You don't think much, then. I must find Nimbulan. Where could he have gone?"

"I don't know. I left early this morning and haven't been able to get back until now."

Lyman paused to look at Bessel more closely. "Strange garb for a magician."

"But proper garb for a fisherman. The agents of Lady Rosselaara search for a journeyman magician."

"Ah, so they decided to take matters into their own hands." Lyman tapped his lip with his index finger. "I should have suspected as much if my mind had been on this existence."

"This existence!" Alarmed, Bessel grabbed the old man's shoulders. "You can't die and pass on to the next existence yet. The University needs you. The Commune needs you. We have to counter Scarface's fanaticism."

"And you need me to reclaim information in the library. Yes, yes, I read your mind. I couldn't help it when you opened it wide to listen to mine. Well, you'll have to find the books and read them on your own."

"Promise me you aren't dying," Bessel pleaded. He'd had too many upsets in too short a time. Lyman was a permanent fixture at the University. He couldn't contemplate losing his mentor and . . . and friend.

"No, boy, the duty I must perform is much more frightening than mere death. I am destined to plague apprentices with reading assignments for a good long time yet. But for now I haven't time to discuss this. I must . . ." He trailed off as he cocked his head.

"What do you hear?" Bessel whispered.

"Everything and nothing." A typical Lyman answer.

"Steeds, a dozen or more." Bessel heard them, too. "All metal shod, some moving quickly, others plodding at a steady pace. . . ."

Anyone who could afford a steed stabled it on the mainland. The crowded city isle with narrow twisting streets put dwelling space at a premium and made clean up of human waste a big problem; adding steed manure to the compost only made the problem worse.

"I fear we are needed." Lyman turned away abruptly and headed through the house toward the front door. Bessel trailed closely on his heels. Mopsie began whining in distress.

The sound of the moving steeds was cut off abruptly as the elderly librarian thrust open the door. Bessel stopped short at the sight of Nimbulan lying weakly on a litter borne between two placid steeds. His master's tall, imposing presence seemed greatly reduced. He barely breathed, as if the effort of living weighed too heavily on his thin frame.

Myrilandel walked beside him, tears streaming down her face. Something terrible must have happened if Myrilandel, the greatest healer in the kingdom, couldn't cure her husband.

Queen Katie rode just ahead of the litter. Her red-rimmed eyes bore more evidence of tears and disaster.

Another clatter of hooves from the opposite direction announced King Quinnault's arrival. He reined in his steed sharply. The beast's hooves skidded on the cobblestones, almost throwing the king. But Quinnault mastered his steed and dismounted in front of the queen's procession. Then he retrieved his daughter from the saddle, cradling her easily in one arm.

"Get a healer, Bessel. Hurry. We need the best healers from the Commune now!" Myrilandel burst into tears once more.

"I can't go back to the University. Scarface has forbidden me," Bessel whispered.

"Then I must delay my quest a little longer." Lyman sighed. "I will summon the healers." He took three regulation breaths to trigger a trance and disappeared.

Chapter 34

Bessel sniffed the air around Nimbulan. He reeked of sweet/bitter Tambootie smoke. Tambootie smoke!

The only ritual calling for burning the tree of magic was the coming of age of an apprentice. He remembered his own trial by Tambootie smoke about two moons after he reached puberty. He'd endured two days and three nights in a sealed stone room with only a Tambootie wood fire for heat and light. The smoke had induced visions of drowning and being eaten by a bemouth—one of the monstrous fish that prowled the outer bay. The only predator large enough and fierce enough to hunt a bemouth was a dragon.

Just the memory of those visions sent sharp pains into all of Bessel's joints. He'd been powerless to fight the monster for three days and two nights. Then, finally, when he fell from the monster's jaws, there was nothing left of his body or soul; he'd fled to the sense-depriving blackness of the void.

Moments later Nimbulan had opened the magically sealed door and drawn him back, lovingly, into the protection of his enclave of Battlemages.

Bessel supposed the continued nightmare of the trial that had introduced him to the void, had given him insight into the extent and limitations of his powers. Those limitations had taught him to take responsibility for his actions and never attempt something he couldn't handle alone.

He'd also figured out how to block any magical assault upon his mind or his person.

Two of his classmates had damaged hearts and lungs after their trials and never practiced magic again. They'd had weak talents even before the trial. Tambootie had been proved poisonous to mundanes. Nimbulan had lost his magic a year and a half ago. . . .

The chain of logic rocked Bessel to the core of his being.

Only one disaster would require the queen and her two best friends to risk exposing themselves to the Tambootie. That risk was also the only disease Bessel knew for certain Myri couldn't cure with her wonderful talent.

"Does he have the plague?" he whispered to Myri as the royal guards passed them bearing the litter.

Bessel's time sense rocked backward and forward, superimposing the image of Jorghe-Rosse's corpse being carried on a litter before the king.

He pushed aside the memory for more immediate concerns.

"Does he have the plague?" he asked again, a little louder.

Myri shook her head, never taking her eyes off her husband.

"Then why couldn't you cure him?" he asked. A note of desperation crept into his voice. He had nothing left if Nimbulan died. No family, no Commune, not even his friend the librarian . . .

Mopsie pressed himself against Bessel's legs and whimpered. The fishermen had given him more consideration than the Commune. He could build a new family with the hearty seamen and their dogs.

King Quinnault rushed up beside his sister. He thrust the baby into Bessel's arms for safekeeping then hugged Myrilandel's shoulders in comfort. "He asks a valid question, Myri," Quinnault said quietly. "The law against women using magic be damned. Please do not let this great man die if you can do anything to help him."

"Do you think I would willingly watch my beloved die if I could help, law or no law?" Myri shook off the king's embrace angrily. "I am newly pregnant. I can't use my talent lest I harm the baby. He stopped me earlier today when I would have corrected the problem. . . ." She broke into sobs, unable to finish her sentence.

King Quinnault cradled her against his chest, rubbing her back helplessly.

Bessel mimicked the motion with the little princess. He'd had enough practice taking care of his younger siblings back home.

"Does he have the plague?" Bessel insisted, still tending the baby. *The plague kills the old, the young, and pregnant women first,* his aunt had said. He had to get Myrilandel and the princess away from here.

"No, he does not have the plague," Queen Maarie Kaathliin said, entering the room. Shorter than anyone else by at least a head, she still radiated authority and commanded respect simply by being there.

"Are you certain?" King Quinnault asked. Even he, the most powerful man in the land deferred to her.

"Yes, I am certain. The Tambootie smoke would have killed the virus if our brief exposure had infected him."

"His skin is waxy and blue like the dragon dream Powwell shared with me," Bessel argued, desperately needing reassurance and not daring to hope for it. "His breathing is ragged just like my mother's was before she died."

"Your mother had the plague?" King Quinnault swung Bessel around, shaking his shoulders as if he had to force the information from him. "Where? When?" Why wasn't I told!"

"Master Scarface said that only the privations of a long winter and the aftermath of so many generations of war ravaged Lord Balthazaan's province, especially the mining villages where they grow very little of their own food. But I remembered the smell. Powwell shared the smell with me telepathically when he shared the dragon dream."

"Stargods, the plague is here for certain, not just a 'perhaps' pushed aside for other concerns. How? When?" Quinnault paced the reception hall. He clenched his hands behind his back and hunched his shoulders. With the afternoon sun pouring through the open doorway, he was outlined in red-gold light like the silhouette of a young dragon.

Bessel stepped away from him. Surreptitiously, he crossed himself in a ward against the evils of the unknown.

"My husband's heart is weak from all those years of warfare that left this kingdom teetering on bankruptcy—a

bankruptcy of people as well as money. He wore out his
heart and himself weaving great magic in battle after battle.
Now he pays the price. Where are the healers? Lyman
promised to summon them." Myri ran to the door, looking
up and down the street anxiously. Then she rushed back
to Nimbulan's side. She knelt beside the litter. The guards
had laid the aging man before the unlit hearth.

Bessel forced his mind to light the fire. No other magicians stalked the room; he could use rogue magic for the
task—so much easier than the increasingly elusive dragon
magic. In a heartbeat the fire leaped high, warming the
large room.

A whoosh of displaced air erupted beside Bessel, nearly
knocking him into the wall. He clutched the baby tighter
to make sure he didn't drop her. As he struggled for balance, Lyman popped into view, much as he had disappeared moments before.

"The healers come," the old librarian announced breathlessly. "Now make yourself useful in the kitchen, Bessel.
Kaariin is here to tend the baby. Stay out of sight, and
keep your mutt quiet. Scarface is hot on the heels of the
medical people. He's angrier than a wet lumbird and looking for a victim." Lyman transferred Princess Marilell to
the arms of the breathless maid who dashed up the steps
from the street.

"Lyman, how did you do that?" Bessel asked, too
amazed to obey. "Dragon magic only allows levitation, not
transportation. And no one could transport a living being
from place to place even when solitary magic was legal."
He dropped his voice as the thought formed into words.
The royal couple and their guards were too occupied making Nimbulan comfortable to pay attention to his almost
accusation.

"Shhush, boy. The answer is in the timing. And if you
ever figure it out, guard the secret with your life. You may
need the spell in the days to come, but never use it carelessly. Now I must be off. The dragons call me."

Another whoosh of displaced air and he was gone, almost
as if he'd never been there.

"Maybe he only sent an illusion along with a powerful
summons," the queen whispered into Bessel's ear.

"Is there anything you don't see or hear, Your Grace?" Bessel asked.

"Very little. Now do as your master says, mull some wine or prepare snacks, or anything you can think of, in the kitchen and out of sight."

Bessel scuttled down the hall to the back of the house just as he heard Scarface's roar of anger in the street.

Chapter 35

Yaala whipped her belt knife upward and held it across Hanassa's throat. With her free arm she pinned the consort's arms. Beside her, Rollett drew his own blade and held it up in a fighting stance. Powwell whipped his staff around to fend off any attackers.

"Kill them, kill them all!" Hanassa cried. She held her body tensely, poised for flight at the first sign of weakness in Yaala's grip.

"If I die, you die, too, Hanassa. I've waited a long time to avenge my father's death." Years of anger, frustration, and loneliness concentrated in Yaala's hand, making the knife blade waver up and down across the great vein of life in Hanassa's throat.

Rollett shot her a strange look.

Her determination wavered a moment. If she killed Hanassa, then she condemned Kalen to a ghostly existence as a wraith. Powwell would never forgive her.

If she killed Hanassa solely to exact vengeance, then she succumbed to the renegade dragon's violence. Rollett would never forgive her.

She'd never forgive herself.

But she couldn't let Hanassa go free either. The tyranny had to end.

The Rover guards lowered their sword tips but did not drop their weapons.

"Tell them to throw their swords and clubs into the pool

of water beside Old Bertha," Yaala commanded her prisoner, loud enough for the Rovers to hear.

"Never. You must die!"

Yaala nicked Kalen's skin. Three drops of blood trickled onto the blade.

A screech of fear and pain echoed around the caverns. Hanassa hadn't uttered a sound. The wraith had.

The Rovers threw their weapons away. All except Piedro.

Cautiously, Yaala edged forward toward the mouth of the tunnel, keeping her prisoner in front of her, the knife still dangerously close to drawing blood.

Piedro took one step forward, raising his sword. "You haven't the guts to take a life," he sneered.

"Perhaps not. But I do," a solemn voice announced from the main cavern.

All the Rovers fell silent, backing away from the frail old man who stood beside Old Bertha. He wore an old-fashioned blue tunic that hung nearly to his knees, belted with a silk sash. The tunic and trews had been dyed Commune blue. He carried a long staff nearly twice his height. The length of wood was so twisted and gnarled from a lifetime of channeling magic, Yaala couldn't see a pattern in the grain that mimicked the man's magical signature.

"Lyman!" Powwell breathed in relief.

"Iianthe! You cannot still live. I felt you die decades ago." Hanassa struggled in Yaala's arms, ready to break free. She looked right and left, up and down, disregarding the knife at her throat.

"Iianthe, the purple-tipped dragon born your twin, died more than twenty years ago, Hanassa," Lyman replied. He swung his staff in a sweeping circle, moving it so fast it blurred in the dim light. A challenging hum followed its rapid passage through the air. "But since you refused to live out your true destiny, I was forced to assume a human body and finish it for you. Now the dragons have sent me to make certain you do not leave here with the knowledge of the machines and how they work."

"You expect to fight me in that frail old body. I, at least had the good sense to choose someone young and strong." Hanassa broke free of Yaala's grip. She thrust Piedro aside as she marched to meet the old magician's challenge.

Yaala stumbled against Rollett. He steadied her with one hand around her waist, never dropping his confrontational stance before the Rover guards. The warmth of his hand and the gentle squeeze of his fingers gave her a sense of rightness.

You did right not to kill. His thoughts came to her unbidden. Something lit deep in his eyes. Respect?

Suddenly her previous attraction to Powwell faded. If she ever loved—truly loved—she would love a man like him: mature, decisive, experienced in the ways of the world. Someone to challenge her spirit and her intellect.

"The wraith fights you for control of the body, Hanassa," Lyman reminded his onetime twin. "This body is mine alone." Lyman crouched in a fighting stance, his staff suddenly still. The artificial lights within the cavern highlighted his body in layers of purple-and-crystal light. The strange aura shaped itself into the outline of a dragon.

Yaala shook her head to clear it of the confusing images. Rollett mimicked the motion.

"Stargods preserve us!" Piedro crossed himself several times. He dropped his sword. It clattered against the rock in an ominous chiming.

Hanassa launched Kalen's body at Lyman with fingers arched into talons, teeth bared, and a snarl erupting from her wide mouth.

Lyman blocked her attack with his staff. He swung it down and around, clipping Hanassa on the temple with one end.

Hanassa staggered back. She stumbled against the rusting hulk of Old Bertha.

Yaala winced as pieces of metal crumbled beneath the impact.

"Get out of the cavern!" Lyman called. He pointed the staff at his opponent. A blast of blinding purple-white light shot forth from the staff with a deafening explosion. Hanassa flew backward, into a wall, slamming her head against the rough stones.

Yaala grabbed for the tunnel walls to catch her balance as the magical attack shook the entire system of caves and tunnels. She missed the wall. Rollett caught her against his side. He wrapped one arm around her shoulders, steadying her—steadying them both.

"We've got to get above ground," he said quietly, almost calmly. "He's filled with dragon magic and will stop at nothing to kill Hanassa, regardless of Kalen's spirit."

"Kalen needs that body. I can't let him kill my sister," Powwell cried, dashing forward.

Rollett and Yaala both grabbed their friend. Yaala caught only a handful of cloth near the neck of his tunic. Rollett had better luck, latching onto his arm.

"Lyman will spare Kalen if he can. If anyone can," Yaala soothed Powwell. "He's a Communal Magician, he values life."

Another magical blast sent Hanassa reeling facedown into the pool of hot water. The tunnel shook. Rocks tumbled from the ceiling.

"We have to save ourselves now!" Yaala dragged Powwell out from under the falling rock.

"Kalen!" Powwell screamed. Tears streamed down his face. His tunic tore as he ripped out of Yaala's grasp.

"No, Powwell," Rollett said. "I can't let you do this." He slammed his fist into the boy's jaw.

Yaala braced herself to catch Powwell as he fell backward into her arms.

The next blast of magic knocked the ground from beneath her feet. They both fell. Rollett crashed on top of them followed by a tumble of rocks.

She couldn't breathe. Something hit her head. Starbursts blinded her. Blood clouded her vision.

She fought for consciousness and lost the battle.

* * *

Afternoon, the pit beneath the city of Hanassa

Powwell struggled to push Rollett off his back. "Yaala, are you all right?" He shook his friend, trapped beneath him.

He heard the Rovers tripping over each other in their mad dash to escape the wrath of Hanassa.

Yaala moaned and rolled her head as if in pain. Then she fell silent.

"Get off me, Rollett." Powwell shoved upward with his elbow.

Rollett groaned and rolled drunkenly to one side. "We ga get oot ah here," he slurred, holding his head and shoulder.

"I've got to help Kalen. Take care of Yaala." Powwell drew his knees up under him. The battle still raged around Old Bertha. Lyman crouched on one side of the old generator. Hanassa drew on Kalen's magical talent and created a geyser directly in front of the old librarian.

In fine Battlemage fashion, Lyman channeled the spurt of hot water back into the broken pipe that passed above the lava core. Boiling water built up within the rusted metal, forcing a new opening. Steam shot out of a dozen rust holes in a variety of directions.

Scalding water struck Hanassa in the face as she crept forward. "Yieeee!" she screamed and dodged back behind the shelter of the machine.

Powwell crawled quietly toward her. He winced for her as she pulled her hands away from her face. A long red weal ran from her left temple to the corner of her mouth. Big tears dribbled from her eyes. She blotted them away from the painful burn, crying more at the pain of touching the wound.

Don't hurt my body. I need it back! The wraith added her own mournful cries to the noise.

Powwell needed to go to his little sister. He didn't know how to force Hanassa out of the body and keep her out short of killing the body. Hot moisture prickled the backs of his eyes.

"Leave her, Powwell," Lyman insisted in a ragged whisper. Exhaustion made his eyes droop and his shoulders sag. "You can't win this battle. The only way I can defeat Hanassa is to kill her—if I can. But I do not yet know the cost. Take your friends and get out of here now."

"The dragongate. It'll open soon. We'll go out the dragongate." Powwell looked longingly toward the little tunnel that opened onto the lava core.

"Over my dead body, boy!" Hanassa jumped up in front of him. Her fingers arched and flexed. Her very long nails looked more like dragon talons than human digits.

Powwell didn't doubt she could render his flesh into slender strips with little effort.

Get it out of my body! The wraith pleaded on a sob.

Powwell reached a tentative hand toward the misty form that circled him and Hanassa.

"Powwell, feel the hot wind!" Rollett called. "The gate is opening again. The gate is opening."

"I'll be free at last! You can't stop me. I'll bleed this world dry." Hanassa turned and ran into the little tunnel.

"Stop her. We can't let Hanassa leave this place," Lyman gasped. He wiped his face wearily with a shaking hand.

Powwell scanned his companions. Lyman was exhausted. Rollett tried staggering to his feet and sat back down heavily. No help from either of them. Yaala, his dear friend, lay unconscious, blood trickling from her temple.

Hanassa skidded to a halt at the edge of the pit. The gate swirled in a kaleidoscope of colors. Green dominated the forming image. The green of Coronnan?

"I'm sorry, Kalen, I've got to close the gate forever. Thorny and I have got to close it."

Noooooooooo! The misty form darted after Hanassa at the end of the tunnel.

Thorny hunched and bristled his spines. Powwell couldn't tell if his familiar reacted in gibbering fear or thought this was another setup for blood magic—the only magic left to them.

"No, Powwell. The gate is our only hope of escape from this hell," Rollett reminded him. The older journeyman crawled toward him, holding out his hand in entreaty. "Please, Powwell, in the Stargods' names, I beg you, don't close the gate. That's home out there. We can be home in two moments."

"Yeeees! I'm free," Hanassa screamed in triumph. She looked up at the wraith rather than forward into the gate. The scene solidified (liquefied?) into storm-tossed waves.

Powwell grabbed one of Thorny's dried spines from his pocket and jabbed it hard into his hand. "Yeeow!" He held his yelp of pain deep inside his chest, letting it grow with the flow of blood from the deep wound.

Power grew with the pain. Each drop of blood increased the magic singing in his veins. He knew every grain of dirt and mineral within the cavern. His magic invaded every crack and crevice. His mind flowed outward, melding with

the cavern until he couldn't tell where the tunnels ended
and he began.

"I'm sorry, Kalen. I'm sorry, but this is the only way
to keep Hanassa or anyone else from controlling you and
your destiny."

He sought the weakest point within the tunnel and
pulled—

The tunnel collapsed upon Hanassa and his sister, sealing
access to the gate forever.

He sensed the weight of the entire cavern system landing
on Hanassa's head, splitting it open. Sympathetic pain
slammed into his own skull. He fell to the ground, screaming at his physical pain and the emptiness in his heart.

Chapter 36

The pit beneath the city of Hanassa

"**W**ake up. You've got to wake up," Rollett pleaded with her. She moaned slightly but didn't rouse.

"Wake up!" He slapped her face lightly, afraid of hurting her, of breaking those fragile facial bones.

Her eyelids fluttered.

A huge boulder broke loose from the ceiling and landed in the middle of Old Bertha. Powwell had upset the delicate balance within the mountain that supported the caves.

"We've got to get out of here, Yaala." He slapped her a little harder. She moaned and rolled away from him.

Rollett risked a glance toward Powwell. The boy had his hands clutched over his head and had rolled into a fetal ball, sobbing uncontrollably. The little hedgehog poked its nose out of his pocket. It trilled a soothing sound.

Lyman seemed to have disappeared again.

"Stargods, I can't carry you both. I'm sorry, Powwell, I've got to save Yaala. The city needs her." He wouldn't admit that *he* needed her.

Rollett hoisted Yaala onto his shoulder and wove his way out of the deep cavern. The roar of multiple cave-ins thundered against his ears. The opening to the lava core adjacent to the dragongate collapsed. Dust exploded in a huge ball, filling the hot air.

He choked and coughed. With one last look of regret toward Powwell, he increased his speed toward the exit.

His last vestige of hope died along with access to the dragongate. He'd climb out of Hanassa tonight. Demons take Piedro and this cursed city. He hoped Yaala would rouse enough to climb with him. Otherwise he'd have to carry her.

Little Liise, the only operating generator, chugged steadily within a side cavern.

That persistent, unwanted hope flowered once more deep inside his gut. His magic talent stirred in response to the emotion.

He set Yaala down beside Liise. She roused a little, flailing about with both hands clenched into fists.

"Wake up, Yaala. You're all right. Wake up." He shook her gently.

Finally, her eyes flew open and she dragged in a deep breath. She coughed the dust-laden air back out again.

"It's getting hotter in here. The volcano is getting ready to erupt!" She bounced to her feet and staggered back into Liise. "My head . . . what happened?" She touched her temple with delicate fingertips. They came away bloody.

"The lower caverns are collapsing. Powwell destroyed the dragongate. I think he killed Hanassa and Kalen when he did it," Rollett explained as he set about examining the generator with minute care.

Should he take the raw energy as it left Liise headed for a transformer, or take the refined 'tricity after it left the transformer?

He opted for raw power. His body would become the transformer. That's what happened when gathering dragon magic.

Which conduit? He reached out tentatively with his dominant left hand and touched one of the wires. A slight spark made him jerk his hand away. His fingers tingled just as if he had tapped a ley line, but the power he tapped was stronger, more intense.

This was what he needed, a renewal of the magical energy contained within the Kardia.

If either Lyman or Hanassa had reverted to natural dragon form, both he and Powwell could have gathered that magic. Yaala could have gathered power from a purple-tipped dragon—anyone could gather from the rare purple-tips, even mundanes.

Lacking a dragon of any color, Rollett had to find other

sources of energy to combat or elude the Rovers who still ruled the city of Hanassa.

He reached again for the wire and the energy he needed.

"No, Rollett," Yaala pleaded. Still clutching her head with one hand she tried to step between him and the generator. She stumbled.

Rollett shifted his reach to hold her upright. Her body fit nicely against his own. "Soon, we'll be free, Yaala, and I'll be able to hold you as long as we both need."

"It's too dangerous, Rollett. Don't touch the 'tricity."

"I have to. It's the only way I'll have enough power to overcome Piedro and get us out of here. I promise that once we're free, we'll make time to explore this thing between us . . . this 'tricity you and I generate all on our own."

"Please, Rollett. We don't know enough about how 'tricity works. No one has ever tried to use it like magic."

"Not too long ago no one had gathered dragon magic either." Resolutely, he separated from her comforting embrace. Out of long habit he stilled his body to make it receptive to the power, reached out and . . .

Energy coursed through his veins. His body became light as it jerked back and forth. Back and forth. His teeth rattled. Back and forth.

He smelled burning flesh. His own. Pain jolted every joint and nerve ending in his body.

"Rollett! Let go. You've got to stop this. It's hurting you," Yaala cried.

"Don't touch me. It's . . . not . . . supposed . . . to be . . . like . . . this!"

He couldn't let go. He couldn't stop the flow.

He couldn't . . .

Chapter 37

Katie looked around the entry hall to Myrilandel's home.
What could she do to help? Bessel and his mutt were
safely out of sight. The healers marched through the doorway. They would repair the initial damage to Nimbulan's
heart. Quinnault comforted his sister.

She eyed the line of healers led by Whitehands skeptically.

"I've been breaking rules all my life. Why should I stop
now?" Katie rubbed her hands together in anticipation of
positive action when she felt so useless to help Nimbulan.
"I need your assistance." She snagged a healer journeyman
as the procession of gray-clad magicians entered the house.

At least she hoped the gray tunic and blue trews signified
a journeyman.

"How may I be of service, Your Grace?" the young man
asked warily. His gaze followed the healers into the reception hall, clearly anxious to be close to the center of action.

"Do you know a plant called Fairy Thimbles?" Katie
asked him.

His eyes glazed over blankly.

"Broad fuzzy leaves tapering to a point. Tall flower stock
filled with purple bells," she described the common *Digitalis purpurea* that had originated on Earth and followed
humanity through colonization of a hundred worlds.

"Fairy Bells, sometimes called foxglove," the young man
responded, his eyes clearing with enlightenment.

"Yes! Can you recognize the plant this early in the season? Can you bring me a specimen now?"

He nodded enthusiastically. "Do you know a medical use for the plant? We know it only as a poison—pretty in the garden but dangerous to ingest."

"Yes. Once the healers have stabilized Master Nimbulan, a drug made from the plant can keep his heart beating regularly."

"I shall return in a few moments." The young man's face brightened, and his eyes sparkled. Katie could almost see the ideas churning in his head.

"Take the plant to the kitchen and tell the young man there to begin making a . . . a decoction of the leaves." She didn't dare name the journeyman in the kitchen lest Scarface at the end of the line of healers overhear. "It must be a very mild decoction, no more than one handful to half a pint of water. Simmer it for about one half an hour. No longer. An effective dose is very close to a lethal one. We must start slow and build up by tiny increments to find the right proportions. We'll need more leaves to dry and use in infusions. That is a better remedy, but we don't have time to dry the leaves. I will join you in a moment to help you."

The journeyman dashed around the corner of the building toward the back of the house just as Scarface stormed up the steps.

"Why must you meddle in affairs that do not concern you, Your Grace?" Scarface demanded. The scar across his face whitened and tightened. "You can't help."

How much guilt from his past haunted him so that he could never find peace within himself and therefore couldn't allow it in another?

"Is aiding a dear friend in his struggle for life meddling?" she retorted with a sarcastic half-smile.

"It is if the Stargods have decreed the man's time to pass on to his next existence," Scarface replied. As usual he looked over her shoulder at the wall rather than directly at her.

"Who are we to know the intent of a deity? We are duty bound to use whatever talents and knowledge we have been given. Myrilandel needs her husband, Her babies need a father, King Quinnault still needs his friend, Coronnan desperately needs Nimbulan's wisdom. I will meddle in whatever way I can to help him."

"Perhaps this is the method the Stargods have chosen to tell us that Nimbulan's guidance is no longer needed or wanted."

"Is that the message of the Stargods or of the Senior Magician who replaced Nimbulan but can never truly replace him?"

"That is not for you to question. You are merely a foreign female who barely hides her illegal magical talent!"

"I am your queen."

"For now. But I know you are also a spy for our enemies. You have lied to the king and all of Coronnan. You cannot possibly be who you say you are." Now he looked directly at her, accusing, unforgiving.

Katie swallowed her rush of fear. How much did Scarface know?

"But I am who I say I am. I do not lie," she countered. "The dragons have blessed me as consort to their king. Quinnault rules by the grace of the dragons. Do you care to argue the matter with Shayla and her nimbus?"

"If I must." Scarface maintained his steady gaze into her eyes. "Dragons have many secrets—secret knowledge they deem dangerous to humans. They recognize the value of some secrets. I do not believe they will honor your secrets much longer, unless you have managed to keep information in your mind hidden from their scrutiny. The plague you carry and the cure you keep secret is clear evidence of your evil intent."

"Take your self-righteous anger elsewhere, Master Aaddler. I have never kept the cure for the plague secret. Only the Tambootie can cure the ailment that devastates my people and may be spreading here." Arguing with him was useless. But he commanded a great deal of power—political as well as magical. If she turned her back on him, he'd presume she fled from guilt and weakness. He'd use that against her. She had to stand her ground.

"Tambootie is poison to mundanes and only mundanes are affected by this disease." Scarface stared back at her, not moving from the doorway of Myrilandel's home. Then he blinked his eyes slowly as if making a decision.

"Terrania, the land you *claim* to hail from is the oldest known country on all of Kardia Hodos. Legend says that men first emerged in that land. But it is now a desert wasteland and has been for many, many centuries. Where do you really come from, wife of my king?"

"We call it Terra now."

"And where is Terra that you and your father can only reach it by flying inside the belly of a mechanical dragon? A mechanical beast that spreads the plague you preach against . . . or have you brought the plague here deliberately to kill us off so you can resettle those who are displaced by the desert sands of Terrania?"

"How dare you!" Katie slapped his face. Red stained his left cheek in the shape of her handprint.

"How dare you!" Scarface raised his right fist as if to slam it into her jaw. "How dare you deceive one and all with your lies, usurping *my* authority by ordering my journeyman to run personal errands when he . . . when none of the Commune even looked to me for confirmation when they received word of *that* man's illness." He pointed to the still form at the center of the healers' circle. "He's not even a magician anymore, and they defer to him in all matters. He steals the respect they owe me."

"Respect has to be earned," Katie held his gaze, daring him to inflict violence upon her. "Nimbulan was your friend. You saved each other's lives numerous times in your escape from Hanassa. Now you wish him and his influence on the kingdom dead."

She didn't know for certain if that last stray thought was her own idea or if Scarface had leaked it to her mind. His ability to guard his psi powers was normally strong.

"Beware of whom you accuse, Your Grace. My magicians may be more concerned with Nimbulan's health than with my permission to leave University Isle, but I can still bring you down and your king with you."

"Scarface!" Quinnault strode to the entry from the reception hall in a few anxious paces. "Why wasn't I told that the plague had already brought Lord Balthazaan's province low?"

"That neglectful lord always loses large numbers of tenants to disease and privation in the spring." Scarface shrugged off the news. But he shifted his eyes away from his king.

He's lying! He knows something dangerous, Katie thought directly into Quinnault's mind.

"This is more than a lord's neglect," Katie countered, trying to peer into Scarface's mind for the truth. "This is a disease that eats the internal organs until you bleed to death from the inside! Bessel watched his mother die of it. He reported dozens of deaths from the same cause. Didn't you listen to him?"

"Bessel is not a reliable witness."

More lies. What was he hiding?

"Why isn't Bessel reliable? He is your senior journeyman." Quinnault stepped closer to Scarface, towering over him. He looked as if he wanted to beat some sense into the magician as well.

"A familiar has sought out Bessel. Familiars fear dragons and will not come to a magician using dragon energies. Therefore Bessel obviously uses illegal rogue magic regularly. Besides, Bessel has never been *my* journeyman. He belongs to Nimbulan and always has. He defies me at every turn. He is a part of this conspiracy to put Nimbulan back into the Commune as Senior Magician even though he is now mundane. I trust no one who has served my predecessor. The mercenaries of Rossemeyer will serve us all well when they assassinate Bessel since you will not condemn him for the murder of Ambassador Jorghe-Rosse."

Katie and Quinnault looked to each other for explanation. Her husband's thoughts, which she could never fully shut out, rolled in chaos as he sought some kind of logic in the last statement.

Then his mind closed, as if he had slammed a door shut upon Katie's link to him. She recoiled in surprise. Never in the year and a half of their marriage had he denied her access to his most intimate thoughts.

Loneliness nearly overwhelmed her need to remain in this conversation.

"I think you'd best retire to the privacy and security of your apartments in the Commune, Master Aaddler," Quinnault said quietly—too calmly.

Let me into your thoughts, Scarecrow! Katie pleaded with her husband. She tried to hold his hand. He jerked free of her tentative touch.

This terrible aloneness frightened her. Without Quinnault, without her brothers, far from the home of her birth and nurturing, she was lost. She needed to become one with him again.

She used to enjoy being alone when her large family became too intrusive, too boisterous. But she always had familiar surroundings and the knowledge that when she wanted she could reach out and touch one of them with her mind, or her hand.

Her father had always respected her privacy when no one else did. And now her father had been exposed to the plague, possibly carried it to others.

Which others? Lord Balthazaan's province already reeled under the impact of the horrible disease. Lord Balthazaan. Something . . .

"Is that a dismissal, Your Grace?" Scarface backed up a step. Surprise almost masked the new surge of anger in his expression and posture.

"It is." Quinnault remained closed to Katie. The easygoing diplomat, always ready to seek a compromise had disappeared inside his head and behind his clenched fists. "I have lost confidence in you as my chief adviser, Master Aaddler. I will ask the Commune to elect a new senior, one whom I can trust."

"Then think on this, King Quinnault Darville de Draconis, before you give your trust and confidence to Nimbulan, the man you call friend: The Rover woman, Maia, has escaped. The only way she could have broken through our wards is with help—the help of someone with Rover blood and therefore access to the mind-to-mind link of Rover magic. Nimbulan has Rovers in his ancestry. He has lied to you when he claims to have lost all of his magic. He still has Rover magic. He was also Maia's lover. She bore him a child. Who else in your kingdom would want to help her escape?" Scarface turned on his heel and marched back the way he had come.

"Lord Balthazaan is Nimbulan's cousin, isn't he?" Katie asked, thinking through the convoluted relationships among the nobility of Coronnan. "He would have Rover blood in his ancestry as well. Could an unscrupulous Rover magician manipulate him? We never found Piedro after he escaped, Scarecrow! A Rover helped him escape a magically sealed prison."

Lord Balthazaan has enjoyed new prosperity of late." Quinnault clasped her hand tightly in his to dispel the lingering nightmare of the night Piedro tried to strangle Katie with the silken tie from Quinnault's robe. "Despite the plague that decimates his population and threatens to close his mines for lack of workers, Lord Balthazaan rides new and expensive steeds. His wife wears the most costly Se-Lenese lace."

"And they both wear a great deal of jewelry," Katie added, thinking again of the Rover ring that Marilell had almost choked on.

"Perhaps Balthazaan's new prosperity results from Rover interference, or possibly your father's manipulation."

"My father carries the plague that has infected Baltha-zaan's province."

"So is the lord the puppet of your father or of the Ro-vers?" Quinnault raised one eyebrow. The solid wall that closed his mind cracked a little.

Katie reached in with her own thoughts, sharing every twisted idea surrounding the issue.

"The vandalism, the riot, the ambush of supply caravans, that strange storm that killed Jorghe-Rosse . . . Balthazaan was always the first to accuse you of incompetence or tyranny, Scarecrow. Perhaps he engineered the incidents."

"Or knew of them in advance to prepare his arguments," Quinnault offered. "Perhaps Kinnsell and Balthazaan used each other and the Rovers ride their schemes to further their own ambitions."

"All of them would like to see an end to our reign for different reasons. I think we need to look closer at Baltha-zaan as a focus for those who oppose you at every turn, Scarecrow."

"The time has come to divide the opposition and thus weaken their resolve."

"But first we must tend to Nimbulan. We need his wisdom now more than ever."

"I hope we are not too late to save him." Quinnault returned to Nimbulan's side, lovingly holding the older man's hand as a bit of color returned to Nimbulan's overly pale face.

"I hope we are not too late to find my father before he infects the entire planet with the plague. There is barely enough Tambootie left to feed the dragons. How can we cure all of our own people without it?" Katie asked herself, the others, and the air.

Chapter 38

*The pit beneath the city of Hanassa, time
undetermined*

Without thinking of the consequences, Yaala punched
a warning button on Liise's control panel and threw
a switch to break the circuit.

The bizarre blue arcing that surrounded Rollett and jerked
him back and forth in a dance of death abruptly ceased.
He dropped to the ground in a boneless heap.

The overhead lights died, plunging the entire cavern system into darkness. Yaala reeled without a sense of up and
down or right and left. Hesitantly, she spread her hands
away from her body for balance. Sparks leaped from Liise
to her fingers. The residual current needed to complete the
circuit. Like a living being, it sought contact rather than die.

She jerked her hand away. At least she knew how far she
stood from the machinery. Rollett should be just there. . . .

She bumped against his unmoving body and dropped to
her knees. "Rollett, wake up!" she pleaded with him for a
sign that he still lived.

He didn't moan. She heard no movement, no rustle of
clothing, no scrape of a shoe on rock, no whisper of air
entering or exiting a pair of lungs.

"Rollett, don't you dare die on me!" She shook him.
Tremors ran through his body.

"I don't know if this will work or not, but Queen Katie
says it should." Yaala stuck a finger in his mouth to make
certain nothing clogged his air passage. Then she tilted back
his head and blew her own breath into his mouth.

"That works better with two people," Old Lyman said from behind her. He held a feeble ball of witchlight in his hand. Powwell staggered beside him, barely outlined in the dim light.

The kardia continued to rumble around them. Dust filled the air, further dimming the tiny light.

"Help me," Yaala pleaded with them. Tears streaked her cheeks. She dashed them away with her sleeve. There was no time for this weakness.

She sensed the constant shifting of the caverns around her. They didn't have much time. She wouldn't leave Rollett, and she couldn't carry him. His life seemed much more important than all of Hanassa right now.

"Breathe into him on the count of five," Lyman instructed as he knelt beside Rollett's still unmoving form. He passed the witchlight to Powwell. The younger magician looked barely able to hold himself up, let alone maintain the dim glowing ball.

Lyman cupped his hands over Rollett's chest and pressed down. "One, two, three, four, breathe."

Yaala followed his rhythm. Two times, three times, and a fourth they forced Rollett's heart to beat while Yaala breathed for him. On the seventh try, or was it the eleventh, Rollett gasped and coughed. He tried sitting up, but Lyman held him down.

"Rest a moment, boy," Lyman said, holding Rollett down with one finger. "We've brought you back from the dead, don't hasten to return there."

The kardia shifted beneath Yaala's feet. She braced herself against the rolling motion. "That was stronger than the last one, and closer," she said. "When was the last one?" She realized she'd been so preoccupied with Rollett, she had forgotten the reason for their perilous route to this situation.

"We have to get out of here before—" A crash of falling stone and a shower of dust in the corner of Liise's cavern punctuated her statement.

The cave system had been her refuge from her mother's tyranny for many years before her official banishment. The machines had been her only true friends. She belonged here.

No longer.

Sadness and regret welled up in her throat and dissipated again as Rollett struggled to his feet. She slid an arm under his shoulders, guiding his rise.

A sense of rightness filled her, replacing the loneliness of many years. She had to find a new family, a new purpose for living. She'd start with these three men.

"This will never be Liise's cavern again. She's dead, and so are all the rest of my machines," she whispered. "No reason to stay."

"Powwell!" Lyman left her to support Rollett alone while he kept Powwell from falling flat on his face.

"What's wrong with him?" Yaala barely spared a backward glance as she half-led and half-carried Rollett up the slope toward the living cavern and the exit.

"I don't think he much cares if he lives or dies," Lyman said, pushing Powwell to follow her. "I know how he feels. We have both lost a sibling today. There is this terrible emptiness." He placed his palm against his chest then resolutely closed his hand into a self-contained fist.

He and Powwell stood together with heads bowed, swaying as they shared the bond of grief.

"I lost my twin centuries ago." Lyman gulped. His voice trailed off and his chin quivered. "I lost Hanassa when he turned renegade, but always I had this faint hope he might be redeemed. Now I have truly lost Hanassa. We will never complete each other again." He bowed his head again, seeming much older than he had when he arrived in the caves.

"I killed her, Yaala," Powwell whispered. "I came here to save Kalen, yet I ended up killing her." Tears streaked his face. The little ball of witchlight flickered, reflecting his waning strength and wandering concentration.

"I'm sorry, Powwell. I'm truly sorry. I know how much you loved Kalen. I know what it is like to lose someone you love dearly, to be helpless as they die before your eyes. But we have to save ourselves now." Yaala led them into the living cavern. They staggered forward. The sounds of collapsing tunnels pursued them the entire distance. The dust grew thicker until they breathed more dirt than air.

For the first time, she became aware of the miles of kardia that rested above their heads. It could all come tumbling down at any time without warning.

At last the large cavern with tons of stored food lay before them. The walls seemed more stable here, the air a little cleaner.

Yaala deposited Rollett on a heap of grain sacks next to a barrel full of pickled meat and vegetables. She gave him and Powwell a handful of each. They nibbled halfheartedly. Lyman dug into the supplies with a little more energy.

The pile of stores showed signs of pilferage—torn sacks, open barrels turned on their side—but more than enough remained to fulfill their immediate needs.

"I'll get water for us all," Yaala said retrieving four carry skins.

"Did Kalen as the wraith survive?" Yaala asked as she knelt by the underground stream, letting the natural flow fill the portable bottles. She held her breath, fearing the answer.

"Doubtful," Lyman replied.

"And . . . and is Hanassa truly gone?"

"I cannot sense my twin within this mountain. I haven't the strength to search farther." A set look came over Lyman's face.

"And the dragongate?" Rollett gasped in whispered tones. "Have we totally lost that exit from this hellhole?"

"Yes," Powwell answered. A tiny spark of animation came into his eyes. Or was it merely a reflection from the ball of witchlight? "I fear the false gate that only opens once each moon is gone as well. We must fight our way out of Hanassa now."

"I can't leave as long as Piedro lives," Rollett announced in a stronger, more resolute voice. "The consort might not guide him anymore, but he's still a bloodthirsty tyrant. My men deserve better."

"The people of Hanassa are outlaws—assassins, highwaymen, and murderers," Yaala argued. "They deserve what they allow to happen here." For the first time, she saw the truth surrounding the city she should have inherited from her mother. A new sense of lightness invaded her being. Her spirit had freed itself of Hanassa, even if she physically remained here.

"Not all of the residents are criminals." Rollett shook off her supporting arm and walked weakly to the creek on his own. He drank deeply of the sulfur-laden water, then continued. "Some of them are political fugitives, some merely mercenaries for hire. Some even still hold a tiny glimmer of honor. They deserve better than Piedro's lust for power without the sense to wield it justly."

"Without the dragongate, Piedro is confined to this city. The city will take care of him. Why should we care as long as we get out?" Lyman asked. Craftiness replaced the grief on his face.

"Because the city will starve before they can oust Piedro. He'll deliberately starve my men, my friends, before he allows them to escape." Rollett's knees wobbled as he returned to the food supplies.

Lyman and Powwell looked ashen in the fading glow of witchlight as they struggled once more to their feet, exhausted and burdened by grief. Their skin seemed grayer than just the dust would account for. "All three of you have got to rest a little longer. Drink deeply and eat as much as you can." She seemed to be the only one strong enough to make a decision. But her head ached terribly with every thought and movement. She followed her own advice.

"No time," Powwell ground out between gritted teeth.

She ached to see the bleak expression in his eyes. Thorny seemed strangely quiet within his pocket. They both suffered from the loss of Kalen and the drain of blood magic.

"Piedro is mine. I claim the right to remove his head." Powwell's words filled the suddenly quiet cavern with dread.

"Not if I get to him first," Rollett replied. He kept moving upward toward the iron gate.

The ground shook again, precursor to another larger quake. As one, they hurried up the slope, eating as they walked.

"I claim blood right for revenge." Powwell stopped moving. His stance challenged them all to contradict him. "Kalen was my sister. Her death is a direct result of Rover manipulation. All Kalen wanted out of life was control of her own life. Piedro is only the latest in a long line of people who used her for their own greedy ends. His head is mine."

"Piedro was as much Hanassa's victim as Kalen was," Yaala insisted. "Let's just concentrate on getting out of here alive. All of us, together." She reached out both hands to include all of them.

"Are we certain that Hanassa died?" Rollett asked.

"Yes," Lyman said sadly. "Through all of these centuries of separation I have been aware of his presence in this existence. Always, no matter what form I took, dragon, human, or ghostly guardian of the beginning place, I knew he waited and brooded and plotted escape. And I hoped. . . . Now there is nothing, only an echo of him in the blood of his descendants, those capable of hosting his spirit within their bodies."

"Kalen, my sister, was descended from Hanassa?" Powwell jerked away from the older man. He stepped backward, as if needing to flee into the lower caverns—flee into the death and destruction that hovered there.

"Through her mother, I believe. Not through your common father," Lyman said. He stared directly at Powwell.

"As long as any of his descendants live, then Hanassa has a body to flee to." Rollett searched the shaky cavern with his eyes. His gaze slid over and away from Yaala. "Do we have to hunt them all down and kill them to prevent Hanassa from wreaking havoc all over Kardia Hodos?"

"Possibly." Lyman hung his head sadly. "Hanassa's exile only included himself. His descendants have been able to leave this city and spread their seed far and wide for seven centuries."

"I am directly descended from the renegade dragon, Lyman," Yaala said, her voice as shaky as the kardia beneath her feet. "Will you kill me for no reason other than that?"

Chapter 39

"No, Yaala, that is not what we mean." Powwell stood up a little straighter, shocked out of his lethargy. How could he have considered killing anyone, ever again—even loathsome Piedro? Kalen's death screams lingered, reverberating in his head.

His sister had made one last desperate attempt to regain her body. For one brief second, both Kalen and Hanassa had been joined. And then . . . and then the collapsing tunnel had crushed their skull.

Sympathetic pain still plagued him, nearly blinded him.

Every time he tried to think of something else, remember the happy times with his sister—there had been precious few—her death cry dragged him back to her last agony. If he ever had to kill again, his mind would lock in a loop of reliving Kalen's death.

He clung to his sanity by a slender thread. Thorny wriggled in his pocket as if to remind him of life.

His lust for vengeance against Piedro died. He sagged with relief, knowing he need not follow through with that particular quest.

"Hanassa died with Kalen," he said as he relived the moment of death once more. "My mind was linked to Kalen's at the last moment. They both died. We do not need to kill anyone for fear they will host Hanassa." He looked pointedly at each of his weary companions.

"Are you sure?" Yaala maintained her aggressive stance.

"I'm certain, Yaala."

She turned back toward the exit, spine a fraction less rigid. "Let's get out of here. The city will kill Piedro eventually. We just have to find a way over the crater walls. Lyman, will any of your dragon friends fetch us?"

"I do not know."

"We'll have to climb, then," Rollett said wearily.

Powwell didn't like the color of his skin. A hint of blue still clung to his lips and the edges of his nostrils. He breathed heavily and had to stop often. His hands looked blistered and swollen from the burns. The symptoms resembled the plague, but the smell was missing.

The Rovers had left the iron gate open when they fled the caverns. Yaala sighed her relief. Without Liise generating any 'tricity, the 'motes would not work.

Powwell breathed easier after passing the boundary of the pit. He'd be better yet when he had left the confines of buildings and caves. That moment of oneness with the kardia just before he collapsed the tunnel on top of Kalen had taught him just how precariously balanced the cave system was. "Stargods, I hope I don't have to go underground again. Ever."

Lyman's steps now seemed a little firmer, too. Rollett still sagged against Yaala for support. She kept her arm around his waist. They fit together as if they had always belonged side by side, two halves of one whole.

Powwell waited for a pang of jealousy. Yaala had been his best friend and constant companion for many moons. At times he had entertained desire for her—when he wasn't consumed by his quest to free Kalen.

His sister had flown free of this existence.

All he had left was Yaala. . . .

No emotion churned within him. He hoped she'd be happy with Rollett.

"Looks as if a lot of people left here in a hurry," Yaala commented as they passed through the corridors of the palace.

Bits and pieces of gilt furniture, costly ornaments, and bolts of silk pilfered from the Kaaliph's stores littered the floor.

"Should we try to rescue the library?" Powwell asked them all. "If Yaala had the right textbooks, she might be able to reconstruct her machines."

"No," Yaala said resolutely. "Queen Katie was right. Technology has no place in Coronnan. We have magic and the Commune. Machines only breed trouble."

They bypassed the entrance to the secret stair without further comment.

"I wonder if Piedro's followers are deserting him?" Yaala mused, pointing to the debris.

"But they still fear what the Kaaliph of Hanassa represents." Powwell pointed to the hideous pictures of torture and depravity. The first time he'd seen the vivid depictions of perverted sexual intercourse beside the bloody executions, his face had flushed with embarrassment. He'd seen too much since then to feel anything but disgust now. He gingerly lifted the tapestries aside, touching only the blood-red borders, unwilling to be tainted by the pictures. The opening behind the wall hangings allowed them access to the Justice Hall once more.

Only the severed heads of Rollett's friends remained. They seemed to mock the living as they passed in front of the altar. Powwell bowed briefly to the departed spirits in respect for the knowledge and the power they had given him the last time he'd passed this way.

They had almost traversed the room when a thunderous roar shook the entire building.

"That wasn't a kardiaquake," Powwell said, bracing himself for the rolling motion he expected but which didn't come.

"It's coming from outside, not beneath us," Rollett confirmed.

They joined the crush of people in the major corridor exiting the palace. No one seemed to notice four more bodies among the hundreds. Most of the servants, retainers, and guards carried at least one artifact looted from the Kaaliph.

Powwell checked Yaala's reactions to the loss of her inheritance, generations of accumulated wealth. She seemed more concerned with protecting Rollett from the jabbing elbows and careless feet of the fleeing populace. She had never wanted her mother's treasure, only her love. When Yaassima had exiled Yaala to the pit, she had turned to her beloved machines for companionship. Now they, too, were dead. Perhaps she had finally found in Rollett someone who would respect her and maybe eventually love her.

The crowd carried Powwell away from Lyman and the others as they neared the main exit. Everyone in the city seemed to be gathering in the open area in front of the palace. They all stopped in their tracks, astounded as a huge mechanical dragon floated down toward the ground. It spat fire from its hind end rather than its mouth and its wings looked far too short and thin to support the weight of the beast in the air. It listed badly to the left while the nose pointed down.

A mighty roar shook the beast as the fire flared, licking the rooftops of nearby buildings.

People screamed and pressed away from the beast, giving it room to land.

Powwell looked frantically for Lyman. Perhaps the elderly librarian could interpret for the beast. He caught sight of the old man's white hair off to his left. Lyman peered upward, seemingly unafraid of this new dragon.

"Is this Hanassa's new form?" Powwell asked, shoving his way over to Lyman's side.

"Doubtful." Lyman shook his head and shielded his eyes from the bright desert sunshine. "I have never seen a dragon so big or awkward as this. And these human eyes have never seen a true dragon so easily. Our gaze should be sliding around the beast, looking everywhere but directly at it. I do not know what this animal is."

"That isn't a dragon, it's a machine!" Yaala yelped excitedly. She pushed and shoved people out of her path as she made her way to the place where the beast settled into the dust. Rollett limped slowly behind her.

"Yaala, stand back!" Powwell yelled. He reached her side just as a hole slid open in the dragon's side.

Maia, the Rover girl the Commune had held hostage, stepped into the opening. Her face looked pale and bloated with worry and tears—or illness. Dozens of Rover guards reached up to help her down to the ground.

"Piedro, help me please," she wailed. "The queen's father is dead. This beast murdered him."

But the smell of the plague clung to her. He and Yaala stood next to her, breathing the same tainted air.

Chapter 40

Midafternoon, city of Hanassa

J oy glowed in Yaala's chest. The Stargods had answered
her prayers. They had given her this wonderful mechanical beast to replace the machines she had sacrificed.

She dismissed her first happy reaction to the machine's presence as the Rover woman's words sank in. King Kinnsell lay dead within the machine's belly. The queen's father was a politically powerful man. What repercussions would follow?

She stopped her headlong rush to dive into the rectangular opening where Maia still stood.

"Yaala, don't go near her. She carries the plague!" Powwell screamed at her.

"Plague?" Fear lanced through Yaala. Powwell had related the dragon dream to her in painstaking detail, including the acrid chemical smell generated by the disease.

Yaala stepped back. Rollett's chest stopped her from running away.

"Can you fly that thing out of here?" Rollett asked.

He sounded so hopeful, Yaala hated to disappoint him.

"I'm an engineer. Given a few days of tearing that thing apart, I might be able to tell you how it works, but to fly it is something else entirely."

"That woman landed it. She must have if the pilot is dead. If Powwell and I can access her mind . . ."

Powwell pushed past them and climbed the two steps that folded out of the machine's portal.

"Powwell!" Yaala protested. "The plague."

"Don't worry, Yaala. I should be immune. The Tamboo-tie in my system from the old days is supposed to protect me from any number of ailments." He turned and grinned at her.

Somehow his reassurance fell flat as he muttered, "If Old Lyman's books are accurate."

"Of course my books are accurate," the old man returned indignantly. "Let's see if King Kinnsell is truly dead, or if you can help him. I'll gladly read his mind while he's still unconscious and undefended. He has much to answer for, bringing the plague, sabotaging King Quinnault's authority. . . ." Muttering further descriptions of Kinnsell's crimes, Lyman disappeared into the machine's interior. Maia continued to stand in the doorway, wringing her hands.

A ripple of disturbance in the crowd revealed the presence of Piedro and his Rover guards, six of them. They surged toward Maia. An evil grin split Piedro's face.

"At last, lovely lady, you return to us." Piedro reached up a hand to help Maia descend, as if she were returning royalty instead of the mistress of their former leader—Piedro's now dead rival. "Our group mind has been lacking since your departure. You must have much to tell us."

"Don't even think about moving," Yaala commanded, stepping up beside Piedro. "I won't let you spread that disease to my city!"

"The Kaalipha! Yaassima's daughter, our true Kaalipha!" the people shouted, surging forward dangerously close to the machine and the plague.

Piedro dropped Maia's hand and stared openmouthed at Yaala. His surprise lasted only a moment.

"Seize her, she's one of the traitors!" he screamed. "I thought we left you dead in the pit," he hissed more quietly.

"Long live the Kaalipha returned from the dead!" the people screamed hysterically. The ones closest pushed and jostled, trying to touch Yaala.

"Open the gates to the city, Kaalipha."

"Save us, Kaalipha."

"Feed us, Kaalipha."

They shoved and pushed uncontrollably, separating Yaala

from proximity with the Rovers. The steps of the machine dug sharply into her legs. She wanted to run back into the protection and the silence of the pit.

All these people, pushing and demanding her attention. All these people shouting at her, robbing her of her privacy. She couldn't think, couldn't breathe.

She stumbled against the steps, clutching at the sides of the portal. Air left her lungs. The bitter taste of the plague filled her mouth.

                    *   *   *

*Midafternoon, home of Myrilandel, Ambassador
from the Nimbus of Dragons, Coronnan City*

"Did you hear the row Scarface just had with the king?" Luucian, a journeyman healer Bessel knew slightly from the old days before dragon magic, rushed into Myrilandel's kitchen. He clutched a pile of greenery against his chest. His breath came in excited gasps.

"I do not indulge in gossip," Bessel said calmly to cover his anxiety. Scarface had been dismissed as chief adviser to the king. His anger could lash out at any moment in any form, catching them all in the backlash.

"But you heard, you were eavesdropping at the servants' door!" Luucian prodded. He dumped his trove of plants on the worktable in the center of the kitchen.

"The kettle is about to boil, there's cheese in the cold cellar, and bread in the pantry. They'll all want nourishment when they're done with the master. Can you handle it?" Bessel marched from his listening post to the outside door.

"Wait a minute, Bessel, where are you going? Didn't you hear that Scarface is out? He's no longer Senior Magician, so you can return to the University. Don't you want to stick around and make sure *they*," Luucian nodded his head toward the interior of the house where master magicians hovered, "remember you are Senior Journeyman, almost ready for elevation to Master status? Promotion is as much politics as merit. You need to keep your face in front of as many masters as possible to get your final quest."

"None of that will matter if Scarface decides to retaliate. Cover for me."

Mopsie pawed at the door, as eager to be gone as Bessel. He whined and yipped anxiously.

"But I've got orders to help Queen Katie prepare the Fairy Bells into a drug instead of pure poison. I need to know how to do it. You fix the food. I need knowledge to earn my promotion."

"You can handle both, Luucian, I have confidence in you." Bessel didn't wait any longer. He had to follow Scarface now, before he destroyed everything dear to the Commune, and to Coronnan.

Yet he wished he could share the communion of magic with the other magicians one more time—with or without Scarface.

A crowd had gathered in front of Myrilandel's home, the dragon embassy, attracted by the presence of the royal couple and their entourage. Bessel slipped through their ranks, keeping his face averted.

His best and safest route lay in anonymity.

Bessel caught sight of Scarface forcing his way through the crowd like a ship plowing through heavy waves with the wind coming from a cross quarter. The anxious people made way for the Senior Magician with only nominal nods of their heads in respect for his rank, not for the man.

Curious. Last year he had been hailed as a hero and welcomed in the city. Now the populace merely tolerated him.

Scarface passed the Rossemeyerian Embassy. A black-clad mercenary still stood vigil on the front stoop. A blood-red banner drooped above his head, limp from the damp river air. Bessel held his breath as he followed the Senior Magician's path. He willed Mopsie to make himself invisible in the crowd. The assassin had seen the dog with Bessel and might look beyond the common fisherman's clothes to find the man blamed for the death of Ambassador Jorghe-Rosse.

But the mercenary looked right past Bessel toward Nimbulan's and Myrilandel's house, keeping one hand on the hilt of his sword, the other hand fingering some unseen weapon beneath his voluminous robes.

Bessel looked directly at the mercenary. No recognition
flickered on the man's face. Bessel smiled to himself. For
once he faded into the background when he really wanted
to. Had his ordeal in the river settled the skill in his bones
as the trial by Tambootie smoke settled a magician's talent?

Once past Embassy Row, Scarface began weaving his
hands in a complicated gesture. Bessel recognized the
movement before he sensed the spell that followed. The
Senior Magician summoned the Commune to attend him
in the tower room. The order contained a subtle, but illegal,
compulsion to obey. Only rogue magic could power a compulsion!

In a flash of insight, Bessel knew that this was the spell
Scarface had been working yesterday during the storm. The
Senior Magician had to tap a ley line in order to compel
people to obey him. That was why he'd noticed when Bessel also tapped a ley line.

Bessel erected his armor before Scarface finished the
spell. No sense in taking a chance it might work past his
natural barriers. He intended to follow Scarface unseen and
counter the Senior Magician's plans with any magic available to him.

They neared the open courtyard in front of the University. Bessel ducked into the shadows beneath the last
bridge. In his mind he envisioned the dark depths blending
with a river fog. He saw no differences in the patterns of
light and shadow with his physical eyes, but the apprentices
and masters who obeyed Scarface's summons looked right
at him without paying him any mind. Even the pesky newcomers who had more curiosity than sense ignored him.

Only Wind-drift looked his way. But he did not linger
and did not inform any of the others of Bessel's presence.

For a brief moment, as their eyes locked, Bessel knew
the tremendous joy of communal magic at work. Bessel
broke the contact, knowing he could not continue within
the Commune. Wind-drift shook his head sadly and returned to the summons.

Bessel's heart ached at the separation.

He reasserted the shadows that hid him. He didn't question the source of the energy that fueled his trick. Scarface
had exiled him from the Commune. His oath to use only

dragon magic had lost validity with that exile. He still served his Commune, Coronnan, and King Quinnault, but he would do so by whatever means he found available against a man who intended to destroy the delicate balance of King, Commune, and Coronnan.

How? What form would Scarface's retaliation take?

Witchlight glowed from the stained-glass windows in the tower room. Bridge traffic in and out of the University ceased. Bessel crept out of his hiding place, keeping the shadows and mist draped around him like a cloak.

He entered through the library. The slightly musty smell of old books, ink, and parchment reached out to welcome him. He drew the comforting scent deep into his lungs, cherishing his return to the familiar sanctuary of learning.

But he didn't have time to linger here in the great room he'd always thought of as home. Silently he crept up the stairs to the tower room. The stone steps muffled his footsteps. His spell of invisibility muffled the shouts coming from the private enclave of the master magicians. Nothing could block out the intense sound altogether.

"The plague is upon us, masters, apprentices, and journeymen," Scarface intoned, as if preaching to a multitude. "The Tambootie is the only cure to this insidious disease. The Tambootie is reserved for dragons and magicians. If we allow the king to harvest enough of the tree of magic to eradicate the seeds of the plague, there will be none left for the dragons to eat or for the Commune to provide the trial by Tambootie smoke for our apprentices as they approach manhood and promotion to journeyman."

A murmur of protest broke out, mostly young voices, probably the apprentices who saw this as a threat to their careers as magicians.

"If the dragons die or desert Coronnan because we allow the destruction of the Tambootie, then we will have no communal magic to bind this kingdom together. We will have to resort to solitary magic and the chaos it brings." Scarface's authoritative tones allowed for no challenge.

But one master spoke up. Bessel thought it might be Saber Cat, one of the former Battlemages turned mercenary who had escaped from Hanassa shortly after Nimbulan and Scarface had last year. He had very prominent canine teeth that stuck out from his upper lip like the predatory cat's. "Master Aaddler, if we do not allow the Tambootie to be harvested and distilled into the remedy for this plague, then we will die too."

"No, we won't," Scarface countered. "The trial by Tambootie smoke makes us immune. We magicians can survive and use our communal magic to heal those who are worthy of healing without the loss of the precious tree of magic."

"What about the apprentices?" another master asked. Bessel couldn't discern which one.

"I order all of them to undergo an abbreviated Tambootie smoke ritual immediately. By tomorrow morning at dawn they will be ready to assist us in the greater task of preserving the Tambootie."

Bessel sensed the compulsion oozing out of Scarface. Instinctively, he drew on a ley line to refuel his armor before he believed the logic behind the master magician's words.

"How do we save the Tambootie?" many voices asked.

"We must destroy the knowledge that Tambootie is the only cure."

A chill ran down Bessel's spine.

"What great magic do you plan, Master Scarface?" Saber Cat asked without hesitation or reservation.

"Wait and see. At dawn we will undertake this great task that will save us."

Bessel drew on every morsel of power he could reach in order to penetrate Scarface's thoughts.

All of the dangerous books in the library will be burned in the central courtyard, above the source of illegal rogue magic. I must control that knowledge to protect myself and the Commune from my enemies. Quinnault, Nimbulan, the Rovers, they all want to kill me because I will not be their tool. I must destroy the knowledge that will give them the power to kill me. Knowledge of solitary magic, Rovers, subverting familiars, and dragon secrets must die forever in the cleansing flames. Then and only then will I be safe.

Chapter 41

"**D**on't you dare get sick on me, Yaala. I'll give you up to Rollett, but I'll be damned if I give you up to the plague," Powwell said, dragging her free of the pressing crowd and their incessant demands.

"You can't heal both Yaala and the queen's father," Lyman reminded him. "You have already exhausted your magic talent. I'm surprised you are still walking."

"I'll survive. But we have to know how to fly this thing to get us out of here. Once we are free, we can dose Yaala with Tambootie. Her dragon heritage should protect her from the toxins in the raw leaves." Powwell brushed the hair out of Yaala's eyes. "You'll be all right, sweetheart. I promise."

"Kinnsell lives?" she asked, looking at the supine figure on the floor.

"Barely. I know I can keep him alive a little longer, but I'm not sure I can cure him. He's pretty far gone." Powwell shook his head sadly.

"I'll check out the controls." Yaala touched Powwell's face briefly, affectionately. "You will always be my best friend, Powwell. I trust you."

Brave words from the woman who trusted machines more than people.

Just then, Rollett dove into the shuttle headfirst. He landed awkwardly on the floor. "Shut the door!" That mob is getting angrier by the minute."

Lyman fussed with a series of buttons set beside the door

until it whooshed shut. Maia remained outside with her Rover clan.

"They're insane," Rollett muttered as the closing door muffled the noise. "Maia is telling Piedro that Rovers must start adding the Tambootie to their food to offset the plague. She's planning recipes spiced with timboor—the berries for Stargods' sake—the most toxic part of the entire tree. She'll kill them all."

"They're all magicians," Powwell said. "They'll give each other immunity from the Tambootie through their strange magic."

The muffled shouts of the mob outside continued to filter into the much quieter machine.

"What about the rest of them out there?" Yaala asked. She thrust out her chin, challenging her companions to give her a solution. "Not everyone in Hanassa is a Rover or a magician. A lot of people will die from the plague unless we do something to help."

"Rollett, go forward with Yaala," Powwell said. "Keep her there while I do this."

"You give orders as if you expect to be obeyed. You've grown up, Powwell." Rollett eyed him curiously.

"That happens when you've killed your sister and undertaken your only option for escape, which may just kill us all." Powwell turned his back on the other two magicians. He sought a pulse in the neck of the desperately ill man. A feeble flutter told him the man's heart continued to beat—irregularly.

Decisively, before his fears could stop him, Powwell sat crossed-legged beside Kinnsell. When he was comfortable, he took three deep breaths to trigger a trance. His focus narrowed to himself and Kinnsell. The edges of his vision darkened. His head lightened as if he floated toward the void.

He removed a sheaf of pages torn from one of Lyman's precious books back home and studied them a moment. When he had the ritual memorized, he took one of Thorny's dried spines from his pocket. He examined it closely for the sharpest point. Thorny hunched and protested inside Powwell's pocket. The little hedgehog crawled out of the protective hiding place, digging his claws into Powwell. His gibbering insisted that Powwell stop.

Powwell ignored the advice of his familiar and stabbed his palm deeply, ripping his palm open in a jagged slash with the spine. He squeezed the edges of the wound until it bled freely. He repeated the procedure with Kinnsell's limp hand.

Thorny jumped off Powwell's lap and scurried away.

"No, Powwell! You can't do this. You don't know for sure it will work. Thorny is frightened. Listen to your familiar." Yaala launched herself onto his back, jerking his bloody palm away from contact with Kinnsell.

"I said, keep her up front and don't interfere," Powwell barked.

"I can't let you kill yourself, Powwell. We'll find another way out of Hanassa." Yaala kicked at Rollett as he dragged her away from Powwell.

"I have to do this, Yaala. It's the only way. Comfort Thorny. He likes you."

"But . . ." Her protests died on a sob.

Powwell took three more deep breaths to bring himself completely into his trance. His vision narrowed again. His hand glowed, the blood taking on a luminescence like a ruby in the sunlight. Or a red-tipped dragon soaring across the Great Bay. The void beckoned Powwell to soar with dragons in the vast nothingness between the planes of existence.

He resisted the urge to flee into the blackness and away from his task. Stinging pain in his hand signaled a weakening of his magic and his resolve.

The aura of power shining around his self-inflicted wound extended to Kinnsell's hand. The king's blood didn't shine or reflect light, a sure sign of the advancing disease.

Resolutely, Powwell placed his palm atop Kinnsell's, aligning the wounds perfectly. Lacking a silk scarf to bind the two hands together he signaled Lyman to wrap his old-fashioned sash belt around them. The moment the cool blue fabric touched his skin, he knew it to be silk. Leave it to Lyman's antique wardrobe to cover all contingencies.

"My blood to your blood," Powwell recited the litany of healing he'd stolen from the library. Behind his eyes he "saw" his blood mingling with his patient's. He pushed the residual Tambootie in his blood to the surface, forcing the essence of the tree to flow into Kinnsell.

"My skin becomes your skin." His entire hand burned with the binding.

"My heart beats for your heart." The rhythm of his pulse stuttered and started up in a new pattern to match Kinnsell's erratic and weak beat.

Slowly Powwell's heart beat stronger, more regularly, forcing healing blood to circulate through Kinnsell, pushing the man's heart to assume a matching rhythm.

Powwell watched his blood seeking out the damage in lungs, heart, liver, and kidneys. At each vital organ he pushed dissolving tissue back into place, binding it to the organs with Tambootie glue and his own healing blood.

Drop by slow drop, Powwell pulled the tainted blood into his own body, replacing it with his own. The Tambootie in his system surrounded the seeds of the disease, making them inert and ineffective. He used every bit of the residual healing properties of the tree of magic and still tainted blood flowed back and forth between his body and Kinnsell's.

The blackness of the void encroached on Powwell's inner vision. He dove deeper into Kinnsell's lungs, desperately trying to repair enough damage for the man to breathe on his own. Powwell's own breathing became ragged, incomplete, clogged with blood. Weakness assailed his heart.

"Powwell, come out of it. You've gone too far," a voice urged him from afar.

Something shook the body he'd left behind on this long journey into another man's life. He didn't care. That body belonged to another existence, another person. He hadn't the strength for anything but to follow the pulses of blood through choked vessels.

*   *   *

Afternoon, inside Kinnsell's shuttle, city of Hanassa

Rollett watched Kinnsell closely for the first signs of rousing from the coma. When his eyelids fluttered in dream sleep, he allowed Yaala to kneel beside Kinnsell and Powwell's now twitching body.

The younger magician remained unconscious. Rollett hoped they'd get out of here in time to rouse him with Tambootie before the plague damaged him beyond repair.

"Your body is younger than mine, Rollett, your mind more receptive to change," Lyman said. "Perhaps you had best do this, while I keep watch on that mob. They sound ugly, near riot."

Rollett nodded his acceptance. If Yaala failed to absorb enough information, he might be able to fill in the gaps.

"I need to keep one hand on your face here." He placed the fingers of his right hand on Yaala's temple. "The other hand will link me to Kinnsell's mind. But you need to touch my temple the same way. That will link our minds together. I am just the vessel for passing knowledge from him to you. Do you understand, Yaala?"

She nodded mutely, never taking her eyes off Powwell. Her right hand kept reaching toward him, in comfort, in love.

"Concentrate, Yaala." Rollett grabbed her reaching hand and placed it on his own head. "If we are ever going to get out of here and get help for Powwell and all the people Maia has exposed to this plague, then you have to concentrate on learning how to fly this strange dragon out of here."

"For Powwell, for my city." She lifted bewildered eyes to his face. "For us, for this strange 'tricity that flows between us."

Several fists pounded fiercely on the portal to the mechanical dragon. The vessel shook violently.

"We haven't much time," Lyman warned them. He left his post behind Powwell to glance out one of the small round windows. "The crowd is turning violent. The Rovers are retreating into the palace under a rain of stones and offal."

"Feed us! Feed us. Feed us," the people chanted over and over. "Save us from the kardiaquakes!" The muffled voices penetrated the walls of the vessel with increasing intensity.

The dragon trembled under the impact of their blows, much as the kardia had shaken within the pit.

Rollett drew on his last reserves of physical strength and took himself into a deep trance. Before the void could claim him, he dove into Kinnsell's mind. A wall of armor repelled his first assault. A second and third try weakened the man's natural defenses but still repelled him.

Slowly. Go slowly and ask politely, Powwell told him. His mental voice was weak and distant.

Rollett didn't question the boy's instructions. He was linked to Kinnsell in a stronger bond of blood and magic than Rollett could hope to achieve with only a touch.

Please, he asked Kinnsell. *Please let us help you. Show us how to fly this strange dragon back to your daughter and help.*

The wall of resistance dissolved. A flood of bewildering images flowed swiftly past Rollett's mind's eye. He opened his connection to Yaala, finding her easier to reach than anyone he'd ever contacted, except when he worked in concert with Commune Magicians, minds and souls mingling and augmenting each other. He tried to organize the rapid pictures filling his mind and failed miserably.

You don't need to understand this. Just pass it on to me. Yaala almost laughed inside his mind. The happy flow within her thoughts showed him that she understood.

He relaxed his vigil over the images and opened himself like a canal.

Repetition brought some sense of information passing through him. He caught glimpses of the control panel at the front of the vessel. Red lights, green lights, flashing lights, and steady burns imprinted on his memory. A negative aura surrounded the strange crown of more blinking lights. Yaala couldn't use that, it responded only to Kinnsell. Then he saw visions of the entire shuttle—the proper name for the dragon filtered past at some point—flying steadily a hundred dragon lengths above the ground. Air, shimmering with heat, but still colorless, flowed out of the "jet engines" at the rear of the ship. Then he saw a hand passing over the control panel in a new pattern. The engines spat red flame and roared louder than thunder, louder than the largest kardiaquake in the pit. The shuttle turned its nose upward and shot into the heavens almost faster than the eye could follow.

The noise of the crowd outside shook Rollett out of contact with Kinnsell and Yaala. His trance fell to pieces.

They all collapsed into a heap.

"The Rovers have turned the mob against us." Lyman pulled Rollett off of Yaala who lay atop Powwell who lay atop Kinnsell. "They are using metal shovels and rakes as well as spears and pikes against the skin of this dragon. They think we have food in here. Maia is trying to open the door from the outside. I'm overriding her commands from in here. I don't know how much longer I can keep them out."

"Did you get enough information, Yaala?" Rollett shook his head to clear it of the last traces of the trance.

"I think so." Her voice shook and so did her hands. She turned frightened eyes up to Rollett. Her mind remained connected to his.

What he saw there scared him. "Yaala, we need to take the ship to the capital. We have to get help for Powwell and Kinnsell—quickly. They are dying. We can send food and healers back here to help the others."

"Hanassa the city is dying. I can't abandon these people."

"You'll burn out the rockets if you use them to blast a hole through the crater wall." The strange vocabulary flowed out of his mouth as if he'd always known the words for this technology. "We won't be able to fly the shuttle afterward. And there is no guarantee you will succeed. We may be stranded here with this very angry and very hungry mob."

"I have to try. I can't condemn a thousand people to a slow and painful death from starvation. Provided the mountain doesn't collapse on them first. Kinnsell thinks the plague has stopped spreading. It has taken those who are weak and vulnerable, the healthy ones are too healthy for the disease to live inside us. I have to free my people, Rollett. This is my legacy as Kaalipha of Hanassa. I have to help my people in the only way I can. I have to."

Chapter 42

Katie watched in amazement as the healers and extra magicians surrounding Nimbulan reared their heads in surprise. The blue glow of their healing spell fizzled and died. Nimbulan lay exposed and vulnerable to his faulty heart once more. Without consulting each other, the magicians rose as one person and walked out the door.

"How dare you desert your patient!" Katie bustled after them. She grabbed the sleeve of the last man in line. He shook off her grip and continued in the wake of his fellows. None of them looked back or heeded her pleas.

"Are you all in a trance?" she yelled at their retreating backs.

"Come back here, every last one of you!" Quinnault ordered in his best parade ground voice.

"I'm sorry, Your Grace, this summons takes precedence. I dare not stay when the others leave," Whitehands said quietly as he trailed after his fellows.

The magicians continued staring straight ahead as they rapidly marched toward the nearest bridge.

"Scarface calls them. They obey a compulsion," Myri said. She looked as if she might also follow the magicians. Then she forced her gaze back to her husband. She sank back onto her heels and lifted his limp hand.

"Compulsion spells are illegal, forbidden by the Commune. Scarface himself wrote that law." Quinnault reached for his short sword. He eased it out of his sheath a few finger-lengths, then rammed it back home. Weapons wouldn't solve this problem.

Katie rushed to kneel beside Myri. "What must we do? We can't leave him like this."

"He breathes on his own. They managed to repair some of the damage to his heart," Myri said listlessly. Her pale blond hair hung limply about her shoulders. She plucked at Nimbulan's hand with anxious fingers. Lavender circles of exhaustion ringed her eyes.

"You must rest, Myri." Katie wrapped her arms around her friend and helped her stand once more. "You must take care of the new baby. Your neighbors will be bringing Amaranth back here soon." Katie chanced a quick glance to Kaariin, sitting in the corner with Marilell. "Think about your daughter, Myri. Bad enough she see her father so ill, but not you, too."

"I can't. I have to stay with him."

"We will stay for now," Quinnault said. He joined his wife in wrapping his arms around his sister. "Go upstairs and rest. I'll send some of my men to find out what is going on at the Commune. I hope I'm not sorry I relied upon Scarface's honor to step down as Senior Magician." He hugged Myri tightly, released her, and stepped to the front door to address the armed men who still stood guard there.

"Bessel is in the kitchen preparing a drug to help Nimbulan's heart beat regularly," Katie offered. A slight grin tugged at her mouth. "I don't think Bessel will obey Scarface's summons. The boy seems to be immune to outside interference."

"My apprentice has never been disobedient," Nimbulan whispered. He breathed shallowly but regularly. A bit of color had returned to his face and the blue tinge to his nostrils and fingernails had given way to a very pale pink.

Myrilandel pressed her fingertips to his neck pulse. "Too rapid," she said after a few moments. "But strong enough as long as you do not exert yourself."

Katie wondered how she did that without a timepiece to measure the pulse against.

"I fully intend to remain alive long enough to see our son born, beloved." Nimbulan captured Myri's hand with his own and pressed his lips to her palm.

"I do not wish to raise a fatherless child, Lan. You will live a long while yet, and father many more children. Shayla has told me so. Dragons do not lie. But you frightened me for a time." Myri pressed Nimbulan's hand to her cheek and held it there a long moment.

Katie's heart swelled with joy at the evidence of the love between her two friends.

Quinnault came up behind Katie, pulling her tight against his chest. He kissed the top of her head. They cherished the moment of togetherness for as long as they could.

A flurry of movement in the back of the house brought Myri's and Quinnault's heads up in an intense listening posture.

"Nimbulan, Your Grace, we have to stop them. Scarface is going to burn the library!" Bessel skidded to a halt on the slick flagstones just short of colliding with his king.

"Is that why he summoned the entire Commune to attend him?" Quinnault held the breathless boy by the shoulders. The whiteness of his knuckles showed his effort to keep from shaking information out of him.

"Yes." Bessel gulped a huge mouthful of air as he nodded his head. "We have to stop him."

"Why does he take such dire action?" Myri asked the question on all of their minds.

"Because knowledge is power," Katie answered.

"So no one else will know that the Tambootie will cure the plague," Bessel added. "Magicians are immune because the Tambootie remains in their bodies from the trial by smoke when they become journeymen. There isn't enough of the tree of magic to cure all of the people of Coronnan as well as feed the dragons. He's more concerned with his supply of magic than with the people."

"He can't do this. We have to make a cure available to anyone who needs it." Myri stood up in protest. "So many suffer." She clutched her belly protectively. "I have to heal those who suffer, but I can't. . . ."

"We need to consult the dragons," Quinnault added decisively.

"There's more trouble, Your Grace." Bessel gulped air a moment then squared his shoulders. "Rovers in the city are extorting protection money from the merchants. They say they've bribed your guards to help them. They set fire to a carpenter's shop earlier today because he wouldn't pay them protection money. The neighbors put out that fire. Then, on my way back here just now, a band of Rovers were beating up the baker in the next marketplace. I've chased them off for now, but they'll be back."

"How did you chase off a gang of Rovers, young man?" Nimbulan asked, trying to raise himself on one elbow. "They don't frighten easily. Especially in groups."

"I set an ember of witchfire in the seat of the leader's pants. Last I saw of him, he was running for the river with flames shooting out of his bum. The others didn't know what to do without him, so they followed him right into the river."

*   *   *

Afternoon, Kinnsell's shuttle, city of Hanassa

Yaala ran her fingertips over the touch pads on the control panel. Kinnsell's memories guided her movements. With a few gestures, her muscles knew how to fly this machine as well as her brain did. She wished she had access to the cyber controls. Just thinking what she needed would be easier than using the panel.

Holding her breath in anticipation of flight, she pressed the ignition sequence.

The jets roared to life. The shuttle vibrated with controlled power, suppressed motion. A thrill ran through her. If the engineers of Hanassa had been allowed to experiment and expand the technology of the generators and 'tricity over the last seven hundred years rather than merely patch and repair, they might have developed mechanical flight. Might have . . . Surely the books in the Kaalipha's library would help dreamers expand their knowledge and their technology. But few, if any, had been allowed to learn the arcane art of reading.

She didn't have time for idle speculation. She had the controls of this shuttle now, for however brief a time.

Her stomach bolted toward her throat as the shuttle lifted free of the kardia. The desperate cries of hunger and anger outside shifted to fear.

"Soon," she promised them. "Soon you will be free." She closed her ears to their pleas as she rotated the shuttle so that the jets faced the partial tunnel through the crater walls to the outside. Slowly, she backed up so that the engines discharged directly into the excavations Rollett had started.

"You did good work, Rollett. The size of your tunnel is a perfect fit," she told him. "And you were nearly through to the outside. Less than a quarter of the way is left."

"There is still time to fly away. We can send food and healers back from the capital," he reminded her.

"They wouldn't come. Hanassa is a city of outlaws. No one cares about this place except you and me. I've got to do this."

"Yaala," Kinnsell called to her weakly. "It won't work. The shuttle has to be vertical when you fire the rockets. You have to be above the planet's atmosphere."

"I know." She closed her eyes and placed her palm on the clear panel she knew would switch power from jets to rockets.

"Warning, the maneuver you are about to execute does not fall within accepted parameters," a strident female voice proclaimed from the depths of the control panel.

"Retract the wings, Yaala," Rollett said. "If you don't retract the wings, you'll break them off."

"Right," Yaala toggled the wing switch. A grinding noise ran the full length of the shuttle. She looked out the windows to make certain the shuttle remained intact.

"Wings tucked up neatly," Lyman called peering through one of the windows.

Yaala closed her eyes. "Please let this work," she prayed. Then she punched the engage button at the same time slamming the shuttle's flight direction into reverse. The shuttle vaulted backward, slamming into the narrow confines of the tunnel. A great shuddering of the hull and screaming of tortured metal pierced her ears as the shuttle scraped the walls of the tunnel. The engine blast backlashed along the sides of the craft within the narrow confines of the excavation. The temperature gauge crept upward.

"Warning, insufficient altitude for rocket engines. Do not proceed," the unnatural voice ordered.

Yaala pushed more fuel to the roaring engines. The temperature gauge crept higher, pushing against the warning red zone.

"Warning, hull temperatures twenty percent above normal." The strident voice rose in pitch to a tinny whine.

Inch by inch the shuttle crept backward toward the outside world and freedom. A tiny viewscreen on the control panel showed the engines eating away at the blockage within the tunnel.

Some of the flames still washed the hull seeking escape.

"The engines can't take much more of this," Rollett shouted above the thunder that surrounded and filled the shuddering shuttle.

"Warning! Hull temperatures sixty percent above normal. Warning! Warning!" the voice squeaked almost beyond hearing range.

The engine noise grew so loud it blotted out all thought, everything but the need to break free of the rock walls that confined and amplified and reverberated against the shuttle.

Yaala pushed more fuel into the engines. The temperature gauge began blinking red.

"Warrrrnnnning . . ." the voice faded, burned out by the stress.

With a tremendous scream and shudder, the shuttle burst through the rock wall. Momentum shot the vessel across the narrow plateau that ringed the crater's exterior.

Silence descended upon them.

"We're free!" Lyman announced. "We're free of Hanassa."

"The rockets died?" Rollett leaned over Yaala's shoulder examining the control panel with a bewildered look on his face.

"I burned them out and used up all of the fuel. Jets not responding," Yaala replied. Her ears still rang in the aftermath of the noise.

"We're flying! Just like a dragon," Lyman proclaimed. He practically jumped up and down in his excitement.

"We're soaring, without wings to hold us up or steer us," Yaala replied.

"Engage the wings. They'll keep us aloft!" Lyman called.

Yaala flipped the switch for the wings. Nothing happened. "We need fuel to open the wings."

"Manual override," Kinnsell murmured, very quietly.

"What!" Yaala nearly screamed above the ringing in her ears.

"Levers, inside the hidden hatch, both sides of the shuttle. Manual override of wing controls." He closed his eyes, looking exhausted from the small effort of speaking.

Yaala and Rollett leaped to the square indentation on the left side of the shuttle. Lyman examined the companion doorway on the opposite side. The two magicians ran their fingertips around the nearly invisible imperfection in the wall.

"Ah!" Lyman's door popped open first. "Pressure point lower right-hand corner."

Rollett repeated the action and his door flew open as well. Behind the door lay a handle that looked like the handgrip of a walking stick with indentations for the fingers. Above and below the handgrip was a narrow channel.

A sudden lurch downward nearly left Yaala's stomach above her head. "Hurry, Rollett. We're losing altitude."

"Pull the handle out and jiggle it until it engages in the track," Kinnsell whispered.

"Yaala, get back to the controls," Rollett grunted as he followed Kinnsell's instructions. The handle did not want to budge. "Look for some kind of manual rudder. We've got to steer this thing once we get the wings out."

Yaala returned to the cockpit of the shuttle. She searched the control panels for something resembling a handle.

A grinding noise irritated the ringing in her ears. She looked over her shoulder, wincing at the sounds. Rollett heaved all of his weight against the handle. Lyman didn't seem to be having much luck getting his mechanism to engage in the track.

The grinding noise repeated itself. Air caught Rollett's side of the shuttle, dropping Lyman's. Yaala braced herself against the sudden tilt in the floor.

Kinnsell and Powwell rolled on top of each other in the direction of the list.

"Let me." Rollett shoved Lyman out of the way as he staggered toward him. He leaned on the handle. Suddenly the shuttle stopped dropping.

"I hope there is a flat place below where we can land," Yaala said.

"Joystick," Kinnsell gasped.

A sudden image of a short walking staff popped into Yaala's head at the mention of the word. Instantly she knew where to find the instrument and how to use it. She sat hastily in the pilot's chair and reached for the rounded top of the stick.

An updraft caught the left wing; she turned into it and felt a lightness beneath the belly of the shuttle. But it wouldn't last. As soon as the air current changed, they'd lose more altitude.

"It's all mountains, ravines, and ridges for hundreds of miles around here," Rollett said flatly. "Even the dragon that brought Nimbulan and me here last year had trouble finding a place to land."

Chapter 43

*Home of Myrilandel, Ambassador from the Nimbus
of Dragons, Coronnan City*

"**Y**our Grace, we can deal with the Rovers later. But
we have to stop Scarface now, tonight!" Bessel insisted. He couldn't let a few narrow-minded men destroy
the precious storehouse of knowledge. Just because they
didn't need a piece of information this moment, didn't
mean it might not prove useful—essential—later.

And Scarface's comment about familiars— He didn't
have time to dwell on that. Any threat to Mopsie was a
threat to Bessel now.

"It is not enough that we know a cure for the plague,"
Nibulan said, trying to rise.

"Don't even think about getting up," Katie and Myri
said in unison, pointing warning fingers at him.

Nimbulan meekly lay back down again.

Bessel took a long look at his master and bit his lip in
sympathetic pain. Nimbulan's gray face and labored breathing hinted at death stalled, not removed.

Don't you desert me, too, Master. I still need you.

"Our first concern is to save the library." Nimbulan held
up his left hand, palm outward, fingers slightly curved while
he thought out loud. The familiar gesture reassured Bessel
a little. "By the law of the Stargods, only magicians, priests,
and healers may learn to read. Surely Commune Magicians,
who can. have no secrets from each other, can be trusted
guardians of knowledge before it is lost? We have lost so
much through the generations. Communal magic is sup-

posed to replace distrust and the willful hiding of precious information."

"Scarface doesn't trust anyone he can't control," Queen Katie mused, tapping her chin.

"He's also afraid that everyone is out to kill him," Bessel muttered. "He has to control everyone around him to make sure they don't kill him. He's using rogue compulsions to keep their loyalty."

Nimbulan winced at him. "For once, I am grateful I no longer have my magic. In my weakened state, I'm not certain I could resist his compulsion."

"All of us in this room have proved to him time and again that he can't control us," Queen Katie continued. "Scarface knows as well as we do that what we *don't* know can hurt us. He's using the library as leverage to stay in power as Senior Magician."

"The time has come to arrest the man." Quinnault squared his shoulders in determination. But Bessel saw his hands grip the hilt of his short sword too fiercely. He didn't like that option.

"Stop and think a moment, Your Grace," Bessel said cautiously. "If Scarface can control the entire Commune—magicians of great power who in concert could subdue him with a thought—what will he do to the mundane guards you send to arrest him? There isn't a prison cell built that could restrain him. There isn't a sword that can touch him."

If I can't return to the Commune with Mopsie, then I'll remain outside, serving Coronnan and the king in secret. But if we can depose Scarface, there's still a chance for me and for Mopsie. The instant of oneness he had shared with Wind-drift haunted him.

"He's right, Scarecrow," Queen Katie agreed. "With the Commune backing him, Scarface could manipulate the entire kingdom into deposing you."

"King Kinnsell manipulates the lords of my Council. Scarface misuses the magical power of the Commune. Rovers incite the people to fear me and my men. The provinces are in near revolt over the plague. What happened to the careful balance we built into this government, Nimbulan? What happened to the honor, ethics, and control you built into the Commune?" Quinnault clenched his fists

as if needing to slam them into something, preferabl
Scarface's jaw.

"Scarface believes he is providing unified leadership fo
the good of the kingdom," Bessel offered. "I slipped insid
his mind. He thinks he's being honorable and ethical i
guiding the Commune and therefore, the kingdom." Mem
ory of the twisted loops and dark caverns of Master Aad
dler's mind made him shudder.

For half a moment Bessel knew the compulsion to follo
Scarface's logic and agree with him. The older magician'
memories of atrocities inflicted on him and by him durin
the Great Wars of Disruption fed his tremendous guilt an
his fear of retaliation. Now he saw every person beyon
his control as his enemy, determined to murder him for hi
past activities.

"Stargods preserve us from righteous tyrants!" Nimbula
muttered. He crossed himself then fell silent.

"Our backs are against the wall, Scarecrow. Our option
are limited. We may have to resort to trickery to ous
Scarface and regain control of the Commune." Quee
Katie reached out and clung to her husband's hand.

"I think we can trust Wind-drift and Whitehands," Besse
mused. "They seem to be aware of what Scarface is doin
and defying him in subtle ways, but they have to appear t
go along with him for their own safety."

"A good piece of information," Nimbulan replied. "W
may call upon it later. But right now, we can trust onl
ourselves."

A long moment of silence stretched out while all of ther
thought furiously.

"Quinnault, the tunnels beneath the central keep of you
palace, is there still access to them?" Nimbulan finall
broke the silence. Unsteadily, he attempted to roll to hi
knees.

Myrilandel urged him back down on his pallet with anx
ious hands. He shook off her help. Bessel offered his ow
hand gently under his master's elbow. Nimbulan accepte
his silent assistance.

"Can we still get to the tunnels?" he repeated his ques
tion as he staggered upright.

"Yes. I have workmen excavating a direct route beneath the river between the palace and the University," Quinnault replied. "If you are thinking of hiding the books down here, the place is much too public at the moment."

"I remember side tunnels and dead ends from the time you showed me the escape route from the royal apartments to a hidden cove on an adjacent island." Nimbulan's face frayed a moment before returning to a more normal, if somewhat pale, color. He leaned heavily against the chimney but remained standing.

"Yes. We've filled some of those dead ends with dirt and rubble from the excavation, others are tool storage and resting places for the workers." Quinnault began to pace, hands behind his back and shoulders slightly hunched.

"A dead end could be walled off, cloaked in magic so it would be ignored." Queen Katie joined him in his thinking ritual, pacing beside him with one hand looped in the crook of his elbow.

"It will have to be an enduring spell, and a subtle one that misdirects. We can't take a chance on Scarface stumbling on the books because he senses the presence of magic," Nimbulan added.

"We can't hide the books forever, Master," Bessel protested. "The books will have to be found someday. Hiding them forever is as bad as burning them."

"A minor detail. We have to take every precaution. We don't know how long Scarface and his conservative faction will remain in power," Nimbulan dismissed Bessel's suggestion. "When will Scarface burn the books?"

"At dawn," Bessel replied sullenly. He didn't like the shortsightedness of his king and his master. "Scarface wants to make a huge public spectacle of the burning. He's planning a speech that will make it seem as if he's doing everyone a favor."

"But he won't burn all of the books," Katie protested. "I don't want to imagine a life without books."

Nor I, Your Grace, Bessel thought. *When ignorance guides people, the innocent suffer.* As he had suffered as a child because his father believed only myths and legends about magicians rather than looking for the truth.

A pang of regret and loneliness made a knot in his gu He had to abandon yet another family, the family of th Commune, in order to maintain control of his own destin

But he would survive. He would find a new family amor the fisherfolk and their dogs.

"Oh, Scarface will keep the volumes he needs or consi ers 'safe,' " Quinnault reassured her. "He's making a spe tacle of the event just to defy me and demonstrate h power and reassert his popularity among the people."

"We'll need help," Nimbulan said. "We might not t able to save all of the books, but we can move a larg number from the library between now and dawn. I wis Lyman and Powwell were here. I can trust them to resi Scarface's manipulation."

"I think I know how to keep Scarface busy." Bessel face brightened.

"How?" Nimbulan raised one eyebrow in query.

"Mopsie and I need to destroy the depth finder."

"The Guild of Bay Pilots will howl mightily in protest Quinnault grinned mischievously. "They'll run straight me and to Scarface demanding someone fix it."

"Once the depth finder is disabled, the pilots will nee their dogs back. I know some men who would gladly tur large packs of water dogs loose on the docks. Scarfac doesn't like dogs, and they don't like him. But the pilo can't afford to let the magicians hurt the dogs. Chaos wi reign for a while."

"What do dogs have to do with the pilots?"

"I'll explain later." Bessel grinned widely. "I've got catch the passenger barge with the depth finder before sails to the port with the afternoon tide." Bessel scoote out the door. He stopped short before stepping down the cobblestones.

Two dozen black-robed mercenaries from Rossemeye stared at him. All of them had covered the lower halves their faces with turban veils. All had drawn their vorp blades at first sight of him.

The man who stood in the center of the semicirc stepped forward one pace. "We besiege this house unt Journeyman Magician Bessel is turned over to us for ju tice," he announced.

Chapter 44

Inside Kinnsell's shuttle, place and time unknown

Kinnsell dragged his aching body toward the cockpit of the shuttle. "Ignorant bushies," he snarled. Pulling himself hand-over-hand, he managed to struggle into the copilot's seat. He settled into it gratefully as his wobbling knees gave way. "I'll show you real flying." Out of long habit, he hit the mayday button to send a distress signal to the mother ship. He also pocketed a portable communicator—something strictly forbidden by the family covenant. Then he overrode the control panel with the joystick. The shuttle's vibrations communicated to him through the length of his preferred tool.

Gradually, he began to sense the air currents and momentum that kept the vessel floating when, for all he knew, it should be a crumpled heap at the bottom of a trackless ravine.

The terrain whizzed backward past the viewscreen. His perceptions distorted. He needed to turn the shuttle around. The helm resisted his control.

Gradually, he was able to maneuver the vessel into the wind. He gained a little altitude and perspective.

Beside him, Yaala clutched the sides of the pilot's cushioned seat with white-knuckled fists. She stared blankly at the mountainsides skidding past the windows. The young man behind her braced himself against her back and held her shoulders while he too stared at the landscape.

Useless. Both useless. Though he had to admit they'd done an admirable job of getting the shuttle airborne and

the wings extended. "You really should have just flown out
of that volcanic crater and not wasted a good shuttle on
blasting an exit through the crater for the rabble," he muttered. "Totally out of fuel. Rockets burned out. Jets disabled. You barely got the wings out in time. At least I have
a rudder to work with."

"The rabble are my people. I had an obligation to free
them from their prison and slow starvation. You brought
the plague to them. I couldn't abandon them. Once we are
safely landed, we can send help. Supplies and medicine can
get into Hanassa." Yaala roused a little from her fear-
induced catatonia.

"You'd make an admirable ruler, girl. Unfortunately,
honor and obligation are only pieces of what keeps a person in power. You also have to balance the political forces.
I don't suppose you managed to kill that Rover person who
manipulated my Maia like a puppet?"

"If you mean Piedro, the last I saw of him he was leading
the mob to kill all of us," the young magician replied.

What was his name? *I should know after that intimate
psychic link,* Kinnsell thought. Rollo . . . Rufus . . . Rollett.
That was it. Rollett—sounded like a stomach remedy or a
chocolate bar. White and dark chocolate in his beard. Good
way to remember his name.

Rollett had probed his mind and channeled information
to Yaala so she could fly the shuttle. Powwell had been the
other one in the link. Powwell, the healer. Powwell had
somehow eradicated most of the disease from Kinnsell's body
and repaired some of the damage. Some, not all. Enough to
keep him alive a while longer.

But Powwell didn't call himself a healer. He thought of
himself as a Bloodmage—whatever that was—and hated
himself for it.

*I can use his self-loathing to make him return to Terra
with me. A psychic healer of that strength is worth a fortune
in both money and power.*

If the boy survived. He'd taken a lot of the plague into
his own system and not neutralized all of it. The boy lay
unconscious in the cabin, maybe dying prematurely because
he had saved Kinnsell.

"I may have done a lot of underhanded things in my life,

but I intend to repay my debt to you, Powwell." He fussed with the long-range sensors, seeking a landing place, any landing place.

"I don't think Maia was manipulated by Piedro so much as she was a willing partner in manipulating you," Yaala said bitterly, returning to the previous conversation. "I know her. She uses men and discards them. Then she blames everyone but herself for the men not returning to her bed when she needs their money, their talents, or their protection. She did it to Nimbulan and to Televarn, the last leader of the Rovers."

"She mentioned Televarn often." Kinnsell wanted to know more, but he needed all of his concentration to get the sensors back online. "Lovely woman, but I'm glad she's out of my life."

"My mother killed Televarn with the poisoned knife Televarn used to try and kill her," Yaala explained. "Maia watched her do it. So did I." She fell into a silent reflection.

"Then almost everything she told me was a lie. Or she blocked out the memory." Kinnsell shrugged. "But then, I knew she lied, and I enjoyed her attempts to manipulate me anyway."

The long-range sensors flashed a terrain map into one corner of the viewscreen. "Got it. There's a plateau ahead. A long way without engines, but we may have enough wind to keep us aloft that long."

"How far?" the old man called from the cabin. "Powwell's in bad shape. I need a dragon to help him."

"Dragons, bah!" Kinnsell hadn't really seen a dragon sitting on top of this very shuttle. He'd been sick, feverish, hallucinating. "Once we land, I'll show you the miracles of modern medicine. I've got scanners and bonesetters and antibiotics. We'll patch him up almost as good as new. I've also got a stash of Tambootie if nothing else works on the boy."

"Our healers can do as much with dragon magic to fuel them and more healers to amplify the magic," Rollett argued.

"Believe what you will, but shut up now. I need all my concentration to land this without a decent runway."

Kinnsell gritted his teeth and memorized the plateau.

Then he closed his eyes and visualized how he had to ease
the shuttle down. He shed altitude and dropped the landing
gear. The vessel slowed to stall speed, except there were
no engines to stall. The control panel beeped at his unusual
command. "I suppose you burned out the vocal control?"
he asked at the third warning beep."

"The voice in the control panel?" Yaala asked, still grip-
ping her seat with white-knuckled fists. "Yes, it is gone
with the rockets, the jets, and the fuel."

"No great loss. My second wife programmed her voice
into it years ago. Time to change it anyway. My current
wife gets jealous every time she flies with me."

He shed more altitude. The wheels bounced off the
rough terrain and hopped back up. Too high. He dipped
the nose and felt the first scrape of dirt beneath the cabin.

"Brace yourselves. This is going to be rough!" he shouted,
clinging to his own chair with what little strength remained
to him.

The shuttle skidded along the narrow ledge. The ceramic/
metal alloy screamed in protest as rocks scraped the belly
and tree limbs lashed the roof and viewscreen.

Kinnsell ducked instinctively.

With a wild screech, the left wheel snapped off. The heavy
tail end of the shuttle skidded around while the nose kept
plunging forward.

"Brakes, I need brakes," he yelled at the controls. A
confusing array of lights flashed on and off. He couldn't
make sense of what worked and what didn't. "How do I
stop this damn ship?" he asked the air.

(You must stop now!) A voice sounded inside his head.
An alien voice he couldn't recognize.

"Who?" he asked the air. "How?"

Before the words finished echoing in his head, the sound
of metal crunching against rock screamed throughout the
shuttle.

Yaala and Rollett held their ears. The old man dropped
to the floor, bracing his legs against a bulkhead while he
draped himself over the still unconscious Powwell.

The sounds of protesting metal wound down to an
annoying whine. The shuttle struck some large obstacle.

For a moment it hopped back into the air. Three seconds of absolute silence deafened him. All he could see out the front viewscreen were rocks and more rocks. The sensors relayed information too quickly for him to comprehend. Then the shuttle dropped again. Kinnsell's stomach lurched toward his throat. He shuddered with the vessel as it struck ground once more. A great tearing sound ran the length of the cabin. The deck split in the wake of the horrendous noise. The cabin canted sharply backward and to the left. Stopped. Suspended. Where?

Kinnsell unclenched his jaw. He rotated the joints a couple of times, fearing he'd cracked a bone or three. When his chin and cheeks stopped popping, he took a moment to appraise the situation.

His sensors and the view outside the window told him the shuttle was precariously balanced upon the edge of the plateau. A tangle of tree limbs kept the stern of the shuttle from teetering into a steep and broken ravine.

A worse fate awaited him out the front viewscreen.

"Not again," he moaned and buried his head in his hands. When he spread his fingers a little and looked out the broken window, he slammed his eyes shut again. "I have to be feverish. I have to be hallucinating."

A huge dragon eye stared back at him through the cracked window.

*   *   *

Midafternoon, home of Myrilandel, Ambassador from the Nimbus of Dragons, Coronnan City

Bessel slipped up the stairs to his room while the royal couple and their friends made plans. He pulled together a disguise out of odds and ends and returned to the kitchen by the back staircase. Luucian's attention was on the servant's spyhole. Bessel tiptoed around him and opened the kitchen door of Myrilandel's house cautiously. A dozen black-clad mercenaries from Rossemeyer lined the alley. They stood tall and formidable, made more imposing by their voluminous black robes that could hide two dozen weapons, and by their elaborate black turbans with one end draped over their faces. Their black eyes glittered with menace as they surveyed Bessel.

He swallowed his fear and opened the door a little wider. As he took the one step down to the stoop, he held his lower back with one hand and balanced his weight to emphasize the large bulge of a blanket wadded up under one of Myrilandel's maternity gowns. His "pregnancy" was held in place by a wide belt. With a kerchief over his hair, he just might pass for a woman nearing the end of a difficult pregnancy.

Provided Mopsie stayed quiet and didn't squirm around too much within the blanket.

Two of the mercenaries stepped forward, hands on the hilts of their swords.

Bessel waddled up to them, keeping his eyes open and frank. He couldn't betray the truth by even so much as a twitch of fear on his face.

"Allow me to assist you, madama." The mercenary on Bessel's left crooked his arm, ready to take Bessel's weight, should he choose to place his hand there.

Bessel suppressed a grin as he leaned heavily against the man. He placed his other hand, still holding the basket, beneath his tummy bulge and moaned a little.

"I'm off to market for some special herbs to ease the birthing pains," he said in falsetto. "I should ever so much appreciate your company on the journey. One never knows when the babe might burst forth." Bessel clutched his belly again and moaned louder. This time he swayed a little.

"Um . . . um . . . shouldn't you stay home and send someone else to market?" His mercenary escort hesitated. The soldier looked frantically toward his companions for inspiration.

Few men, even healers, were comfortable around women in childbirth. Bessel had learned that much through his mother's numerous pregnancies. At the first sign of a labor pain, all the men in the village found urgent work elsewhere.

"There is no one else. They are all held captive in the street. Can't you hear the commotion? I must go now, I can't delay." Bessel moaned again as he took a few mincing steps down the alley.

"Then I fear you must go alone, madama. We cannot desert our posts." All of the mercenaries bowed low.

Bessel took several more steps—a little longer stride this time while they weren't looking.

"Please stay close. I may need you to boil water and fetch supplies by the time I return." Bessel dismissed them with a wave of his hand. The strangers drifted away from Myrilandel's kitchen door in an effort to separate themselves from Bessel.

Bessel fought to keep his steps short and awkward until he had rounded the corner into a wider street. A few people passed him without a second glance. Their attention was fastened upon the commotion at the front of the house on Embassy Row.

The crowd milled. Anger dominated the aura of the gathering. But it had no focus.

Suppressing a grin, Bessel shouted above the noise. "I saw one of the blackmailing Rovers with the foreigners. They're in league with the foreigners." The crowd took up the litany, linking their current troubles with the mercenaries from Rossemeyer rather than with the king.

He wanted to join them, but he had an important task.

Chapter 45

*Inside Kinnsell's shuttle on a plateau deep in the
Southern Mountains*

Yaala stirred cautiously from beneath a pile of seat cush-
ions and broken equipment. When the shuttle came to
a screeching halt, she had been thrown into a bulkhead.
She slipped on the sharply canted deck trying to get her
feet under her.

The shuttle shifted again. The deck tilted more steeply.
She froze in place.

A quick assessment showed Rollett stirring on the other
side of the cabin and Kinnsell staring wide-eyed and gaping
out the window at the baby dragon peering in through the
window. A faint hint of blue along wingtips and horns highlighted the dragon's dark pewter color. Afternoon sunlight
glinted off his fur. He appeared about the size of a small
pack steed, quite young.

"Don't move, Rollett," she commanded. He froze, much
as she had. "We're balanced precariously."

"I think that baby dragon sitting on the nose of the shuttle is all that is keeping us on the ledge," he whispered
back, as if afraid that the sound of his voice would upset
the balance.

"Can you see Lyman and Powwell?" she asked. Wreck-
age blocked her view of the central cabin.

"Lyman's legs. Not much else," Rollett replied.

"I'm alive," Lyman whispered back. "Powwell is burning
up with fever." Yaala picked out the outline of Lyman's

body amid the debris piled around them. He shifted his legs, trying to get his knees under him.

"Don't move," she and Rollett ordered together, much too loud.

The shuttle shifted again.

"I . . . if th . . . that monster is real," Kinnsell stuttered, "can you make it sit on the nose, like a teeter-totter?"

Yaala and Rollett looked at each other and shrugged off the strange words.

"A lever and a fulcrum, dammit! We need a counterbalance on the front to offset the heavy engines in the back." Kinnsell's exasperation broke through his stunned staring.

"Where there is one baby dragon, there will be a dozen more. They don't stray far from the lair at that age. Mama Shayla should be around here somewhere. She'll provide an adequate counterbalance," Lyman said. He lifted his head, cocking it to one side. The gesture was so common to him, Yaala hadn't recognized it as a listening pose until now.

"Do you speak to the dragons, Lyman?" she asked.

"Often. I missed them while I was in Hanassa. The dragons won't let their thoughts penetrate that city," Lyman replied. "The dragonets are too young to communicate with humans. I'm only getting baby screeches from them, no images or words." He tilted his head in the other direction. "Ah, there's Shayla, coming in from a hunt. She understands."

A loud thump vibrated down the length of the shuttle. Metal screeched again as huge talons tore at the strange skin. Then, slowly, the deck straightened.

"She's perched on the roof," Rollett said with a smile. "She wants us to open the hatch and very carefully slide out. The shuttle weighs more than she does, and she can't hold it long."

"I'm not going out there," Kinnsell protested. "I'm not going to become that monster's next meal." He continued to stare at the baby dragon.

Yaala couldn't help giggling. The baby was tiny. Wait until he saw Shayla!

"I—can't—open—the—door!" Lyman said through gritted teeth as he pushed buttons on the control panel and kicked at the hatch.

"There are dragons out there. Can't you gather some magic and force it open?" Yaala asked.

"The air in here is sealed tighter than anything we have encountered before," Lyman reminded her. "The dragon magic can't get in, and I haven't enough reserves to levitate the locking mechanism."

Yaala looked to Rollett for inspiration.

"The engines aren't running. We're going to run out of air very soon," Kinnsell stated calmly.

Yaala wondered if he'd rather suffocate than face the dragons. "Look for a manual override. If the shuttle has them for wings, surely it will have them for the hatch."

They all jerked their heads back to the hatch as a great tearing sound came from the metallic skin of the shuttle. A glimmer of daylight, followed by the tip of a red dragon talon pierced the hatch door.

"I believe rescue is on the way." Lyman grinned.

Seconds later fresh air penetrated the stale chemical tainted odor they'd been breathing since Hanassa. Yaala gulped in the fresh sweet scent of green trees and moisture. Her throat constricted with thirst, reminding her she hadn't drunk in hours—days?

Rollett and Lyman took deep gulps of air. They both sighed in satisfaction.

"Dragon magic!" Rollett opened his arms wide as if to embrace the air. "It's been so long. I didn't think I'd ever fill myself with it again. I didn't think I'd live long enough to find another dragon."

"You can breathe later. We've got to get out of here before the whole shuttle falls into a ravine." Yaala crawled toward the hatch where she could see most of a dark gray dragon paw and some of a red-tipped dragon nose poking through the crack. Blue-tip was still sitting on the nose staring at Kinnsell.

A sudden ripping sound sent the shuttle teetering on the edge again. Back and forth the craft wavered. Up and down.

"Seesaw Marjorie Daw," Kinnsell singsonged on a giggle. He looked and acted drunk. Or frightened to near insanity.

"We all have to get out now," Yaala said, with all of the authority instilled in her by her mother.

The hatch panel vibrated and split. An inquisitive dragon head poked through the opening. Red-tip scraped his budding spiral horn on the top of the hatch and backed out quickly with an affronted squeak. Yaala held her ears against the high-pitched protest.

The shuttle shuddered and tipped backward again. Everyone froze in place until the rocking ceased.

(Hurry!) a frantic voice pounded into Yaala's head.

Rollett and Lyman dropped to all fours and each grabbed one of Powwell's ankles. They dragged him cautiously toward the gaping hole in the bulkhead, keeping close to the deck. They must have heard the voice as well.

That left Kinnsell. *How can I persuade him to leave the dubious shelter of the shuttle?* Yaala asked herself. His skin had paled again and his eyes looked glassy with fever. Powwell's cure must not have been complete.

"I'm not going to let my best friend sacrifice his life for nothing. You come with me easy, or I knock you out and let the dragons drag you to safety!" She yanked him out of his chair and onto his knees.

"Y . . . you w . . . wouldn't," he protested feebly. His skin turned ashen. He swayed to his feet.

"If Powwell gives up his life to save yours, the least you can do is live." Grabbing him by the collar and the seat of his pants, as if he were a dog or a small child, she propelled him toward the hatch.

At least Lyman had persuaded the baby dragon to back away. He held the creature by the sensitive horn bud and peered directly into its eyes. Shayla lowered her long neck to peer at them closely. Lyman might have been a dragon once, but Shayla obviously wouldn't allow him too many liberties with her babies.

Rollett sat nearby on the ground, cradling Powwell's head in his lap.

The shuttle tipped again. Yaala heard a frantic scrambling of dragon talons on the roof. That decided her. Using every last bit of her strength she kicked Kinnsell's butt. He tumbled out the hatch, landing on the rough plateau facedown. He lifted his head and spat dirt.

"You will regret that, young lady. I am a very powerful man," he sneered at her.

Yaala jumped clear, sprawling next to him. "Out here the only power that counts is friendship with the dragons. You are decidedly powerless," she returned.

Behind her, Shayla screeched and flapped her wings in a mighty effort to get airborne. The shuttle creaked and tee-tered on the edge a moment, then tipped. It dropped abruptly down the hundred-foot cliff face, bounced on a lower slope and slid rapidly toward the bottom of a track-less ravine. Huge chunks of dirt and trees broke loose in the wake of the shuttle. Rocks the size of the baby dragons tumbled together in a mighty roar.

Yaala crawled to the cliff edge to watch the shuttle tum-ble down, down, forever down to the forest below.

Several long moments later, it landed. The rockfall con-tinued, on and on until the wonderful machine disappeared in a cloud of dirt and debris.

"It's gone," she whispered. And with it went the last tangible link to her machines, to Hanassa.

"I flew it once." She smiled. "That's all I really needed." Then she stood up, brushed dirt off her trews, assessed the situation, and began issuing orders.

*   *   *

*Late afternoon, home of Myrilandel, Ambassador
from the Nimbus of Dragons, Coronnan City*

"This is ridiculous!" Katie and Quinnault said in unison. They quirked half smiles at each other. The familiar blend-ing of their minds warmed Katie's heart anew.

"I am King of Coronnan. I will not be imprisoned in the home of my best friends by foreigners who do not like my system of justice." Quinnault marched out the door to con-fer with his guards. The dozen uniformed men faced twice their number of mercenary soldiers famed for their fierce thoroughness.

"At least you have a system of justice," Katie whispered to him. She sent him that reassurance mentally as well. Then she turned back to their other business.

"Now, while my husband deals with the soldiers outside, I shall tend to your medicine, Nimbulan." Katie rubbed her hands together eagerly. She had something to do.

"You have the gift, Katie." Myri smiled at her. "People jump to your orders and believe themselves blissfully content. When I give an order, servants look at me as if I were talking to air. It's easier to do the work myself."

Katie shrugged off the compliment. She had work to do.

Much to her surprise, the journeyman healer maintained his vigil over the simmering digitalis in the kitchen.

"You didn't succumb to Scarface's compulsion!" She stopped dead in the kitchen doorway.

"Your orders seemed more important. Besides, I'm only a journeyman. The call went out to masters. Some of the apprentices obeyed because they don't know better. I do." The young man shrugged and continued his chores.

"What is your name?" Katie asked. She moved to the open hearth to inspect his procedure.

"Luucian, Your Grace. Journeyman Healer Luucian, at your service." He bowed slightly, then returned to his remedy.

"Journeyman Luucian, you just became the king's personal healer. And I'll do my best to elevate you to Master Healer before the night is finished."

"Thank you, Your Grace, but only the Commune of Magicians can grant me master status." His face fell a little in disappointment.

"By dawn the Commune may undergo a major restructuring. Right now, His Grace, the king, and Master Nimbulan need people around them who are not influenced by a power-mad crusader." Katie ladled a bit of the raw drug into a clay mug. "It's ready. Take this to Master Nimbulan and make certain he takes all of it, even if you have to pinch his nose to make him swallow it."

"Me? You want me to command Master Nimbulan?" Luucian almost stuttered in his awe.

"Yes. That is your job as his healer. When you have seen to his medication, we'll have a job for you to do. We are all going to be very tired by the time this night is through. But you must make certain Nimbulan only supervises. I don't want him lifting anything."

"I'll take the medicine to Lan," Myri said from the doorway. "Shayla just requested a healer. Powwell and Yaala have rescued Rollett and King Kinnsell from Hanassa. They need a healer. Luucian here seems the only one available."

"Me?" Luucian squeaked again.

"What in bloody blazes was my father doing in Hanassa?" Katie asked in bewilderment. Myri had said "rescued." They needed a healer. Her father was alive. She still had a chance to . . . to . . . She didn't know what she needed to do to him, or for him. She was just very grateful he lived.

"Rouussin is waiting for you on Sacred Isle, Luucian," Myri said. "He'll take you to Shayla's lair and your patients. Gather a little of the Tambootie on the island to take with you. I'll dose my husband and make certain he takes all of his medicine." A look of determination settled over her features. She looked very much like Quinnault when he put on his stubborn face.

"How will I get past the mercenaries out the back door?" Luucian asked as he gathered up his black satchel.

"Nimbulan said you should wrap yourself in shadows and divert their attention with a suggestion implanted in their minds." Myri shrugged and returned to the front of the house with the precious dose of digitalis.

"I'll do my best, Your Grace. Do you have any messages for King Kinnsell and the others?"

"What I have to say to my father, I will say in person. He has a lot to answer for."

Luucian bowed to her again and exited, just one more shadow in a sheltered alley.

Shouting from outside drew Katie back to Quinnault and the mercenaries. Her husband stood with his short sword drawn and a phalanx of uniformed guards around him.

Chapter 46

Late afternoon, Shayla's lair, deep in the Southern Mountains

Powwell opened his eyes to find an unrecognizable face pressed close to his own. His eyes crossed as he tried to focus. His vision swam, and he lost all definition to the pale blob pierced by two bright blue eyes.

"Who?" he asked through dry and cracked lips. He couldn't move anything more than his mouth. His entire body felt as if his joints had been dislocated one by one and put back together wrong.

"I'm Luucian," the face said. The eyes twinkled momentarily and then relaxed, almost glazed over as if they were the center of the man's exhaustion. "Do you remember me, Powwell?"

"Healer?" Powwell couldn't manage more than a single word at a time. His mouth tasted as if he'd eaten sand. Where had a healer come from? Especially one with a bright blue healing aura?

"Yes, I apprenticed to the healers in Nimbulan's battle enclave about a year before you joined him. We met a few times at the University."

"Water." That seemed more important than the identity of the face. Powwell closed his eyes again; the light around him pierced his vision painfully.

Someone pressed a cup to his mouth and dribbled a few drops of blessedly sweet water onto his tongue. He gulped it greedily. No trace of sulfur marred the taste, so they couldn't be in Hanassa. But then, his mouth was so dry even that rancid water would taste sweet.

"More," he demanded.

"Just a few drops at a time, Powwell. You've had a very high fever. Your system is still in shock from it," Luucian replied. "But you'll recover rapidly once you start moving around again. Nothing like a little extra Tambootie in your system to restore your internal balance."

Powwell drank a little bit more this time; enough to roll around his mouth before he swallowed. The muscles in his throat ached and didn't want to work. He tried again and managed to get the water down.

"Thorny?"

"Your familiar is distraught, but still with you." Someone guided his hand until it rested upon Thorny's relaxed spines. The little hedgehog didn't hunch and bristle at his touch. Something must be wrong with him.

Powwell tried to open his eyes again and sit up. He had to take care of Thorny.

"Rest, Powwell. Thorny is fine. He's as worried about you as we are," Yaala said. Her cool hand touched his cheek.

He relaxed a little, but kept one hand on Thorny. A sense of well-being thrummed through his system from his point of contact with his familiar.

"Where?"

"We are in Shayla's lair," Yaala reassured him. "The dragons brought a healer to you from the capital. You are going to be fine."

"Hanassa?" he asked on a cough. Yaala pressed the cup to his mouth again. He took a big swallow but rolled it around his mouth, relieving parched tissue while he allowed only a little to trickle down his throat at a time.

"We escaped," Rollett said. His voice grew distant and loud as if he paced away and then turned back.

Powwell risked opening his eyes again. Sure enough, Rollett paced in front of the source of light—a cave opening? Only his silhouette was visible. Was that boulder by the entrance really a baby dragon watching Rollett?

"And the plague?" Powwell's mouth and throat eased enough to allow three words instead of one. He wanted more water, but Luucian held the cup back.

"You gave Kinnsell enough healing and strength to survive. He still needs some rest and recovery, but he'll live long enough to explain himself to his very irate daughter," Luucian told him. "I doused Yaala with the Tambootie. We don't know if her dragon heritage makes her immune or not. Lyman and Rollett seem to be fine."

When he finished speaking, he lifted the cup to Powwell's mouth again. "Not too much at once. You might bolt it."

Sure enough, the next swallow hit Powwell's stomach like an explosion and threatened to come back up again.

"Did I get the plague?"

"A mild case that I was able to cure," Luucian said. "You went through the trial by Tambootie smoke last winter, and you'd had a few doses of the raw leaves before Nimbulan discovered dragon magic. There must have been enough of the tree of magic still in your system to keep you alive and to heal King Kinnsell, but since you started as an apprentice after magicians gave up heavy doses of Tambootie, you still succumbed to the disease, probably because you passed so much of your natural immunity to King Kinnsell. It's a nasty one, spreads very rapidly. If Rouussin hadn't brought me here to Shayla's lair when he did, you would have died, Powwell."

Powwell smiled at the thought of Rouussin, the elderly red-tipped dragon who viewed humans as willful children who must be indulged.

He looked around the huge cave a moment. Sure enough a dozen baby dragons perched on various rocks and overhangs. A huge nest of sheep's wool, feathers, and moss dominated a slightly raised section toward the back. If Shayla was around, he couldn't see her.

"The plague in Hanassa? Maia?" he asked.

"We don't know yet. The dragons will scout the area and drop supplies, including some Tambootie wood for fires and timboor to add to their food. We have other issues to settle before we send investigators," Rollett answered, still pacing.

"Actually, the population as a whole is not threatened by the plague," Kinnsell added. He was behind Powwell and out of sight.

"Explain?" Luucian looked up. Curiosity overshadowed his fatigue.

"In my world, a haze of pollution alters the light patterns from the sun." He hesitated as if seeking the proper words. "Our bodies adapt to the changes in light. The poisons in the pollution build up in our bodies, triggering more changes. It is these changes along with the toxins in our bodies that allow the plague to attack us. You don't have the pollution, so only the weak and vulnerable—the old, the very young, and pregnant women—catch the disease. Miners might have a problem from coal dust, but the rest of you should be okay. Powwell caught it because of the direct blood contact. My blood in his system carried food for the plague."

"Interesting. I'll relay that information to the queen," Luucian replied.

"Why did Scarface send a journeyman?" Something nagged at Powwell's mind and wouldn't let him take the rest he so sorely needed.

"Scarface didn't send me. Myrilandel did. The dragons have withdrawn from Scarface and his followers."

Silence followed Luucian's words. Rollett and Yaala stared at him in surprise. Powwell did, too. They all waited for an explanation of this dire situation.

"The dragons have been staying away from the capital for weeks now. But today they have withdrawn their magic entirely from the Commune. Now that I know you and King Kinnsell will recover—he took to the Tambootie as well as any solitary magician I've ever met—I must return to the capital." Luucian stood up and dusted the knees of his trews. "Nimbulan and King Quinnault need me."

"What did Scarface do to earn the wrath of the dragons?" Rollett grabbed Luucian's sleeve, swinging the healer around to face him.

"Scarface wants to burn all of the books that mention anything about solitary magic." Luucian kept his eyes on his knees. "He has compelled all of the Commune to agree with him."

"I knew it! I knew he'd go too far in his need to control everyone and everything around him. But this goes beyond all reason, all rationale." Rollett shook his fists in the direction of the capital city.

"He can't burn the books!" Powwell protested. He remembered the precious information about blood magic he'd gleaned from an ancient text. He'd also learned about Rovers, their mind-to-mind magic and ways to avoid being pulled into their traps. Without those books, he'd never have found access to the dragongate. Never have reached Hanassa. . . .

Oh, Kalen, I've failed you once again.

"Nimbulan has a plan, but he needs help," Luucian replied as he stooped to pick up his healer's satchel.

"Scarface must intend to challenge King Quinnault for more than just those books," Rollett mused. "He wants control. Control over every life he touches, not just the Commune. I've got to go back. We can't let him continue his tyranny over the Commune or anyone else."

"Your help is welcome. The plan requires some interesting magic as well as manual labor. Bessel and I are the only magicians who have resisted Scarface's compulsion that we can be sure of, but Bessel is acting strangely and I'm not certain how valuable he will be. Powwell will be all right with Yaala to nurse him for a few days," Luucian replied.

"I'm not leaving without them." Rollett glanced at Yaala. His eyes caressed her. Yaala returned his gaze frankly. An energy nearly crackled between them. "We've been through a lot together. We stay together until we are all safe back home."

"I'll be all right alone," Powwell insisted. He couldn't stand between Yaala and a man who could love her. A part of Powwell would always separate him from Yaala, the part that belonged to Kalen. Dead Kalen.

He gulped back a sob. "The dragons will take care of me."

"I hate the idea of leaving you alone, Powwell, but we're needed in the capital." Yaala looked truly torn between Rollett and her friendship with Powwell.

"I'll stay with the boy. I can't say I'm looking forward to my daughter's tirade. Though I'd like to retrieve my granddaughter from Lord Balthazaan's custody before Katie tears the kingdom apart looking for her," Kinnsell said from the dim interior of the cave.

"Princess Marilell is safe," Luucian replied. His mouth worked as if he choked back a laugh. "The kidnapping attempt failed. Queen Katie and King Quinnault keep the child very close now."

"You bushies aren't as ignorant and helpless as I first imagined." Kinnsell chuckled. "I owe it to the boy to take care of him until you return. Can't say I want to stay here with these monsters, though. Are you sure they won't eat me for lunch?"

"What do I need other than strength to travel with you? I can eat and drink now, and that will restore a lot of my energy." Powwell struggled to raise himself on his elbows. If he stayed here, he'd wallow in his aching grief and never recover. Nimbulan needed him, needed his magic. He couldn't help Kalen anymore. He might as well give his all to the only man Kalen ever respected.

Suddenly his life had purpose. Kalen had spent her life running away from those who had tried to control her and her magnificent talent. He would honor her memory by challenging all those who would victimize other children before they'd had the chance to learn to control their own destinies.

He'd start with Scarface.

*   *   *

Late afternoon, Coronnan City

Bessel crossed two bridges and threaded through a number of streets before he slipped into another alley. He faced the wall of a smithy as he removed Mopsie and the blanket from their hiding places.

The little dog yipped his gratitude and squirmed within Bessel's arms, tired of being confined. He licked Bessel's face before jumping to the ground and running three joyous circles around his ankles.

"Yes, yes, I know you are happy, Mopsie, but we have to keep moving. We have to get to the docks before the tide turns and the barge sails. We have to make sure that by the time Raanald gets the barge to the port, he'll mistrust the depth finder so much he'll destroy it himself." He patted his familiar and set about arranging a new disguise.

After removing the dress and kerchief, he folded them

into the blanket lengthwise and slung the bundle across his back and over one shoulder. He tucked the loose ends into his belt. Then he snapped his fingers and transported his staff and a metal bowl from his room inside Myrilandel's house. The spell was illegal. Dragon magic only allowed levitation, not transportation. But the men of Rossemeyer would have seen the staff floating through the air and followed it.

King Quinnault had told him to use whatever means possible to destroy the depth finder and create chaos on the docks.

Lastly he smeared dirt on his cheeks and chin in imitation of two days' growth of beard.

With bowl in one hand, held out in a classic beggar's stance, and leaning heavily on the staff, he shuffled out of the alley, just another beggar displaced by the wars.

He progressed to the docks unmolested and richer by seven dragini.

"Dinner," he promised Mopsie as he slipped the coins inside his belt pouch. He tucked the bowl into his makeshift bedroll and wound his way through the confusing array of docks and warehouses under construction.

The elaborate passenger barge he had ridden on—was it just two days ago?—rested against a clean ramp. No one bothered to sweep and scrub the more commercial docks. But this one catered to wealthy and elite passengers. A bevy of colorful canopies and padded benches provided those passengers with a place to await the tide and the whim of the pilot.

If he'd worn his magician's robes, Bessel could have walked directly up to the barge and demanded passage free of charge. Dressed as an ordinary fisherman, accompanied by a scruffy dog—who had gotten very dirty again crossing the city—the stewards and crew wouldn't allow him beyond the velvet ropes that separated the passenger area from the common dockside traffic.

He needed another disguise.

What would get him aboard the ship without question and without having to pay an enormous fee? He couldn't board as an ordinary dockhand, and the uniforms of the Guild of Bay Pilots were custom-made for each individual—

no extras. Besides, every man in the Guild knew every other man in the guild.

He'd have to board as a magician needing free passage so he could fulfill some unnamed errand for the Commune. No longer concerned about performing rogue magic, he snapped his fingers again. His formal robe and his best boots from his room in Myrilandel's house landed in a heap at his feet. He ducked behind a pile of crates and rope coils to rearrange himself. The robe covered his ordinary fisherman's clothing. But his bedroll and Mopsie needed a more discreet covering.

He checked the pockets of the robe for his normal assortment of essential equipment. Everything seemed in place.

"With permission to use rogue magic, I can hide the bedroll here and retrieve it later," he whispered to himself and Mopsie. He also needed to change his appearance a little. He didn't want Raanald, the pilot during yesterday's disaster, or any of his crew recognizing him. With just a little magic he made himself appear taller and thinner. The dirt on his face took on a heavier appearance, more like a true beard and mustache.

Mopsie whined in disapproval at the change. "Don't worry, pup, I won't leave you behind. I need you to stand guard while I do what I have to do."

The depth finder was in place. He could see it from here but he couldn't blast it with magic. That would bring down the wrath of the Guild upon the Commune. He needed to make it look as if the machine were defective—dangerous— so the Guild would cooperate with the Commune in the future, not go to war with each other.

He needed to get closer, close enough to touch the machine. Boldly, he stepped up to the steward standing behind the velvet rope.

"Good man, I travel on business for the Commune of Magicians. I need to interview passengers arriving this evening at the port." Bessel gestured expansively toward the four islands far out in the Great Bay at the beginning of deep water. The steward kept his eyes on Bessel's hand and staff rather than on the dirty mutt who hid beneath the journeyman's robes.

"I need a passport." The steward held out his hand for

the bit of slate with symbols scratched on it that outlined Bessel's instructions.

"What you don't know can hurt you," Bessel whispered to himself. He fished in his pocket while murmuring yet another transport spell to bring him the flat scrap of slate he kept with his books. The piece was outdated from his journey to his mother's deathbed. But this man couldn't read—prevented by law from learning the arcane skill.

The steward barely glanced at the passport, then unhitched one of the velvet ropes at the stanchion, allowing Bessel to pass into the waiting area unhindered. "You may board now, but sit somewhere out of the way. We'll sail with the tide regardless, even if that mob of uppity mercenaries and their lady don't show up on time."

"Mercenaries?" Bessel raised one eyebrow at the man as if the issue were of only moderate interest.

"Yeah. The lady sent word. She's taking the ambassador's body back to Rossemeyer for burial. After she executes that other magician, the one who murdered her husband."

Chapter 47

Katie gulped back her immediate fear. Quinnault knew the business end of a sword and how to use it.

So did all of those black-clad mercenaries. But they would not try to find a compromise without violence.

In her fear for Quinnault, the rising noise around them faded from her awareness.

Then she noticed the source of the shouts that had brought her to her husband's side—she must have walked across the cobblestone stoop to stand at his side without being aware of anything but the need to touch his hand and reassure herself he still lived.

Hundreds of people pressed against the foreign mercenaries. They shouted and brandished torches, makeshift clubs, and everyday tools as weapons.

"They're in league with the Rovers," one man shouted. "They steal our money and terrorize our women and children!"

"Kill the Rovers and their helpers!" Another man joined the litany of abuse. "I'll not pay protection money to foreigners."

"Kill all the foreigners!"

"Save the king from the filthy foreigners."

"Stargods bless the king."

The mercenaries looked over their shoulders nervously. They fingered their weapons but kept them sheathed. Their leader, face completely obscured by black veils, backed up two steps. He ran into a solid wall of his own men. They kept pressing forward, away from the murderous crowd. But as they moved away from the crowd, they came closer and closer to Quinnault and his entourage. A few more steps and confrontation was inevitable.

"My people." Quinnault raised his voice above the rabble. He also lifted his hands as a signal for quiet.

The shouts and murmurs stilled closest to Quinnault and spread outward in waves.

"People of Coronnan, listen to me! Once before, you joined to unify against forces that would have destroyed us with civil war. Now I ask you to join me again to save the kingdom. I need your help to unite the crown, the lords, the magicians, and the people. Only you, the people, can bind us together!"

"What do you plan?" Katie whispered. Love and respect flooded her emotions. This medieval man, with a worldview limited by an aristocratic power structure, had just embraced a modern principle of democracy.

He viewed the people as the heart and core of his kingdom.

His mind smiled into hers. She saw his plan. The people would march in triumph to the University and challenge the Commune. Scarface would have to relinquish his hold on the magicians in the face of this determined mob backing their king.

A mighty cheer rose from the throats of the people as they surged forward. The mercenaries looked warily around them. The people pressed against them so tightly they couldn't draw or wield a weapon. Each of the foreigners found himself totally surrounded, cut off from his fellows.

"Hear me, men of Rossemeyer!" Quinnault raised his hands and voice once more. His words echoed in the narrow street. "Honorable warriors, go back to your embassy. Inform Lady Rosselaara that this business is finished. I have investigated and found Ambassador Jorghe-Rosse's death to be an accident. He died honorably fighting the storm and the bay, worthy enemies. No other lives will be forfeited. Take your ambassador home for funeral rites. You are free, all of you, to depart Coronnan with the evening tide."

"And if we doubt your 'investigations'?" the head mercenary asked, fighting to maintain his balance in the midst of the pressing crowd.

"Then your king must send me a new ambassador to negotiate. Now take Ambassador Jorghe-Rosse's body and Lady Rosselaara home for a proper funeral. Would you like an escort to the docks? I'm certain the people of Coronnan City would be happy to see you safely on your way."

The mercenaries melted away. The people closed ranks, jeering at them. A few cityfolk who carried rocks and tools followed them back toward their embassy.

"And now, my people, we must bring back a balance in our government. The Commune, the Council, and the King must once again hold equal power. No one faction can be allowed to dominate the others." Quinnault forged a path through the throng of eager townspeople. They rushed to walk near him, touch him, bask in his glory.

"Excuse me, Your Grace," Luucian appeared at Katie's elbow.

"Luucian, what are you doing here? You are supposed to be at Shayla's lair," Katie gasped in surprise.

"I've been there and back. The dragons know a few shortcuts. The others are trying to work their way through the crowd."

"My father?"

"Well enough, for the time being. He's in the kitchen, eating and drinking to restore some of his vitality. But, Your Grace, I have a message from Bessel, relayed by the dragons. He said to get these people down to the docks. He needs everyone down on the docks."

Katie stared at the mob encircling Quinnault. They were moving toward University Isle. She'd have to divert them. But first. . . .

"Luucian, go with Master Nimbulan and the others and start moving the books from the library into the tunnels below the palace. Master Nimbulan is to supervise only. He is not to lift a single book." Quickly, she outlined the plan for to him. "While you are doing that, I need my father to find Lord Balthazaan and keep him out of the way and misinformed."

Luucian nodded and melted back into the crowd.

Katie had to fight to stay close to her husband as they swept along the city streets in the direction of University Isle.

"Scarecrow, we're needed at the docks. Bessel sent a message."

Quinnault raised an eyebrow at her.

"I've sent Nimbulan and reinforcements on their errand."

"Reinforcements?"

"I'll explain later.

Quinnault nodded. "How am I going to divert this mob?"

"I'm not sure." Katie bit her lip and glanced around at the volatile crowd.

"Stop!" Five master magicians commanded. They stood in a line across the path of the crowd. They linked hands. A dark green aura of power—Scarface's signature color—surrounded them. "Senior Magician Scarface commands this mob to disperse. We place King Quinnault Darville de Draconis under arrest for interfering with the lawful work of the Commune of Magicians."

*   *   *

The docks, Coronnan City

Bessel swallowed his apprehension that Lady Rosselaara would recognize him. He had to trust in his disguises and complete his mission. He nodded to the steward and climbed the ramp to the barge. He chose a seat in the back corner beneath the canopy, deep in the shadows. Here he could relax his delusion spell while he studied the depth finder.

Shortly the crew began moving about the deck, coiling lines and performing other chores indicative of imminent launching. A subtle shift of the water's movement beneath the deck told Bessel when the tide turned and began to recede. Just as a crewman prepared to fling the last line aboard from the dock, a long procession of black-clad mercenaries appeared at the velvet ropes.

Deep within their ranks, Lady Rosselaara stood beside her husband's casket, dry-eyed and angry.

The first of the warriors slashed the rope with his sword and kicked it aside. The steward rushed to stop them and demand their passports. They thrust him out of the way as if he were merely another piece of normal dock debris.

Raanald, the pilot and absolute ruler of the barge, stalked to the head of the boarding ramp. He stood firmly blocking the way, hands on hips, feet spread, and a scowl on his face.

"You're late," Raanald spat, not moving out of the way.

The lead mercenary hesitated. They needed the pilot to guide the barge to the port. He couldn't injure the man, and he couldn't get past him without injuring him.

"We are here now. You have not left without us," the warrior replied from behind his turban veil. His voice remained even and remote through the muffling cloth. A pulse pounded visibly in his temple. Politeness was something these men had little time for.

And yet some of them had been quite gentle and caring toward Bessel when he appeared to be a female in distress.

"You may travel with us, but only because it means we're shut of you for good," Raanald replied. "You'd better hurry. Anyone not in place in five minutes has to swim to the port, or walk across the sucking mud." He turned his back on the newcomers and stationed himself by the helmsman on the elevated platform at the rear of the barge.

The Rossemeyerians proceeded to crowd upon the barge in an orderly fashion, despite their rapid pace.

Bessel allowed himself to be edged out of the sheltering shadows to stand next to the depth finder. The warriors seemed to shun it as if it would contaminate them with its arcane magic. Lady Rosselaara claimed most of the covered area for herself, the coffin, two maids, and a few select warriors. The deck of the barge wallowed a little deeper in the water with so many people aboard.

The oarsmen shoved off. Raanald moved back to the depth finder. He stared alternately at the numbers behind the screen and at the water ahead.

Bessel kept his back to the pilot as much as possible, hoping he had the strength to keep up his disguise throughout the entire procedure. Mopsie had crawled under the nearest bench and watched everything through wary eyes.

When the port islands finally appeared as a hazy blur on

the horizon and the shore remained within clear view, Bessel edged his foot to touch the base of the depth finder.

He plunged his mind into the guts of the machine and met a solid wall of impenetrable lead. He tried again, probing around the edges, seeking a crack in the mechanism, a seam, any point where he could penetrate. Sharp pain bounced back into his eyes along the line of his magical touch. He grimaced and yanked his foot away from the base as if burned. His entire body tingled with backlashed magic.

Quickly, he looked around to see if any of the many warriors around him noticed his discomfort. They all seemed absorbed in keeping their stomachs intact. Not very good sailors, Bessel surmised. Maybe . . .

He sent his next probe into the Bay. The muddy bottom absorbed his magic like a sponge. He tried again, slightly to the left of his original quest for information. A spring bubbled up through the mud. When the tide was completely out, a small freshwater creek would flow away from that spring. Several springs fed the Bay in this manner, making for dangerous sucking mud around the source.

This time his probe sounded different within his mind. The fresh water changed the density of the salt water. He checked the numbers on the depth finder. They spun up and back down again quite rapidly. The change in the water had triggered an inaccurate measurement.

Above him, a dragon bellowed as it flew determinedly around the city. The machine numbers fluctuated again, more drastically than it had with the fresh water.

Bessel smiled to himself and edged over to the railing. He searched for the new wood that marked the spot where Jorghe-Rosse had fallen overboard. He spotted the fresh paint showing a stout replacement to the broken pieces. Two paces away the railing paint peeled and the wood looked worn and weak. He stood beside it.

Bessel here. Please, flying dragon, announce your presence again, loudly, clearly, he called to the nearly invisible beast.

(Rouussin,) the dragon introduced himself. Dragon protocol required names. *(What do you wish?)*

Please, Master Rouussin, will you bellow again? I need the sounds to disrupt an evil machine.

(Shayla has shared with us Queen Maarie Kaathliin's dragon dream. We do not like machines that harbor the seeds of disease.)

The dragon bugled loudly. The expanse of the Bay picked up the sound, amplified it, and bounced it against the cliff walls farther south.

The passengers held their ears and looked at each other in distressed puzzlement.

The numbers on the machine spun out of control. "Hard a port!" Raanald screamed at the helmsman. Panic widened his eyes.

The helmsman leaned all of his body weight onto the tiller.

The barge swung around. The waves slapped the barge sideways. The helmsman kept pushing the tiller. The spring beneath the barge and the conflicting movement of the water created an undertow. The turning barge caught a rip in the tide, spinning it around so the other side of the barge faced the oncoming waves. Then it grounded on the bar.

"S'murghin' machine!" Raanald yelled. He grabbed one of the long oars away from his crew and slammed it into the depth finder. The viewscreen split. The numbers died.

Raanald continued pounding the oar into the black casing. The synthetic black shell cracked, but he did not penetrate to the lead core.

Raanald lifted his makeshift club for one last blow. He looked around him, suddenly aware of the crowd that stared at his anger. They all clutched railings or each other to keep them upright on the uncertain deck.

The pilot's gaze landed on Bessel.

"You!" Raanald stared at him, stunned bewilderment clouded his eyes. "What game are you and that bloody Commune of yours playing this time?"

He advanced upon Bessel, oar raised.

"I did nothing to your machine," Bessel replied, calmly. Suddenly his entire future opened before him. He knew what he had to do.

"You destroyed the machine!" Raanald screamed.

"No, you did." Bessel knew everyone aboard heard him. He only needed a little magic to hold their attention, make them understand. "The depth finder deceived you again with invalid numbers. You destroyed it to regain control of this barge. The Guild can no longer rely on the depth finder."

"But we don't know the channels anymore!" Raanald stared at the vast expanse of water between himself and the port islands, at the oarsmen standing bewildered for lack of direction, at the rudder swinging idly awaiting a guiding hand.

"Trust your Mopplewogger as you have for many generations."

Mopsie yipped and danced on his hind legs. He pranced over to the helmsman. He barked once, quick and sharp.

"That means starboard. You have to go to starboard to get off the bar," Bessel reminded Raanald.

"I know what the dog means. But that ain't a Mopplewogger, and you broke my machine."

"Mopsie is a better Mopplewogger than you'll ever know."

"Don't tell me my business, *Magician*," Raanald spat the last word. "I'm a senior member of the Guild of Bay Pilots." He ran the last few steps to where Bessel stood by the railing. He swung the oar with all his might.

Bessel ducked backward. Raanald's blow landed on the railing, splintering the old wood.

Raanald raised the oar again. Bessel braced himself against the damaged railing. The deck shifted under his feet. His balance twisted.

The club clipped his temple.

Starbursts filled his vision. He fell. The railing gave way.

For a moment the weightless sensation of flying cleared his mind.

Then the cold dark waters of the bay closed over his head.

They'll tell everyone I'm dead, he thought as he shucked his boots and formal robe beneath the waves.

Let them believe I'm dead. I have nothing and no one to mourn me.

Above him Mopsie splashed into the water, barking frantically. His cries and whines took on a note of desperation.

Down here, pup. I'm hiding. Meet me ashore. We'll be together. I have you to live for. We are both free now. Free of our pasts and those who judged us. Our destinies are our own to shape and control.

Chapter 48

Late afternoon, streets of Coronnan City

"**W**e need to stall Scarface until Bessel finishes his chore," Katie whispered to Quinnault.

He nodded curtly in acknowledgment. His gaze remained upon the five magicians facing him across the street.

"I will deal only with Master Aaddler," he announced. "Since he challenges my authority, he must face me directly."

The magicians looked to each other in a moment of confusion.

Katie caught a drift of their stray thoughts.

Scarface said there would be no resistance.

How do we keep the king and his troops away from the island until dawn?

The dragon magic wanes. The dragons have deserted us! Stargods forgive me. The youngest of the magicians went down on his knees, crossing himself repeatedly.

Katie resisted the urge to mimic the gesture. Instead, she watched the shimmer of green power that connected the magicians fade and break apart.

"What breaks our connection to Scarface?" the senior among the magicians asked aloud.

"Nimbulan's people said that even when the dragons deserted Coronnan last year, they had access to *some* dragon magic for a while," one of his fellows replied.

Sensing confusion and weakness among the magicians, the crowd surged forward, pushing Quinnault and Katie to within a few yards of the opposition.

"Fools! Who gave you permission to drop the barrier spell?" Scarface stalked up behind his magicians. "Link up.

Protect University Isle from this mob." His face twisted in anger. The white scar across his brow turned livid, pulsing red.

"Give it up, Master Aaddler," Quinnault called. "You have no authority to arrest me or anyone—*ever.*"

"You can't stop me," Scarface glared at his king.

"Would you care to argue that with my supporters?"

Scarface stared at the dozens, maybe a hundred people, behind the king and queen. They raised their makeshift weapons, shaking them in direct challenge.

"Come," Scarface called to his five compatriots. "We will begin now rather than wait for dawn." He and his magicians backed down the street toward their island.

The crowd became noisy, demanding the end of the Commune's power. They pressed Katie and Quinnault from behind.

"Now what do we do?" Katie asked, fighting to stay afoot. She clung to Quinnault's arm. The dozen armed guards did their best to keep the crowd away.

(Start a fire elsewhere,) a dragon answered out of nowhere.

Shayla circled the crowd low enough for all to see. Then she rose above the city, widening her circle. A moment later she opened her mouth, letting loose a roar followed by a continuous stream of flame. Fire touched the tower roof at the University. The tar holding the slates in place ignited. A second blast of flame exploded the timbers below. Slates flew in all directions becoming deadly missiles.

* * *

Late afternoon, the docks, Coronnan City

Bessel approached the passenger dock from the direction of the fishermen's wharf. He'd exchanged his soaked clothes for a different set of fishermen's togs provided by men who considered him one of them. Raanald and Lady Rosselaara stepped out of a small rowboat within a moment of his arrival.

A dozen boats had been dispatched by royal guards to rescue the passengers from the barge.

"Get me Master Scarface. Now. Bring the interfering bastard here at once!" Raanald shouted above the noise of the curiosity seekers and dock workers.

A dozen or more dogs barked, their excited comments drifting across the bay more clearly than people's voices.

A nice state of chaos ready for the last ingredient.

A new contingent of palace guards appeared on the embankment above the passenger dock. A couple of magicians hovered behind them, but no Scarface. Bessel moved closer to the center of the wordstorm.

Lady Rosselaara looked straight at him without recognition and turned to one of her mercenaries. "Find me another boat. Row it yourself if you have to, but get me out of this city immediately."

"Sometimes hiding in plain sight is more effective than the darkest hidey-hole," Bessel said under his breath as the lady passed him. If she heard, she didn't deign to acknowledge his comment.

He looked up at the line of palace guards arguing fiercely with Raanald and a contingent of magicians. Behind them, King Kinnsell and Lord Balthazaan added their own tirade. Four other finely dressed men followed them meekly.

More dogs crowded onto the docks, barking incessantly.

The babble rose to an uncomfortable crescendo. Confusion reigned, amplifying frustrations and churning anger. But where was Scarface? He needed to be here so that Nimbulan and the others had time to move the books into hiding.

A dragon bellowed from the skies above them. Everyone on the dock ceased speaking and looking up. Bessel could just make out a shimmering outline in a kaleidoscope of all color/no color.

Two dragons in one day? Something wonderful and strange transpired in the city.

A hush fell over the crowd. One of the magicians took an open posture, head turned up, eyes closed. After a few moments of the stillness needed to gather dragon magic, his face crumpled in disappointment. Then he gathered his companions close. They jabbered among themselves and cowered in fear. They kept shifting their gaze between the dragon and back toward the city where a tall column of smoke rose from the vicinity of the University.

Obviously the Commune was out of favor with the dragons if they could not gather precious dragon magic.

Did the smoke have something to do with that?

Shayla! Bessel here, he hailed her.

(Greetings,) the dragon replied. *(Hasten. You are needed. The University burns. The fire will not delay your enemies long.)*

Mopsie nudged him, reminding him of his next chore. "Right, boy. We have to make sure Nimbulan doesn't hide those books permanently."

He whistled sharply. A dozen fishermen looked at him in recognition, then moved to interrupt Lady Rosselaara's tirade. In moments, the diplomatic entourage had been escorted back aboard small fishing boats and headed for the port. Each boat boasted an alert moppelwogger in the bow.

"Coronnan is grateful for your departure, madama," Bessel muttered. "I know I am."

He left the docks whistling. He had his own path to forge; a new destiny to follow. Freedom rode lightly on his shoulders, a comfortable companion.

The magicians turned and hastened back toward the University. The guards ran to follow, Raanald at their heels, still shaking his fist angrily. Kinnsell smiled and followed them more slowly. He kept up a barrage of insults and complaints to the finely dressed men around him. Lord Balthazaan broke off from him to keep up with the magicians. Kinnsell snagged the lord's sleeve, shouting at him and raising his fists. They stood squarely in the path of the mercenaries and dock workers who sought to follow.

The pack of unpartnered water dogs seemed to flow around the obstacle. They nipped at heels as they raced toward this new curiosity.

"We can't delay here any longer, Mopsie. Scarface never showed up. Guess we'll have to try something else to thwart him." Bessel slipped quietly into the crowd, just another anonymous figure watching the antics of the powerful and the angry. But he didn't stay with the throng beyond sight of the docks. As soon as he could, he and Mopsie took off for Palace Isle and the emergency escape tunnels beneath the palace. Mopsie sniffed out shortcuts no human would think to follow.

"Now for the books, pup. We've a lot of magic to weave. Together."

Chapter 49

Near sunset, the streets of Coronnan City

"**S**carface ain't our king. He's got no right to arrest any-one!" a loud-voiced tradesman bellowed over the noise of city crowd.

Katie squeezed Quinnault's hand. They shared a moment of triumph as the crowd surged along the city streets following in the wake of the fleeing magicians.

"Long live King Quinnault!" a hundred voices picked up the cheer. "Stargods bless our king."

She heard a few angry mumbles about ending the tyranny of tax collectors. But mostly the crowd pressed close in order to keep anyone from menacing their king.

They approached Palace Isle, the last major island before Scarface's refuge on University Isle. Smoke filled the air. Ahead, the now roofless tower continued to burn. Flames shot upward, sending sparks outward in a fountain. Most were extinguished before touching ground or landed in the river.

The crowd increased its speed now that their target was clearly visible.

"Dragons bless us," a woman called above the crowd noise. "The dragons bless us." Everyone looked up to the six shimmering outlines that circled the city.

Two dozen more guards swelled the ranks of the throng. In their midst, Katie saw a few familiar but very grimy faces. They all walked heavily as if very tired.

"Myri!" She waved to her friend, signaling her closer.

Old Lyman plowed a passageway through the crowd for

the book rescuers. The crowd made way respectfully for the king's sister and her very dirty entourage.

"Yaala? Is that really you?" Katie grabbed the young woman in a fierce hug. "I've missed you terribly." A dark-haired young man with blond streaks in his thick beard stayed close behind Yaala, not quite daring to approach the queen but seemingly reluctant to let Yaala out of his sight.

"Your Grace, may I present Rollett, Nimbulan's journey-man, recently freed from Hanassa," Yaala introduced the young man, reaching to hold his hand.

Katie nodded her acknowledgment of the introduction, trying not to raise her eyebrows at the intimate gesture.

"Is Nimbulan all right? What about my father?" she asked anxiously, searching the crowd for signs of the others. Nimbulan walked beside Myri, holding her hand. He looked tired, but not in pain. Powwell walked beside them, pale and sad but staying proudly beside his adoptive parents. Luucian was there, too, keeping an eye on Nimbulan and Powwell.

"Where is King Kinnsell?" Katie demanded.

"With Lord Balthazaan," Myri explained. "He'll join us later."

Just then a pack of dogs began barking nearby. They raced forward to University Isle from an adjacent island. Another throng of people, led by Raanald the bay pilot, came into view. The dogs wove in and out of the crowd yapping louder and louder to be heard above the angry shouts. Raanald kicked at a dog to get it out of the way. Kinnsell yanked the man off balance and shouted some-thing unintelligible. Lord Balthazaan and a few of his cro-nies hovered behind Katie's father, looking confused.

"It's useless to talk here." Quinnault shook his head as Katie tried to call to her father. "We'll get the whole story later. Right now, we have to stop Scarface."

And then they faced University Isle. Scarface stood in the center of the courtyard holding a torch aloft. Before him lay a mound of books. Master magicians threw more books out the windows of the adjacent library.

The dogs swarmed over the bridge, baying at the sight of Scarface. They circled him, growling and yapping.

He thrust his torch at them, keeping them at bay.

The dogs backed away, still snarling.

"Hear me, people of Coronnan!" Scarface called. He circled the torch at the dogs, trying to break through their numbers to get to the books. The dogs shifted position, circling but keeping Scarface from his objective.

Finnally one of the dockmen whistled sharply. The dogs backed off.

"Hear me, people of Coronnan!" Scarface repeated.

This time Katie sensed magic behind his words, not a compulsion, but the power to be heard and understood in the farthest reaches of the noisy crowd.

"People of Coronnan, these books harbor evil knowledge. Knowledge of the blood magic and Rovers that brought this land low for three generations of warfare. The books must be purged so that no one can use this knowledge against you ever again."

Murmurs of disquiet rippled through the crowd. They pushed forward to hear more.

Katie found herself and her friends at the edge of the paved courtyard without realizing how rapidly she had been carried forward.

"Stargods, he's going to make the people believe in his madness," Quinnault muttered.

Scarface lowered his torch.

"Who are you to decide what knowledge is evil, which books must be destroyed?" Quinnault screamed.

Scarface hesitated.

"I forbid you to burn any books, Master Aadler," Quinnault said on a calmer note. "I have already dismissed you as my adviser. You cannot be trusted to be impartial."

The magicians gathered around the University courtyard paused to listen. The lords who had gathered behind the magicians looked to Quinnault in puzzlement.

"The art of reading has been forbidden to all but magicians since the coming of the Stargods," Scarface intoned, raising his torch high above his head. "Who else but the Senior Magician can make this decision?" The flickering light cast him in a halo of fire-green light—very close to his signature color of magic.

The crowd of mundane and magician onlookers gasped at the image of sacred blessing he invoked.

"The three brothers who descended upon a cloud of silver flame entrusted a few select, talented people with the forbidden knowledge within these books. As magicians, we carry out that trust by knowing why this knowledge is forbidden to all but us and preventing its use for evil. Rogue magicians who have forsaken the wisdom of the Stargods for personal glory have used it against the good of the common people and the kingdom. We, the guardians of knowledge, decree that the books must be destroyed before more evil is perpetrated by those who refuse the controls of dragon magic and the Commune."

We cannot stop him, Katie moaned to Quinnault. *He doesn't need compulsion anymore. These people will follow him anywhere.*

"How much of our history, philosophy, and law will be lost with those books? That information is as valuable as magic. You can't destroy all of the books just because they might contain information you deem evil," Quinnault protested, as loud and compelling as Scarface's diatribe.

"I can and I will." Scarface lowered his torch to ignite the first books.

"You can't ruin the Commune. I won't let you." A ghostly figure in white trews and yellow shirt launched himself from the edge of the crowd onto Scarface. The two men rolled to the ground. The torch flew out of Scarface's hand onto the paving stone. Silently it rolled toward the books.

"Bessel. The torch!" Powwell bellowed.

"I saw him earlier in the tunnels. He helped move books, but he did it secretly," Yaala added in a quieter tone. "He said he had to disappear. He said . . ."

Rollett dove across the mound of books and grabbed the torch. He thudded into the pavement. Yaala gasped and held her hand to her throat until Rollett rolled to his feet, the torch held away from the precious books.

Beside him Bessel jumped to his feet and disappeared into the shadows. Scarface lay panting where he had fallen.

"Bessel looks more like a ghost than a man," Katie whispered.

"Bessel told me not to believe rumors of his death," Powwell said. He turned a weak smile on his companions.

"Has anyone noticed some of the books disappearing from the mound? He's still helping, but I doubt we'll see him do it. Maybe he is a ghost now." He whispered the last.

"Give it up, Scarface. The dragons burned your tower," Quinnault countered. "Surely, if Shayla seeks to destroy your workplace, then she withdraws her covenant and her blessing from you."

"The priests agree with Scarface," Lord Balthazaan shouted above the hushed whispers of the crowd. "He has the blessing of the Stargods to burn these books. I count the Stargods above a murdering dragon any day. Dragons are monsters to be avoided. We can't trust them." The lord clenched his fist and shook it at the skies where the dragons had flown. His fingers looked naked, devoid of the heavy rings he and his wife habitually wore.

A sudden image splashed in front of Katie's vision. Balthazaan should wear a silver ring of entwined strands on his left hand. His wife wore an identical one—the hereditary betrothal bands of their family. One of those two rings had been left in Marilell's crib. The baby had almost choked to death on a ring normally worn by this lord.

Her father might have prompted the attempted kidnapping of her baby, but this man executed the orders—or tried to.

She flashed the information to Quinnault. He reeled under the impact. *How do we prove it?* Quinnault asked her. Anger stained his cheeks red.

I don't know that we can. Balthazaan will side with anyone who opposes you. He will claim our accusations are merely persecution because of his opposition to your politics, Katie thought.

I thought your father tamed him.

My father has his own agenda. Who knows what thoughts and innuendos he planted in that man's mind. We only asked him to keep the lords out of the way while Nimbulan and his friends rescued a few of the books. Now he's disappeared again.

"Balthazaan." Quinnault gathered himself to speak. "Without the dragons, we cannot fight rogue magic. Do you wish to return to the days of civil war when Battlemages led warlords into battle after battle for no reason other than to prove their superiority over another Battlemage?"

Balthazaan reared back as if he'd been slapped.

"By your own argument, King Quinnault, the books must be burned. They contain knowledge of rogue magic. Once they are destroyed, no one will know how to work any magic but that given us by dragons." The Senior Magician dragged himself to his feet. He kept his eyes on the torch Rollett still held out of his reach.

"Master Aaddler," Katie called aloud. "If other lands with Battlemages who use solitary magic attack us, overtly or covertly, how will we know how to counter them unless we have access to the same knowledge they possess?"

"That cannot happen!" Scarface screamed. His scar whitened, and he scrunched up his eyes, making an ugly mask of his face. "There will be no more rogue magic. I cannot allow any more rogue magic!" Scarface raised his hands to the skies and brought forth a huge ball of witchfire. As suddenly as the flames appeared, he launched them into the middle of the mound of books. They exploded in flame.

Wind-drift and Whitehands lunged for him, knocking him back to the pavement once more. The two magicians slammed their fists into Scarface's jaw alternately, repeatedly.

"How dare you!" they screamed.

"How dare you destroy our heritage?" Tears streamed down Wind-drift's face. "I tried to make you see reason. I tried, but you would not listen," he sobbed.

A dozen hands, led by Rollett and Powwell, rushed to douse the flames with water or blankets. The heat of fire in the tower drove them back before they could get close enough to extinguish more than a few sparks.

Katie hid her face against her husband's chest. She bit her fist to keep from crying out. Quinnault held her tightly. His jaw trembled atop her head with suppressed emotions.

Cheers as well as gasps of dismay rose from the throats of all but a few gathered around the courtyard. The common people who watched from the fringes added their voices to the others.

Allow these few books and shadows of books to burn.

Your helpers have saved many more of them. A masculine voice Katie did not recognize came into her mind.

Who? She looked up to see if a new dragon had joined Shayla and her consorts who hovered above the fire.

None of them responded.

"I can no longer trust you, Master Aaddler," Quinnault said quietly. "While you remain Senior Magician of the Commune, I cannot trust any member of the Commune, except these two brave souls. You are all forbidden the Council chamber until another, more moderate man leads you."

"And so the alien queen will be your sole adviser," Scarface sneered.

"I value the advice of my beloved wife. But I also value the wisdom of a magician. I value the balance in my government provided by magicians, lords, and myself. You would upset that balance in your quest for total control of myself and the lords. Master Rollett and Master Lyman will be my chief advisers, with assistance from Masters Wind-drift and Whitehands."

"Rollett is no master! Only I can confirm a journeyman worthy of master status"

"Incorrect," Lyman intervened. He looked exhausted beneath the layer of grime on his face. "Any master may elevate a worthy journeyman. I am the oldest master among the Commune. Rollett has completed his master's quest set for him by Nimbulan, his mentor and the Senior Magician who sent him on that quest."

"I was not informed of this quest!"

"But you were there in Hanassa with us, when I charged him with certain tasks to facilitate our escape a year ago," Nimbulan added. He and Myrilandel stepped up to stand beside their king. "And you made every effort to ensure I left him behind rather than risk *your* chances for escape. He has returned in spite of you, Scarface."

The old man paused to allow his words to penetrate to the farthest reaches of the crowd. "Rollett survived Hanassa the city and aided in the destruction of Hanassa the renegade dragon. He saved the lives of his companions. I deem him worthy and a master," Lyman declared. "Powwell, too, is ready for elevation, but lacks years and book learning. He is a worthy Senior Journeyman."

"It matters not." Scarface grounded his staff and faced Quinnault proudly. His face and posture took on an air of grim determination. "The books burn."

"I'll not have you in Coronnan challenging my every move, Aaddler," Quinnault said, just as sternly. "I banish you to the same monastery you exiled many aging masters to for the simple reason they owed loyalty to Nimbulan. You will be gone from the capital within the hour."

"I command too many master magicians for you to force me to do anything," Scarface sneered.

"We seem to have reached a stalemate," Kinnsell added from the back of the crowd. Katie's three brothers flanked him, holding blaster pistols. And behind them all stood a dozen armed and armored marines from the mother ship.

"Oh, no," Katie moaned.

"The king doesn't trust the magicians, the magicians don't trust the lords, and the lords don't trust the king. Your balance is destroyed. The only solution is for a new, neutral party to step in and take over. I offer my services to one and all." Kinnsell stepped forward, hands open in a gesture of calm reasonableness. "I have the weapons to subdue you all, including the magicians and the dragons." He waved a hand and one of the marines fired his blaster rifle at the bridge connecting Palace Isle to the University. It disappeared in a shower of sparks and thunderous noise.

"Oh, no, you don't, Daddy!" Katie marched up to face him. "You are the renegade here. You and your total disregard for anything but your own selfishness. Go back to Terra now, while you can. We of Coronnan will never succumb to your tyranny." The knot in her mid-region threatened to explode with anger, with loneliness, with grief.

"Come now, Katie. You are one of us. Surely you are tired of all this magic nonsense by now. I'll bring central heating and indoor plumbing to this benighted backwater." Her father reached out to pat the top of her head as if she were no more than a quarrelsome child.

She backed away from him, standing as tall and proud as she could. Majesty came from more than height.

"There are many more important things in life than those conveniences."

"Like what?"

"Like love," Quinnault said.

"And loyalty," Nimbulan added.

"Like honor." Wind-drift shouldered Scarface aside as he added his voice to his king's.

"And justice," Lord Balthazaan remarked.

One by one all those who had been separated by the issue of the book burning banded together to face this new threat.

Only Scarface remained outside the new circle of unified leaders. A few more books disappeared from the bonfire while everyone was distracted by this new threat.

"You see, Daddy? You'll have to defeat us all to win this war. What will that leave you? A bush world with no one to work the land or mine the resources. Starting up a new colony here will bankrupt you."

Jamie Patrick signaled his brothers to lower their pistols. A smirk brought a twinkle to his eyes. Or was it merely a reflection of the fire that still raged.

"She's right, Pop," he said.

"I'm not actually going to fire on another human being. You said this coup would be bloodless." Sean Michael holstered his weapon.

"Didn't Dad say he saw a dragon?" Liam Francis asked with a mischievous smirk that matched the grin Katie tried to swallow. "When he called the mother ship from his illegal pocket communicator, he said he had flown on a dragon from the mountains to the capital."

"Sounds to me like you are just a little insane, Kinnsell O'Hara," Jamie Patrick agreed. "Let's take him back home for a nice long rest in a secure hospital." The eldest of the siblings clamped a hard hand on his father's shoulder.

"That will take him out of the line of succession. Parliament will never elect him emperor when Gramps dies," Katie reminded them.

"One less to vie for the title." The brothers shrugged in unison. "Two less since you won't be returning with us, Katie."

"Be glad of that, boys. She'd give you all a run for your

money if she decided to leave this benighted backwater," Kinnsell said quietly. A half grin tugged at the corners of his mouth.

"I'll miss you." Katie had to blink rapidly to keep back her tears.

"You know us, Katie. We'll be back to check on you."

"No, you won't. You can't." She sobbed briefly, her next words closing her throat. Quinnault touched her hand and she found the courage to speak on, though tears ran down her cheeks. "Coronnan, all of Kardia Hodos must be off-limits to everyone from Terra. Everyone. We can't take a chance that you'll bring a new mutation of the plague, one that we can't combat. We can't take a chance that you will bring technology and pollution that will give the plague a breeding ground."

Her brothers dropped their heads. When Jamie Patrick looked up again, his eyes looked very moist. "We'll miss watching your daughter grow up. We'll miss you, Katie."

"We love you, Sis," Sean Michael said quietly.

Liam Francis looked decidedly rebellious for a moment, then he stepped forward, gathering Katie in a tight hug. "Good-bye, Katie."

Each of them dropped a kiss on Katie's cheek. Then Kinnsell came forward. "You are right, of course. The most sensible one of the lot of you, and she wants to stay here. She'd make the best emperor, boys. Good-bye, Maarie Kaathliin O'Hara de Draconis." He swallowed convulsively and turned to leave, escorted by his three sons.

Kinnsell turned for one last look at Katie. *In time, Daughter, you will appreciate the gift I leave with you. When you could not unite Coronnan and your balanced government looked about to crumble, you all united against me. You'll bicker for a while, but you will settle your differences. Help Quinnault govern with wisdom and raise a healthy horde of grandchildren for me. Teach them well the lessons of love, loyalty, honor, and justice so that they may pass this legacy through the generations of our dynasty.*

Tears came to Katie's eyes as she nodded her acceptance of her father's gift and final farewell.

What happened, Daddy, to change your mind?

I met some locals who took care of me when they should

have let me die. I owe them. This is my gift to them, to you, and my grandchildren. I leave you to control your own destinies, free of Terran influence. Free of the Varns at last.

Thank you. Katie swallowed a lump in her throat. She'd never see him again.

Call me renegade if you must, but please, give up this nonsense of magic and dragons. They are all illusions and fever dreams, Kinnsell added.

"Live long and well, Daddy." Katie laughed through her tears. "Someday you will realize that dragons are real and magic works. Even on Terra."

Epilogue

Somewhere in Coronnan City, time and date unimportant

*T*here are injustices I must correct as I move through the city like a ghost. I must use my magic sparingly lest the Commune discover my presence.

The Commune still makes rogue magic illegal and maintains the magical border to keep out the unwanted. Winddrift and Rollett will rule them with a more moderate hand than Scarface, but the law was made for a reason and must be enforced.

Mostly, I need to manipulate events only a little to right wrongs perpetuated by those who must control others or destroy them. Whenever possible, I shall eradicate ignorance so that the innocent know their choices. If I have to, I can access the hidden books as well as the magicians' approved library to keep information flowing throughout Coronnan.

Someday I will settle down and make a family of my own among the fisherfolk. Leauman has the most beautiful daughter. Until then, I have a new life among honest boatmen who don't ask about my past. They care only for the strength of my shoulders to haul in nets and the sharp instincts of my Mopplewogger.

Like Hanassa, I have become an exile, a renegade from my own kind. But I choose to work with the dragons and follow the ideals of the Commune, not fight against them just to prove myself in control of my life. I have studied the options, gathered information, and chosen my destiny.

Good-bye, Nimbulan. Good-bye, my friends. You may see me about and we shall each know that the other prospers, but never again will I share with you the incredible intimacy of Communal magic. I miss you.

THE
WIZARD'S
TREASURE

For my Golden Dragon Grandchild,
due to be born the same week this book is released.

Prologue

*T*he cult of the Gnostic Utilitarians bedevils Coronnan.
They proclaim the ridiculous notion that hard work is
the only medium of value. Magic, to them, is anathema.
While they fight for power in the Council of Provinces and
among the common people, the coven has gone into hiding
in Hanassa where they rebuild very slowly. The rogue magicians of the eight-pointed star have patience. They have
waited generations, creating alliances through blackmail, marriage, and coercion.

The numbers within the coven increase slowly. Solitary
magicians prefer to remain solitary and secretive rather than
join with others of their kind. They distrust everyone.

The University of Magicians still hopes that the dragons
will return to Coronnan and restore magic to its honorable
place in society—as if the magical energy they emit will automatically force solitary magicians to work together, under
the law, with no malice, mistrust, or greed guiding them. They
overestimate the honor of men who have tasted power.

And I sit in my lofty fastness, laughing at all of them.
Governments rise and governments fall. This scramble for
power is merely an exercise to satisfy individual greed.

Even Rovers have succumbed to the power-seeking game.
Zolltarn, the current self-styled King of All Rovers, betrays
his own kind as well as the coven and the Commune. After
centuries of seeking nothing more than their own safety
through their separateness, the Rovers have suddenly found
virtue in exploring the disgusting ideas of King Darville of
Coronnan. As if peace, law, and justice mean something.

Zolltarn has stolen the child who should inherit the crowns

of all three of the kingdoms on this continent. This "king" of the Rovers seeks to raise the child to his own traditions, then place him on the thrones, obligated and obedient to Rover will.

I will remove myself from my protected retreat and intervene if Zolltarn succeeds. Zolltarn and a child with so much political and magical power could rob me of all that I hold dear.

Rejiia, who thinks she leads the coven, has the potential to discover my power. She has thrown herself into her perverted rituals with vigor and stamina, using her sexuality to increase the magic. But I sense her distraction from the stated purpose of the coven. She has other, more personal goals and uses the coven to gain them.

The Commune of Magicians grows stronger. I cannot stop them from this distance, but I can eat away at the trust that binds them together.

I must take pains to see that none of these players finds my power. None of them know the true source of power—magical and political. None of them shall have it. Only I. I will, and can, murder my rivals most horribly if they try to interfere with my power. I have done it before, without conscience. I shall do it again.

Men truly seek only the chaos that rules their hearts.

Chapter 1

"So this is the landscape of war," Journeyman Magician Marcus said flatly. "Maybe the dragons should cleanse this battlefield like they did three hundred years ago."

"Dragons cannot cleanse this sinkhole unless they return to Coronnan. We cannot afford to end this war with SeLenicca until the dragons are safely returned from there." Robb, his comrade and also a journeyman magician, argued.

A long moment of silence passed between them as they contemplated the army camp and their possible passage through or around it.

"I think the balladeers need a good dose of reality. I don't see any evidence of glory here," Robb finally broke the silence.

"Just mud and blood, chill and boredom," Marcus confirmed. "Sort of like latrine duty for first-year apprentices." He flashed his friend a smile at shared memories of hardship and mischief.

"Where are we going to find me some new boots in this mess?" He scanned the wide plain at the eastern end of the mountain pass. The once lush river meadows had been churned into a sea of red clay mud.

Marcus shrugged as he wiggled his toes, trying to ease a little of the chill in them from his sopping socks.

The setting sun cast their long shadows against the mudlashed stubble.

"There are too many idle soldiers lolling about. Too much idle curiosity. Beating you in a game of cartes would be easier than getting through this camp," Robb grumbled.

"But not by much?" Marcus' grin widened. "And once we bring the dragons home from the other side of the pass, we won't have to worry about war or illegal magic for a while."

Robb turned his back on the ugly camp and looked out over the green river plains toward home—if an occasional rest in the dormitory of the new University of Magicians hidden in the Southern Mountains could be called home.

"Cheer up, Robb, we've come this far without trouble."

"For a change."

"In a camp this big, we're just two more soldiers out for a stroll. We'll beg some boots and maybe a bed and a meal from the Battlemages." He pointed to the far side of the camp toward a small group of huts made from stout logs where a blue flag with a dragon emblem snapped smartly in the evening breeze.

"Getting to their enclave could be risky. All magicians, including Battlemages and healers—the only legal magicians left in Coronnan—are feared and spied upon. Let's just find a supply shed and steal some boots." Robb fell into his usual lecture mode.

"This shouldn't be harder than crossing the five miles of no-man's-land between our army and the enemy at the far side of the pass. Pickets and patrols from both sides could cut us down with crossbows without bothering to ask identities first. Here, the pickets and patrols will at least ask for a password or something." Marcus thought out loud.

"But we don't know the password."

"We can find out with a tiny probe of magic." Marcus flashed his friend another grin, unwilling to give in to depression at the first sign of difficulty.

"Illegal," Robb warned.

"So is stealing boots from the supply tent," Marcus retorted.

Robb followed closely in Marcus' footsteps.

Marcus shrugged off the difficulties.

"Good thing you are lucky or my infamous bad luck would have gotten us killed a dozen or more times." Robb turned his face away. On this subject he never fell into lengthy lecture mode. He didn't even ask to play cartes anymore to wile away the long lonely hours around the campfire. Marcus always won.

"I have more lives than a cat, and I bet you my new pair of boots that I'll beat you at cartes tonight," Marcus chortled. He slapped his good friend on the back. For a moment he wished Margit, the apprentice magician assigned to spy for the Commune of Magicians within the royal palace, could join them. The tall, sturdy blonde could liven up any game with outrageous stories of the antics of the nobles and royals she watched so carefully.

Marcus longed for the day he and Margit could settle into a little cottage at the University with a dozen children and apprentices. He'd had his fill of journeying.

"Let's skirt the camp rather than cross it. That's a very wide-open space between the officers' tents and the magicians' huts." Robb ran his fingers through his beard in contemplation. A sure sign that he sensed more trouble than he voiced.

Marcus stumbled on a mud-colored rock that seemed to thrust up at him without warning. He limped for a few paces before the pain in his stubbed toes eased.

"Stop hunching your shoulders," Robb ordered. "Soldiers drill and march endlessly. They should have straight spines and firm steps."

"They also need uniforms." Marcus waved away Robb's objections, replacing them with a delusion of a green-and-gold uniform. His twisted magician's staff became a pike. "Now come along, Robb. We aren't getting any closer to the end of our journey standing here."

"We're gathering information," Robb affirmed, cloaking himself in a similar delusion. "Information is the key to power and . . ."

"Safety," Marcus finished. "I heard the same lecture from Jaylor as many times as you did. And as many times before that from Baamin when he was Senior Magician."

"I miss the old coot," Robb replied sadly. "Old Toad Knees will be honored for a long time by all of his apprentices." They both observed a long moment of silence in memory of their first master.

"Look for anything out of the ordinary or too ordinary—

both could be traps." Robb pointed to the first line of pickets near the steed paddock.

"I know, Robb."

"Then why did you step in that pile of steed dung?"

"Camouflage." Marcus paused to scrape the noisome muck from his boot. The worn soles allowed some of the brown liquid to seep through to his socks.

"Some of your luck running out?" Robb quipped.

"Never."

"Let's hope there aren't any Gnostic Utilitarian spies in the area," Robb grumbled. "They'll smell your magic and your boots from half a camp away. Gnuls believe all magic smells like manure—dragon magic or solitary makes no difference to them."

"Another lie that has become accepted as fact." Marcus frowned, no longer willing to keep up the usual banter with his friend. They'd both seen too many atrocities heaped upon innocents because of the unnatural fear of magic spread by the Gnuls. "The sooner we bring the dragons back, the sooner we can help put an end to that all-too-popular cult." Did every mundane in the country truly believe that only hard labor gave work value? That chores accomplished by magic—like transport and communication as well as healing and soil fertility—were evil and deserving of death? Magic was just as hard for a magician as the work was for a mundane.

Robb nodded, his frown quite visible beneath the dark bush of his beard.

They headed boldly through the camp periphery, walking as if they had a purpose. One patrol challenged them. Marcus just shook his head and proceeded. "Orders," he muttered.

The guard shrugged his shoulders and turned his attention back to his patrol.

An invisible line seemed to have been drawn around the magicians' enclave. No one ventured closer than one hundred paces.

"Crossing this barrier could be harder than getting through the pass," Robb muttered.

"Easier," Marcus replied. "The spies watching the magicians never look directly at them. My guess is they don't want to get caught by the evil eye." He grinned at the superstitious nonsense that clung to magicians' reputations.

Despite his bold face, Marcus' neck itched as if one hundred eyes followed every step he made across the untrampled grass that surrounded the ramshackle wooden buildings in a near perfect circle. Each step seemed to make his thin boots heavier and more cumbersome. Was this merely a delusion to keep out uninvited observers?

The blue banner with a dragon outlined in silver seemed to be a beacon, drawing them toward the largest of the buildings. A door beneath the banner stood invitingly open.

Marcus started to step through the doorway without preamble, but Robb held him back.

"For the sake of the Gnul spies all around us, at least look like you are one of the awestruck masses with a message from the generals and knock." He rapped the wooden doorjamb with his list and waited.

"What!" a querulous voice sounded within.

"Message, sir," Marcus replied.

"Leave it and be gone."

Marcus and Robb exchanged a questioning look.

"The message is private and not written," Marcus improvised. Dared he enter without invitation? Slowly he unreeled a thin tendril of magic, probing the doorway and the darkness just inside. A sharp pain behind his eyes made him wince.

"He's armored," he whispered, quickly withdrawing the probe, hopefully before any witch-sniffers could detect it.

"What?" a middle-aged man appeared out of the darkness. His red-veined and pointed nose was the first feature Marcus noted. Gray streaked his red-blond hair and beard. Worry lines made deep crevasses around his eyes. His shoulders drooped.

"Woodpecker?" Marcus asked. He wanted to rush forward and lend his shoulder to support this frail man. A year ago he'd been tall and robust.

"Who?" the Battlemage peered at the two journeymen, blinking in the fading light as if emerging into bright sunlight.

"Marcus and Robb. Jaylor sent us," Marcus said very quietly. No telling who could be listening.

"Get in here, boys, before someone spots you. Your delusion is very thin. Too thin to fool the witch-sniffers that permeate the army. They'll report you in a heartbeat without regard to the validity of your errand. Lucky to get out of here without being stoned." With surprising strength, Woodpecker grabbed each journeyman by the front of their tunics and yanked them inside the narrow entryway.

A wave of prickly magic set Marcus' skin itching and crawling. Then, as quickly as it had come, it left, leaving him in a bright room filled with comfortable furniture, carpets, and a glowing brazier.

"Where are the others?" Robb asked, peering around.

"In their own huts. My turn to monitor the scrying bowl for activity on the other side of the pass. Now what is so all-fired important that Jaylor could not trust a summons sent through a glass and candle flame?" Woodpecker demanded, wringing his hands and pacing the room. He paused to peer out each of the large unshuttered windows.

"Well . . . actually . . . Jaylor sent us on a quest into SeLenicca, and I need new boots before we cross the pass." Marcus found the shimmer of light across the windows that indicated strong magical armor too distorting to stare at for more than a moment.

"A bed and a meal would be welcome as well," Robb added.

"Is that all? Why didn't you just steal a pair of boots and a bedroll from the pickets that sleep on duty day and night? Why didn't you transport supplies from the University? Either course would prove safer than coming here." Woodpecker ceased his pacing and stared at the two journeymen.

Robb hung his head. Marcus wanted to do the same.

I am no first-year apprentice to cower before authority, he told himself sternly.

"To steal essential supplies from one of our own soldiers would be dishonorable. To transport something as trivial as boots a waste of energy. Surely you have the authority to requisition a pair for me from army stores," Marcus replied.

"What stores? Fewer than half our supplies reach us. The merchants in Sambol wear our boots, eat our food, and hoard our medicines. If SeLenicca attacks tomorrow, most of our men will desert to the other side just to get a good meal," Woodpecker grumbled.

"How could conditions get so bad? Does the king know about this?" Rob asked.

"Of course the king knows. Of course Jaylor knows, too. But what can they do about it with the Gnuls overriding every decision made? You'd think they want us to lose the war and let the sorcerer-king rule us!" Woodpecker threw up his hands at that horrible and contradictory thought.

"We hope our quest will end the war and end the tyranny of the Gnuls," Marcus said.

Woodpecker looked at him curiously. "No, I don't suppose you can tell me your quest. That goes against the rules. Well, I hope you have better luck than the last spy Jaylor sent across the pass. He came back to us in pieces. Many of them missing." Woodpecker's normally pale complexion paled further. He swallowed convulsively.

Marcus tasted bile. Rumors leaking out of SeLenicca for years had hinted that King Simeon—the sorcerer-king—made human sacrifices to his winged demon-god Simurgh.

Ignorant Gnuls considered dragons modern incarnations of Simurgh. If only they could experience the glory of shared dragon magic, they'd know how much good the dragons brought to Coronnan. He and Robb had to bring the near invisible creatures back to Coronnan soon.

"Are the enemy troops massing for an attack?" Robb asked.

Leave it to him to ask the practical questions.

"Curiously, no. They're waiting for something. Something big. Something disastrous for us. Well, come along. I'll take you to the supply hut. I'll try to keep the quartermaster from skinning all three of us alive for daring to ask for something. Anything." Woodpecker strode toward the doorway, still muttering.

Marcus and Robb followed the Battlemage across the camp. They passed dozens of men on the way. All of them moved quickly away to avoid any contact with the magicians.

"Fear is a wonderful thing," Woodpecker continued his litany of complaint. "Fear gives us mages all of the privacy we could want and then some. No one interferes with our work. But they won't help either. *S'murghit!* They won't even feed us. Have to do it all ourselves so they don't taint their precious mundane lives with magic. If I didn't know that King Simeon's rule would be worse than putting up with these lumbird-brained fools, I'd desert to the enemy. Or go outlaw. I'd get more respect in Hanassa!"

Marcus resisted the urge to make the ancient ward against evil by crossing his wrists and flapping his hands. No one went to Hanassa voluntarily. No one except mercenaries, outlaws, and rogue magicians—all determined to make trouble for the rest of civilization. King Simeon hailed from Hanassa before he'd married SeLenicca's very young Queen Miranda. And look at the mess he'd made there!

"Stand aside. I have need of a few things," Woodpecker demanded of the three armed men at the supply hut.

"Orders are no one gets anything until the next boatload of supplies comes upriver," the sergeant sneered. Three gold stripes on the sleeve of his green uniform tunic shone brightly in the freshly ignited rushlights beside the door. His collar and cuffs were threadbare and his left elbow nearly poked through the cloth. But his boots were new and shone with fresh polish.

Marcus nearly salivated with greed at the thought of the warm and dry feet those boots would give him.

"You dare give orders to me, Giiorge?" Woodpecker asked. "Didn't I bind up an ax wound on your left side with barely a scar after you dropped your guard and allowed a wounded enemy to sneak up on you?"

"Um . . ." Sergeant Giiorge shuffled his feet and blushed.

"One pair of boots for my journeyman. He might very well be the one to throw the spell that wins the next battle. You and all of your men owe the Battlemages more than your lives."

"Two minutes inside. And don't tell anyone I was the one that let you in." Sergeant Giiorge unlocked the door and then gestured to his men to move forward two paces, just enough room for Woodpecker to get between him and the door. They kept their backs sternly to the doorway and the activities of the magicians.

"Not very grateful, if you ask me," Robb muttered.

"The best we can hope for," Woodpecker replied. He brought a ball of witchlight to his hand and scanned the shelves inside the hut. A few uniform tunics, some blankets, and mess kits. Not much left to supply an army.

"One pair of boots left. Take them and hope they fit." Woodpecker thrust the solitary pair into Marcus' hands and sidled out of the hut.

The moment all three of them were clear of the doorway, Sergeant Giiorge locked it again and resumed his post.

"Follow me back toward the enclave, then leave as soon as no one is looking," Woodpecker ordered as they hurried back the way they had come.

At the edge of the empty circle around the Battlemage's hut, Marcus and Robb veered off toward a clump of trees beside the paddock. Marcus plunked himself down on the ground beneath the spreading branches of an oak. Pale green swelled the ends of the branches with the promise of new life and plenty of shade come summer. He pulled off both his boots and managed to tug on one of the new ones before a commotion on the other side of the paddock interrupted him.

"Ah-ha!" exclaimed a deep voice. "We have the boot thieves! Arrest these men." A burly soldier dressed in a faded green uniform tunic with a single muddy yellow stripe on his sleeves ran toward them brandishing a long dagger and an ax. Three more men with no stripes on their sleeves followed close behind him armed with clubs.

"Run!" Robb exclaimed. He pulled Marcus to his feet.

Marcus grabbed the second boot and followed, limping and off balance.

"Out of the way!" Robb turned to face the enemy, still running backward. He launched a witch bolt that looked like an arrow at the growing number of soldiers in pursuit. Fire fletched and tipped his missile.

"Theft of a comrade's equipment is punishable by hanging," the leader pronounced. His followers screamed more invective.

Marcus couldn't understand a word they said, but their auras displayed intense outrage and bloodlust.

The witch bolt landed directly in front of the leader's

feet. He hopped back, careening into his men. They tumbled backward, like so many stacked game cartes.

"Lucky shot, Robb," Marcus panted as they pelted away from camp toward the dubious cover of a shrub-lined creek.

"Careful aim. I make my own luck."

They had just slid into the chill water of the foaming creek and drawn a deep breath when six men crashed through the shrubs a few paces to their right.

"Keep running!" Robb called, hauling Marcus to his feet.

"How about another witch bolt while I put on my boot?"

"No time."

"We're heading the wrong way." Marcus limped behind Robb as he scrambled up the other side of the shallow ravine. His left sock was soaked and his foot hurt from running across the uneven turf and stones.

"We're heading toward safety."

"But the pass is back that way."

"Later. We'll go after the dragons later."

Marcus dodged a real arrow followed by a knife aimed at his back. "I think my luck just ran out."

Chapter 2

"Three wizards and two Rovers beats your two dragons and three turnips!" Vareena laughed loudly. A deep ripple of mirth warmed her heart. She didn't laugh often enough. "That's the first time I have beaten you at cartes, Farrell. Now hand over your treasure." She peered through the misty light of her witchball at her ghostly companion who faded in and out of her vision.

"My concentration slips, Eena," Farrell excused himself. "Since this last fever, I have become quite forgetful."

"Very forgetful, indeed," Vareena said around her smile. "You seem to have forgotten that you bet three acres of land in the Province of Nunio against my two cows and three chickens." She had no hope of ever claiming her winnings. She and the ghost had played this game before. He always bet the same three acres and she always lost the same two cows and three chickens.

Although her ghost required food and medications, blankets and shelter from the weather, he had no need of her dowry. Once trapped inside this ancient building, her ghosts never left.

"Promise me, Vareena, that when I finally pass into the void between the planes of existence, you will take the amulet from around my neck and carry it to my family in Nunio." Farrell paused a long moment, breathing heavily. His hand stole to his throat where he fingered the leather thong that held the silver-encased amethyst. After a moment he shifted his hand from his only treasure to lay it flat upon his chest. He closed his hand in fierce spasm three times, as if clutching the pain of his worn-out heart.

Vareena saw the pulse in his throat beat more rapidly in an irregular rhythm. She wished she could rest her wrist against his forehead to test for fever. A barrier of stinging energy separated her from each of the ghosts who had found refuge here.

"Tell my sister's sons that you are my heir," Farrell resumed when his breathing and pain eased. "Tell them what happened to me, how you and only you have cared for me these past two years. The amulet is the deed to the land. My nephews will care for you and the land."

A moment of hope brightened within Vareena. When this ghost died, her duties here in this abandoned monastery and within the village would ease. She'd be free to do as Farrell asked.

"I would like that very much, Farrell."

"Promise me, Vareena. Promise that you will leave this cursed place and never return."

Vareena shifted uncomfortably upon her stool. She did not want to lie to her ghost.

He reached out to grab her sleeve. As always, the wall of shocking energy repulsed him before he came in contact with any part of her. 'Twas always the same. He was a ghost and she still human. They were destined never to touch until one of them died.

"Women may not own land." A safe answer.

"King Darville changed that law three years ago."

Vareena lifted her head in surprise. She shouldn't be surprised, though. If such a drastic change had taken place, her isolated village near the western border of Coronnan would be the last to hear of it. The women of the village would hear of it later still. The men here did not like change. They did not like her ghosts. They did not like her. They did not like much of anything.

A measure of hope warmed her heart. She clamped down on it, afraid to allow it to grow and be drowned later.

"I have duties here, Farrell. My family, the village, this monastery. I do not think I will be allowed to leave." She hung her head, refusing to meet his gaze.

"They feed off your generosity, Vareena. They need to fend for themselves. You must leave this place. As you have so often dreamed."

"But . . ." He was right of course.

"For the friendship we have shared these past two years," Farrell pleaded, "promise me that you will leave this place before it curses you, as it has cursed me and countless other men over the centuries. Leave and follow your heart, Vareena."

"My brothers . . . They need me to care for them as my mother did before her untimely death. The villagers . . . I am their only healer."

"They can all tend to themselves if forced to. You do not belong here, Vareena. Your spirit is too bright and loving to be swallowed whole by your family's selfishness. You've given them twenty years since your mama died. Ten of those years ago, you should have married and started a family of your own."

This time she could not avoid his stern gaze. His brown eyes seemed to blaze through the ghostly mist like two dark coals, lit by his fervor. Or his fever.

She sighed a moment in regret. She'd like a family of her own. But none of the men in this village trusted her or honored her because she could see the ghosts and was destined to care for them. None of them had offered for her hand despite her handsome dowry of two cows and three chickens.

"I promise, Farrell. When you pass fully into the void, I will take your amulet and claim the three acres of land in the province of Nunio."

"Good. Now another game, perhaps. With different stakes. I have won your dowry too many times to make it worth anything. Why don't we play for the pile of gold in the library of this place?"

Vareena shuffled the stack of wooden cartes, each one lovingly engraved with a different image and then painted red, black, green, or yellow. "The trick to winning that particular pot is the courage to enter the library to claim the gold. Neither of us will be lucky enough to lose this pot."

"Ah, but what need have I of gold? I am dying, and you will need much money to buy more land in Nunio. Three acres is a fine dowry but not enough to support you."

"Then I will bet a chicken stew, made with the pickled beets that you love so well."

"Not made from your three chickens. Those you must preserve as part of your dowry."

"Those three chickens are sacrosanct. They know it. Even my brothers know it. They refuse to gather eggs lest those haughty ladies peck their eyes out."

"From what I know of your brothers, they deserve whatever fate your chickens hand out."

"Why do you think I always send Yeenos to the coop when his temper is particularly vile?" They both laughed at the image of her tall and lanky brother fighting off the aggressive hens, feathers flying in all directions, squawks and squeals setting the entire coop aflurry.

"I hope Yeenos takes the younger three boys with him as well. They deserve some lessons in humility," Farrell finally said, breaking off his weakening laughter.

In the distance a temple bell tolled twice, long and loud.

"That is the priest calling the shepherds in from the hills for supper. I must go now, Farrell. I'll return in the morning with your breakfast."

"Don't bother, Vareena. There is more than enough stew left. Rest yourself and do something that you never allow yourself the time for."

"I could wash my hair." She smiled, anticipating the luxury of a private bath beneath the waterfall half a league below the village. The cold mountain stream was warmed slightly at the base of the fall by hot springs. All the women of the village went there for bathing and laundry, but never first thing in the morning.

"Use the violet-scented soap. I love the smell of violets on you." Farrell lay back on his cot, one arm thrown across his eyes. "I remember the scent of violets in the spring, how the cows would trample them and the smell would fill the valley." He drifted off into a light doze.

Vareena packed up her mother's precious cartes and tiptoed out of her ghost's cell. He had chosen one in the middle of the southern wing of the old monastery. The rooms were larger here, originally intended for retired magicians and priests rather than novices and journeymen. The south-facing exterior wall warmed the room better than the small rooms of the chill north wing. As she threw her shawl about her shoulders against the spring chill of early evening, something heavy and awkward tangled in her hair.

She batted at the offending thing and danced about, first on one foot then the other, half panicked. Her heart raced in fear of the giant spiders that hid in the dark recesses of this ancient building.

"S'murghit!" she let loose with an unladylike curse as sharp metal stabbed at her fingers. She examined the offended digit for any trace of a spider bite. Satisfied that one of the critters hadn't landed on her, she sucked the tiny cut until the worst of the sting eased.

Only then did she take the time to comb her fingers through the mass of tight blond coils that never stayed in place long, no matter how many pins she used or how tightly she braided it.

At last she freed the long piece of leather that supported a curiously fashioned piece of silver. From the center of the amulet, a bright amethyst winked at her in the setting sun.

"You can't get rid of me so easily, Farrell. I won't leave you until you finally break free of the curse that traps you between this plane of existence and the void. Why is it that only the women of my family can see and care for the ghosts who need us? And there is almost always a ghost here who needs us."

*   *   *

An ill wind blows this way. Does it come from our old enemies in SeLenicca? Partly. I sense chill blasts from Hanassa as well as the capital. My easy life of observation and contemplation is in jeopardy. I must stir myself and resurrect powers I have not used in a very long time.

I do not like change. Yet I must change in order to bring my world back to the way it was before. My safety and the preservation of my power depend upon it. Someone will die. Perhaps many someones. I care not. I must ensure my safety. For the heritage I leave my son and daughter and their descendants, I must ensure my safety.

* * *

"Who among you miserable excuses for apprentices can tell me which elements must be invoked in order to divert water from a free-flowing creek into an irrigation ditch? And which elements must therefore be excluded from the spell?" Master Magician WithyReed intoned to the class.

The short and rotund magician paced in front of his students. He looked the exact opposite of what his working name suggested—as was often the case since most of the nicknames came to magicians while still apprentices.

Of the dozen students gathered on the grassy forecourt of the University, Margit alone raised her hand. She knew the answer. She'd known the answer for weeks. Only if WithyReed offered her the opportunity to answer would she advance through the ranks to journeyman.

Until she passed all of the tests and endured the trial by Tambootie smoke, she was stuck here in the mountain fastness where the University hid from the prying eyes of the rest of Coronnan, and the spies of the Gnuls in particular. Since she had left Queen Rossemikka's employ as a maid, she had no other place to go.

She wondered if WithyReed would pay more attention to her if she and Marcus had announced their betrothal before he disappeared into the wilds of the border country. No one had heard from him or from his partner Robb since . . . since before the dragons came back with Jack.

A stab of fear to the depths of her soul for the man she loved almost shook the answer to WithyReed's question out of her mind. Marcus and Robb often went moons without contacting her. But they always stayed within reach of a summons spell with Senior Magician Jaylor. What kind of trouble had they gotten into this time? She couldn't even hope to chase after them with half-formed plans of rescue until she became a journeyman—journeywoman—magician.

She couldn't became a journeywoman unless she passed the tests set before her by the master magicians. WithyReed refused to so much as let her answer a question let alone take a test.

"Ferrdie?" Master Magician WithyReed called upon a young boy to Margit's right. Ferrdie had been an apprentice for three years now and not passed a single test. But he, too, had nowhere else to go, having been banished from the family homestead by his father because he was left-handed and therefore must be a magician.

"Is . . . is the answer Fire?" Ferrdie stammered. Never once did he lift his eyes to the master.

Margit kept her hand up and tried to capture Withy-Reed's gaze.

"Incorrect." The master magician scanned the rest of the class. "Have any of you studied the treatise written by Master Scarface some three hundred years ago when dragon magic was first discovered and implemented to save Coronnan from three generations of civil war?"

Margit kept her hand up patiently. Learning to read had been difficult for her at the late age of seventeen. But she had mastered the arcane skill and studied all of her assignments thoroughly.

Again WithyReed's challenging stare slid right past Margit and alighted on a moderately talented boy in the back of the group of students seated cross-legged on the grass. "Mikkail?"

"Air!" the boy replied with confidence.

"Such incompetence. I expected better of you. All of you."

"I know the answer, Master WithyReed," Margit said. She thrust out her chin, determined to make the man acknowledge her.

"Since none of you can give me the proper answer, I will give you a hint. Air and Fire are linked as elements. Since the dragons fly through the air and shoot flames to cook their meat and defend themselves—not that anything on Kardia Hodos remains that is big enough to be a danger to a dragon—when a magician gathers dragon magic, he throws spells most closely linked with those two elements."

Margit stood up in the center of the gathering of two dozen students and faced the master. "I know the answer, sir, and the theory behind it."

"When a magician is forced to draw magical energy from the kardia, as we had to do until recently, then our spells must be rooted in the kardia. Now what element is left that would be linked to the kardia?" WithyReed continued to ignore Margit.

Anger boiled in Margit's stomach and heated her face and hands. "Kardia and Water are linked and therefore an irrigation spell must be rooted in the kardia to draw the water from its natural flow in the creek or river to the unnatural channel dug for irrigation." She clenched her fists until her fingernails drew blood from her palms.

"Ferrdie, have you figured it out yet?" Withy Reed acted as if Margit had not spoken at all.

"Why do you ignore me, sir?" she blurted out, thrusting herself directly in front of him. She topped him in height by at least two finger-lengths. He could not ignore her now.

"Sit down, girl. You are here to listen only. Females cannot gather dragon magic, so your presence in the University is temporary. Speak up, Ferrdie, I need you to answer the question."

Margit gritted her teeth and clenched her hands. Oh! to slam one of her fists into the pompous little magician's face. Before she could follow through with her desires, she whipped around and marched out of the forecourt, spine stiff, hands clenched and tears pricking her eyes.

I will not run. I will not give him the satisfaction of running from him.

She met no one between the forecourt and the girl's dormitory on the north side of the quadrangle of timbered buildings. Girls represented over half the apprentices. Females young and old were the most common victims of Gnul persecution. In the last three years, Marcus and Robb had brought more girls here for refuge than boys. Withy-Reed and the other masters had no right to pretend female magicians would evaporate and never bother them again. She fully intended to achieve journeyman status. Only as a journeyman—or journeywoman—could she even hope to accompany Marcus on his treks from one end of the country to the other. Maybe even—she dared hope—they could travel to exotic locations on other continents.

She stepped into the room she shared with Annyia. The dark-haired child/woman had been savagely beaten and raped by her stepbrothers in an attempt to kill the magical talent they thought she possessed. They probably succeeded. The ignorant fools believed the myth that only virgins could work magic. WithyReed and his antique prejudice that demanded male magicians remain celibate until they became masters didn't help the situation.

Jaylor had placed Margit in the same room with Annyia, hoping some of the older girl's confidence and determination would help Annyia break away from her guilt and depression. Margit had little patience with her roommate's tears and frantic starts at every sharp noise.

"WithyReed ignores me because I am female. But if I look like a boy . . . Maybe he'd forget his prejudices for a moment. Just one short moment until he realizes I know what I'm doing."

She marched to the little chest at the foot of her cot where she kept her few personal possessions. The blue tunic and brown trews she had worn on the trek to the University from the capital were on the bottom, cleaned and mended. Beneath them she found her dagger, the one she had used to defend herself in the market square before Jaylor recruited her as his spy.

For a moment her memory put her back in the crowded market square on King Darville's coronation day. She had been selling her mother's baked goods to the hungry throngs waiting for the grand procession after the ceremony. When a foreign spy had threatened her because he did not like the spices in the sausage roll she sold him, Jack had come to her rescue. She'd been more than willing to defend herself with her knife, but Jack had diffused the anger of the crowd and discovered a dangerous plot against the king's life at the same time.

Later that day, as she packed up the last of the unsold food—not much, for the capital citizens and visitors had all been hungry and jovial, quite willing to send money on such an auspicious occasion—Jaylor had come to her, wrapped in an enveloping cloak of magic. She'd seen through his delusion and known him for the head of the now exiled Commune of Magicians. He'd asked her to spy for him and offered to begin training her as a magician in return.

Apparently Jack had noticed something important about her when she stood up to the foreign spy.

Margit appreciated the irony of the Council of Provinces

trying to outlaw magic in Coronnan when their king's best friend from childhood led the most powerful group of magicians in all of Kardia Hodos.

Margit's mother had threatened to lock Margit in the pantry with a cat when she announced that she would give up selling meat rolls, pasties, and baked sweets in the market in favor of serving as the new queen's personal maid. Her mother didn't know that Margit had learned to open every lock in the city years ago. She had only just learned that magic had enhanced her senses to allow her to do that.

Thank the Stargods her three years as Queen Rossemikka's maid had ended. She couldn't stand being cooped up in the palace any longer. She had trouble breathing indoors, especially in the queen's apartments which always smelled of cat.

"Time to improvise." With three swift slashes of the dagger, she cut her blond locks level with her shoulders. Then she bound her hair back into a masculine queue with a bit of blue string. She couldn't get her clumsy gown and shift off fast enough.

"Finding and rescuing Marcus will be much easier if I'm disguised as a boy. I certainly won't remain here any longer than I have to. And I certainly won't babysit any more apprentices."

Chapter 3

A low rumbling ripple along the floor and walls shattered the veil of forgetfulness that encased the woman's mind. She braced herself instinctively against the waving motion and counted to ten. At four, the quake drifted away to a memory. Her mind told her that this was not the first kardiaquake that had rocked Queen's City. Nor would it be the last. Some instinct she did not have the strength to comprehend told her that the intensity had lessened. But she could not remember how or why she knew that.

How long had she been wandering the halls of this damaged palace without being aware of herself?

Her stomach growled. When had she eaten last?

She remembered nothing: not why she wandered these once-magnificent halls; nor why she haunted this huge building like a ghost, alone and lost to everything and everyone she held dear.

Somehow that aloneness seemed almost . . . not quite, but almost . . . right.

She imagined what the passageways must have been like when they were filled with courtiers and politicians, ladies and gentlemen who spent their days—and nights—pretending to agree with the king's demands. Then she imagined herself, a wispy ghost, drifting behind them, eavesdropping, laughing at the truths they would never admit to themselves. The king listened to no one and those who agreed with him, more often than not, met with disfavor.

They were all small dogs chasing their own tails in a

fruitless race. But she was not part of that and never would be.

How did she know that?

A brilliantly colored tapestry on the wall caught her attention. Women sitting at lace bolsters concentrated deeply on their bobbins and the yards and yards of floating threadwork. The scene seemed familiar. She reached out to caress the woven picture. Her broken fingernails snagged a thread. Immediately she halted her quest to touch some part of her past through the picture and worked the jagged edge of her nail free without pulling the entire thread loose.

Something was wrong. She stared at the dirt encrusted in the cuticle and beneath the nail. Never before had she allowed her hands to become so filthy. No lacemaker did.

Lace.

Her hands curved as if lifting two pairs of bobbins for an intricate stitch. The sensuous feel of carved bone and wood crawled through her. Deep satisfaction at the creation of delicate and airy fabric expanded in her lungs and gave her a sense of lightness.

Lace! Her world revolved around lace.

But not a scrap of it graced her night robe, shift, or the tops of her slippers. If she did not wear lace, she must be a worker rather than a noble designer or teacher. She reached up her hand to her silvery blond hair. Her fingers drifted through the long tresses without resistance. She wore no cap, nor had she braided her hair properly.

"I must find the workroom," she resolved. "After I find something to eat and wash. Then I must plait my hair." Two gathered braids from temple to nape that broke free until they reached the center of her back then joined into a single thick rope. That was the proper number for a worker.

"Not two plaits. Three at least." Three plaits belonged to the nobility, and four were reserved for the queen. So if she deserved three plaits, why did she not wear any of the precious lace fabric?

"Three plaits," she repeated. That did not settle in her brain as correct, but better than two plaits or . . . shudder . . . must she revert to the single plait of a peasant or lace factory worker until she knew the truth of her identity?

"Three plaits," she insisted. "But first I must wash and eat."

Her feet automatically headed down three flights of stairs to the long, long dining hall. The central table stretched out with places for fifty people. Remnants of food lay scattered about the table and floor where rodents and other scavengers had left it.

Impatiently, she grabbed one of the discarded serviettes and brushed a place clear for herself. She sat down on the tapestried armchair at the head of the table. The large chair was too large. But she knew this to be her place. The view of the room was correct, but the chair did not fit her.

Why? Why didn't it fit? And why had she presided at the head of the table in this magnificent—but crumbling—palace.

While she puzzled out the problem of where to sit, a series of small crashes brought her awareness back to the palace. Brickwork loosened by the kardiaquake fell throughout the building. Perhaps the impromptu remodeling would allow more light to penetrate the workrooms. She smiled again. An act of nature had defied the pompous king and given her the one thing she wanted most—light to work by.

Well, almost the thing she wanted most. Knowing who she was and why she wandered the palace alone might be useful. But knowledge would come, once she returned to her lace.

More richly colored tapestries hung on the high walls of the hall, from just below the narrow windows near the ceiling, to the top of the sideboards. The one depicting the signing of a long-ago wedding agreement sagged, along with the wall and ceiling. A long rent in the fabric separated the politicians from the bride and groom.

A second tear pushed the couples representing the parents even farther away from the two centers of action.

She almost giggled at the subtle irony created by the rips.

Her stomach growled again. She needed to eat. But . . . but the servants had fled the kardiaquakes. No one would bring her soup and bread. No one remained in the palace but herself. Why had she been left behind in the exodus?

Sitting here would not help. She had to find food. A niggle of pride followed her determination to do something for herself. She'd like to see the politicians in the tapestry fetching anything without help.

Servants always entered through that door to her left and food had always been hot. Therefore the kitchen must be nearby.

Cautiously, she traced the route. Footprints in the dust told her that someone else had passed this way, several times in recent days. She placed her right foot delicately into one of them. For a moment the frayed toes of her embroidered slipper fascinated her. She shook off the thrall of following the patterns of the stitches. Her foot fit perfectly into the indentation in the dust.

A quick scan of the array of prints indicated she had passed this way at least four times in recent days.

Scattered prints next to the wall looked tiny. The impression of heavy toes and light heels indicated someone moved furtively along. A small person. Perhaps a child.

She hastened her steps, suddenly afraid of what she might find.

The end of the passage—longer than she thought necessary to ensure hot food in the dining hall—opened into the cavernous kitchen. A hearth opened from each end of the room. Each fireplace could roast an entire beast. A tall man could stand within without getting soot in his hair.

But no fire burned there now, nor had for some time. Cold ashes, mixed with fallen plaster and bricks from the chimneys, littered the floor before both hearths. Scraps of bone and desiccated meat protruded from the layers of debris. A hole in the exterior wall let in a lot of light. Too much light. She examined the jagged hole, not big enough to crawl through and too many loose bricks to be safe. The kitchen had not fared as well as the rest of the palace.

She seemed to remember a number of passages throughout the palace blocked by collapsed ceilings and bulging walls.

How long before the entire building fell on top of her?

"M'ma!" a tiny voice squealed as a grimy form flung itself at her from the depths of one of the hearths.

She looked carefully at the sobbing bundle of mismatched clothing, dirt, and cobwebs.

"M'ma, you found me. They said you died. They said I'd

never see you again. They said . . ." the child sobbed into her skirts, clutching her knees so tightly she thought she'd tumble forward and crush her baby.

"M'ma? Am I truly your M'ma?" she asked in wonder. She wasn't alone. Someone remembered her.

Then concern for her child overtook her joy. She stooped down to study her baby at eye level. Bright blue eyes looked back at her from a smudged face, still round with baby fat. Probably about three. That number felt right. Three years. Three plaits. Silvery-blond hair scraggled out of three plaits that had started out gathered tightly against the child's head. The end of one plait was still held almost in place by a frayed pink ribbon that clashed with her red hair. The second plait had come undone and hopelessly tangled. The center plait wobbled back and forth as if the little girl had tried to fix it herself and failed.

"Are you hurt, baby?" she asked, soothing tangles away from her child's face. The name eluded her. But that didn't matter. They were together.

"I'm hungry." The little girl pouted.

"What have you eaten these past few days?"

"Some of the roast. I found a turnip!" The child's face brightened as she held up half of a withered root vegetable. Tiny teeth marks showed around the edges. She didn't lisp around missing teeth, so she must still be very young. The number three settled in the woman's mind more firmly.

"What a clever girl you are. Where did you find the turnip?" Her own hunger began to plague her insistently.

"Down there." The child pouted as she glanced at a trap-door and then back to her mother's skirts. A cellar or pantry. More food, assuming the place had not been looted when the kardiaquakes sent everyone in flight from the city.

"You were very brave to climb down there. Will you come with me as we look for more turnips and things?"

"A rat scared me." An almost clean thumb crept toward the little girl's mouth.

The woman allowed the child to find what little comfort she could from sucking. Stargods knew when they'd live a normal life, in a normal home, with a normal schedule again.

Schedules.

The concept of following a routine determined by others sounded oddly comforting and right.

She stood and held her hand for the child. "We'll protect each other from the rat, baby. You and I can do anything together."

"I'm Jaranda. Not a baby anymore." The baby rewarded her with a bright smile and clutched her fingers.

"Of course, Jaranda. How could I forget? You are a big girl now. Big enough to hold the door open for me while I climb down. Be sure you stand so you don't block the light."

"Yes, M'ma." Jaranda stood a little straighter and took her finger out of her mouth.

"I don't suppose you remember *my* name, Jaranda?" she asked her daughter.

"M'ma," Jaranda replied importantly.

"Somehow I thought you'd say that."

Chapter 4

"**W**here have you hidden my son, Rejiia?" Lanciar asked the bottom of his ale mug. He didn't really expect an answer. The steed-piss ale of Hanassa didn't even quench his thirst, let alone show him any truths.

Briefly, he longed for a simpler time when King Simeon still lived to rule SeLenicca and Lanciar had only a minor magical talent. He didn't have to think or make decisions. He only had to obey Simeon, and all the wonders of the coven surrounded him with sex and power and influence. He could love Rejiia in secret and experience the thrill of fathering a son on her while Simeon believed the child his own.

But then Simeon had sent him to seek out the man who wielded enough power within the mines to threaten the coven.

Lanciar had discovered Jack. The young magician was just beginning to recover his memory and his talent after some adolescent trauma.

And then the day came when a deep kardiaquake had collapsed the mine. Jack's newly awakened senses had alerted him to the coming disaster. He, with Lanciar's help, had rescued an entire team of slaves. But Simeon's guards and administrators were caught up in the chaos; the entire complex had to be abandoned. All who survived ran for their lives. Lanciar had attached himself to Jack and his friend as ordered.

On the trail out of the mine Jack had drawn Lanciar deep into a questing spell, seeking the dragon that Simeon had magically wounded and imprisoned. During that long night on a lonely mountain pass, Lanciar's full talent had awakened.

Now he was a master magician having to think and make his own decisions in order to survive, and able to see Rejiia for a selfish, power-hungry bitch who used everyone she came in contact with to augment her own illusion of greatness. Lanciar had to rescue his son from Rejiia's ungentle clutches.

The kardia rolled beneath his feet. He braced himself against the exterior wall of the tavern, momentarily reliving the terror of being trapped underground in the mine with tons of kardia pouring down upon him. He owed Jack his life as well as his respect—probably the only truly honest man he had ever met.

But it was a little quake this time and did not deserve his fear. Almost a daily occurrence here in Hanassa, the city of outlaws. None of the ragged denizens of the city seemed to notice the disruption.

Satisfied that the ground beneath his feet was solid once more, he stared into the last few drops of liquid in his cup. Not enough to scry a vision of Rejiia or the child she had stolen from him. The horrible ale served here was too thick to see through anyway.

Should he drink another? Yes. The dry air within this ancient volcanic caldera that housed the dregs of the world left a constant sour taste in the back of his throat.

"Let's try the next tavern," he suggested to the mug. "Maybe someone there has seen Rejiia with a child. Maybe their ale tastes better."

He strolled casually toward the next outcropping of ramshackle buildings. While he wove a slightly drunken path, he kept his eyes moving, taking in every detail of life among the outlaws, mercenaries, rogue magicians, and criminals. No innocents here, and precious few children.

Where would Rejiia have taken her baby if she didn't keep him with her?

That was a sobering thought. What if she had fostered the child elsewhere? How would Lanciar ever find his son if she had?

A party of richly clad magicians strolled past Lanciar. He knew their profession because they all carried long staffs, some topped with intricate carvings or natural crystals, and they all wore flowing robes embroidered or painted with arcane sigils. At the center of the group strode Rejiia, daughter of the late unlamented Lord Krej, and cousin to King Darville of Coronnan. Under other circumstances, she would be the heir to Darville's dragon throne. But her magic, her illicit alliance with Simeon, the murdered sorcerer-king of SeLenicca, and her own murderous proclivities made her an exile from her native country.

Her father's treason against King Darville didn't help her status either. Lord Krej had thrown one too many illegal spells in a desperate attempt to usurp power in Coronnan. His last piece of magic had been intended to turn Darville into a statue of whatever creature reflected his personality—probably a golden wolf. But the new king had worn his enchanted crown that protected him from all magic. Krej's spell had backlashed into his own eyes, transforming him into a tin weasel with flaking gilt paint.

Rejiia had rescued the statue of her father from Darville's dungeon on the king's coronation day. Simeon had had custody of the tin weasel for a time. But when Jack and his companion from the mines—what was his name?—had murdered the King of SeLenicca a few weeks ago, Rejiia had grabbed the statue and taken it with her in a desperate attempt to murder Jack before he could reunite the dragons with the Commune of Magicians.

She'd failed to do more than enhance Jack's status as a master magician in full command of his powers as she fled that battle scene in disgrace. But she'd managed to keep Krej with her during her escape.

No one knew for sure if Krej lived within the tin casing or not. No one dared probe it lest they be drawn into the statue as well.

As Rejiia toured Hanassa, she levitated the tin weasel behind her in a subservient position, much as Krej had done to her in her youth. Lanciar knew how much humiliation she had suffered under her father. Now she took her revenge.

But she needed Krej animate to fill in the missing ranks of the dispersing coven. Lanciar could stand in only one corner of the eight-pointed ritual star. He was supposed to be anchoring that corner in SeLenicca rather than here, searching for his son.

He no longer trusted Rejiia or any of the other members of the coven. He'd rather work as a solitary magician than ever work magic with Rejiia again.

Lanciar kept his face buried in his mug, pretending to be just another mercenary waiting for a war to break out until Rejiia passed. She shouldn't recognize him with a full beard. He'd added layers of dirt to his hands and clothing to complete his disguise.

The tilt of her head, the sway of her hips, the way her black hair with a single white streak at her left temple fell in enticing waves, curling around her breasts, triggered memories of better times with her. Lanciar felt a stir of his old lust. Pregnancy and childbirth had filled out her breasts and hips without detracting from her long legs and slender waist. She ran long, elegant fingers through the white streak in her flowing mame. The eyes of every man in the vicinity followed the path of those fingers.

She didn't need a staff to focus her magic. She had other tools.

Lanciar's heart ached to hold her one more time. He had loved her once. But then she had tried to pass their infant son off as King Simeon's bastard, possible blood heir to all three kingdoms on this continent. When she discovered that Simeon had been half brother to her father, Lord Krej, she had tried to tell the world that the brat died at birth.

Lanciar knew she lied. Lied more easily than she told the truth.

He hardened his heart against her, likening her to the empty mug in his hand.

Rejiia looked his way.

He raised the mug as if taking a long pull on the sour brew to hide his face from her view. He automatically armored his aura and magical signature and buried them deep inside his gut.

Rejiia and her entourage of magicians passed him by without a second glance. He saw no nannies or servants carrying her infant son. Where had she stashed the boy? Certainly not in the bottom of his mug where he looked for answers.

When he lifted his gaze once more, he noticed that Krej

had dropped into the dust. The statue remained stubbornly still. Had the spirit of the man revived enough to try to defy Rejiia? Lanciar smiled at the thought of the inevitable battle of wills that would ensue.

A moment later, Rejiia paused and scowled at the statue. She sighed heavily and snapped her fingers. The statue rose a hand's span above the dirt and floated behind her once more.

How long before Rejiia turned her full attention to reversing the spell? Krej's magic would give the coven a seventh magician—if Lanciar decided to remain one of them. They needed nine.

She probably would not attempt to revive Krej until she was ready to depose Darville of Coronnan and claim the Coraurlia—the magnificent dragon crown made of precious glass—for herself.

Then she'd set up Lanciar's son as her heir.

Not as long as Lanciar lived. He planned on keeping his boy safe from the machinations of the coven.

He decided to search Rejiia's quarters in the palace while she paraded around the city causing misery.

Rejiia's not-so-dainty footprints showed clearly when he allowed his eyes to cross slightly. She carelessly left her magical signature of deep black and blood red in each of her footsteps. Easy enough to retrace her path. He placed his own foot atop her prints, allowing her magical signature to mask his own.

One hundred steps, and he faced the gaping cave mouth that served as entrance to the palace of Hanassa. A lazy guard propped up the wall while he cleaned his fingernails with his dagger.

He took one more step toward the cave mouth and halted in mid-stride. A band of Rover men emerged from the palace. Their leader, a middle-aged man with distinguished wings of gray in his thick black hair, followed the same footsteps Lanciar traced—but in reverse. The Rovers trailed Rejiia. Why? Up to mischief certainly.

Their leader grinned widely. Sunlight glinted off his teeth, his eyes twinkled and years of care fled his face. Zolltarn. The self-styled king of the Rovers had beguiled the hardest of hearts and wisest of mages with that smile.

Lanciar closed his eyes and still saw that smile though the image of the man behind it faded from memory.

What plot drove Zolltarn to follow Rejiia?

Lanciar's mouth turned dry, and he wished for another drink.

Lanciar waited until the garishly clad Rovers in purple and red over black—obviously all members of the same clan—passed. Then he followed them.

Sure enough, within a few moments, the Rovers caught up with Rejiia as she toured the city. She kept up the pretense of examining every detail of life trapped within the walls of this ancient volcano as if she intended to govern here—or use the denizens as an army to back her claims to more important crowns.

She paused in front of a silk merchant. All of the goods had been stolen from a trading caravan that dared the pass between the desert kingdom of Rossemeyer and Coronnan.

"I want black! Black with silver embroidery. This entire shipment is useless." Rejiia spat and threw two bolts of costly fabric to the ground. She aimed a crystal-topped wand at the merchandise and set it afire.

The tubby little merchant hastened to retrieve the jewel-toned bolts. He slapped at the flames, threw some of the ever-present dust on them, and eventually backed away from the heat generated by Rejiia's witchfire.

Rejiia drew back her substantial foot and kicked the man in the ribs while he bent down. She laughed heartily while he clutched his middle and moaned in pain. The nearby burning cloth sent tendrils of flame too close to his head and spread to his hair. He yelped and scuttled away.

Lanciar sent a quick spell to negate the witchfire—only magic could douse it.

Rejiia whirled to confront the one who dared to interfere with her games. Blotches of red on her white skin showed her outrage.

Lanciar ducked out of sight.

At that moment of distraction, Zolltarn physically grabbed the statue of Krej and retreated. He and his men seemed to disappear before Lanciar's eyes.

But Lanciar knew Zolltarn of old. The Rover used tricks

that mimicked magic, requiring little actual magical energy. Here in Hanassa magicians could not tap the energy of ley lines or of dragons. Both shunned the city of outlaws.

Lanciar allowed his eyes to cross once more and looked for the distortions in light patterns that meant stealthy movement. He had to smile at the trick played upon Rejiia. Her own arrogance had given her a false sense of security. Good. She'd be so outraged at the challenges to her authority she might drop her guard around her son.

Ripples in the light showed all of the Rovers headed for the tunnel exit from the city. The rest of the clan waited just outside the gates with their loaded sledges, and their steeds, ready to flee.

"I expected more subtlety from you, Zolltarn," Lanciar chuckled.

The Rover chieftain flashed his magnificent smile in Lanciar's direction. Zolltarn spoke directly into Lanciar's mind, *The game is not yet finished, young soldier. But time is short. She planned to free Krej this night. The Commune cannot allow that.*

The statue of Krej passed from Rover hand to Rover hand. One wrapped it in silk. Another threw a coarse blanket over it. Then it disappeared inside the round cabinlike structure atop the lead sledge.

Lanciar could find no trace of the statue or the life it contained with either his magic or his mundane senses.

Rejiia whirled and watched the activity.

"After him! I want Zolltarn's head." She stamped her foot, and three magicians ran to do her bidding. "One thousand gold drageen for the return of my father!" she added.

Krej didn't seem nearly as important to her as the blemish to her dignity.

Rejiia's magician entourage wrung their hands in indecision.

Zolltarn turned and saluted Rejiia with his famous smile and a wave of his hand.

"Damn!" Rejiia stamped her foot again.

Was that an aftershock of the previous quake that seemed to drop the Kardia from beneath Lanciar's feet or a measure of her anger?

"When I retrieve my father, I'll have my son back from his Rover wet nurse as well," Rejiia called in the wake of her magicians.

What?

Lanciar burned with anger equal to Rejiia's. Had one of the babies carried by the Rover tribe been his son?

Rejiia drew in a deep breath, held it, and let it out through her teeth three times in preparation for a trance.

Lanciar mimicked her actions. He'd follow both Rejiia and Zolltarn into the void and back if he had to. Quickly, he sought Zolltarn's mind along the path of his earlier communication. This little bit of magic would drain his energy reserves, but he had to try. He needed to know the Rover's next trick.

He met a blankness deeper than the void. All Rovers had impressive and instinctive magical armor.

Rejiia scrunched her face in an ugly scowl of frustration. She hadn't been able to penetrate Zolltarn's mind either.

A peculiar sparkle appeared in the light surrounding the entire Rover clan and their possessions. All of them disappeared in a flash of crackling lightning.

Wind rushed to fill the vacuum left by their transport to elsewhere. It moved so quickly and violently that bits of wood and cloth, ash, leftover food, and broken tools swirled together in a series of tornadoes.

Lanciar threw up an arm to protect his eyes.

Then all became quiet again.

S'murghit! Zolltarn had mastered the transport spell. Lanciar couldn't follow them. He didn't know the secret of coming out the other side *alive.*

Another flash of sparkling light signaled Rejiia's disappearance.

Double s'murghit! She knew the secret, too.

How was he to find his son now?

He stared at the bottom of his empty mug wishing for inspiration. "I need a drink while I think about it."

Chapter 5

Jack inspected long strands of thread dyed in a rainbow of colors. "Katrina said she wanted purple dye," he muttered to the merchant. His neck burned with embarrassment. This arcane feminine errand made him more uncomfortable than the soul-penetrating stare of a dragon.

"This is a lovely shade of lavender," the woman with sparkling eyes said with the slight lisp of a foreign accent. She pulled one long thread free of the bundle and held it against a black cloth for contrast.

"Too pale." Jack suspected his betrothed wanted her threads to match a particular shade. "Amaranth," he said, hoping the plant matched its namesake.

"Ah!" The merchant tossed her dark curls flirtatiously as she retrieved another thread from the bundle. This one had more pink to it and was several shades darker than the lavender.

"That's close. Can I see it against white?"

"White? As in the cream of the queen's new gown or the stark white of SeLenese lace?" Her accent came through thicker with that statement. She must come from Jihab, Jack decided.

Her mouth twitched in laughter.

In another time and place Jack would love to flirt with her.

"Stark white, like lace," he replied.

"Is this for the little lacemaker recently taking refuge as the queen's favorite companion?" The merchant draped the thread on top of a piece of lace. Jack recognized the pattern as similar to one Katrina was working at the moment.

"Yes, I'm sure that's the color she wants. Enough dye for a gown and three skeins of linen thread." He sighed in relief, grateful this chore was complete. "I just hope I did this right." This decision was harder than passing one of Old Baamin's magical exams.

He searched his scrip for the proper coin without haggling. The coin was real. Three years ago he'd paid for goods with illusory coins. He still felt guilty about it and tended to overpay.

"Anything else I can get for you, soldier?" The woman smiled at him as she wrapped three packets of powder into a clean cloth.

"This will do." He wanted to hurry back to the palace and Katrina. Someone might recognize him and remember the cocky apprentice who had terrorized this market square on the day of the king's coronation over three years ago.

Just then, a man wearing brown robes thrust passersby away from him as he descended from the arched bridge. He wrinkled his nose repeatedly, sniffing the air and holding his right arm out in front of him, fist clenched.

"*S'murghin'* Gnul," the merchant muttered behind him. She rapidly packed up her skeins of pretty threads and folded her awning.

"The dye?" Jack asked.

She scuttled away without reply.

Before Jack could search her aura for traces of magic, she disappeared around a corner. But if the man who strode purposefully in this direction was a witch-sniffer from the Gnostic Utilitarian cult, Jack dared not use any of his talent. Even reading an aura could alert some of the more sensitive sniffers.

"You there, soldier!" The Gnul pointed at Jack.

Jack's armor snapped into place in instinctive fear. He put on a bland expression and faced the sniffer. "Me?" He pointed toward his own chest in silent inquiry.

"Yes, you. Apprehend that woman. I must question her. She may be a foreign witch." The sniffer waved obliquely in the direction the dye merchant had disappeared.

"But she didn't do anything but try to sell me some dye," Jack stalled. What made this man think he had the authority to question anyone? Would he go after Katrina next because she was not born in the city and was unmarried?

"Obey me, man! You are obligated to obey the orders of the Council of Provinces."

"I am obligated to obey the orders of my king and no one else, sir," Jack replied. "I do not recognize you as a member of the Council of Provinces. Nor are you one of their retainers." The hair on his spine and nape bristled.

Shoppers and merchants alike began drifting closer, listening avidly.

Jack searched their faces for any sign of an ally. No one looked in the least sympathetic. Their fear of magic gave the witch-sniffers all the authority they wanted. The Gnostic Utilitarian cult had fed that fear with horror stories. Every death within the city—murder, accident, disease, or old age—was caused by a magician's spell. Every financial setback or change in the weather became the revenge of a disgruntled magician. To make matters worse, ritually slaughtered cats, dogs, rats, even goats and sheep were often found laid at the foot of Festival Pylons around the city as if for a magical sacrifice.

Jack knew no magician would leave evidence lying around so openly, even if they needed the blood of the dying animal to fuel a magical talent.

But the Gnuls didn't care about truth, only about instilling fear in the hearts of the innocent so that the cult could take control of their lives.

Nervously, he fingered the short sword at his hip, wishing the weapon were his staff instead. He knew how to defend himself with a magician's basic tool. He'd worn the blade and guard's uniform barely a full moon.

"Are you protecting the witch, young man?" The Gnul continued to press closer to Jack.

The crowd grumbled disapproval of all witches. Two men threw stones where the dye merchant had had her awning. One of them whistled very close to Jack's ear.

"What witch?" Jack faced the accuser, trying to keep his fear out of his voice and posture.

The witch-sniffer had gone from wanting to question the woman to actively accusing her without benefit of trial or evidence. Every accused had the right to a public trial. He wondered if the Gnuls and their witch-sniffers ever bothered with the legal process.

The crowd went silent and closed ranks in a near perfect circle around Jack and the Gnul.

"The woman who just ran away. The woman you were doing business with. What were you trying to buy from her? A love potion, perhaps, or poison to use on our king?"

Jack allowed a laugh to explode at the nonsense. "All I wanted was some dye for my betrothed to use on her wedding gown."

The crowd didn't think this was funny. Angry mutters began rising. The sound nearly drowned out the sound of Jack's heart pounding too rapidly. One stooped, old woman licked her lips. "Gonna have us a witch-burning," she sniggered.

"Seize this man for aiding a witch!" the Gnul shouted.

"Not again," Jack sighed. The last time he'd come to this market square three years ago he'd fled a man bent on destroying him. Must he do so again?

Two burly men grabbed Jack's arms.

Deftly Jack twisted and shifted his weight. His captors lost their grip. While they stumbled forward, he ducked and slid backward. He'd learned something useful during his three years of slavery in King Simeon's mines.

"Catch that man, he's a witch!"

"Not this time, witch-sniffer." Jack ran. He knew this city from years of scavenging the streets before Baamin and the University of Magicians recognized his potential. He knew places . . .

Before he could change his mind, he dove into the river. Cold water closed over his head. He swam deeper, praying to the Stargods that he had enough breath to take him beyond sight of the witch-sniffer.

Lungs burning and eyes smarting, he broke the surface well downstream from the market island. He heard the tramp of many feet on a nearby bridge as the witch-sniffer raised the hue and cry. Coronnan City was made up of hundreds of little river islands connected by bridges.

Within minutes, the current took Jack past a large residential island. The Gnuls would have to wind their way through twisting alleyways to traverse the island. Then they'd have to cross another bridge to catch up to him.

He recognized the blue-painted rowboat tied to the next dock. "Still using that leaking scow, Aquilla?" he asked the absent Bay Pilot who had befriended him many years ago.

He grabbed the gunwale and heaved himself into the little craft. It rocked, threatening to dump him back into the water. He gasped for air and willed the boat to steady. First one leg and then the other over the side. At last he sprawled facedown in the bottom of the boat.

Then, carefully, he sat up and reached for the oars. A deep growl stopped him. A white-and-brown water dog faced him, teeth bared.

"I think I have a problem."

* * *

Wind howled through the trees like a lost soul moaning over separation from its body.

Robb ducked deeper into his cloak.

Marcus threw his cloak hood back and shook his hair free of restraint, glorying in the power of the storm.

"Typical," Robb muttered to himself. "I'm miserable, and he can't get enough of this storm." He plodded a few more steps in Marcus' wake, searching the path for signs of habitation. With each step he dug his staff into the mud. Maybe grounding his tool of focus in the kardia would help him see around the rain.

Too quickly, he chilled and lost strength. The little bit of magic drained him.

He caught up to Marcus and shouted into his companion's ear, "We've got to find shelter. Put up your hood. You'll catch your death of cold! This storm is getting worse." He huddled into himself, trying to keep his body warm. Rain dripped from the edge of his hood onto his chest where the cloak gaped.

Marcus shook his head. "The storm will clear. We have time. With luck we'll be through the pass and out of the rain by nightfall."

They had decided to try passing into SeLenicca in a more obscure location, well south of the armies. Their trek had not been easy, plagued with spoiled supplies, poor hunting, foul weather, and general bad luck.

But Marcus hadn't allowed the miserable conditions to dampen his good spirits. That made Robb grumble all the more.

His feet slid out from beneath him, and he landed flat on his face.

Lightning crackled around them, playing bizarre patterns of light across the thick gray clouds. Marcus laughed out loud at the energy singeing the air. "This is almost as good as gathering dragon magic!"

"Look, there's a light." Robb pointed with his staff toward the meager flicker atop a wooded hill off to their right. The flames burned blue and red rather than natural green.

"It's witchlight! We can spend the evening with another magician," Marcus chortled.

"We're mighty close to the border with SeLenicca. I'm not sure I want to meet another magician around here. No telling if he's friendly or not." Robb shivered as he stood up and tried rearranging his cloak. His hood slipped back in the process. Now he was drenched on the inside as well as without. "Never know it's nearly summer around here. The loss of the dragons combined with the intensive battle magic at the other pass seems to have made a climactic shift."

"Between the two of us, we can take on any magician even without dragons. As long as they don't surprise us. The storm is giving me power."

"Dragons," Robb grumbled. "If we weren't chasing invisible dragons, we'd be home beside a nice warm fire with a mug of spiced wine. Despite the seeming benevolence of dragon magic as opposed to solitary magic, I sometimes think the politics surrounding dragons makes our entire quest worthless."

"If we weren't here, we'd be freezing our bums off as we spy through every corner of Coronnan for Jaylor and the Commune of Magicians. Stop grumbling. Let's see what's up. You said yourself, we need shelter." Marcus marched forward.

"Admit it, Marcus, your infamous good luck has finally run out," Robb grumbled. "I can't remember being colder, wetter, or hungrier on any of our previous quests. Maybe it's time to start planning ahead a little better and making preparations for the next disaster."

"Stop being pessimistic. Of course my luck is holding. There's a light. That means someone with a fire and shelter to keep the fire going. We'll be fine for tonight. Then we can start out new and fresh in the morning, when the storm passes."

"If it passes. Let's just hope that unnatural light isn't marsh gas or a ghost," Robb said. As they pushed up the hill, he checked his dagger and shifted his grip on his staff for better defense.

"We've traveled the length and breadth of Coronnan for three years now while the Commune has remained in exile, and you always look for the worst to happen," Marcus said lightly. "And it never does."

"I don't have your luck. I have found that preparation and forethought work better than waiting to see what happens. Besides, we're too close to the border with SeLenicca. No guarantees that your luck will continue once we cross the border and run out of ley lines to fuel our magic."

"Ah, but over the border we will find dragons. What better luck than to find a dragon and return with it to Coronnan so that the University of Magicians and the Commune of Magicians can gain credibility once more?"

"This isn't dragon weather. It's foul and unpleasant and *s'murghin'* cold. There aren't any dragons nearby. I'll believe we've found dragons when we actually return to Coronnan with them. I'll believe that magicians will regain honor and integrity from dragon magic when the Council of Provinces reinstates the Commune into the University buildings and Council Chamber and not before."

Robb trudged beside Marcus uphill along an overgrown and narrow game trail.

"Look, Robb, there's a building with nice stout walls. The light is coming from a window niche. We'll have you warm and dry and cheerfully lecturing me with a nice cup of something hot to take the chill out of your innards and your mood." Marcus grabbed Robb's sleeve and pulled him forward at a brisk pace.

Trees crowded their path, sheltering them from the wind if not the rain. Robb looked up to scan the walls that towered above them. "I only sense one life," he said through chattering teeth. "I can't smell any magic, but that is definitely witchlight." He gnawed his lip in puzzlement.

"Witchfire won't throw out much heat. Let's hope there's some dry fuel about to turn it into green flame." Marcus lifted each foot carefully in the slick mud on the upward path. His staff kept him balanced, but he leaned on it heavily.

"How tired are you?" Robb asked, concerned. "Don't try to hide it just because I'm in a foul humor."

"One of us has to keep moving. Otherwise you'd crawl into a badger hole and call it shelter. A hot infusion of Brevelan's special blend of spices will taste very good once we get inside and light a real fire."

They hadn't much left of the tasty treat and had agreed to ration it. Robb agreed they really needed it today.

Soon enough, stone buttresses jutted out from the walls, making their path as crooked as Old Baamin's magical staff. —*S'murghit!* He wished the old Senior Magician hadn't passed on to his next existence. Robb would welcome the old man's cranky wisdom now.

The neatly dressed stones fit together snugly.

"I wonder how old this place is?" Marcus reached out a hand to caress the stones. "I can't sense any residual energy embedded in the stone by the mason who shaped it."

"All I feel is the deep cold of many winters," Robb added, mimicking his friend in trying to read the wall. The old cold burned through to his bones. "Old enough to harbor ghosts," he said. He touched his head, heart, and both shoulders in the cross of the Stargods. "I'm not sure . . ."

"Oh, come on. We need shelter and a fire. Let's find the gate." Marcus clumped around the perimeter of the wall. Only an occasional window slit broke the smooth surface between buttresses. The rain eased, but the cloud cover lowered.

"Almost a mile around," Robb stated. His breath made small chill clouds in front of his face. "Wonder if this is an old monastery. There were a number of them during the Great Wars of Disruption. But we only know of one left standing after peace came to Coronnan. Many of them disappeared as people made use of their building stones for other purposes. A few may have been converted into palaces or summer retreats for the nobility." Talking—lecturing as Marcus claimed—kept him from thinking about the thickness of the haze they nearly swam through. All of his senses were distorted, untrustworthy. He felt . . . inadequate.

"Wonder if anyone has lived here in the last three hundred years." Marcus stared up at the top of the wall, a good twenty feet above their heads.

"We'll know soon enough. Looks like a gatehouse tower jutting out from the main wall on the next corner. Of course we walked the long way around before finding it."

"We walked deasil, as we should. Walking widdershins is bad luck."

"First time I've ever known you to care about your luck. Prepare yourself for anything. An entire band of outlaws could be hiding within these walls."

Chapter 6

Robb shifted his grip on his staff and brought it forward, ready to channel magic down its length or flip it and use it as a mundane weapon.

"We'd know if there were hostiles within this building," Marcus said. "I only sense one life. Feels mostly mundane, not a magician at all. Strange. One life with a minimal magical talent I'm guessing; enough power to call a ball of witchlight, but not enough for us to sense."

"Or someone with incredible armor that allows us to sense his presence, but not his magic. Solitary magicians, raised outside the dragon magic tradition, are known to be quite cunning. He could be lulling us into dropping our defenses so as to make us easy prey."

The gatehouse rose out of the walls like a huge malignant growth—nearly a quarter of the wall's width and twice as high. The two young men slowed their steps and crept around the corner.

"This place is defended more like a castle than a monastery," Marcus whispered.

"What do you expect? It was built as a refuge when civil war tore the land apart for three generations."

Marcus shushed Robb with a finger to his lips as he peered around the next corner, staff at the ready.

Robb shrugged and crept forward, peering through the thickening gloom. He kept his larger body in front of his friend. In a fray his brute strength was well teamed with Marcus' agility.

Marcus peeked over Robb's shoulder. The formerly stout

wooden doors hung askew on weary hinges. The wind made them creak with each new gust.

The dense air almost seemed to pour out of that gate. What kind of ghosts and demons hid within it?

Silently, they edged closer. Robb led them through the gap in the doors. Thick oak had shrunk away from dozens of bronze bosses that had reinforced the wood. Green corrosion brushed off on his cloak like soggy mushroom spores. The hinges protested mightily. They both froze in place, waiting, wary.

No one challenged them.

Breathing a sigh of relief, Marcus pushed forward to lead the way across the broad courtyard. They faced a two-story building shaped like a squared-off steedshoe. Thick columns supported the second story where it hung over the first, creating a sheltered passage. Two of the pillars lay broken in the courtyard.

Robb sighed wistfully. He wished people had more respect for these old buildings.

"That way." He pointed to the glimmer of light creeping under the door of one of the ground-floor cells in the southern wing.

A number of long paces took them across the courtyard. They climbed six steep steps from the courtyard to the colonnaded passage. Marcus rested a hand on the wooden panels, seeking. "One life force, barely stronger than the witchlight," he whispered. "Stargods! He's dying!" Marcus pushed hard against the door. It flew inward, banging against the wall to their left.

Robb followed closely, alarmed and ready to defend them both with spells and mundane strength. The sight that met his eyes chilled him more than the storm.

An old man, wasted to skin and bones, lay crumpled upon a stark bed that was pushed right up against the narrow cell's wall, barely made comfortable by a thin pallet and blanket. His image flickered in and out of view, like a dragon in sunlight. His long white hair and beard were matted and yellowed with illness and neglect.

A little ball of blue/white/red witchlight nestled in a window niche high above his head. The light did not flicker or cast shadows. So why did the ancient man fade in and out of reality?

Half the time he looked as transparent as a ghost, but his chest continued to rise and fall with great effort. He hadn't passed into the void between existences yet.

"Start a fire. He needs warmth," Robb ordered. He thrust Marcus aside as he raced to the side of the narrow stone bench that served as a bed. "What ails you, elder?" he asked respectfully as he pulled pouches of herbs from his pack.

Marcus busied himself throwing kindling into the rusting brazier beside the bed. The room was small enough that only a little fire would heat the space nicely. He ignited the twigs and leaves with a snap of his fingers and added larger sticks as quickly as he could. At least the old man had prepared for a fire before illness, injury, or just plain old age felled him.

From the fine cut of his stylish robes and trews, Robb guessed that he had come from a noble and wealthy family. Probably a younger son grown beyond usefulness. He and Marcus would have heard of an heir or lord gone missing. After all, they had spent most of the last three years gathering the gossip of Coronnan.

"Save your medicines for yourself, lad," the ancient waved weakly at Robb's packets. His voice faded and grew with his flickering image. "Leave here. Quickly. This place is cursed. Don't get trapped . . ." His breath gushed out of his chest on a dry rattle like leaves stirred in a drying breeze.

At last his form settled into the current reality, a dry husk that no longer held his spirit trapped between worlds. The witchlight died, leaving only the light from the small fire.

Robb gently closed the old man's staring eyes. "I didn't even have time to ask his name," he said sadly. "I'll hate burying him without a name."

"At least he did not die alone." Marcus looked up from the merrily blazing fire. A little heat spread out from the brazier.

Robb and Marcus set about straightening the old man's limbs. When he lay peacefully on the stone bench, looking comfortable and glad that he no longer struggled through life, Robb searched his pockets for some clue to his identity. His fingers brushed against cool metal disks.

He fished one out and stared at the shiny gold. The soft metal glowed in the gentle firelight. It caressed his fingertips and eyes with an almost living color. His jaw dropped as he recognized the one hundred mark on the old-style coin. The face and inscription did not trigger any memory in him.

"Our fortune is made, Robb. He's got dozens of gold coins in his pockets. Dragons only know how many more are stashed around this lonely monastery." Marcus held up a handful of coins. He gulped as he, too, held them up to catch the light.

Robb's vision fractured into a dozen bright rainbows.

The world tilted.

He fought to retain his balance, eyes focused clearly on the gold coin and nothing else. A fine veil of mist seemed to cover everything.

"The Commune can buy a lot of respectability with these. Not to mention books and equipment for the University," Marcus said. His voice came from a great distance. "This gold will liven up our games of cartes."

"We haven't time to daydream about gold and fortunes," Robb replied as he placed two of the coins upon the ancient's closed eyes. A third rested in his pocket. Keeping one coin for himself would hurt no one. And it might give him an edge against survival during his long treks around Coronnan. Unlike Marcus, he had no desire to settle in one place for a long, long time.

He bowed his head a moment in silent prayer. "This man is very dead, Marcus. And he said this place is cursed. We have to get out of here. We need a plan."

"Not until after the storm passes. We can spend the night searching the place for his stash."

"Marcus," Robb began testily. "Marcus! You're fading into the walls. Marcus, don't you dare leave me and take your good luck with you!"

* * *

"Nice doggy," Jack said quietly. He dared not move.

The beast growled again and showed even more of its teeth. Saliva dripped onto the dock above the boat.

"Nice doggy."

"She doesn't like to be called doggy," a man replied roughly.

"Good mopplewogger," Jack said, still not moving.

The dog pricked her ears and sat.

"Nice mopplewogger," Jack coaxed. "Don't suppose you remember me, doggy?"

The dog rose up on its long legs growling again.

"Different dog. It's been ten years, wharf rat. You don't have to steal the boat. I'd loan it if you asked," the man said with a chuckle.

"Want to call off your mopplewogger, Aquilla?"

"Ten years and you're still running from bullies. Want to trade that prissy uniform for a real one?"

Jack dared to look away from the dog long enough to take in Aquilla's Guild of Bay Pilots uniform of maroon and gold. His weather-beaten face crinkled in laughter.

"I've made oaths of loyalty elsewhere. Want to call off the mopplewogger?"

"Lilly, come," Aquilla said. The shorthaired dog growled at Jack one last time before returning to her master's side. She sat on Aquilla's foot and leaned her head into him. Absently the pilot scratched her ears.

"So what kind of trouble you running from this time, wharf rat?"

"Witch-sniffers. And I have a name now. Old Baamin decided I wasn't too stupid to have a name after all. I'm Jack." Jack scrambled onto the dock. His clothes sagged and dripped. He must indeed look like the wharf rat he had been as a child. Aquilla had rescued him when bullies had stolen his food and beaten him nearly senseless.

"Your loyalty to the University of Magicians was misplaced ten years ago. It still is. You should have come to work for me. Not many men have an affinity for a mopplewogger."

"I don't seem to have any kind of bond with this one." Jack held out his hand for the dog to sniff. She growled again and he jerked his hand away from her all-too-large teeth.

"That's because she caught you trying to steal my boat. You look like you need a meal and some dry clothes."

Aquilla jerked his head toward the cottage above the dock. "Is that a palace guard's uniform underneath all that river muck?"

"Yes." Jack tried to wring some water out of the sodden wool tunic.

"You'll be better off as a Bay Pilot. Every government recognizes the worth of the Guild. Even the Gnuls. Not so the palace guard. Once the Gnuls depose King Darville, you'll be out of a job and quite likely become fuel for their next bonfire. But without the Bay Pilots, no one gets through the mudflats to deep water and the trading ships. We'll always have work." He negotiated the steep path up to his home. Lilly leaped eagerly ahead of him. Jack followed more slowly. His wet boots slipped on the river clay that packed the path.

"The Gnuls had better not find out about your mopplewogger, then," Jack added. "One hint of how these dogs smell the differences in water depth and salinity to show you the way through the channels of the mudflats and they'll burn you all for magicians."

"They wouldn't dare." Aquilla whirled around and faced Jack, eyes wide with horror.

"They'd dare. One of them just accused me of witchcraft because I failed to pursue a woman he chose to question. Her only crime seemed to be that she was single and spoke with a foreign accent." Just like Katrina. "The sniffer had no evidence; no complaints against her; nothing. He just 'smelled' magic in her vicinity."

"Tomorrow there will be another hundred witch-sniffers in the capital. I'm to retrieve them from the port at high tide." Aquilla's face drained of color.

"Make sure your mopplewogger stays hidden below-decks."

"Always do. But, Jack, what are we going to do? Pretty soon there will be more witch-sniffers than mundanes in the city."

"That is going to present a problem."

Chapter 7

Vareena sat before the sparkling fire in the central hearth, contemplating her fate. Not long now. She'd miss Farrell when he passed on. But his death gave her a chance at freedom.

Freedom.

She tasted the word and liked the feel of it in her mouth and her spirit.

Rain spat upon the flames through the smoke hole in the thatched roof. One of the glowing splinters of wood on the edge of the blaze sputtered and died. She didn't bother reigniting it. It had withered to mostly ash now anyway. Like Farrell.

Her spindle lay idle at her feet. She just could not concentrate on keeping her threads smooth and free of slubs while the storm raged and her ghost sat alone up in the abandoned monastery.

He'd pass soon. The fever had returned yesterday, stronger than before. He had no interest in cartes, or tales, or even the chicken stew with pickled beets. A part of her heart sobbed with the coming grief.

But his passing would give her freedom. She fingered the silver amulet through the protective cloth of her shift. Her father and brothers must never find it. They'd confiscate it and sell it for sure. In their eyes women had no rights and could own nothing but the dowry determined at her coming of age.

She'd take her two cows and three chickens with her.

In the outside world, women could own property and select their own husbands. Farrell had promised her that as well as the three acres in Nunio.

Neither she nor her ghost understood what had brought him here to the sanctuary of the monastery. He had wandered in two years ago, seeking a night's shelter after becoming separated from a trading caravan that was headed for the pass into SeLenicca. After that first night he had not been able to leave. He did not remember dying.

She only knew that he brightened her lonely days, made her feel useful and important. And now he offered her freedom.

At a price. His death.

The wind howled around her father's cottage. Vareena shivered and drew her shawl closer about her. She should have gone to the ancient monastery hours ago. Farrell needed her. He felt the cold so acutely. She would take him her extra blanket though he usually refused the little comforts she offered. She should have gone to him before noon, as she usually did. But the storm had come upon them quickly and she had been hard pressed to get the villagers, sheep, and plow steeds under shelter. Already the creek threatened to flood.

The ghost needed her. She sensed him passing into his next existence, finally. He'd lingered between this world and the void for two years, neither here nor there. Neither alive nor dead. A nameless man—he'd admitted that Farrell was but the name of his boyhood hero, a man he wished to emulate—lost to his loved ones. Only Vareena cared for him. Cared about him.

No one, not even a ghost deserved to die alone. Over the years she'd sat beside five other ghosts as they finally gave up this existence. None of them had lasted more than two years. She'd been only seven when she sat the death watch with her first ghost. Her mother had died suddenly and left Vareena the odd destiny to care for the ghosts who periodically appeared in the abandoned monastery, a calling inherited by the women of her family for nearly three hundred years. They were the only ones who could see the ghosts and knew what they needed and how to provide for them.

Suddenly Vareena stood up. "I'm going back up there," she announced to her father and five brothers. Something tugged at her senses. She couldn't sit here listening to the wind any longer.

"Stay, Vareena. The storm," Ceddell, her father, objected. He whittled a toy sheepdog for his four-year-old grandson.

"Let this one go, Eena," Yeenos, the second oldest brother said, looking her directly in the eye. "Your ghost is just a drain on our supplies. No work, no food. That's the rule, for everyone but your *s'murghin'* ghosts!"

"He's lost between here and the void. I can't allow his soul to depart unguided," Vareena stated.

"Maybe there isn't really a ghost at all. You're the only one who can see them. Maybe you're feeding a bunch of outlaws. Why should we take necessary supplies away from our families to feed a bunch of criminals and repair their building? We could use some of those finely dressed stones ourselves," Yeenos continued, his voice rising with his passion. "I say we tear down that cursed building." His fist clenched as if he needed to pound something, or someone.

Vareena backed away from his temper. He'd never hit her before, but a number of men in the village had crooked noses and missing teeth from violent connections with his fists.

"I'll go with you, Eena." Uustass, the eldest of the brood, stood up to join her. "Stargods know, we've never been able to keep you from your duty. Might as well do our best to take care of you when you get a calling."

"Stay, Uustass." She waved him back to his stool and the leather he braided for new steed harnesses. "You'll only catch a chill and be miserable for weeks. Bad enough I'll have to take soup and poultices to half the village in the morning. I don't need to tend you as well. Stay with your children and tell them stories so the storm doesn't frighten them."

Uustass had lost his wife in childbed last winter. He always seemed lost now unless Vareena gave him something specific to do.

"Take him, or you stay," her da commanded. "Lost your mam to a storm. Not lose you." His voice carried the weight of years of experience leading the village, judging misdeeds, and deciding the crop rotation and beast fertility.

No one disobeyed him when he used that tone as if he begrudged each word.

Vareena was tempted.

"Very well. Uustass, take the cloak I oiled yesterday. There's soup in the pot and bread in the hearth oven for supper. Serve yourselves when you get hungry. I don't think this will take long." She fetched her own garment from the row of hooks by the low door. Farrell wouldn't need supper. She knew he would find his way out of his body and into the void this night. Ghosts always passed on during wild storms like this, as if they needed the wind to guide them to their next existence.

As she opened the door, a powerful gust nearly blew her back into the main room of the cottage. "Stargods, I hope I'm not too late."

Uustass took her arm and guided her up the hill to the ancient building on the crest, mostly hidden by trees. His stocky body shielded her from the wind. For her own comfort she blessed him for being so stalwart and ready to aid her when the rest of her people would shun her for her contact with ghosts. Perhaps Uustass hoped to communicate with his recently deceased wife through Vareena's ghosts. Six moons and he still had not accepted the loss of his life mate.

Nothing but ill luck stalked those who communed with ghosts. She'd known that for years.

She fingered the silver amulet again, praying that her luck was about to change. Stargods only knew, her family had suffered their share of grief, with the death of her mother, grandmother, and sister-in-law, with her need to become mother to her family at the age of seven. But they'd been blessed as well. Blessed in ways the villagers rarely recognized. She had five healthy brothers. Two of them were married and helping run their wives' family farms. Her father continued as a wise judge and leader despite his reluctance to utter more than four words at a time. The village prospered most years. Since the war with SeLenicca, trading caravans used the nearby pass more often, bringing trade goods for surplus crops. Even now, when winter stores grew thin and new crops had yet to ripen, they all had enough to eat and more to share with the ghost.

But he'd be gone after tonight. She choked back a sob. The ghosts were her friends. They listened patiently as she explored the problems of growing up the only girl in a household of brothers, the only sensitive in the village, the only woman in a position to care for all those around her, family and villagers alike. The ghosts understood her.

"Almost there, little sister." Uustass helped her up the last few steps of the broken path to the gatehouse.

The wind ceased to pound at her senses the moment she stepped within the massive walls of the building. But then her ears started ringing in the comparative silence. She clutched her temples, trying to make sense of the noise. A hum, deep in her mind, at her nape announced an eerie portent.

"What ails you, Eena?" Uustass clutched both of her elbows.

She leaned into him, using his solid presence to balance the sudden numbness between her ears.

"The ghost is passing. We must hurry!"

"I wish I understood this strange compulsion of yours to tend these bizarre beings. Yet you can't summon the ghosts of our loved ones. You don't even know if these ghosts were once human."

"Whatever they are when they come to me, they were human once. I must help them . . . him. Something is amiss. Hurry, Uustass." She pushed him out of her way and dashed through the relative comfort of the tunnel beneath the gatehouse into the pelting rain of the courtyard. The day seemed darker and heavier here than out in the teeth of the storm.

Her feet automatically took her toward the cell where she had placed the little ball of cold light so that Farrell did not have to pass his last day in darkness.

Natural green firelight flickered beneath the closed doorway. Vareena stopped short, heedless of the cold sheets of water that poured upon her from the leaking gutter of the colonnade.

"Now what ails you?" Uustass sighed wearily.

"I did not light the fire."

"Then the ghost must have."

"But he was too weak to leave his pallet. I left no fire-rock and iron to strike a spark."

Uustass drew his belt knife; the one he used to free young sheep from brambles and cut lengths of rope for various chores around the village. Sharp enough to slice through tree limbs the width of his wrist.

A measure of confidence returned. Whoever had invaded the sanctuary of the ancient monastery must respect her brother's strength and purpose.

Cautiously, Uustass pushed the door open. Rusted hinges creaked. He stood back, peering inward, waiting for an attack.

The fine hairs on Vareena's neck stood up. From the safety of the steps she inspected the small visible portion of the narrow cell. She saw only the slack figure of her ghost, fully formed in this reality, his arms neatly crossed on his chest, legs crossed at the ankles, and shiny gold coins holding down his eyelids. She doubted he had composed himself so peacefully before experiencing his death throes.

"I only see the body," Uustass said, sheathing his knife. "Just like the other times. Once they've died, they are visible to normal people."

"Wait!" Vareena whispered frantically. "There, to the right. Something moved." Her hand went to her throat as she swallowed back a lump of fear. It lodged in her upper chest, constricting her breathing.

"I don't see anything." Uustass shrugged as he stepped into the room. His hands remained at his sides, not reaching for the tempting gold.

"Watch out!" Vareena rushed to her brother's side. She placed herself defiantly between him and the two figures who stood beside the pallet. Suddenly the narrow cell seemed far too crowded.

Two ghosts stared at her in surprise, one tall and broad, the other slighter. The shorter one stared at her from pale eyes that seemed to burn through to her soul, his mouth agape.

As she watched, he faded in and out of her vision, one moment fully formed in this reality, the next heartbeat a pale outline of a human figure that distorted light.

The taller and darker figure seemed a trifle more solid. He kept his hand on the other's shoulder. They belonged together. Both wore magician-blue tunics and carried long staffs that had become as ghostly as they.

Neither had been a ghost long.

"Two of you?"

"What!" Uustass whirled and faced the door. "Where?"

"Over here." Vareena pointed. "We lost one ghost only to add two more. Both young and healthy. I've never seen two ghosts at the same time before."

"Wonderful." Sarcasm dripped from Uustass' voice as he continued to scan the room. His eyes slid away from the two ghosts as if something blocked his mind from settling on that direction. "Now we've got to dip deeper into our dwindling stores to feed two of them. They'll linger for years before they waste away."

"I'll never be free of this place now," Vareena moaned to herself.

Chapter 8

"Look at her, Robb. She's the most beautiful woman I've ever seen!" Marcus held his breath, almost afraid the woman with the crystalline aura would fade before his eyes, like a dragon slipping through the mist. The man with her seemed less substantial, as if he lingered half in the void—sort of like the dead man before he'd gasped his last and emerged from the void.

"Didn't you hear her, Marcus?" Robb asked angrily.

Marcus yanked his concentration away from the slight beauty with blue eyes so vivid they reminded him of Brevelan—Senior Magician Jaylor's witch wife. But this woman had blond hair that kinked and curled in a bright cloud of silver and gold rather than Brevelan's witch-red.

She was a few years older than he was. Her maturity made her much more beautiful than any woman he could remember.

The ghostly man with her, older by almost a decade he guessed, looked enough like her to be her brother rather than a lover. His protective stance with the knife when he first thrust open the door suggested a family relationship, too.

"I wasn't listening. She's so very beautiful, she makes my heart ache. What did you say?" Something important was happening, and Marcus couldn't concentrate, couldn't think. He wanted to go drifting in the void forever with this woman.

"She said that we are ghosts and we will linger as ghosts for a long, long time." Robb's fingers on Marcus' shoulders squeezed painfully tight.

"Ghosts! We can't be ghosts. We're alive. I see you and this room very clearly, I hear the wind and the rain outside, I feel pain where you are bruising my shoulder."

Robb removed his hand, shaking out some of the tension.

Only then did Marcus realize his friend held one of the gold coins in his left hand, rubbing it absently, just as Marcus did with the coins he'd slipped into his pocket.

"Those two are the ghosts," Marcus continued. "They look like dragons, sort of here, sort of in the void."

"Something strange is going on here, Marcus. Something that will delay us a long time from completing our quest and returning to the Commune with the dragons."

"Maybe these people are kin to dragons. Maybe we can gather dragon magic from them," Marcus suggested, his natural optimism replacing the tiny tingles of fear Robb had planted in his mind.

He took three deep breaths, triggering a light trance. Then he stood with his arms to his sides, palms out, feet braced, eyes closed, and opened himself to the energies swirling through the universe.

Robb did the same.

Nothing filled the empty place above his belly and behind his heart where he stored dragon magic.

Robb shook his head.

"They aren't dragons," Marcus admitted.

"This isn't the end of the quest, Marcus. But I fear it is a long and dangerous side trip away from our true mission."

"Not necessarily. We'll just walk out of here. The rain and wind are letting up. We'll find shelter somewhere else. These folks can bury the old man. They probably know his name at least." Resolutely, he stepped around the beautiful woman and her elusive protector. He marched across the courtyard with Robb in his wake. The ghostly pair followed, the woman directing, her companion darting blank looks in every corner.

They entered the tunnel beneath the gatehouse and pushed open the wooden doors.

Two more steps and they would be free of this eerie old building where darkness seemed to gather. Two more steps to return to their quest.

At the exit through the massive monastery walls, Marcus

hit a solid wall of resistance—like running into a magician with incredibly strong armor.

He bounced back into Robb. His friend caught him. Without a word Robb stepped around Marcus and extended his hands to test the blockage.

Marcus jabbed the barrier with his staff. It passed through easily. "I don't sense anything." He tried again to step through the doorway into the outside world. Once more he slammed up against a barrier.

Robb tried and bounced back as well.

"Looks like your luck has finally run out, Marcus. And I don't have a plan. We're trapped."

* * *

Forces are moving against me. I sense the presence of people who will rob me of my power. But I am not the barely talented clerk I was in my youth. I have true power now. I know how to stop my enemies. I am in touch with all four of the elements as none of these modern magicians can hope to be. A little pressure here, a tug against the elements there and we have a kardiaquake. That should delay those who come for me.

* * *

Robb stalked around the perimeter of Hanassa. He knew he'd never been here. Couldn't remember traveling to this remote corner of the world.

It's only a dream, part of him whispered. But the heat of the desert sun, the sour taste of thirst, and the heavy grit that irritated his eyes were too tangible to be merely a dream.

He swallowed heavily, hoping to ease some of the dryness in his throat. Not enough saliva. Not enough strength.

The heavy sand trapped his feet. He couldn't shift them, couldn't think, couldn't plan his next move.

And then the ground rippled beneath him, as if he stood on water like some long-legged bug and the water no longer wanted to support him.

He froze every muscle and gritted his teeth against the waving motion. His stomach tried to turn itself inside out. His eyes refused to focus, and his body wanted to become one with the water.

Arrows rained down upon his head. What could he do? No place to hide. No way to move.

Pain pierced his shoulder. He looked at the source, too stupefied to do anything else. Blood poured down his magician-blue tunic, staining his new, brightly polished boots. He stared at them, aggrieved at the spoiling of the pristine leather.

But he didn't have new boots. Marcus did. Why was he wearing Marcus' boots? But these boots fit. He could barely get his foot inside the ones Marcus stole from the army.

He should throw a spell. What spell?

Sweat broke out on his brow and back. The pain in his shoulder doubled, bringing him to his knees.

Hot oil replaced the onslaught of arrows.

It burned his skin and hair. He held his hands and arms over his head, trying desperately to block the continuing deluge of boiling oil. His sweat turned icy. Blisters on his face and arms froze, burst, and peeled.

The new boots couldn't protect his toes from the icy sand of the desert of Hanassa.

Bright light penetrated his eyes with blinding stabs. He looked up to see what new weapon the outlaws of Hanassa brought to bear.

Dark walls surrounded him. Only a single arrow slit window allowed light to escape Hanassa. The world around him turned to darkness. Intensely cold. An ancient cold born of evil.

Wild screams from above and below him blotted out coherency.

He huddled in on himself. All control of himself, his thoughts, his plans vanished. How could he make his own luck if he couldn't think ahead? There had to be a way out of this mess. He couldn't make it right.

A deep sob wrenched upward from his gut.

The sound of his own moan woke him. Only a hint of starlight penetrated his cell in the ancient monastery, keeping it in deep gloom. The storm had abated.

Vareena and her brother must have trudged home hours ago. They had promised to return to bury Farrell the next day. Robb and Marcus had tried an unsuccessful summons spell to Jaylor that left them exhausted and empty. Then they had selected rooms as far away from the scene of death as possible. They'd eaten their dinners in silence and retired.

Robb hadn't traveled to Hanassa and been assaulted from all sides by unknown outlaws. He rotated his stiff shoulders. Chill and an awkward sleeping position plagued his muscles. An insect bite on his shoulder itched. That must have triggered the dream pain of a poisoned arrow wound.

He heaved a sigh of relief that sounded very much like a sob. He sat on the edge of the stone platform that formed his bed in the corner cell, bracing his elbows on his knees.

The dream had been so real. Almost like a dragon-dream. He shuddered. For years he'd heard stories of how the dragons could impose an illusion so convincing that healthy men wandered in circles for days, not eating or sleeping, ignoring the calls and pleas of friends and family to return, only to die of starvation with a smile on their faces. Always those tales had seemed apocryphal.

Now he wondered what he had done to anger a dragon.

But he wouldn't have awakened from a dragon-dream.

Still shivering with memories of arrows and boiling oil, he called a ball of witchlight to hand and stumbled to the latrine. Best way to banish a nightmare.

Three spiders as large as the largest gold coin crunched under his boots between his cell and the corner latrine. He relished the squishy sound of their deaths. This, he could control.

But when he climbed beneath the blankets again, the dream returned. He forced himself awake and counted the stones in each wall, the floor, and ceiling for the rest of the night.

* * *

"I don't love you anymore, Margit," Marcus stated boldly.

The tall blonde stood before him, hands on hips, feet spread, mouth agape. The setting sun backlit her flowing tresses into a wild halo of indignation. And then she started throwing spells, fire, water, wind, dirt clods.

Marcus ducked, holding up his arms to shield his face. He tried to erect a barrier between himself and Margit's fury. Magic dribbled from his fingers like the last dregs of old ale from the bottom of the barrel.

"Let me explain, Margit." When magic deserted him, he always had words. He could charm the surliest of beldames into giving him a night's shelter, a meal, or a tumble in the hay. "We've had some good times together. We've shared the secrets of magicians spying upon politicos and fanatic Gnuls. I was the liaison between you and Jaylor at the Commune of Magicians. But that wasn't true love. You don't truly love me any more than I love you."

"Explain!" Margit hurled rocks with fists and magic. Only one landed at his feet. The others found her targets, his shoulders, his gut, his head. She'd had a lot of practice warding off ravens and jackdaws from her mother's bakery cart in the market square. "Explain! You call that an explanation? What have you found this time? A more beautiful woman, a wealthier woman, a willing woman on the long, lonely nights in the middle of nowhere? I've heard all of your excuses before, Marcus. But this is the last one. I'll kill you before I let another woman have you."

From empty air she conjured metal throwing stars. She aimed their sharp points at his eyes.

His luck had definitely run out. No more could he count on Margit's love and loyalty waiting for him in the capital when he returned.

Fierce, hot pain in his eyes and head jolted Marcus awake. Darkness surrounded him. Had Margit's aim been true and blinded him? Sweat poured down his face and back. He rubbed at the biting pain in his temple and eye. Insect bites.

Gradually, the faint starlight filtered through the high window of his monastery cell. As his eyes adjusted to the dim light, he remembered where he was. He sighed heavily and brought a ball of cold witchlight to his hand.

"Just a nightmare. I still have my magic and my luck." He rolled over and curled into his bedroll, seeking to warm the chill of sweat drying on his skin.

Images of Margit's fury superimposed themselves on his mind every time he closed his eyes.

"I don't love Margit. 'Tis Vareena who has captured my heart." He tried to conjure her image before him, starting with her cloud of fair curls surrounding delicate features, frail frame, and serene demeanor.

Margit's laugh and well-muscled strength kept trying to mask the pictures he held in his mind's eye.

"I love Vareena. Tomorrow I'll find a way out of here so that we can be together. Forever," he repeated over and over again, until exhausted sleep finally claimed him.

Chapter 9

"**M**arcus, we've tried this before." Robb sighed heavily. "But we haven't tried it this way," Marcus replied. Eagerly he placed his right foot into a crevice in the outer wall. Then he reached for the first secure handhold with a show of confidence he didn't really feel. They'd been trying to escape the old monastery all morning with no luck.

No luck. The words rang ominously around his head. He gritted his teeth and hauled himself up to find the next toehold. The chipped crevice he sought eluded him. As his balance teetered and his arms threatened to give way from the strain of holding his weight so precariously, he pressed his back against the gatehouse tower and wedged his body in the tight corner between it and the main curtain wall.

This would be easier if he'd slept better last night. Even after he'd banished the nightmare of Margit trying to kill him, he had not slept. Every time he'd turned over on the stone bench of a bed, the bed itself had seemed to roll and reshape itself to be more uncomfortable. Good fortune would never return until he escaped this cursed monastery.

From the looks of the deep shadows beneath Robb's eyes, he hadn't slept any better.

They had to set out of here. Today. Now.

"Your theory is flawed, Marcus. Whatever magical barrier holds us here is most thorough. Even the scattered ley lines within the courtyard do not reach the wall. They end abruptly and never do they cross. Our summons spell to Jaylor last night did not leave this complex. I think the thick cloud cover kept it within the walls. The confinement spell must have been constructed to surround the entire wall, not just the obvious exits and easily climbed points. Actually from the way you are bracing yourself there, I believe this to be the most obvious place for a climber to escape." Robb droned on with his logical assessment of their predicament. He held his grounded staff so that the top made little circles at the end of each sentence.

"But Vareena comes and goes with her brother. Why them and not us?" Marcus returned. "She brought us food and blankets this morning. She talks to us. She sees us. But her brother doesn't. Not once could I make eye contact with him while we dug Farrell's grave. Why can Vareena and her brother leave and we can't?" He didn't add that he wanted to follow the lovely blonde. He'd follow her to the ends of the kardia if he had to, giving up his dreams of a snug cottage and never wandering more than a few leagues from there ever·again.

Margit's image reared up before him. She'd never forgive him for deserting her. She'd hunt him down and kill him . . . No that was the nightmare. Margit might make life miserable for him, but she'd never . . . or would she?

He had a nagging feeling that his infamous good luck wouldn't solve this problem for him.

But he had to have Vareena— He caressed the name in his mind as he climbed. Vareena needed his protection. She stood barely as tall as his shoulder. Her willowy figure looked too fragile to withstand a light breeze, let alone stand up to her strapping brother. And yet, from their conversations, Marcus gathered that the entire family of strong brothers and an implacable father listened and obeyed her. She'd remained a spinster to care for them.

"Perhaps Vareena and her brother have the freedom to leave because they are mundane," Robb mused. He stroked his dark beard, eyes crossing in thought. In another time and place, Marcus might expect a spell to bounce from the end of his staff. But those ley lines curved and twisted away from each other as if repelled. Neither he nor Robb had been able to tap into their energy for more than the most rudimentary spells.

The summons spell had not exited the walls.

"What does talent or lack of it have to do with escape?"

Marcus wormed his way up the wall a little higher. His right foot slipped just as he shifted his balance to move his other foot. Rough stone rasped his palms and cheek while he scrabbled for a better position. "*S'murghit!* That stings." His breath whistled through his clenched teeth.

Time was, he could set his mind to any task, and luck would carry him through to the end. He always found a way to come through unscathed no matter how difficult or dangerous the chore.

Robb bore a number of scars from their adventures. They enhanced his rugged appeal. Marcus had no scars to blemish his fair skin and lithe body—yet.

Doggedly he climbed higher, doing his best to ignore the painful scrapes that made him want to curl his fingers tightly over the wounds.

"This would be a lot easier if the builders had put in a parapet and walkway for guards or lookouts. This exterior wall must have been added for protection after the main building was constructed," Marcus mused rather than think about his luck and his magic draining away.

"We must consider the possibility that this monastery was converted to a prison for rogue magicians at the end of the Great Wars of Disruption." Robb continued his lecture. "If such were the case, then the Commune would need a powerful spell to keep the criminals in. Something in the nature of the magical border around Coronnan. Until recently it prevented enemies and undesirables from entering the country."

"Flawed logic, Robb. The border broke down when the number of dragons that supplied our magic decreased. When Shayla flew away and took her mates with her, the border dissolved completely. Why didn't this spell?" He didn't want to think what kind of sorcery kept the dragons in SeLenicca. Who could be stronger than a dragon?

Robb made no reply. A quick glance over his shoulder told Marcus that his friend's eyes crossed almost to opposite sockets as he stroked his beard.

"Another puzzle that I must think on," Robb replied after several moments.

"If you don't let your eyes straighten out, Robb, they will remain crossed forever," he chided his friend.

Robb apparently didn't hear him, but remained deep in contemplation.

Marcus reached higher. His shoulders and back ached and his face burned from the previous scrape. If he didn't have an audience, he just might give up and go find a dark corner where he could vent his frustration by stomping a few of the monstrous spiders that thrived in this place. Then he'd nurse his hurts in private.

He edged closer to the top of the wall where it joined the taller gatehouse tower.

At last his left hand clutched the rounded top. Then he pushed high enough to fling his right arm over the top stone and brace his weight. A shout of triumph burst out of his laboring lungs.

It died before it passed his lips. Magical power jolted up his arm to his neck and head. His ears rang and a numbness grew in his head. The blankness spread and he lost his grip. He couldn't find the other wall with his back. His feet went slack.

He knew he fell, but he couldn't feel a thing.

He *did* hear Robb droning on about *his* theory of how one would create such an enduring protective spell that would not disintegrate with the loss of the dragons.

"That *s'murghin'* containment spell is killing my luck," Marcus cursed.

* * *

These men who seek to steal my power are either too stubborn for their own health or too stupid to survive. They have not responded to the dreams of portent I sent them, nor to the subtle persuasion of a kardiaquake. I must think anew. I have time. I am not going anywhere.

* * *

"Your Grace?" Jack hissed to King Darville and Queen Rossemikka from the cover of a flowering shrub in the queen's private garden.

The king stopped quickly, gaze darting for the source the whisper. His hand reached for the ceremonial short sword he always wore on his right hip.

Queen Mikka's fingers arched away from the arm of her husband that she had clung to as they walked. She opened her mouth in a silent hiss, revealing small pointed teeth.

Her eyes narrowed, and the pupils showed as definite vertical slits. Jack suspected that her back arched as well and the hairs on her neck stood up. But her richly textured gown fell in wide folds all around her, disguising her posture.

The gown hung too heavily on her thin frame. Since her last miscarriage—a very dangerous one that had required Brevelan and Jaylor to transport to the capital to heal her—Mikka had been listless and pale with little appetite. If Jack did not succeed with his special project soon, she might die of a broken heart.

"Your Grace, it's only me." Jack half rose from his crouched position, then ducked quickly back within the broad leaves and abundant red blossoms. He wanted to sneeze away the heavy perfume of the flowers, but didn't dare. Even here, guards trailed behind the royal couple. Two of them, Jack suspected of being at least spies for the Gnuls, if not actual witch-sniffers. And they closed in upon the royal couple, alerted by Darville's startlement.

After his conversation with Aquilla, he suspected more people than he had this morning. He dared not use even the tiniest of spells as long as any of these men were present.

Darville soothed his wife with a gentle hand to her mane of multicolored hair. She leaned into his caress and kissed his palm.

"I need to speak with you privately, Your Grace."

"My office. You are on duty later today."

"This won't wait, and there are too many curious people hanging around the barracks. I can't get in there yet to change to a clean uniform," Jack insisted. He'd dried his tunic and trews as best he could before Aquilla's fire, but the uniform was crumpled and stained, not fit to be worn in the king's presence.

"Your Grace, what do you fear?" Sergeant Fred asked. He held his functional battle sword at the ready while he scanned the bushes and tree branches for signs of an enemy. Equally alert, his five attending soldiers spread out in a wide circle.

Jack trusted Fred. The slightly older soldier had been with the king for a number of years as personal bodyguard and confidant. Of all the palace guard, only Fred knew Jack's true reason for being in the capital disguised as another trusted soldier.

"Only a bird scuttling in the bushes after a worm, Sergeant," Darville dismissed the six hovering attendants.

Fred gestured to the men to retreat the required ten paces to grant the king and queen an illusion of privacy.

Rossemikka bent to sniff at the red blossoms that concealed Jack from mundane eyes. Her fingers relaxed and when she blinked, her eyes had returned to a normal round pupil.

Darville rubbed the back of his wrist idly. Were the red weals beneath his fingertips cat scratches? The queen must be in a high state of agitation if she allowed the cat persona trapped within her to rise to the surface so readily. She hadn't scratched her husband in weeks.

"Are you any closer to finding a cure for me?" the queen asked in her slightly accented voice. She hailed from the desert kingdom of Rossemeyer where the land was so harsh, the people traded for all of their food and most of their household goods with mercenaries and the fiery liquor called *beta'arack*. "I would be rid of this cat."

"Alas, Your Grace, no. I wish I had found the proper spell. I came today to warn you both of extreme danger. A boatload of witch-sniffers arrived at the port islands this morning." Three islands at the edge of deep water in the Great Bay marked the sailing limit for large vessels. Only shallow draft barges piloted by Guild of Bay Pilot members could negotiate the mudflats of the inner bay. "They await transport into the city. Another one hundred are due to arrive next week. Some of these foreign seekers are extremely sensitive. They may 'smell' the cat within you since it was put there by magic."

Jack checked the position of the soldiers. The two he suspected had inched forward, right arms slightly extended and circling. They kept the signature gesture of a witch-sniffer subtle. But Jack knew they sought him.

Darville must have seen them as well. He shifted his position so that he stood between his beloved queen and the sniffers. Years ago, before he ascended to the throne, Darville had been kidnapped by his cousin, the rogue magician Krej, and ensorcelled into the body of a golden wolf. When Jaylor had rescued him and exposed the plot, Darville had fallen ill from the effects of too many spells being cast upon a mundane within too short a time. The illness had given the Council of Provinces reason to deny him the crown for many moons.

He could always claim that the sniffers smelled him and not his queen who did have magic in her blood even before the cat had joined her in that body.

"Why don't you just dismiss those men?" Jack mused, not realizing he had spoken until he heard his words.

"Because the Gnuls control my council. Any retaliation against them brings worse reprisals against innocents. I am only the first among equals, not a tyrant. I must defer to the wishes of the lords who help me govern," the king said sadly. "I thought I had pounded some sense into them, but apparently not."

"What will we do, Darville?" Rossemikka turned wide, frightened eyes up to her husband. Her fingers curled again. The cat wanted dominance.

"What we always do. Dissemble, divert, claim they persecute us with unfounded accusations merely to overthrow me and claim the throne for themselves."

"They can't depose you, Your Grace. Your coronation was dragon-blessed. Thousands witnessed B—" he couldn't say the true name of the blue-tipped dragon out loud. The secret of Baamin's origins must remain secret a while longer. "They all saw the same thing I saw. The dragons blessed your crown and your queen."

"But no one has seen a dragon since. Before and after my coronation, the dragon nimbus remained in exile. Baamin returned only long enough to show himself at the coronation." The king grinned widely, letting Jack know that not much remained secret from him.

"Our enemies have grown in strength while the dragons remained in SeLenicca. They now discount the reality of the dragons you returned to Coronnan. The Gnuls will try to kill any dragons who show themselves, claiming them the spawn of Simurgh."

"But what do you want me to do about the influx of witch-sniffers?"

"Can you whip up a storm that will strand them in the port for a time?"

"I don't dare with those two watching everything in the palace so closely."

"Then we must invent a disease that will close the port to all people, but not goods."

"That I can do, Your Grace. I have a friend who will gladly dispense a convincing rumor." Jack eased backward through the clump of bushes until he stood on a path well hidden from the view of the guards. Within moments he was running back to Aquilla, just like when he was nothing more than a scullery lad and wharf rat needing protection from bullies. Gnuls, bullies, what was the difference?

Chapter 10

Lanciar tried hard to think in convoluted circles like a Rover. The more he drank, the straighter the path his mind followed. In the end, logic prevailed. Lanciar left Hanassa by the same dizzyingly steep path he had entered the haven for outlaws—on foot.

Zolltarn could not have transported his entire clan and all of their goods far. That much magic was unprecedented, even if the entire Rover clan joined the spell. Logic also told Lanciar that the Rovers must head for Coronnan and the Commune of Magicians. No one else would value the statue of Lord Krej. And no Rover would steal something unless it held value to someone. Besides, Zolltarn had deserted the coven for the Commune three years ago.

Was the entire adventure merely a ploy to lead Rejiia to the Commune? If so, then he had a better chance of claiming his son by following the Rovers into Coronnan than treading in Rejiia's footsteps.

Rumors claimed the dragons had returned to the Commune. Neither Rejiia, nor the entire coven—especially with its depleted numbers—could stand against a Commune united by dragon magic. Dragon magic had its limits when wielded by a single magician. But unlike the coven's blood rituals that enhanced power, or the Rovers' secret ceremonies, dragon magic allowed talented men to join their talents, augmenting the strength of every spell by orders of magnitude. With this united power they could impose laws, ethics, and honor upon their members, and overcome all those who opposed them.

Fortunately for the Rovers, the coven, and solitary magicians, their honor and ethics kept them from going to war against their own people to wrest political power from the Gnostic Utilitarian cult.

Once more he wondered if his old adversary Jack had managed to return the dragons to Coronnan or if he had died beneath the rubble of Queen's City. "We'll have to see if Jack awakened the ability to gather dragon magic as well as my other magical powers," Lanciar mused.

If it would help regain his son, Lanciar would join the Commune and submit to the limitations and laws of dragon magic in order to negate the power of Rejiia and the coven and the Gnuls.

Once outside the volcanic crater of Hanassa, Lanciar found a thin ley line deep within the surface of the kardia. He drew its meager energies into him. Weak power infiltrated his blood. He needed to get farther away from the mountain fastness before he'd have access to more power.

Three deep breaths triggered his light trance. He used his power to levitate himself down the zigzag path of stairs cut into the steep cliff's side. He kept his eyes firmly on the steps rather than evaluate the deadly drop-off into the ravine below. One false step would send him careening down the mountain. Levitation—exhausting though it was—was less daunting than walking.

A simple thing like looking down this near vertical cliff should not make his stomach queasy and detach his head from his shoulders. He'd spent most of his life training to be a soldier. He should be able to tackle any physical challenge. He'd faced death in battle many times. He'd killed men before, in battle and in magical sacrifice. Still his head reeled if he looked beyond the path.

At the bottom of the cliff, some three hundred feet below Hanassa's plateau, the land leveled out and showed signs of a little more rainfall than on the desert plateau. Scrawny shrubs and a few fistfuls of grass clung to precious bits of dirt beside the path. Indeed, the path became a road broad enough for men to walk two and three abreast with pack steeds. Two miles farther on, an inn perched precariously atop another cliff beside a thundering waterfall. Caravans and their beasts camped across the river from the inn. A wobbly bridge strung together with odd bits of rope and mismatched planks spanned the rushing stream.

Lanciar's head spun at the thought of crashing through the bridge into the river and then plummeting over the cataract onto the broken rocks one hundred feet below. He gulped and turned his eyes and attention away from such thoughts.

Three pairs of men wrestled in the inn's forecourt, exchanging blows. The pointless brawl spread to several of the spectators. Lanciar spat in the dust in disgust. "Waste of energy and discipline. If you were part of my army, I'd have all of you flogged."

Rejiia might aspire to the title of Kaalipha of Hanassa, but she didn't have the discipline to organize the city, only to terrorize it. Lanciar could do it. If he wanted to. The people of Coronnan, SeLenicca, and Rossemeyer would rise up in rebellion against her tyranny. She'd not last long as queen of any place. Lanciar had to retrieve his son before Rejiia put the boy in the way of vengeful assassins.

Lanciar walked a little way past the inn. He paused, drinking in the colors of the place and the clean smell of the air. Green grass beside the river, red tile roof, bright yellow mud walls, a shrub or two, and bright tents in a variety of colors—red, purple, green, and blue. But mostly the tents were the red and purple with black trim of Zolltarn's clan. A dozen or more dark-haired men and women, dressed in the same colors as the tents, worked hard to rig the tents and start cooking fires.

Indeed, the Rovers had not gone far.

How to approach them undetected? And how to find his son among the numerous babies he'd seen in packs on the backs of the clan women?

He went into the inn and ordered an ale. The first one slid down his throat in welcome relief. He needed to replenish his bodily reserves after the long levitation down the mountain with only a faint and spindly ley line to fuel his talent. Another ale and a meal sent the magic humming through his body once more.

He took his third ale outside while he watched the Rover camp. A pleasant buzz accompanied him. A placid smile spread through him as he sought a place to sit.

"This is too nice a day to do more than watch other people work." He settled onto a bench at the back of the inn beside the corral, beneath a spreading hardwood tree. He didn't know the variety and frankly did not care since it bore plain blue/green leaves rather than the pink-veined, thick and oily foliage of a Tambootie tree.

He could eat a few leaves of the Tambootie to enhance his magic. No. He wasn't that desperate yet. King Simeon's insanity near the end had been caused by addiction to the leaves. He suspected Rejiia's instability stemmed from an overuse of Tambootie as well.

But where the Tambootie grew, dragons flew. Tambootie provided essential nutrients to the huge, winged beasts. Those nutrients allowed them to emit magical energy magicians could gather.

Lanciar opened himself to the air, as if drinking in the power contained within the ley lines that crisscrossed the planet. Nothing.

He'd try again later, deeper into Coronnan where dragons might fly once more.

At first the tents and activity across the rapid stream seemed all a jumble. He might have dozed a bit, lulled by the buzz of insects, the warm air, and the ale. Bright colors flowed behind his closed eyes like the umbilicals of life one saw in the void between the planes of existence.

Travel in the void was dangerous, both physically and mentally. He'd known fledgling magicians who went insane and killed themselves after viewing unspeakable truths about themselves in the void.

He jerked awake and saw anew the arrangement of tents. The black, brown, and dusty green shelters clustered together with their backs to the more garish Rover tents. As in the rest of life, ordinary travelers had turned their backs on the Rovers.

The Rovers gathered their tents and sledges in a large circle around a common cook fire with smaller campfires before each flapping opening. A few of the round huts atop the sledges—bardos, he'd heard them called—had been pressed into service as small dwellings to complete the circle.

Lanciar smiled to himself. Zolltarn must reside in the largest purple tent with red-and-black trim.

Lanciar hunted for some sign of the statue of Krej in the vicinity of that tent. Surely Zolltarn would want to display his trophy.

The tin weasel with flaking gilt paint remained elusive.

A middle-aged woman with streaks of gray in her hair directed a myriad of younger women who scurried about the big tent. She could only be the wife of the chieftain.

Three of the five young women—two still teenagers—bore the signs of pregnancy; one barely showing, one about midway along, the third about to pop. Zolltarn's wives or daughters? The other two girls remained youthfully slim and unburdened with children.

"I doubt I'll find my boy there." He turned his attention to the next tent in line. Three women, three infants. His eyes focused more closely on this campfire. All three infants bore the dark hair common to Rovers—but then so did Rejiia. He dared not hope any child of his union with the witch would result in a blue-eyed blond of the true-blood of SeLenicca. Two of the infants toddled out of their mothers' laps to play in the dirt. The third appeared the size of a child somewhere between three and six moons old. The proper age for Lanciar's son.

He sent a tendril of silvery magic across the bridge and into the Rover encampment.

At that moment Rejiia walked through his magical thread, breaking the connection. She paused before the woman cradling the infant.

Lanciar cursed and tried again to listen to the conversation. He caught only a few words.

"I seek . . . wet nurse . . . Kestra. . . . told to ask . . . claim my son," Rejiia commanded. She stood straight and tall, as regal as the queen she claimed to be.

The Rover woman laughed out loud. Lanciar heard her all the way across the rushing stream without magic. "Kestra, first daughter of Zolltarn, disappeared nearly twenty years ago. Have you not heard the legend of the missing girl and her miracle child? Rovers still seek them."

"Simurgh shit on you! Where is my son?" Rejiia screamed and stamped her foot. Enough magic compulsion accompanied her words to threaten a kardiaquake.

Lanciar braced himself, but the land absorbed Rejiia's frustration.

"If you gave us a child, Lady Sorcerer, then the child is ours. Now go back to your schemes and your politics. As for the child, if he did not die of disease or malnutrition or was not stoned by fearful *gadjé*, then he is lost to you forever." The woman continued to smile, but her eyes narrowed and her muscles tightened in defense.

"Take me to Zolltarn! He cannot steal from me. I'll have the statue of my father from him, now. And my son. The time has come to find a new wet nurse. Zolltarn owes me for his betrayal of the coven. He must not refuse. If he does, he will suffer the wrath of the coven!"

"Zolltarn can refuse anyone. Rovers have no fear of your coven. Zolltarn owes what he chooses to owe. Our debts are not always honored as *gadjé* sluts would. Go away, Lady Sorcerer. Run back to your broken coven."

Bloody Simurgh's hell! thought Lanciar. Rejiia had alerted the Rovers to her pursuit. They'd hide the baby as well as the statue of Krej where no one without Rover blood could find them. Lanciar would never get close enough to separate his son from all of the other children running around the camp.

He'd not take just any child. He wanted his own son, blood of his blood.

Blood.

The boy's blood would shine through his life force when viewed from the void.

Simurgh take them all, I'll have to go into the void by myself, without an anchor to this world. I never thought I'd want to see you again, Jack. But I could use your help right now.

"*S'murghit*, I think I need another drink of this steed-piss ale."

Chapter 11

From Aquilla's boat, Jack hastened back to the palace. He trusted the Bay Pilot to pick out one passenger with cool clammy skin and wobbling balance from sea sickness—there was always at least one even in the calmest of seas—and proclaim him ill from some exotic plague. Aquilla had the authority to quarantine all of the passengers. By sunset, the entire load of witch-sniffers would be back aboard their boat and headed out to sea flying a yellow flag of quarantine.

Jack did not trust the witch-sniffers already in the city to cease their torment of innocents. Katrina, his betrothed, was a prime target for Gnul persecution because she hailed from a foreign land and had no legal spouse to protect her.

Once changed into a decent uniform, he sneaked through the palace toward the inner courtyard that caught and held the sunlight. It was there Katrina chose to work at her lace pillow.

He couldn't allow her to delay their marriage any longer.

"Name the day, Katrina." Jack kissed his love on the forehead. He brushed his fingers along the long plaits of silver-gilt hair. She dropped her head onto his chest, hiding her face. He tugged on the plaits where they joined into a single thick rope below her nape, bringing her eyes up to meet his again.

Fear of the witch-sniffers made him jumpy. He had to keep a calm face and manner so Katrina would not panic.

The drone of bees flitting from flower to flower in this private courtyard within the palace sounded loud in his ears, but not as loudly as the pounding of his heart.

"Just tell me when, and I will meet you in any temple in Coronnan City to say my vows to any priest. Just name the day," he pleaded. Once they were married, he might convince King Darville to hasten his promised appointment as ambassador to SeLenicca. Then he could leave the witch-sniffers and their rabid accusations behind before they threatened Katrina.

"I . . . I . . . Jack, I'm afraid," she replied as she turned pale blue eyes up to him.

He wanted nothing more than to wrap his arms around her and protect her from her inner demons as well as from the Gnuls for the rest of their lives.

Since the death of his familiar—a cranky jackdaw with tufts of white feathers over his eyes that looked like Old Baamin's bushy white eyebrows—he'd been empty, emotionally lost. Only Katrina made him feel whole again. With her beside him, he might not need another familiar.

What he needed was to get her out of town.

"You led me across Queen's City during a massive kardiaquake." He brushed a light kiss across her brow. "You bandaged a dragon wing with a special piece of magic lace." He kissed both of her cheeks. She started melting into him, losing the rigidity in her spine. "And you helped me battle the coven with tremendous courage, Katrina. What could you possibly fear after that?"

"I . . . I fear you, Jack." She looked pointedly at his palace guard uniform. The uniform must remind her of the violence inflicted upon one and all by palace guards in Queen's City. The inhabitants of her home tolerated, almost encouraged, that violence. They claimed it kept them safe from contamination by outlanders.

"I fear the intensity of your love for me," Katrina admitted. "I'm not certain I can return it. After Brunix . . . You know what he did to me. How can I love any man after that?"

Jack held her face protectively against his chest rather than look at the tears in her eyes. Neeles Brunix, half-Rover, opportunist, and unscrupulous businessman, had owned Katrina and her lacemaking talent for three years. The coven had murdered Brunix and framed Jack for the crime.

"Brunix loved you, too, in his own twisted way," Jack cajoled. "He loved his possessions because he owned them rather than owning them because he loved them. He did not touch you out of anger, Katrina. In time, the scars he left on your heart will fade. When you are ready, I will be waiting for you."

"I fear you must wait a very long time. I can't ask you to do that, Jack. I love you too much to keep you from finding someone who can return your love." She broke away from his embrace and turned her back on him.

Suddenly the little courtyard where she had set up her lace bolster seemed too small to contain all of Jack's panic. How could he get permission to take her away from here unless they were married?

"I'll always love you." He reached out for her but let his hand drop back to his side before he touched her. If she did not marry him, how could he protect her?

"Perhaps by the time you figure out how to separate the queen from the cat spirit that also inhabits her body, I will be ready to love you properly." That project had occupied the finest magical minds for over three years without success.

She fingered the wide piece of lace she had been working on when he sneaked into the courtyard.

"I'm nearly ready to try the spell, Katrina." He had a few ideas but not yet enough to try the spell. Right now, though, he'd try anything to get Katrina out of the city. "As soon as we know the queen is back to being one person in one body, King Darville will dispatch me to SeLenicca as ambassador. I need you to come with me as my wife. Only together will we be able to help rebuild your country."

She looked over her shoulder at him, a hopeful smile tugging at her lips. "Home."

"Barely. SeLenicca is changed, torn apart by war and natural catastrophe. Your family is gone. The lacemaking industry is in tatters. Nothing will be as you remember. But it is your home. You belong there. Here you will always be a political refugee, no matter how much the queen favors you." One foray into the marketplace could bring the witch-sniffers down on her as it had on the dye merchant.

"Will you be able to use your magic to revive Queen

Miranda from her coma?" Katrina asked. Hope shone from her eyes for the first time since Jack had pressed her to marry him. "With our queen restored, SeLenicca will rebuild, stronger than ever before." She rushed back into his arms. "On the day after you cure Queen Rossemikka of Coronnan, I will marry you. Then we will go home, together."

Jack sealed her promise with a fierce kiss. His first assault on her mouth softened, explored possibilities, deepened to a mutual sharing. They were getting good at this. He kissed her again, pulling her tight against his chest.

She fit snugly against him, as if they were two halves of the same mold. A tremendous ache built within him. He deepened the kiss, needing more of her, all of her, forever.

"Home." Katrina repeated when she came up for air. Then she renewed the kiss with vigor and promise.

A playful squeak in the back of Jack's mind alerted him to new observers. He opened one eye and stared into the silvery muzzle of a baby dragon perched on the courtyard wall. Bricks sagged and mortar crumbled beneath his purplish talons. Jack's ungainly tag-along might be only a baby—barely two full years old—but he already exceeded a pack steed in size and weight. He'd grown rapidly in the past months since Jack had first made contact with the dragons.

The stub of his slightly-askew spiral forehead horn also glowed with the identifying color—the rarest of all dragons. That all-important horn might never grow to its full length the way Amaranth kept stumbling and falling on it.

Jack had tried to match the dye to Amaranth's pinky-purple-tipped wingtips, and talons. What had happened to the dye merchant?

He took a long deep breath, anticipating the dragon magic that would soon fill him, augmenting the power he drew from the ley lines that wove a lacy network beneath the kardia in Coronnan.

"Where did you come from, Amaranth? And where is your mama?" Jack asked aloud, reaching to touch the baby. He could communicate with this dragon mind-to-mind, but Katrina could not. He'd developed a premature rapport with Amaranth when he'd tried gathering dragon magic from him in order to heal the mother dragon's injured wing. The spell had failed, but the bond with Amaranth was sealed long before the baby was mature enough to understand it or cope with the emotions evoked. He barely had the vocabulary to communicate more than his emotions—which he broadcast loudly in a wide band.

At the moment, happiness with a touch of mischief radiated from the baby dragon.

"You must not be seen here, Amaranth. While the Gnostic Utilitarians dominate the Council of Provinces, magic and dragons remain illegal." Jack tried discouraging the dragon. Dragon safety had always come from their elusiveness and near invisibility. Amaranth had trouble understanding the concept of danger.

"Amaranth?" Katrina squealed in delight. She jumped away from Jack and hurried to the wall where she reached up to scratch the baby's muzzle. He opened his mouth and drooled in ecstasy. His meat-ripping fangs bent slightly backward, curved over his lower jaw at a near useless angle—damaged from one too many stumbles while the teeth were forming and vulnerable. Amaranth hadn't made much success as a dragon.

A dozen bricks from the top of Amaranth's perch tumbled to the ground at Katrina's feet. She dodged them neatly.

"Amaranth, where is Shayla, your mama?" Jack asked again, worried about the safety of the wall as well as the baby. More mortar broke away from the courtyard wall as he watched. Six bricks on the top tilted precariously, ready to fly in odd directions.

He placed his hands on the wall just beneath Amaranth. His fingertips touched the dragon's talons; enough contact to allow the dragon energies to flood him. He used the magic to shore up the wall and replace the discarded bricks.

He hoped the legend that witch-sniffers had more difficulty detecting dragon magic than solitary powers was true.

The dragon nibbled delicately on Jack's hair. At the brief contact more magic dusted him. But it would evaporate the moment Jack ceased touching the dragon.

Amaranth squeaked something in juvenile dragon talk.

Jack interpreted his emotions rather than the scattered images. He caught a glimpse of Shayla soaring over the Bay on a never-ending hunt to feed her twelve voracious babies. Amaranth had seen his mother's absence as permission to find Jack for a romp in the Bay. And he'd only fallen on his nose twice trying to launch into flight.

"No swimming today, Amaranth." Jack joined Katrina in scratching the dragonet. The magic filled his being. As long as he touched a purple-tipped dragon, he could use the power that traditional magicians gathered from the air. His inability to gather dragon magic in the normal way would always isolate him from his fellow magicians, despite his master status and membership in the Commune.

The flood of magic allowed him to find another weak spot in the wall. He used some of the power to strengthen more of the stressed mortar and bricks.

The magic and contact with Amaranth also told him how much the bruised horn hurt. He wanted to reach up and soothe it, find a way to straighten and restore it to normal size. But the dragon had to learn from his mistakes or he would not survive long.

Jack feared that his friend would not survive at all. According to dragon lore, only one purple-tipped dragon could live at any one time, and they were always born twins. Iianthe, Amaranth's twin, exhibited a great deal more grace, caution, and intelligence than this enthusiastic toddler.

But Jack loved this baby and hated the idea of him being sacrificed merely to satisfy dragon tradition. If only there was some way to adopt this baby, to take him to SeLenicca along with Katrina . . .

Amaranth lowered his head for attention to his itchy horn.

"Yes, I see how big the horn grows," Jack cooed. Though it looked more swollen than growing. "But you can't stay here, Amaranth. You need to go home until your mama brings you to the city. You could get hurt if one of the Gnuls sees you."

The Gnuls used the same tactics of fear as the coven to gain followers.

His years of slavery in King Simeon's mines had taught

him that violence only begets more violence and the innocent are the ones who are hurt the most. Innocents like the dye merchant and Katrina.

The next squeak from Amaranth sounded like a pout.

"I have work to do for King Darville, Amaranth," Jack apologized to the dragonet for not joining his games in the Bay. "Katrina has lace to make. We can't play today. I'll come to the lair soon and we'll spend some time together."

(Lace?) The human word formed decisively in Jack's mind. A picture of the lace shawl that Katrina had used to patch Shayla's wing after Jack's healing spell had failed followed. Though Shayla's magically damaged wing had grown back whole and strong, the lace bandage had left its imprint permanently in the membrane.

(Make lace for my wings?) The dragonet spread and flapped his stubby wings. *(Make my wings pretty with lace?)* Jack translated for the dragonet.

"Your wings are beautiful as they are, Amaranth," Katrina reassured the baby. "You don't need lace. Though I wish I could find a dye to match you for my newest lace pattern. For now, you just need to grow big and strong like your mama, safely back in your own lair."

Another pout.

"Where's your twin brother, Amaranth? Iianthe must be lonely without you." Jack tried to persuade the dragonet to leave.

(Don't want Iianthe. Want Jack.)

Already the twins must sense the separation soon to come.

An idea hit Jack like one of the dislodged bricks from the wall.

A grin spread across his face and lightened his soul. Some of his problems crumbled like the wall where Amaranth perched.

"Amaranth, there is one way you can stay and play with me forever."

The dragonet and Katrina cocked their heads in curiously similar gestures of acute listening. Jack's heart swelled with possibilities and love for them both.

He smiled fondly at them and the image they presented. Family. His family.

"As a purple dragon, a very rare and special being, either you or Iianthe must give up your dragon form soon."

The dragon nodded sagely, suddenly more mature and experienced than any two-year-old had a right to be.

"If you transform into a catlike creature, you can help me entice Rosie the cat out of Queen Mikka. Then you can stay with me forever as my familiar. As a dragon, you must make a lair of your own and live alone."

Perhaps, as a cat, Amaranth would lose a little of his awkwardness. Jack had never known a clumsy cat.

"This is a really important task, Amaranth. I really need your help."

As long as Rosie remained joined to Rossemikka, the queen's body would be unbalanced and she could not produce the heir that the country needed so badly for stability. The Gnuls preyed on that instability to spread their litany of fear.

(An elegant solution to our problems, Jack,) Shayla said from a great distance.

Jack sensed her presence, high above the city as she soared on a thermal. He knew she would not be too far away while one of her brood explored the world.

"You agree with the plan?" he asked.

Katrina struck an acute listening pose as well. Ever since she had bandaged Shayla's wing with the unique lace shawl woven of Tambrin thread spun from the Tambootie trees, she had shared a rapport with the dragon.

(How did you know that one of the two forms a redundant purple dragon may take is the flywacket?)

"Flywacket? What's a flywacket?"

(A creature that has not been seen in this land in many generations of humans, but thanks to you, one will once again grace us with its wisdom and life force.)

Somehow grace and wisdom did not fit Amaranth.

"Flywacket, huh? If everyone agrees, we can try it tonight."

"So soon?" Katrina's eyes grew wide with just a touch of panic.

"Tonight! In the central grove on Sacred Isle. There should be enough space there for Shayla and Amaranth and everyone else."

He remembered with joy the day he had found his magician's staff within one of the sacred oaks there. Performing the greatest spell of his life should take place in the same sacred grove. A few weeks ago he thought bringing the dragons home and defeating Rejiia should have been the magical achievement of a lifetime. What awaited him after this?

"Why wait another day? Queen Mikka has been waiting three years to be rid of that cat. Tonight I perform the spell. Tomorrow we will marry. The day after we journey to SeLenicca." He kissed Katrina soundly, wanting to linger. But the logistics of the magic pulled at his concentration. "I have to leave now, love. A spell of this magnitude requires a lot of preparation."

Amaranth squealed in delight. His dragon language rose shrill and piercing. Jack and Katrina both covered their ears rather than linger with another kiss.

"Uh, Shayla, will you call your dragonet? He's making a shambles of this wall and our eardrums."

A dragonlike chuckle sounded in the back of Jack's head. A moment later Amaranth cocked his head and obediently, but clumsily, flapped his ungainly wings for a launch. The dragonet tilted dangerously forward, nearly brushing his nose against a prickly rosebush.

Jack dashed forward to make sure the dragonet didn't bump his muzzle and sensitive horn bud—again—when he crashed into the paving.

At the last minute, Amaranth got enough air under his wings and cleared the courtyard by a talon length. Moments later he disappeared into the air, one more silvery distortion of light on this bright spring day.

"Tonight, my love. I'll do the spell tonight. Trust me, everything will be all right. Then we'll go home to SeLenicca." Jack promised.

"I trusted you with my life when all of SeLenicca conspired against me," she replied, looking at her threads rather than him.

"Tomorrow we will wed." He kissed her again, cherishing the warmth of her body in his arms. "Trust me. We will be happy together. I'll never hurt you. Ever."

Chapter 12

Vareena opened the sagging gates of the monastery. She must remember to send Yeenos with a work party to repair the hinges.

The villagers grumbled about the extra—and to them unnecessary—work of keeping the old site in good repair. Some, led by Yeenos himself, had refused outright when she'd requested repairs to the broken gutters last moon. She wondered how many more times she could command them.

If the orders had come from Lord Laislac, they would obey without question. But since they came from her, a spinster no man wanted, they questioned their duty constantly.

Did her mother and grandmother have the same trouble with recalcitrant villagers?

What she really needed right now was a bolt of lightning, judiciously aimed at a few reluctant backsides.

Instead, she had two new ghosts to cater to, just when she thought she'd get a rest from her duties and a chance to escape.

The silver-and-amethyst amulet weighed heavily against her neck. It seemed to taunt her with broken promises of freedom; from her duties, from the scorn of the villagers, from her brothers.

She kept the amulet hidden beneath her shift lest her family steal it from her.

Early sunshine barely penetrated to the monastery court-yard through the ever-present haze. The mist seemed thicker today. "Good morning!" she called cheerfully. In all this

haze she'd not see her ghosts easily. They'd have to come
to her today. With direct light or within the building, she
could see them quite easily as misty outlines with hints of
color in their clothing. Hair and eye color tended to bleach
out with only vague suggestions of fair or dark. Out here,
with the light scattering in all directions and lingering nowhere, even those brief hints of their presence evaporated.

If she couldn't see them, could she pretend they did not
exist and make her escape to the promised acres in Nunio?

No. These two new ghosts had only recently passed into
their amorphous existence. They needed her.

She took a moment to stand beside the fresh grave
among the foundation stones of the original temple in the
southeast corner. When the magicians and priests abandoned this place, they had dismantled the house of worship
to prevent desecration. "Stargods, watch over your servant
Farrell as he passes to his next existence. Guide him with
your wisdom. And grant his family peace in accepting his
death though they have heard nothing from him in over
two years."

Silence hung so heavy in this corner that she wondered
if her prayer had escaped any better than any of her ghosts.

Prayers complete, she searched for traces of Marcus'
magician-blue tunic, trews, and sash. She suspected the
color matched his eyes exactly. Robb on the other hand,
with dark, hooded eyes that brooded mysteriously, favored
black for all but his identifying tunic and cloak.

She worried about him. He hadn't accepted his transition
to ghosthood with Marcus' good humor and optimism.

"Over here, Vareena," Marcus called to her.

Without seeing him, she sensed the smile behind his
voice. Her own lips curved upward in response. He told
wonderfully funny accounts of their journeys. He made her
laugh when her life seemed so hopeless. She searched the
curtain wall on the other side of the gatehouse tower for
signs of his vague outline.

"No, I'm over here by the well," Marcus called again.

Vareena turned toward the stone circle that enclosed the
pool of water. It had once provided for over one hundred
men. Now it served only two. She trusted Marcus to direct

her correctly. She'd never had a ghost trick her. Or lie to her—unlike the people of her village.

"I brought you breakfast," she said to the air, hoping she directed her words in the proper direction. She'd waited four days to come back. Ghosts never needed to eat more than once or twice a week.

"Thanks, I'm hungry." The trencher of bread and cheese covered by a plain linen cloth floated from her hands. Ghosts could touch inanimate objects in this world, but not a living being. Life energies generated a barrier that repelled ghosts from humans and humans from ghosts.

"Did anyone ever tell you how beautiful you are, Vareena?" Marcus asked. "I would compose poetry to you, but you defy the limitation of words."

She dismissed his admiration. Other ghosts had told her as much. They had no one else to speak to, share their thoughts with, or pass the idle hours. Of course they fell in love with her, or her mother before her, or her grandmother before that.

If she were as beautiful as they claimed, then some normal man would have claimed her as his wife by now.

Nothing could come of Marcus' flirtations. These men were ghosts, after all. And she must cater to them until they died. Quite likely these two could last for the rest of her life rather than a bare two years.

"Step into shadows, so I can see you, please." She continued to search the area around the well for some trace of distorted light or a wisp of mist.

There! The outline of Robb, the dark and brooding one, materialized on the far side of the well as he slumped to sit on the ground with his back against the stone circle.

"Why bother eating," Robb grumbled. "We're trapped here until we die. Might as well hasten the process and get on into our next existence."

His dark eyes burned through the mist of the gloaming into her soul.

"I wish I could help you," she murmured. Her entire body ached for him, trapped here with no hope.

And then she realized that she ached for herself as well.

"Coronnan is doomed. We'll never find the dragons and

return magic to the Commune. Without dragon magic and controls, the lords will tear the country apart. Three hundred years of peace will evaporate like mist in sunshine. I wonder if this gloom ever evaporates. Everything is lost because we sought shelter here during a storm." Robb buried his face in his hands.

"Is he always so gloomy?" Vareena asked, wary of her own sensitivity to his emotions.

"No. I can usually persuade him to look on the bright side." Marcus moved around the well until he crouched beside Robb. "We'll find a way out of this, friend. We always do. My luck will return. It always does."

"And if your good luck has deserted us permanently? As the dragons deserted Coronnan?" Robb thrust Marcus' placating hand off his arm.

"Then you will develop a plan, like you always do."

"I told you yesterday and the day before, and the day before that, your luck has run out and I never had any."

"There has to be a way out of here. I don't know how or why yet, but there has to be," Vareena said. Did she truly believe that? She must, or she would not have said so.

Her mother had taught her that lies—even those said in comfort—served no purpose. Vareena had never knowingly lied before.

Tentatively, she reached to touch Robb's shoulder, offering what comfort she could—as she would to any living person in the village. Her hand tingled as she neared him. Resolutely she pushed herself closer, resisting the urge to jerk her hand back. The strange sensation in her hand and arm did not really hurt. Felt more like the pinpricks when she lay too long with her weight on a hand or foot.

At last she made contact with him—almost. Her hand did not so much pass through as curve around a soft mass, not quite liquid, not quite solid. Then the barrier of energy broke through her willpower and thrust her hand aside.

Her hand and arm had not faded when she touched the ghost, however briefly.

Robb looked at her. All of his hurt and despair poured from him into her. Her heart twisted and found a new rhythm.

The world seemed to shift beneath her feet as she sought a new destiny. One that included this sorrowful man.

"I brought a deck of cartes to help pass the time." She proffered the painted sheets of pressed wood.

Robb took them from her. He shuffled them idly. "Maybe I can finally win a game with Marcus now that his luck has deserted him. That's about the only good that's come out of this mess."

"I will help you find a way out of this," Vareena vowed. Her heart ached for the sadness that made Robb's shoulders slump and his mouth frown. "I promise on my sacred duty to serve the ghosts that haunt this place, that I will find a way to help you back into this existence. We will end the curse of this place so that no one becomes a ghost here again." *Perhaps then I will finally be able to claim my acres in Nunio and be free.*

       *   *   *

Robb stood in the shadows of the north tower above the kitchen and refectory watching Marcus watch Vareena. After hours playing a complex three-handed game of cartes—which Marcus won quite handily—Vareena had left on errands (she said for the night but only a few hours had passed) and returned again while the sun still rode high in the sky.

Part of his heart rejoiced every time Marcus sighed with longing directed at Vareena. If Marcus did truly love the woman—her maturity might give Marcus the steadying influence Robb thought he needed—then Marcus would forget his longtime passion for Margit. Margit would be hurt, of course. But when she healed, then perhaps, if he courted her very carefully, perhaps Robb could win her heart.

Another part of him coiled in anger against his best friend. How could Marcus be so callous? How could he forget Margit so easily? How could he hurt her thus?

He remembered the first time he'd seen Margit. She had met them in the market square near where her mother sold baked goods.

"Tell Jaylor that the queen swears she will educate any daughters she bears in the ways of Rossemeyer. I presume that means she will bare her breasts and cover her hair.

But the Gnuls in the city whisper that magic is not illegal in Rossemeyer and the queen wants her daughters to learn to throw magic." Margit's harsh whisper reached Robb's ears before he realized that Jaylor's spy in the palace had found him before he'd spotted her.

He honed in on the direction of the whisper and spotted several of the queen's maids examining the produce in the cart where Marcus and Robb lounged in seeming idleness. All of the maids were dressed alike in fine green brocade with low bodices and skirts that fell in wide folds to completely cover their shoes. All five of the women had veiled their hair as well. But one of them, the tallest among them, wore her finery awkwardly. She tripped upon the long skirts, had trouble keeping her blond braids confined beneath the gauzy veil and slouched her shoulders in an attempt to hide the vast expanse of her upper breast exposed by the lack of gown.

Robb nudged Marcus with his elbow. They both stared at the girl with open admiration until she eased away from her companions and sent them a withering glance in reprimand. Robb had lowered his eyes in apology. A brief nod of his head acknowledged her whisper as she reached across them to examine a ripe melon.

Marcus continued to stare at her with mouth slightly open. "I think I'm love," he said quietly when the women had moved on.

"You are always in love," Robb returned. A flare of jealousy burned through him. Marcus attracted any number of women and fell in love with most of them in turn. His rejects found solace in Robb's arms.

He'd never loved anyone. But Margit . . . this new apprentice of Jaylor's intrigued him. Margit. He caressed the name in his mind. Margit.

He could love this girl.

But as their friendship developed, Margit clearly preferred Marcus. Robb's best friend had remained faithful to Margit—as faithful as he was capable of being—for nearly three years, never declaring his love for another until now.

Robb had kept his love for Margit a secret for all that time. He heaved a weary sigh, wondering if something good might come of this disastrous quest after all. If he could return to Margit with comfort and companionship while Marcus chased after Vareena . . .

Vareena emptied her carry basket of firewood and kindling at Marcus' feet. Her brother stood in disapproving silence at the gate. But his stern posture broke frequently as he cast weary glances about the courtyard, seeking what he did not have the talent to see.

Robb allowed his eyes to cross slightly as he sought the aura of the man who escorted his sister so diligently. Spikes of orange fear shot through the multiple layers of fire green. A man of passion without a single hint of magical talent.

Vareena, on the other hand, sparkled around the edges of her aura of bright pink and pale yellow. A minor talent that would go unnoticed anywhere but in this haunted monastery.

Then Vareena lifted her eyes from the firewood to search the courtyard. Her gaze rested on Robb for a long moment. He looked away first. The longing that burned in her gaze embarrassed him. He had no interest in her as a woman, only as a helper in this dilemma. His heart truly belonged to Margit and Margit only.

Reluctantly, Vareena turned to her brother and retreated back to her normal world in the village.

Normal. What was normal anymore?

For years he had trained to work only dragon magic and revile anyone who dared tap rogue powers. As magicians had believed for centuries, Robb had held to the tenet that any use of rogue, or solitary magic, had its roots in evil. That had been normal. Then the dragons had left Coronnan, taking their communal magic with them. Over the last three years Robb had come to accept solitary magic as normal. The wandering life he and Marcus led as journeymen carrying out Jaylor's missions had become normal.

How long would he and his best friend be stuck here before this half existence between reality and the void became normal?

He couldn't allow that to happen. Coronnan needed dragons so that honor and respect could be restored to magic and magicians. Only with dragons could magicians combine their powers, have them amplified by orders of magnitude to overcome any solitary magician. The Commune of Magicians was dedicated to enforcing law, ethics, honor, and justice among themselves and throughout Coronnan. He and Marcus were Jaylor's last hope for bringing the female dragon Shayla and her mates home.

Yaakke had failed, having gone missing some three years ago.

Now he and Marcus must remain missing in this hazy gloaming indefinitely.

Didn't that half-haze ever dissipate from the sky? He kicked the stone wall of the tower in his frustration. All he wanted right now was to see honest sunshine reflecting off Margit's blond braids.

In the center of the courtyard Marcus arranged the kindling and wood into an efficient campfire. He snapped his fingers and brought a flamelet of witchfire to his fingertip. It leaped from his hand into the kindling, chewing hungrily at the fuel.

They were ready to try a summons spell again, in broad daylight, when they had a better chance of someone being awake at the University to respond. Possibly the containment spell around the monastery weakened the spell to the point a sleeping magician would not notice the faint hum in the recipient's glass.

Robb moved to Marcus' side, staying slightly behind so he could feed the fire without distracting his friend from his spell.

Marcus acknowledged him with a slight nod as he breathed deeply, in three counts, hold three, out three, hold three. His eyes glazed over, and he stared into the flames, seeing something far, far away. Slowly, deliberately, he brought his square of precious glass up to eye level and recited the ritual words that would summon Jaylor, Senior Magician of the Commune.

Robb fought the urge to dive into his own trance and participate in the spell. If dragon magic were available, he could combine his own talent with Marcus' and boost the power of the spell far beyond the sum of their two talents. Without dragons, he could only monitor his friend and keep the fire going for as long as the spell took to reach across Coronnan to the protected Clearing near the University.

"Flame to flame, glass to glass, like seeking like," Marcus chanted over and over again.

Robb grew cramped sitting cross-legged on the hard-packed surface of the courtyard. He shifted uneasily and fed yet another log onto the fire. The sparks leaped high, greedy for more fuel.

His back ached. He reached out with a tiny magical probe and checked Marcus' pulse. He'd been in trance a long time. Surely Jaylor would answer the thrumming vibration of his glass no matter what time of the day or night. If he couldn't, then an apprentice or another magician would intervene with his own glass and flame. He could not imagine a situation that would keep every magician in the Commune and University away from communication at the same time.

The probe lost contact with Marcus' pulse. Robb risked touching his friend. His skin was cool and had taken on the waxy pallor of exhaustion and hunger.

"Wake up, Marcus. Return to your body and your thoughts. Come back slowly, easily." Robb held his friend's hand, infusing warmth and strength into the chill skin.

Marcus slumped and sighed heavily. His eyelids fluttered. He looked up bleakly. "I couldn't get through. I don't think the spell climbed the walls any better than we did."

"My plan didn't work."

Chapter 13

"**D**id you feel that?" Margit asked Ferrdie and Mikkail. She touched the little shard of glass in her scrip. A moment ago it felt as if it vibrated with a summons. Now it lay quiet again.

For years, during her time as Queen Rossemikka's maid and Jaylor's spy in the capital, the summons spell was the only bit of magic she could work. She had mastered all nuances of that spell very well and should know that characteristic thrumming in her glass.

But now the sensation had dissipated like mist in a fog. A summons did not work that way. The glass should continue to vibrate until the one summoned found a flame and a bit of privacy to answer.

She'd known a spell to linger in her glass for the best part of a day.

"Feel what?" Mikkail returned. He looked up from the text he studied at the long library table. Darkness had driven them inside, otherwise Margit would have insisted they continue their reading beneath a tree in the fresh air. She had chosen a table beneath a shuttered window, which she opened to the night air.

Ferrdie looked around anxiously as if expecting to be beaten for doing his homework.

Since she'd adopted masculine clothing and hairstyle, the boys in her class accepted her more readily, asked her to study and practice with them. WithyReed still did not call upon her in class, but the other masters took her more seriously. Almost as if a gown set up a barrier between them.

Or a challenge. Dressed as a boy, she did not threaten their preconceived ideas about females and magic. She wondered briefly how Brevelan, the wife of the Senior Magician, coped with the archaic attitude.

In asking the question, she knew the answer. Brevelan ignored the masters who treated her as subhuman. That irritated the masters immensely because their lofty opinions meant nothing to the wife of their Senior Magician.

Briefly, Margit explained the strange half-sensation that her glass had interrupted a summons to someone else. Both boys touched their glasses within their scrips. Both shook their heads. Mikkail shrugged his shoulders and returned to the treatise written by the ancient magician named Scarface.

"What's this word, Margit?" He turned the scroll so she could see it.

"Complementary," she replied.

"So the elements of Fire and Air are 'com-ple-men-tar-y'." He sounded each syllable carefully as Margit had taught him, so he'd remember the word next time he saw it.

"And Kardia and Water are complementary. I wonder if one could negate a spell by invoking opposing elements?" she mused.

"An interesting theory you may explore as part of your next advancement test, Margit," Jaylor said from the doorway.

All three apprentices jumped to their feet in respect for the Senior Magician.

"Sit, sit, return to your studies." He waved them back to their stools and their books. He carried his younger son under one arm and a cat on his other shoulder. Lately, he was rarely seen without at least one of his two sons and some of the overflow of animals attracted to the shelter of Brevelan's Clearing. The first Senior Magician in many generations to have a family, he took his duties as a father very seriously—especially now that his wife Brevelan was heavily pregnant again. She needed a break from the excessive energy of her two sons and husband.

"Have any of you seen Master Librarian Lyman?" Jaylor asked, looking about the jumbled shelves of the library. They'd lost a number of books in their years of running from refuge to refuge before building a new University in exile. But they'd retrieved many more books from unexpected sources as silent sympathizers found circuitous ways to send the treasures. Not everyone was willing to consign books to Gnul bonfires. Lyman, the ancient librarian, hadn't managed to sort and shelve them all properly. Nor had he appointed an assistant to help him.

Perhaps Ferrdie? Margit thought the job perfect for her meek friend.

"Dozing in the corner," Margit whispered to Jaylor.

"I'll not wake him then. He needs his rest." Jaylor started to back out of the room.

"Master Jaylor?" Margit stopped him. "Did you just sense a summons gone astray?" Her hand automatically went to her scrip, testing the glass again for residual vibrations.

"Did you?" Jaylor's eyebrows rose nearly to his dark auburn hair.

"Aye, sir. But it . . . evaporated. I've never had anything like that come through my glass before."

"Neither have I. Keep alert, Margit. And work on the paper about opposing elements to negate a spell. You'll find some preliminary explorations on the subject over by the last window on the right. Don't wake Master Lyman. He's getting old and needs his rest." Jaylor quietly left the library.

"Master Lyman was born old," Mikkail muttered.

"I heard he doesn't eat. He just inhales the dust from the books," Ferrdie offered.

Margit had to smile. The boy just might break away from the trap of his fears if he could repeat a joke that had followed apprentices for—forever.

"No, I don't breathe book dust, little boy, I eat apprentices who disturb my nap!" Lyman called from the corner. His wrinkled skin and wispy silver hair almost blended into the shadows as if he were as invisible as a dragon.

Ferrdie cowered behind his book.

"And I was born older than I am now. I don't age, I young," Lyman tugged his beard and winked at Margit. "Now, come along, Margit. Get the study on your topic. Only way you'll make journeyman in time to answer that distress summons you intercepted is to get the paper written and impress the masters that you aren't just a girl."

"Distress summons?" Margit's voice came out on a squeak. The only person she knew who might send a distress summons that would reach her but not Jaylor was Marcus.

Once again she knew a stab of hot fear that her love had been lost and out of communication for many moons.

"Nothing to worry about just yet. He's safe for the moment. But you must push forward to be ready when you need to be."

"How did you know it was a distress summons, Master Lyman?"

"Because I'm older than the oldest dragon, and I've seen it all," the frail old man retorted. "A distress summons that is interrupted is the only summons that hits more than one person like a stab in the side and then evaporates into mist. The sender is lucky someone caught it and is willing to prepare for it. Now, research and write that paper. You don't have enough knowledge and talent to plan ahead as Robb does or to trust in your luck like Marcus does."

"Then I'll have to improvise." She flashed the old man an impish grin.

*   *   *

These intruders have one hundred days. That is all. One hundred days and they die. They will not figure out how to steal my power in that time.

*   *   *

"Tell me a story, M'ma," Jaranda demanded. The regal, imperious tone of the three-year-old lost a lot in translation around the thumb she sucked. Her eyelids drooped.

Mother and daughter had consumed every scrap of food they could scrounge from the kitchen and pantry. For the moment they were replete and happy.

What about tomorrow?

All around them, they heard small crashes and groans as weakened walls and ceilings gave way. How much longer could they safely stay here? With atavistic fear, she resisted going forth into the city.

"Come sit in my lap, baby. I'll tell you a story." She opened her arms where they sat on the floor of the workroom. Round bolster pillows spilled yards of soft lace around them. Straight-backed chairs by the pillow stands offered the only seating in the room. So she and Jaranda sat on the floor where they could be together. They had found elegant withdrawing rooms with comfortable furniture, bedrooms with lace curtains, and little private salons all over the palace. All of them had breaches in the walls or ceilings and offered little protection. The workroom remained intact and felt like home. How long? What about food tomorrow?

"Once upon a time, in a country far, far away . . ." she began the story.

"How far away?" Jaranda asked as she snuggled her head into her mother's lap. She sucked her thumb again.

Part of the woman knew she should do her best to discourage the little girl from the baby behavior, but with life so unsettled, their future so uncertain, she allowed Jaranda whatever comfort she could find.

"Many days' travel by barge up the river, farther away than you or I have ever been. Farther away than either of us would want to travel."

"Hmm," Jaranda agreed.

"In this far, far country, there lived a . . . a princess who made lace. And her name was . . . Jaranda."

"That's me," the little girl sighed and shifted deeper into her mother's lap.

"And she lived in a crumbling palace that had been deserted by one and all when an evil sorcerer with dark eyes and hair made the land tremble and the skies shoot flame. Everyone was very afraid. Everyone except the princess. She knew that the only defense against the evil sorcerer was to make enough lace to cover the walls of the palace and heal them. The little princess searched the palace high and low for all of the Tambrin thread she could find. For Tambrin has special magic spun into it . . ."

Jaranda drifted into sleep, a smile on her face.

The woman looked around the workroom with new hope. Tambrin.

If she could find some of the silky thread spun from the fibers of immature Tambootie trees, perhaps she could heal herself, remember her name. Maybe then she would know where to look for family or friends to shelter and feed her and her daughter.

Without disturbing Jaranda, she reached to the nearest strand of lace dangling from a work table. She fingered the fine threads woven into an airy pattern.

Silk. Lovely. But not Tambrin.

She reached a little farther to the table behind her. Linen. The finest spun linen in the world, but still not Tambrin.

She reached again, across her to the left. The lace eluded her. She stretched farther and touched—a hand!

A scream lodged deep in her throat. She wanted to scream, needed to shout her fear to the rooftops.

But that would awaken the baby.

"Nice story, Lady. Tambrin lace is worth six times its weight in gold in Coronnan right now." The man's deep voice flowed around her in soothing tones. "Show me which of these is Tambrin, and I'll show you a safe place to stay in the city."

Just then the floor rippled beneath them, and the ceiling dropped chunks of plaster on top of her head.

"I think I'd rather take one of these pillows to Coronnan and make my fortune there," she replied.

Only then did she look at the intruder. Tall, black-haired, with eyes as deeply dark as a well, he smiled at her with a mouth full of gleaming teeth. A small pack steed stood patiently behind him. Not a true pack steed. One of those odd little creatures from the mountains of Jehab with exceedingly long ears and shaggy coat. It opened its mouth and brayed long and loud as if it laughed at her, at him, at the world. It displayed an amazing number of oversized square teeth—a lot like its master.

His clothing certainly deserved a smile, black trews and shirt brightened by a garish vest of purple with red trim and silver embroidery. His fringed sash of bright blue hung nearly to his dusty black boots. A dozen or more coins hung from the sash at his waist, from rings in his ears, and dangling from his purple, billed cap set at rakish angle.

Something in the back of her mind whispered "Exotic, interesting." She thought perhaps it should have shouted "Dangerous!" But it didn't.

"I should fear you, but I don't."

"Prejudices have to be learned. Not much to fear from me. I'm just a simple trader trying to make a living. You and a lace pillow filled with Tambrin lace could set us up in a nice palace all our own in Coronnan. No kardiaquakes in Coronnan." A mischievous twinkle in his eyes made his offer nearly as attractive as the man.

"I don't suppose you know my name?"

"Never met you before, Lady." He shrugged, setting the coins to jingling. They formed an almost recognizable melody played on silver bells.

"I suspected you'd say that."

Chapter 14

"What was this room used for?" Marcus asked Vareena. They had reached the corner room beneath one of the two large watchtowers. Two smaller towers at the end of the residential wings of the monastery contained latrines and staircases but no observation platforms on their roofs. These corner towers were massive—larger than four of the individual rooms combined. They topped the courtyard walls by at least another story.

Vareena paced the colonnade beside him, thrusting open doors as they passed. He wanted to hold her hand as they explored, but the barrier of energy repulsed him every time.

Robb slunk along behind them, lost in his own grumbling. He'd sat by the well for hours shuffling the deck of cartes. But as soon as Marcus and Vareena neared the tower, he had joined them.

"Looks like an office or study," Vareena said, staring at the slanted writing desk, tall stool, stone visitor's bench, and rank of empty bookshelves along one wall. The desktop and the shelves held only dust.

They explored a bed niche behind a half-wall at the back of the room. In the corner, steps spiraled up into the tower. Indentations in the shallow risers showed the wear of many feet climbing those stairs over the course of centuries of use.

Robb stared at the stairs without mounting them. "Maybe the bathing chamber is up there. Haven't seen any signs of a bath. How did they keep clean?" he muttered.

"At least they have convenient privies in every corner

and every level. They're dry. No one has used them for centuries. Maybe we can crawl down one and out of the monastery." Marcus began looking for the private closet that should be behind the stairs.

"What if they drain directly into the river, or into a pit beneath the ground with no exit? Besides the holes are too small for either of us to squeeze through," Robb reminded him.

"We've found nothing. Nothing at all in this place." Marcus slammed one fist into the other. He'd learned not to try putting it through the wall. He had several bruises and raw knuckles to remind him.

"I have a vague recollection of Mam saying that when the numbers of priests and monks declined to only three men, they packed up everything, including the temple stones, and moved elsewhere," Vareena continued. "But that was long, long ago. Before the first ghost came three hundred years ago."

"We need information," Marcus interjected. He wanted to slam his fist into something in his frustration, again. Fear replaced his certainty that all would come out right.

And he could not touch Vareena, the one person he longed to take comfort from.

"Can you bring your mother here for us to talk to?" Robb looked up, hope shining in his eyes rather than his usual pessimism. "Always best to get information as close to the source as possible."

"No." She stared off into the distance, refusing to look at them, all her friendliness and helpfulness faded.

For once, Robb respected her silence and did not press her to comply with his request. Instead, he reached out one of his hands as if to caress her hair in comfort. But he dropped it before he even came close.

Marcus let out a long, uneasy breath. Unwanted jealousy flared hot. He and Robb had never competed for a woman before—they'd both had a number of liaisons—but always with the other's blessing. They took care to seek out women who did not interest the other. But where Marcus fell in and out of love quite easily, Robb had always kept his heart slightly aloof.

For the past two years Marcus had loved Margit, Jaylor's

spy in Palace Reveta Tristile. He thought perhaps this attachment would last forever since it had lasted so long.

Then they'd come here.

He should remain faithful to Margit's memory. He shouldn't begrudge Robb's attraction to Vareena.

But Vareena was so very beautiful, resilient, wise, and mature. And their only hope.

Marcus' heart twisted in silent agony.

"Guess it's natural we'd both want the only woman who can see either of us," he muttered under his breath. He tried to reassert his natural good humor, without much luck.

The endless empty rooms of the monastery depressed him. He and Robb had searched the place, of course, looking for another exit. But he'd hoped Vareena could show them something they'd overlooked. She seemed more ignorant of the layout than they.

"My mam died twenty years ago. She tried to come up here to sit with her last ghost during a wild thunderstorm. Like the one that brought you here. Lightning hit a tree as she was making her way here. It fell on top of her and killed her. I inherited the duty to tend the ghosts that night."

"How old were you, Vareena?" Marcus asked gently.

She held up her hand displaying all five fingers plus two from the other hand while she swallowed repeatedly, working to avoid the strong emotions that gripped her.

"Stargods!" He slammed his right fist into his left palm. Unsatisfied with the explosive gesture, he looked for something else to hit. Robb would do. He caught his breath and closed his eyes in shock. "This place is truly cursed. And all three of us along with it. We've got to get out of here!"

"That is what I have been trying to tell you for two days, Marcus," Robb said quietly. Too quietly. Had he sensed Marcus' earlier anger and jealousy, his need to lash out at his best friend because he was a handy target?

"What's in the other corner room?" Marcus nearly ran the length of the colonnade where he kicked the door open, letting it slam against the stone wall behind it. The bang did nothing to alleviate his frustration.

"The kitchen with storage behind and refectory above."

Vareena looked inside. Her posture told him nothing of her thoughts.

He considered probing her mind, letting her memories give him as much information as she possessed—even the deeply buried bits about her mother. Something repelled him. He wasn't even sure his magic would work on her since she seemed partially in the void. The summons spell he'd tried last night had lain dormant within the fire, never passing through his glass. He'd tried three times since coming here to no avail. Maybe all of his magic had died the moment they passed through these walls. He certainly had not had any luck trying to tap the erratic ley lines that passed through the courtyard. They never seemed to rest in the same place two heartbeats in a row.

And the constant haze in the sky distorted his planetary orientation. He had slept only two nights in this place. Well he hadn't really slept all that much what with the nightmares and all.

His latest nightmare involved losing at endless games of cartes, until he finally bet with University money entrusted to him by Jaylor. In a desperate play to salvage his losses he'd bet everything, including Margit.

And lost.

He shuddered and tried to think the problem through—as Jaylor and Baamin before him had taught him.

His connection to the wheel of the stars, the spin of the planet, and the shift of the season told him more time had passed than the two nights he thought he'd spent in the monastery. Much more time. On top of that, his sense of *where* they were in relation to the nearest magnetic pole shifted every few hours.

Perhaps the way the ley lines broke just before meeting the exterior walls had something to do with his reactions. He got a headache every time he tried to puzzle it through. He just wanted out. Now.

He breathed deeply, trying to master his emotions. The failed summons spell had left him frightened and afraid to try again lest he fail and know for certain that all his magic was lost along with his luck.

"Look, Marcus," Robb said in hushed tones. "Look at this!"

Marcus turned his attention away from his fears and looked where Robb had stopped at the center of the central wing of the monastery. He stomped over to his friend and peered inside.

Large and larger. Like the University, this three-story room took up one entire wing of the building, dominating the lesser rooms.

"A library," Robb whispered.

"An empty library." The last of Marcus' optimism slid out of him, into the cold paving stones. "No books, no journals. Not even a cobweb. The rest of this building is filled with spiders and cobwebs, but not here. Only dust and empty shelves."

"Not entirely empty. This bank of shelves in the center is filled with sacks of gold," Robb dribbled a handful of coins out of a rotting canvas sack. He moved around to the back of the shelving unit and reappeared with another sack. "As many back here as in front."

Marcus paced around the massive unit. It could easily hold one hundred or more books on each side. The entire thing was filled with sacks of gold coins and several bullion bars.

"What sunlight penetrates through the gloaming and then through the windows seems to concentrate in this spot." Robb circled the unit in the opposite direction. With each pass the two of them made, the gold seemed to glow more brightly.

"Maybe whoever put the gold here wanted to spend his hours staring at it," Marcus mused.

"Kind of a boring existence," Robb added.

"Who would collect all this gold and just leave it?" Marcus reached out to touch the shiny metal. The coin warmed under his touch. Light reflected off it in warm shades. It almost begged him to pocket it along with the few coins he'd taken from Farrell's corpse.

His heartbeat and breathing slowed. He focused only on the gold. Time seemed to stop . . .

Some moments later he shook himself free of the enthrallment. "Gold doesn't do anyone any good just sitting here in isolation. We need to get it back to Jaylor and the Commune." Hope blossomed again in Marcus' chest. "Think of all that the Commune and University can accomplish with this much gold. New buildings. Books. Tools. Food and clothing for apprentices and journeymen."

"Bribes to nobles to legalize the Commune again." Robb grinned from ear to ear. His previous depression seemed to have eased.

"Stargods save us!" Vareena crossed herself, paused and signed the ward against evil again. "Money is evil. Put it back, Robb."

"Nonsense. The world economy depends upon the free circulation of coins." Robb fell into lecture mode. "Some coins may be cursed by an individual. But the coins themselves are not evil. Evil exists only in the hearts of certain humans. A magician of unusual strength and evil design might place a curse upon coin. But the curse would die with the magician. Since ghosts have been coming here for generations, these coins cannot be cursed."

"Put it back. You have no need for gold. I will provide all that you need while you are here. We do not use gold or silver in our village. We trade for everything we need with the caravans that use the pass, or the Rovers that wander through. The priests have told us that coins are the source of all evil. We grow and make all else that we need ourselves. Put it back! Before you die, put it back."

* * *

These amateurs slept through the kardiaquake I caused. They ignored the nightmares I gave them as if they were of no consequence. What will it take to be rid of them?

They should tremble in their boots at thought of the power I command. I was the first to employ a blending of traditions. Dragon magic is limited in scope for all the strength it employs. Ley line magic cannot be combined with other magicians to enhance the power by orders of magnitude. Blood magic requires a unique personality to endure the pain and to relish the fear and blood sacrifice of others.

But I discovered how to use all three disciplines at once. My offspring continue experimenting with my discoveries. I sired two of the strongest magicians ever. The older is even more innovative than I. The younger is warped by early rejection. She has not the emotional strength to use that trauma to enhance her magic. But the warping in her person-

ality makes her very creative in inflicting pain. She is truly a master of blood magic. She also taps ley lines as a spigot in a cask of wine. But being female she cannot draw upon dragon magic, unless she remains in physical contact with a purple dragon. I think she may have solved that little problem on her own.

I will bring my two children to me. They will know how to find me with only a little prompting and a few clues.

With their help, I can deal with these matters and be free to enjoy my power.

Chapter 15

"**D**o you have a name, my dark-eyed friend?" the unnamed woman asked.

"Outside my clan, I am called Zebbiah," the Rover merchant replied, nodding his head. "And do you, my new business partner, have a name?"

"If I have one, I have forgotten it." She sighed heavily. "Do you happen to have any idea what I might be called inside or outside my clan?"

"True-bloods of SeLenicca do not have clans," he replied succinctly. "Your blond hair and blue eyes proclaim you a true-blood."

Jaranda had red hair. Did that make her other than a true-blood of SeLenicca? The woman couldn't remember if that held import in society or not.

"But what am I called?"

He shrugged and set about removing the panniers from his pack beast. He'd neatly evaded her question. She had a feeling he was good at evading issues rather than lying. Good. She trusted him not to lie outright to her even if he did not speak the truth.

"Why did you bring that animal inside the palace?"

Jaranda stirred from her nap. The woman soothed her with a gentle caress through the baby's tangled hair.

"This is not a true palace anymore. More ruins than building. Besides, I didn't dare leave him alone. Beasts are valuable in this city. Someone would steal him."

"Is theft so rampant that the city guards cannot control it?" Something fearful clutched at her heart and throat.

"Aye, Lady. The city guard fled along with all the others.

No one rules here now. Law is enforced by the strongest bully who makes his own rules as benefit him and him alone." Panniers off the beast, Zebbiah set about lighting a fire in the nearby brazier. He squatted on his heels, looking comfortable making camp in the workroom of the ruined palace. He looked as if he could make himself comfortable anywhere, any time.

She wished she knew enough about herself to find comfort within her own mind and heart. In this state of not knowing, only Jaranda anchored her.

With a half smile she suddenly realized that her lack of memory offered her a kind of freedom. She and her baby could make a home for themselves anywhere they chose. They could set the rules and style of their home to suit themselves. They need please no one else—except possibly Zebbiah if he stayed with them.

The heat quickly penetrated her bones, and her mind lightened. "I didn't realize I was cold until I touched heat again," she mused.

"Cold can be like that. When it gets really bad, it almost feels like warmth and then you fall asleep and never wake up."

"Will you protect me and my baby from the cold?"

"If I can."

"And from the bandits and bully gangs?" She shuddered.

He paused a moment before answering. "My word as a Rover. I'll do my best to protect you from harm of any kind."

"Even from yourself?"

He grinned, flashing a huge number of teeth, just like his pack beast "My word of honor, Lady. You are as safe from me as you want to be."

A long silent moment passed between them. The woman looked away first.

"You hungry?" Zebbiah asked.

The woman shook her head. "We scavenged in the pantry. But we will need to eat again by nightfall."

"I've food for the three of us. We'll leave at dawn." He fished a pot and some packets wrapped in oiled cloth from one of the panniers. "Is there water?"

"The well behind the kitchen still tastes sweet."

He nodded abruptly and rose from his squat in one graceful motion, without using his hands to brace himself.

"You need anything while I'm out?"

The pack beast shifted his head and began nibbling her tangled hair.

"If you could find a hairbrush or comb?"

He nodded again and left without complaint.

"We'll deal well together, Zebbiah," she whispered. "I'm not sure why I trust you, but I do."

Oversized teeth nipped her ear. She batted the pack beast away. It then began grazing on a piece of lace dangling from a corner pillow. "But you'll have to teach this beast of yours some manners, Zebbiah." She settled Jaranda on the floor and followed the beast to rescue the priceless ornament.

"I don't suppose you know my name?" she asked the beast as she pulled half a yard of lace free of its jaws

"Heeeeeee haaaaaaaw," the beast brayed in answer, or protest.

"Somehow I thought you'd say that."

* * *

Jack waited outside King Darville's private study, impatiently shifting from one foot to the other. He pretended to stand guard while listening with every sense available to him. He needed to speak to the king and queen alone. How much longer before Darville and Rossemikka freed themselves from the increasingly loud political conversation?

Lord Laislac had spent the last hour haranguing his king. Lord Andrall, the king's uncle by marriage, had spoken a couple of times. Laislac's daughter Ariiell had whimpered occasionally. Jack had seen Andrall's and Laislac's wives enter the room, but so far they had remained silent.

Darville had said little, asking only an occasional question. Queen Mikka probably sat in the window embrasure, basking in the afternoon sunshine, stroking the sensuous texture of her gown with long fingers. She said little during these sessions, but she observed everything and counseled Darville afterward.

Jack did not have to open his magical listening senses to hear the scandal in the making. Long ago, when he'd been a kitchen drudge, considered too stupid to even have a name, he'd learned to listen carefully with all of his senses before entering a room. He'd also eventually learned how to make himself seem invisible in order to avoid the local bullies.

Today invisibility came from his plain guard's uniform and his presence outside the king's study. No one noticed him because he belonged there.

But Jack had to stand still, at attention, hoping his impatience for a moment of privacy with the king and queen did not alert anyone that something unusual was about to happen.

He needed absolute secrecy to summon the Commune for tonight's spell. One whisper of the king and queen involved with magic would bring the wrath of the Gnuls and the lords they controlled down on their heads. None of them would be safe for a moment if the Gnuls found out what Jack planned to do tonight.

He shuddered every time he thought about this morning's adventures in the market square. Fear of magic grew by the day. The dye merchant wasn't the only innocent to be accused and judged upon the spot. Stoning had become a favorite form of execution. It required no preparation and could be carried out before palace guards could interfere. That the Gnuls had grown so bold as to accuse Jack while he wore a guard's uniform told him how strong the Gnuls had grown.

King Darville and Queen Mikka kept bodyguards close to them all the time now. Jack and Sergeant Fred pulled the duty more often than others. Fred was an accepted presence and trusted by king and council alike. Jack was new and unknown to the council, but the king and queen relied upon his magical talent for their safety as well as secret communication with Jaylor and the Commune of Magicians.

"She must marry the boy. He's responsible for this—this outrage!" Lord Laislac screamed within the king's study.

Any mention of marriage piqued Jack's interest.

"The boy is not responsible for his own actions," Lord Andrall replied mildly. "My son was born with only half his wits and never found the rest. For him to marry anyone would be a mockery of the Stargods."

"Well, he certainly managed to become a man long enough

to sire a child on my daughter. My daughter who was a virgin when she came to your household for fosterage after her mother died," Laislac sneered this time. But his agitation showed through his wavering voice.

Jack leaned a little closer to the door. He'd been very young and frightened when news hit the capital that Lord Andrall's son, first cousin to then Prince Darville, had been born damaged. The court went into mourning for the beloved lord and his lady, sister to Darville's father, King Darcine.

Jack had rejoiced because at last there was someone more stupid than him. Upon the few occasions the childlike young man came to court, Jack had grown to love and honor him as the Stargods commanded. Few people realized how much love, patience, and truth they could learn from the special people marked by the Stargods.

"But I don't want to marry him, P'pa. He's repulsive! He's ugly. And he smells." That must be Ariiell, she of the whining voice.

Jack had seen her around court a couple of times, frail, pale, and uninteresting. No personality to go with the fair prettiness.

"Well, you certainly found him attractive enough once to take him into your bed," Andrall replied mildly.

"You don't understand! 'Twas but a game. A teasing game, and I . . . he lost control." A long pause followed her slip of the tongue. "He's strong. He overpowered me. I had no choice." She babbled on, trying to make excuses for herself.

Jack doubted that Andrall's son had been much more than a passive participant. He knew the young man too well. But he also knew how often his own patience had been taxed by Katrina, and he had his full wits. Mardall didn't have the reasoning power and emotional control of an adult.

"Gentlemen, ladies. I do not believe a forced marriage is the answer to this dilemma," Darville said in a soothing tone. "Surely a retreat into the country for a year or so, a discreet adoption by a childless couple of good family would serve all of us and no scandal need accompany either party."

" 'Twould serve you, Your Grace. You would not have

to acknowledge your cousin's child as your heir," Laislac replied, sarcasm dripping from every word. "Since you can't manage to get the queen pregnant yourself." The insult brought a painful silence.

Jack suddenly turned his full attention to every breath within the room. Lady Ariiell sought to make her child legitimate with a hasty marriage to Darville's only blood heir—discounting the exiled Rejiia and her equally exiled sisters. Should Darville die heirless, then Laislac was the logical choice as regent for his young grandson as monarch. Kings had been killed for less.

This made Jack's errand doubly important. He knew how to stabilize Queen Mikka's body so she could carry a child to full term and give the country an unquestioned heir.

"I would welcome the stability a legitimate heir would bring to Coronnan," Darville replied. Jack could almost see him pacing back and forth behind his massive desk like a wolf stalking his territory. The king rarely sat still and then only when Queen Mikka held his hand.

"We will discuss this further, when all of us have had time to reflect on all of the options." More likely when Darville had a chance to discuss the alternatives with Mikka. "Remember, Laislac, the plight of Lord Andrall's son is well known. This marriage and his impending paternity would generate more scandal than were Lady Ariiell to give birth to an illegitimate child. Do you really want this?"

"I insist that Lord Andrall and his son honor their obligations to my daughter. They will marry!" Laislac screamed loud enough for the entire court to hear.

A few moments later all of the combatants exited. Lady Lynnetta in tears, comforted by the supporting arm of her husband, Lord Andrall. Their son, Mardall, tripped along in their wake, drooling slightly, smiling happily at Jack's familiar wave. He clutched a stuffed toy—perhaps a well-worn spotted saber cat—and seemed oblivious to the storm that had threatened his quiet, predictable world away from the court. He'd been so quiet, Jack had not realized he'd been in the room.

Lord Laislac looked as if he'd spit thunder and lightning. His wife, Ariiell's stepmother, held her chin up and pursed her mouth in a disgusted pout.

But Lady Ariiell smiled and patted her slightly swollen tummy.

She was up to something.

Jack needed to follow her and find out what.

He also needed to inform the king and queen that he had a possible answer to Mikka's problem. After tonight, Queen Mikka might very well negate Lady Ariiell's ambitions.

Jack slipped into the study and locked the door behind him, both physically and magically.

"Something *else* that requires my attention?" King Darville asked impatiently, lifting one golden eyebrow. He barely looked up from the documents that he read most intently. His leather queue restraint had slipped, and he looked in need of a shave. The last confrontation had taken its toll on him since Jack's witch-sniffer report a few hours ago.

Still the king maintained his gentle smile and politeness while his eyes narrowed in slight disapproval. Better to risk the king's irritation than brave the wolflike smile and bared teeth that betrayed his anger. He glanced at his wife, clearly anxious for a moment alone with her to discuss that touchy situation Laislac had thrown at his feet.

"Your Grace, I believe I have a solution to a recurring problem."

Darville half rose from his chair, his full gaze intent upon Jack's face. "Do we have privacy?" he asked quietly.

Mikka came to his side and clutched his arm. Darville tucked her neatly against his side in a loving and companionable gesture. Her eyes became huge in her too thin face; not daring to hope.

Jack closed his eyes and breathed deeply, listening to all of the small sounds around the palace with extra as well as mundane senses. He heard the shuffle of many feet within the building and out in the courtyards. The murmur of many conversations drifted close to his ear. He sorted through them and dismissed all but one. Just above the subtle shift of stones and kardia settling into each other, he detected a whisper, two heartbeats, the sputter of a rushlight . . .

He held up two fingers and pointed beneath the floor.

Darville cocked his head and pursed his lips in consternation. "The tunnels," he mouthed the words and pointed to his massive desk.

Jack had heard about the numerous secret passages that riddled the residential wing of the palace. They dated to the earliest construction of the old keep, intended to give the original lord of the islands an escape in time of war. Only one tunnel remained open and well known. It provided a quick trip between the palace and the University complex on an adjacent island. Now that the University served as a barracks, the guards used the tunnel to move quickly between duties, protected from the weather.

But the other tunnels. The older ones were supposed to remain secret from all but the king's closest family and confidants.

Jack drew his sword, actually his staff in mild disguise.

"Fred?" Darville said quietly.

"No time," Jack replied equally quiet.

"Ready?"

Jack nodded.

The king pressed a hidden lever. The desktop slid sideways. He withdrew from the opening quickly, taking Mikka with him.

Unnatural yellow flame tinged with blue lighted the dark hole where the desktop had been. Witchlight!

Mikka gasped and held her hand over her mouth to stifle any further sound. Darville pushed her behind him as he reached for his short sword atop the desk.

A magician eavesdropped on the king. Only a member of the coven would have the audacity to do that.

Chapter 16

Jack reached down with his sword/staff, with his free hand, and with his magic to yank a startled scullery maid through the hole.

She squeaked a protest, her eyes wide.

Jack detected no magic in her aura. He'd heard a second heartbeat.

The witchlight torch continued to gleam. The magician who had lighted it could not be far. The coven had grown as bold as the Gnuls if they eavesdropped within the palace.

Jack thrust the maid toward Darville. The king stumbled with his unexpected burden. The two landed in a heap on the floor. Feminine giggles erupted from the froth of flying petticoats.

Mikka grabbed the girl by the back of her bodice and hoisted her away from the grinning king with a ferocious yank. The queen did not return the smile.

Jack reached again into the hole, only slightly distracted by the sight of feminine legs protruding enticingly from the tangle of lacy petticoats—too much expensive lace for a mere scullery maid.

This time his hands came up empty. He peered deeper. The witchlight retreated rapidly.

Should he follow?

"Who was with you?" Jack demanded angrily.

The maid continued to eye the king while patting and shifting her clothing. She giggled as Queen Mikka possessively brushed dust off her husband's tunic. Darville did not look overly distressed at the attention of two attractive women.

"Why, no one, my lord," the maid replied. She preened and fussed with her mussed gown, making certain Jack saw how low her bodice dipped.

The king kept his eyes discreetly on his wife's face.

"Don't lie, girl. I saw the witchlight within the torch." Jack advanced on the girl until his sword tip touched her throat just below the chin. He hated using violence to intimidate the truth out of her, yet he knew of no other safe way to interrogate her. She'd report magic coercion to the Gnuls and the Council of Provinces.

"Witchlight!" she gasped, crossing herself, then making the older warding gesture of right wrist crossed over left and flapping her hands—a symbolic banning of Simurgh, the ancient winged demon who thrived upon blood. "I never . . . He never . . ." She drifted off into panicky choking noises as she looked pleadingly at Jack and then at the king. "He said we'd just listen . . . gather gossip . . . harmless, he said . . ." the maid stammered her explanation.

"I'll send Sergeant Fred to search the tunnels from both ends," Darville said as he marched toward the door, pointedly keeping his back to the maid. He tried the door.

It resisted.

He turned the key.

It still wouldn't budge.

He looked at Jack, lifting one eyebrow again in a maddening gesture.

Jack blinked hastily, three times and recited the trigger words that would remove the locking spell, hoping the maid was too concerned with her own hysteria and Jack's sword point to notice the delay.

The door flew open at Darville's touch. Three guards, led by Fred, almost fell into the room, swords and daggers drawn. Three steps, two turns, double over, and balance on one foot. The maid dove into their clumsy dance for balance, further upsetting them. More laughter and delay.

She knew more than she admitted.

"A little late, aren't you, Sergeant?" Jack said, working his cheeks to keep from laughing at their antics.

"Fred, take one man into the tunnels and search for anyone who might have carried a torch of witchlight within the past few moments. And you." Darville thrust the maid into the all too willing arms of the third guard. "Take her to an interrogation room. No one talks to her until I get there. No one. Do you hear me?"

The guard gulped and nodded. His fair skin turned blotchy red in embarrassment.

"I didn't mean no harm . . . only gossip about Lady Ariiell being in the family way. No harm in gossip," the maid protested as the guard dragged her from the room.

"And dispatch some men to search the tunnels from the barracks end and the cove three islands over where His Grace keeps his private boat," Jack added. No doubt the listener had brought the maid along so that she would be caught while he escaped.

The soldiers scrambled to obey Jack's orders as if he were the lieutenant and not merely a new recruit.

Jack smiled to himself. Authority came from within and not from a rank arbitrarily assigned. That had been one of the hardest lessons he'd had to learn.

When the room cleared again and the desk closed, King Darville sat down heavily in the window seat. Mikka curled up against him, like a cat seeking a lap in the waning sunlight. "I am tired of all these plots," Darville said upon a weary sigh. "Let's put your plan into effect as soon as possible. I think we need to summon Jaylor," he said while leaning his head back against the precious glass covering of the window.

"My thoughts exactly," Mikka added, stroking her husband's cheek. The she touched her abdomen, just above where she had carried five babes and lost all of them before they quickened. "I am willing to share this body only with the children my husband and I conceive out of love. The cat has to go. I have long lost all affection for the pet I once considered the other half of myself."

"I'll need at least three other master magicians, two purple dragons, and you, Your Grace, in the clearing on Sacred Isle tonight as the moon crests the oak trees."

"And is my presence required?" Darville asked. Again that half-ironic gesture of one raised eyebrow.

"Advisable, but not required."

"Is the clearing large enough to accommodate all of those you do require. You must include Shayla in your entourage. I cannot imagine the mother dragon allowing you to play with two of her precious babies without her. And Brevelan, too. She won't want to miss something this big involving her best friend, her husband, and *her* dragons," Mikka added with a smile. She and Darville had shared a number of adventures with Jaylor and Brevelan before duty and responsibility had weighed so heavily upon all their shoulders.

"We may be a bit crowded," Jack admitted. "But I believe Brevelan must stay home tonight. She's expecting again, very soon."

"Yes, she is. Twins this time, I believe." Mikka looked at her hands where she plucked at the satiny texture of her brocade gown. "Even for my best friend, I will not postpone this ceremony. We will have to perform it without Brevelan's supervision."

"Lock the door again and armor the desk against eavesdropping." Darville roused from his seat, leaving his wife there to stare at her own inner thoughts. "Send your summons to Jaylor from here."

"Should be the safest place in the palace for a while. The man with the witchlight speeding away from here should draw the witch-sniffers after him." Jack pulled energy from the nearest ley line to fuel his spells. The magic tingled through his body in welcome waves. He drank it in, relishing the power that fed his talent and energized his mind. The pattern of tingles was different from dragon magic, but more familiar. He knew how to mold this power precisely.

Besides he didn't have a purple-tipped dragon at his fingertips to give him power.

If he'd been able to gather dragon magic from the air, he'd have been accepted by the University and Commune as a child. But if he'd been accepted and nurtured, he'd not have learned the strength and resilience his adventures had taught him. He'd not have met Katrina, or found the lair of the dragons to bring them home.

Katrina wouldn't be planning their wedding for tomorrow if . . .

Breathing deeply in the early stages of a trance, he set a candle upon the desk and sat in the king's chair. He couldn't settle comfortably in the furniture custom-made for the tall and lanky man who paced the room like a caged wolf.

Jack moved to the smaller visitor's chair. It wasn't exactly comfortable either, made that way to discourage visitors from lingering unnecessarily. But the size was better suited to Jack's shorter, stockier figure.

Only then did he retrieve a special shard of glass hidden deep within his scrip. Possession of the precious and rare piece marked him as a magician. As a master magician, he was entitled to a much larger, gold-framed piece. Even journeymen used a larger piece than this. But they were harder to hide. And other than an occasional summons to Jaylor, or a bubble of armor to ensure privacy, he wasn't supposed to work any magic while in the capital.

A middling trance settled on his mind. His eyes crossed slightly, and the flame doubled and wavered in his sight. He looked through the glass into the flame.

"Flame to flame, glass to glass, like seeking like, follow my thoughts to the one I seek," he murmured in a singsong. His talent flew along the path of his chant through the glass into the flame. In his mind he watched a tiny flamelet jump from the candle, fly along the desk, drop to the floor and travel along the carpet without igniting the fibers.

King Darville watched the candle, oblivious to the movement of the ghostly flame. It traveled to Mikka's gown, across her lap, and out the closed window in the space of three heartbeats. The queen shifted position restlessly three times during that brief moment. Her own magical talent might make her aware of the spell, but she couldn't participate.

Jack breathed easily again when the flame passed onto the roof of the wing below the study tower. In his mind he followed the tiny spark on its journey far to the south. It gained speed as it traversed the land, uphill, jumping rivers and creeks, through forests, over pastures and plowed fields. At last, it found a nameless little village perched on a cliff above a treacherous cove. It paused a moment as if catching a breath near the triple festival pylon, still decorated with flowers, new foliage, and grasses from the spring celebrations. Then off again, steeply uphill along a narrow but well-trodden path. At the boulder split by a tree, the path seemed to pass to the left. Jack's mind and the flamelet pressed to the right. He saw the iridescent shimmer of the magical barrier that protected Brevelan's Clearing. No human could pass through this barrier without Brevelan's or Jaylor's express wish. But the flame did not live, and Jack's body remained in Coronnan City.

A sudden thrumming in Jack's mind told him the flame had found a piece of glass and sent a signal to the owner that a summons awaited. The vibration of the signal set Jack's teeth on edge. It had set his fingers twitching before a second flame appeared in his glass. Then Jaylor's familiar face emerged, as close and clear as if he sat on the opposite side of the desk.

"What?" Jaylor asked abruptly. His gaze wandered to his left and stayed there. Worry shadowed his eyes and drew his mouth into a deep frown. His beard looked untrimmed, and his hair had pulled loose from his queue restraint.

"Jaylor, I have a solution and need help. Shayla has agreed to meet us with the twin purple-tips on Sacred Isle tonight," Jack replied. Jaylor's distraction worried him. The Senior Magician of the Commune did not allow his students anything but full concentration on any spell and taught by example.

"Not tonight. No time." Jaylor raised his hand in the time-honored signal that he closed the communication.

"But it has to be tonight!" Otherwise Katrina might find another excuse to delay their wedding.

Otherwise Ariiell and Laislac might find a way to grab the position of heir to the throne.

"Not tonight. Brevelan is in labor. It's not going well. I can't leave her, and I won't delegate this chore."

"What's wrong?" Darville asked. "Tell him we can go to the Clearing instead of to Sacred Isle. Tell him about the eavesdroppers. Tell him that Mikka . . ."

"Do you want to do this?" Jack looked at his king, slightly exasperated.

"You know I can't. Tell him . . ."

"Jaylor, we can come to the Clearing. I can transport Their Graces and Katrina and myself."

"Not tonight!" Jaylor nearly screamed. Then he took a deep breath, composing himself. "Give us three days to recover from the birth. Then we will meet you in Shayla's lair. All of us." He ended the summons abruptly.

"I'd better tell Katrina she has a three-day reprieve,"

Jack murmured sadly. Three days for her to think up new excuses for delay.

Suddenly, he knew she did not need the three days to find an excuse. She'd make one of her own today.

Without bothering to extinguish the candle or take leave of his king, Jack pelted out of the room, down the stairs, across three corridors, and out into the sunny courtyard where she usually worked. He gasped for breath, seeking a trace of her presence.

Gone. Lace pillow, patterns, and herself. She might never have been here an hour ago when he left her. The ragged wall still showed marks from Amaranth's talons. Jack hadn't dreamed Katrina's agreement to marry. She had promised.

Where would she go?

Back inside, he traced the route to the honored servants' quarters where she slept or sometimes worked by rushlight when rain threatened.

Not a cloud in the sky, he thought to himself. *Why would she retreat indoors on such a fine day? Not too hot, nor too windy. The sun will shine another candle mark at least.*

The other servants nodded to him as he passed, a now-familiar presence in the palace, as was Katrina. He paused outside her door. He knocked quietly. The door swung open at his first touch.

He knew before he looked with his eyes that the room was empty. It looked as if she had never been there.

Gone.

Pillows, lace, patterns, her clothes, and the little trinkets he'd given her to make the stark room a home.

Gone.

He searched the wardrobe, the chest at the foot of the bed, beneath the bed. She had taken the magical lace shawl they'd used to patch Shayla's wing. Katrina had planned to use the airy lace as her wedding veil.

Perhaps she had merely gone to the dressmaker for her wedding gown.

But he knew she had fled.

She'd run away rather than marry him. Run into danger from the Gnuls, and he couldn't protect her.

Chapter 17

Vareena picked her way over the muddy paths that wound through the village. Rain had made the packed dirt slick and left puddles in every indentation. The summer sun had not climbed high enough to remove the shadows and evaporate the water. The haze that shrouded the monastery seemed to be spreading.

What would happen to her village if the gloaming spread here and deprived them all of light, distorted time, and trapped them forever? She'd never break free, trade caravans would cease coming . . . They'd all become ghosts.

She shuddered and wished she were back in bed where she could pull the blankets over her head and pretend none of this was happening.

But the baker's son had burned his hand and arm badly, stoking the fire beneath the huge bread oven. Cold water and lard had not eased the boy's pain, so the family had summoned Vareena out of her warm bed.

She'd have liked to take her time gathering the eggs herself and preparing breakfast for her brothers. Her chickens never pecked her when she reached for their treasures. She sang soothing songs to them, talked to them, treated them as important assets to the farm. They responded in kind.

"What kept you?" snarled the baker's wife. She thrust her hands behind her back, crossing her wrists and flapping her hands. The old ward could not keep Vareena from entering the cottage. The huge mud-and-brick oven that served the entire village heated the place almost beyond tolerance in this bright summer weather.

A low moan coming from behind the curtain at the back

of the low-ceilinged room grabbed Vareena's attention.
Rather than reply to the surly woman, so typical of the
villagers, Vareena thrust her way past her. She tore aside
the curtain to the dark lean-to that normally contained
firewood and food stores for the family.

The baker had set his son Jeeremy on a rough pallet
here before returning to his oven. From the grimace of pain
that crossed the boy's face, Vareena guessed he had been
unable to climb the ladder into the sleeping loft above the
cottage's only room.

"What witchcraft you gonna work on my boy?" the
baker's wife demanded as she inserted herself between
Vareena and her son.

"No witchcraft," Vareena replied, holding herself rigid
rather than flinging herself out of the cottage without so
much as looking at the boy. The ghosts might trap her in
this hated place, but they at least appreciated her, thanked
her for the small services she gave them.

"I'll have no witchery, Vareena. Headman's daughter
you might be, but I don't have to tolerate your evil ways."

"If you do not want me to heal your son, why did you
send for me?"

"Baker made me send for you. He needs the boy up and
working, not languishing here screaming his heart out. Had
I my way, I'd have treated him myself and let him heal
slow. Burns heal better slow."

Jeeremy did not seem to be screaming, merely moaning.
His pain reached out and squeezed Vareena's heart. She
couldn't abandon him because of his mother's rude intol-
erance.

"I have a salve made of barks and berries," Vareena said
quietly through her clamped teeth. "But first I must cleanse
the burn of the lard you slathered on. That might have
cooled it a little at first, but such a treatment offers no
lasting relief."

"You saying I don't know what is best for my boy?" The
woman's voice rose to near hysteria.

"I'll fetch some water." Vareena ducked out of the dark
and dusty lean-to rather than issue the angry retort that
nearly choked her.

Outside the cottage she breathed deeply, holding each

breath within her lungs before letting it out. The cool morning breeze taunted her with hints of other places it had visited before blowing here. It tasted cool and tangy, like salt, everblue trees, and rich loamy dirt. Bits of the mist and haze scattered to reveal patches of blue sky.

A tear stung her eyes. If only she could follow the breeze wherever it led her. She clutched the silver-and-amethyst amulet beneath her shift. If only she could claim the acres Farrell had bequeathed her. If only she and Robb could leave this place together. If only . . .

But none of that would happen. She had to fetch fresh well water and tend to Jeeremy's burns under the hostile stare of his mother. Then she had to take fresh food up to her ghosts. Tomorrow and the next day and the next promised her no difference in her routine. Her freedom fled with the breeze.

* * *

They think to keep me in darkness. But I do not need light. I need only my magic to keep safe what is mine. The kardiaquake did not stop them. The nightmares did not stop them. I must try something else. As I send out my senses, seeking another diversion, I see others gathering. They come from many directions. Diverse people with different priorities and warring ideals. An idea planted here. A whisper there.

Soon they will fight among themselves rather than bother with me and mine.

* * *

"Just hold that lace pillow nice and gentle, Lady, while I strap it on tight," Zebbiah said.

The nameless woman did so while she took one last look at the palace where she had wandered aimlessly for . . . at least five days before she awakened and two days since then.

"Zebbiah, do you think I have the right to give myself a name, since neither you nor my daughter remembers my true name?" she asked intently.

Yesterday, while she'd packed the lace, he and Jaranda had scavenged food and other journey supplies. They had tried to leave at dawn as planned. An explosion outside the palace walls had frightened the pack beast. It sat and brayed as if in pain for a long time. It did not understand that the terrible noise was probably only someone clearing rubble. The beast would not rise again, no matter the enticement or provocation, for almost two hours until the city that surrounded them on three sides had quieted.

Now they seemed about to set forth. Into danger? Perhaps only adventure. But she still had no idea who she was or why she and her daughter had been abandoned in the palace. Something about her daughter having red hair rather than the blond of a true-blood?

"Choose whatever name you like, Lady," Zebbiah said as he secured more straps on his pack beast. The obnoxious creature let out a mournful bray, extending its neck and laying back its ears as the Rover cinched the girth strap tighter. It shifted its rear hooves restlessly. Both the Rover and the woman moved out of range of those dangerous feet.

It kicked back once and arched its back. But since it had not connected with anything, or anyone, it settled again.

"I'll think about a name as we walk to the docks. Are you certain the ferries are still running upriver?" The traffic on the river she had observed from the palace windows was sporadic at best.

"Sure as sure. My uncle's cousin's nephew has a boat waiting for me. We can pay them with that linen doily you found tucked inside your favorite pillow," he answered, still concentrating on the packing. "Lace still has some value here, mostly to people trading outland, but hard work and sharp weapons have more. We'll save the Tambrin lace for trade in Coronnan."

From the palace windows she had watched the river. Some people left on outland barges, others moved back into the city in small groups. In the city, she had watched a few people trying to clear away rubble and start new buildings, others attempted to rebuild their damaged homes and businesses. No one stopped the looters or bully gangs that robbed at will. No one traveled alone. Almost everyone, men, women, and children, carried weapons.

She knew that was wrong. Weapons had no place in this peaceful city. She had never carried a weapon, wouldn't know how to use one if she had. What little crime prowled around the edges of civilization should be handled by the city guard—or in extreme cases by . . . She couldn't remember who judged the more serious crimes, only that a feared authority existed.

None of the returning citizens or gangs came near the palace. No one came to check on the unnamed woman and her child who had been abandoned in the palace—except this itinerant trader. She trusted his strong arms and his politeness. Mostly she trusted his greed. He could have stolen the lace and sold it outland at a profit. But that would be the end of that market. By taking her under his wing, he guaranteed a continuing supply of lace. As long as she gave him a valuable product to sell, he would protect her and her daughter.

"Have an eye to everything around you as we walk, Lady. I don't think anyone will accost you on the way. Rovers still have a reputation in this land." He flashed her a smile that bordered on vicious. "I'd like to concentrate on protecting the beast and the lace. So keep one eye on your daughter and the other on everyone and everything around you. Once aboard the ferry, my people will keep you from harm."

As if to emphasize his warning, the sounds of harsh words, blows exchanged, a scream, and running feet came from just outside the walls.

The woman shuddered and closed her eyes a moment. Her people should be working together to rebuild, not fighting and stealing.

"And these relatives of yours will take us all the way to the headwaters of the River Lenicc? All the way to safety?"

"He said so. There's a caravan gathering to go over the pass into Coronnan. We'll be safe with them, but we have to get going. The journey is long. As it is, we might have to spend the winter in an abandoned monastery I know of on the other side of the pass. Find your daughter, Lady, and let us leave."

The ground shook once again as if to emphasize his order. The roof above the lace workroom collapsed, sending bricks and beams spraying over the courtyard. Zebbiah crouched down with his arms over his head and neck until the avalanche of debris ceased.

"Jaranda!" the woman screamed. "Where are you, baby?" Panic filled her heart.

The pack beast brayed again in protest at the disruption. It kicked out and then threatened to park its rear end down on the cobbles.

Zebbiah cursed and kicked the creature to keep it on its feet.

"Jaranda!" she called again. She whirled about, desperately seeking a sign of her child.

"Here I am, M'ma." The little girl skipped over loose cobblestones and fallen bricks from the far side of the courtyard, seemingly unconcerned despite the recent danger. She bounced a ball from the royal nursery.

The woman nearly sagged with relief. She crouched down and hugged her daughter close.

"Lady, you have never questioned traveling so far with me. You, a woman alone and unprotected. Me, a man you don't know, have no reason to trust."

"You have not given me a reason not to trust you. As you said, prejudices must be learned. I have forgotten everything."

They stared at each other for a long silent moment, assessing, weighing, enjoying.

He looked away first.

"Jaranda, my love, I think I would like the name Trizia. Do you like that name? It means noble lady." She pulled the little girl against her leg in a fierce hug, unwilling to let her stray again, even for a moment.

"You are M'ma," the little girl insisted. She stamped her foot in irritation. "M'ma."

"Trizia doesn't fit," Zebbiah added. He yanked the pack beast's halter to start it moving.

"I thought you'd say that."

*   *   *

"Twelve, thirteen, fourteen," Marcus counted out loud the number of bags of gold on the first bank of shelves.

He counted because Robb had told him to count. He could not think beyond the straight sequence of numbers, could not plan. If he stopped counting, he'd fall into deep despair.

Yet the more he counted, the heavier he felt. Each movement and thought became an effort. The gloaming pressed against all of his senses. Soon he'd not be able to hold his head up, stand, talk, eat.

"Fifteen, sixteen, seventeen." He gulped back a sob.

The monastery trapped them. His luck and his magic had drained out of him. The future looked hopeless.

"Snap out of it, Marcus," Robb barked. He spoke slowly as if he, too, swam through the thick air.

"It all seems so hopeless." Marcus rubbed two gold coins together in his pocket while he paused. "All this gold stashed away, gathering dust. It could be put to such good use—rebuilding the University, stabilizing the economy, increasing trade."

"Bribing nobles to make magic legal again," Robb added with a grin. But his smile looked false. As false as the hazy light that dominated the entire monastery.

"And the gold just sits here! And we can't get out to put it to use."

"Every bit of information we gather is a step toward finding an exit." Robb placed a comforting hand upon Marcus' shoulder. "We're magicians, trained to think, to plan, and solve problems. We can't always trust in luck. If we plan it right, we'll get out of here."

Warmth and reassurance spread from Robb's touch. Marcus absorbed it, fighting for a small glimmer of hope.

"We've got to make our own luck, Marcus. Maybe there is significance in the number and arrangement of bags. Perhaps these isolated shelves in the center of the room mask an exit we haven't discovered yet. We won't know until we investigate."

"What is happening to us, Robb? I'm supposed to be the one who gives you cheer and encouragement. That's why we work so well together. You think, I plow forward with infinite optimism, making up the plan as we go." Marcus covered his friend's hand on his shoulder with his own and squeezed to show his undying friendship—even in this terrible time.

"We've been in worse scrapes before. Remember that

time in Hanic when that farmer caught us hiding in his byre with his daughter? He chased us bare-assed through his fields for almost a quarter league before we got our wits together enough to throw up magical armor?" They both chuckled at the memory. "Think about something pleasant for a while, rather than what we can't do. Think about Margit. Margit always brings a smile to your face."

"Margit." Marcus tried to conjure her image in his mind's eye. Bold and forthright, she had a minor magical talent and had used it in good stead as Jaylor's spy in the royal household. Her dark blond braids bounced with life as she strode strongly through each task.

But she hated living indoors. And she hated cats; said they robbed her breath. When Marcus had seen her last, she had not known the nature of Queen Rossemikka's problem—that a cat spirit shared her body.

But she had known her own heart and pledged it to Marcus.

A daintier blonde, more mature, milder of temperament and smaller of body superimposed herself upon Marcus' inner vision.

Vareena.

"I bet Vareena likes cats as much as I do," he said to himself.

He shook his head to clear it.

"I wonder if Jaylor has found a solution to the queen's problem?" he mused rather than admit his sense of guilt and betrayal of Margit. He'd loved her and been faithful to her for two years and more. He'd never loved anyone for that long before.

"We won't know what is going on in the capital or the University until we find a way to break the spell trapping us. Now count the bags. Count the pattern of their arrangement. Count the coins themselves."

"And what will you be doing while I count?"

"Counting the graves of the ghosts. Searching the temple foundation stones for another exit. I have this odd feeling that something is missing. Something I should have noticed."

Robb turned to retreat from the bookless library and froze in his tracks.

Alerted to danger, Marcus opened his senses and stared

in the direction Robb looked—toward the back of the room into deep shadows from the overhanging gallery and more empty shelves.

And something else. A glittering mist that gathered and coalesced into a vague human shape. Dressed in old-fashioned robes of gold and brown, the figure carried a bloody sacrificial knife and a magician's staff.

"Do you see what I see?" Robb whispered.

"I hope I don't. That . . . that looks like a ghost. A real ghost." His balance and perceptions twisted. He stumbled and clutched the gold-laden shelves for balance.

"That ghost looks very angry indeed!" Robb wasn't standing easy on the roiling floor either.

"Run!"

Chapter 18

Marcus skidded to a halt on the slick paving stones at the end of the colonnade. He had to bend over to catch his breath. Still, icy bugs seemed to climb his spine. He imagined the ghost slicing into his back from the base of his spine upward.

Robb careened into him. They looked at each other, eyes wide. Marcus' heart beat loudly in his ears.

Without a word spoken, they took off again, away from the buildings toward the graveyard and the foundations for the old temple.

Vareena stood just inside the gates, holding a covered basket—probably full of food.

"What ails you, Marcus, Robb?" Vareena gasped, clutching her throat in alarm.

b "A—g–gho–ghost!" Marcus panted. He leaned heavily against the gatehouse wall as he drew in deep draughts of air.

"But you are the ghosts here. No one else," she protested. She furrowed her brow in puzzlement, tilting her adorable little nose down.

Marcus reached out to smooth tight worry lines from her face. A barrier of burning energy repulsed his hand. He clenched it into a fist instead.

"We. Are. Not. Ghosts," Robb stated breathlessly. "We did not die, leaving our spirits behind."

"You only forget your passing, Robb. You are both truly ghosts," Vareena insisted.

"No, we aren't," Marcus agreed with his friend. "That—thing—haunting the library is a real ghost. And it is royally pissed . . . um . . . I mean perturbed by our presence."

"If there is truly another ghost in this place, why have I not sensed his presence? Why have I not seen him in all these past twenty years? I assure you, you two are the only ghosts currently residing here." She placed her hands upon her hips and pursed her lips as if reprimanding errant children.

"I beg to differ, my dear." Robb assumed his normal preaching tone, so obviously missing earlier today. "The entity we encountered in the library has most certainly staked a claim there. You admitted that you had not explored any part of the monastery other than the rooms occupied by your guests. The villagers shun the place unless required by you to make repairs, and even then they usually restrict themselves to the residential wing. Why should anyone have disturbed that thing other than your other guests who examined the building out of boredom, or seeking an exit. I can only presume they, too, were frightened away by this true ghost and did not explore further. Therefore, I must conclude that the answer to our quest for escape lies within the library." Robb finally paused to breathe.

"I am not going back to that library!" Marcus trembled. "It wanted to carve out my heart with that sacrificial knife. Didn't you see how much blood it dripped, how it reeked of the grave, and carried the chill of the void between existences?" Had he truly felt all that, or had his imagination filled in the gaps from old stories passed around apprentice dormitories late at night on Saawheen Eve?

"Yes, I did see all that and felt the same unnatural chill," Robb said thoughtfully, tapping his teeth. He began to pace a serpentine path around Marcus and Vareena. "That is how I know it to be a true ghost."

"A ghost is a ghost!" Vareena protested. "I shall prove it to you. You two are the only ghosts here." She set down her basket, pushed past the two magicians, and marched back along the colonnade toward the library. Her footsteps echoed against the flagstones.

Marcus suddenly realized that he and Robb made no noise as they moved about the old place. Their boots with sturdy leather soles and hard wooden heels should clomp noisily with every step.

The gloaming seemed to absorb the sounds of their passing. He wondered if they stood on the edge of the void between the planes of existence. The sense-robbing blackness of the void when one first entered could also rob a man of his sanity if he did not have a purpose, a question to ask. Only when he held that purpose or question firmly in his mind did the multicolored umbilicals of life become visible. If one had patience and courage, a man could sort through the life forces that surrounded him in the void that represented all those important to him in reality.

Perhaps . . . If he could summon enough magic for a trip into the void, he could find a way home.

"Robb." He stopped his friend from following Vareena with a hand upon his shoulder. No barrier of energy repulsed his touch as it did with Vareena. "Robb, maybe we are ghosts of a sort. Our boots make no noise, we can touch each other but not her. Perhaps we are at the edge . . ."

"True. Our condition is not normal. But we cannot pass through walls, we require food and drink—we both eliminate bodily wastes regularly. And we have no memory of injury or death. None of that indicates that we have left our bodies behind as we would in death or on a trip through the void. We have bodies. We just aren't truly in one reality or another, but trapped halfway between."

"Isn't that what happens to a ghost? His body is in one reality and his spirit in another."

"Our spirits and bodies remain intact. 'Tis reality around us that wavers."

"You've got a point there. Let's follow and see what Vareena conjures up in the library."

"An apt description, I believe."

Together they caught up with Vareena as she pushed open the door to the library.

"I don't remember closing the door. Did you close it, Robb?"

Robb shook his head and scrunched his face in a puzzled frown. "I believe the ghost wishes to be left alone."

Marcus tasted the air with his magical senses. Dust, mold, stone older than time, staleness, and . . . and something sour tingling on his tongue that did not belong there.

"It's waiting for us," he whispered.

"Stuff and nonsense. I'd know if another ghost had come here. I'm a sensitive." Vareena resolutely pushed the door open and stepped into the vast room. "Yoohooo! Anybody home?"

Her words echoed around the nearly empty room. Silence followed.

Marcus and Robb poked their heads around the door, Robb above, Marcus slightly stooped. Diffuse sunlight filtered through the dust in broken shafts. "The dust should have settled by now. There isn't a breeze to stir it," Marcus whispered.

"I know," Robb replied.

"Look for the sparkles, for movement."

Vareena walked around the free-standing bookshelves. Her skirts raised clouds of dust in her wake. It swirled and eddied, drifting to new locations. But none of her dust stayed in the air more than a moment or two.

The other dust—the stuff that lingered in the corner far away from her circuitous path—took on a vaguely human shape, the glint of red and metal showed the knife now tucked into his old-fashioned belt sash over yellow tunic and orange sleeveless robe. Brown trews and boots faded into the shadows, making him look almost legless. He made mocking faces at Vareena, waving his arms in a parody of drawing attention to himself.

Eventually, Vareena climbed the spiral staircase to the second-floor gallery. The gloating dust followed her only within touching distance of the cold iron structure. Then it jerked back as if burned.

"Behind you," Marcus hissed at her.

"What?" Vareena turned on the sixth step, looking over her shoulder at them.

"The ghost. In the dust. Behind you." Marcus held his breath, not daring to come closer, yet fearful for her well-being.

"I see nothing." Firmly she marched up the stairs.

"She didn't even look," Robb protested.

"Perhaps she truly cannot see this ghost. Her sensitivities are limited, as is her magic."

"I wonder if all of her other ghosts have been mundane," Robb mused.

"If so, they might not have seen this ghost. If mundanes couldn't find a way out, perhaps the solution lies in magic."

Hope brightened Marcus' heart for the first time since coming here.

"But our magic has become quite limited by whatever force holds us here. Without a dragon to combine and enhance our powers, we may not have enough magic to break the spell."

* * *

Ariiell loosened the ties of her gown and shifted the pillows behind her back. She sighed at the relief of pressure on her swelling belly.

Outside her bedchamber her father and stepmother continued to argue over her plight. Her father's second wife wept more than she spoke. "Think of the disgrace of bringing that monster into our family. Everyone will know 'tis not a love match. 'Tis not even a good political move." Lady Laislac choked out the words between sobs. "Better we send her to a convent overseas for a year and foster the baby elsewhere. It's likely to be as hideous as the father."

Ariiell frowned. Her stepmother repeated some of the arguments Ariiell had put forth against the marriage to Mardall. Arguments she expected and hoped to lose.

"My honor is as much at stake as the girl's. She'll never be able to make a more advantageous marriage. Whoever we pawn her off on will know she's not a virgin and will renounce the marriage on the wedding night." Lord Laislac's boots pounded the floor rushes into a distinctive path from his repetitive pacing.

Her father always won family arguments regardless of the wisdom or lightness of his position.

The best way for Ariiell to get what she wanted was to counter her father with the opposite of her goal. In four years of marriage, her stepmother had never learned that little trick. Her father's wife deserved the unhappiness Lord Laislac dealt her every day.

"To bring that . . . that thing into the family!"

"That *thing* is blood heir to the throne," Ariiell's father reminded his wife.

"Precisely," Ariiell whispered to herself. "Mardall will never take the throne. But as long as Queen Rossemikka remains barren, my child is next in line." She smiled hugely, rubbing her tummy.

The baby kicked in response to the slight pressure. A good sign of the child's health and vigor. Her mentor had promised the child would be normal.

"I will be the mother of the next king of Coronnan," she whispered to herself. No sense in losing the battle with her father by stating the truth. "As soon as the marriage takes place and the child is declared legitimate, I must find a way to eliminate Darville. I'll certainly be more successful than those idiots from the coven and the Gnuls who have bungled every attempt these last three years."

She reached beneath the mattress for the book of poisons she had recently acquired. She wasn't supposed to be able to read—no person other than the now outlawed magicians were allowed to learn the arcane art of reading and higher mathematics. But Ariiell had watched the family magician priest as he sounded out the letters and words on letters and reports. The priest was supposed to consign written communications to the fire as soon as he read them to the lord. A little sleight of hand had brought most of those messages into Ariiell's possession.

Careful study had brought the words to life.

So now she plotted out ways to coat the inside of Darville's riding gloves with a fast-acting poison. She'd need time to gather all the necessary ingredients. Time to insert herself into court life. After the wedding.

By this time next year, she intended to be regent for her infant son and the coven.

Earlier today, her guardian from the coven had tried another assassination upon the king. But this one was intended to fail. The coven needed Darville alive until Ariiell's child was born. But they needed him frightened of dying without an heir so that he would name Ariiell's child as next in succession. The man must have failed. He hadn't reported back to her, and the king had not sent word to hasten the marriage.

Time for a change of tactics. In a few hours she'd summon her nameless guardian and give him a new task—the poison ingredients would work just as well on Queen Rossemikka.

*   *   *

"I think I have a problem, Jaylor. I can't throw the spell. I can't come to the lair in three days or even tonight." Jack schooled his voice and his face to slip through the summons spell on a note of calm. Panic gibbered inside him, demanding he pace, he pound, he seek Katrina in any way possible. He'd even travel into the void by himself, without an anchor, in order to find her.

He sent this summons alone, deep in the night. As he had always been alone. He'd hoped Katrina would be the one to fill the aching void in his life. Now she was gone, too!

He intended to fight to bring her back.

Moonlight filtered through the rare glass window of the king's study tower. Hours of searching had resulted in no new information as to Katrina's direction or means of transportation. The scrying bowl had revealed only that she fled away from him.

The king had had less luck in interrogating the scullery maid from the tunnel. She had disappeared from her locked room before anyone could question her, and no one from the kitchen remembered her ever working there. And yet Jack knew he'd seen her there just the day before . . . a puzzle he did not have time for.

Jack's only hope of finding his beloved lay in Katrina's lack of magical talent. She couldn't transport herself and had to travel on foot or steedback. She'd not get beyond the reach of his transport spell. But he had to have a landmark, something recognizable to home in on.

And every minute he prayed that the Gnuls had not captured her. Their witch-sniffers had ways of shielding their prisoners from searches conducted by mundanes and magicians alike—much as Journeymen Marcus and Robb had disappeared some moons ago.

He wouldn't think about that. He knew he could find Katrina anywhere, any time, once he calmed down. Their souls were linked. His last journey through the void had shown him how the white and gold of her life force had entwined with his silver and purple.

"Calm down, Jack," Jaylor ordered. "What happened?" He looked more relaxed and coherent than the last time

Jack had summoned him. The twin girls had made their entrance into the world. One came screaming, kicking, and protesting the transition. The other was much smaller and more placid, almost listless. Not all of Jaylor's worries had ended, just the worst of them. Brevelan and the new babies slept . . . for the moment.

Jack took three deep breaths, almost triggering a deeper trance that would take him into the void then and there. A haunting *Song* drifted through the blackness of the void, tempting him.

(Answers can be found in the void. Are you ready to learn and accept what you find, pleasant or distressful?) Baamin asked. In his current existence Baamin wore magician blue on the tips of his dragon wings. He had befriended Jack more than once.

Jack couldn't see the wise dragon at the moment, but would recognize his voice anywhere.

He held himself tightly to this world.

"Talk to me, Jack. Don't revert to your old habits of silence. In this case, keeping your mouth shut will not solve the problem," Jaylor coaxed. He'd known Jack when he was a nameless kitchen drudge. He'd stood by Jack when he became an arrogant apprentice magician who chose the magnificent name Yaakke out of history. But Jaylor was not there when Jack had to live up to the name he chose. Jack had learned most painfully that the humbler shortening of the name suited him much better. Jaylor could not know how important Katrina had been to his survival through that long and grueling process.

"She's gone," Jack choked out. Slowly, he found the words to explain how and why Katrina had fled rather than face the intimacy of marriage. "I have to bring her back!"

"You need to follow her, certainly," Jaylor replied. "But believe me, you can't force her to come back to you. All you can do is wait patiently by her side and allow her to make the first move." The Senior Magician smiled. His attention drifted as if he remembered something wonderful.

Jack had to remind himself that Jaylor might hold authority over all members of the Commune of Magicians, but he was only a few years older than Jack. And a new father, for the third and fourth time. Balladeers had been singing of his deep and abiding love for Brevelan for four years now.

"Then I'll follow Katrina now."

"No. You will complete your duty to Coronnan, the Commune, and our king! That is our oath as members of the Commune."

Jack's sense of duty to Coronnan, Commune, and king had seen him through years of slavery, terrible dangers, and persecution. It had brought him many rewards, including Katrina's love.

"She's not safe. I can't fulfill my duties to anyone as long as she's in danger."

"I'll send Margit to catch up with her. My apprentice is most anxious to get out in the world. She says that she finds life at the University or at court stifling—she can't breathe properly indoors. But I suspect much of her anxiety centers around the missing Marcus and Robb—Marcus in particular."

"Margit has no training. The only spell she can work is a weak summons. How can she protect Katrina?"

"Margit has learned a lot in the last few moons, and as long as her breathing isn't stifled while indoors, she does have more magic than we thought. She's the best person to be with Katrina right now. They are the same age. They are both in love and having difficulty with the relationship. Margit can talk to her. They can share female secrets, where a man will just frighten your ladylove."

"But . . ."

"No buts. Do your research and planning. Then transport Mikka and Darville to the lair three days hence."

"But . . ."

Jaylor broke off the summons.

Jack slumped against the king's desk. His spine no longer had the stiffness to hold him up.

"Be safe, Katrina. Be safe until I can come to you."

Chapter 19

"**B**ut I haven't finished writing the paper you requested," Margit half-protested Jaylor's exciting news. Dawn had barely crested the horizon. She hadn't expected anyone to be out and about so early. The Senior Magician had surprised her in her favorite study perch in an oak tree on the edge of the University compound.

A quest! A chance to journey like a true journeyman . . . er—journeywoman. Could she be considered a journeywoman if she had not undergone the trial by Tambootie smoke?

She both dreaded and welcomed the ritual. Well . . . she welcomed the advancement the ritual offered. But to endure three days in a windowless room, the only door sealed by magic, with only a Tambootie wood fire for light and warmth, strapping huge bands of pressure around her lungs, squeezing the breath from her. Rumor—almost legend—proclaimed that when Jaylor had undergone the trial, the master magicians had had to battle the demons he conjured for three days before sending them back beyond the void.

To be trapped in the room for three days would be bad enough. To be trapped with the monsters of her worst nightmares would kill her. She'd die of suffocation before the monsters could take form.

"Have you finished the research for the paper?" Jaylor asked. He kept looking back toward the clearing, eyes clouded, worry making deep creases beside his mouth. Then he finger-combed his beard and turned those deep brown eyes fully on her.

Margit felt as if her skin peeled away, revealing more

than just her bones and organs. Her very soul was exposed to this man. He had to know how her heart skipped a beat and pounded relentlessly, how her skin jumped and her toes wiggled, eager to begin the journey this very instant.

Her tree branch became very uncomfortable.

"I think I've read everything others have written about opposing elements and complementary elements. But I need to conduct some experiments before I can know for sure that the theory works."

"You can do that on the road. I suggest simple things like a compulsion on your steed to make it travel faster to appease Katrina's need to flee, then negate it when you find her to delay until Jack can catch up to you."

"Is this quest so very important?" She tucked her book inside her tunic and swung down to face the Senior Magician on his own level. She had to look up at the man who held her career in his hands as easily as he held the reins of the entire Commune and University. Not many men topped her by more than half a hand's span.

"I, the queen, the entire kingdom, have need of Jack's special talents and skills. He is worthless unless he knows for certain that Katrina is safe. Can you do that?" The earnestness of his question lost some of its effect as his attention wandered back to his home in the clearing.

She'd heard that one of the newborn twins was small and sickly, her sister having enough strength and energy for two. Too often, twins were born early—too early for both, or either, to survive. She wished she'd paid more attention to how long Brevelan had carried the babies.

"Are Brevelan and the babies all right?" she asked, rather than speculate. The Commune thrived on rumors and gossip, most of it wrong. If the kingdom needed Jack free of concern and fully concentrating on his tasks, likewise the kingdom and the Commune needed Jaylor free of problems in his personal life.

"Nothing you need worry about. Now, have you ever scried in a bowl of water?" Jaylor avoided answering. His eyes remained fixed on the trees in the direction of his home.

"Uh . . . not officially, sir." How much experimentation should she have done on her own?

WithyReed discouraged apprentices from working any spell unless directly supervised by him. Slippy and Lyman, on the other hand, applauded initiative, even competition, among their students.

"Unofficially, then, how much success did you have?"

"None at all." Margit hung her head.

"Come into my study and show me how you worked the spell."

"Uh, can we try this out-of-doors, sir?" She stared at the closed door of his private workroom on the back side of the library. Only one entrance and one window, both facing north, toward the clearing and his beloved wife and children.

Margit didn't care which direction the openings faced. There weren't enough of them.

"Is this unnatural fear you have of being within four walls going to interfere with your ability to work magic?"

"No. I survived three years in the palace as the queen's maid."

"Survived, but did not flourish. Your magical talent has blossomed well beyond our initial test results since we brought you here. What bothers you so about being indoors?"

"There isn't enough air to breathe. Besides, you always have a cat with you. They suck out all the air in confined places."

"Cats." Jaylor stared at her long and hard. "Cats. Very well. Fetch me the bowl on my desk and draw some fresh water from the well. We'll enjoy the sunshine under this tree. I have to admit, I prefer fresh air myself." He lifted a drooping everblue branch and ducked beneath it to the open place beside the trunk, as private a place as one could have this close to the classrooms, library, dormitories, and workrooms of the University.

"Uh, sir, wouldn't the spell work better with fresh water from a free-flowing creek and a crockery bowl rather than silver?"

"You have been studying! Amazing." He sounded very much like old Lyman. "You are correct, of course. The bowl on my desk is crockery. Take it to the creek and fill it half full. What about a crystal to trigger the spell?"

"Only if it's uncut. Otherwise, an agate works better."

"And you absorbed the entire lesson. Will miracles never cease?" he added on a chuckle. He sounded so much like Old Lyman, Margit wondered if the Commune still needed the ancient librarian now that he slept so much and avoided work even more.

A few moments later, Margit settled on the carpet of everblue needles, the bowl nestled into a little depression before her. She crossed her legs beneath her and began the deep breathing necessary to focus her concentration.

"That's it, breathe deep, one, two, three, hold on three, release on three, hold, one, two, three," Jaylor chanted quietly. "Let the light trance slide over your mind, concentrate on the water. Focus all of your senses on the water. Now think of whom you seek. Picture Katrina firmly in your mind. If you can't remember her features, think of her most dominant characteristic."

"Silver-blond hair and a lace pillow," Margit mumbled as the picture of Katrina, the last time she had seen her, formed within her mind.

"Yes, the lace pillow. Almost inseparable from her. Now drop the agate into the center of the bowl and watch the ripples, not the agate. See how the ripples reach out from the center, seeking, seeking . . ."

"There!" Margit breathed. In the water she watched the refugee from SeLenicca riding across the river plains away from the capital. Her lace pillow, barely covered with a bright kerchief, and a small pack rested precariously behind her saddle. Her steed plodded, Katrina's shoulders drooped, and her head sagged. Had she ridden all night and fallen asleep while riding?

"Do you recognize any landmarks?"

"Yes, the queen used to like riding across that meadow. I've followed her up that barren hill and around those boulders many times."

"Good, now withdraw from the images slowly."

Margit allowed her eyes to blink rapidly several times while she let loose her breath that had become pent up with excitement. The pictures faded from the water. Sleepiness fogged her mind and made her head too heavy for her neck to support.

"Wake up!" Jaylor clapped his hands sharply right beneath her nose.

Margit shook herself and focused on the tent made by drooping everblue branches. She seemed to return to herself from a great distance. Her stomach growled.

"Now, Margit, think carefully. What did you do differently from the time you tried this on your own?"

"Nothing."

"Something was different. This time it worked very well. Last time you saw nothing. What is different?"

Margit scrunched her eyes closed reviewing the entire procedure. "I've tried several times to find Marcus. Every time, the water ripples and the agate falls and nothing happens."

"Marcus? You've tried to find my missing journeyman?"

"Yes, sir. We—ah—we . . ."

"Are in love. Yes. I recognized the symptoms."

Margit blushed. "I did not think our feelings had become so obvious to others."

"Love is something that cannot hide, Margit. It needs to shine forth and grow. Now go get your breakfast. You'll need to refuel your body while I arrange for riding and pack steeds. You'll need journey food and camping gear for several days, perhaps a week. Master Lyman, Master Slippy, and I will transport you to the place you recognized when all is ready. When Jack catches up with you in a few days, I want you to stay with Katrina, make sure that both of them get safely into SeLenicca and report back to me every night." Jaylor stood up and lifted one of the branches for an exit.

"What about Marcus and Robb?" Margit stayed stubbornly beside the bowl.

"Keep your eyes open for signs of them. I expect they headed for one of the passes to the south of Sambol. Try to steer Jack and Katrina in that direction. I suspect those roads are less well guarded and safer than through two armies at the headwaters of the River Coronnan." He left her alone.

"Oh, and return the water to the creek and the bowl and agate to my desk before you eat."

"Am I a journeywoman yet, Master Jaylor?"

"Probably. But we haven't time for the trial by Tambootie smoke. We'll worry about that later. Find yourself a staff anyway. We'll discuss this further when you get back to me tonight." He hurried back toward the clearing and his family.

"I'm going to find you, Marcus, no matter how much I have to improvise," Margit said to the empty air. "No matter what magical and mundane barriers stand between us, I will find you. Then the two of us will spend the rest of our lives together, traveling the world on missions for the Commune."

*   *   *

"Come, daughter." Lord Laislac grabbed Ariiell's hand and dragged her off the bed. "A priest and the imbecile await us."

"P'pa?" Ariiell sat down on the edge of the high mattress, resisting his efforts to propel her out the door. "What has come over you? Why the sudden hurry?"

She knew the reason well enough. All day the king and queen had withdrawn from court, smiling longingly into each other's eyes. Rossemikka's pale skin had developed a rosy glow, she wore her hair loose about her shoulders, disguising the strange white streaks in the auburn, brown, black, blond hair. The royal couple laughed and smiled secretly at each other as they held hands.

They acted like newlyweds, in the first flush of love. Disgusting.

They were up to something. Something devious and detrimental to Ariiell.

Rumors flew through the capital. Half the court were certain the queen had conceived again. The other half gleefully named a secret mistress who would produce a child that the royal couple would substitute for the queen's many failed pregnancies.

If Ariiell and her father had any hopes of having her child named heir to the throne, they had to insure its legitimacy as quickly as possible.

"Lord Andrall agrees with me. The kingdom is too unstable to rely on the queen to produce an heir. If she miscarries again, it could well kill her. The brat you carry is the only hope." Laislac yanked hard on Ariiell's arm, nearly dislocating her shoulder before she had a chance to balance on her own two feet. The folds of her gown twisted to outline the huge swell of her baby.

"How far along are you?" Laislac stared at his daughter. "You told your stepmother only four moons."

"Closer to seven," Ariiell dropped her eyes, feigning embarrassment.

"We've no time to waste, then, do we?" her father stated.

She cringed away from him, expecting a hard slap, or a burning bruise on her upper arm. When the hurt did not come, she chanced a glance at him. A wry smile tugged at her father's lips.

"Stargods, I wish your brothers were half as cunning as you. How often did you have to endure the imbecile in your bed before you arranged to be found?"

"Only three times." Mardall, for all of his slow mind and stalled emotional growth, had been a rather considerate lover. More so than some. Mardall wanted to please. Her other lovers—usually within a ritual eight-pointed star of the coven—wanted only their own pleasure and the power of domination. "When I knew for certain that Mardall's seed had found fertile ground, I deliberately made mistakes in arranging the next tryst." Ariiell returned her father's smile. "You'll be the grandfather of the next king, P'pa. 'Twill be easy enough to arrange a joint regency between you and Lord Andrall."

"Tell me, daughter, did you choose to foster with Andrall after your mother died and before I remarried with this in mind?"

Ariiell smiled at her father, letting him draw his own conclusions. If she allowed him to guess part of the truth, he'd not look further for the entire truth.

"Lord Andrall and Lady Lynnetta are very kind and trusting. Too bad they have withdrawn from court so often this last year and more." Ariiell kept her eyes on the floor—she couldn't see her toes anymore for the bulk of the baby. Let her father think what he liked. She'd never tell him that she had anchored the eight-pointed star in Nunio. She'd never tell him how the coven had arranged for her fosterage and her pregnancy.

"Everyone knows Andrall retreats to the quiet of the country because his heart has weakened. Too much distress over keeping his nephew safe on the throne." This time Laislac laughed heartily. "Rumor claims he has not long to live. Perhaps someone can hasten to give truth to the rumor, eh?" He cocked his head and smiled with half his mouth. His eyes glittered with malice and greed.

Ariiell rearranged her gown to once more draw men's eyes away from her belly to the more enticing swell of her breasts. Then she draped a filmy veil over her hair and shoulders. The belled fringe fluttered in another off-center illusion. Each step created a delicate chiming of the silver ornaments.

"We'll leave for home directly after the ceremony," Lord Laislac pronounced. "You'll deliver safely within the confines of our castle. I shall control the time and place of the announcement of the birth."

"But, P'pa, won't our presence be more advantageous at court, where we can watch Darville and his foreign queen, make certain he does not survive long enough to father a child that the queen might carry full term?"

"We have time. The queen has lost five babes before the fifth month. The last miscarriage nearly killed her. She won't risk another pregnancy so soon. The servants will pack for you. Come. Your groom awaits you."

"Perhaps you are right, P'pa. If Darville witnesses the marriage, he cannot later deny the legitimacy of my child. Best he be born in safety. At court the Gnuls might kill me and the child just to make sure we do not succeed Darville." She clenched her fist in her gown, praying to Simurgh that her father would remain true to form and immediately counter her wishes.

"Precisely. Now come along so the servants can get busy packing."

"But, P'pa!" She couldn't allow servants to dismantle her room. They'd find the book beneath the mattress. She had only had time to acquire half the ingredients for the poison she wanted to use. She had not had time to memorize the entire spell and components to recreate it without the book.

"Stop acting the fool and come, before Andrall changes his mind and takes the imbecile back to Nunio." Laislac grabbed her arm once more. This time his grip threatened to leave large bruises. "He can do that after the wedding. We won't need him once he says the vows. I hope Andrall prompts his son correctly. I don't want any doubts about the legality of the marriage or the birth."

Ariiell dropped to her knees. If her father dragged her farther, he'd ruin her gown so that she appeared at the wedding reluctant and disgraced.

"What now?" he stared down at her, hands on hips. The lines around his mouth clearly showed his need to release his temper.

"I . . . I lost my balance. The babe . . ." Ariiell heaved herself upright, using the bed as a crutch. With her back to her father, she slipped the precious book from beneath the mattress into a secret pocket within an extra fold of her skirt. She redraped the scarf to further conceal it. The fluttering bells would disguise and distract anyone from looking too closely at any misalignment of her gown.

Darville would not long survive the birth of her child even if she had to steal the transport spell from Rejiia to return to court.

Chapter 20

"**Y**ou may now kiss the bride," the red-robed priest intoned. His clean-shaven face showed not a trace of emotion.

Ariiell stared equally stone-faced straight ahead at the tapestry icon of the Stargods descending upon a cloud of silver flame. The metallic embroidery had been cunningly worked to take on the outline of a dragon in certain lights. The flickering candles on the altar gave her tantalizing glimpses of the magical creatures.

She wished a dragon would swoop down and whisk away her bridegroom.

"Go ahead, kiss her, Mardall," Lord Andrall prompted his son.

King Darville looked away, his upper lip curled in a feral snarl. He looked as if he'd like to retreat from the dais where he stood beside the priest. Queen Rossemikka was notably missing from the ceremony.

Mardall blushed slightly as he pursed his lips and leaned vaguely in Ariiell's direction. She turned her head so that his damp mouth touched only her cheek. At least he didn't drool. She'd almost cured him of that in the time she was actively trying to get pregnant. One more spell and she thought she'd eliminate the problem.

Ariiell batted her eyes at the king and tried to look hurt at his rebuff. Inside, she nearly shouted in triumph. The marriage ceremony was complete. Her child legitimate and likely to sit on the throne wearing the Coraurlia as soon as Darville died. The coven had achieved their primary aim:

one of their own would be heir to the throne of rich and powerful Coronnan.

Power! She did this for power. Political power. Magical power. All she had to do was endure until the baby was born strong and healthy.

The coven would place her at the center of every ritual because of the power and the fulfillment of their dearest and most ancient goal.

"Toast to the royal couple, Your Grace," Lord Laislac suggested. He snapped his fingers to summon his steward.

The servant stepped forward carrying a tray of jewel-encrusted cups and a matching decanter of wine.

"Ohhh," Lady Laislac moaned. She wept loudly into her handkerchief.

"Must we heap hypocrisy upon scandal?" Darville snarled.

Lord Andrall and his lady both gasped. Lady Lynetta clung to her husband's arm, chin quivering.

The bridegroom, Mardall, looked happily around at the marvelous wall paintings and tapestries in the royal chapel.

Ariiell was getting tired of his lighthearted mood already. Nothing seemed to upset him for more than a moment.

"Take the wine away," Darville commanded. "This ceremony may be necessary, but I do not have to like it. There will be no celebration. And there will be no announcements or discussion at court until *I* decide."

"Your Grace, please . . ." Laislac protested.

"We will see how long you can keep this secret," Ariiell told herself silently.

King Darville cocked his head and frowned at her from his position beside the priest. His aunt, Lady Lynnetta, had a similar gesture. With their identical golden-blond hair and golden-brown eyes, they could have been mother and son.

The king's frown deepened.

Had he heard her whisper? She doubted it. He and his line were notoriously mundane, with no trace of magic in their blood at all. He couldn't have learned any listening tricks from Jaylor. They had spent most of their dissolute youth together. But tricks were useless without a magical talent to fuel them.

And Darville's queen, who might or might not have magical power, depending upon which rumor you believed, had not graced the ceremony with her presence. A deliberate snub that Ariiell intended to revenge as soon as she became regent for her baby.

Ariiell smiled at the king, with an expression she hoped beguiled him with innocence. Tradition required him to preside over and bless the marriage since the idiot Mardall was his closest blood relative. Darville needed to appear in accord with the marriage that might produce his heir.

Rossemikka's absence kept Ariiell's hopes and aspirations in a shadowy realm. The marriage was legal, but the royal couple strongly disapproved. She'd have a hard time gaining acceptance at court until she killed Darville.

Never mind. The king would not long survive the birth of the baby.

"You all have leave to depart for Laislac Province," King Darville said. "You still have four or five hours of daylight."

"Leave!" Ariiell choked. "Surely, I cannot travel now." She thrust back her shoulders emphasizing the full extent of her bulging belly.

"By your parent's reckoning you can't be more than four months gone. The best healers in the country tell me you may travel safely," he insisted, daring her to admit the child had resulted from a long-term affair rather than a single incident.

Such an admission would put the blame and disgrace on her shoulders and remove Mardall from all responsibility. She couldn't allow that. She had to appear the victim here to gain the sympathy of the court and the Council of Provinces.

"But . . . but . . ." She couldn't think of a single argument against the king's stern order.

"Surely you wish your cousin to be born at court, Your Grace," Lord Andrall argued. "Surely you want the Council of Provinces to acknowledge the legitimacy of the birth. Our country will gain a great deal of stability with this birth and acknowledgment."

King Darville looked aghast at Lord Andrall, his most

loyal supporter and uncle by marriage. Mardall's father nodded sadly.

The king's jaw firmed and his golden-brown eyes narrowed. Wolf eyes. Ariiell suddenly saw herself reflected in those eyes as a small rabbit, easy prey. She shrank away from him, making certain the book of poisons hidden within the folds and pleats of her gown remained out of sight.

"The child will be born away from court. If it survives and displays normal intelligence, I will acknowledge it in the line of succession. Bad enough I have to preside over this mockery of a marriage. I will not endure the constant reminder of events that should not have happened. All of you are dismissed." He turned on his heel and exited through the private door behind the altar.

A dozen guards appeared at the main door, as if summoned by the king's departure. "Your sledges and steeds await you in the postern courtyard, my lords," the sergeant said. "We will escort you beyond the city limits now." His hand rested easily on his sword.

*   *   *

Lanciar postponed his trip into the void in search of his son. As a military tactician, he knew that intelligence was more important than troop numbers and superior weapons.

So he sat outside the tavern day after day, drinking the sour ale until it began to taste good and watching the Rover encampment. Then he drank some more, relishing the soft haze around his vision. For the first time since he'd left Queen's City in SeLenicca, he did not thirst from his very pores and he did not need to shield his eyes from an overly bright sun.

Day after day he memorized the movements within the Rover encampment. Day after day he learned the faces of the women and the children, which tent or bardo they inhabited, which man they waited for at the end of the day.

Always, he counted more women than men in each dwelling. His heart beat faster at the thrill of two or three women in his bed. Then he clamped down on his emotions and returned to the task at hand.

The dearth of men puzzled Lanciar. Fewer angry and

armed men to pursue him when he chose to retrieve his son. But where had they all gone? Only old men and young boys, barely mature enough to mate remained. He saw nothing of men in their prime.

He learned that laundry, cooking, and minding the children were communal chores shared by all of the women. Men and women alike hunted and foraged to feed the entire community.

Visitors from the inn and nearby campground came to the Rover camp to have their fortunes told, their pots mended, or to buy unique silver jewelry and embroidery. Their few coins bought the things the Rovers could not find in the nearby forest or field.

He guessed that the statue of Krej resided with Zolltarn in the largest tent, for it was guarded night and day. Zolltarn rarely emerged from the fabric shelter, and then only when a dispute disturbed the usual quiet of the camp. He did not linger with his clan, did not join in the singing or dancing or storytelling. But once disturbed he would flash his smile and his people settled into their chores without protest. Whatever had caused the noisy disagreement, it dispersed like mist in sunshine.

"Which child are you, son?" Lanciar asked the air repeatedly. All of the children were treated equally with love and respect. All of the children were tended by at least three adults at all times.

Even if he knew which child to snatch, he'd not travel more than three steps before encountering a vorpal dagger wielded by a very angry Rover. Both men and women carried the nasty rippled blades.

Lanciar trusted his own ability to wield a weapon, but not while carrying a precious baby in one arm.

He knew that Rejiia also watched the Rover enclave, but from the relative comfort of the upper window of the inn. She had commandeered their best and biggest room for herself.

And then the day came when the Rovers broke camp.

Lanciar had seen nothing unusual in their movement. One night they went to bed after singing and dancing around the campfires until nearly midnight—as was their custom— and the next morning they were gone at sunrise.

But this time, they had not used the transport spell. Lanciar found their tracks easily. With an illusory coin, he hired a sturdy steed without much energy and only one speed—slow. But it would walk at that plodding pace all day and half the night without pause.

"Saddle that steed for me, peasant," Rejiia sneered right behind Lanciar. Rejiia gestured to a high-stepping black steed with a blaze of white on its nose and mane that matched her own raven locks streaked at one temple with white.

"I'll see the color of your coin first," the hostler replied calmly.

"You'll see the color of my magic first." Rejiia flung a ball of witchfire into his face.

He screamed and stumbled to a watering trough. Batting at the flames, he plunged his head beneath the water.

The steed pranced and snorted and wheeled, its eyes rolled.

"*S'murghit*, stand still!" Rejiia cursed loudly and let a spell fly. The beast froze in place. Two grooms scurried out of the stable with saddle and tack. They prepared him for riding in record time.

Lanciar sensed the beast straining at the spell. She'd not keep it on a tight rein for long. When it bolted . . .

He hoped Rejiia landed on her lush bottom in the dirt.

For the next three days, Lanciar followed the caravan. The first two nights, the clan camped within shouting distance of villages with inns. He and Rejiia each hired a room. But on the third night, they had passed into Coronnan. The natives here rarely traveled outside their own lands—except for magicians and the occasional trader caravan—and thus had no need for inns. None of their taverns had guest facilities. He made a rough camp beyond the reach of Rover firelight and perimeter guards.

He kept his own fire low, and his noise to a minimum. He'd learned the basic skills of camping behind enemy lines in his first years as a recruit in the SeLenese army.

Of Rejiia, he saw no sign. Perhaps she commandeered lodging at the nearest manor. Perhaps she retreated and watched Zolltarn through a scrying bowl. He found no trace of her within a league of the Rovers with his magical or mundane senses and hoped she had given up the chase.

With his back against a tree, Lanciar munched on dry
journey rations. He watched the Rovers prepare a rich stew
of hedgehog and root vegetables, flavored with a fruity red
wine. The enticing aromas wafted on the breeze like a compulsion spell. His mouth watered, and his stomach grumbled.

His bedroll already took on the dampness of dewfall. The
fire sputtered from damp wood and threatened to die.

All at the Rover camp seemed warm and dry and friendly.

Lanciar took comfort that his son ate well and slept in a
dry cot.

Ah well, he'd endured worse in rough bivouacs while on
patrol behind enemy lines.

"Spy," a woman spoke from directly behind his tree.

"*S'murghit!* Where did you come from? I didn't hear
you," he cursed to cover his startlement. His magical and
military trained senses should have alerted him to her presence the moment she left camp.

"Watch your language, spy. We have children nearby."
She glared at him, hands on hips, eyes blazing with outrage.

"Sorry. You surprised me." Good thing the darkness hid
his flaming cheeks.

"Spy, you have followed us diligently. You might as well
join us. We offer you comfort this rough camp cannot
give you."

"Wh–what?"

"You heard me. You've watched us and followed us,
learning all you can of our people and our habits. We have
nothing to hide. You might as well join us."

"J–join you?" He'd never heard of an enemy openly inviting a spy into their camp. Never heard of Rovers inviting
gadjé adults into their camp either. Children they welcomed, not strangers over the age of ten.

But the invitation made a twisted kind of sense. They
could observe him and control the knowledge he gained
under their supervision.

He could get a closer look at each of the children, see
which might have fairer skin or lighter eyes than those born
to the clan.

"I'll be with you as soon as I put out the fire and gather
my bloody bedroll."

"Watch your language or you will never be allowed near your son." She frowned at him sternly.

Lanciar closed his eyes and dipped his head a fraction in acknowledgment of the rules.

She smiled at him and twitched her hips as she returned to the protection of her clan.

"I've heard they have good wine and ale in Rover camps."

"I brew the best ale of all the Rovers," the young woman replied. "Come and join us. If we learn to trust you, perhaps we will introduce you to your son."

"My . . . my son. How did you know I sought my son?"

"Zolltarn knows everything." She flashed a smile as big and enchanting as the Rover chieftain's.

"Lead me to the ale. I think I'm going to need it."

Chapter 21

Jack came out of the transport spell inside Shayla's lair. He landed with a jolt to his spine and foot-numbing abruptness. His mind had remained drifting in the void a heartbeat too long. He stumbled and grabbed the closest object to steady his balance.

He hoped Mikka and Darville had arrived in the dragon lair ahead of him and with more grace.

Amaranth let out a squeak of distress and jerked away from Jack's grasp.

"Sorry, Amaranth." He petted the bruised and stunted spiral horn bud on the baby dragon's forehead. "This will all be over soon."

The dragonet nuzzled Jack's side, keeping his sensitive forehead lowered and out of reach. He radiated bewilderment, excitement, and just a touch of fear. Jack cuddled Amaranth a little closer.

Emotional distraction kept him from adding any other reassurance. He needed to be on the road following Katrina. Jaylor had confidence in Margit's ability to take care of Katrina. Jack didn't trust anyone but himself where Katrina's well-being was concerned.

Amaranth almost purred under his caresses. Magical power flooded Jack's being. The dragonet opened his mind to Jack. Vivid images of the dragonet's daily hunt and swim in the Bay with his brothers filled Jack's head.

For a moment he felt like part of the group, a member of the family. He pushed it aside; the only family he wanted now was Katrina.

But the premature bond he had inadvertently awakened

in Amaranth did not allow him to shut out the images or the emotions. Nor could he forget his preparation for the spell with Baamin, the blue-tipped dragon who had been his mentor at the old University in a previous life. He'd always have a family with the dragons.

"Amaranth, where is Baamin, the elder blue-tipped dragon?"

(Here, son,) a new voice replied. Soothing, confident, wise.

Jack breathed deeply, more comfortable with himself just hearing the voice of his mentor. His father—though neither of them had known of the relationship while the old man lived in his human body.

For Jack, just knowing that Old Baamin lived on in the dragon body gave him a sense of continuity with the past, something that had been missing most of his life. But at the moment he could not comprehend his life extending forward to new generations, not until he and Katrina found a way to overcome her fears.

"Are you here in the lair, Baamin? Or here in my head?" Jack asked.

(In your head, Jack. There isn't room for me in the lair tonight.)

"Can you check on Katrina for me? Is she safe? Is she lonely?"

(Yes, and yes. You have time to complete your tasks and then catch up with her. She needs this time alone.)

Jack nodded his acceptance of the dragon's words, knowing the old man would read his emotions. Other than himself, he trusted Baamin more than anyone on Kardia Hodos. As long as Baamin watched Katrina, no one would beset her intending harm.

(Stop feeling sorry for yourself and get on with your spell, boy,) the dragon reprimanded him, sounding very much like the master magician in charge of exuberant and inattentive apprentices.

"Is everyone here?" Jack asked the assembly in the lair. He counted noses: at least ten master magicians and a horde of journeymen and apprentices, Shayla and the two purple dragonets, Jaylor and Brevelan near the slightly raised platform that usually held Shayla's nest. Brevelan sat on a boulder that seemed molded to her slight frame. She held one of her newborn twins, the tiny quiet one that everyone feared might not live, a small scrap of life who held everyone's heart and concern. Queen Mikka sat beside her on another boulder holding the other baby, a squalling, squirming bundle of aggressive humanity with an aura big enough for two. King Darville leaned over his queen inspecting the baby. A look of wistful regret passed between the king and queen. They'd lost five babes before Mikka could carry them to full term. The cat spirit within the queen's body caused an imbalance that affected her ability to produce the long hoped-for heir.

"After tonight, maybe you'll have your own brood of sons and daughters," Jack whispered.

Shayla must have banished the other ten dragonets to keep them from interfering with the spell. Ten curious dragon babies could wreak havoc on the simplest of activities. He almost chuckled at the antics that had greeted him the first time he'd encountered the dragons in a cave hidden behind a waterfall deep within the mountains of SeLenicca.

Jaylor came out from behind his wife with an outstretched hand, greeting Jack like an equal. He beamed proudly. Of his two sons, Jack saw no sign. Good. Amaranth's clumsiness created enough chaos in the lair. Two rambunctious and under-cautious young boys would only add to the confusion Jack was about to create.

Jack did not envy the four apprentices assigned to sit with the boys this night. They needed four adults to handle the two boys. Four apprentices or Brevelan.

With one arm draped around Amaranth's neck—to keep him from falling into the campfire ignited for the humans' benefit, Jack nearly stumbled again with an awesome sense of having done this before. And failed.

No. He forced himself to remember that this time he had the backing of the full Commune of Magicians. He had a purple dragon to give him extra magic that he normally could not gather. Never again would he be as alone or lonely as he had been before he met Katrina.

He'd needed Katrina and her Tambrin lace to truly heal Shayla's wing. Tonight he needed Katrina by his side to anchor him, give him reasons for succeeding.

"Your Grace, time to convince your pesky cat to find a

new body." Jack bowed to Queen Mikka. "Is everyone ready?"

"Will it hurt?" Mikka asked.

"Perhaps. I don't know, Your Grace." Jack shrugged his shoulders.

"Very well. Let us proceed." Mikka stood up and handed the bawling baby back to Brevelan. As she turned to face Jack, she presented a regal calm. Her multicolored hair, like a brindled brown cat's fur, flowed smoothly about her shoulders. As tall as Brevelan was short, she radiated authority and determination as well as acceptance of tonight's procedures—complete with risks.

Precisely the queen Darville needed to help him govern the fractious lords who sat on the Council of Provinces. The couple ruled by the grace of the dragons. But the lords no longer respected the dragons.

Jack sensed the other magicians arranging themselves around Amaranth in a circle. Shayla nudged Iianthe, the second purple-tipped dragonet to join them. Iianthe held back. He'd always been shy around Jack.

That other time Jack had used a purple dragon to give him extra magic to heal Shayla's wing, Amaranth had willingly joined him. The spell had awakened their unique rapport before the dragonet was mature enough to understand or control it. Iianthe had hidden rather than participate in something new.

"We need symmetry with the original spell that bound the queen and her cat into the same body," Jack announced. He tapped several of the master magicians on the shoulder and indicated they should leave. "That means eight men working around a center point. Your Grace, if you will take the center with Amaranth." He beckoned the queen over. Jaylor followed her.

Four years ago, Jaylor had been the center of the spell. The Rovers had agreed to straighten out his warped magic. Their massive working had involved an eight-pointed star, dance, music, and fire. Mikka and her cat had been on the sidelines then, along with Brevelan and Darville. As the Rovers unraveled Jaylor's talent and then bound it back into his body, the cat had crawled into her mistress' lap and the two had been caught in the spillover of magic.

Jack couldn't let that happen again. Carefully, he positioned two journeymen in front of Brevelan and the babies. Then he beckoned Darville to stand behind them as well. "I want a full bubble of armor around the nonparticipants the entire time," he whispered to the journeymen as he returned to his core of magicians.

Quietly he chalked the important points and junctions of an eight-pointed star on the ground. "We'll need a second fire over there, to balance this one. I don't want the fire in the middle. That will destroy the balance."

Amaranth obliged by igniting the pile of reserve firewood. It blazed merrily and the dragon bounced back to Jack's side.

The spell was taking shape.

"Where's Zolltarn? He needs to be here." Jack looked around, blinking slightly as he roused from his deep concentration and memories.

"He did not respond to our summons." Jaylor shrugged.

The Rover Chieftain obeyed his own rules—rules he made up as he went along.

"He designed the original spell," Jack half protested.

"He's your grandfather, boy," Old Lyman half sneered. "The blood tie is complete." The elder librarian hobbled about the cave with the aid of his staff. Jack was glad he'd kept the old man out of the spell.

Three years ago the Rover spell had put too much strain on Baamin's heart and hastened his death. Jack did not want to be responsible for that happening with Lyman.

Old hurts. He needed to put them aside and make new memories. With Katrina.

"Let's get started." Jack squared his shoulders with new resolve. The sooner he completed this duty, the sooner he'd be on the road, following his love. No matter that departing abruptly, without explicit permission would look like a repeat of his youthful misdeeds that had led him to SeLenicca and Katrina the first time.

Jaylor could not hold him. Only Katrina could do that.

"Amaranth, into the center with Queen Mikka." Jack pushed the dragonet from behind.

Amaranth hung his head and dragged his tail. He knew something strange was about to occur and feared it. Jack was afraid, too. Afraid of failing yet again, afraid of losing Katrina forever. Afraid of hurting his friend, the baby dragon, and the queen.

He couldn't let his fears govern his actions. He had to impart some measure of reassurance and love to Amaranth.

"I need you to help the queen, Amaranth. Only you can do that." The dragonet's head came up, and he emitted a bit of pride. "Remember, when this is over, you get to stay with me forever, as my cat."

(Be your familiar?) The baby dragon looked at him with hope and adoration.

"My familiar?" A peculiar warmth untied itself from his inner knot of loneliness. "Yes, if you like." He half smiled. Something good might come of this night's work after all. He'd have Amaranth's help while he tracked Katrina. He'd have another to share his hopes and fears, to plot and plan, to dream with.

Reluctantly, tail and muzzle drooping, Amaranth trudged to the center of the circle. He paused to look back at Jack three times before he settled on his haunches at the queen's side.

"Touch the dragonet, Your Grace. You need a conduit for the cat to follow out of your body."

She rested her left hand on Amaranth's head, behind the stubby horn, and gently scratched his ears. He began to hum, just like a cat purring.

"Iianthe, here, beside me."

The other purple-tipped dragon slunk behind his mother.

"Shayla." Jack looked toward the mother dragon. Exhaustion seemed to feed upon every little setback in this procedure. He needed to be gone, in search of Katrina. He took a deep breath and continued addressing Shayla. "If Amaranth is to become the flywacket, I won't be able to gather magic from him. I can only gather magic from a purple-tipped dragon, unlike my companions. I need Iianthe to complete this spell. We need the augmented power of dragon magic to make this work. Solitary magic isn't enough."

The other master magicians looked at Jack with small frowns of disapproval.

By the laws of Coronnan and the Commune, he must be

able to gather dragon magic or go into exile. But the situation had changed and Jack's solitary magic had saved the Commune more than once.

He frowned back at them. All but elder Librarian Lyman looked away in embarrassment. That old man made his own rules and set his own standards of acceptability. He slammed his staff into the dirt as a prompt to get the spell moving.

Iianthe retreated farther behind his mother. Amaranth began to shift his weight uneasily beside Mikka.

All of the magicians looked at each other blankly.

"I'll get him," Jaylor heaved a sigh. He might be Senior Magician, but except for Jack, he was the youngest and strongest among them.

Shayla nudged Iianthe forward with her muzzle. A touch of her long spiral forehead horn applied judiciously to his rump brought him abruptly to Jack's side.

"Everyone get ready. We may not have a lot of time once I start," Jack warned.

"Perhaps one of us should take over the managing of this spell," Slippy said. He'd taken his name from the eels that nestled near the shore of the Great Bay. Cooked properly, they had a sweet nutritious meat. Handled incorrectly, they poisoned all they touched.

"None of you were there during the original spell. None of you have the *feel* of what happened," Jack asserted.

"Jaylor was there," Slippy corrected him.

"Jaylor was the object of the spell. As such, he was a passive participant."

Silence greeted his assertion.

"Look, nothing would please me more than turning over the entire procedure to one or all of you. I have business elsewhere. Pressing business. But you chose me for this spell. Me. The rogue who was too stupid to have a name, and too irresponsible to follow orders. Me. I developed the transport spell. I saved the entire Commune from Rejiia. I found the dragons and brought them home. You chose me for a reason." Jack clenched his fists in a serious effort to keep from shouting and throwing flashes of fire from his staff.

"What do we do?" Jaylor asked. He ignored the tension that grew almost tangibly among his master magicians.

"Link together, Jaylor to my right with Iianthe between us. Each of you stand on a point of the eight-pointed star." Jack forced his hands to relax as he gently caressed Iianthe's horn bud. Unlike Amaranth's, this one had grown. It had started to spiral into a sharp point.

Shayla crooned in the background. The baby dragon coiled his tail around himself. At least it wasn't sticking straight out and elevated in preparation to bolt.

"Rovers induce a trancelike state through music and dance. They then draw magical energy from all life by reaching out and touching it with their heightened senses," Jack reminded the other magicians. "That's how the original spell began."

There'd be no dancing to recreate a Rover spell tonight. Jack had to remain rooted beside Iianthe in order to gather dragon magic.

But the men of the Commune could sing and move their feet while standing in one place.

Jack gave out his instructions quietly. No sense in spooking Iianthe. He reached for the shoulder of the man to his left. Jaylor placed one hand on Jack's shoulder to complete the circle of eight magicians.

They chanted the poetry of the Rovers, words Jack had dredged up from his memory and sent to the other men to memorize earlier in the day.

And then they marched in place, keeping time with the rhythmic repetition of the song.

Iianthe shifted uneasily beneath Jack's hand. He sped up the chant and the march. His eyes crossed as the power rose within him. It grew, expanded, writhed like a living being in a myriad of colors representing each of the magicians in the circle.

Jack drew a deep breath and grabbed the power, molding it to his will. Between one heartbeat and the next the auras of every being within the circle took on the lavender-and-silver overtones of his magical signature.

Amaranth responded to the compulsion within the chant, shrinking, collapsing in on himself, absorbing all the light his silvery hide normally reflected. He darkened as he shrank until . . . until . . .

A black cat, so dark its fur reflected purple lights stood beside the queen. It yowled loudly and fluttered black-feathered wings. A flywacket. A creature of legend and prophecy.

In that instant, Jack grabbed at the source of the queen's double aura and yanked.

Amaranth yowled again.

Iianthe reared up, breaking Jack's contact.

The circle of magic dissolved.

Jack doubled over in exhaustion with a curious pain in his gut. Strange afterimages showed around everything he tried to focus his eyes upon.

"I'm free!" Mikka shouted as she sank to her knees. Her head looked too heavy for her neck to support. "I'm free of that blasted cat." Tears of joy streamed down her face. Her husband rushed forward and knelt beside her, scuffing the marks of the eight-pointed star. He cradled her against him, kissing away her tears.

"Are you hurt?" Darville cupped her face in his long-fingered hands.

"A curious emptiness. Tired. A little dizzy—disoriented." Her strength gave out. She collapsed in a faint. Darville caught her.

"Thank you, young man." Darville looked up from his wife's peaceful countenance. "We—all of Coronnan—owe you a debt of gratitude. Hopefully, now we can stabilize the succession without Lord Laislac and his daughter."

"I'd best send you home, Your Grace, before you are missed," Jaylor said. He took a deep breath. His face still looked a little gray.

"No more magic until you all eat!" Brevelan proclaimed.

"Food," Jack murmured, recognizing the cause of some of his disorientation. The afterimages continued to plague his vision like half-formed ghosts. His skin felt clammy, and his knees wobbled. "I need food."

An unknown journeyman stuffed a hunk of bread into Jack's hand, followed by a thick slab of cheese.

Jack ate hungrily, methodically. He had to restore his energies quickly.

"Jack, I'll see you in my study in the morning. We need to discuss security within the palace." Darville swallowed convulsively.

"SeLenicca," Jack croaked. "You promised to send Katrina and me to SeLenicca as ambassadors."

"Later. I need you in Coronnan City more than I need you across the border now that the war is over. We still have an eavesdropping rogue to find." Darville dismissed the suggestion.

"I've got to take Katrina home, Your Grace. Now."

Three deep breaths and the void beckoned him. "Come, Amaranth." The flywacket leaped into his arms. Three more breaths and he sent them both into the void in search of his true love.

Chapter 22

Zebbiah hustled Jaranda and the pack beast onto the sailing vessel amidst shouts for haste from the captain and crew—who all looked amazingly like the Rover except they wore blue and green on their black clothing instead of purple and red. The pack beast protested the plank up to the ship's deck vehemently and tried to sit down again in the middle of it.

The woman pushed the animal from behind with a sharp stick, trying her best to keep it from parking its rear anywhere but on the deck. Zebbiah called no orders to her, nor did he look to see if she followed. They had made a bargain; therefore, he must presume she followed.

Eight passengers, all dressed in rough clothing, moved abruptly to the far side of the open-decked vessel giving the Rover and his beast more than enough room to settle for the long voyage upriver.

The woman inspected the other passengers openly. All of the women but one wore a single plait that started at the crown and gathered closely to the head to the nape where it broke free into a thick rope of a braid. Two of them had not bothered with the complex four strand plait but sufficed with the simpler three strand braid. The other woman wore two plaits that started at her temples and stayed close to her head to the nape, then swung free for a short space and joined into a single thick plait halfway down her back. She must come from a merchant family. The others were all peasants.

Not knowing who she was or what her status was, the

unnamed woman had gathered her own hair into a thick knot at her own nape. Jaranda's hair, she had tied back with a green ribbon to match her dress. They, like their fellow passengers, wore sturdy dark skirts and vests with white, long-sleeved shifts beneath.

She caught the eye of the woman wearing two plaits. The merchant's wife turned up her nose and spun on her heel to face the water on the other side of the vessel. The peasant women followed suit.

The men talked amongst themselves and paid no attention to the newcomers.

Jaranda did not seem to care about the people. She skipped about looking at everything, watching the crew as they cast off the lines and set the sail.

"Zebbiah, what plagues them?" the woman whispered to her traveling companion.

He looked up from tending to the stubborn beast that carried all their worldly wealth and supplies.

"We made them late. They are displeased." He shrugged and returned to the beast's reins, tethering them to a brass ring embedded into the decking.

" 'Tis more than that, Zebbiah. Displeasure at our tardiness would evoke curses and grumbling, not this silent disdain." Why did she know that? An image, a very old image, flashed across her mind's eye. She stood and watched a parade of noblemen and courtiers as they exited the king's audience chamber. One of them turned and faced her squarely. "This war with Coronnan will benefit no one. No one. We'd be better off governing ourselves than submitting to *his* demands for more money, more war, more slaves, more sacrifices."

She tried to put a name to the man's face. She tried to place herself in the crowd. She tried to remember who *he* was.

The images faded to mists.

"You remembering something?" Zebbiah asked.

"Not quite. Has our country been at war long?"

"Over three years." No further comment good or bad. No information as to the cause. Just that war had become a part of life.

"And is all this devastation a part of the war?" She swept a hand to include the city behind the docks that drifted farther and farther away.

"Partly."

She raised her eyebrows, waiting for more information. He sat down on a cargo bale and began plaiting a piece of leather he drew from the panniers.

Slightly miffed, she marched over to the women crowding against the far railing. "Good morning, ladies. Are you traveling all the way to the end of the river?" she asked politely.

Two-plaits sniffed as if she smelled something rancid. "Riffraff, tainting true-blood with dark-eyed outlanders," she spat.

"Wouldn't have this problem if the council hadn't made mixed marriages legal so Queen Miranda could marry an outlander," a stout woman added. She wore a clumsy braid that looked as if it had not been washed or combed in a month.

Two-plaits looked pointedly at red-haired Jaranda.

"I don't suppose you know my name, ladies?"

"A name that's too good for you, if you ask me," two-plaits replied and moved as far into the bow as she could, away from them all.

"Somehow, I didn't expect you to say that."

* * *

"Stargods, they make a lot of demands for ghosts!" Yeenos, Vareena's older brother protested. "Bad enough we have to feed two more of them with no respite from the last one. Now they want special herbs and minerals, crystals, and our soap-making cauldrons. I say no. We feed them because the Stargods decree we must. But no more!" He swung his shepherd's crook in a wide circle before slamming the crook against a watering trough.

"Yeenos, calm down." Vareena ducked the staff, well used to her brother's temper. She had seen Marcus do the same thing with his staff. Robb seemed to have better control of his temper and treated his staff more gently. "These new ghosts claim that another ghost, a true ghost of a man who has died, haunts the monastery and causes live men

to become trapped there, halfway between here and their
next existence."

"What else is a ghost?" Yeenos sneered, then he whistled
for his dog to run the sheep farther uphill from the farm-
house.

"I don't know. But they refuse to believe they are true
ghosts, and they need these things to work a spell that will
lay the other ghost to rest and free them from the trap."
Vareena rubbed her hands together nervously. She'd have
gone to Uustass for help, but he had led a dozen men to
the river this morning with scythes. The village needed
fresh grass and reeds to repair the thatch on several dwellings and byres.

Jeeremy Baker had gone with them, his burns heavily
bandaged but no longer in pain.

"I agree with Yeenos," Vareena's father Ceddell said,
coming over to them from the byre. "We owe the ghosts
food. That was the curse laid on this village three hundred
years ago for refusing hospitality to a benighted traveler.
S'murghin' magician." He crossed his wrists and flapped his
hands as he spat onto the ground. "But we owe them nothing more. I'll not be spending our resources to find these
odd ingredients for a useless bit of magic." He kicked the
water trough and called his dog to his heels, away from the
flock Yeenos worked with his own dogs.

"But, Papa, if we can end this curse once and for all . . ."

"We've had priests and magicians alike trying to end the
curse with no luck."

"But these ghosts are magicians trapped by the curse,
not magicians working outside of it. They might have a
chance . . ."

"You've gone and fallen in love with one of them,
haven't you!" Ceddell raised his voice and his hand in
anger.

Vareena stepped back but did not duck. She faced her
father, refusing to submit to his violence. She might be as
trapped here as the ghosts, but she refused to lessen herself
by accepting any man's abuse.

"Your mother did the same thing, before I showed her
the wrong of it."

"Showed her with your fists, no doubt." Vareena schooled her voice and features to betray none of her fear or her disgust.

"I'll find you a husband this night. Then you'll give up this nonsense."

"No man in this village wants me. I'll have none you bribe or coerce into the act."

"You'll marry the man I choose for you. The law of the land and the laws of the Stargods decree that you must obey your father." Ceddell raised his clenched fist once more.

Vareena stood her ground. "Touch me, and I move into the monastery permanently. The villagers will have to bring food, clothing, and bedding to me there. They will have to come to me for healing. How far will your authority stretch Ceddell, once the Ghost Woman removes herself and her witch healing from your household?"

"Enough!" Yeenos nearly screamed at them. His nostrils pinched white and his mouth pursed to a thin lipless line. "This village has borne the burden of this curse too long."

Both Vareena and her father stared at the young man as if he had lost his reason.

"You say these new ghosts are magicians, Vareena?"

"So they claim. I have seen no evidence of their talent other than lighting a fire from a distance. But I can do that."

"Lord Laislac sent around a newscrier three years ago," Yeenos said, almost gloating. "Magic is illegal in all of Coronnan now. I'm going to the capital to talk to the priests and to the Council of Provinces. I'll get the obligation removed from us. Ghosts or no ghosts, there will be no more food and supplies wasted upon those who haunt the monastery."

"You can't!" Vareena gasped.

"You can't stop me, Eena. It's time."

He whistled one last time to his dog and turned his crook over to his father. Then he stalked into the house and began throwing journey rations into a pack.

Vareena took off running for the hill crested by the abandoned monastery.

"Vareena!" her father roared. "Come back here."

"Never. I have to save my ghosts. I can't let them die of neglect." She had to find a way to bring Robb back to life. Marcus, too. If the Stargods showed any mercy at all, they'd allow her to kiss her love just once in this existence. She'd give up the freedom Farrell promised her for one kiss from Robb.

* * *

"How much time do we have?" Robb asked at Vareena's breathless news.

She shrugged her shoulders, inhaled deeply, and spoke. "A week. Perhaps two. Depends if Yeenos changes steeds along the way, or if he talks his way onto a barge."

"We're doomed." Marcus slid to a heap in the corner of the refectory. He wrapped his arms around his knees and began rocking.

Robb wanted to do the same, but refused to give in to the despair that his friend exhibited.

" 'Tis a long way from here to the capital and back." Robb finger-combed his beard. Years ago he had copied the thinking gesture from Jaylor. Now he'd done it for so long that it had become a part of him. "We've walked from the capital to the border often enough in the past three years. Even with magic urging a steed to greater speed and endurance, the trip always took at least a week each direction. Once Yeenos reaches the capital, he'll need to gain an audience, first with the priests at the Royal Temple, then with the Council of Provinces. That could take weeks. Moons. Until he returns with an edict withdrawing village responsibility for us, we have food and supplies. We have time to trap that ghost in the library and get some answers."

"Papa has agreed to village responsibility to feed you two until Yeenos returns. But he refuses you the supplies you need for the spell." Vareena turned her face away from him.

Robb wished he could watch her eyes, know what she hid. But the mist that separated her from the two magicians veiled her eyes and her mind from his probes.

Strange how physical objects retained their crisp outlines, but the people looked as insubstantial as a dragon. He could touch physical objects, lift them, probe them for long-lost memories, but a kind of armor prevented him from touching other people—except Marcus.

Perhaps if they probed the walls rather than trying to climb them, he could discern the nature of the spell that kept them within. Later, when he was alone and could concentrate. Hard to do since the entrapment.

"Can you find these supplies for us?" Robb asked Vareena.

"Some of them. The herbs are common enough. Some of the minerals, but crystals and the cauldron . . ."

"We've got little crystals in our supplies. We've got a little cooking pot. They will have to serve for now. A smaller spell. Less chance of success, but perhaps enough to show us what *can* be done."

"I'll bring you what I can." She rose up on tiptoe as if to kiss his cheek, then reared back, repulsed by the energy barrier. "I'll go now." A tear formed in the corner of her eye, like a perfect dew drop glinting in the sun. Then she ran off on her errand.

"Stargods! She's in love with you," Marcus choked on a sob. "I might as well curl up and die. I've lost everything."

"What are you talking about?"

Marcus moaned and buried his head in his knees. "I can't do anything right, can't even love the right woman!"

"Marcus, stop wallowing in misery and help me. We have a ghost to trap."

His friend only moaned again.

"Marcus." Robb stalked over and shook him by the shoulder. "What are you talking about? Until we got here, you were madly in love with Margit—and she with you. Before Margit, you loved that little dairymaid in Hanic. You are always in love with someone. Now you *think* you love Vareena, and you *think* she loves me. You aren't thinking straight."

"I can't think of anything else but Vareena. This place twists everything back to her." Marcus clutched Robb's hand in a painful grip that bordered on desperation.

"Perhaps this place does cloud our thinking." Robb had kept visions of Margit in his heart and his dreams for a long, long time. He focused hard on her each night before sleeping to stave off the recurring nightmares of attack and fruitless defense. But she obviously had strong feelings for Marcus. He did not want to come between his two best friends if their affection was genuine.

Now?

"What a tangled mess." He slumped down beside Marcus and draped an arm around his friend's shoulders.

Marcus rested his head on Robb's shoulders and sobbed.

"Vareena loves me," Robb mused. "I love Margit, Margit loves you, you love Vareena . . ."

"I love you, too, Robb," Marcus sobbed. "You are right. My feelings for women are temporary. Illusions. My love for you will last forever."

Horror shuddered through Robb. He stood up jerkily, putting as much physical distance as he could between them.

"Snap out of your adolescent hero worship, Marcus. I'm going to climb the tower, see if a summons spell works from there—above the level of the walls."

Chapter 23

Unlike my son, those who seek to capture me are bumbling beginners. My son would have known how to break my spells and leave this cursed place. My daughter, too. They did not need this paltry dragon magic to bring them anything they wished. Nor did they need the convoluted and time-consuming rituals of the Rovers.

And yet these amateurs do not panic easily. They have been trained to think a problem through—as Nimbulan did. I could have trained them better.

Let us see how they handle my next little trick. Their own fear will force them to leave me alone long before I finish with them. They shall die in another ninety-seven days if they remain here. Soon I will be alone again with my power.

* * *

The nameless woman surveyed the long line of pack steeds, sledges, merchants, and other travelers who had banded together to cross the pass safely into Coronnan. Every traveler had to be wary of bandits, out-of-work mercenaries, and rogue magicians. They were too close to the border of Hanassa for comfort.

A flash of memory lanced her mind right between her eyes. Images of battles, war, displaced families, hungry people, noble and peasant alike, fire, flood, kardiaquakes without end.

She clutched the mane of Zebbiah's beast for balance as the world spun around and around, taking her with it.

"M'ma!" Jaranda screamed.

She fought her way through the maze of images to find the coarse, mottled brown-and-gray hide of the pack beast.

It brayed loudly, threatening to sit again in protest of her fierce clutch on its mane.

Her memory flashed again to another steed, one she rode, a docile little mare that was greatly intimidated by the mighty war stallion beside her. Her husband sat atop that horse, surveying the battle below. She had eyes only for the red-haired man who commanded the troops. "I was too young to see beyond the glamour of being in love with the notion of love," she whispered. "I worshiped him." He was a powerful general with tangled political connections, a strong and handsome man: what more could an idealistic young girl ask for in a man? He took care of her, protected her from . . . she couldn't remember from what, only that she cherished his domineering presence.

And she thanked him daily for the child he had given her.

"Jaranda," she whispered.

"M'ma!" Jaranda tugged on her gown. "Wake up, M'ma. I'm scared," the little girl implored.

"Jaranda," she said again, louder, firmly. "Jaranda, my love. Do you remember your father?"

Strange, she felt no sense of loss at the man's absence. No regret. She focused entirely on her daughter, stooping to put herself on the same level as the child.

Jaranda shook her head. Her thumb crept toward her mouth.

The woman gently restrained her from the baby habit of insecurity. "This is important, Jaranda. If I know your P'pa's name, I might remember my own."

"You're M'ma. You don't need 'nother name." Jaranda thrust out her lower lip. A tear trembled in the corner of her eye.

"I am your M'ma, little one. But these other people need to call my by another name. I'm not their M'ma, after all." She touched the edge of her hem to her daughter's eyes, blotting the half-formed tears.

"I don't remember P'pa. 'Cept he was big. He filled the doorway when he came to watch me at night. He thought I was asleep. He wouldn't have come if he knew I was awake." Jaranda flung her arms around her mother's neck and hugged her tightly, nearly strangling her.

"We don't want P'pa. He scared me. I like Zebbie better."

"Yes, I like Zebbiah, too, Jaranda," she choked out, fighting the pressure on her throat from the little girl's enthusiasm. She stood up and gently held her daughter's hands.

She turned to find the dark-eyed man watching her.

"You remember something." His usually expressive eyes took on a hooded look, and he refused to meet her gaze.

"Where is my husband, Zebbiah? Why did he not come for us in the palace when everyone deserted me?"

"Many men died in the war." He bent to fuss with the harness on his pack beast.

"Dead?" A huge weight seemed to lift from her chest. "I'm a widow." She had to restrain herself from jumping in glee. "I guess the marriage was not happy," she whispered to herself. Jaranda renewed her stranglehold, on her knees this time.

"Serves you right." A bulky man, managing the sledge behind her spat into the dirt. "Can't trust outlanders. Especially those with dark eyes. Brown or blue as dark as midnight, don't matter, they's all signs of outlanders," he sneered. "Best you don't remember the man what give you a child with outland hair. Best you take her and your dark-eyed lover out of SeLenicca. We don't need no outlanders tainting our blood or telling us what to do."

"And yet you travel outland. By the looks of the goods on your sledge, you intend to stay there a long time." She raised an eyebrow at him in irony at his hypocrisy.

"Prejudice has to be learned, Lady," Zebbiah said quietly.

"And I have forgotten my prejudices along with my name."

"Common enough name," the bulky man snarled again.

"Do you know my name, traveler?"

He turned his back on her, refusing to answer.

"Somehow I thought he'd say that. But I'll remember eventually. I've started to remember. The rest will come." She brushed Jaranda's dress free of dust. "Let's get started. The day is too beautiful to waste on the past and regrets and prejudices." She whistled to the pack beast. It brayed in an obnoxious imitation of an agreement and plodded along behind her. The other steed riders and sledge drivers followed her lead.

"Your M . . . Your Ladyship, get back in line," the caravan leader snarled, pushing ahead of her. But he kept marching, no longer finding excuses to delay.

"Excuse me, do you happen to know my name?" she asked the leader, assuming a place just behind his left shoulder.

"That ain't your place in line, Lady. Get back with your outland lover."

"Why did I know you'd be as evasive as the others?"

* * *

Jack stood on a promontory overlooking the vale where Margit and Katrina made camp. Even after three days, he struggled to reconcile the double nature of his vision. The massive spell to separate the queen from her cat had sapped his energies to a dangerously low point.

Amaranth balanced easily on his shoulder. Corby used to perch in much the same spot. Amaranth was heavier, but more willing to please and become an extension of Jack's magic and personality. A friend. His rich fur brushed Jack's face and they both leaned into the caress, needing each other.

Jack had cried the morning he could not wake Corby, but he'd accepted the loss. Corby had been his only—if somewhat reluctant—friend for a long time; much longer than jackdaws normally lived. Corby deserved his rest. Hopefully, he'd pass peacefully into his next existence, into a life without the wild adventures reserved for a magician's familiar.

Amaranth chattered his teeth in anxious anticipation of the coming adventures.

"They've come a long way in so short a time," Jack mused as he stroked Amaranth's fur. He'd stalked the two women for three days, not daring to approach closer lest Katrina reject him. He'd also husbanded his strength. That last spell had drained him of more energy than usual. More often than not, he was so tired he saw double.

"We're very near the border with SeLenicca. I don't like them camping without a bubble of armor."

But if Katrina would *Sing* as she had *Sung* in SeLenicca, she might create her own spell of invisibility that Margit couldn't duplicate. Jack had to chuckle at how many villages and homesteads had eluded him on his quest, all because the women unconsciously *Sang* spells of protection for their loved ones as they went about their daily chores.

The flywacket ruffled his feathered wings, getting used to their size and the skin flap that hid them when at rest. He rubbed his cat's muzzle against Jack's chin, eager for more caresses.

(Steeds.) Not so much a word as an image of two fleet and one pack steed picketed beyond Margit's fire, but sheltered by an outcropping of rock. Jack could not have seen the animals without Amaranth's help.

"They've stopped early. Still hours of daylight left," he mused. As he watched, Katrina and Margit both rubbed the insides of their thighs through their journey trews. Riding had taken its toll on unfamiliar riders.

"Is it time to let the girls know we've followed them?" Jack asked Amaranth, not really expecting an answer.

Amaranth purred, devoid of opinion. Jack supposed the true cat spirit he'd liberated from Queen Mikka vied with the dragon intelligence for dominance inside the flywacket. They'd compromise soon enough. Then Amaranth would reawaken his true telepathic communication with Jack.

Something alien churned inside Jack, and the base of his spine itched as if it needed to twitch. The smell of Margit's roasting hedgehog filtered up to his nose in hundreds of component odors. He grew dizzy trying to sort them.

"I guess you are channeling your heightened senses into me without knowing it, Amaranth," he commented.

The flywacket perked his ears and continued purring.

"Maybe I'll stay up here one more night. I'll join them tomorrow," Jack mused.

"Mew," Amaranth agreed.

The wind shifted to the east, behind Jack. It smelled of rain with a slight tang of salt. Another storm approached from the sea.

Margit sneezed three times in quick succession.

Katrina draped a blanket over the apprentice magician's shoulders.

Jack crouched down to observe closer. Margit getting sick was not in his plans. She'd delay them. He hoped that once in her own land, Katrina would learn to trust him again, learn that he'd never hurt her, even if they must remain celibate the rest of their lives—a fate he certainly hoped to avoid.

(Not sick,) Amaranth insisted.

"Well, nice to hear you speak again, friend," Jack murmured, stroking the flywacket's neck and back. His fingers lingered on the slight bump of the extra skin that had rolled back to release the wings.

(Lonely for Katrina. She lonely, too.) Amaranth launched into a long glide down the rock face. He landed beside Katrina, tucked his wings neatly away and began an obligatory bath.

Both women squealed, Margit half-frightened, Katrina half-delighted, at their visitor. Margit shifted her bottom to a rock on the opposite side of the fire from the flywacket.

"I hate cats!" Her words came distinctly to Jack's ears, despite the wind that blew in the opposite direction.

True to the perverse nature of all cats, Amaranth followed Margit. He rubbed up against her arm and attempted to crawl into her lap. Margit jumped up with a yelp and began walking circles around the camp. The flywacket followed her lazily.

Katrina tried luring the black cat into her lap. Amaranth crouched on the other side of the fire, shifting his front paws in hunter mode, ready to leap.

But Jack saw the cat's trajectory in his mind and Amaranth's. He'd land directly on Margit's shoulder, not Katrina's lap.

"Thanks for making my decision for me, Amaranth." Jack climbed down to retrieve his familiar and restore order in the camp. "I just hope you haven't created more problems than you solved."

Chapter 24

Lanciar threaded his way along the line of march toward Zolltarn's sledge. The stern and wily clan chieftain popped a whip just above the left ear of the lead pack steed. The animal quickened its pace a bit. The other steeds followed suit.

The tin weasel, perched on the raised front of the sledge, seemed to wink and drool at the evidence of Zolltarn's control of the dumb beasts. Its tail lost some of its rigidity and bristled.

Lanciar quickly crossed his wrists behind his back and wiggled his fingers in an abbreviated ward against evil. The statue was inanimate. It couldn't move. Could it?

Zolltarn smiled and so did everyone else in the caravan, including Lanciar, the tin weasel forgotten. That happened a lot. Whatever mood sat on Zolltarn's shoulders infected the entire clan. Was this part of their connected magic; all of them subtly linked so that what one experienced the others shared? Lanciar hoped not. If that were the case, he was falling under their spell. He needed independence and privacy to steal his son. If he ever found the boy.

"You have something to ask me?" Zolltarn spoke before Lanciar could open his mouth or even frame his question.

"You lead us in a strange direction," Lanciar said.

"The road leads us. We follow it," Zolltarn replied in typically cryptic Rover fashion.

"The road branched three ways less than an hour ago. You could have chosen any one of those directions."

"This road seemed more enticing."

"This road leads to the mountains. The pass into SeLenicca is haunted by demons and ghosts as well as bandits."

"Ghosts have no reason to trouble Rovers. Bandits have learned to leave us alone. And as for demons? Demons can be our friends." The Rover leader smiled and squinted his eyes in an expression that looked like mischief personified.

Lanciar refused to repeat the ward behind his back. He'd have to learn to deal with Zolltarn and his smile sooner or later, hopefully later, after he left the clan with his son.

"Rovers are not welcome in SeLenicca," Lanciar argued. "The land has been stripped of resources. Why borrow trouble, when you can roam Coronnan and live off its lush bounty?"

"My grandson travels this way. I sense that he needs me." Zolltarn lifted his head and sniffed the air. His eyes took on a glazed expression.

"Who calls you, Zolltarn?" Lanciar asked.

"As I said, my grandson."

"You have so few men in the clan. I'm surprised you allowed the man to leave."

"In the way of the People, the man goes to his wife's clan. For my grandson to marry within the clan would violate our laws against incest. He will rule his wife's clan one day, as I rule my wife's."

"You have not brought in new husbands for the many women here. Instead you indulge in polygamy."

"You have been brought into the clan. As have many orphaned children."

"I travel with you. There is a difference." But his senses became suddenly alert to the nuances in Zolltarn's tone. There was only one child that interested him.

"Is there a difference? We take in the son, so must we take in the father."

"I will leave when I have accomplished my mission."

"Will you?"

"*S'murghit,* I will."

Watch your language! He distinctly heard Maija's reprimand in his mind.

Lanciar looked around for Zolltarn's youngest daughter. She frowned at him from three sledges behind him. For once he did not look away and feel ashamed, but boldly held her gaze until she smiled and nodded.

Only then did Lanciar turn his attention back to the

Rover Chieftain's challenge. Inwardly he shuddered against
standing in such close proximity to a dark-eyed outlander;
having his son raised by outlanders. Prejudices pounded
into him as a child remained firmly rooted in his gut and
the back of his mind.

At one time he'd loved Rejiia. By that time, he'd spent
enough time in the company of foreign soldiers and diplomats to overlook many things about outlanders. But still he
resented them, felt dirty having to touch one. He'd overlooked Rejiia's black hair because she had an incredibly lush
body and an insatiable sexual appetite. True-blood women
were notorious prudes. She also had piercing and beautiful
blue eyes—the blue of an endless night sky in deep winter.
True-bloods of SeLenicca always had blue eyes (though several shades lighter than Rejiia's) and blond hair.

But she and her lover King Simeon, Queen Miranda's
red-haired consort, had stolen the crown from Simeon's
meek little wife. Rejiia had claimed that her son was fathered by Simeon, hoping to put the child on the throne
of SeLenicca as well as Coronnan with claims to Rossemeyer and Hanassa. But Simeon had turned out to be her
father's half brother. Then she claimed the boy died at birth
to avoid the taint of incest.

But Lanciar knew the child to be his, sired during a particularly passionate coven ritual when The Simeon had occupied himself exclusively with Ariiell. She'd been a
simpering virgin at the time and screamed loudly enough
to satisfy even The Simeon. Rejiia had never screamed during sex and always participated with all of her strength and
emotions—even during her first ritual when Simeon claimed
her virginity.

Lanciar wondered if she'd indeed been a virgin or merely
used her magic to create that illusion.

You can't trust a dark-eyed outlander. The oft repeated
phrase burned into Lanciar's mind.

"I'll leave when I accomplish my mission," he reiterated.

"You have met my daughter Maija," Zolltarn continued
as if Lanciar had not spoken. "A comely girl."

"She's a good cook." Lanciar wasn't about to admit how
beautiful he found the girl with her flashing eyes, bright
smile, long legs, and lush bosom. He didn't really mind her

reprimands about his soldier-bred language. From that first night when she'd asked him to abandon his campsite and join the clan, he'd admired her.

But the promise of a romp in her bed had remained an elusive taunt between them. All he wanted from her was a romp. A commitment for more would tie him to the clan and he did not want to stay with them any longer than necessary. He wanted his son free of Rover ideas and morals—or lack of morals.

He sensed a trap in Zolltarn's words and the girl's seduction. And he'd witnessed almost no immoral conduct or indiscretions.

"Maija has no husband. She has courted a number of suitable men from other clans but found none of them to her liking. Not all of the men are willing to follow me because I am a powerful magician and have ties to the Commune of Magicians. They know that once they mate with one of mine there is no escape. They remain part of my clan even if their bride dies."

"I presume, then, that the choice of mate belongs to the women in your clan." Lanciar found himself edging away from Zolltarn, off the road, away from these people and their alien customs.

"'Tis the way of the Rovers. Once she chooses, she must be faithful. Before she chooses, she must remain untouched. Upon occasion we have relaxed that rule and met with disaster. My eldest daughter Kestra died and her child was stolen from us because we sought a different solution to our needs. Never again."

"I'm surprised you have not pushed Maija to choose sooner, bring new blood, another man into the clan."

"Ah, but now she has chosen. And she will take your son into her household as soon as he is weaned." Zolltarn stared directly at Lanciar.

"I think I need a drink."

"Maija brews the best ale of all the Rover clans."

* * *

Eight black articulated limbs quested outward from the slime-coated, bulbous body of the spider. Vareena stared at the malevolent creature, frozen by fear.

Poison dripped from the clacking pincers on the forward

limbs. Its eyes, positioned near the joint of each leg, flashed demon red. The thing could easily enclose her fist within its eight arms.

Her heart pounded as loud as festival drums. Cold sweat trickled down her back.

The spider inched forward, tasting the air with each leg-tip, glowing as redly as its eyes.

"Stargods protect me," she whispered, trying to edge away from her stalker. The stone walls on three sides of her hard bed within the monastery stopped her retreat.

The spider moved forward faster than she could edge away from it.

Could she run for the doorway before it swung out on its web and latched onto her vulnerable neck?

Surely Robb must sense her fear, hear her thudding heartbeat, and come to her rescue.

The door remained stubbornly closed. The entire monastery was wrapped in the preternatural silence of the gloaming.

The spider came closer.

Panic propelled Vareena out of bed and across the room. She tugged at the door. It remained firmly closed and latched. She kicked it and bruised her toes. She pulled with both hands. It did not even rattle.

Something heavy and hard landed on her hair.

She screamed . . .

And awoke in bed drenched in sweat.

Cautiously, afraid to move lest she bring the spider upon her, she brought a wisp of witchlight to her fingertip.

Search as she might, she could not find the spider. An empty and torn cobweb hung from the far corner of her cell. She'd thrown witchfire at it before claiming the room as her own.

The sweat beneath her shift chilled rapidly. She needed to move or wrap the covers more tightly about her. But if she did that, she might disturb the spider.

The door burst open. Marcus and Robb, both bleary-eyed with sleep-tousled hair stood side by side. Each carried a large ball of witchlight. The directionless light illuminated every corner of the room.

"Spider!" she hissed at them, almost daring them to search her blankets.

Marcus strode forward with confidence and whipped the bedcovers away from her. He shook them vigorously.

Nothing scuttled away from his search.

"You must have had a nightmare," Robb said behind a yawn. "We've both had them since coming here. Go back to sleep. The dream will fade with the dawn."

"I can't go back to sleep." She wished one of them, either of them, both of them, would hold her tight and banish the fear with their strength. Their ghostly energies kept them from touching her.

"Then get up and do something. Best way to banish a dream is to use the privy and let it drain away. Bake some bread, clean something, count the bricks in the wall. You'll be sleep again in moments." Robb backed out of the room.

"He's right, Vareena. You need to do something to shake yourself free of the dream." Marcus shrugged and exited as well.

"He's right." Vareena stood up and took stock of her cell. No shadows hid from her witchlight. "Childish fears. I won't let them rule me." With determination, she dressed and went to find flour and yeast. Time to start baking bread for breakfast.

* * *

My powers are weakening! My enemies have weathered every disaster I throw at them. Yet still they gather. Still they plot against me.

Once, long ago, when I was just beginning, all others thought me weak and of little consequence. But I showed them. I gathered secrets as a miser gathers gold. I gathered power and I learned to use it subtly, so that they never knew from whence the attack came. I taught my children to do the same. They became almost as powerful as me.

To protect myself and the source of my power, I must delve deep into my memories for a spell that will drain away all that these thieves hold dear. Then, when they are weak and vulnerable, I will scatter them, make them wander lost and alone, powerless. If that fails, I must murder them all.

Chapter 25

The unnamed woman sat staring into the crackling fire. Zebbiah and Jaranda had left her alone while they made a game of fetching water and washing the roots he had gathered earlier today. Her heart warmed whenever she saw the two of them together. Zebbiah would make an admirable father for the little girl.

Would he make as fine a husband?

She nudged the notion aside while she concentrated on the flames. Images from her past flitted in and out of her view.

She tasted a name on her tongue. *Miranda.* A common enough name since a former king and queen of SeLenicca had given the name to their only child nineteen years ago.

Miranda. The name tasted smoky, like the air on this crisp and clear night in the middle of a remote mountain pass.

Miranda.

Could that truly be her name?

She stared into the green-and-yellow flames, seeking answers, wondering if she'd asked the right questions.

Images danced with the flames, teasing her mind. The strong, red-haired man with deep blue eyes, older than she by many years, dominated every scene she managed to mine from the deep recesses of her fragmented memory.

Jaranda's eyes. Her daughter had inherited those midnight blue eyes. True-bloods tended to have eyes as pale as their hair and skin. Washed out. As depleted of color as the land was depleted of vitality and resources.

She heaved a sigh and tasted the name again. She heard

it whispered behind her back by the other travelers. It reso-
nated within her as if it belonged.

Queen Miranda had married a red-haired outlander: Simeon the sorcerer-king. In her youth and naïveté, Queen
Miranda had granted him joint ruling powers. Then she had
turned over the government to him so that she could spend
all of her time making lace—the proper place for a woman
in her culture.

But Simeon had imposed crushing taxes on her people.
He had forced a war with Coronnan. He had enacted strin-
gent laws. For even the tiniest infraction of the new laws
he had exacted the extreme punishment, slavery or execution. The executions had been carried out as sacrifices to
his blood-thirsty demon god Simurgh.

And yet Simeon himself had broken every law he enacted. He'd taken several mistresses—one of them, Rejiia,
his own niece. He'd consorted with foreigners. He'd paid
no tithes to the temple as required, yet he stole temple
funds for his own bizarre religion.

And then he had outlawed the ancient and beautiful worship of the three Stargod brothers.

SeLenicca had crumbled under his crushing rule.

Change had come to SeLenicca. Dramatic, catastrophic,
and none too soon.

The SeLenese had long believed that they were the Chosen of the Stargods. The land was theirs to exploit. Nurturing the land, growing crops, and raising livestock had been
delegated to lesser peoples in other countries. By the time
Miranda came to the throne, the Chosen of the Stargods
had bled SeLenicca of all her natural resources. They had
nothing left except their arrogance, their prejudices, and
their lace.

Dared she believe that she and the meek woman who
had allowed all that to happen while she closeted herself
with her lace were one and the same. Did she want to be
that woman?

What other reason for one and all to desert her and her
young daughter in the palace when they fled the kardiaquakes and the fires and the flooding? What other reason
than to condemn her for their troubles?

Miranda.

"I'll do better when I return. But first I have to find the strength to be the kind of queen my people need. I need to remember everything, not just bits and pieces glued together with supposition."

A noise alerted her to the presence of another. She wasn't ready to face Zebbiah and Jaranda yet, so she continued staring blankly into the fire. Part of her senses remained focused on the shuffling steps and wheezing breath of the intruder.

Not Zebbiah.

She listened more closely and shifted her eyes, but not her head, to catch a glimpse of whoever hovered behind her, near the pack beast and the panniers; the panniers filled with her lace pillow and countless yards of priceless lace.

"You there!" She stood abruptly and whirled to face the caravan leader.

He held a long strand of lace, as wide as two joints of her pointing finger.

"Thief!" she screamed as loud as she could.

The leader took off running, trailing the lace behind him.

"Stop, thief!" she screamed again.

Loud footsteps ran closer. Men crowded close to her. Off to the side she caught a glimpse of Zebbiah running in pursuit.

"The leader stealing?" someone whispered behind her.

"What have we let ourselves in for."

"We can't continue with a thief for our leader."

"Is it truly theft to steal from a Rover and his mistress?"

The thief stumbled, tripping over the long strand of lace he tried desperately to gather as he ran. Zebbiah tackled him. They both landed facedown in the dirt.

"Leader, I accuse you of theft from the queen!" Miranda announced. She fought the hole in her gut that felt like he'd stolen her soul as well as her identity when he stole the lace. "The presence of Tambrin lace in your hand is all the evidence we need to convict you."

Stunned silence rang around the campfires at her pronouncement.

"You are sentenced to exile. Escort him from the camp," she ordered.

"But who will lead us? Who will guide us?"

"You caused this!" the stout merchant woman with two plaits from the boat shouldered her way to Miranda's side. "You and your slutty ways. If you'd married a true-blood we'd not have had your outland husband bring the wrath of the Stargods down on our heads. If you'd acted the queen and ruled rather than surrendering to your sorcerer husband, he'd not have ruined our beautiful land. Now you consort with another outlander. Aren't true-bloods good enough for you? We should exile you!" She raised a fist as if to hit Miranda.

The former queen stood straight, facing her accuser.

Excited whispers broke out among the men and the few women in the caravan. They retreated a step or two, leaving Miranda alone in the circle with her accuser.

Jaranda broke into wild cries.

Zebbiah wrestled the purloined lace from the thief.

"It seems to me, I am headed into exile, as are you and the rest of these people. What more can you do to me?" Miranda finally spoke. "But thievery from me is only a symptom of this man's dishonesty. Do you truly wish to risk traveling so far with him? Do you truly wish to be led by a man who will steal from each of you as easily as he does from me? I am no longer your queen. Decide for yourselves how you will treat a thief. I am going to eat my dinner." She sat down on her rock beside the fire once more.

"Somehow, I thought you'd find a rod of iron in your backbone once you started to remember," Zebbiah said quietly. He cuddled Jaranda close to his side.

Miranda took the lace from him and began rolling it into a neat coil, brushing dust from it as best she could. "How long have you known who I am?"

"Since the beginning. Who else would haunt the palace like the most beautiful ghost this world ever saw?"

"Why did I know you'd say something lovely like that?" She smiled up at him, welcoming his open admiration of her.

*   *   *

Marcus waited until the faint sounds of Robb settling back into his bed filtered through the wall separating their

rooms. Barefoot, he crept across to the doorway and waited
again. Vareena had quieted, too. The chill of the ages
seeped from the stones into his feet. But he dared not put
on his boots. He needed quiet and privacy. Not even the
ghost must hear him.

He was convinced the ghost had given or augmented
Vareena's nightmare. He had to be stopped. And Marcus
had to be the one to stop him.

He'd oiled the leather hinges of his door this afternoon
with a bit of fat from his breakfast bacon. The door opened
silently. He closed it again behind him, leaving it just
slightly ajar so that even the click of the latch would not
alert another to his movements.

A tiny bit of light showed around the edges of Robb's
door, as it did most nights. For some reason the absolute
darkness within the monastery bothered him. He set a ball
of witchlight in his window each night and let it fade as he
fell asleep.

Vareena's room was dark, but a little light glowed from
the refectory.

Marcus welcomed the dark tonight. He needed stealth.

Thirty paces down the colonnade brought him to the
doorway of the corner master's suite. No one else seemed
to have noticed that this room remained unused by those
seeking sanctuary here. The previous prisoners should have
sought the relative luxury of the larger room with its own
privy. Even he and Robb had instinctively chosen rooms
at the end of the wing of the building rather than bunk
in here.

Why?

In asking the question, he knew the room must contain
answers to the entrapment puzzle. But the answers were
hidden and not easily ferreted out.

The door opened easily and silently at his touch. He'd
greased these hinges as well as his own. Once inside, with
the door closed, he brought a ball of cold light to his palm
and held it aloft.

Nothing seemed changed, or out of place. An ordinary
room reserved for the most senior magician who would
administer the place from the office portion of the room.
The bed niche behind the half wall would allow him to rest

in relative privacy. From here he had easy access to the tower observation platform where he would monitor the movements of the stars and moon in the endless wheel of time.

Marcus had seen many towers and many observation platforms in his career. Answers might lie in the stars, but those patterns were subject to interpretation. What he needed was communion with the ancient spirits who had lived here long ago, when the first ghosts came here to die.

Inanimate objects could absorb strong emotions. Stone walls might reveal things that people forgot.

He placed the ball of witchlight in a niche beside the tower stairs. It nestled in there as if born to the place. The builders must have placed the small opening there as a night light for weary magicians moving up and down the staircase when they watched the stars for omens and portents of the future as well as answers to the present.

Breathing deeply, Marcus stared at the wall that adjoined the library, seeking a vulnerable place; some stone that might have been struck in anger or frustration, a place where a weary man had leaned for a moment of rest.

A trance settled on his shoulders, and the light in the room seemed to magnify. The tiny chinks and crevices blazed forth. The stones and the mortar took on a luminescence. He could see every fleck of minerals on the surface.

There! The stone a little below shoulder height, five blocks away from the doorway, seemed to have a handprint outlined in tiny glowing dots of white marble within the granite. Marcus placed his own left hand over the handprint. His longer and narrower fingers spread beyond the print, but his palm seemed an almost perfect match.

Already, he got a sense of the man, shorter than himself, probably stouter. And there, a darker splotch, about his nose level, where he had rested his head. He mimicked the posture.

Beneath his ear, the stones seemed to pulse. He let his trance fall deeper, penetrate the wall taking him . . .

* * *

Betrayed! The one who has claimed to be my friend our entire lives has betrayed me. He knows nothing of the reality of politics or economics, nothing of the greed of men. He knows only magic, the theories and techniques. Now he expects me to step aside and allow him to govern all magic and magicians in Coronnan. He'll botch the job for certain. Without me working beside him to keep lords and merchants honest in their dealings, he'll be bankrupt and disgraced before a moon has transpired.

But I will not be there to drag him out of the muck of politics and economics. This time his insults and disdain go too far. I shall take myself and my meager savings to another. Another man will pay me well to be his Battlemage. My so-called friend will have to face me in battle. He shall come alone and unprepared, because I am not there to do the work for him beforehand.

But first I must secure what is mine! No one shall find it in three hundred years.

* * *

Marcus jerked away from the wall as if burned. The anger of the man scorched the very walls of this monastery. His palm continued to tingle and radiate heat. He'd learn nothing more tonight.

"Ackerly. I think his name was Ackerly," he whispered as he made his way back to bed.

Chapter 26

Robb sat atop the open northwest watchtower above the kitchen and refectory, watching the stars. The haze thinned up here, giving him a clearer view. Many hundreds of years ago, hundreds of magician priests, and retired magicians, healers, and Battlemages had taken turns sitting up here watching the same stars. He found the familiar constellations, noting their position in the sky automatically. His planetary orientation told him that his observations were correct—something he couldn't discern down in the courtyard. The great wheel of stars around the moon had moved seventeen days since he and Marcus had arrived.

And yet they had only slept three nights. Time as well as magic became distorted within the monastery.

Another storm massed clouds to the west. But it would not arrive until tomorrow or the next day in real time, depending on the winds that pushed it. He didn't think it would hit with as much severity as the last one, if it reached them at all. The time distortion might very well push the weather elsewhere. Only one storm in a thousand hit the forgotten enclave, and then only those storms of unusual fierceness.

The scent of yeast bread rising wafted up to him from the refectory. What was he to do with Vareena and her obvious infatuation with him? "She loves the idea that I might take her away from here more than she loves me," he decided.

Idly, he tossed pebbles off the roof thinking of nothing

and everything. Mostly he avoided thinking of Marcus and his declaration of love.

How could he ever feel close to his comrade again?

They had traveled the length and breadth of Coronnan several times these last three years. Many times they had faced danger together. Many more times they had fled from it. Never had they questioned their friendship or their dependence upon each other. But that need had never crossed over the unspoken sexual boundaries Marcus now teetered on.

They both enjoyed women, looked forward to the day they could commit to just one. That they both wanted Margit hadn't seemed to matter. Margit loved Marcus. Robb had convinced himself he'd learn to love another someday.

But now? He'd rather watch the pebbles he threw, feel the rhythm of his shoulders and arms as he got the knack of aiming them to different parts of the monastery.

The stones landed in the packed dirt of the courtyard with tiny *plunk* sounds. He cast the next pebbles farther, aiming for a peculiar twist in the silvery-blue ley line. It landed on the slate paving stones around the well with a satisfying *thwack*. The next six pebbles also landed anywhere but on top of a ley line. Curious. The lines might be illusory, part of the confinement spell. He put more energy into the next pebble, a slightly larger piece of rubble from this rooftop observation post. It soared over the walls of the monastery to land silent and unseen.

"So, things can get out of here. People with magical talent can't." But could a spell?

Shrugging his shoulders, he lit a candle and dug out his shard of glass. He went through the motions of setting up the summons spell without thinking. Just before he sent his mind through the glass into the candle, he sat back and looked up at the stars once more. They twinkled at him invitingly.

"It's worth a try." He moved the candle to the parapet and sat below it, aiming his spell upward. Three deep breaths sent him halfway to the void. Another three breaths and the stars sang in his blood. All of his senses hummed in harmony with the world. He drew power from the stars, from the stones, from the ancient trees.

"If this doesn't work, I'll try probing the walls."

He took another three breaths for courage. "Like seeking like, flame to flame, glass to glass, my mind to a receptive mind. Heed my call of distress. Hear my plea for release." The rhythmic words poured from his mouth and his mind through the glass into the flame.

Reluctantly the flame pried itself loose from the candle and soared upward, much diminished in size and intensity. It flew beyond the walls, beyond the spell that bound it to Robb. It arced high and wide, flying on and on until Robb lost all trace of it in his glass and in his mind.

The candle guttered. The glass fell from his nerveless hands. He collapsed in a heap upon the stones, utterly exhausted.

The chill of morning dew awoke him. Automatically, he reached for the precious piece of glass. Pain slashed across his fingers. He yelped and jerked his hand away from the glass, sucking on the bloody cut. His glass had shattered when he dropped it.

His glass. The very symbol of his magical talent. His most precious tool along with his staff. A part of him. Broken. Shattered into six fragments too small to use for even the simplest of spells.

"S'murghit!" he yelled at the top of his lungs. *"Bloody, tartarian Simurgh!"* He threw the largest piece as far and high as he could, then the next shard and the next. When he still needed to release more energy, he grabbed the piece of gold in his pocket and threw it.

The world shattered. Light blazed. The stones at his feet tilted and whirled. Two heartbeats later his senses righted and he looked out at the world with a new clarity.

The gloaming retreated downward, leaving him above the haze.

"What the . . ." He retreated cautiously back down the staircase to the ground level. The coin glinted at him from the vicinity of the gate, enticing him to return it to his pocket where it belonged.

Robb raced down the stairs to retrieve the coin before he lost it. He paused in the arched entryway of the stairs. No one yet stirred in the monastery. He could retrieve the coin without observation.

He took fifty silent paces across the courtyard. Then stooped, about to place the little bit of treasure in his pocket—protected, out of sight. Hoarded.

The rising sun glinting through the crack in the sagging gate caught his attention.

"Just once more. I'll try the gate just once more." Holding his breath he pushed against the heavy panels. They creaked open.

Hastily, he looked over his shoulder to check if Marcus or Vareena came to investigate. The courtyard remained empty.

One more deep breath for courage and he—

Stepped through the gateway into the outside world.

Astonishment kept him pressed against the gate, afraid to step away lest his knees give out.

"I'm free?" he whispered to the winds. Two steps away from the stout walls confirmed it. He could walk away from here. Send help back for Marcus and Vareena. He could tap the formerly crazy ley lines that now ran straight and thick. He could . . .

He had to go back.

Marcus would disintegrate, physically and emotionally without him. He owed it to Marcus to go back.

The coin greeted him upon his return.

"So you are the culprit." He gritted his teeth and picked up the shiny piece of gold. "And my guess is your original owner was a miser. A miser who refused his next existence rather than give you up."

Once more the world tilted and light flashed, momentarily blinding him. When he opened his eyes again, a misty veil lay over everything.

"Coronnan has waited years for the return of the dragons. A few more weeks will not make so much difference."

"Robb, is everything all right?" Marcus appeared at the doorway to his cell, running his fingers through his tangled hair and blinking sleepily.

"Yeah, Marcus, everything's going to be fine." *If I can figure this out, so can you. You need the success to bolster your luck more than I do. I'll wait until things get really desperate to show you the truth—if you haven't figured it out by then.*

*　　*　　*

"Get that cat away from me!" Margit screamed as she jumped away from Amaranth for the fifth time.

"What a sweet creature," Katrina gathered Amaranth into her lap. "Such a *big* cat. Did you truly fly here or did you just jump from the rocks above us?" She petted him with enthusiasm.

"He's with me," Jack said quietly as he scrambled down the last of the rocks. He had to work hard to retain his balance, never quite certain which image was real and which a ghost.

Margit jumped again, startled. "You're supposed to let your armor down when approaching the camp of a magician. I could have blasted you with . . . with . . ."

"With what, Margit? What spell could you devise that would catch me off guard?" Jack smiled, trying hard to keep any sense of triumph out of his voice. From what he'd seen, Margit would make a competent journeywoman someday. Master status would elude her talents.

"I—I'd have thought of some—something." Margit worked her nose and mouth in peculiar gyrations.

"Jack," Katrina said quietly, still stroking Amaranth.

"Ahhhchooo!" Margit sneezed strongly enough to nearly extinguish the fire. "Get that cat away from me."

"Katrina," Jack acknowledged the woman he loved, ignoring Margit completely.

"I suppose you've come to take me back," Katrina said quietly, burying her face in Amaranth's blacker than black fur.

Did she sound accepting or defiant? Jack couldn't tell while Margit continued to sneeze her head off right next to him.

"No, Katrina, I've come to join you, keep you safe on this journey you've chosen."

"I thought that was Margit's job."

The apprentice magician sneezed again, three times in quick succession.

Katrina shifted to a rock on the far side of the fire, taking Amaranth with her. She looked up at Jack with hopeful eyes.

Margit continued to sneeze.

"I hope you will welcome my company," Jack said tersely.

Katrina looked up at him without answering, eyes huge in the firelight.

"Something is different about you, Jack. You are . . . almost vulnerable. Like you were when I first met you."

"Lonely. Missing you as I would miss my breath or the beat of my heart."

Her chin quivered slightly. She bit her lip.

Jack waited a moment, hoping she'd say something, anything to reassure him. "I'll not press you to marry me, Katrina. I know you fear it. But I need to know you are safe. I need to be close to you, look at you, touch you." He stroked her long, silky plaits.

Margit might not have been there except for her sneezes. Which tapered off as Jack moved away from her.

The funny feeling churned in his gut again, and his tailbone needed to twitch. He knew a sudden compulsion to wash his hands and face—especially behind his ears—in the nearby creek.

"And who is this new companion of yours, Jack? I know you miss Corby, but I never thought I'd see you with a cat," Katrina continued, as if their future together did not lie between them like an open wound.

"That is Amaranth." Silently, Jack sent the flywacket an image of rubbing his black fur against Margit's trews.

"Amaranth?" Katrina looked up at him, love and trust shining in her eyes.. Could this be just another ordinary conversation catching up on the news?

"The redundant purple dragon has taken a new form. He's truly my familiar now." Jack perched on a rock next to Katrina; close enough to reach out and hold her hand, but not so close as to threaten her.

"It's as if he now absorbs all of the light he used to reflect." She tried to stop the black cat from hopping off her lap, but he wriggled free of her grasp and slunk over to Margit. She had her back to the fire and for a moment her sneezes had abated.

"Amaranth," Katrina called him back.

Under Jack's prodding the flywacket circled Margit three

times, each circuit bringing him closer to her until he rubbed his face against her boots and then her knees.

"Get away, you awful creature." Margit hopped and jumped farther away from the fire. But she did not sneeze.

Jack sent Amaranth another mental command to return to Katrina and stay with her. Amaranth arched his back and stretched, leaning first backward, tail up, front legs extended. Then he leaned forward, stretching his back legs one at a time. At last he shook himself and leaped over the fire, extending only the tips of his wings for balance. He landed next to Katrina and sat. He accepted a few ear scratches, then began to lave his front paws.

Jack wanted to fish the soap out of his pack and join his familiar in the cleansing ritual.

Margit whirled to face him, eyes huge, hands fishing within her scrip. "Did you feel that? You must have. It was stronger this time, more urgent."

Then Jack put aside his own horrible fears and opened his awareness. His glass thrummed, very lightly; almost as if he had already answered the summons that had brought it to life.

"What?"

"A distress call. From that direction." She pointed. "West by southwest."

"I barely felt it before it was gone."

"That's the nature of a distress call, sent out to any magician who might intercept it."

Jack looked at her quizzically.

"That's what Lyman says. And I'm betting it's Marcus. I'm following it. Now." She stooped to pick up her pack at her feet. "You two don't need me anymore."

"Wait, Margit. You can't go now. It's dark. The road is uncertain, and we're very near the border. Who knows what kinds of bandits lurk in the foothills." Jack gritted his teeth and grabbed Margit's arm to detain her. His insides coiled in mistrust and an urge to flee.

The moment he touched her shoulder, Margit sneezed three more times in rapid succession.

He whirled quickly and sought Amaranth's aura, clearly outlined in the firelight. Only the pale purple signature color outlined his black body with energy. Jack sought Katrina's single aura of crystal and white, like her lace. Margit shone three shades of yellow between sneezes that shifted all her energy to orange while she purged himself of some foreign humor in the air.

Then Jack took a deep breath and sought the first stages of a trance. He stared at the silvery umbilical of life that trailed from his body.

Very few master magicians could see their umbilical anywhere but in the void. Fewer still ever had a glimpse of their true signature colors in the umbilical.

Along with Jack's signature silver and purple—darker than Amaranth's—he saw a strange coil of life entwined with his own. Red, black, yellow, brown, and a touch of white.

The same colors he'd sensed around Queen Mikka. The same colors as the cat she had lost when she absorbed her pet's spirit.

"Ladies, I think I have a problem."

Chapter 27

Lanciar shifted the bundle of kindling under his arm for better balance. Satisfied that he'd not drop the load of small sticks and dried grasses, he swung his free arm jauntily and whistled a gay tune as he strolled through the line of trees bordering a chuckling creek. This simple life of trekking across the countryside with the Rovers appealed to him. Almost like being back in the army without the worry and responsibility of seeing to the discipline and well-being of a thousand men under his command.

Indeed, discipline never seemed to be a problem with the Rovers. Their mind-to-mind links with Zolltarn gave them a sense of unity and purpose he'd never achieved in the army.

For a moment he felt very alone and left out of the clan. The whistling tune died in his throat. Alone. As he had always been alone except for those few brief hours when he and Jack had sat on a cold mountain trail while they traversed the void together seeking a way to center and awaken Lanciar's magical talent. Linked to Jack by mind and magic, he had known a short time of belonging with the universe at large and with one other person.

The next morning he and Jack had parted with hostility. And then, because of his misguided loyalty to the coven, Lanciar had betrayed Jack. Lanciar had never heard if the young magician had survived. He hoped so, even though they belonged to opposing forces on both the magic and mundane planes. Jack's honesty and unwavering loyalty deserved better than Rejiia had given him.

Guilt made him long for a tall mug of Maija's ale.

"What troubles you, spy?" Maija asked from directly behind him.

Lanciar gasped and whirled, ready to defend himself with his staff and magic. He'd never get used to the Rover's ability to creep up on him unannounced. Inanely, he was still clutching the kindling, recognizing its importance to the camp as a whole.

"What do you want?" he asked rather curtly. His irritation at his own failings suddenly became her fault.

"I thought you might like to meet your son, spy."

"I am not a spy. I have a *s'murghin'* name." He couldn't allow hope to overshadow his caution.

"Watch your language," she replied curtly. "Until you are one of us, we do not acknowledge your name. When you join us, we will give you a name worthy of our clan."

"When will I join you—if I decide to join your clan?"

"When you and I are married. When you and I soar through the heavens on a cloud of bliss on our wedding night. Then you will know the ecstasy of belonging to a clan." She moved closer. Her scent—soap, berries, and feminine allure—filled Lanciar's senses with longing.

Lanciar swallowed against a suddenly dry mouth.

"Come with me now, spy, and I will introduce you to your son. For the sake of your son, you will marry me. For the sake of your son, you will moderate your language, you will join with us, strengthen our clan with your strength, with your weapons, with your magic." She drifted closer yet. Her sweet breath fanned his cheek.

Slowly he shifted his mouth closer to hers. Closer until his lips brushed hers ever so lightly. Fire lit his veins and blanked his mind to all but Maija.

"Come," she whispered, taking his hand and leading him back to the encampment.

Men and women alike erected the circle of tents and bardos with swift efficiency. Trained soldiers didn't set up camp any better.

Still holding his hand, Maija led him to the small red tent with black trim beside Zolltarn's huge purple one. Together they ducked inside the long strands of wooden beads that served as a curtain. The aromatic incense of Tambootie wood greeted him from the beads as well as the fire. His senses reeled under the onslaught of hypnotic humors.

Lanciar blinked rapidly for several heartbeats, waiting for his eyes to adjust to the gloom of the tent interior and for his senses to balance. Maija continued to hold his hand. A fine layer of sweat moistened his palms. His mouth continued to dry. He swallowed convulsively several times, wishing he had a mug of Maija's very fine ale.

At last he spotted the curtained cradle swinging between two upright stands set beside the narrow pallet where Maija slept alone each night. A series of gurgles and coos came from the depths of the gauzy linen drapes over the peaked half roof of the cradle.

Lanciar dropped the bundle of kindling in his haste to reach his son. The Tambootie smoke had heightened his magical senses. One glimpse of the child's aura told him that he had sired this fragile scrap of humanity. He slid to his knees beside the cradle, fumbling with the coverings. Desperate to see the boy, afraid that Maija would hide the baby again if Lanciar took too long, he ripped away the fine linen.

His son stopped wiggling and cooing for one long breathless moment while father and son studied each other. Then at last the boy smiled, revealing toothless gums. He drooled and waved his hands about, happy with his life, with his full tummy, and his clean diaper.

"He is the most beautiful baby in the world," Lanciar gasped.

"Because he is your son." Maija beamed at him.

"Have you given him a name?" Lanciar spoke in hushed tones lest he startle the babe and set him crying. He offered the boy a finger to grasp.

A tiny fist wrapped around the digit with amazing strength and pulled it toward his mouth. Instantly, the baby began gnawing on it.

"Is he hungry?" Lanciar kept his finger where his son wanted it.

"No. He just needs to taste you in order to fix you in his tiny mind," Maija replied. She continued smiling hugely. "He's also beginning to grow teeth. His gums itch."

Lanciar finally gathered enough of his wits to look the boy over. Fine black hair with just a hint of a curl in it. Pink skin, much fairer than the olive tones of the Rovers. And incredibly deep blue eyes, the color of midnight at the full moon.

Rejiia's eyes.

Lanciar allowed his eyes to cross so he could study his son's aura. Undistinguished layers of purple, blue, red, green, and yellow frothed about him. He hadn't yet developed enough personality to push one color through to dominance.

"Marry me, and we will raise the boy together. You need never be separated from him again," Maija said. She lifted the babe into her arms, one hand beneath his bottom, the other supporting his head as she held him close against her shoulder.

"And if I choose to take my son back to my own land?"

"You will never see him again," she replied sternly.

"Then I will marry you." He swallowed, trying to get rid of his increasingly dry throat.

And then he noticed, eyes still crossed, how Maija's aura completely engulfed his son's, replacing it with her own dark purple-and-red coloring, extensions of Zolltarn's colors. The boy would never have an identity or personality of his own as long as he remained with the clan.

Lanciar had to get him away from here and soon.

"But first I need a drink. A very long and cold drink. Let me hold the boy while you fetch the ale."

"I will take him with me to the wet nurse. He will be hungry again soon."

"But . . ."

"When we marry, you may hold him all you wish. Until then, he belongs to the wet nurse."

"I'll get my own ale. And lots of it."

* * *

Jaranda fretted and cried. Her face flushed with fever. Her mother held her on her shoulder, gently rubbing the child's back.

"Hush, baby. Hush," she murmured over and over.

Jaranda pouted and stuck her thumb into her mouth.

"Zebbiah, she's feverish," Miranda called to her traveling

companion. "We have to find someplace warm and dry. My baby needs rest and nourishing broths. We have to stop!"

Zebbiah frowned, looking up and down the line of march. "We need to stay with the caravan. These parts aren't safe," he said quietly. "Look, she's fallen asleep. I'll carry her for a while. She's just not used to traveling."

"It's more than that, Zebbiah. I remember a time of great sickness the winter she was born. I remember the funeral pyres—the terrible smell. Most of all I remember the fear every time someone spiked a fever in a matter of moments. I will not let my baby die because you refuse to leave the dubious safety of these thieves and vagabonds."

"Lady, if I take you to a place where you can rest, will you make lace for me to sell?" Zebbiah asked in a whisper.

"Travel dust kept me from working the pillow by the campfire. These thieves and vagabonds have already tried to steal the lace. They'd steal the glass beads, silk threads, and bag of lace for the price of a meal. If you find me a quiet place with a roof and a fire pit and proper food, I'll gladly sit and make lace every day as long as the light allows." Until she remembered everything.

She'd gladly separate from this caravan to get away from their fellow travelers. None of them had spoken civilly to her since they'd ousted the leader. And they kept their distance, making sure each evening to light their fires well away from Miranda, Zebbiah, and Jaranda.

She had pieces of her memory, her name and that of her husband, flashes of faces from the past, but little else.

"Lady, where I plan to take you, I'll have access to witchlight come winter. You'll be able to make lace in the darkest corner in quiet privacy."

"Witchlight?" she gasped, frightened and exhilarated by the danger of sorcery. Often enough on this long trek through the mountains she'd seen the other travelers make the ward against witchcraft and evil whenever Zebbiah passed. She knew the motion of crossed wrists, right over left, and then flapping hands from a deep memory that seemed a part of her from her very beginnings. She wished she knew the origin of the gesture. Then perhaps she could understand the nature of the magic it warded against.

Something flapping, like a bird's wings . . .

She yanked her mind back to the immediate problem. Letting herself drift with minor remembrance often led to a true memory. But she didn't have time for that now.

"Yes, take me to this place, and I will make lace for you to sell while my baby recovers. Turn the place into a home, and I might stay there forever, content to make lace and raise my child in peace." Easier than returning to SeLenicca to take up the reins of government.

"Peace I cannot guarantee for long. But not many people know of this abandoned monastery. Most who know of it shun it because it is haunted. I have yet to meet a ghost there. It is not far from here, a day at most. We will break away from the caravan at the first bird chirp."

Jaranda stirred in Zebbiah's arms, snuggling close to him. She slept peacefully, thumb slipping free of her mouth. Something solid and honest about the man soothed her more than her mother's presence.

"We leave before dawn," the woman agreed.

"Take your baby now. I will make sure we camp close to the hidden path within the hour. I don't want to have to backtrack. Not on the open road. These vagabonds and thieves might well follow and attack us as soon as we are out of sight. I need to make plans to divert them."

Chapter 28

"We've only the one room above, the rest of you must take pallets in the great room—or the stable. Take your pick," the innkeeper announced. "Caravan came through from the pass yesterday and ain't left yet." She stood with fists atop her broad hips and a frown making deep creases in her heavy jowls. A thick wooden rolling pin with numerous dents sprouted from one of his fists. She looked as if she'd used it often to keep order in her tavern.

"I will have the private room to myself!" Ariiell stated firmly.

"I am the lord of this province, daughter. I shall have the room, with my wife, of course." Laislac glared at her with equal stubbornness. His face darkened. He'd explode with flying fists in a moment.

"I am a new bride and I carry the heir to the throne of all Coronnan. I believe I take precedence here."

Mardall giggled beside her. A bit of drool escaped his lips. His mother gently wiped it away with a lace-edged handkerchief.

"Protocol is useless in a situation like this." Andrall shouldered his way between Laislac and Ariiell. "If truth be told, Lady Lynnetta is senior in nobility to all of us. She is the daughter of one king, sister to another, and aunt to the current one. The only sensible thing to do is for all six of us to share the room above. Our retainers will bed down here and in the stable."

"Oh, why couldn't we have waited to leave Coronnan City? Then we could have traveled by our usual route, taking hospitality from minor lords who treat us as we deserve.

Instead we have stayed with ungrateful merchants. Now we must spend tonight in this foul inn that breeds disease and crime," Lady Laislac wailed and sobbed into her own handkerchief—not nearly as fine as Lady Lynnetta's.

The innkeeper frowned more deeply. She looked as if she'd gladly throw them all out to fend for themselves in the nightly drizzle.

"We left in midafternoon because the king commanded it," Andrall reminded them all. "If we had gone to my own castle at Nunio, we'd be there by now. 'Twould be more seemly for the child to be born in his father's ancestral home."

"I want my daughter comfortable, in familiar surroundings, where *I* can protect her and the babe." Laislac faced his new great-brother, his face darkening further. "You know the threats by the Gnuls. They want Darville to die heirless so the kingdom will fall into chaos. My daughter and her child will be safe in Laislac. Nunio is too close to the capital and the Gnuls."

"The Gnuls are everywhere, even in Laislac. Ariiell and the child would be safer in Nunio where *I* can protect them," Andrall returned. "I, at least, have some battle experience."

Ariiell motioned her maid to take her bag up the rickety staircase to the attic room. She slipped away, leaving her elders to their arguments.

Once inside the drafty space between the main floor and the roof, she dismissed her servant—a spy for her stepmother and probably the king as well—and locked the door. She shoved a table and chair in front of it for good measure.

"Alone at last!" She dug a small candle and piece of glass out of her personal bag of toiletries. The wick burst into flame with a thought. Then she settled down to summon her mentor. Rejiia would find a way to force Darville into recalling her to court. The mission of the coven was at stake.

"Flame to flame, like seeking like," she intoned the ritual phrases as she breathed deeply. The flickering green bit of fire drew her focus deep within the many layers of color, so like an aura, but more primitive and pure. She was content to sit there staring at the light magnified by her bit of glass.

A hazy yellow/green/blue glow rippled across the clear surface, vibrating slightly with the thrumming magic she had channeled through it.

Her spell must be weak and diffuse because she did not know where Rejiia hid. An answer might take a long time in coming . . .

"What!" Rejiia's explosive reply burst through the glass before her image solidified. Anger and impatience blazed in her midnight-blue eyes. Her black hair crackled about her puffy face in wild disarray. Dark shadows ringed her eyes.

Ariiell had never seen her in such disorder. She could almost smell the Tambootie leaves on Rejiia's breath. The drugs within the tree sap might enhance magical power, but also led to certain insanity.

"Rejiia, I need your help . . ." she began.

"Of course you do, you inept little . . ." Rejiia clamped her mouth shut and closed her eyes for a brief moment. When she returned her attention to Ariiell, she appeared calm, gentle, patient, and wise. Her eyes were clear and the familiar lean planes had returned to her cheeks and chin. A demeanor befitting the Center of the coven, a position Rejiia guarded jealously. Even though pregnancy should allow Ariiell to anchor the eight-pointed star rituals, Rejiia had not relinquished her place since her own pregnancy had ousted the late King Simeon from the center.

"What troubles you, child?" Rejiia asked. An aura of love and forgiveness flowed through the glass. But her hair still needed a good brushing.

Ariiell didn't trust that projected image any more than she trusted Rejiia to do anything except advance herself and the cause of the coven.

"Darville has exiled my entire family from court, Lord Andrall and Lady Lynnetta as well."

"Did the marriage take place?" Rejiia asked anxiously.

"Of course. Darville presided beside the priest. The entire ceremony was duly witnessed and recorded. The child is legitimate. But Rossemikka did not attend. 'Twas not a state event. I doubt anyone outside the family knows of it." Ariiell allowed herself a small smile.

"And the idiot?"

"With us."

"Good. Keep him, close. Sleep with him if you must. We need him alive and well until the child is born."

"I must return to court, Rejiia. That is the plan. I must be there to poison Darville and his foreign queen as soon as my child is acknowledged the legitimate heir."

"Plans change. I leave the poisoning to your guardian who is still in the capital." Rejiia lifted her hand in the gesture to end the summons.

But Ariiell had the book of poisons. Her guardian—whatever his name and status in the coven might be—had asked for it several times. She smiled to herself.

"The plan will not change. My son will rule Coronnan and I shall be regent. The coven will rule Coronnan through me," Ariiell replied sternly.

"Plans change," Rejiia stated firmly. Her eyes narrowed with secrets.

Suddenly Ariiell did not trust Rejiia to work in the coven's best interests. She worked only for herself.

"There may be another heir. I must investigate," Rejiia continued. "I am needed elsewhere."

"The coven has decreed that I must remain at court. Now help me return there. Shall I summon the full coven in council?" Ariiell asserted her rights.

"Very well, where are you?" Rejiia sighed and rolled her eyes upward. Dark shadows made her brilliantly blue eyes look as deep and fathomless as the Great Bay at midnight.

Ariiell shuddered with a sudden chill. Rejiia's anger could be formidable. She wasn't certain her own magic was strong enough yet to challenge the black-haired, black-hearted woman for the Center of the coven.

Quickly, Ariiell gave Rejiia a brief accounting of her location, still about five hours' hard steed ride east and south of Castle Laislac, not too far from the small pass through the mountains into SeLenicca.

"Really?" Rejiia's smile brightened. She laughed loud and long. The echoes of her mirth rippled through the glass to bounce off the walls of the attic room. Rejiia might have been next door. "How interesting. At dawn, you must proceed south on the main road for approximately one league, then turn north by northwest on a drover's track until you reach the small village perched on a rolling meadow by the river. Above the village at the top of a wooded hill is an abandoned monastery. Go there and wait for further instructions."

"But that is out of the way! What excuse can I use to separate myself from all these people? They guard me closely." As they should, since she carried the heir.

"You'll think of something. Just get there before noon. The entire fate of the coven depends upon you arriving in time . . . Never mind what for. Just do it. You'll know why when you arrive." Rejiia ended the summons with a snap of her fingers.

The glass turned cloudy with soot from the candle flame. It ceased vibrating with rippling colors and became once more inert.

The sounds of Rejiia's misplaced laughter still vibrated in Ariiell's ears.

Deflated by hunger and exhaustion from the spell, Ariiell fell back upon the single bed. Sleep wanted to claim her, but her mind spun with possibilities and plans.

* * *

"I don't like the smell of this," Zebbiah said quietly.

Miranda started out of a drifting sleep at the pressure of his hand over her mouth. She nodded briefly to acknowledge her understanding of the need to say nothing. He removed his hand slowly. Reluctantly? Did his fingertips truly caress her cheek and mouth?

"Our former caravan leader is scouting the perimeter of the camp. I don't want him to see which way we travel."

"The pack beast?" Miranda mouthed the words.

"Tethered away from the other animals."

"Will he protest?" They both grinned at the thought of the trouble the stubborn beast could cause them if he chose.

"I know a few tricks."

Miranda rose from her bedroll, careful not disturb her still sleeping daughter. Gently, she wrapped the baby in the covers and carried her to where Zebbiah indicated the pack beast waited.

At first she couldn't see the animal, only smell his dusty hide. Then, in the predawn stillness, she heard the click of teeth snapping at a tuft of grass just ahead of her, on the other side of the scraggly bush of d'vil's weed. The thorny vines had a tendency to reach out and grab unwary passersby and cling, and twine, and choke, and infect. The stuff grew everywhere that men had not burned it out and poisoned the roots.

How to get through the bush to the pack beast? Serve the obnoxious creature right for getting caught in the mass. It might starve before they could untwine all the branches and drop them in the campfire.

A flash of eldritch blue fire brightened the entire sky to the south. Miranda ducked, putting her back between the fire and her baby. She tried to cover her head from the unholy beings that might swoop down on them out of that fire. She tried to make the cross of the Stargods, but found her movements hampered by her burden.

Jaranda whimpered from being clutched so tightly.

Miranda settled for flapping her crossed wrists, hoping the antique ward against evil was sufficient protection.

The camp erupted in screams and flailing limbs. Men ran in opposing directions. Women crashed into each other as they tried to escape the eldritch light.

The former leader stumbled into their midst thrashing his arms about, his back aglow with blue flames that did not consume his shirt or skin.

Miranda wanted to run, too. Where? Masses of d'vil's weed blocked her path. She could escape only into that terrible blueness.

The Zebbiah was beside her. "Good girl. You didn't panic."

Swallowing the lump in her throat, she glared at him. "Why didn't you warn me this was but a Rover trick?"

"Didn't want to spoil the surprise." He grinned, flashing his magnificent white teeth. "This way." He waved toward the pernicious vines that grew thick between them and the pack steed.

"How?"

He grinned again and swept the vines aside with one arm. Strangely, they did not cling to his shirt or dig sharp spines into his flesh.

"Another Rover trick?" She eyed the vines suspiciously.

"Rover magic."

This time she did cross herself, no longer sure she could trust him. Or wanted to.

Chapter 29

"**D**o you think we should go back to the library and investigate?" Marcus asked Robb and Vareena. They were lounging around the well, listening to the bees feast on the blossoms of hundreds of overgrown herbs and flowers. No other sound penetrated the high walls. Marcus' fingers itched to get in there and start pulling weeds, pruning, and thinning.

He decided that when he had a place to call his own, he'd spend lots of time in an herb garden, meditating as he worked.

Maybe his restlessness pushed him to work among the growing things. Maybe this half-death made him long for contact with living things.

He needed to confront the ghost, throw the name of Ackerly at it, give it a chance to tell its story. But he also wanted Robb to be the one to find the answers. He deserved that. He'd been right. They had to make their own luck and opportunities.

The villagers, led by Uustaas, had left them enough food for a week. They didn't need extra blankets in the warmer weather, and the villagers had no reason to leave their work just to amuse two ghosts and their keeper. Vareena had turned her back to her brother and refused to speak to any who tried to break down her wall of silence.

When the outsiders had left—most of them with unseemly haste—Marcus had seen tears in her eyes. He wanted to hold her in his arms and chase the tears away with kisses. But the barrier of energy had repulsed him quite effectively.

Confronting the ghost seemed the only way to end this half-existence.

"Promise me, Robb and Marcus, promise me, that when you find a way to break the spell that holds you here, you will take me with you." Vareena seemed to be looking far beyond the restrictions of the monastery walls.

Both magicians nodded mutely.

"Have you noticed that the big spiders crawl everywhere but inside the library," Marcus added as a challenge to his partner.

Robb's head came up abruptly. He stared at Marcus a moment, then grinned with half his mouth. He knew something.

"Poking around the library has to be better than sitting out here doing nothing." Robb heaved himself to his feet.

Marcus followed suit, curious as to what Robb hid.

"Have you figured out how to avoid the true ghost?" Vareena asked.

"We need information," Marcus stated firmly. How many times had Jaylor, and before him Baamin, pounded that idea into his thick head? Information was the key to power. Information was the key to problem solving. Depending upon luck only worked when backed by information to point him in the right direction. He squared his shoulders, swallowed his instinctive fear of the ghost and marched in Robb's wake. He knew something, too.

Vareena shuffled along behind him, still shredding the petals from a daisy. She hummed a tune with a catchy repetitive rhythm under her breath. He'd heard that song before. It played itself over and over in his mind without end, like an obsession. Even the bees in the herb garden around the well seemed to buzz in time with it.

"You know what I miss most in this place?" Marcus remarked.

Robb kept walking. Vareena caught up with him and rewarded him with a smile. The haze seemed suddenly thinner, and the bees hummed louder.

"I miss music. We have no instruments. We don't sing

or dance to pass the too many idle hours. Even the birds are silent here." He continued staring at Vareena, hoping to lock her gaze with his own. If only he could look deeply into her eyes, he could convey all of his feelings.

"I thought I heard music on the wind, last night," Vareena said. "I thought it was the villagers."

"The wind was from the wrong quarter," Robb announced as he grasped the latch on the library doors. "This place plays tricks on your mind and distorts truths." He paused a moment for a breath and then thrust both sides of the double portal open.

"Hey, you, Ghost of this library. I'm not afraid of you. What are you going to do about it!" he called into the echoing emptiness.

"Who are you, Ghost? Does the name Ackerly mean anything to you?" Marcus grinned at Robb's look of surprise.

"Where'd you come up with that name?"

Marcus shrugged. "I probed a wall last night."

"Do you know who Ackerly was?" Rob's eyes remained wide and fixed on Marcus rather than on the gathering of mist under the gallery.

"I read it somewhere in a history book."

"You read it in Nimbulan's journals. The founder of the Commune of Magicians had an assistant named Ackerly who betrayed him. They fought with magic, and Ackerly died. No magician since has been named Ackerly."

"Ah, that explains some things." Marcus started backing out of the library as if afraid. He needed Robb to find the next clue. He needed his friend to succeed.

"First time I've ever known you to be the timid one, Marcus."

"That was before my luck ran out."

"Then make your own luck." Robb marched into the library and stood in the precise center of the room, legs spread sturdily, hands on hips, head thrown back in defiance.

The gold lay temptingly to his right and left.

"Stargods, Robb, you don't even have your armor up." Quickly, Marcus brought forward his own magical shields and extended them to his friend.

No sooner had his protection snapped into place than

the misty form drifted forward. It glowed with a dark yellow, almost goldenrod color, around the edges. The dripping sacrificial knife pulsed with preternatural colors, seemingly growing sharper and hungrier by the moment.

Marcus gulped but stood his ground. Robb still stubbornly refused to armor himself.

"Come and get us, Ghost of Ackerly the traitor," Robb taunted. "Kill us so you won't be alone. Kill us and you will share this monastery and all its secrets with us as we become true ghosts as well."

The ghost reared back, stopping three arm's lengths from the two magicians.

"What are you afraid of, Ackerly?" Marcus asked, trying very hard to make his voice strong and assertive. "Afraid that if we join you as ghosts, you'll have to share something?"

The ghost moved his head back and forth, looking first at the knife, then at Robb and Marcus.

"Well, I guess he won't interfere if we take some of this gold to the villagers to pay for our keep." Robb said.

"Gold!" a new voice exclaimed from the doorway.

Marcus looked over his shoulder, keeping the ghost and Robb still within his perceptions.

Vareena tugged on the hand of a tall, dark-haired man with wings of silver at his temple. He wore black garments trimmed with garish purple and red. He smiled, and all the light in the room seemed to sparkle off his teeth.

"Please, sir. You must leave here at once before you are trapped by the ghost," she protested, trying desperately to keep him out of the library. "The gold is but an illusion. Gold is the source of all evil," she added another argument.

"Gold by itself is the source of much pleasure and joy. Only a curse can make the gold evil. Only a curse cast by a Rover can harm a Rover, child," the man gently disengaged Vareena's hands from his arms. "Gold!" He turned his attention back to the bags dripping coins of many nations and denominations. "Gold to ensure our freedom, and our welcome wherever we might wander. Now I will truly be king of all the Rovers in Kardia Hodos. We must have a celebration and a coronation!"

Almost quicker than thought he dashed to the shelves and grabbed a handful of coins. A dozen or more people trooped into the room behind him and each also grabbed as many coins as they could hold in both hands. All of them hummed that obnoxious little tune that still repeated endlessly in Marcus' head.

Lightning flashed. The world tilted. The veil of mist flew from the chieftain and the rest of the Rovers, bringing them all sharply into Marcus' view and dimension. Even the ones who had not yet touched the gold shifted.

"Oh, no," Marcus groaned. The gold was indeed cursed. And he and Robb had fallen into its alluring trap. He fingered the gold in his pocket, longing to cast it aside and be free again.

Then he remembered what he had read about Ackerly, confirmed by the emotions trapped within the wall: a miser who loved his gold more than his life, his magic, or his honor.

Marcus looked to see if Robb had been watching.

But his friend's attention remained entirely on Ackerly.

The ghost, in turn, stared at the intruders, eyes wide in shock and horror.

"You have to make your own luck, Robb," Marcus whispered. "I can keep the secret a little longer until you figure out the answer. You deserve this triumph, if for nothing else than to prove yourself right and me wrong."

Chapter 30

"**S**top staring at the dumb steed and mount it!" Margit ordered Jack from atop her own mount. "We go through this every morning and every morning, for the last three, you stare at the beast an hour before you get up the courage to mount. I'm tired of waiting for you. We've a long way to travel yet."

Margit's steed pranced closer to Jack. He shied away from the animal as well as from the placid pack steed he had ridden yesterday. At least he'd learned to cope with the double vision and now knew which image of the steed might step on his foot and which was only an illusion.

Morning had passed halfway to noon. Jack had tried mounting the beast four times and had not yet come close to touching the animal.

He eyed the steed warily. "I never used to be afraid of these critters. I've ridden wilder beasts over the years. Why now?"

The cat inside him squirmed uncomfortably. Amaranth swooped low upon Margit, laughing at her discomfort as well as Jack's.

"Surely you can master the spirit of a cat, Jack. You have the strongest soul of any man I have ever met." Katrina sidled her steed close enough to Jack to ruffle his head.

He inclined his neck to lean into her caress. A deep thrumming sound began in his chest and climbed to his nose.

Why didn't he retreat from this beast? Because Katrina

rode it. He trusted Katrina more than himself at the moment.

The thrumming deep inside him matched the tingle in his fingers and behind his eyes, almost like the summons spell gone astray. He'd tried for three nights running to anchor the distress call that both he and Margit had intercepted and failed. He sincerely hoped the alien presence in his body hadn't interfered with his magic.

The cat—Rosie, as it thought of itself—purred in accompaniment to Katrina's caress.

At least Rosie liked Katrina. He remembered a time when Rosie was still within Queen Mikka that the cat took a sudden and unexplained dislike to her husband. Darville had worn scratch marks repeatedly.

The pack steed sidled and shifted closer to Jack. He jumped back hastily.

Margit laughed again.

"You didn't sneeze when Amaranth touched you because he isn't a true cat," he grumbled at the apprentice magician. "But you sneeze every time I think about coming near you."

"My instincts are true, Jack. I have the purrrrfect defense against you." With another chuckle she dug her heels into her steed. "Now, let's go find Marcus. We can't delay any longer." Her beast lunged forward at a rapid clip.

"I'll walk." Jack decided, handling the reins of the extra steed to Katrina.

"She's right, Jack. We have a long way to go to Queen's City."

"A long time for me to figure out what to do with this troublesome cat. At least the queen is free of it. My spell didn't completely fail." He smiled up at her as he trudged up onto the road from their campsite. He'd spent quite a bit of time obscuring all traces of their presence. Most of that time he'd been merely stalling.

"Why didn't the cat go to Amaranth as you directed? I would think it would want to return to a cat's body after all this time." Katrina kept her mount walking at Jack's pace. Margit trotted ahead of them.

"I'm guessing that Rosie has gotten used to the superior intelligence of humans. She—it—recognizes the difference between being a pet and controlling a human." Jack stuffed his hands in his pockets to keep from licking them and laving his ears.

"I'm sorry, Katrina, but I think we'll have to postpone our wedding again until I solve this problem."

Katrina half-frowned but didn't say anything.

"I do still want to marry you, when you are ready," he reassured her.

"I know, Jack. Strange, now that you want to postpone the wedding, I want it more than anything."

They both chuckled.

"We'll work it out, love. By the time we get to SeLenicca, we'll work it out."

Amaranth flew past them, nearly brushing Jack's head with his extended talons. He dropped onto the pack saddle of the steed Jack should be riding and set about preening his wings.

"I take it you like the body you inherited," Jack said to his familiar. He wanted to caress the soft black fur of his friend, but Rosie prevented him from coming any closer to the steed. How had the queen managed to ride so fearlessly these last three years?

Amaranth purred his contentment while continuing his bath. As he lifted his hind leg to wash the fur along that quarter, his talonlike claws embedded into the pack saddle for better balance. But he missed the saddle and clutched the steed's mane. The steed spooked and reared, rolling its eyes and screaming its outrage.

Amaranth shrieked and flopped around, trying desperately to disengage his claws.

With a long and frightened neigh the steed bolted. Katrina tried to hang onto the leading rein. It whipped through her fingers, cutting deeply as it burned free of her grasp. Her steed pranced wild-eyed and nervous at the strange noises and the smell of blood. It gathered its legs under it, ready to bolt after its companion.

* * *

Lanciar watched as one by one the Rovers winked out of sight, including the children—including *his* son. His jaw dropped. A fly buzzed around him. He knew he should close his mouth and yet. . . .

"I wish I hadn't drunk so much." He had trouble think-ing clearly. His head buzzed and his eyes ached.

Beside him, the unknown blonde woman sobbed as she dropped his arm and buried her face in her hands.

"Oh, no," she moaned, rocking from foot to foot. "Not more ghosts. More ghosts for my people to feed. They'll surely forsake the Stargods now and let us all starve."

The air smelled strange, slightly acidic, slightly rancid sweet, like a spell gone wrong. The wind rushed into this bizarre building, filling the vacuum left by the disappearing people. But not enough wind to account for the loss of all these people.

He remembered the fierce gusts that rushed through Ha-nassa when the Rovers had transported out. Then the Ro-vers had disappeared all at once from one heartbeat to the next. Now, they vanished one at a time like links in an anchor chain disappearing beneath the water.

They'd stumbled onto something strange—to say the least.

He wished Rejiia had accompanied them so that she could explain the phenomenon. His former love had an instinctive grasp of otherworldly puzzles.

Jack, too, would be a great help.

He had to find his son and flee. Now. Before things got worse.

Feeling almost blind with numb senses and numb magic, he grasped the doorjamb for balance. A burning energy repulsed his hand. He peered more closely at the spot. His magic kicked in, opening all of his senses.

"What?" The dim outline of another hand—almost invis-ible, like a dragon sliding in and out of view—shone with a silvery energy. He traced with trembling fingers the almost-visible hand up a black-clad arm to a shoulder and a black vest trimmed in bright purple and red. An abundance of silvery embroidery shone through the misty veil that seemed to separate him from the man.

"Zolltarn?" Lanciar gasped.

"Of course. Who else would I be?" the Rover leader sneered, then flashed his amazing smile. Lanciar immedi-ately felt more comfortable, ready to listen to the older man's wisdom. But his voice sounded as if it came from a great distance.

"What happened to you? You—you're as transparent as a ghost," Lanciar said.

"Nonsense, boy. You are the one fading in and out of view. Come in, come fully into the room. Then you will be one of us. You must be one of us if you hope to marry my daughter." Zolltarn opened his arms as if to embrace Lanciar, an all too familiar and disarming gesture. The curious burning energy kept them apart.

Lanciar breathed a little easier. He knew Zolltarn's charm all too well, knew how he lulled suspicions with the little deceptions of friendship.

"One of the clan." Lanciar stated flatly. He'd resisted all attempts by the Rovers to draw him into their direct mind-to-mind connections by ritual or coercion. He'd postponed his marriage to Maija for days, keeping his individuality for as long as possible by sheer force of will.

He wanted a drink. Desperately.

"Can you help me?" He turned to the sobbing blonde.

"Stay out of the library. Stay away from the other ghosts, the true ghost as well as all these new ones. Just turn around and walk out the gate before you, too, are cursed and trapped here forever." She gulped back her tears and faced him resolutely. "Get out now! And take me with you. I forsake my destiny though I'll be cursed through all my future existences. I cannot be responsible for all of these ghosts." She gulped back a new round of sobs and stiffened her spine. "I'm sorry, Robb. I must also forsake my love for you."

"I'm not leaving without my son," Lanciar told her. He looked for a trace of the smallest children among the Rovers. They should be too young to be linked with the Rover magic. But each one had been in the arms of a Rover woman. If touch or proximity to the library turned one into a ghost, then he'd lost his son, too. Forever?

"What do you know of this curse, woman?" He grabbed her arm, shaking her gently. "I've got to find my son among them. Help me find my son. Then I will leave and take you with me. Not before."

" 'Tis my destiny to serve the ghosts, not to understand them. They cannot leave here and must be fed. Your son is lost. Leave now before you too are cursed." Her eyes widened in horror. "I've never had more than one ghost before Marcus and Robb came. Now there are dozens. Dozens! Where will I find enough food for them all? Now I will never be allowed to leave this cursed place."

The statue of Krej sat in the place of honor at the front of the lead sledge—Zolltarn's conveyance. The hideous visage seemed to wink and grin at Lanciar in silent laughter as yet more gilt paint flaked off its tin hide. One front paw seemed to shed its metal coating and become true fur.

"I'll think of something. I need some ale in order to think." Lanciar wove through the scattered sledges seeking Maija's bardo. She did indeed brew the best ale he'd ever tasted.

But maybe he'd had too much already.

*   *   *

What strange being is this who stares at me from his perch atop the Rover conveyance? I can see the true nature of a man as a ghostly aura around the tin statue with the flaking gilt paint that renews itself only to flake off once more. Another ghost, as I am. Another with a mission. Shall I release him from his tin prison so that his gold will become real and cease to flake? I could possess the gold then. But that would deprive him of his life.

I sense that soon this ghostly man will separate from the tin statue that traps him. If he is not released before then, both the inert beast and animated spirit will drift forever in time, unanchored in any reality. He will cause havoc in all realities if that occurs. He has not much time.

But this place is a strange meeting of vortexes. Anything can happen, and time moves differently here. That is how I know my children live though three hundred years have passed. They must survive. Otherwise all I did for them is worthless.

I will know this man's true heart so that he can not betray me as others have.

As long as I have the gold, I can accomplish anything. Gold is power.

Chapter 31

"**K**atrina!" Jack sent a magical probe into the steed's mind, forcing it to remain in place. He gulped down his fear and grabbed the reins, yanking them down hard to keep the steed under control. His stomach heaved in fear of the steed and for Katrina's safety. His magical bond with Amaranth stretched thin to the breaking point.

"I am stronger than this!" he muttered through gritted teeth. "First things first." He lifted Katrina free of her skittish mount. He cradled her in his arms, soothing her shock and pain. A cursory examination of her bleeding hand showed him deep cuts from the leather.

"I don't have the healing touch, love, but I'll do what I can," he apologized. "It's going to hurt terribly, but I have to wash it."

She nodded, white-faced. "I trust you," she whispered so softly he wasn't certain he heard her as she clung to him with her free hand, resting her head upon his shoulder.

He kissed her temple and carried her to the creek beside the road.

Margit wheeled her horse and galloped back to them. "I'll take care of her. You go after that demented cat of yours." she said. "We can't afford to lose the supplies on the steed." She swung her leg over the saddle horn and dropped to the ground in one swift movement.

Jack released Katrina reluctantly. He took off running after the steed that was rapidly disappearing in the distance. "Stop, *s'murghit*," he panted. He couldn't call up his Far-Sight or enter the beast's mind while he put all of his energy into running. He didn't dare stop running lest the steed and Amaranth got too far away.

The steed would not cease its blind flight until Amaranth stopped shrieking and flopping about in panic. He could still hear his familiar protesting in the distance.

Quiet, my friend. Quiet, he whispered directly into the flywacket's receptive mind. The bonds between them guided his words. *Hush, little one.* He repeated the lulling words over and over, all the magic he could muster while maintaining his ground-eating lope.

At last, winded and nearly doubled over, gulping in huge draughts of air, he sensed that Amaranth worked his talons free of the tangled mane and the padded leather of the pack saddle. But the steed plunged on and on.

Jack repeated his quiet litany, seeking the equine brain. Steeds usually responded to humans, being nearly as physically compatible as cats. This one's panic blocked all of the normal channels of communication and control.

He sensed Amaranth launching into flight, having had enough of the steed's wild thrashing through the thickening woods.

Track it Amaranth. We can't afford to lose it! he called to his friend.

Amaranth swooped onto Jack's shoulder instead, barely digging in his claws at all. He kept his feathered wings half engaged, flustered, frightened, and bewildered. His voice reverted to baby shrieks. No telepathy at all.

"Go after the blasted steed, Jack!" Margit ordered him with mind and voice.

"Go, Amaranth. You can do this. The steed did not hurt you. Hunt it and show it to me as you fly."

Amaranth rubbed his face along Jack's cheek, heaved a sigh, and pushed himself into the air.

The absence of his weight on Jack's shoulder left him feeling terribly alone, almost empty. He stared after his familiar for several long moments, then returned to the women.

Katrina sat on the creek bank with her head between her knees, and her left hand held out for Margit's ministrations. Margit knelt beside the water rinsing a bloody rag. Mud and everblue needles stained the knees of her leather trews.

"I can't make it stop bleeding, Jack," Margit said. A touch of panic edged her voice. "It's stiffening up, like there's a tendon damaged."

Katrina gasped, then bit her trembling lip.

Jack knew her thoughts without reading her. She feared she'd never hold her lace bobbins again.

Margit closed her eyes, then spoke without looking at either of them. "Jaylor's going to kill me if I fail in this mission. He told me specifically to take care of her." She worked her cheeks in an effort to control her own panic. "Even last night when I reported that I was an unnecessary extra on this mission, he ordered me to stay with her."

"Let me see," Jack took her place beside Katrina. He concentrated on sending out an aura of calm authority to both of them.

When Margit's eyes quit darting about, he took Katrina's hand gently, probing the wicked cut across the palm, just below the finger joints. His eyes saw torn flesh and new puddles of blood. His magic found the severed blood vessels and gashed tendon. He took three deep breaths to trigger a trance.

"Are you going to cauterize it?" Margit rested her hand on his shoulder as she watched.

"Sort of." Jack narrowed his focus. "A healer would do this without effort and without pain to the patient. Just bear with me, Katrina." A nearby ley line winked at him with silvery-blue energy. He tapped it to fuel his work.

A little magic bound him to his love. A little more opened his TrueSight to the layers of tissue and energy in her hand. Flesh became translucent. Beneath it, he saw the pulsing vessels, the twitching joints, the binding tendons and cartilage.

"Sing something, Katrina. Sing your magic to match my own," he breathed, still within the throes of his trance. "You knew how to heal burned-out ley lines with your *Songs. Sing* to heal yourself now."

"I—I can't." She grimaced. Her pain became a visible layer of blackened red infiltrating all the layers of her aura. She kept trying to tug her hand out of his grasp.

"Trust me?"

"With my life."

He caught her frightened eyes with his own gaze. In a moment she quieted. Her breathing slowed to match his own.

A small *Song* of magic worked its way out of his heart into his voice. Their song. The little lullaby she'd sung in their prison cell. The one that had spawned tiny, spidery ley lines of energy where no ley lines had existed for many centuries. Together they had discovered the magic all women invoked when singing over mundane tasks. Unconsciously, they set up layer upon layer of protection for those they loved.

He'd tapped the ley lines Katrina had brought to life to release their shackles and aid their escape while Queen's City shook and crumbled in the aftermath of multiple kardiaquakes.

Slowly, gently, with the *Song* still lighting his mind and his magic, he sent a needle-fine probe of magic to the first small blood vessel. He encouraged it to mend. Then the next, a larger one this time. He needed a second, hotter touch to make it seal off.

Katrina gasped and tried to wrench her hand away.

He held her tighter, seeing precisely how much pressure he exerted with his solid hand against her seemingly transparent flesh.

A moment more and the last vessel closed. He encouraged the tendon tissue to knit and expel foreign matter so tiny only Jack's magic could see it. Then he brought the muscle and skin together, binding them loosely with magic. Best if they finished healing on their own.

At last he sat back on his heels and withdrew from the intimate contact. Sweat poured from his brow and his heart pounded erratically. Too tired to eat, he just wanted to curl up and sleep. He closed his eyes and still saw the pulses of energy and layers of color in the hand he kept within his own.

"You did it, Jack," Katrina said quietly. "I knew all along you had the healing touch. It only hurt a little."

Judging by the quieting layers of energy in her aura, that was a lie she almost believed.

She brushed a stray lock of hair off his forehead. Her

fingers lingered and traced his cheek. He turned his face just enough to kiss her palm.

"It will be stiff for a few days, while it finishes healing. But you'll be handling bobbins with ease after that," he reassured her.

"Time to get moving," Margit said brusquely. She stood up and brushed her trews clean of the creekside debris. "Has your cat found the pack steed yet?"

"He's working on it." Flashes of images began to penetrate Jack's mind. Tall trees, rising terrain as they neared the mountain barrier between SeLenicca and Coronnan. A scatter of small buildings at the base of a hill. More trees and then—atop the hill a jumble of stones with many pack steeds and sledges milling among the stones. A great deal of black with purple-and-red trim adorned the saddles, packs and rounded huts atop the sledges. He knew who owned them.

He sat up straighter, pushing Amaranth to focus more closely on the stones.

Not jumbled haphazardly. Worked stone stacked carefully and mortared into thick walls. A steedshoe-shaped building—squared off at the corners—with an exterior wall connecting the two outthrusting wings and forming a wide courtyard.

And there, quietly nickering to one of the smaller beasts harnessed to a sledge, stood Margit's white pack steed.

"Found him!" Jack stood up, dragging Katrina with him. "Only a mile or two off, that way." He pointed west and slightly south where they could see the beginning of the rising ground and the dense forest around the hill. The line of everblues blocked their view of the building.

Margit threw dried meat and journey bread at Jack from her pack as she leaped astride her mount. "Eat as we ride. You need to replenish energies lost while working magic. We need that steed and its supplies. If we delay, it may wander farther."

More slowly, Katrina stuck her foot into a stirrup. Jack pushed her into the saddle. Then, closing his eyes and forcing Rosie to the back of his consciousness, he clambered up behind her.

The cat within him roiled and wanted to spit. He fought it. His need to remain close to Katrina overcame the cat's hissing fear. More like a need to have its own way than a real fear.

Jack almost laughed out loud at this insight. "I'll match you stubborn for stubborn, cat," he said to himself.

Katrina looked over her shoulder at him in question.

"I think I found a solution to my problem," he whispered into Katrina's ear as he wound his arms around her waist. "Our steed found a bunch of Rover steeds. I believe they belong to my grandfather. The original spell that bound the queen to her cat was danced by Rovers. We'll have my grandfather's people reverse it for me and put the cat into Amaranth's body where it belongs."

"Rovers." Katrina gulped and stiffened in his arms. She did not urge her mount forward.

Neeles Brunix, the man who had owned her for three years; used and abused her for his own gain, had flaunted his half-Rover connections, the same blood mix as Jack.

Chapter 32

"**T**here's a village," Margit whooped. "We'll purchase supplies and a new pack steed here. No sense going off on a wild lumbird chase after the other one." She set her heels into the sides of her mount.

Katrina did likewise.

Jack bounced uncomfortably on the spine of the animal, clinging to Katrina for dear life. The cat spirit rose sharply to the front of his senses. His back arched, the hair on his nape and along his backbone stood up. A curious itch in his bottom felt as if a tail twitched in agitation. He swallowed the angry hiss that climbed from his gut to his throat like a too-long-suppressed cough. Rosie *really* did not like this steed.

"I am stronger than you," he hissed at the cat.

"What?" Katrina spared him a look over her shoulder while she gripped the reins firmly with her right hand, fully in control of her mount. She rested her bandaged left hand in her lap.

"Nothing, love. Take this path angling off to the south." He relived the course Amaranth had flown in pursuit of the errant steed. Even now the flywacket perched atop a high stone tower, trying to make sense of the images that wandered in and out of his vision. Jack couldn't make sense of them either. He hoped the confusion came from Amaranth's youth and lack of experience and not what he feared.

"But Margit . . ."

"Margit will follow. Her mission is to take care of you. She won't let us stray too far without her."

"Her true mission is to find Marcus. She can do that a lot easier without me. And now that you have come to see me safely into SeLenicca she will go off on her own, no matter what Jaylor orders."

"And leave you without a chaperone? Not likely. She knows her best chance of finding Marcus and Robb is to stick with me. Just guide this monstrous beast up that path to the top of the hill. I have a feeling we'll all find answers up there."

He blinked rapidly trying to sort the curious double vision. Amaranth's continuous feed of bizarre images, much clearer now that he perched atop a tower than when he flew, overlaid his own sensory view. He had to fight for balance the entire time. Then Rosie had to add her own confused perceptions, relying more on scent and sound than sight. Jack nearly lost his meager breakfast.

Amaranth sensed Rosie's need to understand through her other senses, and he began to relay scent impressions more than visual. Too many bodies confined together. Too many bewildered steeds. Strange cooking smells that relied heavily upon timboor, the fruit of the Tambootie tree, and something very old on the verge of decay.

And then Amaranth focused sharply on a curious statue perched atop the largest and gaudiest of the Rover bardos. A tin weasel. At one time the statue had been dipped in gold and the outermost layer had begun to flake off. The flywacket knew the weasel form, but could not understand why the statue did not smell of weasel.

Krej. Jack's heart fell. Another problem for him to deal with before he could take Katrina to SeLenicca.

(Gold!) the flywacket proclaimed.

At one time the dragons had told Jack that they valued gold and jewels almost as much as humans. Gold represented the power of the kardia, a symbol of the beauty of life.

Rosie recognized the value humans placed upon gold and reared up, ready to make Jack pounce.

Hold back, Amaranth. Do not announce your presence or betray your wings. I will be there, in a few moments. We can investigate together, he ordered his familiar.

Ruthlessly, he forced Rosie away from the front of his consciousness. It fought him every finger-length of the way.

Amaranth reluctantly folded his wings but continued to peer avariciously at the statue.

Jack closed his eyes again, reducing the onslaught of sensations. His stomach slid back down from his throat to about the middle of his chest. Manageable.

Silently he called Amaranth to him. Maybe if he could reduce the number of perspectives, he could conquer the queasiness.

Amaranth remained stubbornly in place. *(Must keep the gold from disappearing like funny men,)* the flywacket returned.

"What funny men?" Jack muttered.

Katrina pulled on the reins and looked back at him questioningly. He motioned her forward.

Then another view of the monastery with a thick haze over all. The vague outlines, as if viewing them through a thick fog, of mingling steeds and Rover bardos superimposed onto his already distorted visions. This one came from high above them. Briefly he caught a glimpse of himself and Katrina atop the lumbering steed. He watched them climbing the long trail that circled the hill half a dozen times before ending abruptly at the tree line a few yards from the gatehouse tower.

His stomach lurched again. "Don't fly, Amaranth," he pleaded with his familiar. Then he realized that the new view came from yet another source. A dragon flew above.

"Shayla?" he asked the unseen observer.

"Shayla?" Katrina looked up in delight.

(Baamin,) the blue-tipped male dragon replied with a chuckle. *(Shayla's son fares better than you do, young Jack.)* Another laugh rippled across Jack's consciousness. *(You can sever the link between your minds upon occasion.)*

"I don't want him to feel lost. We need this time of constant contact to solidify our bond." Jack looked up trying to catch a glimpse of the magician turned dragon who had been his mentor and father figure as well as father in another life. "You taught me that with Corby, my first familiar."

Katrina patted his hand. "How sweet, Jack. I hope you are as considerate of our children." She must have heard the dragon. Unusual. Normally, only Shayla communicated with her.

"I'm glad you are still thinking of our future." Jack nuzzled her neck, drinking in her unique smell and the silkiness of her hair.

(There will be many times when you do not wish a third participant in your life, Jack. Amaranth will wait for you.) Baamin broke off his verbal and visual contact. Abruptly, Amaranth's contribution ceased as well.

Jack sensed a tiny squeak of protest from his familiar just before his vision centered upon what his eyes could see alone.

Relief came to his stomach with a sense of emptiness. The cat settled into a contented purr within him. The vibrations centered at the base of his spine. Since his attention was no longer divided between the cat and the flywacket, Rosie had nothing further to contribute.

Jack almost panicked at the loss of Amaranth's familiar presence in his mind. They'd been linked constantly since before the purple dragonet's transformation. He took a deep breath and accepted the temporary separation. Temporary, he reminded himself and the cat.

You know, if you had gone into Amaranth's body as planned, you wouldn't have anything to be jealous of, he reminded Rosie.

The cat continued to purr without further comment, setting up an almost sexual satisfaction within Jack as the vibrations radiated out from his spine. His bottom stopped itching, as if his invisible tail curled around his hips in contentment.

"What was that all about?" Katrina asked.

"Did Baamin show you the view from above?"

"I only caught bits and pieces through a thick fog. My contact with him is not as—as complete as it is with Shayla. But I sense his approval of me. He wants to deepen our contact. What is that strange building atop the hill that he seemed so concerned about?"

"I'm guessing from the shape it's an abandoned monastery from long ago. People who aren't supposed to be there have recently taken up residence."

"What people?"

"Rovers." The bardos atop the sledges were distinctly Rover in construction and painted design. But why had the owners neglected the sledges and pack beasts? Rovers always attended to their animals very carefully before seeing to their own needs. Always. Steeds carried nearly as much value to them as the gold coins they wore on their sashes and caps. Only children represented more wealth than gold and steeds.

The distinctive purple and red that dominated the colors of those bardos proclaimed them the possessions of Zolltarn, self-styled king of all Rovers, member of the Commune of Magicians, and Jack's grandfather. That clan had an abundance of babies born in the last four years—to replace the men who had died quite suddenly the year before Zolltarn changed his loyalties from coven to Commune. The dragons had a hand in the loss of those men, and the Rovers had never quite trusted them as a source of magic or as a benign presence since.

Zolltarn used dragon magic and his membership in the Commune to serve his own ends. Only he of all master magicians dared ignore a summons from Senior Magician Jaylor.

"I might have known that Zolltarn would end up with the statue of Krej," he muttered.

"Amaranth. I need you to look again. Where are the children, where are the Rovers for that matter? They wouldn't abandon their steeds and bardos." He relinquished the moments of quiet single vision in favor of information.

He saw again the bardos still harnessed to the steeds; the riding steeds wandering about the large courtyard, grazing on the overgrown herb garden; a woman he did not know sitting on the step beside the well, face buried in her hands, her shoulders heaving with sobs. Beside her stood a familiar and unwelcome figure. He sensed more than recognized the aura of his old enemy Lanciar from SeLenicca. What was *he* doing in Coronnan? And if Lanciar was about, Rejiia could not be far behind.

Then the Rovers and several other figures emerged from inside the building. They looked nearly transparent, outlined in silver like a dragon. All of them had become ghosts!

At that moment Katrina stopped their steed abruptly at the gate tower. Jack slid from her back, half planning to dismount, half falling from distorted balance and perception.

"We've got some real problems here. Stay outside the walls, Katrina. Whatever happens, you and Margit stay outside the walls." He walked quietly through the gate, keeping to the shadows.

"Your problems are my problems, Jack." Behind him, Katrina dismounted and followed closely on his heels.

* * *

Vareena rose from her seat by the well and marched out into the courtyard. Steeds milled about, placing their burdensome sledges at odd angles. She stumbled over an abandoned pack, slipped in a fresh pile of dung and landed heavily against the sledge cabin. A tin weasel with flaking gilt paint grinned down at her as it teetered on its porch.

"*S'murghit!*" she cursed in very unladylike tones. "I refuse to be responsible anymore. I'm leaving." She righted herself and aimed for the gate.

"Wait, you can't abandon us. You're the only one who knows what's going on," the blond man who remained human grabbed her sleeve and kept her from retreating out the gate.

Another steed—taller and stockier than the beasts that had come with the Rovers—blocked the exit. Its sides heaved as if it had run a long distance. She'd not shove it aside without help, not for a while yet anyway.

"You can leave this cursed place with me," she said flatly, shoving her way through the crowded courtyard. Ghosts began appearing among the steeds. She bounced away from them into more animals, dogs and chickens as well as the pack beasts.

"No, I can't leave. They have my son. I can't find him without your help, and I won't leave him with these people."

"A child?" Vareena stopped short, heart aching for the lost souls condemned to this place. Why had this man been spared but not his son?

"My son is still a baby, a tiny baby with black hair and brilliant blue eyes. Please help me find him. Please help me to hold him one more time before this terrible curse takes him from me forever." The man who had appeared so confident when he walked through the gate looked helpless now. A great deal of pain and longing poured out of his eyes.

"Vareena!" Marcus pelted out of the library into the courtyard. "Vareena, don't leave me, please. I need you. I love you," he panted as he skidded to a halt scant inches from her.

"Marcus?" Vareena peered at his insubstantial form, not certain she had heard him correctly.

"Yes, Vareena. I love you. I have from the moment I first saw you. Please stay. I can find an answer to this problem. I know I can." He rammed his right fist into the pocket of is trews while his left hand reached out tentatively as if to brush a stray lock of hair from her brow. A sharp tingle of energy repulsed him before he made contact with her.

"No, Marcus, you do not love me. You can't." *Not Marcus,* her heart wailed. *Why couldn't it be Robb? 'Tis Robb I love. Will always love.*

Having acknowledged her attraction to the dark-haired magician, she knew she could not abandon Robb or his friend now. She needed to see this through to the end, even if she remained here the rest of her life, like her mother, and her mother's mother before her.

Once cursed by the monastery and the hoard of gold, the women of her family were cursed forever.

Her last hope of freedom slid away.

Chapter 33

"**M**aking your own luck doesn't always work," Marcus said as he trudged back to the library from Vareena's side. She'd stay to help. Now he needed to stay by Robb until his friend also figured out the source of the curse.

He watched the Rovers step through the constant veil of mist into his reality. His heart lodged in his throat. How could he push Robb to discover the secret with all of these Rovers complicating things?

"This is bad luck for all of us," Robb agreed.

The hair on the back of Marcus' neck stood on end. An unnatural chill climbed his spine. He whipped around to face the ghost of Ackerly. The misty form coalesced into a nearly solid being. His aura pulsed brighter as he sped across the massive library, sacrificial knife raised over his head.

"He's a Bloodmage," Robb hissed. "He gains power from inflicting pain and drawing blood!"

"Zolltarn, look out!" Marcus called. He dove for the Rover, knocking him to the ground. Ackerly's knife sliced through the air where Zolltarn's neck had been. In the same movement, Marcus drew Zolltarn's long dagger and turned on the ghost.

"Eat iron!" he yelled, stabbing at the air around him.

A wail of pain and frustration pierced his ears. He wanted to clutch his ears and curl into a fetal ball but dared not shift his attention away from the knife. The ghostly sound faded.

An eerie silence fell upon the library. No one moved. No one breathed.

"M–my thanks, young magician," Zolltarn said. He remained on the flagstone floor staring about him, eyes wide, showing more white than black. He tried working his mouth into one of his engaging smiles and failed. "I owe you my life and my soul."

Marcus nodded but kept searching for the ghost.

"Best we all retreat," Robb said, ushering the Rovers away from the gold.

One young man sneered at Robb, still clutching an awkward double handful of coins.

"Go!" Zolltarn said, resuming his natural authority over his people. "The gold will still be here tomorrow."

"And many tomorrows after that," Marcus muttered. "Unless my luck changes."

"Make your own luck," Robb reminded him, patting him on the back.

Together they retreated, blades at the ready.

But the ghost remained quiet and out of sight.

"I think saving the life and soul of a Rover chieftain is a bit of luck," Robb continued when the haze separated them from the darkness in the library. "Rovers have power, and Zolltarn is more powerful than most. He's indebted to you."

"What did he mean that I saved his soul?" Marcus asked quietly.

"I meant that for a Rover to lose his life to a Bloodmage binds his soul to the murderer. When that Bloodmage is a ghost . . ." Zolltarn shuddered rather than complete the sentence. "My debt to you is immeasurable, young magician. I offer you any of my daughters as your wife."

"Uh . . . no thanks. I may have spent the last three years wandering, but the Rover life is not for me. I want a nice little cottage with a wife and a dozen children and a dozen more apprentices." He felt immeasurably lighter for having voiced his longtime dream. The possibilities seemed firmer.

Robb raised his eyebrows at him. A big grin tugged at his mouth. "By any chance did you ever tell Margit this is what you want out of life?"

Marcus shrugged. Had he? No matter. He loved Vareena now. He'd likely never see Margit again.

"We will be on our way, young magicians," Zolltarn dismissed them. "We had planned to spend some time here and celebrate the marriage of my daughter Maija to soldier

Lanciar. But we do not willingly share space with the ghost of a Bloodmage." He bowed deeply, all the while edging toward the gatehouse.

"Good luck getting out of here," Marcus snorted, keeping his attention on the library.

"What?" Zolltarn stared at him with eyes narrowed in speculation.

"Explain the situation to Zolltarn, Robb. I'm going to see if we can persuade the ghost to drop his knife." Marcus took a deep breath and stepped back in the direction of the library.

An unholy screech from atop the walls interrupted Robb before he could speak. Lumbird bumps raced up Marcus' arms and spine. Both he and Robb turned toward this new menace, blades at the ready for the ghost.

"Stargods, save us all!" Zolltarn crossed himself three times, flapped his wrists in the ward against Simurgh and crossed himself again. "An evil creature out of myths! What strange place is this?"

A black cat swooped down on black-feathered wings. Its blacker than black fur seemed to absorb all the sunlight. The beast let loose with another of its eerie cries, half yowl, half the screech of an enraged éagle.

Everyone ducked as it passed.

Marcus heard many strange invocations against the ancient winged demon Simurgh. As soon as he felt the passage of air on his hair from the cat's flight, he glanced up to follow its trajectory. Surprisingly it landed neatly on the outstretched arm of a Rover-dark man standing in the archway to the gatehouse. He might have the coloring of a Rover, but he dressed like a Commune magician in blue tunic and trews. Behind him stood a blonde woman. The misty veil of unreality separated them from the rest of the milling crowd of Rovers. Marcus was certain neither of them had been in the courtyard a few moments before. Neither of them was dressed in the garish purple and red on black. But the man's eyes bore the same shape and intensity as Zolltarn's.

He'd seen those eyes before.

"Stay out of this cursed place," Vareena ordered, marching quickly up to the newcomers.

"We seek only a night's shelter," the stranger said.

"With the spawn of Simurgh on your shoulder you seek more than that," Zolltarn challenged. But his smile returned full force, driving away the sense of foreboding that hovered among his people.

"Perhaps I seek my grandfather," the stranger returned the smile. He clutched the hand of the young woman behind him and strode forward.

"Jack, have you returned to the clan at last?" Zolltarn asked, striding to meet him. The Rover spread his arms wide intending a fierce embrace. Jack remained in place, arms firmly at his side. Zolltarn bounced off him before Jack could rebuff him. Zolltarn frowned deeply. Jack merely nodded with a grimace.

"You look like a ghost, Grandfather," Jack said, peering at all of the Rovers with curiosity.

"I know that man." Robb whispered to Marcus.

"He does seem familiar, but I've never met Zolltarn's grandson. I know a lot of men named Jack, none of them magicians. A magician would change his name to something more lofty to command respect," Marcus replied. "Jack doesn't seem like a Rover name either."

"Perhaps you knew me under another name, before I learned of my heritage. Before I earned Master status in the Commune," Jack said.

Marcus searched his memory for any apprentice or journeyman with Rover heritage.

"Um . . . Yaakke had very dark hair and eyes," Robb reminded him.

"Yaakke? The lost journeyman?"

"One and the same. And this is my betrothed, Katrina of SeLenicca."

"You escaped SeLenicca?" Lanciar pushed his way toward them—of all the Rover party, he alone remained fully human. "Thank the Stargods you survived."

Vareena followed Lanciar, shaking her head.

Marcus moved to Vareena's side. "It will be all right. We'll get this fixed soon," he whispered to his love.

She had eyes only for Robb.

"Aye, Lanciar, no thanks to you, I survived," Jack said, ignoring the others. His voice and face remained calm, almost devoid of emotion. But his eyes took on a haunted look. "I survived. With Katrina's help, I escaped Rejiia's foul prison, and the kardiaquakes and the destruction of Queen's City. The last I saw of you, you were meekly obeying her orders and boasting of your membership in the coven." Both men's auras flared with wild and violent emotions.

"But did you find the dragons?" Marcus moved to stand between the men before they engaged in a physical, or worse, a magical duel. The barrier of energy around him repulsed them in opposite directions.

Vareena tugged on Katrina's hand, urging her toward the gate. But Katrina held firmly to Jack, or Yaakke, or whoever he was now. Older, more mature and sure of himself with only a trace of the cockiness of his youth.

"Yes, I found the dragons and returned them to the lair, again with Katrina's help."

"Then magic is legal again in Coronnan?" Marcus asked. His dream of a home and family at the University shifted slightly from a cottage in the woods to a suite of rooms in the massive stone building in the capital.

"Not exactly," Jack and Zolltarn replied at the same time.

"Marcus!" a new voice announced herself from the gateway. Margit raced across the crowded courtyard, bouncing off of one ghostly Rover after another, heedless of the angry voices and offended travelers. "So this is where you've been hiding. This is where you came just to get away from me!" She raised her fist and slammed it into his jaw.

The anger behind her blow pushed her through the energy barrier and knocked Marcus flat on his bum.

* * *

Iron! They fight me with iron. I have no defense against that base metal. So cold. And yet it burns. Not like my gold that warms to the touch and invites me to caress it. The young whelps must have watched when I could not follow our keeper up the iron staircase.

The iron cannot push me into my next existence. I want no other than what I have. I have the gold and that is all I need. I do not even need my children—proud of them as I am—as long as I have the gold. But iron will give me terrible pain that will not go away. Ever.

I must make them flee. None of the others who have vis-

ited me have given me so much trouble. The others were company of sorts. I was content to let them fondle a piece or two of gold. They could not leave with it. And so I retrieved it upon their deaths. Quiet deaths mostly, with a peaceful passage into their next existence. They can only last one hundred days or less living under my curse. And I still had the gold.

But these magicians tax me greatly. They have the gift to undo three hundred years of protecting my gold. I shall whisper the secret into their dreams. 'Tis their greed that keeps them here. Tonight, I shall whisper into their dreams. All of them. By morning they will either flee or kill each other. One way or another, I shall be free of them all.

* * *

Ariiell eyed the side trail with suspicion. Why would Rejiia send her up there? This must be the wrong road.

But they'd passed no others. She had watched diligently for signs of the place Rejiia needed her to go. With just a touch of TrueSight she discerned the signs of many steeds passing this way recently. Steeds and sledges.

No respectable trading caravan would travel up this narrow and nearly overgrown path. They would seek the village up ahead.

She sniffed the trail with her mundane nose, made more sensitive by magic and pregnancy. This was a talent Rejiia and the coven did not know about. She could identify individuals by smell from one hundred paces, she could tell what Cook prepared for dinner before the dishes began cooking. And she knew that the passing steeds pulling the sledges had left a great deal of dung on the path.

She would not traverse this trail. No matter what Rejiia ordered. She would not go there!

"I'll not follow orders blindly anymore. I carry the heir. I shall make all my own decisions." She kicked her placid mare into a sprightly trot, leaving the noisome trail behind.

"Why did you tarry there, daughter?" Lord Laislac asked as she rode alongside him.

"I thought it might lead someplace interesting." She dismissed the topic.

Lord Andrall immediately looked back over his shoulder at the trail and up the hill. As his gaze came to the crest, his eyes widened. "I do not like well-traversed trails branching off to old ruins. They speak of outlaw hideouts."

"An abandoned monastery." Laislac kept his voice light, but his eyes remained fixed on the same spot as Lord Andrall's. "The locals proclaim it haunted and do not go near. Outlaws heed them."

Ariiell squinted and called up her FarSight. Nothing but a pile of old stones shrouded in mist.

"Tales of haunting are often spread by outlaws and bandits to keep the locals away. I'm going to investigate." Andrall yanked his reins so his steed would make the tight turn onto the trail. Mardall steered his own mount to follow his father.

"Milord, you cannot go there alone!" Lady Lynnetta protested, hand to her throat.

"Half of the men with me, weapons at the ready. The rest stay close to the ladies," he called to the troop of retainers behind them.

"Not without me," Laislac muttered.

"No, P'pa," Ariiell protested. Amazing, just when she decided not to obey Rejiia's orders, her father proceeded to force her to follow them. "You cannot leave us with such meager protection." She waved to indicate her stepmother and Lady Lynnetta. Then she placed her hand on the bulge of her belly in silent reminder of the importance of the child she carried.

"No one will disturb you on the main road. Go up to the village if you are frightened." Laislac pushed his steed onto the side trail.

Lord Andrall looked as if he would protest the safety of the road and village. Then he firmed his jaw and turned in the wake of his great-brother. The men at arms followed. The retainers and servants milled about, uncertain of which way to go.

Ariiell rolled her eyes up in exasperation. "I'm not going to be left behind." She joined the trek up the hillside. Behind her the others followed her lead.

"This had better be good, Rejiia."

In the back of her head she heard a malicious chuckle.

Chapter 34

"**W**here'd he go?" Margit stared at the space where Marcus had just been. She shook her hand to free it of the curious burn on top of the bruising from connecting so firmly with his jaw. "The bastard must have used the transport spell to disappear on me again. *S'murghin'* coward couldn't tell me to my face he expects me to sit quietly at home bearing his brats and babysitting his apprentices! What makes him think I want that kind of life? What makes him think . . ."

"I'm right here, Margit, right where you dumped me on the ground." Marcus' voice came to her from a great distance.

"Where?" She looked around for the source of his voice. Only Jack and Katrina with the blasted flywacket and another man and woman and a lot of steeds and sledges stood in the courtyard. "Where?" she repeated.

"Right here!" the once-beloved voice sounded angry now. "You could have told me your dreams. Instead you let me ramble on about my hopes for the future and you never said a word. You could have told me you don't really love me. You only wanted to use me as a means to wander the world."

The thickening fog distorted the air into a vague manlike shape, like looking at a dragon, but . . . but dragons had more solidity.

"You never said anything to me about settling down. All you did was retell your adventures on the road. I thought you wanted to keep traveling, take me with you on your journeys." Margit gulped back a sob, trying to rekindle the anger that had propelled her. "Jack, what's going on?" She looked to the one magician who might figure out this puzzle.

"Your anger must have heightened your senses for you to see him in the first place," Jack sighed. "Engage your TrueSight, Margit. Then look slightly to the side of the distortion. Do you see him?"

"I'm not sure. He looks sort of like a scrying image gone awry, almost there but not quite."

"I'm here, Margit. And our betrothal is off. I've found another. Vareena." His voice caressed the name. The figure that might be Marcus reached out as if to embrace the short woman standing off to the side. But he didn't touch her.

Vareena heaved a weary sigh and stepped away from him. She'd be pretty if she weren't so old. Nearly thirty. Past being a spinster. Margit classified her as a maiden aunt, destined to care for her brother's families, if she had any.

"Robb, tell him that I do not love him," Vareena said wearily. "I cannot love him." She sounded more exasperated than aggrieved.

"I can't tell him anything, Vareena." Another ghostly voice that sounded like Robb but not quite, from somewhere near the largest of the sledges.

Margit looked closely. Definitely another man shape within the light distortion. And beside him another and another. The flutters and fluctuations in her perceptions made her dizzy.

She closed her eyes to regain her balance. When she opened them again, the wavering light remained.

"What's going on, Jack?" She looked at his solid body rather than at all of the almost-people who milled around the courtyard. Katrina looked as bewildered as she. Only Vareena and the other man who did not seem a part of the entire proceedings acted as if all was normal.

"I was just about to find out when you interjected with your rather—um—forceful opinion," Jack replied. The corners of his mouth twitched even though he kept them in a stern frown.

Just then a caterwauling rose all around them, like a

thousand cat fights all at once. Chills ran through Margit, but she didn't sneeze.

"Now what?"

"They're all fighting over the gold," Marcus said. He sounded as if a great weight pressed against him.

Margit's heart almost moved in empathy with him.

But the hurt was too great.

How could he have just presumed she wanted a home and children? Kardia Hodos was a big planet, and she intended to see all of it.

No, he hadn't heard. He hadn't listened. He never listened to anything but what he wanted to hear because he presumed his luck would make everyone agree with him.

"Your luck just ran out, Marcus," she muttered as Jack and two blobs of watery light moved toward the loudest of the disagreements.

And then she heard something that chilled her even more than the screeching fights and arguments by unseen ghosts: the distinctive hiss of long metal blades sliding out of wooden scabbards.

She whirled around to find a new party of a dozen steeds ridden by nobles and men at arms.

* * *

"Whatever happens, do not touch the gold," Robb whispered to Jack. He slammed his weight into two Rover men who grabbed each other by their shirts, clutching fingers far too close to the vulnerable throats of their opponent.

"Zolltarn!" he yelled at the top of his lungs. "Zolltarn, control your people!"

Jack bounced off two women, one heavily pregnant. They separated, mouths agape, panting for breath as they stared at the man who had the audacity to interfere. The burning energy that must separate the women from the normal world kept Jack from touching them directly, but his impact against the barrier should have been unpleasant enough to force them apart.

Someone grabbed the back of Robb's shirt and spun him around. Then a fist connected with his jaw and stars spun before his eyes.

"Robb!" Vareena screamed. And then she was kneeling

beside him, hands reaching out to examine the huge ache in his teeth that spread from his chin to his eye. This time she forced her hand through the burning energy. Her fingers caressed his jaw, feather-light. The sharp pain eased to a dull ache.

For a moment his gaze caught hers. Suddenly his heart raced in his chest, opening him to new emotions, new truths about himself. A kind of serenity filled him. All because she touched him.

"We'll discuss this later. Right now, I have a brawl to break up." He heaved himself to his feet, wishing he could return her caress, perhaps kiss her cheek in tentative promise. "Later," he affirmed to them both.

The world seemed suddenly brighter and all of their problems surmountable.

And then the world tilted, light flashed, and the misty veil around the world expanded.

A gaggle of newcomers at the gate flashed swords. "Where'd she go?" Lord Andrall shouted.

Robb felt his skin grow cold as he recognized the king's adviser and his lady and their simple son astride the magnificent steeds clustered around the gatehouse. The other lord and lady could only be Lord Laislac and his second wife—his first wife had died quite mysteriously, and with a scandal Robb couldn't remember, some years ago. Their attention all focused on a very pregnant young woman—now in the ghostly reality—wrestling with a Rover woman over a scarf heavy with gold coins.

"Give it to me, you ignorant slut. I need that gold. In the name of the coven, give me that gold!" she shouted.

"Get out of here now, Vareena," Robb implored. "Run as far and as fast as you can. Save yourself from the coven."

*   *   *

Everyone and everything in the courtyard stilled. The name of the coven had that effect on people.

Marcus looked around to see who had invoked them. The band of magicians was dedicated to the overthrow of every peaceful government in all of Kardia Hodos. His gaze lighted on the young woman in elegant velvet riding clothes. Hints of red glistened within her blond hair. Her aura almost shouted magical power within the orange-and-yellow layers.

He blinked and looked again, more closely. She had touched the gold a Rover woman had fastened to a sash. In touching the gold-laden sash she joined the growing crowd of those trapped in this other reality. She broadcast greed to any receptive magician within a league's distance. So did the Rovers.

"Did I hear someone say gold?" One of the lords at the gatehouse dismounted hurriedly. If he wasn't careful, he'd trip over one of the Rovers and become a ghost himself.

"Lord Laislac." Vareena dipped a hasty curtsy to him.

He ignored her.

Marcus already knew Lord Andrall and his lady. He'd heard tales of their simple son. The other woman in the party must be Laislac's wife. The one he'd married in haste after his first wife quite conveniently fell from the castle ramparts. Or was pushed. The scandal had circulated in the capital for a few weeks and then disappeared in the wake of newer gossip. Laislac had married a much younger woman the day the official mourning period ended.

Marcus peered around Zolltarn's sledge to see if any of the Rovers acknowledged the presence of nobility. They didn't seem to care. But the statue on top of the sledge, the tin weasel with flaking gilt paint, began to rock and shift. Both front paws and about half of the tail seemed to have shed its tin coating. A spot of drool dripped from the exposed teeth—real teeth, not metal castings.

"Robb, Jack, look at Krej!" he called, fascinated by the partial animation. At one time Krej had been the most powerful lord of the land—first cousin to Darville's father and regent during Darville's magically induced illness at the beginning of his reign.

"Krej and Lanciar in the same area?" Jack held his staff out, prepared to use it as a defensive weapon, physical and magical. "Rejiia can't be far away."

Katrina touched Jack's shoulder and pointed to the top of the southwest tower. Marcus followed her pointing finger with half his attention, keeping one eye on Krej.

Atop the tower the light sparkled with new magic. The

wind blasted outward and down into the courtyard whipping dust into everyone's eyes. Marcus forced himself to keep his gaze trained on the area. He didn't know the secret of the transport spell, but he'd witnessed it often enough to know when someone used it.

Black and red dominated the spot. The light coalesced into the figure of a black-haired woman with a silver streak running from one temple down the length of her waist-length tresses. Her black gown molded to her tall figure, outlining all of her curves and emphasizing the length of her legs.

"Rejiia," Jack confirmed.

Marcus' armor snapped into place. Beautiful, deadly, vicious. Krej's daughter. She'd learned a lot from her father before the lord had thrown one spell too many and had it backlash off King Darville's sword and crown. He'd been captive in the weasel statue ever since. Without Krej's disdainful supervision, Rejiia had learned a lot more about magic and about evil than her father had ever dreamed of.

She would continue to menace Coronnan until she sat on the throne with the Coraurlia—the magically charmed glass crown in the shape of a dragon—on her head; or until someone managed to kill her.

"Release my father!" she called in an imperious tone. But there was a tightness in her neck muscles and the way her hand clenched around a small wand set with a black crystal on the end. She must use the wand as most magicians used a staff. A pretty and feminine affectation. And undoubtedly just as deadly as the woman who used it. She pointed the crystal directly at the statue of her father.

The tin weasel rocked again, but it remained firmly anchored atop the sledge.

Then Marcus noted that Zolltarn rested his hand on Krej. He flashed his brilliant smile at Rejiia. She flinched ever so slightly.

As long as Zolltarn had some of the enchanted gold in his possession and touched the tin statue, the statue traversed both realities and was subject to the magic of neither. A dark aura surrounded the statue, as black as the void.

Something was terribly wrong with Krej.

Rejiia must have sensed it, too. She disappeared in another flash of light and swirl of wind. Just as suddenly, she reappeared directly in front of Zolltarn and the statue.

The black aura moved higher. The statue rocked harder, puffing up to almost twice its normal size.

Marcus jumped to stand between Margit and Vareena and the magic about to go awry.

Chapter 35

"**G**ive him back to me!" Rejiia said through clenched teeth. Her body seemed as tightly controlled as her jaw.

"And what of our son, Rejiia?" Lanciar asked. "Don't you care anything at all about the child the Rovers hide from you?" The mass of Rovers and newcomers separated for him as he marched over to her side. Outrage poured from him like a leaking bucket. Magic power raced from his fingertips up his arms to his shoulders. He wanted nothing more than to backhand the woman and knock her clear out of his life into her next existence.

"The child is just one more crime for which Zolltarn and his Rovers must answer to the coven. My father is in greater danger. Release him!" Rejiia reached out with her hand and her magic to encircle the tin weasel.

Light flashed, and the world tilted. Rejiia joined the Rovers and the others trapped in some reality different from Lanciar's.

Part of Lanciar wanted to laugh. Disgust invaded a bigger part of him.

"Is this place truly safe?" A new voice asked from the gateway. A feminine voice speaking Lanciar's native language.

Only Katrina turned to look at this newest additions to the mob. Rejiia continued to struggle with Zolltarn for possession of Krej.

"Your Majesty," Katrina gasped as she bent her knees into a full curtsy. In the same motion, she tugged on Jack's sleeve to bring his head respectfully lower than the trail-weary woman.

Miranda cradled a small child in her arms. Yet another Rover held her arm at the elbow.

This new Rover wore the same red-and-purple trim on his black clothes as Zolltarn's clan. Lanciar did not recognize him from his weeks on the road with the Rovers.

Lace spilled from the panniers on the back of their pack steed. But it wasn't quite a steed. Then the beast opened his mouth and extended his neck, bellowing an obnoxious braying sound around a mouthful of big, square teeth. A team of trumpeters could not have attracted more attention.

Everyone in the compound turned to face this new greeting.

"Who?" Zolltarn asked.

Lord Andrall and Lord Laislac immediately bent a single knee to her presence. Their wives followed suit—sometime during the fray they, too, had dismounted.

"Your Majesty, may I present your new ambassador from Coronnan," Katrina said, daring to raise her head a little. She pushed Jack forward. He stumbled to one knee. The flywacket remained firmly on his shoulder, flaring his wings just enough for them both to catch their balance.

"Your Majesty, my position as ambassador to SeLenicca has not been confirmed by the Council of Provinces, only promised by His Grace King Darville."

"Miranda," Lanciar breathed. "When did she come back to life?" In asking the question, he knew the answer. The moment Simeon died, his spells would have dissipated. The sorcerer-king had kept his wife—the hereditary ruler of SeLenicca—comatose for weeks to keep her from revoking the edict of joint monarchy. She had planned to strip him of power and divorce him. His blatant affair with Rejiia had pushed her beyond forgiveness.

"Queen Miranda," Marcus gasped. "What in the name of the Stargods is *she* doing here, dressed as a peasant and in the company of a Rover? I thought the SeLenese did not acknowledge outlanders as human."

"They don't," Lanciar confirmed. "It seems some changes are happening in SeLenicca."

"Rise up, all of you," Queen Miranda said. She blushed and looked to her escort. "I am queen no longer. SeLenicca is in ruins. I have no government. Today I am no more than this trader's partner. I make lace for a living."

Katrina smiled brightly. "So do I, Your Majesty."

"You will have a government again," Jack affirmed. "King Darville is committed to helping you rebuild your country."

"With what? The land is bankrupt. My people are scattered and disillusioned."

Rejiia seemed to have been forgotten in this new development. Lanciar spared her a probing glance. She raised her wand as if to strike Zolltarn on the head with it. Did she have any magic to accompany the blow? Her emotions were out of control and so must her magic be. She reeked of Tambootie.

Lanciar guessed the dragon weed was pushing her into insanity, just as it had Krej and Simeon before their downfalls.

"We have a vast hoard of gold here, Milady Queen," Zolltarn announced with all the enthusiasm of a minstrel at an Equinox Festival. "You have only to claim it."

"No!" a dozen or more voices protested. "The gold is mine."

And then the ghost of Ackerly erupted from the library. His misty white form flew broad circles around the courtyard, slashing with his sacrificial knife at all who held his gold.

Rovers and armed guards alike in both realities beat at the wraith with daggers and cook pots and anything else made of cold iron that came easily to hand. One Rover slashed the sleeve of another open with a dagger. He received a fist in his jaw in return. Another dozen brawls erupted, spilling over to the newcomers who had not yet had a chance to claim any of the hoard.

Still the ghost circled the compound, screaming and slashing with his dripping ritual blade. Two men fell to the ground screaming, dripping blood from scalp and back wounds.

Lanciar waved his hands at the being. Just as it flew past him, knife aimed at the great vein of his neck, Lanciar dove beneath a sledge. The wraith howled his disappointment but kept circling, seeking a new victim.

"Maija, if you love me even a little, you will help me

make sure Rejiia does not escape justice this time," Lanciar pleaded with whoever might hear him. A second later the weight of a gold coin rested firmly within his palm.

Black stars clouded his vision and his head felt as if it floated somewhere around the tower roofs. The ground beneath him seemed to slant sideways.

He braced himself to keep from sliding out from beneath the sledge and into the extended brawl. Quickly everything settled and Maija lay beside him, eyes wide and moist.

He kissed her lips lightly. "Thank you, Maija. Now help me make certain none of these people leave until we sort this all out. We have to stop Rejiia from stealing my son or reanimating her father. Stop her forever."

"I knew you loved me," Maija cried, throwing her arms around his neck and returning his kiss most soundly.

"Later, Maija. I promise that once this is over we will marry and I will stay with you. We will raise my son together with any other children we happen to have." He held up the coin she had given him and smiled. "What happens if we drop a coin deep in the undergarment pockets of all these people?"

Maija returned his grin. "I have listened to all these people argue. The gold is what traps them here in a ghostly existence."

"Then we must keep them all here for a time. Especially Rejiia. She must not leave, and she must not liberate her father from the statue."

"With your promise to marry me, with my clan as witness, we are already married and bound to each other for all time." Another kiss with her body pressed tightly against his distracted him a moment.

"Then we must work together for the safety of the clan. Help me keep all these *s'murghin'* people here."

"Watch your language around the children!" Maija's eyes, sparkling with mischief, belied her stern frown.

"Will you please help me keep everyone here?"

"Even the *gadjé* nobles and their retainers?"

"Especially the *s'mur*—um—*gadjé* nobles and their pregnant daughter. If she escapes before we sort this all out, she will alert the coven and bring them here from the far corners of Kardia Hodos." He kissed Maija's cheek—her mouth was too dangerous with its open invitation to linger with her. Then he extricated himself from her arms.

Maija crawled over to the nearest Rovers who rolled on the ground punching each other. She lightly removed a coin from the discarded cap of one of the men.

"Is it one of the ghostly coins?" he asked as she handed it to him.

"Aye. See how old it is?"

He nodded as he picked out the outline of a long dead monarch. The date on the inscription connected it to the province of Faciar before the unification of Coronnan and the foundation of the Commune of Magicians.

"Only the ghost's hoard is that old."

Rejiia had both hands upon the tin weasel. Zolltarn worked to keep her from wrenching it away from his grasp. Sweat dripped from both of their brows. The statue retained all of Krej's mass as a full-grown man. Neither of them could lift the thing easily. Both of their magical talents seemed depressed by the ghostly reality of the gold.

Lanciar crawled out of his cover, careful to avoid the swooping ghost. He walked right up to Rejiia and Zolltarn. Neither took any notice of him. The weasel was more tin than gilt these days and the front legs and all of the tail seemed to have lost most of the metal, taking on a decidedly furry texture. The backlashed spell was wearing off.

Would Krej survive? Would he emerge as a man? Or did the spell have to be reversed instead of wearing out in order for him to become other than a weasel?

Lanciar didn't care. He was about to irrevocably sever all of his connections to the coven. Perhaps break it apart once and for all.

"This is for deserting our son, Rejiia, and for not giving me the right to raise him as I choose." He dropped the antique coin down the front of her bodice. It lodged neatly between her ample breasts.

Rejiia screeched in her most annoying voice. She clutched her temples and reeled. Zolltarn tumbled backward in full possession of the heavy statue. He landed flat on his back with Krej sitting on his chest.

Then Rejiia's already ghostly form dissipated more. Lanciar could barely make out an outline of her or her aura.

Both had been clearly visible while she merely clutched Krej on the other side of Zolltarn's ghostly grasp.

"Neatly done, my boy. You'll make an admirable Rover!" Zolltarn proclaimed around heavy gasps for air. He remained a silvery outline. The Bloodmage ghost and his wicked knife were more substantial.

"Zolltarn's had the wind knocked out of him," Lanciar said. "Marcus, Robb, somebody help him up."

Lanciar had difficulty seeing the men he called to for help. But Jack and Katrina remained clearly visible, along with Vareena and Queen Miranda and her party. He must have slipped back into reality when he let loose the coin into Rejiia's bodice. Rejiia's violent transition had kept him from noticing the sense-shattering shift.

One by one the nobles became opaque ghosts. Strange that the mundanes were more visible than those with magic. Rejiia and Zolltarn were the hardest of all to see.

Then Maija popped back into full view. She smiled at him. The sun seemed to burst through the clouds and brighten his day. She had definitely inherited that smile from her father.

"Let's hope you have a few more scruples than your father," he muttered as he moved to join her.

"Changing sides again, Lanciar?" Jack confronted him, keeping him from Maija. He leveled his staff, aiming the tip directly at him.

"Trust me, Jack. Please, trust me just this once. I know which side offers me the best hope of regaining my son and raising him in a loving family, learning to use magic responsibly."

"I don't believe you any more than I did back in King Simeon's mines. You were a spy for him and the coven then. I know you still spy for them."

"Traitor!" Rejiia aimed her wand directly at Lanciar.

Lanciar saw two brief blasts of fire, one purple and silver, the other red and black, then there was nothing.

*   *   *

"Enough," Marcus said. "I've had enough." He took a deep breath and fingered the three gold coins in his pocket.

Robb, Jack, Vareena, and Margit looked at him strangely. He smiled at them. Only half his mouth turned up.

"I'm sorry, Robb, you really deserved to figure this out first, but I can't take any more of this. I'm getting out." Deliberately, he sank his hand into his pocket and retrieved the three coins.

He held them up to the sunlight. They glinted enticingly, begging him to hold them, caress them, keep them forever.

He closed his eyes and gathered his strength. With a mighty effort he threw them at Ackerly. "Take these back, you cursed ghost. I have no more use for your hoard. I want to live poor rather than remain trapped here with your riches."

Ackerly snatched the gold out of the air as he circled the compound once more. He juggled his bloody knife while he fumbled to hold onto this returned wealth. For a moment he looked as if he might drop them both. Then he sighed and disappeared into his library.

Light flashed blue and white and red. The world tilted. Up and down exchanged places three or four times. And then Marcus found his feet firmly planted on the ground. The misty haze that had covered his vision for so long lifted and he could see Vareena and Margit quite clearly along with Queen Miranda and her party. Robb, the Rovers, Rejiia, and the pregnant woman and her party remained insubstantial forms.

But the heavy fog remained across the top of the courtyard.

A moment later Robb emerged from his haze to stand before him with a big silly grin on his face. "I was waiting for you to figure it out."

Marcus hugged him tight and slapped his back.

Robb returned the comradely embrace.

"Now what do we do?" Marcus asked them all.

Chapter 36

"It seems to me that part of completing a quest is cleaning up the messes along the way," Jack said quietly. Guilt immediately heated his face. He'd left a terrible mess in SeLenicca.

But he was going back there, with Katrina, to do what he could. And the gold seemed to be one of the answers to that country's many problems. If they could convince Ackerly to give it up and remove the curse.

At least he'd temporarily stunned Lanciar enough to keep him from interfering.

"Our quest is a bit redundant," Robb replied. "We were sent to bring the dragons home and possibly find you. You seem to have completed both of those tasks quite handily. Our duty to the Commune is to return to the University for a new assignment." His face fell, as if that were the last thing he wanted to do. His eyes strayed to Margit and Vareena.

"Marcus and Robb, do you intend to leave this situation unsettled?" Jack asked. "These Rovers and the others trapped between the void and reality, with a ghost to haunt them, need a solution. So does the village that will impoverish itself trying to feed them." Jack needed to prod them into making their own decisions. He couldn't do it for them. They'd never become master magicians if they relied on others to make their decisions.

That had been a hard lesson to learn and one the cat within him truly resented. Rosie was more interested in watching than leading. He had to get rid of this cat and 'soon. He had enough problems without Rosie complicating things.

"I've never known a Rover to willingly give up anything they possessed. Why did Zolltarn offer a fortune in gold to a foreign queen?" Marcus interjected.

"Why give away the gold, Zolltarn?" Jack raised his voice over the sounds of many people arguing. Even the lords and their ladies fought over who could bow the lowest to the improbable queen in their midst even though the queen remained substantial and the nobles had become ghosts.

The Rover chieftain opened his mouth in a toothy grin. Jack continued to look at him questioningly rather than succumb to the seduction within that smile. He knew his grandfather too well.

"With a Rover sitting beside the queen of SeLenicca." He nodded to their kinsman holding Miranda's hand and guarding the pack beast and its treasure trove of expensive lace from the light fingers of a number of the combatants. "And Rover gold to rebuild the country, my clan will have a homeland. We will have the freedom to roam there forever."

"You won't end a thousand years and more of prejudice against dark-eyed outlanders with a little bit of gold," Jack reminded him.

"And the people of SeLenicca may not allow their queen to marry another outlander. Look what the last one did to us," Katrina added. "With the help of that black-haired bitch." She almost snarled as she jerked her head toward Rejiia.

The coven witch had returned her attention to Zolltarn and the tin statue.

"Katrina?" Jack had never seen her so aggressive, or so angry. But then, Rejiia had made her watch Jack's torture. Afterward, she had left Katrina to share his dank and miserable cell and die chained apart as the city collapsed around them.

Memories of that awful night pushed Jack closer to Katrina. Silently he reached for her hand. United, they had defeated Rejiia and her lover, King Simeon. Together they could conquer the world.

"I need to return to the University to find a way to lay Ackerly to rest and lift the curse from the gold," Marcus said.

Jack almost didn't hear him.

"What about us?" Margit asked belligerently. Her fist clenched as if she intended to knock him flat once more.

"I don't know, Margit. We need to talk. We need to find out if our dreams for the future can ever find a common ground. But first, I need to solve this problem." He captured her gaze for a long moment. Margit looked away first.

If a breaking heart could make a sound, Jack heard it in her sigh. But no tear touched her eyes.

"Come on, Robb. Let's pack and get out of here. We have a long walk back to the University."

"I think I'd best stay here, Marcus," Robb replied. "Vareena and I have much to discuss. And someone needs to try to restore order to this mess."

"Yeah, maybe the time has come for us to work alone. We've always relied on each other and that is a good thing. But some things can only be done alone."

"I can't give you the secret of the transport spell until you are confirmed a master magician, Marcus, but I can send you on your way in a matter of heartbeats rather than weeks. We don't have time to wait for you to walk there and back," Jack offered.

"And my brother Yeenos may return at any time with an edict from the priests and Council of Provinces removing our responsibility to these ghosts," Vareena reminded them. "We have to free all of these people before then."

"And free yourself as well," Robb added. "As long as there is a chance someone will wander in here and become a ghost, you will feel honor-bound to remain here. I can't allow you to do that, Vareena."

Jack took a moment to assess the status of the captured people. Marcus and Robb had returned from the gloaming. Katrina, Margit, Zebbiah, and Queen Miranda had never transferred into a ghostly state. All of the Rovers seemed to be gone, as well as Rejiia. Rejiia and Zolltarn continued to tussle over possession of Krej. The Rovers and the nobles continued to argue and brawl.

The noise began to make his head spin.

Amaranth screeched and flapped his wings, not liking the loud chaos much either.

"I'll take the offer of the transport spell." Marcus firmed his chin. "Though the way my luck has been running lately, I'll probably get lost in the void."

"I did that once, Marcus." Jack could smile now at the devastating mistake that had begun his adventures. But he'd been young and too arrogant of his talent then. "Have you undergone a trial by Tambootie smoke?"

"Of course. We all do upon advancement to journeyman from apprentice. It centers the talent and opens true life paths," Marcus replied.

"And protects young magicians from the inconsistency of raging growth and change when we reach puberty," Jack confirmed. He hadn't undergone the important magical trial when he'd become lost in the void. His body and talent had rebelled against each other. "I'll make sure you don't get lost. But just to be sure, I'll send Amaranth along with you to guide you home."

And that way, he'd also have some privacy with Katrina. If this mob would ever settle down.

"One problem at a time," he told himself.

                    *   *   *

Vareena joined the Rover girl kneeling beside the blond man Jack and Rejiia had reduced to immobility.

Rejiia, who seemed to be everyone's enemy, had time and attention only for the hideous statue. But the Rover chieftain had secreted it once more inside one of the funny looking hovels atop the sledges. Vareena had watched him hand it over to a subordinate who in turn passed it to another and another until she'd lost track of who had it.

"Where have you hidden my father?" Rejiia screeched, much like the flywacket. With magic, she blasted open the door of the closest bardo. While the wooden panels smoldered, she began pawing through the possessions inside. She discarded clothing and boxes, cooking pots and camp furniture in her desperate search.

"Get away from my things!" a Rover woman howled at Rejiia in protest, louder than the ghost of Ackerly had. She launched herself at Rejiia's back, fingers arched to claws and teeth exposed to bite.

Rejiia flicked her wrist and her assailant landed on her back in the middle of the compound. Rejiia continued her disorderly search.

"Murderer!" Maija screamed. She dove after Rejiia. "You murdered Lanciar for no reason." The two women rolled out of the bardo, the Rover clinging to Rejiia's back, fingernails raking the fine, white skin of Rejiia's neck and face.

"But he's not dead," Vareena said quietly. Beneath her fingertips, the pulse on Lanciar's neck pounded in a regular rhythm. Surely Maija had felt the same life sign.

Lanciar opened his eyes a crack. "Wha . . . what?" he croaked.

"Hush. I'm trying to sort this out," Vareena whispered.

Then Jack, Marcus, and Robb joined the attack on Rejiia. First one, then the other aimed their staffs at the woman.

"Get off me!" Rejiia fought Maija with one hand while her other plucked at something invisible that seemed to be encircling her.

If only the brawling Rovers would be quiet, she could figure out more of the complex relationships in this strange group. For a moment she understood Marcus' disgust with the entire situation. She wanted little more than to leave the mess and let these people sort it out themselves as best they could.

"You cannot bind me," Rejiia proclaimed. "I lead the coven. My magic is stronger than yours." She bucked backward, much as a plow steed rejects a rider. Maija sprang free of her victim, a sly smile on her face.

Jack directed Marcus and Robb with his staff. The three men circled Rejiia three times, each chanting something slightly different in a language Vareena did not understand. She was only aware of the fact that they did not speak in unison.

"Three different spells to break, each with a different solution," Maija told her. "Even Rejiia will have a hard time getting out of their bindings."

With each circle, Rejiia's movements became more restrained. Her hands and arms pressed tightly against her sides, immobile. Only her mouth remained free and she spewed invective on every head.

"Oh, shut up," Vareena finally exclaimed. "I'm sick and tired of all this noise and chaos in *my* monastery."

"*Your* monastery? My dear young woman, this entire province belongs to me and only me!" Lord Laislac said. He puffed out his chest and attempted to look down his nose.

"At the moment, milord, you, your lady, and your daughter are all ghosts trapped within these walls. I have inherited the responsibility for this place and the ghosts it holds. Therefore, you belong to me at the moment, and I said, 'Shut up!' "

Stunned silence followed her words. One by one the Rover brawls stilled. The combatants dusted themselves off and offered a hand up to the people they had been fighting only moments before. Only the pregnant girl continued to tussle for possession of a coin-laden scarf.

"That goes for you, too." Vareena shoved herself between the two women. The energy barrier that separated her from the ghosts forced the last combatants apart. The scarf tore and both women moved to attack Vareena. They bounced off her into the arms of their families, waiting to receive them.

"Now, Robb, see that Rejiia is locked in one of the towers," Vareena ordered. "Please."

"One of the lesser towers, I think." Robb grinned back at her, still anchoring Rejiia with magic from his staff.

"Jack, you and Marcus go to his room and do whatever it is you have to do. Zolltarn, see that your people find places to settle. Lord Laislac, I suggest you do the same for your party. And as for you, Ackerly, you'd better stay in the library where you belong."

Surprisingly, everyone obeyed her.

Satisfaction nestled comfortably on her shoulders.

"You can't have the big room," the pregnant girl said imperiously to Zolltarn. "I carry the heir to all of Coronnan. Therefore I am entitled to the biggest room with the private facilities."

Zolltarn snarled at her. The expression carried almost as much weight as his smile.

The girl backed away from him, but she did not bow her head or lower her eyes.

"You, Lady whoever you are, can have the scriptorium above the south wing all to yourself. I'll stand guard at the foot of the stairs if necessary to keep you there and out of mischief." Vareena glared at her.

"That will not be necessary, miss," the other lord said. "The six of us will settle into that same scriptorium. My daughter-in-law will not disturb you." He bowed slightly and offered his arm to his lady. They retreated in silent dignity.

Lord Laislac and his lady followed suit. The moonfaced young man with a little drool at the corner of his mouth copied the men in offering his arm to the pregnant girl. She batted it away and huffed in the wake of her elders. The simple boy shrugged and flashed a smile to one and all.

"Good luck," Vareena called to him, utterly charmed. "I wish I could do something for him," she said to herself.

"Perhaps we can do something for him," Jack said. "But that is a plan I cannot implement without some serious consultation with the Commune. Marcus is ready. Do you want to see him off?"

"I . . . uh . . ." What did she want? Marcus had earned her respect as a clear thinker and leader in this adventure, but he wasn't Robb. "I think I'll remain out here and keep order. My eldest brother has just arrived at the gate looking very puzzled. I'd best inform him of this newest crisis and arrange for food for all of these people. You and I may have to go hunting later."

She picked up her skirts and rushed to the gate to confer with Uustass. She hoped he had some better ideas for provisioning two dozen Rovers, two lords and their retinues, an exiled queen, and a host of magicians.

"Hurry back, Marcus. We need whatever answers you can find quickly."

She'd never wanted to leave this place more. Freedom beckoned to her just beyond the room where Jack and Marcus had firmly closed the door against intruders. She fingered the silver-and-amethyst amulet. Boldly, she pulled it from beneath her shift. She needed to see it in the sunlight as a symbol of the future freedom she only dared dream of.

*   *   *

These invaders with their iron and their greed do not frighten me. But the wounds I suffer from their iron will plague me forever. For that they must pay.

They have betrayed me, as Nimbulan did. As my son and daughter did when they rejected me as their father, preferring Nimbulan to raise them.

They will all die before another night passes, or they will wish themselves dead. In this place, such wishes come true.

Chapter 37

Marcus stuffed his few possessions into his pack. Excitement fluttered in his belly, making his movements jerky and imprecise.

"Be sure to check on Old Lyman," Margit said, throwing open the door to his room with a bang.

Marcus jumped a little at her abrupt entrance. Then he settled into his packing once more.

"He was ailing when I left. Sleeping more than waking and acting a little confused when he did bother to open his eyes."

"Lyman is older than dirt and always acts confused. Untangling his cryptic statements is one of the best learning tools at the University," Marcus countered.

"Ask about Jaylor's newborn twins as well," Jack added right on Margit's heels. He caressed his ever-present fly-wacket, murmuring to it. "Gossip among the Masters said that one of the twins was too small and weak to survive long. Such a loss will devastate Jaylor and Brevelan. We need them both hale and thinking clearly as long as the Gnuls have power in Coronnan."

"Yeah, I noticed Jaylor was acting distracted, always wanting to be back at the clearing rather than in the University," Margit confirmed. "But there wasn't the triumphant shout announcing the births either."

"I'll check on both of them—not that I can be of any help. Now can we get on with this? Is there anything special I should know or do to survive the transport spell?"

"Marcus, good, I caught you before you left," Robb burst

into the little room, Vareena right behind him. It was getting crowded in here.

Presumably Katrina was helping Queen Miranda settle in with her daughter and Rover escort. Otherwise, she'd be pressed as close to Jack as Vareena was to Robb.

"I'll be back as soon as I can, Robb." Marcus indulged in one last back-slapping hug with his friend and partner. "Thanks for showing me how to take responsibility and not trust in my luck so much."

"I think today is my lucky day," Robb looked into Vareena's eyes for one long adoring moment before turning back to Marcus. "Check out Nimbulan's diaries for any reference to Ackerly. There has to be a clue there as to how we can separate him from the gold."

"Look in the library for early references to exorcism of ghosts and blood magic," Jack added. He began his deep breathing in preparation for a trance. "Just think about the courtyard of the University. There's a big everblue tree with a bank of calubra ferns at the base on the north end."

"I know the place." Marcus breathed deeply on his own, fixing the memory of the University firmly in his mind as he'd seen it only a moon or so ago. "I always pictured Margit nestled in among the lower branches for a shady study place."

"How did you know?" Margit asked.

The sense-robbing blackness of the void closed around him before he could answer.

Before he could register the mind-numbing cold and the tangle of colored umbilicals that entwined with his own life force, a sharp jolt through his feet brought him into the exact spot he had visualized.

"Merawk!" Amaranth protested in the branch above with a flutter of wings and scraping of talons on bark. Then the creature flapped his wings and flew up the cliff face behind the library toward Shayla's lair. He had his own errands to run.

Marcus took a deep breath that smelled of home.

"Marcus, you are the last person I expected to invade our meditation session," Master Slippy exclaimed. The lanky magician gestured to the silent students sitting cross-legged all around the compound. The leaves on the trees around them had faded and begun to change color and the sun angled quite low.

"How—how long have I been gone?" He had meticulously counted the days in the monastery—difficult because of the perpetual twilight the gloaming had imposed upon him. High Summer should still brighten the courtyard.

"Many moons. Since early last spring." Slippy looked puzzled.

"The ghost was right. Time does move differently in his domain."

"Time cannot be distorted, boy," Slippy reprimanded him. "I thought I taught you better than that."

"Maybe time isn't distorted, but our perceptions are. I need to report to Jaylor, right away."

"Not today, young man. Our Senior Magician is sorely troubled at home. I could have told him that families interfere with magic. But he wouldn't listen. No one listens to me anymore."

Marcus noted the increased amount of white hair in Slippy's faded strawberry-blond queue. The hairline on his forehead had receded another finger-length since Marcus had last seen him as well.

"This will not wait, Master Slippy." Marcus kept his voice down in deference to the apprentices hard at work within their own minds. "There is great trouble brewing in Laislac near one of the minor passes."

"Another invasion? I thought SeLenicca broken and beyond organizing anything."

"That is probably true since their queen has taken herself into exile at an abandoned monastery. No, the trouble involves the coven, and the Rovers, and a ghost, and . . . it's too complex to relate all at once."

"Then come into the library. These pesky students can survive without supervision for a while. In the absence of Jaylor and Lyman—he's truly ill—I guess I am the most senior of the masters and the one you should report to."

"Is . . . is Master Lyman truly so ill?" Marcus had difficulty imagining the University without the elderly librarian. But then everyone grew old and died eventually, even Old Baamin, Jaylor's predecessor as Senior Magician.

Everyone died eventually and passed on to the next existence. So why hadn't Ackerly passed on? What chained him other than his lust for gold?

A sense of urgency drove him to ask one last question before diving into his research.

"Master Slippy, have you heard any rumors from the capital about the priests or Gnuls breaking the sanctuary of that abandoned monastery?"

Slippy stopped his slow steps toward the library abruptly. "How did you know that Hanic's successor is mounting an armed force to guard a party of engineers that are supposed to tear the place apart stone by stone and kill anything that lives within?"

Marcus had to stop and breathe deeply.

"What ails you, boy? You are as pale as a ghost." Slippy clutched his arm.

"An apt description," Marcus mumbled. He welcomed the extra support while he fought for balance. "When are the engineers leaving the capital?"

"Two days ago, riding with all haste, guided by a local. A young man petitioned to destroy the place, the village too, if they encounter resistance."

*   *   *

Lanciar woke abruptly. He opened his eyes to dim stone walls and a fierce stabbing pain pounding in his temple. The ache in his lower back competed with the burning sensation on his wrists and ankles for dominance.

"Am I alive?" His words came out in a dry whisper. He grimaced at the increase in the knife stabs behind his eyes.

"You'd probably hurt less if you had drunk a whole barrel of ale," Jack said. His tone offered no sympathy and certainly no mercy. "From what Maija tells me, that is not usual for you."

Lanciar tried to lift his hand to rub his eyes, his temples, his aching hair. The burning sensation on his wrists increased.

"You are restrained, by magic as well as mundane manacles," Jack informed him. Still no easing in his tone.

Lanciar risked lifting his head to look and wished he hadn't.

"Where's Maija?" he asked, knowing she'd soothe his hurts with cool towels, kind words, and ale.

"Waiting outside, wringing her hands and wailing to her father. Hard to believe that beautiful girl is my maternal aunt." This last piece of news came out in a confused mutter.

"Then you are the legendary child of the missing Kestra," Lanciar repeated the gossip he'd heard while traveling with the clan. Zolltarn's oldest daughter had been ordered to conceive a child with the most powerful magician in all of Coronnan. The resulting child should have prodigious magical talents to open the dragon magic barrier that had surrounded Coronnan at the time. But Kestra and her escort had disappeared before she could rejoin the clan. All of the Rover clans had searched for her and the child ever since.

"My father tells me that Kestra was my mother, and therefore Zolltarn is my grandfather," Jack added no details to satisfy Lanciar's curiosity.

"Then we will shortly be family, Jack. I intend to marry Maija and raise my son with the Rovers—honorable rogues that they are." A sense of satisfaction settled upon Lanciar. He wasn't certain he loved Maija, not like he had loved Rejiia. But his affection for the sprightly Rover girl would endure a lot longer. He'd work hard to be sure of that.

He'd even watch his language around Maija. And he'd drink a lot less ale. Maija wouldn't have to brew so much and would have more time for him . . . and dared he hope? . . . for their children.

"Your son?" Jack asked.

"Rejiia rejected him at birth. I won't allow her to kidnap him away from me again."

"I thought Simeon fathered her child and that it died at birth. Not unusual, considering Simeon was her uncle. The close blood tie could damage the child."

"Lies. Rejiia lies as naturally as she breathes. She wanted the child to be a secret. When she brought to fruit all her convoluted plans to conquer all of Kardia Hodos through magic, she'd produce the child as heir to the three kingdoms. But she didn't want the responsibility of raising him. She can't love anyone but herself."

"And possibly her father."

"Not much longer if the spell keeping him within the

statue isn't reversed soon. I think Krej is dying. Let me up, Jack. I'm no longer a threat to you."

"You've lied to me before. You were the coven's spy in King Simeon's mines where I was enslaved for three years. You betrayed me to Rejiia and Simeon. You gloated over me while she tortured me."

"I have renounced my membership in the coven. And I truly regret my misguided loyalty to Rejiia. She and Simeon coerced me into betraying the only truly honest man I have ever known." He caught Jack's gaze with his own, imploring him to understand.

Jack remained stone-faced and unforgiving.

"My son needs me, needs the family the Rovers have offered us. You, Jack, are a part of that family whether you want to be or not."

Jack blanched a moment. Then he firmed his jaw. "What makes you think you can be a father to the child? From what I hear, you look for too many answers in the bottom of your ale mug and never find them, so you have to refill the mug until you pass out."

Lanciar had no answer for that. Even now his mouth watered for the taste of Maija's ale. He knew he drank too much, had drunk too much ever since he'd discovered the depth of Rejiia's betrayal of him and the coven. "I need the clan as much as my son does. Their petty thefts and chicanery are minor irritations. I would like to reform them, but doubt anyone could. Throw a truth spell on me if you must to determine my intentions."

"You know as well as I do that if you lie while under a truth spell, you will die—quite horribly." Jack breathed deeply. For the first time since this terrible interview had begun, his eyes relaxed.

"Yes, I know that. I also know that you awakened my magical talent, so you have delved into the depths of my soul. You can ferret out my secrets easier than I can. Throw the spell and know that I have renounced the coven once and for all."

"I wish I could take your word for it. But I've dealt with the coven too many times. I know from experience how they gain power from pain, their own or what they can inflict upon others." Jack flinched as he spoke.

Lanciar understood how deep his scars must run.

"I speak the truth, I have no need to fear your spell, Jack."

"Just be glad Katrina is not here to take fright and thus weaken my resolve." With a simple gesture blue sparkles shot from Jack's fingers.

Lanciar just had time for a single breath before numbing cold settled over his entire body. A veil of blue haze covered everything—not unlike the few moments when he'd held the gold in his hands. And then all of his aches and pains disappeared, replaced by that terrible cold. His mind drifted free of his body and he looked down upon himself and Jack from somewhere near the narrow window at the top of the room.

His perceptions expanded. He wanted to drift into the haze, free of hurt, free of tangled emotions, free of . . .

Off in the distance he sensed things that he thought he'd left behind in SeLenicca: Many steeds pounding the kardia as they raced forward, men cursing and sweating as they drew weapons, fear, excitement, determination. All the things that accompanied men as they rode to battle. They rode here to the monastery. When would they arrive? Where did they come from?

"To whom do you owe allegiance, Lanciar, soldier of SeLenicca, member of the coven?" Jack asked.

Lanciar's attention returned to the little room in the monastery. He had to answer every question correctly and end this interview quickly. He had to make preparations to protect the ones he loved. "I owe allegiance to my son, to myself, and to Maija, daughter of Zolltarn, chieftain of his clan of Rovers." His voice came from a great distance. And then he realized that his body had spoken what was in his heart.

"And what will you do when the coven commands you?"

"I will fight them with every tool at my command. I will fight anyone who seeks to harm Maija and my son," he answered rather fiercely. How long did he have to prepare for the coming attack?

"Why have you turned upon the coven?"

"Because they threaten my son." But the coven did not employ armies. Who commanded the troops coming here?

"Do you still love Rejiia?"

"No." The answer came more readily than he expected. He'd loved Rejiia passionately, devotedly. He'd schemed with her to cheat Simeon of the son he craved. He'd lied and stolen for the coven. He had betrayed Jack, possibly the only true friend he'd ever had. But no more. His son and Maija claimed him now. And the rest of the Rovers, and the motley band trapped here.

"And if Rejiia kidnaps her son from you?"

"I will follow her to the ends of the Kardia Hodos and do all I can to protect my boy from her manipulations."

"How will you revive Lord Krej?"

"I won't unless asked to by you and Zolltarn, backed by whomever you take orders from."

Suddenly Lanciar was sucked back into his body. Before he could register what was happening, he blinked and the blue haze disappeared. His extremities took longer to warm up, but the burning pain around his wrists and ankles ceased.

Jack looked depleted, almost as badly as he had on that lonely mountain pass where the two of them had traveled the stars and awakened Lanciar's latent talent. Jack ran a shaking hand across his eyes and then dropped onto the stool in the corner of the room.

"There's an army on its way here," Lanciar blurted out.

"How far?"

"I don't know. But I sensed them during the spell. They ride hard, have ridden hard for a time."

"We'd best make plans."

"I'm best qualified to do that."

Jack nodded. "We still have to settle the matter of the gold. We have to have a plan before we go into battle.

Lanciar nodded. His mind quickly reviewed the layout of the monastery and their limited weapons.

"Marcus and Robb found it. They should determine who deserves it, if anyone. But only after they remove the curse. If they are able to do so."

"I'd like it to go to Queen Miranda. SeLenicca does not deserve what we did to it." And if the approaching army came from SeLenicca the gold might appease their anger. They needed Miranda's cooperation. "The people of SeLenicca are arrogant, determined to remain superior and separate from the rest of the world. But most of them are innocent of the evil the coven brought there. We need to help them rebuild."

"Somehow, I didn't expect that from you, Lanciar," Jack said after a long moment of silence. "I have to admit I half-hoped you'd try to lie and I could watch you die. For both our sakes, I'm glad you told the truth. Now I know why Katrina is so frightened of me. I scare myself sometimes. You can get up whenever you feel strong enough."

Lanciar wiggled his toes and rotated his hands. A bit of chafing remained. "Where'd you get the manacles, Jack?"

"Left over from my days as King Darville's bodyguard."

"We might need them on Rejiia." She could complicate the battle plan taking shape in his head.

"I doubt they'd hold long. She has one formidable talent."

"What are we going to do with her? Now that she knows the transport spell, she can't be kept out of Coronnan."

"I have some ideas. But they are dangerous. Thanks to her, we all have a very big problem."

"On top of many other problems. Perhaps the combined might of the Rovers will hold her until Marcus returns with some answers—if he gets back in time. Your Rover blood will allow you to join with them. Maija assures me that once she and I are married, I will be able to join her clan in their mind-to-mind link."

"I've resisted that link," Jack replied, staring blankly at the floor. "I worked too hard to find out who I was and what was important to me to risk losing myself in the clan. I'll work with Andrall and Laislac as we plan a defense. You can work with Zolltarn."

"I look forward to losing myself in the clan rather than in the bottom of a mug of ale. I'll need a clear head to get through the next battle."

Chapter 38

"**W**here are you going Lord Andrall?" Ariiell asked in panic.

How could she have been so stupid as to reveal her connections to the coven? Something about the sight of all that gold in the hands of filthy Rovers. Something compelling. The gold was enchanted. That was the answer. She had to possess it, learn its secrets. Then she could use it to buy influence, bribe and coerce the rest of the coven to give her the center position of power.

For now, she sat huddled before a small fire burning in the hearth against the outside wall of the scriptorium of this ancient and chill monastery. She didn't believe for a moment that some enchantment trapped her here. She could overcome any curse laid upon her. Her magic was strong and growing stronger because the baby anchored her more firmly to Kardia.

She shivered despite the heat thrown out by the fire she augmented with magic. These old stone walls held the chill of the ages, a chill that burned all the way to her soul. She had to get out of here, quickly, before the ancient cold hurt the baby.

But everyone—her parents, Mardall, his parents, and all of their retainers—watched her with suspicion and fear.

"I am going to consult with the resident magicians. King Darville must be informed of these latest developments," Andrall stated coldly. "He may have exiled me because of your behavior, Ariiell, but I still support him as my king, my wife's nephew, and . . . and my friend." He rose from his camp stool and walked resolutely to the door.

"You intend to rob me and my child of our rightful place in the succession," she accused bitterly.

"If necessary." He stalked out of the large room without bothering to bow to anyone.

"You owe me respect. I carry the heir to the throne. I carry your grandchild!" Rage propelled her off her own uncomfortable camp stool—all their luggage could provide. She kicked the offensive piece of furniture into the fire. This Simurgh-cursed place did not have so much as a chair to ease the pain in her back.

"My husband owes you nothing, slut," Lady Lynnetta sneered. "You seduced my boy. You brought this exile upon us. And now you profess loyalty to the coven. You will never hold power within Coronnan. I hope the Star-gods punish you appropriately."

Lady Lynnetta's reputation for sweetness might have won her the respect of the court, but Ariiell suspected no one had ever heard her speak with so much malice.

The idiot continued to smile and laugh and drool, taking pleasure from helping the servants unpack.

Ariiell marched to the door in Andrall's wake. She refused to remain in this room any longer.

She'd keep Andrall from contacting King Darville. She had the magic at her fingertips. And when all was in place, she would release Rejiia from her prison in the small tower across the compound. Rejiia would be so grateful she'd give up her position in the center of the coven rituals.

"Are you forgetting, Lord Andrall, that magic and magicians are still illegal in Coronnan? If you deliberately use magic to contact our king, you violate numerous laws and put King Darville in jeopardy of losing his crown," she whispered to him in a malicious hiss at the foot of the tower stairs. She knew her words would carry up the stairwell to any of the avid listeners in their party.

"By your own admission of ties to the coven, you make yourself and your child illegal as well." Lord Andrall looked down his long patrician nose at her.

"Have you ever seen me throw a spell, Lord Andrall? Do you have any evidence that I *belong* to the coven? Perhaps I merely used their name to invoke fear and obedience in a woman of an inferior race," Ariiell replied sweetly.

She hated following on his heels, pressing her arguments. He should stand respectfully still and hear her out.

"The chaos your accusations cause cannot help anyone but the Gnostic Utilitarian cult. And they will hunt you down and torture you without mercy. You and any other followers of the coven they find." Andrall turned his back on her again and proceeded into the courtyard.

Ariiell refused to admit defeat. She stamped her foot angrily and followed closely.

The magician named Robb and the older woman who seemed to be in charge stood by the wall conversing. Their rapidly waving hands and slightly hunched posture broadcast their anxiety.

A veil of mist made them look like ghosts. Who was alive and who dead in this place? Another reason to leave as soon as possible.

Ariiell studied them closely as she and Andrall came closer to them. She'd be able to think more clearly if this *s'murghin'* mist didn't cover everything.

How could she use their upset to her own advantage? Robb was certainly ripe for loss of concentration if he tried a summons. And just who would receive the summons? Who in the king's court had enough magic to be in constant communication with the Commune of Magicians?

She intended to eavesdrop and find out. The Gnuls would pay handsomely for that information. The coven would also receive the news with delight. She must escape this horrible place—alone—before Andrall's overblown sense of morality revealed her untimely admission. News of a magician in close contact with the king would set the Council of Provinces to depose Darville and put her child on the throne. Possibly before the birth!

Lord Andrall stopped short, staring at the older woman beside Robb. She was handsome in an aging sort of way, but not worth this mouth-agape stare. Ariiell alone in this hodgepodge of captives should have invited such open admiration.

Ariiell stamped her foot in frustration. Lord Andrall continued to utter incomprehensible choking sounds rather than come to the point of his mission. Ariiell needed Lord

Andrall and Robb to discuss a summons to Darville so she could learn the name of the king's magical confidant.

"Wh . . . where . . . who . . . that amulet . . ." At last Andrall pointed to the rather clumsy and ugly jumble of silver and amethyst hanging around the woman's neck.

"This is mine." Vareena immediately clasped the jewelry defensively.

Robb put an arm around her shoulders in a touching display of affection. Disgusting!

"Then . . . then that amulet can only be yours because you stole it," Andrall spluttered. "What have you done to my brother? He would not have parted with that symbol of inheritance while he lived!" He reached to tear the amulet from her neck.

Magical power tingled through Ariiell. *Yes!* This is what the coven had tried in vain to teach her. She could feed off strong emotions, drain people of power by absorbing all of their energy. She longed to let a spell, any spell, fly from her fingertips before it dissipated. But what? What could she do that would not get her into more trouble?

She wiggled her fingers and the knot in the leather thong that held Vareena's amulet loosened. The thing dropped into Andrall's outstretched hand.

"Farrell gave that to me on his deathbed. I nursed him for two years while he resided here in this monastery. With the amulet comes a bequest of acres in the Province of Nunio," Vareena replied proudly. Her spine looked like it was lashed to a broom handle or her magician lover's staff.

"Farrell? So that's the name he gave you," Andrall mused, tracing the silverwork on the amulet lovingly with his fingertip. "Farrell. He always wanted to be a hero. But poor Iiann never had the courage to do anything but run away." The lord closed his eyes and grimaced as if in great pain.

Ariiell had heard that he had suffered from a weak heart recently, that he'd kept to his home more frequently because of it. What would happen to her plans if she encouraged his heart to fail?

Without his accusations, she had a better chance of gaining the crown for her child. Without his testimony, no one else would have the courage to remember her untimely confession to membership in the coven.

"She murdered your brother for the land," Ariiell whispered into his ear. She used the last of the magic from his anger to fuel her words with compulsion. He had to believe her. He had to condemn this spinster on the spot. And then she'd feed off his pain and give him more.

"Your bother died of the effects of age and loneliness and grief that he could not return home one last time." Vareena reached a placating hand toward Andrall and the amulet.

"Where is he buried? I'd like to pay my respects."

"No!" Ariiel bit her tongue to keep from saying more out loud. She raised her hand to push some of her own outrage into Andrall, to keep his anger at a fever pitch.

Red trails of magic compulsion dribbled from her fingers, dissipating uselessly in the dust.

Robb finger-combed his beard. Laughter sparkled in his eyes.

"How dare you laugh at me!" she hissed at him.

He merely raised his eyebrows and pointed to his chest in mock surprise.

Ariiel suppressed a snarl.

"Over there," Vareena pointed to the far corner of the herb garden, ignoring Ariiel. *How dare she!* "He's with the other ghosts who have perished in this cursed place. The foundations of the old temple seemed appropriate for their last resting place."

"Don't believe her!" Ariiell had no more magic to push Andrall into drastic action. If only the coven had taught her to tap a ley line. But her fellows did not believe the ley lines worth bothering with. They relied on rituals filled with music, dance, nudity, and sexual perversion to enhance their powers. Ariiell had no power to tap unless she could push these strangely placid people into violent emotions again.

"My lord," Robb interrupted, "I was with your brother in his last moments. He died peacefully, anxious for his next existence. Will you honor his bequest to Vareena?"

"Of course."

"No, you can't! You have to condemn her for murder right here and now!"

"Oh, shut up, Ariiell. Go back to the room and behave like the lady you want to be." Andrall dismissed her with a bored wave of his hand.

The trio ignored her as they approached the graves in the corner by the wall.

"You can't do this to me," she murmured quietly. "I still have the book of poisons. I can still take control." A nice little demon let loose within these walls ought to liven things up. Rejiia would know how to conjure one.

* * *

"Stay with me, Zebbiah," Miranda called anxiously to her friend. His face faded into mist and then reformed in this reality followed by his body. Twice now, he'd drifted off into the strange haze with the rest of his clan. Both times she'd been able to call him back. But this time he seemed to have difficulty getting all of him to step free of the engulfing mist.

Her lace pillow lay forgotten beside her. She dared not lose herself in the lace she loved. The entire purpose of their long journey had been for her to sit and make their fortune with her work. Zebbiah's anchor to this reality was still too tenuous for her to concentrate on anything but him and her daughter.

She rocked Jaranda gently in front of the little fire Zebbiah had built in one of the large second-story rooms. Possibly this had been a smaller scriptorium, possibly a classroom. It covered nearly half of one wing with an identical room adjoining it.

The pack beast brayed obnoxiously and Zebbiah freed himself from the gloaming. He'd had a time coaxing the pack beast up the circular stairs, but he refused to be separated from it or the packs loaded on its back.

"I never thought I wanted to sever my link to my clan before," Zebbiah said, dropping his head into his hands. "Their blood calls to my blood. It is a comfort and an asset most of the time."

"Except when danger to them threatens you as well." Miranda reached out and touched his hand.

His expression brightened and the last little bit of mist around him seemed to evaporate.

"In times of danger, the mind-to-mind link and access to magic helps the entire clan. Each of us has all the others to draw upon for help, for strength, for courage. This time, they draw upon me as an anchor to life outside this fog. They drain me."

"This . . . this link, does it allow all of you to participate in the . . . the activities of one of your numbers?" Katrina asked. She'd been pacing the room while she examined the lace and the pillows that Miranda had liberated from the palace. Her fingers constantly tangled the lengths of edgings and she nearly shredded one particularly fine cap while moving about the room. Curiously, she kept to the edges, looking out of the row of windows at every pass.

"Sometimes. Why do you ask?" Zebbiah watched her carefully, as if he saw something more than a normal eye could discern. The strange mist started to gather around him again.

Miranda grabbed his hand, and the mist went away. For a time. Fatigue clutched her heart. How long could she keep him here before he fully joined the others? She wished she could see them as easily as the magicians seemed to. If even a dim outline appeared to her, she'd feel more comfortable with their looming presence. As it was, she constantly looked to see if an unseen eavesdropper hovered nearby.

Her back itched as if a thousand eyes watched her every breath, waiting, ready to attack her.

"Was Neeles Brunix, the owner of a lace factory in Queen's City, one your clan?" Katrina ceased her pacing for a moment at the cost of the linen lace doily that unraveled beneath her anxious fingers.

"Brunix, *bah!*" Zebbiah spat the name. "His mother was of our clan. Technically that makes him one of ours. But his father's people raised him to despise us. He took what he wanted of our rituals and customs and perverted them to suit his needs. We never admitted him to our special link."

"Yet you did business with him." Katrina held up the remnants of the doily.

"Rovers trade where the trade is best. Brunix provided

us with the best lace. Brunix gave us many unique designs. The palace lacemakers had not enough imagination to try new things." He grinned at Miranda in a sort of apology.

"I designed this piece and several others in your pack. He stole the patterns from me during the three years he owned me. My lace." Katrina nearly shook with the emotions that racked her.

Miranda sympathized with her. Designing and working a pattern required a great deal of diligence, dedication, and devotion to the art. To have it stolen represented almost a sacrilege to a true lacemaker.

Except that the women who designed lace for the palace workers had been locked into specific forms and techniques, never taking a chance on something new and different.

Miranda wanted nothing more than to let the world pass her by while she made lace now. She wouldn't even mind the invisible watching eyes as long as she had the bobbins in her hands and the rhythm of the pattern in her body and mind.

"Whatever happened to you, the clan did not participate in, or sanction the actions of Brunix," Zebbiah comforted Katrina. "Too often have our people been enslaved over the centuries by those who do not understand our ways, who fear anything they do not understand. We deny anyone the right to own another. All should be free to rove as they choose. As we choose."

"But your people steal. You hide behind half truths and you take children from their rightful parents!" Katrina resumed her pacing. Her words sounded more a recitation of oft told tales than an accusation.

"When people refuse to sell us things we need to survive, we often take those things, but we leave something of value behind in payment—just not always what the original owner thinks has value. Half a truth is better than a lie. Parents often give us unwanted children—those who are deformed or simple or sometimes just one too many mouths to feed. The only children we steal are those who are beaten and treated as less than dirt by their parents." Zebbiah answered each of her accusations in turn with resignation.

Katrina nodded. "Jack says much the same thing." She resumed her pacing. This time she alternately touched the walls and ran her fingers through her already disheveled hair.

"I never thought about slavery before," Miranda mused. She brushed damp hair off Jaranda's brow. She seemed cooler, sleeping easier than before. Perhaps the fever had broken. "I never thought about my people before. All I cared about was my lace. I was happy to allow Simeon to take the burden of rule from my shoulders. I was happy not to have to think about the hardship of others. I can't let that happen again. Slavery in SeLenicca must end."

A hole opened in her heart. If she took over the responsibilities of the crown—responsibilities she had inherited but never been allowed to exercise by her parents or husband—then she'd never have the time to work the lace as she had before. She'd never have the concentration to design new patterns or lovingly recreate old ones.

But then, SeLenicca must never again become dependent upon lace, only one export, to support the entire economy. Her people must be trained to other tasks. The land must be nurtured rather than exploited. Her people must become self-sufficient, as the Rovers were self-sufficient. Only she could change the entire culture of SeLenicca. She had to go back.

Jaranda whimpered in her sleep. She thrashed in her mother's arms. Her movements mimicked the rhythm of Katrina's pacing.

"Katrina, what ails you?" Zebbiah asked before Miranda could.

"This place." Katrina hugged herself. "The cold follows me. My arms are all lumbird bumps. If I were trapped here, as your clan and nobles are, then I do not think I would want to live."

"Come sit by the fire. Let it warm you," Miranda urged, trying to ignore the chill that climbed her spine and set the hairs on her neck standing straight up. " 'Tis your fatigue talking, nothing more."

The invisible eyes seemed to increase and move closer, sensing her unease, ready to pounce at the first sign of weakness.

"No!" Katrina protested too violently for the nature of the suggestion. Then she breathed deeply, forcing calm. "Fire. The ghost of Ackerly fears fire." Slowly she walked closer to the cheery blaze, as if she forced one foot in front of the other.

"No, P'pa, no," Jaranda whispered in her sleep. "Don't kill me, P'pa. I'm too little to sacrifice."

"Wake up, Jaranda." Miranda shook her baby. Memories of Simeon and the tortures he delighted in crowded around her vision, forcing out the present. "Wake up, baby. It's only a dream. Wake up."

"M'ma, don't let P'pa take me to the fires."

"We must leave this place, *cherbein* Miranda." Zebbiah stood up, grabbing the packs in one graceful movement. "The ghost will poison all of us if we do not leave. Now."

Jaranda's eyes opened and she stared over her mother's shoulders. "Go away, P'pa. Go away. You are dead," she sobbed.

"Don't leave me alone here!" Katrina protested. Her eyes darted frantically all around. "Do not leave me with Simeon's ghost. If he haunts this place, then Brunix will, too."

"I would say let us all leave immediately, but we have nowhere else to go," Miranda reminded them.

Chapter 39

"**F**ound it!" Marcus whispered excitedly. He looked around the library for someone to share the good news with. The place was deserted. All the apprentices seemed to prefer taking their books outdoors to study. Had Margit started that tradition? He had had more than enough of the out of doors to last a lifetime.

At least now he knew how to lay the ghost to rest. He even had an idea of how to remove the curse from the gold. But he needed help.

This information should go to Jaylor first. Marcus gathered the texts he had studied repeatedly for days. Too many days. How long before the army reached the monastery?

Moments later he knocked upon the door to Jaylor's office. The wooden panels echoed emptily within. He rapped again, a little louder and longer.

Jaylor always spent the midafternoon in his office while the children napped and he could guarantee at least a little time without familial interference. Puzzled, Marcus sent an inquisitive probe into the room. It circled aimlessly, encountering only empty air and dust.

"You won't find our Senior Magician anywhere near the University, Marcus," Slippy said coming toward him from the direction of the courtyard. "One of the twins is dying. He's with his family."

"Where he belongs," Marcus replied. "But I need to talk to him. Now. It's important."

"I doubt he wants anyone near except his wife and his sons." Slippy shook his head. "I sent a message to our representative in the king's court to inform His Grace. Jaylor and Brevelan may want to share their grief with their oldest friends, but no one else."

"I wondered why everyone was so quiet today." Actually he hadn't noticed the lack of activity or the conversations in unusually hushed tones until now. His concentration had all been on his research. He looked at his books, weighing them in his hands. Now what? He had to get back to the monastery soon. He'd wasted too much time already.

"May I be of assistance?" Slippy looked pointedly at the books Marcus carried.

"Do you know anything about time travel?" Marcus asked.

"Never! Impossible." Slippy sniffed with disdain.

"I didn't think I'd be lucky enough to find the help I need right off." Marcus excused himself and went in search of Old Lyman. If anyone had ever traveled through time and lived, Lyman was the most likely candidate.

Marcus hadn't seen the ancient librarian in any of his usual haunts about the library. He turned his steps toward the master's quarters on the opposite wing of the sprawling University. But that didn't feel right. Lyman loved his library and his books. Even if he were dying, he'd want to be there, not in some sterile bedroom.

Marcus found him in a deep recess at the back of the second gallery, near an open window that looked at the cliff face, between his books and the dragons. The best place for the old man.

Lyman turned rheumy eyes on Marcus as he tiptoed closer. "Who?" His question came out of tired lungs almost like a whistle, or the call of a baby dragon.

"It's Marcus, sir. I have a question that only you can answer." He knelt beside the old man's pallet.

"Marcus? You can't be here. You are lost between here and there, now and then."

"I found my way back home, sir."

"That is hard to do, boy."

"Easy enough once you have the scent in your mind. In spirit I've never left." In that moment he knew that the one hearth to light his days and cook his meals and the one bed at the end of the day that he craved was here, at the University. But the one smiling face to greet him at the door, cook his meals, warm his bed? He'd loved Margit. He'd loved Vareena. Did either woman belong to his heart and his life forever?

The image of a smiling woman with a cloud of blond curls and a twinkle of mischief in her eyes while she dealt cartes came to mind.

Expelling a huge, pent-up breath, he shed a lot of the weight of indecision.

Lyman closed his eyes and turned his face toward the window. "My time is nearly come, boy. I must leave this body behind very soon. Ask your question and let me get on with this."

"Master Librarian, I need to lay a ghost to rest and remove the curse he placed upon a hoard of gold."

"Ghosts are easy to get rid of. Curses are not."

"How do I trick Ackerly into telling me how he laid the curse so that I may reverse it?"

"Ackerly, eh? Always knew that man would not give up his gold even in death. He'll not tell you, boy. He invented the tricks you plan to turn on him. The gold must remain cursed even after you lay him to rest."

"Won't the curse dissipate once his presence no longer nourishes it?"

"If the curse has lasted three hundred years beyond his death then it will not fade in time to save those now cursed by the cursed gold."

"Then how do I . . . ?"

"You must go back in time and watch him throw the spell. Ackerly was tricky. He probably used a mixture of solitary, blood, and dragon magic. You'll have to use an exact reversal of his ritual. One slip and you fail. One slip and you and the gold become one."

"Trapped in the gloaming forever," Marcus finished for him. "How do I travel back in time?"

"Jack will have to guide you. He's done it before. I'm too tired." Yet he heaved himself to his knees.

Marcus offered him an arm for support. Surprisingly the old man leaned heavily upon him. Lyman had always asserted his ability to get around in fierce defiance of his age.

"Brevelan's child is nearly ready to give up the fight. I must be there when she does. Take me to the Clearing, boy."

"Shouldn't you rest, sir? Here, where you are at home, between your books and the dragons?"

"Ah, to be a dragon again," Lyman sighed. For a moment his face took on a vacant expression as he looked far into his past. "I had hoped to tell my story to Jack. He's the one who deserves to know this, but there isn't time. Be sure to repeat this to him word for word."

"Save your words, Master Lyman. You are too weak to walk and talk." Marcus didn't know how to handle the stubborn old man. Surely, if he were indeed dying, he'd want to conserve his strength and remain in this existence as long as possible.

Unless he looked forward to his next existence.

"Let me call for some help. We'll carry you, Master."

"Nonsense. I'll not have my story repeated among the apprentices like some ancient legend that grows with each telling. This is for you and for Jack. Jack earned the right to hear the truth. You, my boy, are merely the messenger." Lyman fixed him with a fierce gaze. For an instant, his watery old eyes blazed forth in silver-and-purple lights, whirling in a hypnotic stare.

The world faded from Marcus' perceptions. All that existed was the elderly librarian's voice.

"Listen and learn, young Marcus. Learn that many aeons ago, before weak and insignificant humans learned to harness the power of dragons, or cared to, when the Stargods were but pups dreaming of their first outrageous adventures, I was born Iianthe, twin purple-tipped dragon to Hanassa."

"But only one purple-tip can live at any one time," Marcus heard himself protest the old man's litany. Somehow, in the process of speaking, they had descended three staircases to the ground level.

" 'Twas the destiny of my twin Hanassa to choose another life form or to die. In choosing, he must find a new life path that would benefit all of Kardia Hodos. He chose to become human. But he was weak and envied the power of the Stargods. He wanted to control all that he touched.

And so he sought to mimic the gods and awakened many dark powers. Plagues followed in his wake and eventually the humans, with the power of the Stargods to back them, exiled my twin to the land we now know as Hanassa. There he ruled for many generations, choosing to inhabit the body of one of his descendants as each body wore out."

"Hanassa, the home of outlaws and rebels and rogue magicians." Marcus nearly whistled on his exhalation. "How did he take new bodies?"

Lyman waved away the question. "Hanassa became the home of the outcasts and misfits of society. That city of outlaws was, and is, a bloodthirsty place and saw many terrible tortures before Hanassa finally died. But seven hundred years passed before he gave up his last body. That is a tale you will find in the journals of a magician named Powwell. It is hidden in my room, beneath a loose board in the flooring. Only Jack should read it, but you will have to take it to him. I know you will read it. You were always a curious one. If you or Jack chooses to share the tale, think long and hard about who can safely carry the knowledge." The old man's voice cracked with dryness and he ceased walking while his knees sagged. "Powwell was Ackerly's son. His journal may help you lay the ghost to rest."

They had made it as far as the path to the Clearing.

"Rest, Master. I'll take the journal to Jack."

"No time to rest. Jaylor's daughter is eager for her next existence. She is tired of fighting to retain possession of her body." Lyman took a deep breath and continued his tale and his final journey.

"When Shayla birthed a new pair of purple-tipped dragons, my existence as Iianthe had to come to an end. I should have passed into the void and gone on without memory of my past. But Hanassa had not completed his destiny. I had to live out the life he had forsaken. So I chose the body of an old man and joined Nimbulan in his search for a way to control magic and make it ethical."

"But that was three hundred years ago!"

"Haven't you been listening, boy? I already said I had lived over seven hundred years as the purple-tipped dragon Iianthe. I have worn out dozens of aging bodies in the past three hundred years. Always, there was one more task to complete, one more life to save, one more apprentice to guide forward. Now this body is giving out and I still have work to do."

"Jaylor's daughter! You plan to take the baby's body the moment she gives it up." Inspiration dawned in Marcus at the moment Lyman's knees gave up the fight to walk all the way to the clearing.

"The little girl has not the determination to fight for her life. If she would hang on only a while longer, her body would heal. But she will not. So I must."

"Climb onto my back, Master. I'll carry you the rest of the way."

Marcus draped the old man's arms over his shoulders and hoisted his legs near his hips. Old Lyman weighed next to nothing.

"Be sure to tell the tale to Jack word for word, except for the last. No one else must know where I send my spirit next."

"I'll tell Jack to look for you in the most unlikely place, right under his nose."

"He'll think I've given Amaranth a little sense and grace." The old man wheezed heavily in something approximating a chuckle.

"Only a little way to go, Master." Marcus could see the eldritch shimmer of the protective barrier that surrounded the clearing. They'd not get through it without Jaylor's or Brevelan's permission. And they were undoubtedly distracted at the moment.

"Close enough. The spirit knows no boundaries imposed upon frail bodies. Remember Powwell's journal." Lyman grew limp, slipped down, and breathed his last in Marcus' arms.

Chapter 40

Jack awoke in a cold sweat. His heart beat in his chest. He lay on cold stone, without so much as a few rushes to ease his sleep. He dreamed of the time Rejiia had sent a magical probe through his eye in that noisome dungeon cell. Memory relived the shafts of pain. Only by massive willpower had he kept the probe from stripping his mind and leaving him a brainless hulk. But he had babbled endlessly about the transport spell. Thanks to him, Coronnan's greatest enemy could now travel anywhere she chose without restraint.

The ancient stone walls of his cell too closely resembled the prison beneath King Simeon's palace. Disoriented, he lay on his pallet for many long moments, desperately afraid he had not broken free of that dank and miserable death-trap.

Then sanity returned. He knew he rested in the old monastery near a small mountain pass between Coronnan and SeLenicca. He knew that Katrina rested just the other side of this wall in her own cell. They had survived Rejiia's tortures once. He'd not let the witch capture him again.

He sent out a probe automatically, seeking Rejiia's location. Surprisingly, she remained in the tower prison he and Robb had made for her yesterday. Why hadn't she used the transport spell to free herself from this prison?

Because one of Ackerly's coins remained on her person and the curse on the gold kept her here. She hadn't been able to remove her magical restraints either.

Why?

Because the gloaming—that frightful place that traversed

two realities while retaining part of the void that lay between them—limited the amount of magic that could leave
a magician. Jack, Robb, and Marcus had not fully entered
the haze at the time of the spell since they had none of the
cursed gold on them, so their magic might be stronger than
Rejiia's. She was still in her ghostly form.

He hoped. He feared she might use hidden talents to
overcome any of the obstacles in her way. She'd done it
before, popping up in odd places without warning at moments when she could inflict the most damage.

Resolutely, Jack threw off the bedroll and placed his feet
on the stone floor. The midnight chill banished the last fog
of his nightmare.

While he slept, the approaching army had days to travel
closer. If he hadn't sent Amaranth back to Shayla, he could
send the flywacket in search of them.

"Best check on Rejiia. Make sure those magical chains
still hold her." Though the chains that held Rejiia had been
woven by three separate magicians, none of them would be
as strong as he liked.

He ran a hand through his sweat-damp hair and heaved
himself upright. This old building never seemed to warm
up. He threw on his clothes and boots, pulling on extra
thick stockings to ward against the chill, and made his way
into the colonnade. A faint glow of green firelight flickered
beneath the doorways all along the outdoor passageway.
The others must feel the chill as badly as he did.

Out in the courtyard he could almost see the stars in
their slow dance across the universe. He drank in the crisp
night air, grateful that his nightmare had been merely a
memory dream and not reality. His planetary awareness
centered and he knew precisely where and when he was
despite a slight time distortion caused by the gloaming.

He opened his senses, seeking a similar awareness of Rejiia. His magic shied away from contact with her. Ever since
her mind probe had debilitated him, he'd fought coming in
contact with her again. Surely she must sense his presence
and draw power from his discomfort.

His mind touched hers. She dreamed restlessly, thrashing
within her bonds and the fears that plagued her. Jack shied
away from intruding on her privacy.

But this is Rejiia, he reminded himself. The safety of many people relied on knowing what she planned and what she feared.

From across the courtyard he slid into her thoughts. Seeking. Endless seeking. Her quarry always just beyond her reach. She ran. She stumbled and fell. The gray weasel with gold tipping the ends of its fur slipped easily through her hands. And behind her, danger loomed. Every time she failed to capture the weasel, the unnamed danger came closer. Her life depended upon capturing the weasel.

And then she woke on a cry, sweating as badly as Jack had.

He pulled back from her dreams before her waking thoughts sensed his presence.

And then the dreams of all the others descended upon him with equal clarity. Everyone in this cursed building dreamed their greatest fears. They saw their closest friends as deadly enemies. More than dreamed, relived their most vivid horrors. Almost like a dragon-dream.

Despair haunted them all. Many considered death a relief from their misery.

Anxiously he searched the skies for the presence of a dragon. Who among the nimbus would visit this kind of terror upon innocents?

None. He knew that.

Baamin! he called. *Baamin, what transpires here?*

He knew the answer before the blue-tipped dragon had a chance to reply. The ghost tried to drive them to kill each other or to suicide before Marcus returned with a spell to remove the curse from the gold.

"Jack!" Katrina cried in panic. He dashed the few steps to her doorway. She threw open the door as he skidded to a halt before her.

Clad only in her shift, she trembled with more than cold. He wrapped his arms around her. "Wake up, Katrina. It was only a nightmare."

"Jack, he was here. Brunix was here and he grabbed hold of me. He still owns me. I'm still his slave! I'll kill myself before I live as his slave again."

"Hush, Katrina. Brunix is dead. I watched him die. His last words commanded me to take care of you. He loved you in his own perverted way. He'd never truly hurt you alive or dead. It was only a nightmare, preying on your worst fear."

I'll have my revenge on you, Ackerly, he swore silently. *I'll make sure you rest silently in a deep, deep grave. You will never haunt my Katrina again.*

Others have tried and failed. You will fail as well. You will always fail, the ghost taunted him.

Jack shut out the ghost's voice.

"Just hold me, Jack." Katrina clung to him until her trembling ceased.

"Go back to sleep now, Katrina. 'Twas only a dream and can't truly hurt you." Gently he kissed her brow and eased away from her. He'd gladly go on holding her all night. Now was not the time to discuss her reluctance to marry him.

"Stay with me, Jack. I don't want to be alone." She pulled him close again, burying her face in his shoulder. Her fingers clutched his tunic with fierce strength.

"Katrina, is that a good idea?" He tried to hold her away, allow them both to gain some perspective, and keep his desire under control.

"Yes, Jack, this is a very good idea. Together we can keep the dreams at bay. Besides, tomorrow may never come and I want to die with you beside me." She kissed him soundly and pulled him down onto her bed.

* * *

Robb approached the baker's hut cautiously. Vareena kept close to his heels. Her hand constantly touched the silver-and-amethyst amulet she wore on a thong around her neck.

"That thing won't protect you from mundane dangers," Robb said testily. He had not slept well, the old nightmare coming time and time again no matter what he did to banish it. Vareena's eyes looked hollow with dark circles beneath them. She had probably spent the night searching for spiders in her bed.

From the wary jumpiness of all of the Rovers and extra guests around campfires in the courtyard before dawn, he presumed they, too, had had nightmares of their greatest fears. Except Jack and Katrina. Those two had emerged from their room holding hands and smiling at each other as if they'd just discovered the greatest secret in the world.

Maybe they had.

"I think the baker and his son are more likely to give us extra bread than his wife." Vareena directed him around to the oven and away from the nearby hut.

"Unusual. In my years on the road, I've always found the women more interested in charity than the men."

"Charity to handsome young men is different from charity to the ghost woman no one fully trusts even when they depend upon her for healing." The stony blankness that came over her face betrayed more of her hurt than any amount of anger or tears.

Robb pulled her close against him. "She's just jealous of how beautiful you are."

"I'm a spinster, available, and therefore I must be a whore as well as a witch."

"No one will say those thing about you once I take you away from here. Besides, you'll be too busy marveling at the wonders of our world. I'll show you bemouths swimming in the Great Bay. They are as big around as the baker's oven and longer than two of them put together. And their hide is so tough spears bounce off it. But they are the most beautiful iridescent blue. You can see every color of the ocean in their hides. And then there are the dragons flying above. You have to look very close to see them at all. I saw one at King Darville's coronation three years ago. It was a blue-tip. Light slides around them, challenging the eye to look anywhere but at them, but they are so magnificent, elegant, graceful, and perfectly proportioned that you can't look anywhere else. There are gold mines deep in the kardia, black holes where no light shines at all and towers in the capital that look like they are climbing to the sky—or to the dragons. If you want, I'll even take you to the jewel markets in Jihab where you can find the finest loose gems as well as stones set in gold and silver. Or maybe you fancy the spice traders in Varnicia?"

Robb painted the pictures in his mind of all the places he wanted to see for himself and show her. Let Marcus settle in his little cottage with a wife and a dozen children.

Robb still needed to see more of the world. He liked the idea of sharing his adventures with someone.

His breath caught for a moment. Vareena would make a comfortable traveling companion. But then, so would Margit, or Jack, or even some of the Rovers. He wondered if his attraction to Vareena was merely part of her talent to soothe and calm those in need.

"Robb." Vareena looked up at him with puzzled eyes. "Robb, I thought you would take me to my land in Lord Andrall's province."

"We'll go there to make your claim. But you've been trapped in this village all your life. Now you have the opportunity to view the world." Why were people so fond of one hearth, one bed, one life mate when the entire world awaited them?

"I want to live on my land, work it, nurture it, know where my place is in this world. Can you understand that?"

"Yeah." But he didn't really. He withdrew his arm from her shoulder. "I think I understand. Marcus has the same dream."

"I'm sorry, Robb, but I think I love the idea of owning something permanent more than I love you."

"And I was just so grateful for all you've done for us, that I mistook it for love." He had to look away from her.

After a moment he had the courage to face her again. "We'd best get the extra bread and head back. We're still needed back at the monastery before we can pursue our dreams." Separately.

Somehow removing Vareena from his view of the future didn't hurt as much as he thought. Jaylor and the Commune still needed him in the field. *He* still needed to be in the field.

"I knew we should have talked last night," he mumbled.

"If we had, we would still have ended up going our separate ways, but I would not have had the hope of you beside me in the morning to get me through that night of terrible dreams. Twice I considered killing myself—or someone else—just to end the dreams." She wrapped her arms around herself and shivered.

"Me, too. Thank you for that little bit of hope." He kissed her temple and stepped up to the baker's oven.

A wiry man turned from the opening where he shifted several loaves around with a wet wooden paddle. A young boy held out his arms, covered with thick padded cloths to receive any finished loaves the baker retrieved.

"Master Baker, we appeal to your charity and your sense of responsibility to those in need," Robb said quietly by way of introduction.

"Be off with you, filthy Rover!" Baker turned on him waving the massive paddle at his head.

Robb leaned away from the blow but held his ground. "I am no Rover," he said quietly.

"Thieves all of you!" Baker advanced with the paddle once more. His bellows had attracted the attention of others in the village. Some of them handled shepherd crooks and belt knives as if they intended to use them.

"Stop this all of you! Stop and think what you are doing. We need bread for the monastery. Nobles and warriors have come there as well as Rovers." Vareena tried to step between Robb and the baker.

Robb held her back. He hadn't her confidence that the locals would not attack.

"Mercenaries from SeLenicca," a man with a crook shouted. He swung it like he knew how to use it for defense.

Robb brought his own staff to the ready. He didn't want to blast these people with magic. Magic had a bad enough reputation in Coronnan without him adding more distrust and fear. But he'd bash a few heads if he had to.

"Why should we feed the enemy?" An older man with an air of authority stepped forward. He carried no weapon. He didn't need to.

"Who told you Rovers and mercenaries from SeLenicca came to the monastery yesterday?" Robb asked.

"Didn't need to be told. We saw them all arrive. Thieving Rovers can feed themselves." The village elder stepped forward, fist raised. His people followed.

All of them had red-rimmed eyes and their gazes darted about warily. Some jumped in alarm as they brushed against their neighbors.

Could the ghost have sent his terrible nightmares this far?

If so, there would be no reasoning with these people until they'd had a good night's sleep.

"Get away from here, Vareena," Robb whispered as he pushed her behind him.

"I will not run from my own people. From my own father." She stood her ground.

"Then you die with your Rover lover, for you are no daughter of mine." The village elder advanced. He grabbed a knife and crook from his neighbor.

"You would kill me, P'pa?" Vareena still did not move out of range of the rocks some of the children picked up. Robb knew from experience that children often had the best throwing aim.

Sure enough a rock flew through the air directly at his head. He ducked, but it grazed his temple. Fire followed its path across his skull. Warm moisture oozed down his cheek.

"Robb!" Vareena screamed.

"Run, Vareena." Robb threw up his magical armor around himself. But he couldn't extend it to Vareena and fend off the press of bodies that followed the rocks.

He lashed out with his staff, tripping the closest man. He fell forward into Robb's armor and bounced backward into his comrades. They clutched and scrambled for balance.

Robb used the diversion to put several arm's lengths between himself and the irate villagers.

Stupidly, Vareena stood rooted in place. She held up her hands, begging her people to listen to reason. Her eyes showed her bewilderment at their actions.

"Just because you would never hurt a soul, doesn't mean they won't," Robb muttered. His armor snapped into a wider circle to include her. He grabbed her around the waist and threw her over his shoulder.

He took off running, back to the haunted monastery. Back to all of the problems and anxious demands that had sent him out in search of bread.

"Time for a new plan," he muttered.

Chapter 41

Margit sat in the shadowed ell between the lesser tower at the south end of the west wing and the exterior wall. She braced her feet against one of the few remaining foundation stones of the little temple that used to serve the monastic community. She needed the tension in her thighs and calves to maintain control of the emotions roiling in her gut.

Marcus didn't love her.

She pushed harder against the stone before a tear could shatter her control.

One of the shadowy rovers—she could almost see these "ghosts" if she crossed her eyes and drew on every bit of magic she possessed—stood guard at the only ground floor entrance to the round structure at her back. More Rovers guarded the second-story and roof-top entrances. This lesser tower topped the exterior wall by only a few handspans and did not rise above the gloaming—the great towers on the western corners rose a full story above the defensive walls and pierced the constant haze. Inside the circular room at the base of the tower, Rejiia paced around and around her prison. Her footsteps and heavy sighs filtered through the stone to Margit's extended senses. Sometimes she heard Rejiia climb the turret stairs and pound on the doors. Mostly she just paced.

She'd done this all night long after waking screaming from some pain or nightmare. Margit had listened from the observation platform atop the northwest tower where she had attempted to sleep. Never one to remain indoors if the weather were anything but the most hostile, Margit had rejected the tiny cells available. Better to fall asleep under the stars than trapped by four walls.

But sleep had eluded her. When she wasn't crying over the loss of Marcus, a sense of airless dread had pursued her even to the open air. So she had listened with her magic to all of the inhabitants, looking for the source of her unease.

Everyone within the compound seemed to have awakened screaming, in a cold sweat at one time or another. And yet, even with her senses wide open, Margit couldn't isolate the cause.

A loud thud within the lesser tower where Margit sat now sounded as if Rejiia had thrown her entire body as well as her magic at the door of her prison. The woman had a fierce temper if she still beat aimlessly at anything and everything that defied her.

Margit withdrew any lingering magic from her mundane sense to avoid touching the witch or being touched by her.

Yet she sympathized with Rejiia. Many times during her three years as Queen Rossemikka's maid she had railed at the confinement of the palace. The only thing that kept her there for so long was the dream of advancing to journeywoman magician so she could wander the world at Marcus' side.

But Marcus had had his fill of wandering. He also, it seemed, had had his fill of Margit.

She refused to be bound by his dream of hearth and home and dozens of children and apprentices. She had her own dreams.

She'd accept whatever quest Jaylor chose to give her, alone or in the company of another, as long as she did not have walls confining her or cats fouling the scant air within a building.

The ache in her heart spread to her head. Marcus had never considered her wishes in his plans. He'd never even asked what she wanted out of life. That betrayal hurt as much as the idea of spending the rest of her life indoors, cooking and cleaning for him and his brats. And he loved cats, frequently trying to arouse her sympathy for some stray whenever he visited the capital.

Some subtle variation in the light caught her attention.

She sensed more than saw the Rover at the doorway shifting restlessly from foot to foot. He'd been there since before dawn. Margit would be restless and tired by now, too. Something about the changes in light around his ghostly outline made her open her magical senses again, straining to see his posture and possibly an aura.

At the same moment, she became aware of a subtle difference in the way Rejiia and her magic moved. The witch focused her beating against the magical and mundane chains that bound her. The wall at Margit's back no longer vibrated from her assault. And yet a great deal of magic beat at her senses.

A subtle voice in the back of her mind suggested that the lock was open. She needed to shift it. She needed . . .

"Compulsions are illegal, Rejiia," Margit chortled as she recognized the nature of the magic drifting around her. "The lock is in place. Shifting it will merely open it for you. Commune magicians are trained to be immune to magical coercion. But that Rover isn't."

She stood up, alert to any other changes in the compound. No more time to feel sorry for herself or worry about sleep loss. The best cure for a broken heart was action. She smiled, anticipating a fight. She twirled her staff, seeking the best defensive grip.

But if Rejiia relied on magic, Margit needed help. Marcus had not returned—probably wouldn't for days. Robb had gone to the village with Vareena. That left Jack and the Rovers. By his own admission, Jack was half Rover, Zolltarn's grandson. Her prejudices told her not to trust either man. But both had sworn oaths of loyalty to the Commune.

The Rover at the doorway drifted closer. His hands reached behind him. Margit couldn't tell more because of the blasted haze that made the man nearly invisible. But she knew that no lock could resist a Rover for long.

She placed two fingers against her teeth and blew. A sharp whistle reverberated through the courtyard. Several shadowy outlines lifted their heads to look in her direction. Jack and Katrina among them.

At least Margit could see those two along with Miranda,

her Rover lover, and Lanciar, the soldier from SeLenicca. None of them had passed into the gloaming.

With her magical senses extended, Jack and Katrina's auras became fully visible to her. They complemented each other in shades of purple, silver, and white. Except . . .

Jack's aura had a strange double layer; a reversed reflection of the purple and silver that could also be bronze and black depending upon how the light hit him. Queen Rossemikka's aura also had a bizarre reflection that doubled the layers of energy about her. Jack did indeed have a problem.

He only took about three heartbeats to assess the position of the Rover. He turned his head toward the Rover guard. One of the indistinct outlines raised a hand and pointed at the figure outside Rejiia's prison door.

Instantly the guard jerked as if coming awake from a doze.

Rejiia's magic recoiled, too, as if she'd been stung by a bee.

That strange mind-to-mind link all Rovers seemed to share at work again. So why wasn't Miranda's lover a ghost, too?

And then Margit felt the faintest brush of tingling air against her arm. Instinctively, she swatted at the butterfly-light touch. Her hand encountered a barrier of energy extremely close. One of the ghosts stood next to her. She peered closer, letting her eyes cross, looking for distortions of light, a remnant of an aura, anything that might tell her who stood so close, so quiet she couldn't even hear him/her breathe.

Jack and the ghost who was probably Zolltarn approached the guard. They stood for several moments talking to him in heated whispers in a language Margit did not understand. The ghost who stood next to her must be someone different. An unwanted eavesdropper.

One of the nobles or their servants? Jack and Lanciar had made certain they had all passed into the gloaming to keep them here until the situation was resolved.

"Why didn't Rejiia try this earlier, while we slept?" Jack's words came to Margit quite clearly.

"Time is distorted here," Zolltarn said. His worried voice

sounded as if it traversed a great distance, but was more distinct than his body. "If I have lost my planetary orientation, then so must Rejiia. She might not know what time it is. She might not have been able to control her temper until now."

"I know what it's like when the loss of one's sense of where and when goes askew." Jack shuddered visibly. "But Rejiia has always been able channel her temper into ruthless cunning. Why not now?"

"Because Ackerly has invaded all of our dreams and made us react without thinking," Zolltarn replied.

"Who needs to think?" the invisible one next to Margit said on a breath. "Don't think. Just turn your backs for one long moment."

Margit almost didn't hear her, but as soon as the words penetrated her consciousness she recognized the petulant tones of Ariiell, the pregnant one who thought the world owed her adulation.

Ariiell almost floated between the Rover guard and the door. She must have cloaked herself in some kind of invisibility spell for Jack and Zolltarn not to notice her. But the spell probably kept her from noticing anyone not in the gloaming.

Ariiell hunched over the lock and proceeded to fiddle with it.

"Oh, no, you don't, you conniving bitch." Margit launched herself at Ariiell in a full body tackle. She bounced against the barrier to the gloaming. Her entire front burned. But Ariiell stumbled away from the lock. A tiny bit of the mist that surrounded her faded along with her invisibility spell.

"Get away from me, you filthy peasant!" Ariiell screeched. She arched her fingers as if to claw at anyone who stood in her way.

"You won't get that door open, Lady." Zolltarn hauled her to her feet without regard to her delicate condition or sensibilities.

"Do not touch me, Rover." Ariiell spat at Zolltarn's feet. "And I am more than a lady. I carry the heir to the throne of Coronnan. I'll have your head when I am regent."

"You'll have to wait for King Darville to die first. And now that we've been warned, we'll protect him." Margit inserted herself between the door and the guard, making sure Ariiell could get no closer.

"But . . . but you can't. I have the coven backing me," Ariiell spluttered. Her haughty demeanor drained out of her, leaving a greatly diminished and confused young woman.

"Oh, shut up, you ignorant twit!" Rejiia's harsh voice came from behind the sealed door.

Just then Robb pushed his way through the crowd. "If you want your child to inherit the crown, then you have to stop using magic now, Ariiell." He leaned close to her, speaking each word distinctly. "Do you know what happens when a child's magic is awakened prematurely because the mother thoughtlessly throws spells—if the child survives the ordeal of birth? Usually a premature birth." Anger suffused his face with bright color.

Margit had never seen him display such passion. Usually he fell into a long pedantic lecture. Interest pricked, she noted that Vareena hung back from the confrontation. The air of possessiveness she'd displayed when they left this morning seemed to have blown away.

"Well, I'll tell you what happens—what happened to Brevelan's first child," Robb continued with barely a pause for breath. "The child never speaks. He doesn't need to because he has direct mind-to-mind communication with anyone who has a bit of magical talent. But he is totally incapable of communicating with mundanes. How can a king rule if he can't communicate with his Council or the vast majority of his subjects? Those of us with magical talent grow up surrounded by other magicians, we seek out others of our kind when we are away from our comrades. So we expect everyone to be able to do what we do. But only one in one thousand is born with any magical talent at all. Only one in one thousand of those have enough talent to qualify for admission into the University. Only one in one hundred of those will ever reach master status."

"Mundanes mean nothing." Ariiell dismissed his tirade with a disdainful wave of her delicate hand.

"You've been working magic your entire pregnancy. I can smell it on you." Rob did not let up. His eyes almost glowed with intensity.

Margit gritted her teeth. She knew there was a reason

she shouldn't settle down with Marcus to produce baby after baby—as Brevelan had. She wasn't ready to give up her magic yet. She had too much more to learn. Too many more places to go and sights to see.

"Any one of the Rover midwives will be able to tell you the child's awareness is awakened very early in the womb. It grows eager to be out in the world, to see what all of the magic is about." Robb finally breathed. He stood straight again and relaxed his shoulders. But Margit suspected his words were intended to reach more ears than just Ariiell's. "The child will come early, before you are ready. He'll tear up your insides in his eagerness to be out in the world before he is ready to breathe air and eat food. If you survive, you'll never bear another child."

"Is that the fate of my son? Will he ever learn to speak? Will he be able to lead a normal life?" Lanciar, the soldier from SeLenicca asked. His slender cheeks took on new hollows and shadows. "Stargods, Rejiia ate the Tambootie while pregnant. What did that do to her?"

"Your son is too young to know the extent of Rejiia's folly while carrying him," Zolltarn said. He reached out a hand as if to pat the man's shoulder in reassurance. But of course he couldn't bridge the energy barrier that separated him from the real world where Lanciar remained. "Rejiia has always been indiscriminate with her spells and her concerns for others. That is why her Rover wet nurse spirited him away from the witch. With our special links, we hope to give him a home and family that will protect him from the violent prejudice of the outside world."

"I knew I had decided to join you for a good reason." A half smile lighted the soldier's face.

"King Darville has already been alerted that the child you carry is no longer qualified to succeed him," Marcus said, strolling into the group.

Margit's heart skipped a beat in joy at sight of him, but then slowed to its normal dull thud. She would always love this man, but her destiny lay elsewhere. A deep sigh heaved its way up through her chest. When it was gone, she felt lighter, more confident. She was in charge of her destiny for the first time in a very long time.

"When did you get back?" she asked, keeping her tone neutral and polite.

"Just now. I heard most of what Robb said so eloquently." He looked at her longingly, then shook himself free of any lingering ties.

"No! You can't do this to me." Ariiell's eyes went wide. Her pupils contracted to mere dots. Her mouth pinched. White showed around her nostrils. "I am to be queen. The coven promised. I will have all of your heads."

No one answered her.

"You will obey me this instant. I am to be queen. My son will be king. Darville will be put to death. The coven promised." Her voice grew louder, more shrill.

The crowd drifted away, tired of her tantrum.

"Come back here," she screeched, tearing at her red-blond hair. Crimson splotches showed on her neck and cheeks. The whites of her eyes dominated her face. "I am queen!" She lifted her hands in a classic gesture to throw a spell. Blue-and-yellow witchfire streamed from her fingertips toward Zolltarn's retreating back. The flames fizzled and lost energy a mere arm's length from her hands. Dull sparks flowed to the ground and winked out. "Where is my magic?" Ariiell fell to her knees moaning. "I have to have my magic. Oh, baby, lend me some magic." She clutched her belly and rocked back and forth continuing her self-absorbed litany.

"Come, Ariiell. I'll take care of you." Lord Laislac knelt beside her, lifting her gently to her feet. "I feared this might come to pass." He looked around at the others in apology, especially Lord Andrall and Lady Lynnetta. "Her mother succumbed to insanity. She threw herself from the top of the tower of Castle Laislac, convinced she could fly. My daughter seems to have inherited the same weakness in her mind. Her use of the Tambootie in coven ritual may have hastened her infirmity."

Sadly, he led Ariiell back toward their second-story room in the opposite wing.

"She is welcome to shelter in our home until the child comes. We will raise it, love it, as our only grandchild." Lady Lynnetta reached an imploring hand toward them.

"We are used to caring for . . . well, for our son." Lord Andrall gestured toward Mardall who led the Rover children in a quiet game that involved drawing complex patterns in the dirt.

"I have an idea that might help you with that, Lord Andrall." Jack grinned from ear to ear. "I have a rather pesky, but intelligent cat who needs a good home."

"Before we do anything, I have to let you know that some very angry villagers are on their way here. They plan to dismantle this place stone by stone to end the tyranny of the ghost once and for all," Robb said.

"They will be aided by a troop of soldiers with a commission from the priests in the capital," Marcus added. "They are led by Gnuls and employ three witch-sniffers. With or without permission, they intend to capture and burn any magicians they find here."

Jack and Lanciar nodded to each other in confirmation of that statement.

Why hadn't they told her? Margit fumed for a bit, wishing these men had more confidence in her. She could help. She knew she could, if they'd just let her.

"We have work to do, folks," Marcus continued. "That ghost has to be laid to rest and the curse removed from the gold before the others arrive."

"What can I do to help?" Margit leaped at the chance to finally *do* something. They wouldn't think to ask her unless she volunteered.

"That depends upon how friendly you are with dragons." Marcus cocked his head and raised his eyebrows in an endearing gesture.

Margit needed to run to him, hold him tight, kiss him one more time. Maybe they could work things out.

But he turned his gaze elsewhere. No longer interested in her love.

The joy at her sense of freedom battled with the heavy ache in her gut. "I'll just have to improvise to get through this."

Chapter 42

"**T**he good news is that Jaylor's daughter is gaining strength and vitality by the hour," Marcus told his companions from the Commune as they closeted themselves in the large suite Zolltarn had appropriated for himself. "The bad news is that Master Lyman has gone to his next existence."

That statement felt quite strange. Marcus knew where Lyman had gone. He'd chosen a new existence but not necessarily in the way one expected.

Jack sank down on the floor in the corner. "I wanted to be there with him. He . . . he and I had a kind of kinship."

The blank mask that descended over Jack's features told Marcus how close the young master magician and the elder Librarian had become.

"He wanted you there, Jack," Marcus consoled. "He said to look for him where you least expect."

"Probably right under my nose." Jack's laugh became choked. He swallowed deeply and then remained silent.

There is more to his story. I'll tell all, later, in private. Marcus sent his telepathic message on a tight line. With all of these other magicians in the room anything more might be intercepted. Lyman had been most emphatic that his story was for Jack alone.

"This feels almost as bad as when Old Baamin died." Robb sank to the floor beside Jack as if his legs would no longer support his weight.

"About time the old coot gave up and let someone younger and more vital govern his beloved collection of books." Zolltarn stretched within his comfortably padded chair—the only piece of furniture in the room besides the built-in bed platform and slanted writing desk that was either too heavy to move or anchored to the floor. The chair and the bedding had come with the Rover.

"I really liked Old Lyman," Margit said. "He understood why I preferred to study outdoors rather than in his stuffy library. He even showed me a little spell that would keep the rain off the books so I wouldn't have to come inside."

Marcus touched the book tucked into his tunic that Lyman had directed him to in his last moments. One of these days, when life had settled into a pattern again, he'd have to ask Jaylor if any of his ancestors had been named Bessell. That young companion of Powwell—the author of the book— had developed an attitude of benign defiance very similar to Jaylor's before he'd become Senior Magician. He also had an almost identical magical signature to Jaylor.

Old Lyman had known every word in every book, the name of the author, and where he'd shelved it. He probably suspected the family connection. He would indeed be missed.

"Speaking of Old Baamin." Marcus jumped back to the subject he needed to follow. He took a moment to survey all of their faces and to make sure he had all of their attention. "The old blue-tipped dragon who brought me here is named Baamin." He closed his eyes a moment as he relived the exhilarating, stomach-dropping moments of flight. The sight of the thick gray fog that surrounded the monastery had troubled him at first. But the view from above had also given him a bit of understanding. The building existed halfway into a different dimension from the rest of the planet. That explained the time distortion and the weakening of magic within its walls.

He waited a moment for the others to absorb the hint he'd given them about Baamin's new existence. Robb looked up from his fascinated gaze at his hands in his lap. He cocked his head and winked one eye. Margit didn't seem interested at all—but then she had never known the rotund little magician who had governed the Commune and the University for decades.

Zolltarn chortled aloud. "I knew the bas . . . the master would find a way to come back to haunt me!"

Jack merely looked blank again. He was very good at that. He'd learned early and well to hide his true emotions in silence.

"You knew that one of the dragons is named Baamin, Jack," Marcus said, almost accusingly.

"He rescued me from SeLenicca," Jack said quietly. "He was also my father in his previous existence." His last words sounded so softly Marcus wasn't quite sure he'd heard him correctly.

"Your father?" Robb asked. He rolled to his knees and peered at their comrade. He used his standard pin-you-in-place-with-my-eyes look. A lecture usually followed that ploy. But this time Robb waited for an answer.

"A long story of a Rover girl seducing a very powerful magician the night before his installation as Senior Magician of the Commune. Her clan wanted a child who could break down the magical border that kept them out of Coronnan." Jack recited the tale as if it had happened to someone else. "The woman died protecting her baby as she escaped from Hanassa. The baby disappeared. It took the dragons to find him again."

Marcus wondered briefly if Master Baamin had known of his son. He was the only one who believed Jack as a child had any intelligence at all when the rest of the world considered him too stupid to even have a name.

"Kestra," Margit supplied. "I've heard legends for years about the missing Kestra and her miracle child. We all believed them to be Rover myths with no basis in reality."

"Kestra was my oldest daughter," Zolltarn admitted proudly. "Jack is my grandson. And a mighty magician he is. Who else but my grandson could have brought SeLenicca to its knees, killed The Simeon, defeated Rejiia in open battle, and returned the dragons to Coronnan!" More a statement than a question.

"I had a lot of help from the Commune and from the dragons. Katrina's love saw me through the worst of it. Simeon's and Rejiia's arrogance didn't help them any either," Jack retorted. "Don't forget we still have to battle Rejiia and do something about her father in the tin statue."

"With a heritage like that, no wonder you made master

magician before you turned twenty." Marcus slapped his forehead with his hand. No one knew for sure exactly how old Jack was. Well, maybe Zolltarn knew.

Robb shook his head and ran his hands across his eyes. "What does a dragon named Baamin have to do with laying the ghost to rest before the villagers and soldiers arrive to tear this place—and us—apart, stone by stone?"

"Old Lyman told me just before he died that in order to remove the curse from the gold we have to travel back in time to watch Ackerly lay the spell upon the gold. He said Jack knew how to do it."

"The only time I did it, I had the help of a dragon." Jack grinned. "We'll have to solicit his help again."

"A blue-tipped dragon named Baamin, by any chance?" Robb asked.

When had Robb become so succinct of speech?

"A dragon named Baamin helped me go back in time to view my beginnings." Jack eased himself up, keeping his back in the corner, using the walls as a brace. "There are dangers. We may not have time to do this."

Marcus touched the book beneath his tunic superstitiously. "It's the only way, Jack. We have to know his ritual down to the last detail in order to reverse it. And we have to reverse it. We can't afford to leave the gold tempting people into the gloaming. I surveyed this place meticulously before Baamin landed. There is a thick fog around it. Even without touching the gold, a person enters the edges of the gloaming whenever they walk through the gatehouse. And it is spreading, reaching down to the village."

He let them think about that for several long moments. "Besides, if Robb and I succeed in this and in laying the ghost to rest, Jaylor will promote us to Master Magicians," he ended on a more optimistic note.

"Going back in time is worse than being trapped in the gloaming, Marcus." Jack looked him directly in the eye.

"Nothing is worse than that half-existence," Robb insisted.

"Nothing is worse than having the rest of the world pass you by, where an entire week of real time feels like only a day in the spell fog. We will end the curse or die trying," Marcus insisted.

"You may very well die. Your time in the past is very

limited. The longer you stay, the harder it is to return. You fade and fade into mist until there is nothing left of you to return. You have to pick the exact time on the exact day. Lingering is not an option. Nor is repeating the process."

"And the cost of the spell?" Robb asked.

"You become part dragon in order to go back in time. You are never fully content afterward to remain merely human. The longer you stay in the past, the more the dragon in you takes of your soul."

"Well, then, let's hope that Ackerly's son recorded accurately the time and day Ackerly fought with his superiors and disappeared from the first University." Marcus held up the little book in triumph.

A heavy vibration traveled through the floor slates. Jack blanched and braced himself as if anticipating a kardiaquake.

"We haven't much time," Zolltarn warned. "Do you hear that banging? That is a very angry mob trying to break down the gates to our refuge."

*   *   *

"This won't hold them long," Lanciar said as he helped Lord Andrall shove one of the bardos in front of the outer gate. The angry shouts from the villagers on the other side of the meager barrier echoed menacingly around the gate-house tunnel.

The noise made his head ache worse than the nightmare sounds made by the ghost last night. He'd dreamed repeatedly that Rejiia had stolen his son and was using the baby as a focus for her tortuous rituals to raise power. Rather than have the dream—vision almost—repeat endlessly he had walked the colonnade until the others roused at dawn. They, too, had wandered about heavy-eyed and listless.

"Do you have a better suggestion?" Lord Andrall sat on the sloped edge of the sledge, adding his weight on the barricade. He had discarded his single piece of gold to free himself of the gloaming. But he hadn't told Lord Laislac or any of the others in his party how to emerge from the perpetual mist.

Lanciar found the man much easier to work with when he could see him and a barrier of energy did not separate them.

The sound of men and tools ramming into the gate pounded in his ears. The wooden planks of the outer door buckled under the pressure.

"We don't have much besides these bardos to block the outer gate. This one is all that will fit in the gatehouse. We'll have to close the inner portal—if it will still close—and push the rest of the sledges in front of it." His military training quickly assessed the situation and made his decisions almost before he thought them through.

"Weapons?" Lord Andrall tilted his head.

"A few of your retainers have swords. Most of us have daggers and eating knives. We also have five magicians." He shrugged his shoulders.

"You . . . you will kill my people?" Vareena looked ghostly pale. She swayed slightly as she wrung her hands.

"Please sit somewhere, Vareena, before you fall down," Lord Andrall suggested. "We will do our best to spare these frightened villagers while defending ourselves."

"Let's just hope our magicians find a solution to the problem of the curse before they break through," Lanciar added. Then he began directing the closing of the inner gate.

The assault on the gate came again, stronger this time. More of the wooden planks screeched and buckled. Lanciar dragged Lord Andrall off the sledge and into the courtyard. "Get that inner gate closed now. Use magic if you have to. Two more bardos ready to move in front of it!"

Just then, the flying black cat—had he heard Jack call it a flywacket?—swooped into the courtyard. It landed neatly on the stonework around the well. Before it could begin to preen its wings, it caught Lanciar's gaze.

A blurred and confused image of mounted soldiers racing through the foothills to this lonely spot on nearly blown steeds flashed before his mind's eye. The scene repeated itself twice more, becoming clearer each time.

Just then the four other magicians emerged from Zolltarn's lair.

Jack stretched his arm for the flywacket to perch on. The bird/cat (or was it dragon/cat) pushed down with his wings once and glided over to his companion. They stared deeply into each other's eyes for a moment. "I think I need a drink," Jack said as if cursing.

"Somehow I thought you'd say that," Marcus replied. His eyes had the same half-glaze as Jack's. He'd probably shared the information.

"*S'murghit!* I think we have a problem," Lanciar muttered.

"Watch your language around the children," Vareena hissed at him.

"We haven't time to do all that we need to," Marcus protested.

"Then we'll have to improvise," Robb replied.

"Time to make our own luck, people," Queen Miranda insisted upon hearing the news. "Magicians, get to work on whatever spells you have to cast to lay the ghost to rest and remove the curse of the gloaming. Lanciar, you and Lord Andrall devise and direct a battle plan. I shall keep you informed of the attack from the top of the tower."

Lanciar didn't wait for Andrall to finish bowing to the queen. "Rovers," he shouted, "on the ramparts with any loose rubble you can find. Start tearing the walls down yourselves if you have to. Throw it at the attackers, but watch your aim. We want to scare them off—not kill them. Ladies, boil water to pour down on the villagers. That should hurt and discourage without seriously maiming and killing."

Everyone hopped to obey as if he were truly a general and not just a middle-rank officer.

Lanciar nodded his head to his queen. She didn't know how run a battle, but she knew how to delegate to someone with experience. She might have been a flighty, self-absorbed teenager when she turned over the rule of her country to Simeon, but now she showed the makings of a true leader. He looked forward to negotiating with her for the free passage of Rovers through her country.

The pounding on the gate increased, followed by a shriek of shattering wood.

Chapter 43

Marcus pulled the book out of his tunic and stared at the plain leather cover for a moment. He bit his lip while he prayed for the strength to complete the next task.

He called to mind the passages Powwell had written about his father, Ackerly.

A memory of the night he had read Ackerly's emotions in the stone wall of the master's suite flashed through him. Emotions he had dismissed because he did not understand them became clear. Ackerly was proud of his son.

His son, Powwell, had not been proud of the man who sired him but had never acted the father.

"Maybe, if we do this right, we won't have to take a dangerous trip through time," he said. "Maybe . . ."

"Your guess is as good as mine," Jack replied after communing with his flywacket for a moment.

"We can't allow the greed the gold inspires to go beyond these walls. I believe it possible that once the stones are torn down the gloaming, and the spell, will spread as far as the stones are scattered." Robb had returned to his normal lecture mode.

Marcus felt better with this one return to normal. "Then let's do it. All of you, Zolltarn and Lanciar, Margit, Robb, anyone with a bit of magical talent, cóme with me."

"My Lord Andrall, will you direct the defenses according to our plan?" Lanciar called to the lord.

Andrall saluted him and began tossing orders right and left.

Satisfied, Marcus took two firm steps toward the library. Vareena blocked his path resolutely.

"Vareena, this could be dangerous. You'd be more help trying to soothe the villagers," Robb said gently.

"All the ghosts within this monastery are my responsibility. All of them," she insisted. "That includes Ackerly. I will be there to guide him into his next existence. I must."

Marcus shrugged his shoulders and smiled. "When this is all over, may I escort you to your lands in Nunio, and perhaps call upon you upon occasion?" Stargods! He loved her strength and determination.

Vareena bit her lip, then jerked her head up and down once in assent.

Marcus suddenly felt much more confident of the outcome of this day's work. "Come along, then, all of you. Just be prepared to duck on command and avoid that ritual knife of his. He may be a ghost, but his weapon isn't."

In single-file, they moved into the shadowed coolness of the library. Diffused sunlight streamed through the high windows around the gallery, highlighting the centuries of accumulated dust. Instantly, the dust motes beneath the gallery began to swirl and concentrate. Ackerly formed more quickly than usual. Marcus saw the knife first, just before the ghost sped toward him, aiming the blade for his eyes.

"Scatter," Marcus called as he dived beneath Ackerly. A preternatural chill ran down his spine. Childhood fears of monsters beneath the bed made his teeth chatter.

He clamped his jaw shut as he read one of the final passages in the journal he carried. Still lying prone, he turned the book so that it caught some of the light from the gallery windows.

"Listen to what happened to your son, Ackerly," he said with what little control he had left. "Listen to how you tainted everything you touched, especially the lives of your only two children—bastard children at that. 'I shall not accept a new existence when this one passes. Life hurts too much. Love hurts more. When my sister Kalen died in the pit beneath Hanassa, a large hole ripped open in my gut and it has never healed. Her death was as filled with torment as her life. Her ghost has haunted me since. When I die, her spirit will be free, not before. I have never wanted to inflict that kind of curse upon anyone. My years of seeking the best forms of healing—even though they dipped into rogue magic—have not been enough to remove the curse laid upon us by our father. I have not truly loved anyone since Kalen died. I have not fathered any children. Ackerly's line and his curses die with me. There will be no reincarnation for any of us.' "

Marcus sensed stillness throughout the library.

"By the Fire of my body, the Water of my blood, the Air that I breathe, and the Kardia of my bones, I call forth the restless one who dwells only in sadness and refuses to live!" Zolltarn shouted to each of the four corners of the room, the four cardinal directions.

Vareena repeated his chant four times facing each of the four walls.

Margit followed suit. As did Jack.

"That sounds like a coven ritual," Robb whispered.

"Who cares, as long as it accomplishes something positive," Marcus replied.

LIES! Ackerly's voice boomed through Marcus' mind.

He clamped his hands over his ears in a futile effort to block out the reverberations and the need to crawl out of the monastery in abject defeat.

"It's just the ghost. There is nothing to fear. We can handle him," Marcus muttered to himself over and over.

"Lies! You wish to steal my gold. All lies. Everything is lies." Ackerly flew around the room so rapidly Marcus couldn't separate the trail of dust from his ethereal robes from the cloud of dust around his hair. His voice had become audible to mundane senses. His emotions must be roiling and totally beyond control.

Lanciar kept the ghost from fleeing to the courtyard with wild slashes of his iron sword at the doorway.

"Your life and your death have all been lies," Marcus announced. He noted that Ackerly stayed away from Zolltarn, Lanciar, Margit, and Vareena. The haze seemed to thicken around them, a misty veil deeper than the half existence Ackerly had created for himself and his gold.

"What good is the gold, Ackerly? What good did you accomplish by hoarding it all these centuries?" Marcus had to keep the ghost occupied until Zolltarn finished his conjure.

Gold is power. I have power as long as I have the gold.

"You have nothing. Power exists only when it involves other people. Hidden away here you have power over nothing. Not even yourself."

I have the gold.

"Hoarding the gold makes you a failure. You won't use it to buy land or trade with foreign countries. You can't buy influence in politics. You can't help the poor. You are a failure, Ackerly. A failure in your life and in your death. You can't even get to your next existence properly. And your greed kept your son and daughter from seeking their next existence. You denied them their due. You FAILED!" Marcus taunted the ghost.

You know nothing. Without the gold I am nothing. Ackerly's wails became shriller, more desperate.

"With the gold, you are less than nothing," a new voice said softly.

Everyone in the room turned to look at the figure that stood at the top of the spiral iron stair. More fully formed than Ackerly, the light still shone through the man. His curly dark hair stood out around his head in a kind of halo. Old-fashioned blue robes, similar to what master magicians still wore for formal occasions, fluttered as if in a breeze. He anchored his staff against the first stair.

Vareena took a step closer, staring at the man's tired gray eyes. Compassion, as well as inner pain, radiated from those eyes. Those eyes had seen more pain and destruction than a man three times his age. Marcus doubted he'd seen more than thirty summers. And yet he seemed ageless, timeless. He held his twisted staff in his right hand, a miniature hedgehog in his left. A familiar that had followed him into death.

The hedgehog bristled and wiggled in response to Powwell's emotions.

A curious shadow stood behind his left shoulder, a darker, shorter, duplicate of himself.

Not too different from Jack's double aura, or the one that Queen Rossemikka possessed.

What strange entity haunted him?

"We could not have conjured your son if his soul resided anywhere but drifting aimlessly in the void," Marcus said quietly. He knew Ackerly heard him.

"I am Powwell, of the Commune of Magicians. You called me across time for a purpose," the new entity announced.

"We called you to confront your father." Marcus found the courage to speak first.

"My father is not worth the time and trouble. Your true need and purpose must be great indeed to risk calling me forth from the void."

"Your father has also refused his next existence. He and his gold have cursed this place for nigh on three hundred years. We have called you to heal him," Zolltarn answered the man's plea. He had, after all initiated the spell.

"You were the greatest healer of your time," Jack added. "And you could not heal yourself because you never had the opportunity to confront your father. I thank the Stargods that the dragons gave my father the opportunity to continue his destiny as a dragon so that I could confront him and find myself in my heritage. We give you the same chance."

"For all of our sakes, acknowledge Ackerly and guide him to his next existence," Vareena concluded.

"I hate to interrupt this sentimental reunion, folks, but the door around Rejiia's tower is smoking," Lanciar hissed from the doorway. "She'll be drawn to the magic swirling around us all like iron to lodestone."

"I repeat, the man who sired me is not worth the trouble and danger you face when drawing me across time and distance." Powwell turned away.

I refute your accusation! Ackerly screamed. The cloud of dust approached the iron stairway. *I dedicated my life to making Nimbulan's life easier, more organized. I fed him when he was too exhausted to think. I made sure all of his equipment was at hand while he waged battle on the enemies of Coronnan. I supported him all our lives and he betrayed me. As you, Powwell, and your sister Kalen betrayed me.* He stopped short at the bottom step.

Once before the iron in the stairway had repulsed him. He could approach no closer to his son.

Could Powwell cross the barrier iron placed between them? There were higher and thicker barriers to contend with first.

"You betrayed Nimbulan, the greatest magician of his age, perhaps of any age. You tried to kill him with an overdose of Tambootie, and then you usurped his position in the University. You sold the services of half-trained apprentices for gold. You manipulated and coerced the lords of the land for gold. You did nothing for others, only for your own selfish greed," Powwell accused. He kept his back to his father.

The gold was to be your inheritance. I did not want either you or Kalen to be left destitute and dependent because of the wars. Ackerly held out a hand to his son in entreaty.

"Then why did you secrete the gold here where no one could find it? Why didn't you acknowledge your two bastards and at least give them names? You did nothing for us. Kalen died barely two years after you did. She was still a *child*. The victim of yet another who sought to use her talent for their own gain and without regard for her soul."

I left clues. If only you had sought them. You were both children when I departed Coronnan. If I had left the gold in an obvious place, it would have been stolen from you. You might have been murdered for it.

Powwell turned back to face his father. He took two steps forward only to stop, or be stopped by the iron stairs.

Marcus sensed something important was going on. He needed to listen and learn, perhaps heal his own hurts by their example.

The scent of woodsmoke drew his attention to the doorway. Flames shot upward across the courtyard. The door to the lesser tower exploded outward.

Rejiia stalked through the fire, free of her bonds.

Chapter 44

Jack watched as Rejiia, with a deceptively subtle gesture, knocked flat three determined Rover women armed with rolling pins. Black-and-red spikes of magic radiated from her aura. Everything that came in contact with those layers of energy was in danger.

How had she overcome the magical dissipation of the gloaming? Then he realized he could see her quite clearly. She had discarded the coin that trapped her between dimensions as soon as she broke the bonds he, Marcus, and Robb had wrapped around her.

And she reeked of Tambootie. The leaves of the tree of magic, which she probably kept about her person at all times, could temporarily enhance her powers. But once the effects of the drug wore off . . .

Three more women, Zolltarn's head wife in the lead, jumped to attack the renegade witch with pots full of boiling water. Everything they threw at the determined woman bounced off her armor and back in the faces of her attackers.

The women cowered away from her, covering their eyes.

Around them, Rovers, nobles, and the others confronted the villagers with whatever weapons came to hand. Miranda stood on the observation platform of the northwest tower calling to Lord Andrall the activities of each attacker still outside the walls. The noise of that battle distracted Jack from the impending magical duel with his old enemy.

Rejiia's eyes burned with her need for revenge. Flames nearly shot from her gaze. But her hands shook. With pent-up emotion or a side effect of the Tambootie?

Jack wanted to cower away from Rejiia and the memory of what she had done to him in the prison cell in Queen's City. The last time he'd battled her, she'd been calm and controlled, almost mocking in her superiority.

But she'd fled in defeat when confronted by a united Commune.

The weasel statue of her father, Lord Krej, rocked on top of the bardo as she passed. The muzzle and ears had joined both front legs and the tail in becoming realistically furry. His mouth opened, and he drooled. More of the tin casing dropped away from his head. Not a trace of humanity touched his features.

Before Jack could think of a ploy to stop or delay Rejiia, the inner gate split and tumbled forward on top of the jumble of bardos. Hopefully, the maze of sledges and cabins, of milling steeds, squawking flusterhens, and bawling children would slow them down until Ackerly's angry influence had been negated.

Where were the soldiers and Gnuls from the capital? How much time did they have? Amaranth didn't know and didn't care. He only wanted to hide his head under a wing and pretend all this chaos and noise would go away.

Jack sent him safely into the air to search.

He had no idea how the breach in the defenses of the monastery would affect the curse on the gold. Would it spread or dissipate? Maybe nothing at all would affect it but a true reversal of the curse. Whatever, they had to finish before the army with the Gnuls and witch-sniffers arrived.

His fellow magicians looked anxiously back and forth between the melee at the gate and Rejiia's advancing menace.

Jack waved them over to the gate. "Take care of Katrina for me. I'll be with you shortly," he said. "Rejiia is mine."

"And mine," Lanciar added. He took up his position shoulder to shoulder with Jack. "We may have been enemies once, but in this we are allies."

"We forged some interesting bonds on that frigid mountain pass . . . comrade," Jack replied.

"Friend. And kin."

Jack needed more time to forgive Lanciar. He nodded

his acceptance that one day they might walk side by side as friends. One day. Not yet.

Together they faced their foe.

"Jack, Rejiia's element seems to be fire," Margit said almost breathless.

Jack raised an eyebrow at her.

"I did some research on opposing elements for Jaylor. Air and Fire are linked. Water and Kardia oppose them. Use Water and Kardia. You can negate her magic without harming the others around her. Trust me."

Across the courtyard the other magicians joined the Rovers and nobles in shoving obstacles in front of the invading villagers. Queen Miranda moved atop Zolltarn's large bardo with Lord Andrall for more immediate observation and direction of the defenses.

Amaranth showed Jack images of the soldiers led by Vareena's brother on the far side of the river. They were still almost a league from the ford. Without the professionals backing the locals and urging them to battle, Jack and his companions had a chance to end this without giving or receiving serious injury.

With the transport spell, he could then evacuate all of the magicians from the place and keep them safe from Gnul persecution. Zolltarn could tend to his own people quite nicely.

Rejiia raised her hands, fingers arched, fire at her command, murder in her eyes.

"Let's see if your research works, Margit, because I don't have any other ideas," Jack muttered. He took a deep breath and began his spell. "Gather together, drop by drop, seek your like, find the path," he chanted calling upon the element of Water to oppose Fire. "Gather to a trickle, spread to a stream, climb to a wave."

All the water in the courtyard that had been flung at friend and enemy alike responded to his plea, willingly bonding with its own kind. It gathered in puddles that traveled quickly to join with other rivulets streaming from the well. Then the puddles piled on top of each other, fed by the deep underground spring, forming a wall of water traveling forward toward Jack.

"Air rush to fill the emptiness," Lanciar chanted beside him. "Join with Water, swell the wave. Oppose each other in battle, aid the brave."

The wave grew and spread wide. A strong wind pushed it higher yet. The two elements raged where they met, churning each other, adding pressure to the path they followed.

At the moment the wall of water reached Rejiia's back, Jack and Lanciar both dropped their hands. "Water seek your complement. Ground in the Kardia taking Fire and Air with you," they chanted together.

The wave crested over the witch. For a moment Rejiia was lost within the roaring water, pushed forward, off balance. She thrashed about, spluttering for air.

Water retreated. Fire sought its opposite, ready to do battle, and fled her fingers to ground itself harmlessly in the Kardia.

"Aid me, Air, reignite my Fire," Rejiia called, still spitting water from her mouth. She emerged sputtering from the rapidly dissipating Water, hair drenched and scraggling in thin and tangled tendrils. Her once elegant black-and-silver gown hung upon her body in ugly, misplaced lumps. Her skin looked pasty. The boost to her magic given by the Tambootie was wearing off.

Air ignored her, rushing onward.

"From North, South, East, and West and the lesser points between, I call upon the coven to come forth. Aide me, brethren. Defeat our enemies now and forever," she called, turning a full but wobbling circle with her arms outstretched.

Again the magic fizzled as soon as it left her body.

"They aren't coming, Rejiia," Lanciar taunted her. "Your summons never left the compound."

She raised a fist and shook it at him in anger. Some of her lumpy padding dislodged and settled near her waist.

Lanciar giggled slightly. "All those tempting curves were nothing more than cotton padding," he said. A touch of magic projected his words to the farthest corners of the embattled courtyard.

More giggles rippled around the crowd, many of them

from the throats of villagers. Much of the anger that had propelled them dissipated, much like the water retreating toward the well.

"You can't do this to me!" Rejiia screamed. Frantically she pushed at the lumps in her clothing, only misplacing them more. Her hands trembled. A convulsive shudder vibrated her entire body. She looked as if her knees would no longer support her.

At that moment Jack realized that humiliation was the one weapon Rejiia could not fight—especially not with her magic drained and an exhausted body. She'd not restore herself soon without more Tambootie. He detected no more leaves in her possession.

"She couldn't even bother enhancing her appearance with a magical glamour. She just used the common artifice available to any *mundane* woman," Jack chortled.

"I'll show you magic!" Rejiia raised her hands again. This time she held half a dozen metal stars in each palm. When accurately thrown, the wickedly sharp points could take out an eye, or penetrate to the heart.

Jack sobered immediately. He needed to be in the courtyard, standing atop one of the ley lines to command enough magic to wrap Rejiia in a bubble of armor strong enough to contain those stars. He edged forward, Lanciar in his wake.

"Merawk!" Amaranth screeched from atop the tallest tower. He spread his wings and swooped down, talons extended. Sunlight hit his feathered wings, making them glisten purple. He seemed to grow, to shed the light his black body absorbed. He skimmed over Rejiia's head, grabbing several tufts of her dripping hair.

"Yieeeeee!" Rejiia's screech echoed and amplified as it bounced off the stone walls that confined them all. She dropped the throwing stars to clutch her scalp.

Amaranth shrank back to normal size as he swooped about, displaying his trophy.

The weasel rose up on its hind legs and nipped at the flywacket's tail feathers.

Amaranth screeched, compounding the noise. He flew higher, scattering tufts of Rejiia's hair.

A bald spot showed clearly just off center of her head.

"Krej is nearly free of the spell," Zolltarn gasped. "We must stop him from running."

"Or transforming back to a man," Jack added.

"I don't want to go back to the days when he was regent," Robb said as he ran up from the gate area. The fray at the entrance had given way to astonished gasps and stares.

"I don't think he can become a man again," Lancier said, pointing to the now animate animal. "His humanity is so deeply buried within the tin, it will take magic to bring it forth again. He's been a weasel for three years. A weasel he will stay."

Jack had the impression of dozens of people frozen in mid-scramble across the barricade of bardos. Their anger dispersed, much as Rejiia's magic had.

Some of the villagers scuttled away, crossing themselves repeatedly, making the flapping wrist ward against Simurgh in between each invocation of the Stargods.

Then he realized that the Rovers were much easier to see. The haze had thinned. Sunlight began to penetrate to the courtyard.

"The gloaming is fading. We have to finish this now, before Rejiia manages to escape again," he said to Lanciar and anyone else who cared to help. He raised his hands once more to find a spell, any spell that would trap the witch.

Just then the weasel broke free of the last of its tin casing and leaped from its perch on the bardo.

Lancier flung his arm forward as if launching a spell or an invisible spear.

"Come back here," Rejiia screamed and dove for the slippery animal. It eluded her grasp. "Don't you dare leave before I'm ready. I am your master as long as you are enthralled. I will be your master when you live." She crawled after the elusive animal into the midst of the sledges.

A pain ripped across Jack's gut, leaving him dizzy and disoriented. What was he about to do? He touched his temples, trying desperately to ground himself. His eyes crossed and lost focus.

Then his vision cleared of the afterimages he'd seen ever

since Rosie took up residence in his body. His bottom no longer itched as if to twitch a tail.

"Rejiia and Krej, Krej and Rejiia, father and daughter, daughter and father, bound together by blood and by magic, cling to each other in the chase," Lanciar said quietly as he traced a sigil in the dirt with his toe. He followed with more words, spoken too rapidly in a language similar to Rover, but . . . Jack didn't have the concentration to think through a translation.

More pain attacked every joint in Jack's body. He needed to fall to his knees. He didn't dare.

And then Katrina was there, holding him, giving him the strength he needed to continue, as she had done in that dank and miserable dungeon cell beneath Queen's City.

But this time the weakness that assailed him felt like a kind of freedom.

Rejiia continued to crawl after her father, coaxing now rather than screaming. She stopped to groom her wet and straggling hair. Then she returned to her determined chase.

"Did I see her lick her hand and wash her ears?" Jack asked. Feeling suddenly lighter, he patted his gut, his backside, all of his joints in turn. Rosie did not respond. He risked a minor trance to search his inner being.

"Katrina, I think I've just lost one of our problems." He couldn't help grinning.

Then Rejiia did pause in her mad scramble beneath the sledges to rub dust off her hands and lick them.

"What?" Jack eyed Lanciar carefully.

"I just put a compulsion upon her."

"Compulsions are illegal," Marcus reminded him.

"I'm not a member of the Commune and not bound by their conventions. Yet."

"What did you do to her?" Jack asked again.

"She'll follow the weasel until one or both of them dies. And until she catches it—alive—she can't throw any magic."

"She'll be tracking that thing for years before she realizes she's under a compulsion!" Marcus chortled.

"All Lanciar did was enhance her own inner demons," Jack added. "She's been obsessed with her father since before his spell against Darville backlashed and turned him into a weasel. I think that was why she embraced Simeon as a lover. He looked so much like her father, and Rejiia controlled that relationship from the beginning." He didn't add that with the cat persona embedded with her own, the compulsion would compound. No one could outstubborn a cat.

"Even when Simeon thought he commanded the world, Rejiia gave him the commands," Lanciar mused. "She controlled him as she never could her father."

"How long does a weasel live?" Marcus asked. "What happens when Krej dies? Are we back to battling Rejiia?"

"I don't think so." Lanciar whistled a jaunty Rover tune. "That compulsion won't go away unless she captures the weasel *alive!* She'll search for him even after he dies."

"I think we need to get back into the library," Robb reminded them. "The gloaming is lifting, but not gone. Vareena needs our help."

Chapter 45

Vareena watched and listened as Powwell and Ackerly continued their bitter litanies against each other. Over and over, she tried to project love and peace into their hearts. She'd done this for every ghost who came under her care. She had to show these two lost souls the lighted path through the void to their next existence.

'Twas her destiny, her purpose in staying so long in this cursed and unforgiving place. If she could not help these two, she would never have freedom, even if she left.

Ackerly and Powwell rejected every offer.

"Stop it, both of you!" she finally insisted. "Stop and listen to yourselves. You just repeat the same arguments over and over, phrased a little differently, but accomplishing nothing." She stomped her foot in frustration.

Both ghosts paused and looked at her, acknowledging something outside their own bitterness for the first time.

"You have both been trapped in this half-life, this nothingness, for three hundred years. You've accomplished nothing in that time, a true reflection of the nothing you accomplished in life."

Both opened insubstantial mouths to protest.

"What did you achieve?" she asked Powwell.

"I was the greatest healer of my time. I researched the healing arts and brought new techniques to ease the pain and suffering of many," Powwell intoned. The little hedgehog perched on his palm bristled as if protesting the statement.

"According to this journal, written in your own hand, Powwell, many of those techniques were borrowed from rogue and blood magic. All of them have been rejected by the Commune since then. Your legacy is forgotten." She held up the little book.

I taught many new magicians in the University while Nimbulan wandered aimlessly in search of something that eluded him all his life, Ackerly returned.

"Our histories tell us that Nimbulan found dragon magic and brought an end to the Great Wars of Disruption. You died opposing him in the final battle of the war." Vareena allowed the silence to stretch for another endless moment. "We remember Nimbulan with love and adulation. No one remembered either of you until Nimbulan's journals were found."

Nimbulan found peace with his wife and family. He died at the age of ninety, content with his life and his death. I was there. I guided him to the void that final time. Powwell almost choked on this thought/words. His words and form faded to a mere echo inside Vareena's mind. If he faded much more, she'd lose contact with him altogether. *He was the greatest man of his time. More a father to me than you, Ackerly. He loved me, nurtured me, wept with me when Kalen died.*

"Then accept him as your father and seek a new existence. Continue his greatness by passing beyond your misery and seeking happiness and good in a new life." Vareena sensed Powwell's hesitation. His form wavered, strengthening and fading in his indecision.

"And you, Ackerly. Give up your gold, give up this illusion of power. True power is in the kind of love Nimbulan gave his family, his apprentices, and his country. You are reviled as a traitor by those who do know of you. You can have the kind of power Nimbulan had in your next life if you only try. You can have a family to nurture and love next time. But you have to give up the gold."

Powwell reached out a hand to Ackerly. *Join me, Father, in this new quest. Begin your healing alongside me.*

Ackerly lifted his hand as well.

The solid iron of the staircase blocked them.

Tears in her eyes, Vareena ran to the first step. She had to brush Ackerly's ghostly robes. Chills racked her body at the unnatural touch. Just a small taste of what was to come, if she succeeded.

She couldn't turn back now. She had to succeed. She had to end this here and now.

One at a time she mounted the steps until she stood halfway between the two ghosts. "Let me guide you both forward." She held out a hand to each. Bare finger-lengths separated her hands from theirs. "You have to try harder. You have to reach beyond your fears, beyond the limitations of this existence."

Both ghosts leaned forward, bending around the iron barrier.

Still they could not reach her.

Then Powwell shifted his staff. He grasped the butt end and pushed the crystal-studded head down. It dropped on the second step.

Ackerly couldn't reach it without touching the deadly iron. Vareena grasped the crystal at the end of the staff. Ackerly held out the hilt of his knife for her questing hands. She clutched them both tightly.

Light, power, love pulsed through the staff and the knife. They washed over Vareena in endless, daunting waves. The onslaught of emotions drained the strength from her knees. The intricate pattern of the iron stair pressed through her gown, bruising her mortal flesh. She fought to remain conscious, to keep the tunnel of light open for the two souls who must take the first steps toward their next existence.

The magical tools burned her palms. The iron stairs seared her knees. Light pierced her eyes, until she knew she must close them or be blinded for life. Her aching need for freedom intensified. How could she leave if she couldn't see? How could she work her meager acres without her sight? Who would love her, a blind spinster with burn scars hampering her grasp and her walk?

Still she clung to the tools, binding father and son together.

"Vareena!" Marcus and Robb cried.

She couldn't see them. The staff and the knife continued to vibrate, continued to bind her to her ghosts. She sensed Ackerly and Powwell lifting free of the confines of their half-existence. Sensed their spirits joining, melding, leaving her behind.

Their joy flooded her. "Take me with you," she whispered. "Take me away from the hurts of this life, from the weight of my duty and responsibility."

"Not yet, Vareena. You have too much life to live and love to give." Marcus eased the staff from her hands. "I'll help you heal. I'll take care of you, if you let me."

She heard the wooden staff land on the stone floor with a clatter. The knife followed, its blade shattering.

Robb lifted her free of the staircase. Both magicians held her close, crooning soothing words. Each loving her in his own way.

"You're safe now. The Rover women are coming to heal you." Marcus kissed her temple, smoothing tangled hair out of her eyes.

"Lord Andrall has pledged his protection of you and your acres."

"You are safe now."

She couldn't tell which man spoke, only that they both took care of her as she had taken care of them and all the ghosts of this place. She leaned into Marcus, cherishing the strength of his arms supporting her.

Thank you, Vareena. Thank you for your gift of love and healing, Powwell and Ackerly both whispered across her mind.

She opened her eyes. Too much light still blazed around the edges of her vision. The gloaming lifted. She could see only a few dark figures at the center of the brightness. But she could see.

She saw a tiny hedgehog scuttle away from the staff under her skirts, seeking protection and love. She stooped to cradle it in her burned hands.

Thorny, the creature announced his name to her.

"I guess that makes you a magician after all," Marcus said around a huge smile. "Powwell left you his staff and his familiar."

A gift of love and healing for a gift of love and healing. Powwell's voice echoed around the library, spreading to the courtyard.

The mist of Ackerly's spell lifted from all around. The gold lay inert and uncharmed upon its shelves, ready and waiting to be put to use.